Time is the Simplest Thing

Without setting foot on another planet, people like Shep Blaine were reaching out to the stars with their minds, telepathically contacting strange beings on other worlds. But even Blaine was unprepared for what happened when he communed with the soul of an utterly alien being light years from Earth. After recovering from his experience, he becomes a dangerous man: not only has he gained startling new powers – but he now understands that humankind must share the stars.

Way Station

Enoch Wallace survived the carnage of Gettysburg and lived through the rest of the Civil War to make it home to his parents' farm in south-west Wisconsin. But his mother was already dead and his father soon joined her in the tiny family cemetery. It was then that Enoch met the being he called Ulysses and the farm became a way station for space travellers. Now, nearly a hundred years later, the US government is taking an interest in the seemingly immortal Enoch, and the Galactic Council, which set up the way station, is threatening to tear itself apart.

A Choice of Gods

The Earth's population had been more than eight billion. One day they were there, the next they were gone – all except the guests at a family birthday party, a small tribe of American Indians and, of course, the robots. Technology disintegrated, the Indians went back to nature, and the rest developed new and extraordinary powers. As for the robots, some went to live with the remnants of humanity, others gathered in their own community. Then one day a traveller returned from the stars – and the idyllic existence of the last of Earth's humans was threatened.

Also by Clifford D. Simak

Cosmic Engineers (1950)
Time and Again (1951) (aka First He Died)
Empire (1951)
City (1952)
Ring Around the Sun (1952)
Time Is the Simplest Thing (1961) (aka The Fisherman)
Trouble with Tycho (1961)
They Walked Like Men (1962)
Way Station (1963) (aka Here Gather the Stars)
All Flesh Is Grass (1965)
Why Call Them Back from Heaven? (1967)
The Werewolf Principle (1967)
The Goblin Reservation (1968)
So Bright the Vision (1968)
Out of Their Minds (1969)
Destiny Doll (1971)
Prehistoric Man (1971)
A Choice of Gods (1972)
Cemetery World (1973)
Our Children's Children (1974)
The Enchanted Pilgrimage (1975)
Shakespeare's Planet (1976)
A Heritage of Stars (1977)
The Fellowship of the Talisman (1978)
Mastodonia (1978) (aka Catface)
The Visitors (1980)
Project Pope (1981)
Where the Evil Dwells (1982)
Special Deliverance (1982)
Highway of Eternity (1986)

Clifford D. Simak

SF GATEWAY OMNIBUS

TIME IS THE SIMPLEST THING
WAY STATION
A CHOICE OF GODS

GOLLANCZ

LONDON

First published in Great Britain in 2013 by
Gollancz
An imprint of the Orion Publishing Group
Orion House, 5 Upper St Martin's Lane,
London WC2H 9EA

An Hachette UK Company

A CIP catalogue record for this book
is available from the British Library

ISBN 978 0 575 12232 1

1 3 5 7 9 10 8 6 4 2

Typeset by Jouve (UK), Milton Keynes

Printed and bounded by CPI Group (UK) Ltd, Croydon, CR0 4YY

The Orion Publishing Group's policy is to use papers
that are natural, renewable and recyclable products and
made from wood grown in sustainable forests. The logging
and manufacturing processes are expected to conform to
the environmental regulations of the country of origin.

www.orionbooks.co.uk
www.gollancz.co.uk

CONTENTS

ENTER THE SF GATEWAY . . .

Towards the end of 2011, in conjunction with the celebration of fifty years of coherent, continuous science fiction and fantasy publishing, Gollancz launched the SF Gateway.

Over a decade after launching the landmark SF Masterworks series, we realised that the realities of commercial publishing are such that even the Masterworks could only ever scratch the surface of an author's career. Vast troves of classic SF and fantasy were almost certainly destined never again to see print. Until very recently, this meant that anyone interested in reading any of those books would have been confined to scouring second-hand bookshops. The advent of digital publishing changed that paradigm for ever.

Embracing the future even as we honour the past, Gollancz launched the SF Gateway with a view to utilising the technology that now exists to make available, for the first time, the entire backlists of an incredibly wide range of classic and modern SF and fantasy authors. Our plan, at its simplest, was – and still is! – to use this technology to build on the success of the SF and Fantasy Masterworks series and to go even further.

The SF Gateway was designed to be the new home of classic science fiction and fantasy – the most comprehensive electronic library of classic SFF titles ever assembled. The programme has been extremely well received and we've been very happy with the results. So happy, in fact, that we've decided to complete the circle and return a selection of our titles to print, in these omnibus editions.

We hope you enjoy this selection. And we hope that you'll want to explore more of the classic SF and fantasy we have available. These are wonderful books you're holding in your hand, but you'll find much, much more ... through the SF Gateway.

www.sfgateway.com

INTRODUCTION

Clifford D. Simak (1904–1988) was a US writer whose primary occupation 1929–1976 was newspaper work, and who worked full-time for the *Minneapolis Star* from 1939 until his retirement, when he became a full-time writer of sf, some years after his early prime. He had been in fact a prolific and increasingly popular sf figure – after some stories in the early 1930s – from the true beginning of his writing career in 1938, and remained prolific from that date until his death. His first published stories, beginning with 'The World of the Red Sun' for *Wonder Stories* in December 1931, were less individual than his later work; significantly, however, that first tale deals with Time Travel, which became his favourite sf device for the importation of Aliens into rural Wisconsin, always his venue of choice. Other early work of interest included 'The Voice in the Void' (1932), about the desecration of a sacred tomb on Mars which possibly contains the relics of a Messiah from Earth; 'Hellhounds of the Cosmos' (1932), in which defenders of Earth who, in order to fight a monster in another Dimension, combine into a gestalt; and *The Creator* (1935; book form 1946), in which humans and other races travel by Time Machine in order to combat the creator of the universe, who has become bored with his/her handiwork.

In 1938, inspired by John W. Campbell Jr's editorial policy at *Astounding*, Simak began to produce less melodramatic, more maturely couched stories like 'Rule 18' (1938) or 'Reunion on Ganymede' (1938). He swiftly followed with his first full-length novel, *Cosmic Engineers* (1939; book form 1950), a Galaxy-spanning throw-back in the vein of E. E. Smith and Edmond Hamilton. While continuing to write steadily for Campbell, his work gradually became identifiably Simakian – constrained, intensely emotional beneath a calmly competent Genre SF surface; tales deeply Pastoral in the sense that his idylls, his Edens, were almost inevitably supported by some superior civilization, sometimes urban (though his distaste for the City marred his efforts at verisimilitude), sometimes Alien. Two circumstances may be noted: Millville, Wisconsin, where he was born, could be described as a Polder, occupying as it does a protected enclave – a valley that, almost magically, escaped the last Ice Age; over and above the fact of this paradisal exemption, the nostalgic intensity of his vision of rural Wisconsin is typically exilic in that he spent most of his adult life in Minneapolis, Minnesota, a large city almost 200 miles away.

Stories like 'Rim of the Deep' (1940), 'Tools' (1942) and 'Hunch' (1943) were further signs of his development, though the full Simak did not 'arrive' until the appearance of 'City' (1944) and its sequel, 'Huddling Place' (1944), the first two segments of *City* (book form 1952), a collection of closely linked stories that deals initially with the Near-Future exodus of mankind from the Cities and the return to a quasi-suburban existence aided by a benign Technology. As the tale progresses, Earth is abandoned by all humans, who escape the Arrested Development inherent in the physical nature of *Homo sapiens*, and find Transcendence on Jupiter. They leave behind a Keep in Geneva, where a few humans remain in Suspended Animation; some mysterious Mutants; and Jenkins, an excellently depicted Robot (though his behaviour in earlier sections is uncomfortably Stepin Fetchit-like), who is left to monitor the forced evolution (or Uplift) of the intelligent Dogs destined to inherit the Earth. Gathered into Club Story format as a set of tales the Dogs tell each other around the campfire, *City* won an International Fantasy Award. It remains Simak's best known early work.

In 1950 Simak found another market in the new magazine *Galaxy*, which serialized his novel *Time and Again* (1950; book form 1951). A trickily plotted Time Travel story, with a Changewar on the verge of transforming reality, and a sympathetic Android, it proved to be very popular – though ominously prefiguring some over-plotted works from the late 1970s. After the less compelling *Empire* (1951), a tale of Near Future intrigue involving a new Power Source, he published a second *Galaxy* serial, *Ring Around the Sun* (1952–1953; book form 1953), which involves the discovery of a chain of Parallel Worlds and the machinations of a secret society of Mutants who are plotting to subvert the world's economy by producing everlasting goods. Its anti-urban and pro-agrarian sentiments were by now a standard part of Simak's work; in stories like 'Neighbor' (1954) he became sf's leading spokesman for rural, Midwestern values. His stories in general contain little violence and much folk humour, and stress the value of individualism tempered by compassion – 'good neighbourliness', in short. Throughout the 1950s, he produced dozens of competent short stories, many assembled in *Strangers in the Universe* (1956), *The Worlds of Clifford Simak* (1960) and *All the Traps of Earth* (1962), all of these issued in various editions under various titles. Two high points were the stories 'The Big Front Yard' (1958), which won a 1959 Hugo Award, and 'A Death in the House' (1959). Many of these tales appear in the retrospective *Skirmish: The Great Short Fiction* (1977), in various retrospective volumes published after his death, and in the first two volumes of a projected Collected Stories: *The Collected Stories 1: Eternity Lost* (2004) and *The Collected Stories 2: Physician to the Universe* (2006).

After 1960 Simak began to produce novels at the rate of roughly one a year, the first few being among his very best work. *Time is the Simplest Thing* (1961; book form 1961) is strongly told (see below) and *They Walked Like Men* (1962) is workmanlike and entertaining, and *Way Station* (1963; book form 1963) (see below) is perhaps his finest single novel. *All Flesh is Grass* (1965), *Why Call them Back from Heaven?* (1967) and *The Werewolf Principle* (1967), featuring Werewolves are enjoyable, if essentially repetitive. *The Goblin Reservation* (1968; book form 1968) seemed at first glance to be innovative, striking out into new territory; but in fact turned out to be a Wisconsin-valley fantasy in a new and whimsical guise. Simak had always wrestled with such whimsy – notoriously paired with nostalgia in many authors of his emotional bent – and by the start of the 1970s whimsy seemed to be winning. Its triumph may have derived from the fact that the venues for which he felt genuine emotion were now forty years past (and, as noted above, elsewhere), and the world had irrevocably repudiated and scummed over the rural clarities dear to his memories: but although the temptation to dodge change and Decadence by sidestepping them seemed increasingly sentimental. Novels like *Destiny Doll* (1971), *Cemetery World* (1972 –1973; book form 1973), *Enchanted Pilgrimage* (1975), *Shakespeare's Planet* (1976), *Catface* (1978), *Special Deliverance* (1982) and *Highway of Eternity* (1986), his last novel, contain only flashes of the old talent, mingled with a good deal of sheer silliness.

There were exceptions, however: *A Choice of Gods* (1972) (see below); and *A Heritage of Stars* (1977), a quest novel set in a post-technological society, is another compendium of Simak's old material, but cagily expressed. Though he seemed generally to need the relative discipline of sf to achieve his best effects, *The Fellowship of the Talisman* (1978) is a reasonably effective Fantasy; another, somewhat weaker fantasy is *Where the Evil Dwells* (1982). *The Visitors* (1979; book form 1980), in which Aliens once again visit Earth bearing enigmatic gifts, may be the finest novel of his last active decade, for a vein of irony is allowed some play. The strengths of *Project Pope* (1981), about the devising of an AI to serve as the ultimate pope, are somewhat vitiated by Simak's visible reluctance to understand Computers.

Simak's late short stories are less variable, and tales like 'The Ghost of a Model T' (1975), or 'Grotto of the Dancing Deer' (1980) which won both the Hugo and the Nebula awards, retain all the skill and much of the resilience of his prime. He was a man of strong moral convictions and only intermittent concern for ideas, and perhaps surprisingly for a man of such professional attainments he rarely tended to stray outside his natural bailiwick. Wisconsin in about 1925 – or any extraterrestrial venue demonstrating the same rooted virtues – was his true home, and when he was in residence there Simak reigned as the finest pastoral elegist of his genre. He received the SFWA Grand Master Award in 1977.

*

Time is the Simplest Thing (1961; book form 1961), the first of three central Simak novels here assembled, may have seemed unduly harsh on its first publication half a century ago; but it now reads as prophetic in its depiction of a future America under the sway of a cynical corporation whose monopolistic behaviour has created a dystopia even in Simak's beloved rural mid-West. The protagonist, though, gives us hope. After a mind-melding experience with an alien, which massively increases his powers, he realizes that to survive in the galaxy Earth must co-operate with those who co-inhabit it. The message is exhilarating, and – though more calmly – is reiterated in *Way Station* (1963; book form 1963), the second novel here presented, which won the 1964 Hugo Award. The tale impressively focuses on Simak's favourite kind of protagonist and venue: a lonely but wise Wisconsin farmer has been given Immortality in return for his services as a galactic station-master, his house having been, long before the tale begins, transformed into a way-station or Stargate – a resting place for Aliens who travel from star to star via Matter Transmission. Its warmth and imaginative detail, its finely rendered, almost Edenic vision of the good life, and its powerful insistence that *Homo sapiens* must co-operate or perish, make this probably Simak's best novel.

A *Choice of Gods* (1972), the final novel in this omnibus, came at a point in Simak's career when he was perhaps writing too much too quickly, but stands out from its fellows. It is a tale of summing up, in which Simak returns to his most deeply felt early works, especially the slow plainsong of *City*, and reworks their elegiac message in 1970s language. So we encounter once again the venues and characters for which Simak was science fiction's most eloquent spokesman: the depopulated world, the sage old man gazing at sunset, the liberated Robots, the 'haunted' house, Teleportation to the stars, harmony. Simak's wisdom may seem too simple for the new world we now inhabit; but almost certainly that is our loss. These books are here to remind us.

For a more detailed version of the above, see Clifford D. Simak's author entry in *The Encyclopedia of Science Fiction*: http://sf-encyclopedia.com/entry/simak_clifford_d

Some terms above are capitalised when they would not normally be so rendered; this indicates that the terms represent discrete entries in *The Encyclopedia of Science Fiction*.

TIME IS THE SIMPLEST THING

1

Finally there came a time when Man was ready to admit that he was barred from space. He had first suspected it in that day when Van Allen found the radiation belts that encircled Earth, and the men at Minnesota used balloons to trap the solar protons. But Man had dreamed so long that even in the face of this he could not forsake the dream without giving it a try.

So he went ahead and tried – and he kept on trying even after astronauts had died to prove he couldn't do it. Man was too frail for space. He died too easily. He died either of the primary radiations hurled out by the sun or of the secondaries to which the metal of his ship gave birth.

At length Man knew the dream had failed and there was a bitterness and a disillusion in looking at the stars, for the stars were farther now than they had ever been.

After many years, after great thundering in the sky, after a hundred million heartbreaks, Man finally gave up.

It was just as well he did.

There was a better way.

2

Shepherd Blaine sensed that he was in some sort of house, or, if not a house exactly, in something's dwelling place. For there was an orderliness and a sense of proportion and of form which did not occur in nature, even in an alien nature on the planet of an unknown star far removed from Earth.

His treads left no tracks upon the floor as they had left tracks upon the sand dunes before he had come upon this dwelling place, if that was what it was. The wind was a whisper only as compared with the howling of the desert storm through which he'd forged for hours.

The floor was hard and smooth and of a bright blue color and very easy for him to roll along. There were forms scattered here and there that might have been furniture or equipment or artifacts of some aesthetic value and they all were blue as well and the shape of them was not the wild, haphazard shape of a surface carved by wind or sun or weather, but the clean-cut lines, straight or curved as they might be, of functional apparatus.

And yet the stars still shone and the distant sun was there, dim as it might be, and so this place he had stumbled on was certainly no enclosure.

Blaine moved forward slowly with all his sensors out, turned up to full capacity, and the sense of *house* persisted and, a little after that, the sense of life as well.

He felt a thin thread of excitement mount inside himself. For it was not often that one found life at all. It was a memorable occasion when one found intelligence. And here, from the smoothness of the bright blue floor, from these artifacts, was intelligence.

His pace slowed to a crawl, his treads whispering on the floor, his sensors out and working, and the whirring of the tape that sucked up sight and sound and shape and smell and form, recording temperature and time and magnetics and all the other phenomena which existed on this planet.

Far off he saw the life – the thing that sprawled limply on the floor, as a lazy man might sprawl, not doing anything, not expecting to do anything, but just lying there.

Blaine moved toward it, still keeping his slow pace, and the sensors gathered in the knowledge of this sprawling life and the recorders sucked it up.

It was pink; an exciting pink, not a disgusting pink as pink so often can be, not a washed-out pink, nor an anatomical pink, but a very pretty pink, the kind of pink the little girl next door might wear at her seventh birthday party.

It was looking at him – maybe not with eyes – but it was looking at him. It was aware of him. And it was not afraid.

Finally he reached it. He came up to within six feet of it and there he stopped and waited.

It was a fairly massive thing, twelve feet high or so in the middle of it, and it sprawled across an area twenty feet or more in diameter. It towered above the smallness of the machine that happened to be Blaine, but there was no menace in it. Nor a friendliness. There was nothing yet. It was just a lump.

And this was the tough part of it, Blaine reminded himself. This was the moment when you could make or break. The move that he made now might set the pattern for all his future relationship with this thing he faced.

So he stayed perfectly still and did not a single thing. The sensors pulled back in and barely kept alive, the tape scarcely moved at all.

And it was tough to wait, for he was running out of time. There was very little left.

Then he sensed the flutter, picked up by the sophisticated electronic innards of the machine which for the moment was his body; the flutter of the being that sprawled pinkly on the floor – the flutter of a thought half-formed, the beginning of communication, the breaking of the ice.

Blaine tensed, fighting down the elation that surged inside of him. For it was foolish to become elated yet – there was no certain indication of telepathic power. Although the flutter had the feeling of it, a certain connotation …

Hang on, he told himself, hang on!

Hold onto that time!

Just thirty seconds left!

The flutter stirred again, louder and sharper now, as if the creature squatting there before him had cleared its mental throat before attempting speech.

It was seldom that one contacted a telepathic creature. Other abilities and traits and idiosyncrasies that made telepathy seem a pallid thing were not at all uncommon, but only rarely did they prove as useful as the plain, old-fashioned telepathic art.

And the creature spoke.

Hi, pal, it said. *I trade with you my mind.*

Blaine's mind screamed soundlessly in outraged surprise that came very close to panic. For, suddenly, without warning, he was a double thing – himself and this other creature. For one chaotic instant he saw as the creature saw, felt as the creature felt, knew what the creature knew. And in that same

5

instant he was likewise Shepherd Blaine, Fishhook explorer, a mind from out of Earth and very far from home.

And in that same instant, as well, his time clicked to an end.

There was a sense of rushing, as if space itself might be thundering past at a fantastic rate of speed. Shepherd Blaine, protesting, was jerked across five thousand light years into one specific spot in northern Mexico.

3

He crawled upward from the well of darkness into which he had been plunged, groping his way with a blind persistence that was almost driven instinct. And he knew where he was – he was sure he knew – but he could not grasp the knowledge. He had been in this well before, many times before, and it was familiar to him, but there was a strangeness now that had never been before.

It was himself, he knew, in which the strangeness lay – almost as if he were another, as if he were only half himself, and the other half of him were tenanted by an unknown being that was backed against a wall and spat in overriding fear and mewled in loneliness.

He clawed his way upward from the well, and his mind fought in frantic urgency against the mewling strangeness in him even as he sensed that it was no use to fight, that the strangeness was a thing that had come to live with him and be a part of him so long as he existed.

He rested for a moment from the climbing and tried to sort out himself, but he was too many things and in too many places and it was utterly confusing. He was a human being (whatever that might be) and he was a scurrying machine and he was an alien Pinkness sprawling on a bright blue floor and he was a mindlessness that fell through aeons of screaming time which finally figured out, when one nailed down the mathematics of it, to the fraction of a second.

He crawled out of the well, and the blackness went away and there was soft light. He was lying flat upon his back and he finally was home and he felt the old, old thankfulness that he'd made it once again.

And finally he knew.

He was Shepherd Blaine and he was an explorer for Fishhook, and he went far out in space to nose out stranger stars. He went out many light years and at times he found certain things of some significance and other times he didn't. But this time he had found a thing, and a part of it had come back home with him.

He sought for it and found it in the corner of his mind, rolled tight against its fear, and he tried to comfort it even as he feared it. For it was a terrible thing, he told himself, to be caught inside an alien mind. And, on the other hand, it was a lousy deal to have a thing like this trapped inside his mind.

It's tough on both of us, he said, talking to himself and to this other thing which was a part of him.

He lay there quietly – wherever he was lying – and tried to put himself in

7

order. He had gone out some thirty hours before – not he, himself, of course, for his body had stayed here – but his mind had gone out, and with it the little scurrying machine, to this unguessed planet that spun around an unknown sun.

The planet had been no different than a lot of other planets, just a howling wilderness, and that was what a lot of them turned out to be when you came stumbling down upon them. This time a howling wilderness of sand although it could just as well have been a jungle or a desert of ice or a bare and naked place of nothing but primeval rock.

For almost thirty hours he had roamed the sand and there had been nothing there. Then suddenly he had come upon the great blue room with the Pinkness sprawling in it, and when he had come home the Pinkness, or a shadow of the Pinkness, had come back with him.

It crawled out from where it had been hiding, and he felt the touch of it again, the knowing and the feeling and the knowledge. His blood crawled like icy slush gurgling in his veins, and he went rigid with the musty smell and the slimy feel of alienness, and he could have shouted in pure terror, but he did not shout. He lay there, quite unstirring, and the Pinkness scurried back to its nook once more and lay there tightly curled.

Blaine opened his eyes and saw that the lid of the place in which he lay had been tilted back, and the glare of brightness that was a hooded light bulb was stabbing down at him.

He took inventory of his body and it was all right. There was no reason for it not to be all right, for it had lain here and rested for all of thirty hours.

He stirred and raised himself so that he sat up, and there were faces, staring at him, faces swimming in the light.

'A tough one?' asked one face.

'They all are tough,' said Blaine.

He climbed from the coffinlike machine and shivered, for he suddenly was cold.

'Here's your jacket, sir,' one of the faces said, a face that surmounted a white smock.

She held it for him, and he shrugged into it.

She handed him a glass, and he took a sip of it and knew that it was milk. He should have known it would be. As soon as anyone got back they gave him a glass of milk. With something in it, maybe? He had never thought to ask. It was just one of the many little things that spelled out Fishhook to him and to all the others like him. Fishhook, in its century or more, had managed to accumulate an entire host of moldy traditions, all of them fuddy-duddy in varying degrees.

It was coming back – familiar now as he stood there sipping at his glass of milk – the great operations room with its rows of glistening star machines, some of which were closed while the rest stood open. And in the closed ones lay others like himself, their bodies left behind and their minds far out in space.

'What time is it?' he asked.

'Nine P.M.,' said a man who held a clipboard in his hand.

The alienness was creeping in his mind again, and the words were there once more: *Hi, pal. I trade with you my mind!*

And now, in the light of human reason, it was crazier than hell. A form of greeting more than likely. A sort of shaking hands. A shaking of the minds. And when one thought of it, a lot more sensible than the shaking of the hands.

The girl reached out and touched him on the arm. 'Finish up your milk,' she said.

If it were a mind-shake, it was a lasting one, for the mind was staying on. He could feel it now, an alien dirtiness, lurking just below the level of his consciousness.

'The machine got back O.K.?' he asked.

The man with the clipboard nodded. 'Not a bit of trouble. We sent down the tapes.'

Half an hour, Blaine thought calmly, and was surprised that he could be so calm. Half an hour was all he had, for that was the length of time required to process the tapes. They always, he knew, ran through the exploratory tapes as soon as they came in.

It would all be there; all the data would be down, telling all the story. There would be no question of it, no doubt of what had happened. And before they read it, he must be out of reach.

He looked around the room and once again he felt the satisfaction and the thrill and pride that he had felt, years ago, when he'd first been brought into this room. For here was the heartthrob of Fishhook itself; here was the reaching out, here the dipping into distant places.

It would be hard to leave, he knew; hard to turn his back upon, for much of him was here.

But there was no question of it – he simply had to go.

He finished up the milk and handed the waiting girl the glass. He turned toward the door.

'Just a minute,' said the man, holding out the clipboard. 'You forgot to sign out, sir.'

Grumbling, Blaine pulled the pencil from beneath the clip and signed. It was a lot of foolishness, but you went through the motions. You signed in and you signed out and you kept your mouth tight shut, and all of Fishhook acted as if the place would fall into a heap of dust if you missed a single lick.

He handed back the board.

'Excuse me, Mr Blaine, but you failed to note when you would return for evaluation.'

'Make it nine tomorrow morning,' Blaine told him curtly.

They could put down anything they wished, for he wasn't coming back. He had thirty minutes left – less than thirty minutes now – and he needed all of it.

For the memory of that night of three years ago was becoming sharper with every passing second. He could remember, not the words alone, but the very tone of them. When Godfrey Stone had phoned that night there had been a sound of sobbing in his breath, as if he had been running, and there had been a sense of panic.

'Good night, everyone,' said Blaine.

He went out into the corridor and closed the door behind him, and the place was empty. The flanking doors were closed, although lights burned in some of them. The corridor was deserted and everything was quiet. But even in the quietness and the emptiness there was still a sense of massive vitality, as if all of Fishhook might have stood on watch. As if all the mighty complex never slept at all – all the laboratories and experimental stations all the factories and the universities, all the planning boards and the vast libraries and repositories and all the rest of it never closed an eye.

He stood for a moment, considering. And it all was simple. He could walk out of here and there was not a thing to stop him. He could get his car out of the parking lot just five blocks away and head northward for the border. But it was, he told himself, too simple and direct. It was too obvious. It was just the thing that Fishhook would figure him to do.

And there was something else – the nagging thought, the clinging, monstrous doubt: did he really need to run?

Five men in the three years since Godfrey Stone – and was that evidence?

He went striding down the corridor, and his mind was busy sorting out the doubts, but even as he sorted he knew there was no room for doubts. Whatever doubt might rise, he knew that he was right. But the tightness was an intellectual rightness and the doubt emotional.

He admitted to himself that it all boiled down to a single factor: he did not want to flee from Fishhook. He liked being here; he liked the work he did; he didn't want to leave.

But he had fought that out with himself many months ago. He'd reached a decision then. When the time came, he would go. No matter how much he might want to stay, he'd drop everything and run.

For Godfrey Stone had known and in his desperate fleeing he had taken out the time to make one desperate call – not a call for help, but a cry of warning.

'Shep,' he had said, sobbing out the words as if he had been running. 'Shep, listen to me and don't interrupt. If you ever should go alien, take it on the lam. Don't wait around a minute. Just take it on the lam.'

And then the receiver had crashed down and that was all there was.

Blaine remembered how he'd stood there, with the phone still in his fist.

'Yes, Godfrey,' he had said into the silence at the other end. 'Yes, Godfrey, I'll remember. Thank you and good luck.'

And there'd not been word again. He had never heard from Godfrey Stone again.

If you ever should turn alien, Godfrey Stone had said. And now he had turned alien, for he could feel the alienness, like a lurking second self crouched inside his brain. And that had been the manner in which he had turned alien. But what about the others? Certainly not all of them had met a Pinkness, five thousand light years distant. How many other ways might a man turn alien?

Fishhook would know that he was alien. There was no way to stop them knowing. They'd know when they processed the tapes. Then they'd have him in and turn a peeper on him – for while the tapes might say that he was alien, they could not tell in what manner or to what extent he might have turned an alien. The peeper would talk very friendly to him even sympathetically, and all the time he would be rooting out the alien in his mind – rooting it out of hiding to find out what it was.

He reached the elevator and was punching at the button when a door just down the hall came open.

'Oh, Shep, I see it's you,' said the man standing in the door. 'I heard you going down the hall. I wondered who it was.'

Blaine swung around. 'I just got back,' he said.

'Why don't you come in for a while?' Kirby Rand invited. 'I was getting ready to open up a bottle.'

There was no time to hesitate. Blaine knew. He either went in and had a drink or two or he gave a curt refusal. And if there were a curt refusal, Rand would become suspicious. For suspicion was Rand's business. He was section chief of Fishhook security.

'Thanks,' said Blaine, as unruffled as he could. 'For a short one only. There's a girl. I shouldn't keep her waiting.'

And that, he told himself, would block any well-intentioned invitation to take him out to dinner or to go out and see a show.

He heard the elevator coming up, but he walked away from it. There was nothing he could do. It was a dirty break, but there was no help for it.

As he walked through the door, Rand thumped him on the shoulder in round good fellowship.

'Good trip?' he asked.

'Not a bit of trouble.'

'How far out?'

'About five thousand.'

Rand wagged his head. 'I guess that's a foolish one to ask,' he said. 'They all are far out now. We've just about finished off all the near-by ones. Another hundred years from now, we'll be going out ten thousand.'

'It makes no difference,' Blaine told him. 'Once you get going, you are there. Distance seems to be no factor. Maybe when we get way out we may pick up a lag. Halfway across the galaxy. But I doubt it even then.'

'The theoretical boys think not,' said Rand.

He walked across the office to the massive desk and picked up the bottle that was standing there. He broke the seal and spun the cap.

'You know, Shep,' he said, 'this is a fantastic business we are in. We tend to take it in our stride and it becomes at times a bit humdrum to us. But the fantasy is there.'

'Just because it came so late to us,' said Blaine. 'Just because we passed up the ability so long. It was in us all the time and we never used it. Because it wasn't practical. Because it was fantastic. Because we couldn't quite believe it. The ancients grabbed the edge of it, but they didn't understand it. They thought that it was magic.'

'That's what a lot of folks still think,' said Rand.

He rustled up two glasses and got ice out of the wall refrigerator. He poured out generous helpings.

'Drink up,' he said, handing Blaine a glass.

Rand lowered himself into the chair behind the desk.

'Sit down,' he said to Blaine. 'You aren't in that much of a rush. And you lose something in the drinking when you stay standing up.'

Blaine sat down.

Rand put his feet up on the desk, settled back in comfort.

No more than twenty minutes left!

And sitting there, with the glass clutched in his hand, in that second of silence before Rand should speak again, it seemed to Blaine once more that he could hear the throbbing of the huge thing that was Fishhook, as if it were one great sentient being lying here against the nighttime Mother Earth of northern Mexico, as if it had heart and lungs and many throbbing veins and it was this throbbing which he heard.

Across the desk Rand crinkled his face into a gracious mask of geniality.

'You guys have all the fun,' he said. 'I sometimes envy you.'

'It's a job,' Blaine told him carelessly.

'You went out five thousand years today. You got something out of it.'

'I suppose there was some satisfaction,' Blaine admitted. 'The intellectual thrill of knowing where you were. Actually, it was better than the usual run. I think I rustled up some life.'

'Tell me,' said Rand.

'Not a thing to tell. I found this thing when time was running out. I didn't have a chance to do anything at all before I was jerked back home. You've got to do something about that, Kirby. It can get damn embarrassing.'

Rand shook his head. 'I'm afraid that's out,' he said.

'You should give us some discretion,' Blaine insisted. 'The time limit should not be so arbitrary. You keep a man out the total length of time – the entire thirty hours – when there is no earthly reason for him staying on. Then you yank him back when he's on the very verge of something.'

Rand grinned at him.

'Don't tell me you can't do it,' said Blaine. 'Don't pretend that it's impossible. Fishhook has cords of scientists, stacked up in solid rows –'

'Oh, I suppose it's possible,' Rand told him. 'We just like to keep control.'

'Afraid of someone staying?'

'That's possible,' said Rand.

'What for?' demanded Blaine. 'You're not a man out there. You're nothing but a human mind caged in a smart machine.'

'We like it as it is,' said Rand. 'After all, you guys are valuable. We must take safety measures. What if you got into a jam five thousand years from home? What if something happened and you were unable to exercise control? We would lose you then. But this way it's automatic. When we send you out, we know you're coming back.'

'You value us too highly,' Blaine told him dryly.

'Not at all,' said Rand. 'Do you realize how much we have invested in you? Do you realize how many men we sift through before we find one that we can use? One who is both a telepath and a rather special kind of teleporter, one who has the mental balance to stand up to the impact of some of the things he finds out there, and, finally, one who is capable of loyalty to Fishhook.'

'You buy the loyalty,' said Blaine. 'There is no one of us who ever claimed he was underpaid.'

'That,' Rand told him, 'is not what I am talking about and you know it isn't.'

And you, Blaine asked inaudibly – what are the qualifications for security? Peeping could be one of them – the ability to look into another's mind – but there'd never been any evidence in all the years he had known Rand that the man actually was a peeper. If he were a peeper, then why should he use men in his department whose sole purpose consisted of their ability to peep?

'I can't see what all this has to do,' said Blaine, 'with not giving us some time control. We could—'

'And I don't see why you should fret yourself,' Rand countered. 'You'll be going back to your precious planet. You can pick up where you left off.'

'Of course I'm going back. I found it, didn't I? That sort of makes it mine.'

He finished off the drink, put the glass down on the desk.

'Well, I'm off,' he said. 'Thank you for the drink.'

'Of course,' said Rand. 'Wouldn't think of keeping you. You'll be back tomorrow?'

'Nine o'clock,' said Blaine.

4

Blaine walked through the massive, ornate entrance that fronted on the plaza and under ordinary circumstance he would have stopped there for a moment to soak in this best part of the day.

The street lamps were soft blobs of light, and the fronds were rustling in the evening breeze. The strollers on the walks seemed disembodied shadows, and the cars went sliding past in a sort of breathless haste, but quietly, very quietly. And over all of it hung the magic haze of an autumn night.

Tonight he did not stop. There was no time to stop.

Eight minutes now. Eight little lousy minutes.

Five blocks to get his car out of the parking lot and he didn't have the time. He couldn't take the chance. He had to leave the car.

And there was something else – there was Kirby Rand. Why, on this of all nights, had Rand popped out his door and asked him in to have a drink?

There was nothing that he could put his finger on, but he felt a vague disquiet at his talk with Rand. It was almost as if the man had known he was stealing time from him, as if he might have sensed that there was something wrong.

But all of that was past, Blaine told himself. It had been hard luck, of course, but it was not disastrous. In fact, there might even be some advantage to it. If he had got his car, Fishhook would have known exactly where to look for him. But forced to stay within the city, he could vanish in a matter of ten minutes.

He strode swiftly down the walk and turned in a direction away from the parking lot.

Give me ten minutes more, he told himself, almost as if it were a prayer. With a ten-minute start, there were a dozen places he could hide himself – hide himself to gain a little breathing space, to do a little thinking and to make some plans. For now, without a car, he simply had no plans.

He'd get those ten minutes, he was sure, if he only could be so lucky as to meet no one who might recognize him.

He felt the terror welling up as he strode along, a terror rising like a froth foaming in his skull. And it was not his terror; it was not human terror. It was abysmal and black, a screaming, clawing terror that had its origin in a mind that could hide no longer from the horrors of an alien planet, that could no longer huddle inside an alien brain, that finally found it unbearable to face up to a frightening situation that was made almost unendurable by a total lack of background.

Blaine fought against the terror, teeth gritted in his mind, knowing with one thin, undulled edge of understanding that it was not himself who had tripped the terror, but this other, this lurker in the brain.

And realized, even as he thought it, that he could scarcely separate the two of them – that they were bound inexorably together, that they shared a common fate.

He started to run but forced himself to stop with the last ounce of resolution in him. For he must not run; he must in no wise attract attention to himself.

He lurched off the walk and collided with the trunk of a massive tree, and his hands went out to grasp and hug it, as if by the mere act of contact with something earthly he might gain some strength.

He stood there against the tree, hanging on as best he could – and hanging on was all. Slowly the terror began to drain back into some inner recess of his skull, crawling back into its hole, hiding piteously again.

It's all right, he told the thing. You stay right where you are. Don't worry. Leave everything to me. I will handle this.

It had tried to get away. It had tried its best to burst free of where it was and, having failed, now was pulling back into the one safe corner of the pen in which it found itself.

No more of this, Blaine thought. I can't afford another one like this. If another came, he knew, he could not stand against it. He could not keep himself from running from the terror, slobbering and screaming in horror as he ran. And that would be the end for him.

He let loose of the tree and stood stiff and straight beside it, forcing himself to stand stiff and straight against his weakness and his rubber legs. He felt the chill dampness of the perspiration which had started out on him and he was panting like a man who had run a race.

How could he run and hide, he asked himself; how could he get away with this monkey on his back? Himself alone was bad enough. He could not hope to do it if he had to drag along a frightened, whimpering alien.

But there was no way to lose the alien, no way he knew of at the moment to shake it loose of him. He was stuck with it and he must get along with it the best way that he could.

He moved out from the tree and went on down the walk, but more slowly and less surely, trying to still the shaking in him, trying to pump some strength into his wobbly legs. And through it all, he suddenly realized that he was ravenous with hunger. The wonder was, he told himself, that he had not sooner been aware of it, for except for the glass of milk, he had had no food for more than thirty hours. Rest – rest that had amounted to a deep, unbroken sleep – but not a bite of food.

The cars went sliding past, whispering on their airjets, with the soft, low murmur of the nuclear engines like an undertone.

One pulled to the curb just ahead of him, and a head stuck out.

'Shep,' said the head, 'how lucky! I was hoping I would find you.'

Blaine stood in panic for an instant and he felt the alien terror rising once again, but he crammed it back into its corner with every shred of mental power he had.

He made his voice calm and fought to keep it even.

'Freddy,' he said. 'It's a long time since I've seen you.'

For it was Freddy Bates, man of no apparent occupation, although it was vaguely understood that he represented someone or other in this place where almost every other person was a lobbyist or representative or petty diplomat or undercover agent.

Freddy opened the door.

'Hop in,' he said. 'We're going to a party.'

And this might be it, thought Blaine. This might be the way to start where he was going. It was better, certainly, than anything he had in mind. Fishhook would never in a million years think to find him at a party. And another thing: a party would be an easy place to slip away from. There would be so many people that none of them would notice when or where one of them might go. There would be, he was almost certain, at least one car with the key left carelessly in its ignition lock. There would be food – and he needed food.

'Come on,' said Freddy. 'It is one of Charline's parties.'

Blaine slid into the car and sank into the seat. The door hissed shut, and Freddy swung the car into a traffic lane.

'I told Charline,' said Freddy, settling down to chatter, 'that a party simply could not be a party without a soul from Fishhook. I volunteered to go out and snare a Fishhook personage.'

'You goofed,' Blaine told him shortly. 'I am no personage.'

'Except,' said Freddy, 'you travelers have such horrendous tales to tell.'

'You know,' said Blaine, 'that we never tell them.'

Freddy clicked his tongue. 'Secrecy,' he said.

'You're wrong,' said Blaine. 'It's rules and regulations.'

'Of course. And that's the reason rumor is a rampant wildfire in this town. Let something happen in the afternoon up here on the hill and by evening it is being told in the finest detail in the lowest dives.'

'But usually not correct.'

'Perhaps not in its more lurid and exact description, but at least in principle.'

Blaine did not answer. He settled back in the seat and turned his head toward the window, watching the lighted streets slide past and above the streets the massive, terraced blocks of buildings that were Fishhook. And marveled at the unfailing wonder of this sight which after all the years never failed to thrill him. Knowing as he thought it that it was not the sight itself, for there were grander in the world, but the fabulous significance which fell like a mantle on the city.

For here, he thought, in fact, if not in name, was the capital of Earth. Here lay the hope and greatness of the future, here was the human link with other worlds deep in outer space.

And he was leaving it.

Incredible as it seemed, with all his love of it and all his devotion to it and all his faith in it, he was running from it like a frightened rabbit.

'What are you guys going to do with all of it?' asked Freddy.

'All of what?'

'All the knowledge, all the secrets, all the concepts that you are raking in.'

'I wouldn't know,' said Blaine.

'Regiments of scientists,' said Freddy, 'working happily away. Corps of technologists doping out new angles. How far ahead of the rest of us are you – a million years or so?'

'You're talking to the wrong man,' said Blaine. 'I don't know a thing. I just do my job. And if you're needling me, you should know that I don't needle.'

'I'm sorry,' said Freddy. 'It's an obsession with me.'

'You and a million other people. Bitching at Fishhook is a worldwide pastime.'

'Look at it my way,' said Freddy, earnestly. 'I'm sitting on the outside. I'm not even looking in. Here I see this great monstrosity, this human paragon, this superhuman project, and I feel an envy of everyone who's in it and a sense of not belonging and distinctly second-rate. Do you wonder the world hates Fishhook's guts?'

'Do they?'

'Shep,' said Freddy, solemnly, 'you should get around.'

'No particular need. I hear enough of it without going anywhere. My question was: Do they hate Fishhook really?'

'I think they do,' said Freddy. 'Maybe not right here. All the talk in this town is mostly fashionable. But get out in the provinces. They really hate it there.'

The streets now were not so closely hemmed nor the lights so bright. There were fewer business places and the residences were thinning out. The traffic had diminished.

'Who'll be at Charline's?' asked Blaine.

'Oh, the usual crowd,' said Freddy. 'Plus this the usual zoo. She's the crazy sort. Without any inhibitions, scarcely with a social sense. You might bump into almost anyone.'

'Yes, I know,' said Blaine.

The thing stirred inside his brain, almost a sleepy stir.

It's all right, Blaine told it. Just settle down and snooze. We have got it made. We are on our way.

Freddy swung the car off the main road and followed a secondary that went winding up a canyon. The air took on a chill. In the dark outside one could hear the trees talking back and forth and there was the smell of pine.

The car turned an abrupt curve, and the house was shining on a bench above – a modernistic cliff dwelling plastered in the canyon's wall like a swallow's nest.

'Well,' said Freddy, joyously, 'here we finally are.'

5

The party was beginning to get noisy – not boisterous, but noisy. It was beginning to acquire that stale air of futility to which, in the end, all parties must fall victim. And there was something about it – about the sour smell of too many cigarettes, the chill of the canyon breeze through the open windows, the shrill and vacant sound of human chatter – that said it was getting late – late and time to go, although it really wasn't. It wasn't midnight yet.

The man named Herman Dalton stretched his long legs out, slumping in the chair, the big cigar thrust into one corner of his mouth, and his hair like a new-built brush pile from his running hands through it.

'But I tell you, Blaine,' he rumbled, 'there's got to be an end to it. The time will come, if something isn't done, when there'll be no such thing as business. Fishhook, even now, has driven us flat against the wall.'

'Mr Dalton,' Blaine told him wearily, 'if you must argue this, you should find someone else. I know nothing about business and even less of Fishhook despite the fact I work there.'

'Fishhook's absorbing us,' said Dalton, angrily. 'They're taking away our very livelihood. They're destroying a fine system of conventions and of ethics built very painfully through the centuries by men deeply dedicated to the public service. They are breaking down the commercial structure which has been built so carefully. They're ruining us, slowly and inexorably, not all of us at once, but surely, one by one. There is the matter, for example, of this so-called butcher vegetable. You plant a row of seeds, then later you go out and dig up the plants as you would potatoes, but rather than potatoes you have hunks of protein.'

'And so,' said Blaine, 'for the first time in their lives, millions of people are eating meat they couldn't buy before, that your fine, brave system of conventions and of ethics didn't allow them to earn enough to buy.'

'But the farmers!' Dalton yelled. 'And the meat market operators. Not to mention the packing interests ...'

'I suppose,' suggested Blaine, 'it would have been more cricket if the seeds had been sold exclusively to the farmers or the supermarkets. Or if they were sold at the rate of a dollar or a dollar and a half apiece instead of ten cents a packet. That way we'd keep natural meat competitive and the economy safe and sound. Of course, then, these millions of people—'

'But you do not understand,' protested Dalton. 'Business is the very lifeblood of our society. Destroy it and you destroy Man himself.'

'I doubt that very much,' said Blaine.

'But history proves the position of commercialism. It has built the world as it stands today. It opened up the new lands, it sent out the pioneers, it erected the factories and it—'

'I take it, Mr Dalton, you read a lot of history.'

'Yes, Mr Blaine, I do. I am particularly fond of—'

'Then, perhaps, you've noticed one other thing as well. Ideas and institutions and beliefs in time outlive their usefulness. You'll find it in page after page of all our history – the world evolves and the people and their methods change. Has it ever occurred to you that business as you think of it may have outlived its usefulness? Business has made its contribution and the world moves on. Business is just another dodo ...'

Dalton came straight out of his slump, his hair standing straight on end, the cigar dangling in his mouth.

'By God,' he cried, 'I believe you actually mean it. Is that what Fishhook thinks?'

Blaine chuckled dryly. 'No, it's what I think. I have no idea what Fishhook may be thinking. I am not in Policy.'

And that was the way it went, Blaine told himself. No matter where you went, that was the way it was. There was always someone who tried to root out a hint, a clue, a tiny secret that might pertain to Fishhook. Like a group of hopping vultures, like a bunch of peeping Toms – athirst to know what was going on, suspecting, perhaps, much more was going on than was actually the case.

The city was a madhouse of intrigue and of whispering and of rumor – filled with representatives and operatives and pseudo-diplomats. And this gent in the chair across from him, Blaine speculated, was here to place a formal protest against some new outrage perpetrated upon some proud commercial unit by some new Fishhook enterprise.

Dalton settled back into his chair. He got a fresh and deadly grip upon the big cigar. His hair fell back again, it seemed, into some semblance of once having known a comb.

'You say you're not in Policy,' he said. 'I believe you told me you are a traveler.'

Blaine nodded.

'That means that you go out in space and visit other stars.'

'I guess that covers it,' said Blaine.

'You're a parry, then.'

'I suppose you'd call me that. Although I'll tell you frankly it is not a name that is regularly employed in polite society.'

The rebuke was lost on Dalton. He was immune to shame.

'What's it like?' he asked.

'Really, Mr Dalton, I cannot begin to tell you.'

'You go out all alone?'

'Well, not alone. I take a taper with me.'

'A taper?'

'A machine. It gets things down on tape. It is full of all sorts of instruments, highly miniaturized, of course, and it keeps a record of everything it sees.'

'And this machine goes out with you—'

'No, damn it. I told you. I take it out with me. When I go out, I take it along with me. Like you'd take along a brief case.'

'Your mind and that machine?'

'That's right. My mind and that machine.'

'Think of it!' said Dalton.

Blaine did not bother with an answer.

Dalton took the cigar out of his mouth and examined it intently. The end that had been in his mouth was very badly chewed. The end of it was shredded, and untidy strips hung down. Grunting with concentration, he tucked it back into his mouth, twirling it a bit to wind up the shreds.

'To get back to what we were talking about before,' he announced pontifically. 'Fishhook has all these alien things and I suppose it is all right. I understand they test them rather thoroughly before they put them on the market. There'd be no hard feelings – no sir, none at all – if they'd only market them through regular retail channels. But they don't do that. They will allow no one to sell any of these items. They've set up their own retail outlets and, to add insult to injury, they call these outlets Trading Posts. As if, mind you, they were dealing with a bunch of savages.'

Blaine chuckled. 'Someone, long ago, in Fishhook must have had a sense of humor. Believe me, Mr Dalton, it is a hard thing to believe.'

'Item after item,' Dalton raged, 'they contrive to ruin us. Year by year they take away or cancel out commodities for which there was demand. It's a process of erosion that wears away at us. There's no vicious threat, there's just the steady chiseling. And I hear now that they may open up their transportation system to the general public. You realize what a blow that would strike at the old commercial setup.'

'I suppose,' said Blaine, 'it would put the truckers out of business and a number of the airlines.'

'You know very well it would. There isn't any transportation system that could compete with a teleportive system.'

Blaine said: 'It seems to me the answer is for you to develop a teleportive system of your own. You could have done it years ago. You've got a lot of people outside of Fishhook who could show you how it's done.'

'Crackpots,' said Dalton viciously.

'No, Dalton. Not crackpots. Just ordinary people who have the paranormal powers that put Fishhook where it is today – the very powers you admire in Fishhook but deplore in your own people.'

'We wouldn't dare,' said Dalton. 'There's the social situation.'

'Yes, I know,' said Blaine. 'The social situation. Are the happy little mobs still crucifying them?'

'The moral climate,' conceded Dalton, 'is at times confusing.'

'I should imagine so,' said Blaine.

Dalton took the cigar from his mouth and regarded it with something like disgust. One end of it was dead and the other badly frayed. After considering for a moment, he tossed it into a potted plant. It caught on the lower part of the greenery and dangled there obscenely.

Dalton leaned back and clamped his hands across his gut. He stared up at the ceiling.

'Mr Blaine,' he said.

'Yes?'

'You're a man of great discernment. And of integrity. And of a great impatience with fuddy-duddy thinking. You've brought me up short on a couple of matters and I liked the way you did it.'

'Your servant,' Blaine said, coldly.

'How much do they pay you?'

'Enough,' said Blaine.

'There's no such thing as enough. I never saw a man—'

'If you're trying to buy me, you're out of your ever-loving mind.'

'Not buy you. Hire you. You know the ins and outs of Fishhook. You know a lot of people. In a consultive capacity, you'd be invaluable. We'd be willing to discuss—'

'Excuse me, sir,' said Blaine, 'but I'd be entirely useless to you. Under the present circumstance, I'd be no good at all.'

For he'd been here for an hour and that was much too long. He'd eaten and he'd had a drink and he'd talked with Dalton – he'd wasted a lot of time on Dalton – and he must be getting on. For the word that he was here would filter back to Fishhook and before it did he must be far away.

There was a fabric rustle, and a hand fell on his shoulder.

'Shep,' said Charline Whittier, 'it was nice of you to come.'

He rose and faced her.

'It was good of you to ask me.'

She crinkled impish eyes at him. 'Did I really ask you?'

'No,' he said. 'Leave us be honest. Freddy dragged me in. I hope that you don't mind.'

'You know you're always welcome.' Her hand tightened on his arm. 'There's someone you must meet. You'll forgive us, Mr Dalton.'

'Certainly,' said Dalton.

She led Blaine away.

'You know,' he said, 'that was rather rude of you.'

'I was rescuing you,' she told him. 'The man's a frightful bore. I can't imagine how he got here. I'm sure I didn't ask him.'

'Just who is he?' asked Blaine. 'I'm afraid I never did find out.'

She shrugged bare and dimpled shoulders. 'The head of some business delegation. Down here to cry out their broken hearts to Fishhook.'

'He indicated that much. He's irate and most unhappy.'

'You haven't got a drink,' said Charline.

'I just finished one.'

'And you've had something to eat? You're having a good time? I have a new dimensino, the very latest thing …'

'Maybe,' said Blaine. 'Maybe later on.'

'Go and get another drink,' said Charline. 'I must say hello to some other of my guests. How about staying after? It's been weeks since I have seen you.'

He shook his head. 'I'm more sorry than I can tell you. It was nice of you to ask.'

'Some other time,' she said.

She moved away, but Blaine reached out and stopped her.

'Charline,' he said, 'did anyone ever tell you you're an awfully good egg?'

'No one,' she told him. 'Absolutely no one.'

She stood on tiptoe to kiss him lightly on the cheek.

'Now run along and play,' she said.

He stood and watched her move away into the crowd.

Inside him the Pinkness stirred, a question mark implicit in its stirring.

Just a while, Blaine told it, watching the crowd. *Let me handle it a little longer. Then we'll talk it over.*

And he felt the gratitude, the sudden tail-wag of appreciation for being recognized.

We'll get along, he said. We've got to get along. We're stuck with one another.

It curled up again – he could feel it curling up, leaving things to him.

It had been frightened to start with, it might become frightened again, but at the moment it was accepting the situation – and to it the situation, he knew, must seem particularly horrific, for this place was a far and frightening cry from the detachment and serenity of that blue room on the far-off planet.

He drifted aimlessly across the room, skirting the bar, pausing a moment to peer into the room which contained the newly installed dimensino, then heading for the foyer. For he must be getting on. Before morning light he either must be miles away or be well hidden out.

He skirted little jabbering groups and nodded at a few acquaintances who spoke to him or waved across the room.

It might take some time to find a car in which a forgetful driver had left the key. It might be – and the thought came with brutal force – he would fail to find one. And if that were the case, what was there to do? Take to the hills, perhaps, and hide out there for a day or two while he got things figured out. Charline would be willing to help him, but she was a chatterbox, and he would be a whole lot better off if she knew nothing of the matter. There was no one else he could think of immediately who could give him any help. Some of the boys in Fishhook would, but any help they gave him would compromise themselves, and he was not as desperate as all that. And a lot of others, of course, but each of them with an ax to grind in this mad pattern of intrigue and petition which surrounded Fishhook – and you could never know which of them to trust. There were some of them, he was quite aware, who would sell you out in the hope of gaining some concession or some imagined position of advantage.

He gained the entrance of the foyer and it was like coming out of some deep forest onto a wind-swept plain – for here the surflike chatter was no more than a murmuring, and the air seemed clearer and somehow a great deal cleaner. Gone was the feeling of oppression, of the crowding in of bodies and of minds, of the strange pulse beat and crosscurrent of idle opinion and malicious gossip.

The outer door came open, and a woman stepped into the foyer.

'Harriet,' said Blaine, 'I might have known you'd come. You never miss Charline's parties, I remember now. You pick up a running history of all that's happened of importance and—'

Her telepathic whisper scorched his brain: *Shep, you utter, perfect fool! What are you doing here? (Picture of an ape with a dunce cap on its head, picture of the south end of a horse, picture of a derisive phallic symbol.)*

'But, you—'

Of course. Why not (a row of startled question marks)? Do you think only in Fishhook? Only in yourself? Secret, sure – but I have a right to secrets. How else would a good newspaperman pick up (heaps of blowing dirt, endless flutter of statistics, huge ear with a pair of lips flapping loosely at it)?

Harriet Quimby said, sweetly, vocally: 'I wouldn't miss Charline's parties for anything at all. One meets such stunning people.'

Bad manners, said Blaine, reprovingly. For it was bad manners. There were only certain times when it was permissible to use telepathy – and never at a social function.

To hell with that, she said. Lay bare my soul for you and that is what I get. (A face remarkably like his with a thin, trim hand laid very smartly on it.) It is all over town. They even know you're here. They'll be coming soon – if they're not already here. I came as fast as I could immediately I heard. Vocalize, you fool. Someone will catch on. Us just standing here.

'You're wasting your time,' said Blaine. 'No stunning people here tonight. It's the poorest lot Charline has ever got together.'

Maybe. We have to take our chance. You are on the lam. Just like Stone. Just like all the others. I am here to help you.

He said: 'I was talking to some business lobbyist. He was an awful bore. I just stepped out to get a breath of air.' *Stone! What do you know of Stone?*

Never mind right now. 'In that case I'll be going. No use to waste my time.' *My car is down the road, but you can't go out with me. I'll go ahead and have the car out in front and running. You wander around awhile, then duck down into the kitchen (map of house with red guideline leading to the kitchen).*

I know where the kitchen is.

Don't muff it. No sudden moves, remember. No grim and awful purpose. Just wander like the average partygoer, almost bored to death. (Cartoon of gent with droopy eyelids and shoulders all bowed down by the weight of a cocktail glass he held limply in his hand, ears puffed out from listening and a frozen smile pasted on his puss.) But wander to the kitchen, then out the side door down the road.

'You don't mean you're leaving – just like that?' said Blaine. 'My judgment, I can assure you, is very often bad.' *But you? Why are you doing this? What do you get out of it? (Perplexed, angry person holding empty sack.)*

Love you. (Board fence with interlocked hearts carved all over it.)

Lie. (Bar of soap energetically washing out a mouth!)

'Don't tell them, Shep,' said Harriet. 'It would break Charline's heart.' *I'm a newspaperman (woman) and I'm working on a story and you are part of it.*

One thing you forgot. Fishhook may be waiting at the mouth of the canyon road.

Shep, don't worry. I've got it all doped out. We'll fool them yet.

'All right, then,' said Blaine. 'I won't say a word. Be seeing you around.' *And thanks.*

She opened the door and was gone, and he could hear the sound of her walking across the patio and clicking down the stairs.

He slowly turned around toward the crowded rooms and as he stepped through the door, the blast of conversation hit him in the face – the jumbled sound of many people talking simultaneously, not caring particularly what they said, not trying to make sense, but simply jabbering for the sake of jabber, seeking for the equivalent of conformity in this sea of noise.

So Harriet was a telly and it was something he would never have suspected. Although, if you were a news hen and you had the talent, it would make only common sense to keep it under cover.

Closemouthed women, he thought, and wondered how any woman could have managed to keep so quiet about it. Although Harriet, he reminded himself, was more newsman than she was woman. You could put her up there with the best of the scribblers.

He stopped at the bar and got a Scotch and ice and stood idly for a moment, sipping at it. He must not appear to hurry, he must never seem to be heading anywhere, and yet he couldn't afford to let himself be sucked into one of the conversational eddies – there wasn't time for that.

He could drop into the dimensino room for a minute or two, but there was danger in that. One got identified with what was going on too quickly. One lost one's sense of time; one lost everything but the situation which dimensino created. And it often was disturbing and confusing to drop into the middle of it.

It would not be, he decided, a very good idea.

He exchanged brief greetings with a couple of acquaintances; he suffered a backslapping reunion with a slightly inebriated gentleman he'd seen no longer than ten days before; he was forced to listen to two off-color stories; he went through a mild flirting routine with a simpering dowager who came charging out of ambush.

And all the time he moved steadily toward the door that led down to the kitchen. Finally he arrived.

He stepped through the doorway and went casually down the stairs.

The place was empty, a cold, metallic place with the gleam of chrome and the shine of high utility. A clock with a sweep second hand hung upon one wall and its whirring sound hung heavy in the room.

Blaine placed his glass, still half full of Scotch, on the nearest table, and there, six strides away, across the gleaming floor, was the outside door.

He took the first two steps and as he started on the third a silent shout of warning sounded in his brain and he spun around.

Freddy Bates stood beside the huge refrigerator, one hand jammed deep into a jacket pocket.

'Shep,' said Freddy Bates, 'if I were you, I wouldn't try it. Fishhook has the place tied up. You haven't got a chance.'

6

Blaine stood frozen for a second while wonder hammered at him. And it was surprise and bafflement, rather than either fear or anger, that held him frozen there. Surprise that, of all people, it should be Freddy Bates. Freddy, no longer the aimless man-about-town, the inconsequential mystery man in a town that was full of such as he, but an agent of Fishhook and, apparently, a very able one.

And another thing – that Kirby Rand had known and had allowed him to walk out of the office and go down the elevator. But grabbing for a phone as soon as he had reached the corridor to put Freddy on the job.

It had been clever, Blaine admitted to himself – much more clever than he himself had been. There had never been a moment that he had suspected Rand felt anything was wrong, and Freddy, when he picked him up, had been his normal, ineffectual self.

Anger soaked slowly into him, to replace the wonder. Anger that he had been taken in, that he had been trapped by such a jerk as Freddy.

'We'll just walk outside,' said Freddy, 'like the friends we are, and I'll take you back to have a talk with Rand. No fuss, no fight, but very gentlemanly. We would not want to do anything – either one of us – to cause Charline embarrassment.'

'No,' said Blaine. 'No, of course we wouldn't.'

His mind was racing, seeking for a way, looking for an out, anything at all that would get him out of this. For he was not going back. No matter what might happen, he wasn't going back with Freddy.

He felt the Pinkness stir as if it were coming out.

'No!' yelled Blaine. 'No!'

But it was too late. The Pinkness had crawled out and it filled his brain, and he was still himself but someone else as well. He was two things at once and it was most confusing and something strange had happened.

The room became as still as death except for the groaning of the clock upon the wall. And that was strange, as well, for until this very moment, the clock had done no groaning; it had whirred but never groaned.

Blaine took a swift step forward, and Freddy didn't move. He stayed standing there, with the hand thrust in the pocket.

And another step and still Freddy barely stirred. His eyes stayed stiff and staring and he didn't blink. But his face began to twist, a slow and tortured twist, and the hand in the pocket moved, but so deliberately that one only was aware of a sort of stirring, as if the arm and hand and the thing the hand clutched in the pocket were waking from deep sleep.

And yet another step and Blaine was almost on him, with his fist moving like a piston. Freddy's mouth dropped slowly open, as if the jaw hinge might be rusty, and his eyelids came creeping down in the caricature of a blink.

Then the fist exploded on his jaw. Blaine hit where he was aiming and he hit with everything he had, his torso twisting to follow through the blow. Even as he hit and the pain of contact slashed across his knuckles and tingled in his wrist, he knew it was all wrong. For Freddy had scarcely moved, had not even tried to defend himself.

Freddy was falling, but not as one should fall. He was falling slowly, deliberately, as a tree will topple when the final cut is made. In slow motion, he crumpled toward the floor and as he fell his hand finally cleared the pocket and there was a gun in it. The gun slipped from his flaccid fingers and beat him to the floor.

Blaine bent to scoop it up and he had it in his hand before Freddy hit the floor and he stood there, with the gun in hand, watching Freddy finally strike the floor – not actually striking it, but just sort of settling down on it and relaxing in slow motion on its surface.

The clock still groaned upon the wall, and Blaine swung around to look at it and saw that the second hand was barely crawling across the numbered face. Crawling where it should have galloped, and groaning when it should have whirred, and the clock, Blaine told himself, had gone crazy, too.

There was something wrong with time. The creeping second hand and Freddy's slow reaction was evidence of that.

Time had been slowed down.

And that was impossible.

Time did not slow down; time was a universal constant. But if time, somehow, had slowed down, why had not he been a party to it?

Unless –

Of course, unless time had stayed the way it was and he had been speeded up; had moved so fast that Freddy had not had the time to act, had been unable to defend himself, could under no circumstances have gotten the gun out of his pocket.

Blaine held his fist out in front of him and looked at the gun. It was a squat and ugly thing and it had a deadly bluntness.

Freddy had not been fooling, nor was Fishhook fooling. You do not pack a gun in a little game all filled with lightness and politeness. You do not pack a gun unless you're prepared to use it. And Freddy – there was no doubt of that – had been prepared to use it.

Blaine swung back toward Freddy and he was still upon the floor and he seemed to be most restful. It would be quite a little while before Freddy would be coming round.

Blaine dropped the gun into his pocket and turned toward the door and as he did so he glanced up at the clock and the second hand had barely moved from where he'd seen it last.

He reached the door and opened it and took one last glance back into the room. The room still was bright with chrome, still stark in its utility, and the one untidy thing within it was Freddy sprawled upon the floor.

Blaine stepped out of the door and moved along the flagstone walk that led to the long stone stairway that went slanting down across the great cliff face.

A man was lounging at the head of the stairs and he began to straighten slowly as Blaine raced down the walk toward him.

The light from one of the upstairs windows shone across the face of the straightening man, and Blaine saw the lines of outraged surprise, as if they were sculptured lines in a graven face.

'Sorry, pal,' said Blaine.

He shot his arm out, stiff from the shoulder, with the palm spread flat and caught the graven face.

The man reeled backward slowly, step by cautious step, tilting farther and farther backward with each step. In another little while he'd fall upon his back.

Blaine didn't wait to see. He went running down the stairs. Beyond the dark lines of parked vehicles stood a single car, with its taillights gleaming and its motor humming softly.

It was Harriet's car, Blaine told himself, but it was headed the wrong way – not down the road toward the canyon's mouth, but into the canyon's maw. And that was wrong, he knew, because the road pinched out a mile or two beyond.

He reached the bottom of the steps and threaded his way among the cars out into the road.

Harriet sat waiting in the car, and he walked around it and opened the door. He slid into the seat.

Weariness hit him, a terrible, bone-aching weariness, as if he had been running, as if he'd run too far. He sank into the seat and looked at his hands lying in his lap and saw that they were trembling.

Harriet turned to look at him. 'It didn't take you long,' she said.

'I got a break,' said Blaine. 'I hurried.'

She put the car in gear and it floated up the road, its airjets thrumming and the canyon walls picking up the thrumming to fling it back and forth.

'I hope,' said Blaine, 'you know where you are going. The road ends up here aways.'

'Don't worry, Shep. I know.'

He was too tired to argue. He was all beaten out.

And he had a right to be, he told himself, for he had been moving ten times (or a hundred times?) faster than he should, than the human body ever had been intended to. He had been using energy at a terrific rate – his heart had beat the faster, his lungs had worked the harder, and his muscles had gone sliding back and forth at an astounding rate.

He lay quietly, his mind agape at what had happened, and wondering, too, what had made it happen. Although the wonder was a formalized and an academic wonder, for he knew what it was.

The Pinkness had faded out of him, and he went hunting it and found it, snug inside its den.

Thanks, he said to it.

Although it seemed a little funny that he should be thanking it, for it was a part of him – it was inside his skull, it sheltered in his brain. And yet not a part of him, not yet a part of him. But a skulker no longer, a fugitive no more.

The car went fleeing up the canyon, and the air was fresh and cool, as if it had been new-washed in some clear mountain stream, and the smell of pine came down between the walls like the smell of a faint and delicate perfume.

Perhaps, he told himself, it had been with no thoughts of helping him that the thing inside his brain had acted as it did. Rather it might have been an almost automatic reflex action for the preservation of itself. But no matter what it was, it had saved him as surely as itself. For the two of them were one. No longer could either of them act independently of the other. They were bound together by the legerdemain of that sprawling Pinkness on that other planet, by the double of the thing that had come to live with him – for the thing within his mind was a shadow of its other self five thousand light years distant,

'Have trouble?' Harriet asked.

'I met up with Freddy.'

'Freddy Bates, you mean,'

'He's the one and only Freddy.'

'The little nincompoop.'

'Your little nincompoop,' said Blaine, 'was packing a gun and he had blood within his eyes.'

'You don't mean—'

'Harriet,' said Blaine, 'this is liable to get rough. Why don't you let me out –?'

'Not on your life,' said Harriet. 'I've never had so much fun in all my life.'

'You aren't going anywhere. You haven't much road left.'

'Shep, you may not think it to look at me, but I'm the intellectual type. I do a lot of reading and I like history best of all, bloody battle history. Especially if there are a lot of campaign maps to follow.'

'So?'

'So I've found out one thing. It is always a good idea to have a line of retreat laid out.'

'But not up this road.'

'Up this road,' she said.

He turned his head and watched her profile and she didn't look the part – not the hard-boiled newspaper gal that she really was. No chatter column writer nor a sob sister nor a society hen, but one of the dozen or so top-notch reporters spelling out the big picture of Fishhook for one of the biggest news-papers in North America.

And yet as chic, he thought, as a fashion model. Chic, without being sleek, and with an air of quiet assurance that would have been arrogance in any other woman.

There was nothing, he was sure, that could be known of Fishhook which she didn't know. She wrote with a strangely objective viewpoint, one might almost say detached, but even in that rare atmosphere of journalistic prose she injected a soft sense of human warmth.

And in the face of all of this, what was she doing here?

She was a friend, of course. He had known her for years, ever since that day shortly after she had arrived at Fishhook and they had gone to dinner at the little place where the old blind woman still sold roses. He had bought her a rose, he remembered, and being far from home and lonesome she had cried a little. But, he told himself, she'd probably not cried since.

Strange, he thought, but it all was strange. Fishhook, itself, was a modern nightmare which the outer world, in a century's time, had not quite accepted.

He wondered what it had been like, that century ago, when the men of science had finally given up, when they had admitted that Man was not for space. And all the years were dead and all the dreams were futile and Man had finally ended up in a little planetary dead-end. For then the gods had toppled, and Man, in his secret mind, had known that after all the years of yearnings, he had achieved nothing more than gadgets.

Hope had fallen on hard times, and the dreams had dwindled, and the trap closed tight – but the urge to space had refused to die. For there was a group of very stubborn men who took another road – a road that Man had missed, or deserted, whichever you might choose, many years ago and ever since that time had sneered at and damned with the name of magic.

For magic was a childish thing; it was an old wives' tale; it was something out of nursery books – and in the hard and brittle world of the road that Man had taken it was intolerable. You were out of your mind if you believed in magic.

But the stubborn men had believed in it, or at least in the principle of this thing which the world called magic, for it was not actually magic if one used the connotation which through the years had been placed upon the word. Rather it was a principle as true as the principles which underlay the physical sciences. But rather than a physical science, it was a mental science; it concerned the using of the mind and the extension of the mind instead of the using of the hands and the extensions of the hands.

Out of this stubbornness and this belief and faith Fishhook had arisen – Fishhook because it was a reaching out, a fishing into space, a going of the mind where the body could not go.

Ahead of the car the road swung to the right, then swiveled to the left, in a tightening curve. This was the turnaround; here the road came to an end.

'Hang on,' said Harriet.

She swung the car off the road and nosed it up a rocky stream bed that ran along one of the canyon walls. The airjets roared and blustered, the engines throbbed and howled. Branches scraped along the bubble top, and the car tilted sharply, then brought itself aright.

'This is not too bad,' said Harriet. 'There is a place or two, later on, where it gets a little rough.'

'This is the line of retreat you were talking about?'

'That's exactly right.'

And why, he wondered, should Harriet Quimby need a line of retreat? He almost asked her but decided not to.

She drove cautiously, traveling in the dry creek bed, clinging close against the wall of rock that came down out of darkness. Birds fled squawling from the bushes, and branches dragged against the car, screeching in their agony of tortured wood.

The headlights showed a sharp bend, with a barn-size boulder hemming in the wall of rock. The car slowed to a crawl, thrust its nose into the space between the boulder and the wall, swiveled its rear around and went inching through the space into the clear again.

Harriet cut down the jets, and the car sank to the ground, grating on the gravel in the creek bed. The jets cut out and the engine stopped and silence closed upon them.

'We walk from here?' asked Blaine.

'No. We only wait awhile. They'll come hunting for us. If they heard the jets, they'd know where we had gone.'

'You go clear to the top?'

'Clear to the top,' she said.

'You have driven it?' he asked.

'Many times,' she told him. 'Because I knew that if the time ever came to use it, I'd have to use it fast. There'd be no time for guessing or for doubling back. I'd have to know the trail.'

'But why, in the name of God—'

'Look, Shep. You are in a jam. I get you out of it. Shall we let it go at that?'

'If that's the way you want it, sure. But you're sticking out your neck. There's no need to stick it out.'

'I've stuck out my neck before. A good newsman sticks out the neck whenever there is need to.'

That might be true, he told himself, but not to this extent. There were a lot of newspapermen in Fishhook and he'd drunk with most of them. There were a few he could even call his friends. And yet no one of them – no one but Harriet – would do what she was doing.

So newspapering by itself could not be the answer. Nor could friendship be the entire answer, either. It was something more than either, perhaps a good deal more than either.

The answer might be that Harriet was not a newswoman only. She must be something else. There must be another interest and a most compelling one.

'One of the other times you stuck your neck out, did you stick it out for Stone?'

'No,' she said. 'I only heard of Stone.'

They sat in the car, listening, and from far down the canyon came the faint muttering of jets. The muttering came swiftly up the road, and Blaine tried to count them and it seemed that there were three, but he could not be sure.

The cars came to the turn-around and stopped, and men got out of them and tramped into the brush. They called to one another.

Harriet put out a hand and her fingers clamped around Blaine's arm.

Shep, what did you do to Freddy? (Picture of a grinning death's-head.)

Knocked him out, is all.

And he had a gun?

Took it away from him.

(Freddy in a coffin, with a tight smile on his painted face, with a monstrous lily stuck between his folded hands.)

No. Not that. (Freddy with a puffed-up eye, with a bloody nose, a cross-hatch of patches on his blotchy face.)

They sat quietly, listening.

The shouts of the men died away, and the cars started up and went down the road.

Now?

We'll wait, said Harriet. Three came up. Only two went back. There is still one waiting (a row of listening ears, all stretched out of shape with straining for a sound). They're sure we came up the road. They don't know where we are. This is (a gaping trap with jagged rows of teeth). They'll figure we'll think they went away and will betray ourselves.

They waited. Somewhere in the woods a raccoon whickered, and a bird, disturbed by some nighttime prowler, protested sleepily.

There is a place, said Harriet. *A place where you'll be safe. If you want to go there.*

Anyplace. I haven't any choice.

You know what the outside's like?

I've heard.

They have signs in some towns (a billboard with the words: PARRY, DON'T LET THE SUN SET ON YOU HERE). *They have prejudice and intolerance and there are (bearded, old-time preachers thumping pulpits; men clad in nightgowns, with masks upon their faces and rope and whip in hand; bewildered, frightened people cowering beneath a symbolic bramblebush).*

She said in a vocal whisper: 'It's a dirty, stinking shame.'

Down on the road the car had started up. They listened to it leave.

'They gave up finally,' said Harriet. 'They may still have left a man behind, but we'll have to chance that.'

She started the engine and turned up the jets. With the lights switched on, the car nosed up the stream bed. The way grew steeper and the bed pinched out. The car moved along a hog's back, dodging clumps of bushes. They picked lip a wall of rock again, but it was on the left side now. The car dipped into a crevasse no more than a paint-layer distant away from either side and they inched along it. The crevasse pinched sharply out, and they were on a narrow ledge with black rock above and black emptiness below. For an eternity they climbed, and the wind grew chill and bitter and finally before them was a flatness, flooded by a moon dipping toward the west.

Harriet stopped the car and slumped in the seat.

Blaine got out and fumbled in his pocket for a pack of cigarettes. He finally found it and there was only one left in the pack. It was very badly crumpled. He straightened it out carefully and lit it. Then he walked around the car and stuck it between Harriet's lips.

She puffed on it gratefully.

'The border's up ahead,' she said. 'You take the wheel. Another fifty miles across country. Very easy going. There's a little town where we can stop for breakfast.'

7

The crowd had gathered across the street from the restaurant. It was clustered thickly about Harriet's car and it was watching closely and it was deadly silent. Ugly, but not noisy. Angry, and perhaps just slightly apprehensive, perhaps just on the edge of fear. Angry, more than likely, because it was afraid.

Blaine pressed his back against the wall of the restaurant where, a few minutes before, they had finished breakfast. And there had been nothing wrong at breakfast. It had been all right. No one had said a thing. No one stared at them. Everything had been normal and very commonplace.

'How could they tell?' asked Blaine.

'I don't know,' said Harriet.

'They took down the sign.'

'Or maybe it fell over. Maybe they never had one. There are some that don't. It takes a lot of belligerence to put up a sign.'

'These babies look belligerent enough.'

They may not be after us.'

'Maybe not,' he said. But there was no one else, there was nothing else against which they would be banded.

Listen closely, Shep. If something happens. If we are separated. Go to South Dakota. Pierre in South Dakota (map of the United States with Pierre marked with a star and the name in big red letters and a purple road that led from this tiny border town to the city on the wide Missouri).

I know the place, said Blaine.

Ask for me at this restaurant (the facade of a building, stone-fronted, big plate windows with an ornate, silver-mounted saddle hanging in one window, a magnificent set of elk antlers fixed above the door). It's up on the hill, above the river. Almost anyone will know me. They can tell you where I am.

We won't get separated.

But if we do, you mind what I say.

Of course I will, said Blaine. You have lugged me this far. I'll trust you all the way.

The crowd was beginning to seethe a little – not actually moving, but stirring around, beginning to get restless, as if it might be gently frothing. And a murmur rose from it, a sullen, growling murmur without any words.

An old crone pushed through it and shambled out into the street. She was an ancient thing. What could be seen of her – her head, her hands, her bare and muddy feet – was a mass of wrinkles. Her hair was dirty, ragged white and it drooped in wisps all about her head.

She lifted a feeble arm, from which flabby muscles hung like an obscene pouch, and she pointed a crooked, bony, quavering forefinger straight in Blaine's direction.

'That is him,' she screamed. 'He is the one I spotted. There's something queer with him. You can't get into his brain. It's like a shining mirror. It—'

The rest of what she said was drowned out in the rising clamor of the crowd, which began moving forward – not rapidly, but foot by foot – edging along toward the two against the wall, as if it might be fearful and reluctant but pushed along by a civic duty that was greater than its fear.

Blaine put his hand into his jacket pocket and his fingers closed around the gun he'd scooped up in Charline's kitchen. But that was not the way, he knew. That would only make it worse. He pulled his hand out of the pocket and let it dangle at his side.

But there was something wrong – he was standing all alone, just his human self. There was no Pinkness in him, no stir inside his brain. He was a naked human and wondered wildly, for a moment, if he should be glad or not. And then he caught it peeping out of one corner of his brain and he waited for it, but nothing happened and the questioning segment of it pulled out of consciousness again.

There was fury and loathing in the faces that floated atop the mass of human bodies moving in the street. Not the night-shrouded baying of the mob, but the slantwise, daylight slinking of a pack of wolves, and in the forefront of the press, borne along on the edge of this wave of human hatred, was the withered crone who had pointed with her finger to set the pack in motion.

'Stand still,' Blaine said to Harriet. 'That is our only chance.'

Any moment now, he knew, the situation could hit a crisis point. The mob would either lose its nerve and waver, or some slight incident, some smallest motion, some spoken word, would send it forward with a rush.

And if that happened, he knew, he would use the gun. Not that he wanted to, not that he intended to – but it would be the one thing left to do.

But for the moment, in the little interval before violence could erupt, the town stood petrified – a sleepy little town with shabby, two-storey business buildings, all in need of paint, fronting on a sun-baked street. Scraggy trees stood at infrequent intervals, and there were faces at the upstairs windows, staring out in astonishment at the potential animal padding in the street.

The mob moved closer, circling, still cautious, and mute; all its murmur quieted, all its hate locked tight behind the savage masks.

A foot clicked sharply on the sidewalk, then another foot, and still another one – the rugged, steady sound of someone's stolid walking.

The footsteps came closer, and Blaine turned his eyes a second to catch out of the corner of them the sight of a tall, angular almost cadaverous man who strode along deliberately, for all the world as if he were out for a morning stroll. The man reached Blaine and stood to one side of him and then he turned and faced the mob. He never said a word; he just stayed standing there. But the crowd came to a halt and stood there in the street in a dreadful quietness.

Then a man said: 'Good morning to you, Sheriff.'

The sheriff didn't stir; he didn't say a word.

'Them is parries,' said the man.

'Who says so?' asked the sheriff.

'Old Sara, she says so.'

The sheriff looked at the crone: 'How about it, Sara?'

'Tom is right,' Old Sara screeched. 'That one there, he has a funny mind. It bounces back at you.'

'And the woman?' asked the sheriff.

'She is with him, ain't she?'

'I am ashamed of you,' the sheriff said, as if they all were naughty children. 'I have a mind to run you in, every one of you.'

'But them is parries!' yelled a stricken voice. 'You know we don't allow no parries here.'

'Now, I tell you what,' the sheriff said. 'You all get back to business. I'll take care of this.'

'The both of them?' a voice asked.

'Why, I don't know,' the sheriff said. 'The lady ain't no parry. I just kind of figured we'd run her out of town and that would be enough.'

He said to Harriet: 'Are you with this man?'

'And I'm staying with him!'

No! said Blaine. *(A sign for silence, finger to the lips.)*

Fast, hoping that no one would catch it, for in a town like this even a telepath might be in for trouble.

But the warning must be sounded.

'That your car across the street?' the sheriff asked.

Harriet shot a questioning glance at Blaine.

'Yes, it is,' she said.

'Well, I tell you, miss. You just trot over to it and get out of here. The folks will let you through.'

'But I don't intend—'

Blaine said: 'You better do it, Harriet.'

She hesitated.

'Go ahead,' he said.

She stepped slowly off the sidewalk, then turned back.

'I'll be seeing you,' she said to Blaine.

She glanced with contempt at the sheriff. 'Cossack,' she declared.

The sheriff didn't mind. He'd never heard the term.

'Beat it, lady,' he said, and his voice was almost kindly.

The crowd parted to let her through, but buzzed angrily. She reached the car and turned to wave at Blaine. Then she got into the seat and started the motor, gunned the jets and swung the car sharply out into the street. The crowd fled, shrieking, tumbling over one another to get out of the way, blinded by the screaming dust that was spun up by the jets.

The sheriff watched with monumental calm as the car roared down the street.

'You see that, Sheriff!' roared an outraged victim. 'Why don't you run her in?'

'Served you right,' the sheriff said. 'You started all of this. Here I was getting ready for a restful day and you got me all stirred up.'

He didn't look stirred up.

The protesting crowd pushed toward the sidewalk, arguing violently.

The sheriff waved his hands, as if he were shooing chickens.

'Get along with you,' he told them. 'You have had your fun. Now I got to get to work. I got this guy to jail.'

He turned to Blaine. 'Come along with me,' he said.

They walked down the street together toward the courthouse.

'You ought to have known better,' said the sheriff. 'This town is hell on parries.'

'No way to tell,' said Blaine. 'There wasn't any sign.'

'Blew down a year or two ago,' the sheriff told him. 'No one had the gumption to set it up again. Really should have a new sign. Old one got pretty rickety. You could hardly read the lettering on it. Sand storms scoured off the paint.'

'What do you intend to do with me?'

The sheriff said: 'Not too much, I reckon. Hold you for a while until the folks cool down. For your own protection. As soon as it is safe, I'll get you out of here.'

He was silent for a moment, considering the situation.

'Can't do it right away,' he said. 'The boys will be watching mighty close.'

They reached the courthouse and climbed the steps. The sheriff opened the door. 'Straight ahead,' he said.

They walked into the sheriff's office, and the sheriff closed the door.

'You know,' said Blaine, 'I don't believe you've got the grounds to hold me. What would happen if I just walked out of here?'

'Nothing much, I guess. Not right away, at least. I certainly wouldn't stop you, although I'd argue some. But you wouldn't get out of town. They'd have you in five minutes.'

'I could have left in the car.'

The sheriff shook his head. 'Son, I know these people. I was raised with them. I am one of them. I know how far I can go with them and when I've got to stop. I could get the lady off, but not the both of you. You ever see a mob in action?'

Blaine shook his head.

'It ain't a pretty sight.'

'How about this Sara? She's a parry, too.'

'Well, I tell you, friend. Sara has good blood behind her. Fell on evil times, but her family's been here for more than a hundred years. The town just tolerates her.'

'And she's handy as a spotter.'

The sheriff shook his head and chuckled. 'There ain't much,' he said, with local pride, 'that filters past our Sara. She has a busy time of it, watching all the strangers that come into town.'

'You catch a lot of parries that way?'

'Tolerable,' said the sheriff. 'Every now and then. A tolerable number, I would say.'

He motioned at the desk. 'Just dump your pockets there. The law says I got to do it. I'll fix up a receipt for you.'

Blaine began digging in his pockets. Billfold, card case, handkerchief, key ring, matches and, finally, the gun.

He lifted it out rather gingerly and laid it with the other stuff.

The sheriff eyed it. 'You had that all the time?'

Blaine nodded.

'And you never reached for it?'

'I was too scared to reach for it.'

'You got a permit for it?'

'I don't even own it.'

The sheriff whistled softly through his teeth.

He picked up the gun and broke it. There was the coppery shine of cartridge cases.

The sheriff opened a desk drawer and tossed it in.

'Now,' he said, as if relieved, 'I've got something legal I can hold you on.'

He picked up the book of matches and handed them to Blaine.

'You'll want these for smoking.'

Blaine put them in his pocket.

'I could get you cigarettes,' the sheriff said.

'No need,' Blaine told him. 'I carry them sometimes, but I don't do much smoking. Usually I wear them out carrying them before I get around to smoking.'

The sheriff lifted a ring of keys off a nail. 'Come along,' he said.

Blaine followed him into a corridor that fronted on a row of cells.

The sheriff unlocked the nearest one, across the corridor from the door.

'You've got it all alone,' he said. 'Ran the last one out last night. Boy who came across the border and got himself tanked up. Figured he was as good as white folks.'

Blaine walked into the cell. The sheriff banged and locked the door.

'Anything you want,' he said, with a fine show of hospitality, 'just yell out and say so. I'll get it for you.'

8

It had gone by many names.

Once it had been known as extrasensory perception. And then there had been a time when it had been psionics, psi for short. But first of all it had been magic.

The medicine man, with the oxides that he used for paint, with his knucklebones to rattle in the skull, with his bag of nauseous content, may have practiced it in a clumsy sort of way before the first word had been written – grasping at a principle he did not understand, more than likely not even knowing that he did not understand, not realizing there was anything he ought to understand. And the knowledge was passed on, from hand to inept hand. The witch doctor of the Congo used it, the priests of Egypt knew it, the wise men of Tibet were acquainted with it. And in all these cases it was not wisely used and it was not understood and it got mixed up with a lot of mumbo jumbo and in the days of reason it became discredited and there was scarcely anyone who believed in it.

Out of the days of reason rose a method and a science, and there was no place for magic in the world that science built – for there was no method in it and there was no system in it and it could not be reduced to a formula or equation. So it was suspect and it was outside the pale and it was all stupid foolishness. No man in his right mind would once consider it.

But they called it PK now for paranormal kinetics, which was too long to say. And the ones who had it they called parries and shut them up in jails and did even worse than that.

It was a queer business, once one thought of it – for despite the strange gulf which lay between PK and science, it had taken the orderly mind which science had drummed into the human race to make PK finally work.

And, strange as it might seem, Blaine told himself, it had been necessary that science should come first. For science had to be developed before Man could understand the forces which had freed his mind from the shackles in which they had been bound, before mental energy could be tapped and put to work by those who quite unsuspectingly had always carried with them that power and energy. For even in the study of PK there had been a need for method, and science had been the training ground in which method had developed.

There were those who said that in some distant past two roads had forked for mankind, one of them marked 'Magic' and the other 'Science', and that Man had taken the 'Science' road and let the 'Magic' go. Many of these people then went on to say that Man had made a great mistake in the choosing of the roads. See how far we'd have gone, they said, if we had taken 'Magic' at the first beginning.

But they were wrong, Blaine said, talking to himself, for there had never been two roads; there'd only been the one. For Man had had to master science before he could master magic.

Although science had almost defeated magic, had almost driven it into limbo with laughter and with scorn.

And would have driven it had there not been stubborn men who had refused to give up the dream of stars. Men who had been willing to do anything at all, to brave the laughter of the world, to accept derision, if they only could lay hands upon the stars.

He wondered how it must have been in those days when Fishhook had been no more than a feeble hope, a glimmer of the mind, an article of faith. For the little band of hopeful, stubborn men had stood entirely by themselves. When they had asked for help, there had been no help, but only scornful chuckling against such errant foolery.

The press had made a field day of it when they had appeared in Washington to ask financial aid. There had, quite naturally, been no such aid forthcoming, for the government would have naught to do with such a wildcat scheme. If science in all its might and glory had failed to reach the stars, how could there be hope that such as these might do it? So the men had worked alone, except for such pittances as they might be given here and there – a small grant from India, another from the Philippines and a little from Columbia – plus dribbles that came in from metaphysical societies and a few sympathetic donors.

Then finally a country with a heart – Mexico – had invited them to come, had provided money, had set up a study center and a laboratory, had lent encouragement rather than guffaws of laughter.

And almost from that day, Fishhook had become reality, had developed into an institution which did credit not to itself alone, but to the country which had opened up its heart.

And I am a part of it, thought Blaine, sitting in his cell; a part of this virtually secret society, although secret through no fault of its own. Made secret, rather, by the envy and intolerance and the surging superstition of the entire world. Even though I am running from it, even though it be hunting me, I am still a part of it.

He got up from the tiny bunk with its dirty blanket and stood at the window, staring out. He could see the sun-baked street and the scraggly trees staggered on the boulevard and across the street the sad, defeated business houses with a few dilapidated cars parked against the curb, some of them so ancient they were equipped with wheels which in turn were driven by internal combustion engines. Men sat on the steps that led up to the store fronts, chewing tobacco and spitting out onto the sidewalks, creating little pools of sticky amber liquid which looked like old bloodstains. They sat there languidly and chewed and occasionally talked among themselves, not looking at the courthouse, looking nowhere in particular, but being very nonchalant about their deadly loafing.

But they were watching the courthouse, Blaine knew. They were watching him – the man with the mirror in his mind. The mind, Old Sara told the sheriff, that bounces back at you.

And that had been what Kirby Rand had seen, that had been what had tipped him off and set Fishhook on the trail. Which meant that Rand, if he were not a peeper, then certainly was a spotter. Although, Blaine thought, it didn't really matter whether Rand was a peeper or a spotter, for a peeper would have little luck in reading a mind that bounced right back at you.

And that meant, Blaine realized, that he carried in his mind the equivalent of a flashing warning light for anyone with the ability to see. There'd be nowhere he'd be safe. There'd be no place he could hide. He'd ring a loud and angry bell for any peeper or any spotter or any hounder that came within his range.

He'd not been that way before. He was quite certain of it. Someone would have mentioned it or it would have been on his psych report.

You, he said to the hider in his mind, *come out of there!*

It wagged its tail. It wriggled like a happy dog. It did not come out.

Blaine went back to the bunk and sat down on the edge of it.

Harriet would be back with some sort of help. Or maybe the sheriff would let him go before then, as soon as it was safe. Although the sheriff didn't have to, for the sheriff had good grounds to hold him – the possession of the gun.

Buster, he said to his boon companion, *it may be up to you again. We may need another trick.*

For the thing inside his mind had come up with a trick before – a very trick in time. Or metabolism? There was no way of knowing which, whether he had moved faster than was customary or whether time had been slowed down for everyone but him.

And when he got away, what then?

Up to South Dakota, as Harriet had said?

He might as well, he told himself, for he had no other plans. There had been no time in which he could make any plans. It had been a bare, bald matter of getting out of Fishhook's clutches. Years ago, he told himself, he should have laid his plans, but it had seemed a far thing then. It had seemed a circumstance that could never happen to him. So here he was, stuck inside a jail cell in a little town of which he did not even know the name, with no more than fifteen dollars and that locked in the sheriff's desk.

He sat and listened to a gasoline car come stuttering down the street, and somewhere a bird was chirping. And he was in a jam, he admitted to himself – he was in an awful jam.

The men were waiting out there, sitting on the steps, trying very hard not to seem to watch the courthouse, and he did not like the looks of it.

The door in the sheriff's office opened and banged again, and there was the sound of feet moving on the floor. Voices came indistinctly, and Blaine didn't try to listen. What was the use of listening? What was the use of anything?

Then the sheriff's deliberate tread moved across the office and out into the corridor. Blaine looked up as the sheriff stopped just outside his cell.

'Blaine,' the sheriff said, 'the Father's here to see you.'

'What father?'

'The priest, you heathen. The pastor of this parish.'

'I can't understand,' said Blaine, 'why he'd be interested.'

'You're a human being, aren't you?' said the sheriff. 'You have got a soul.'

'I will not deny it.'

The sheriff regarded him with a stern and puzzled look. 'Why didn't you tell me that you were from Fishhook?'

Blaine shrugged. 'What difference would it make?'

'Good God, man,' the sheriff said, 'if the folks in this town knew you were from Fishhook, they'd be in to string you up. They might let just a simple parry slip through their fingers, but not a man from Fishhook. They burned down the Trading Post three years ago last month, and the factor got out of town just ahead of them.'

'And what would you do about it,' Blaine demanded, 'if they decided I needed stringing up?'

The sheriff scratched his head. 'Well, naturally, I'd do the best I could.'

'Thanks a lot,' said Blaine. 'I suppose you contacted Fishhook.'

'I told them to come and get you. Take you off my hands.'

'That's a pal,' said Blaine.

The sheriff proceeded to get sore.

'Why did you come blundering into this town?' he demanded, with quite a lot of heat. 'This is a quiet, peaceable, decent place until folks like you show up.'

'We were hungry,' said Blaine, 'and we stopped to get some breakfast.'

'You stuck your head into a noose,' the sheriff told him, sternly. 'I hope to God I can get you out of it.'

He started to turn away and then turned back.

'I'll send the Father in,' he said.

9

The priest came into the cell and stood for a moment, blinking in the dimness.

Blaine stood and said to him: 'I am glad you came. The best I can offer you is a seat here on the bunk.'

'It's all right,' said the priest. 'I thank you. I am Father Flanagan and I hope I'm not intruding.'

'Not in the least,' said Blaine. 'I am glad to see you.'

Father Flanagan eased himself to a seat upon the bunk, groaning a little with the effort. He was an aged man who ran to corpulence, with a kindly face and withered hands that looked as if they might be crippled by arthritis.

'Sit down, my son,' he said. 'I hope I don't disturb you. I warn you at the outset that I'm a horrible busybody. It would come, I would suspect, from being the shepherd to a group of people who are largely children, irrespective of their years. Is there anything you would like to talk about?'

'Anything at all,' said Blaine, 'except possibly religion.'

'You are not a religious man, my son?'

'Not particularly,' said Blaine. 'Whenever I consider it, I tend to become confused.'

The old man shook his head. 'These are ungodly days. There are many like you. It is a worry to me. To Holy Mother Church as well. We have fallen on hard times of the spirit, with many of the people more concerned with fear of evil than contemplation of the good. There is talk of werewolf and incubus and devil, and a hundred years ago all fear of such had been washed out of our minds.'

He turned his body ponderously and sat sidewise the better to face Blaine.

'The sheriff tells me,' he said, 'that you come from Fishhook.'

'There is no use,' said Blaine, 'of my denying it.'

'I have never talked with anyone from Fishhook,' the old priest said, mumbling just a little, as if he might be talking to himself rather than to Blaine. 'I have only heard of Fishhook, and some of the stories I have heard of it are incredible and wild. There was a factor here for a time before the people burned the Post, but I never went to see him. The people would not have understood.'

'From what happened here this morning,' Blaine agreed, 'I rather doubt they would have.'

They say you are a paranormal ...'

'Parry is the word,' Blaine told him. 'No need to dress it up.'

'And you are really one?'

'Father, I am at a loss to understand your interest.'

'Just academic,' said Father Flanagan. 'I can assure you, purely academic. Something that is of interest to me personally. You are as safe with me as if you were in a confessional.'

There was a day,' said Blaine, 'when science was deeply suspect as the hidden foe of all religious truth. We have the same thing here.'

'But the people,' said Father Flanagan, 'are afraid again. They close and bar their doors. They do not go out of night. They have hex signs – hex signs, mind you, instead of the blessed crucifix – hanging on their gates and the gables of their houses. They whisper of things which have been dead and dust since the Middle Ages. They tremble in the smoky chimney corners of their minds. They have lost much of their ancient faith. They go through all the rituals, of course, but I see it in their faces, I sense it in their talk, I glimpse it in their minds. They have lost the simple art of faith.'

'No, Father, I don't think they have. They're just very troubled people.'

'The entire world is troubled,' said Father Flanagan.

And that was right, Blaine told himself – the entire world was troubled. For it had lost a cultural hero and had not been able to acquire another for all that it had tried. It had lost an anchor which had held it against the winds of illogic and unreason and it was now adrift upon an ocean for which there was no chart.

At one time science had served as the cultural hero. It had logic and reason and ultimate precision that probed down into the atom and out to the farther edge of space. It spawned gadgets by the millions for the comfort of its worshipers and it placed the hand and eye of Man upon the entire universe, by proxy. It was something you could trust in, for it was the sum of human wisdom among many other things.

But principally it was translated into machines and machine technology, for science was an abstract, but machines were something that anyone could see.

Then there came the day when Man, for all his wondrous machines, for all his famed technology, had been driven back from space, had been whipped howling from the heavens back to the den of Earth. And that day the cultural god of science had shone a bit less brightly, had died a little in the people's minds.

And that other day, when Man had gone to the stars without the benefit of machines, the worship of technology had died for good and all. Machines and technology and science itself still existed, still were in daily use, still were of vast importance, but they no longer formed a cult.

For while Fishhook used machines, they were not machines as such – not machines that could be accepted by the common mass of mankind. For they had no pistons and no wheels, no gears, no shafts, no levers, not a single button – they had nothing of the component parts of a commonplace machine. They were strange and alien and they had no common touch.

So Man had lost his cultural hero, and since his nature was so fashioned that he must have some abstract hero-worship, because he must always have an ideal and a goal, a vacuum was created that screamed aloud for filling.

Paranormal kinetics, for all its strangeness, for all its alien concept, filled the bill exactly. For here, finally, were all the crackpot cults completely justified; here, at last, was the promise of ultimate wish-fulfillment; here was something exotic enough, or that could be made exotic, to satisfy the depth of human emotion such as a mere machine never had been able.

Here, so help us God, was magic!

So the world went off on a magic jag.

The pendulum had swung too far, as always, and now was swinging back, and the horror of intolerance had been loosed upon the land.

So Man once again was without a cultural hero, but had acquired instead a neosuperstition that went howling through the dark of a second Middle Ages.

'I have puzzled much upon the matter,' said Father Flanagan. 'It is something which naturally must concern even so unworthy a servant of the Church as I. For whatever may concern the souls and the minds of men is of interest to the Church and to the Holy Father. It has been the historic position of Rome that we must so concern ourselves.'

Blaine bowed slightly in recognition of the sincerity of the man, but there was a fleck of bitterness in his voice when he answered: 'So you've come to study me. You are here to question me.'

There was sadness in the old priest's voice. 'I prayed you would not see it in this light. I have failed, I see. I came to you as to someone who could help me and, through me, the Church. For, my son, the Church at times needs help. It is not too proud to say so, for all that it has been charged, through all its history, with excessive pride. You are a man, an intelligent man, who is a part of this thing which serves to puzzle us. I thought that you might help me.'

Blaine sat silent, and the priest sat looking at him, a humble man who sought a favor, and yet with a sense of inner strength one could not help but feel.

'I would not mind,' said Blaine. 'Not that I think for a moment it would do any good. You're a part of what is in this town.'

'Not so, my son. We neither sanction nor condemn. We do not have facts enough.'

'I'll tell you about myself,' said Blaine, 'if that is what you want to know. I am a traveler. My job is to go out to the stars. I climb into a machine – well, not exactly a machine, rather it's a symbolic contrivance that helps me free my mind, that possibly even gives my mind a kick in the right direction. And it helps with the navigation. Look, Father, this is hard to say in simple, common terms. It sounds like gibberish.'

'I am following you with no difficulty.'

'Well, this navigation. That's another funny thing. There are factors involved that there is no way to put one's tongue to them. In science it would be mathematics, but it's not actually mathematics. It's a way of getting there, of knowing where you're going.'

'Magic?'

'Hell, no – pardon me, Father. No, it isn't magic. Once you understand it, once you get the feel of it, it is clear and simple and it becomes a part of you. It is as natural as breathing and as easy as falling off a log. I would imagine—'

'I would think,' said Father Flanagan, 'that it is unnecessary to go into the mechanics of it. Could you tell me how it feels to be on another star?'

'Why,' Blaine told him, 'no different than sitting here with you. At first – the first few times, that is – you feel obscenely naked, with just your mind and not your body ...'

'And your mind wanders all about?'

'Well, no. It could, of course, but it doesn't. Usually you stuff yourself inside the machine you took along with you.'

'Machine?'

'A monitoring contraption. It picks up all the data, gets it down on tape. You get the entire picture. Not just what you see yourself – although it's not actually seeing; it's sensing – but you get it all, everything that can possibly be caught. In theory, and largely in practice, the machine picks up the data, and the mind is there for interpretation only.'

'And what do you see?'

Blaine laughed. 'Father, that would take longer than either of us have.'

'Nothing like on Earth?'

'Not often, for there are not too many Earth-like planets. Proportionately, that is. There are, in fact, quite a lot in number. But we're not limited to Earth-like planets. We can go anywhere it is possible for the machine to function, and the way those machines are engineered, that means almost anywhere ...'

'Even to the heart of another sun?'

'Not the machine. It would be destroyed. I imagine that the mind could. But it's not been done. So far as I know, that is.'

'And your feelings? What do you think?'

'I observe,' said Blaine. 'That is what I go for.'

'You do not get the feeling you're lord of all creation? You do not have the thought that Man holds all the universe in the hollow of his hand?'

'If it's the sin of pride and vanity you're thinking of, no, never. You sometimes get a thrill at knowing where you are. You're often filled with wonder, but more often you are puzzled. You are reminded, again and yet again, of how insignificant you are. And there are times when you forget that you are human. You're just a blob of life – brother to everything that ever existed or ever will exist.'

'And you think of God?'

'No,' said Blaine. 'I can't say I ever do.'

'That is too bad,' said Father Flanagan. 'It is rather frightening. To be out there alone ...'

'Father, at the very start I made it plain to you that I was not inclined to be a religious sort of man – not in the accepted sense, that is. And I played square with you.'

'So you did,' said Father Flanagan.

'And if your next question is going to be: Could a religious man go out to the stars and still retain his faith; could he go out and come back full of faith; would traveling to the stars take away something of the true belief he held? Then I'd have to ask you to define your terms.'

'My terms?' asked Father Flanagan, amazed.

'Yes, faith, for one thing. What do you mean by faith? Is faith enough for Man? Should he be satisfied with faith alone? Is there no way of finding out the truth? Is the attitude of faith, of believing in something for which there can be no more than philosophic proof, the true mark of a Christian? Or should the Church long since—'

Father Flanagan raised a hand. 'My son!' he said. 'My son!'

'Forget it, Father. I should not have said it.'

They sat for a moment, regarding one another; neither understanding. As if we were two aliens, thought Blaine. With viewpoints that did not come within a million miles of coinciding, and yet they both were men.

'I am truly sorry, Father.'

'No need to be. You said it. There are others who believe it, or think it, but would never say it. You at least are honest.'

He reached out and patted Blaine slowly on the arm.

'You are a telepath?' he asked.

'And a teleporter. But limited. Very limited.'

'And that is all?'

'I don't know. I've never dug around.'

'You mean you may have other abilities you are not aware of?'

'Look, Father, in PK you have a certain mental capacity. First, you are the simple things, the easy things – the telepath, the teleport, the huncher. You

49

go on from there – or there are some who do. You grow. Some stop growing after a time and others keep on growing. Each of these abilities is not a separate ability; the abilities themselves are simply manifestations of a wholeness of the mind. They are, lumped together, the mind working as it always should have worked, even from the very first, if it had had its chance.'

'And it is not evil?'

'Certainly. Wrongly used, it's evil. And it was wrongly used by a lot of people, a lot of amateurs who never took the time to understand or to analyze the power they had. But Man has misused his hands, as well. He killed, he stole—'

'And you are not a warlock?'

Blaine wanted to laugh – the laugh was rising in him – but he could not laugh. There was too much terror for a man to laugh.

'No, Father, I swear to you. I am not a warlock. Nor a werewolf. Nor a –'

The old man raised his hand and stopped him.

'Now we're even,' he declared. 'I, too, said something I should not have said.'

He rose stiffly from the bunk and held out his hand, the fingers twisted by arthritis or whatever it was that might be wrong with them.

'Thank you,' he said. 'God help you.'

'And you'll be here tonight?'

'Tonight?'

'When the people of this town come to take me out and hang me? Or do they burn them at the stake?'

The old man's face twisted in revulsion. 'You must not think such things. Surely not in this—'

'They burned down the Trading Post. They would have killed the factor.'

'That was wrong,' said Father Flanagan. 'I told them that it was. For I am certain members of my parish participated. Not that they were alone in it, for there were many others. But they should have known better. I have worked for years among them against this very sort of thing.'

Blaine put out his hand and grasped the hand of Father Flanagan. The crippled fingers closed with a warm, hard grip.

'The sheriff is a good man,' said the priest. 'He will do his best. I will talk to some of them myself.'

'Thank you, Father.'

'My son, are you afraid to die?'

'I don't know. I have often thought I wouldn't be. I'll have to wait and see.'

'You must have faith.'

'Perhaps I will. If ever I can find it. You'll say a prayer for me?'

'God watch over you. I'll pray away the blessed afternoon.'

10

Blaine stood at the window and watched them gather in the dusk – not quickly, but slowly; not boisterously, but quietly, almost nonchalantly, as if they might be coming into town for a program at the schoolhouse or a meeting of the grange or some other normal and entirely routine function.

He could hear the sheriff stirring quietly about in the office across the corridor and he wondered if the sheriff knew – although assuredly he did, for he had lived in this town long enough to know what it was apt to do.

Blaine stood at the window and reached up and grasped the metal bars, and out beyond the bars, somewhere in the unkempt trees on the courthouse lawn, a bird was singing his last song of evening before cuddling on a branch and going fast asleep.

And as he stood there watching, the Pinkness crept out of its corner and floated in his mind, expanding until it filled his mind.

I have come to be with you, it seemed to say. *I am done with hiding. I know about you now. I have explored every nook and cranny of you and I know the kind of thing you are. And through you, the kind of world you're in – and the kind of world I'm in, for it is my world now.*

No more foolishness? asked that part of the strange duality that continued to be Blaine.

No more foolishness, said the other. *No more screaming, no more running, no more trying to get out.*

Except there was no death. There was no such thing as death, for the ending of a life was inexplicable. It simply could not happen, although dimly, far back in memory, there seemed there had been others it might have happened to.

Blaine left the window and went back to sit down on the bunk and he was remembering now. But the memories were dim and they came from far away and from very long ago and one could not be sure at once if they were truly memories or if they were no more than quaint imagining.

For there were many planets and many different peoples and a host of strange ideas and there were jumbled bits of cosmic information that lay all helter-skelter like a pile of ten billion heaped-up jackstraws.

'How are you feeling?' asked the sheriff, who had come so quietly across the corridor that Blaine had not heard him coming.

Blaine jerked up his head. 'Why, all right, I suppose. I have just been watching your friends out across the street.'

The sheriff chuckled thinly. 'No need to fear,' he said. 'They haven't got the guts to even cross the street. If they do, I'll go and talk with them.'

'Even if they know that I am Fishhook?'

'That's one thing,' the sheriff said, 'that they wouldn't know.'

'You told the priest.'

'That's different,' said the sheriff. 'I had to tell the father.'

'And he would tell no one?'

'Why should he?' asked the sheriff.

And there was no answer; it was one of those questions which could not be answered. 'And you sent a message.'

'But not to Fishhook. To a friend who'll send it on to Fishhook.'

'It was wasted effort,' Blaine told him. 'You should not have bothered. Fishhook knows where I am.'

For they'd have hounders on the trail by now; they would have picked up the trail many hours ago. There had been but one chance for him to have escaped – to have traveled rapidly and very much alone.

They might be in this very town tonight, he thought, and a surge of hope flowed through him. For Fishhook would scarcely let a posse do him in.

Blaine got up from the bunk and crossed over to the window.

'You better get out there now,' he told the sheriff. 'They're already across the street.'

For they had to hurry, naturally. They must get what they had to do done quickly before the fall of deeper night. When darkness fell in all obscurity, they must be snug inside their homes, with the doors double-locked and barred, with the shutters fastened, with the drapes drawn tight, with the hex signs bravely hanging at every opening. For then, and only then, would they be safe from the hideous forces that prowled the outer darkness, from banshee and werewolf, from vampire, goblin, sprite.

He heard the sheriff turning and going back across the corridor, back into the office. Metal scraped as a gun was taken from a rack, and there was a hollow clicking as the sheriff broke the breech and fed shells into the barrels.

The mob moved like a dark and flowing blanket and it came in utter silence aside from the shuffling of its feet.

Blaine watched it, fascinated, as if it were a thing that stood apart from him, as if it were a circumstance which concerned him not at all. And that was strange, he told himself knowing it was strange, for the mob was coming for him.

But it made no difference, for there was no death. Death was something that made no sense at all and nothing to be thought of. It was a foolish wastefulness and not to be tolerated.

And who was it that said that?

For he knew that there was death – that there must be death if there were evolution, that death was one of the mechanisms that biologically spelled progress and advancement for evolutionary species.

You, he said to the thing within his mind – a thing that was a thing no longer, but was a part of him – *it is your idea. Death is something that you can't accept.*

But something that in all truth must surely be accepted. For it was an actuality, it was an ever-presence, it was something that everything must live with through the shortness of its life.

There was death and it was close – much too close for comfort or denial. It was in the mumble of the mob just outside the building, the mob that now had passed from sight and quit its shuffling, that even now was massed outside the courthouse entrance, arguing with the sheriff. For the sheriff's booming voice came clearly through the outer door, calling upon those outside to break up and go back to their homes.

'All that this will get you,' yelled the sheriff, 'is a belly full of shot.'

But they yelled back at him, and the sheriff yelled again and it went back and forth for quite a little while. Blaine stood at the inner bars and waited, and fear seeped into him, slowly at first, then faster, like an evil tide racing through his blood.

Then the sheriff was coming through the door and there were three men with him – angry men and frightened, but so purposeful and grim their fright was covered up.

The sheriff came across the office and into the corridor, with the shotgun hanging limply from his hand. The other three strode close upon his heels.

The sheriff stopped just outside the bars and looked at Blaine, trying to conceal the sheepishness he wore.

'I am sorry, Blaine,' he said, 'but I just can't do it. These folks are friends of mine. I was raised with a lot of them. I can't bear to shoot them down.'

'Of course you can't,' said Blaine, 'you yellow-bellied coward.'

'Give me them keys,' snarled one of the three. 'Let's get him out of here.'

'They're hanging on the nail beside the door,' the sheriff said.

He glanced at Blaine.

'There's nothing I can do,' he said.

'You can go off and shoot yourself,' said Blaine. 'I'd highly recommend it.'

The man came with the key, and the sheriff stepped aside. The key rattled in the lock.

Blaine said to the man opening the door, 'There is one thing I want understood. I walk out of here alone.'

'Huh!' said the man.

'I said I want to walk alone. I will not be dragged.'

'You'll come the way we want you,' growled the man.

'It's a small thing,' the sheriff urged. 'It wouldn't hurt to let him.'

The man swung the cell door open. 'All right, come on,' he said.

Blaine stepped out into the corridor, and the three men closed in, one on either side of him, the other one behind. They did not raise a hand to touch him. The man with the keys flung them to the floor. They made a clashing sound that filled the corridor, that set Blaine's teeth on edge.

It was happening, thought Blaine. Incredible as it seemed, it was happening to him.

'Get on, you stinking parry,' said the man behind him and punched him in the back.

'You wanted to walk,' said another. 'Leave us see you walk.'

Blaine walked, steadily and straight, concentrating on each step to make sure he did not stumble. For he must not stumble; he must do nothing to disgrace himself.

Hope still lived, he told himself. There still was a chance that someone from Fishhook might be out there, set to snatch him from them. Or that Harriet had gotten help and was coming back or was already here. Although that, he told himself, was quite unlikely. She'd not had time enough and she could not have known the urgency involved.

He marched with steady stride across the sheriff's office and down the hall to the outer door, the three men who were with him pressing close against him.

Someone was holding the outer door, with a gesture of mock politeness, so he could pass through.

He hesitated for an instant, terror sweeping over him. For if he passed that door, if he stood upon the steps outside, if he faced the waiting mob, then all hope was gone.

'Go on, you filthy bastard,' growled the man behind him. 'They are waiting out there for you.'

The man put a hand behind his shoulder blades and shoved. Blaine staggered for a step or two, then was walking straight again.

And now he was across the doorway, now he faced the crowd!

An animal sound came boiling up from it – a sound of intermingled hate and terror, like the howling of a pack of wolves on a bloody trail, like the snarling of the tiger that is tired of waiting, with something in it, too, of the whimper of the cornered animal, hunted to its death.

And these, thought Blaine, with a queer detached corner of his mind, were the hunted animals – the people on the run. Here was the terror and the hate and envy of the uninitiate, here the frustration of those who had been left out, here the intolerance and the smuggery of those who refused to understand, the rear guard of an old order holding the narrow pass against the outflankers of the future.

They would kill him as they had killed others, as they would kill many more, but their fate was already settled, the battle already had been won.

Someone pushed him from behind and he went skidding down the smooth stone steps. He slipped and fell and rolled, and the mob closed in upon him. There were many hands upon him, there were fingers grinding into muscles, there was the hot foul breath and the odor of their mouths blowing in his face.

The many hands jerked him to his feet and pushed him back and forth. Someone punched him in the belly and another slapped him hard across the face and out of the bull-roaring of the crowd came one bellowing voice: 'Go on, you stinking parry, teleport yourself! That's all you have to do. Just teleport yourself.'

And that was most fitting mockery – for there were very few indeed who could teleport themselves. There were the levitators who could move themselves through the air like birds, and there were many others, like Blaine, who could teleport small objects, and others, also like Blaine, who could teleport their minds over many light years, but with the help of weird machines. But the true self-teleport, who could snap his body from one location to another in the fraction of an instant, was extremely hard to come by.

The crowd took up the mocking chant: 'Teleport yourself! Teleport! Teleport! Teleport yourself, you dirty, stinking parry!' Laughing all the time at their cleverness, smirking all the time at the indignity thus heaped upon their victim. And never for a moment ceasing to use hands and feet upon him.

There was a warmness running down his chin, and one lip felt puffed and swollen, and there was a saltiness in his mouth. His belly ached and his ribs were sore, and the feet and fists still kept punching in.

Then another bellowing voice roared about the din: 'Cut that out! Leave the man alone!'

The crowd fell back, but they still ringed him in, and Blaine, standing in the center of the human circle, looked around it and in the last faint light of dusk saw the rat eyes gleaming, and flaked saliva on the lips, sensed the hate that rose and rolled toward him like a body smell.

The circle parted and two men came through – one a small and fussy man who might have been a bookkeeper or a clerk, and the other a massive bruiser with a face that looked as if it were a place where chickens scratched in their search for grubs and worms. The big man had a rope coiled on one arm and from his hand he dangled one end of the rope fashioned very neatly into a hangman's noose.

The two of them stopped in front of Blaine, and the small man turned slightly to face one segment of the circle.

'Gents,' he said, in a voice that any funeral director would have been proud to own, 'we must conduct ourselves with a certain decency and dignity. We have nothing personal against this man, only against the system and the abomination of which he is a part.'

'You tell 'em, Buster!' yelled an enthusiastic voice from the fringes of the crowd.

The man with the funeral director's voice held up a hand for silence.

'It is a sad and solemn duty,' he said unctuously, 'that we must perform, but it is a duty. Let us proceed with it in a seemly fashion.'

'Yeah,' yelled the enthusiast, 'let us get it done with. Let's hang the dirty bastard!'

The big man came close to Blaine and lifted up the noose. He dropped it almost gently over Blaine's head so that it rested on his shoulders. Then he slowly tightened it until it was snug about the neck.

The rope was new and prickly and it burned like a red-hot iron, and the numbness that had settled into Blaine's body ran out of him like water and left him standing cold and empty and naked before all eternity.

All the time, even while it had been happening, he had clung subconsciously to the firm conviction that it could not happen – that he couldn't die this way; that it could and did happen to many other people, but not to Shepherd Blaine.

And now death was only minutes distant; the instrument of death already put in place. These men – these men he did not know, these men he'd never know – were about to take his life.

He tried to lift his hands to snatch the rope away, but his arms would not stir from where they hung limply from his shoulders. He gulped, for there already was the sense of slow, painful strangulation.

And they hadn't even begun to hang him yet!

The coldness of his empty self grew colder with the chill of overwhelming fear – fear that took him in its fist and held him stiff and rigid while it froze him solid. The blood, it seemed, stopped running in his veins and he seemed to have no body and the ice piled up and up inside his brain until he thought his skull would burst.

And from some far nether region of that brain came the fleeting realization that he no longer was a man, but mere frightened animal. Too cold, still too proud to whimper, too frozen in his terror to move a single muscle – only kept from screaming because his frozen tongue and throat could no longer function.

But if he could not scream aloud, he screamed inside himself. And the scream built up and up, a mounting tension that could find no way to effect release. And he knew that if no release were found in another instant he would blow apart from the sheer pressure of the tension.

There was a split second – not of blackout, but of unawareness – then he stood alone and he was cold no longer.

He stood on the crumbling brick of the ancient walk that led up to the courthouse entrance, and the rope was still about his neck, but there was no one in the courthouse square. He was all alone in an empty town!

11

There was less of dusk and more of light and there was a quietness that was unimaginable.

There was no grass.

There were no trees.

There were no men, nor any sign of men.

The courthouse lawn, or what had been the lawn, stretched naked down to the asphalt street. There was no grass upon the lawn. It was soil and pebble. Not dried-out grass or killed-out grass, but not any grass at all. As if there had never been such a thing as grass. As if grass never had existed.

With the rope still trailing from his neck, Blaine slowly pivoted to look in all directions. And in all directions it was the self-same scene. The courthouse still stood starkly against the last light of the day. The street was still and empty, with cars parked at the curb. The store fronts lined the street, their windows staring blindly.

There was one tree – lone and dead – standing at the corner beside the barber shop.

And no men anywhere. No birds or song of birds. No dogs. No cats. Nor an insect humming. Perhaps, thought Blaine, not even a bacteria or a microbe.

Cautiously, almost as if afraid by doing so he might break the spell, Blaine put up his hands and loosened the rope. He slipped it over his head and tossed it to the ground. He massaged his neck carefully with one hand, for the neck still stung. There were little prickles in it, where tiny pieces of the fiber had broken off and still stuck in the skin.

He took a tentative step and found that he could walk, although his body still was sore from the casual beating it had taken. He walked out into the street and stood in the middle of it, and looked up and down its length. It was deserted so far as he could see.

The sun had set, and dark was not far off and that meant, he told himself, that he had come back just a little time.

And stood astounded, frozen in the middle of the street, that he should have known.

For he did know! Without a doubt he knew exactly what he had accomplished. Although he thought he must have done it without a conscious effort, almost instinctively, a sort of conditioned reflex action to escape the danger.

It was something that he had no way of knowing how to do, that a short minute earlier he would have sworn would be impossible that he do. It was something that no human had ever done before, that no human would have ever dreamed of trying.

For he had moved through time. He had gone into the past a half an hour or so.

He stood in the street, attempting to recall how he might have done it, but all he could remember was the mounting terror that had come rolling, wave on wave, to drown him. There was one answer only: he had done it as a matter of deep-seated knowledge which he had not been aware of having and had accomplished it only as a final, desperate, instinctive effort – as one might, without thinking, throw up an arm to ward off an unexpected blow.

As a human it would have been beyond his capability, but it would not, undoubtedly, have been impossible for the alien mind. As a human being he did not have the instinct, did not have even the beginning of the necessary know-how. It was an ability even outside the pale of paranormal action. There was no question of it: the only way he could have snapped himself through time was by the agency and through the courtesy of the alien mind.

But the alien mind, it seemed, had left him; it was no longer with him. He hunted it and called it, and there was no trace and there was no answer.

He turned to face the north and began to walk, keeping to the center of the street, marching through this ghost town of the past.

The graveyard of the past, he thought. No life anywhere. Just the dead, bare stone and brick, the lifeless clay and wood. And where had gone the life? Why must the past be dead?

And what had happened to that mind the alien on the distant star had exchanged with him?

He sought for it again and he could not find it, but he did find traces of it; he found the spoor of it, tiny, muddy footprints that went across his brain; he found bits and pieces that it had left behind – strange, chaotic memories and straws of exotic, disconnected information that floated like flecks of jetsam in a frothy tide.

He did not find it, but he found the answer to its going – the instinctive answer that suddenly was there. The mind had not gone and left him. It had, rather, finally, become a part of him. In the forge of fright and terror, in the chemistry of danger, there had been a psychologic factor that had welded the two of them together.

And yet he still was human. Therefore, he told himself, the answer must be false. But it kept on persisting. There was no reason to it and there was no logic – for if he had two minds, if he were half human and half alien, there would be a difference. A difference he would notice.

The business part of the street had dwindled to shabby residences, and up ahead of him he could see where the village ended – this village which half an hour ago (or a half an hour ahead?) had been most intent upon the killing of him.

He halted for a moment and looked back and he could see the courthouse cupola and remembered that he'd left everything he owned back there, locked in the sheriff's desk. He hesitated a moment, wondering if he should go back. It was a terrible thing to be without a dollar to his name, with all his pockets empty.

If he went back, he thought, he could steal a car. If there were none with the keys left in the lock, he could short-circuit the ignition. He should have thought of it before, he told himself. The cars were standing there, waiting to be taken.

He turned and started back. He took two steps, then wheeled about again.

He didn't dare to go back. For he was safely out. There was nothing that could persuade him – money or car or anything – to go back into the village.

The light was waning and he headed northward, settling down to rolling up some distance – not running, but walking fast, with long, loose strides that ate up the very road.

He passed out of the village and came into the country and here there was an even greater loneliness, an even greater barrenness. A few dead cotton-woods lined the stream that ran down the valley, and ghostly fence posts stood in ragged rows – but the land was naked, without a weed, with-out a blade of grass. And the wind had a crying in it as it swept across the wasteland.

The darkness deepened and the moon came up, a blotch-faced mirror with the silver cracked and blackened, to cast a pallid light upon the arid stretch of earth.

He reached a rough plank bridge that crossed the tiny stream and stopped to rest a second and glance back along his trail. Nothing moved; there was nothing following. The village was some miles behind, and up on the hill above the stream stood the ramshackle bones of some forgotten farm – a barn, what looked like a hog pen, several dilapidated outhouses and the house itself.

Blaine stood and sucked the air into his lungs, and it seemed to him that the very air itself was dead. It had no sparkle in it. There was no smell in it and hardly any taste.

He reached out a hand to rest it on the bridge, and his hand went through the plank. It reached the plank and went into the plank and through it and there was nothing there. There wasn't any plank; there wasn't any bridge.

He tried again. For, he told himself, he might have missed it, he might have reached out for it and fallen short of it and only imagined his hand going through the plank. Moonlight, he reminded himself, is tricky stuff to see by.

So this time he was very careful.

His hand still went through the plank.

He back away from the bridge for a step or two, for it suddenly had become a thing – not of menace, perhaps – but a thing of which one must be very careful. It was nothing to depend on. It was a fantasy and delusion; it was a ghost that stood spraddled on the road. If he had walked out on it, he told himself, or tried to walk upon it, he would have been tumbled down into the stream bed.

And the dead trees and the fence posts – were they delusions, too?

He stood stock-still as the thought came to him: was it all delusion? For an illogical moment he did not dare to stir, scarcely dared to breathe, for any disturbance he might make might send this frail and unreal place crashing down into the dust of dreary nothingness.

But the ground was solid underneath his feet, or it seemed quite solid. He pressed one foot hard against it, and the ground still held. Cautiously he lowered himself to his knees and felt the ground with spread-out hand, kneading his fingers against it as if to test its consistency, running his fingers through the dust down to the hardness of the earth.

This was foolishness, he told himself, angry with himself – for he had walked this road and it had not shattered beneath the impact of his footsteps; it had held up beneath him.

But even so this was a place where one could not be sure; this was a place where there seemed to be no rules. Or at least a place where you were forced to figure out the rules, like: *Roads are real, but bridges aren't.*

Although it wasn't that, at all. It was something else. It would all basically have to do with the fact there was no life within this world.

This was the past and it was the dead past; there were only corpses in it – and perhaps not even corpses, but the shadows of those corpses. For the dead tree and the fence posts and the bridges and the buildings on the hill all would classify as shadows. There was no life here; the life was up ahead. Life must occupy but a single point in time, and as time moved forward, life moved with it. And so was gone, thought Blaine, any dream that Man might have ever held of visiting the past and living in the action and the thought and viewpoint of men who'd long been dust. For the living past did not exist, nor did the human past except in the records of the past. The present was the only valid point for life – life kept moving on, keeping pace with the present, and once it had passed, all traces of it or its existences were carefully erased.

There were certain basic things, perhaps – the very Earth, itself – which existed through every point in time, holding a sort of limited eternity to provide a solid matrix. And the dead – the dead and fabricated – stayed in the past as ghosts. The fence posts and the wire strung on them, the dead trees, the farm buildings and the bridge were shadows of the present persisting in the past. Persisting, perhaps, reluctantly, because since they had no life they could not move along. They were bound in time and stretched through time and they were long, long shadows.

He was, he realized with a shock, the only living thing existing in this moment on this Earth. He and nothing else.

He rose from his knees and dusted off his hands. He stood looking at the bridge, and in the brightness of the moonlight there seemed nothing wrong with it. And yet he knew the wrongness of it.

Trapped, he thought. If he did not know how to get out of here, then surely he was trapped – and he did not know.

There was nothing in all of human experience which gave him any chance or any hope to know.

He stood silent in the road, wondering how human he could be, how much humanity there still might be left to him. And if he were not entirely human, if there still were alienness, then he had a chance.

He felt human, he told himself – yet how was he to judge? For he still would be himself if he were entirely alien. Human, half-human, or not human in the slightest, he still would be himself. He'd scarcely know the difference. There was no other outside point from which he would stand and judge himself with anything like objectivity.

He (or whatever he might be) had known in a time of terror and of panic how to slip into the past, and it stood to reason that, knowing that, he likewise should know how to slide back into the present, or what had been his present – back to that point in time, whatever one might call it, where life was possible.

But the hard, cold fact was there: he had no idea of how it might be done!

He looked about him, at the antiseptic coldness of the moonlight-painted land, and a shudder started at the core of him. He tried to stop the shudder, for he recognized it as the prelude to unreasoned terror, but the shudder would not stop.

He gritted mental teeth, and the shudder kept on growing and suddenly he knew – with one corner of his mind, he knew.

Then there was the sound of wind blowing in the cottonwoods – and there'd been no cottonwoods before. Something, too, had happened to the shudder, for it was there no longer. He was himself again.

There were insects, fiddling stridently somewhere in the grass and bushes, and there were flecks of light moving in the night to betray the lightning bug. And through the shuttered window of the house up on the hill came thin, strangled shafts of light.

He turned off the road and walked down into the stream bed, stepped through the foot-deep water and up the other bank among the cottonwoods.

He was back again, back where he'd started from. He'd come from past to present and he'd done it by himself. For a fleeting moment, at the very end of it, he had caught the method, but it had slipped from him again and he did not know it now.

But that did not matter. He was safely home.

12

He woke before morning light, when the birds first began to chirp, and made his way up the hill to the garden patch just below the house. He got three ears of corn, he dug into a hill of potatoes, he dug up a butcher plant and noted with some satisfaction that it had four steaks upon it.

Back in the grove of cottonwoods, he searched through his pockets until he found the book of matches the sheriff had let him keep of all the stuff he had. He flipped back the cover and saw there were three matches left.

Regarding the three matches gravely, he thought of that day long ago when he had to pass a Boy Scout test by the lighting of a fire with a single match. Was he that good now? he wondered, chuckling at the thought.

He found a dead tree trunk and dug into the heart of it to get punk that was powder-dry. He selected dead, dry twigs. He rustled up some bigger wood, still paying close attention to its dryness, for the fire must be as smokeless as it was possible to make it. There was every reason he should not advertise his presence.

On the road above him the first car of the day went past, and far off a cow was bellowing.

The fire started on the second match, and he nursed it carefully, building it bit by bit with the adding of more twigs and finally larger twigs until there came a time when he could put on some of the bigger wood. The fire burned clear and smokeless, and he sat down beside it to wait for it to burn into a bed of coals.

The sun was not yet up, but the light in the east was growing brighter and there was a coolness on the land. Below him the creek ran chattering across its bed of pebbles. Blaine drew in a deep breath of the morning air and it tasted good.

He was still alive and in the land of other people and he had food to put into his belly – but what did he do next? He had no money – he had nothing but a single match and the clothes he stood in. And he had a mind that would betray him – a mind, the old crone had said, that would bounce back at you. He would be a sitting duck for any peeper, any spotter, that should chance across him.

He could hide by day and walk by night, for it would be safe to be abroad at night when others kept inside. He could raid orchards and gardens for his food. He could keep alive and make a few miles every night, but it would be slow going.

There must, he told himself, be some other way.

He put more wood on the fire and it still burned bright without any smoke. He went down to the stream and lay flat upon his belly and drank from the singing water.

Had he been mistaken, he asked himself, to run away from Fishhook? No matter what had awaited him in Fishhook, the situation in which he now found himself probably was worse. For he was a fugitive now from everyone; there was no one he could trust.

He lay staring down into the stream bed, looking at the pebbles – looking at one pebble, a red one that gleamed like polished ruby. He took the pebble into his mind and he saw what it was made of and the structure of its crystals and he knew where it had come from and he could trace its wanderings through millennia.

Then he tossed it from his mind and took in another pebble, a shiny bit of quartz.

There was something wrong here!

This was something he'd never done before!

And yet he had been doing it as if it were a commonplace performance and nothing at which one should wonder.

He pushed his body up and hunkered by the stream, his human sense aghast, but still not entirely startled – for he was still himself, no matter what he was.

He sought the alienness again and it wasn't there; it did not reveal itself, but he knew that it was there. It still was there, he knew, with its grab bag of senseless memories, with its cockeyed abilities, with its crazy logic and its topsy-turvy values.

In his mind's eye he saw a strange parade of purple geometric figures lurching across a desert of pure gold, with a blood-red sun hanging in a sulfur sky and nothing else in sight. And in the fleetness of that moment he knew the location of the place and the meaning of it and coordinates of a fantastic cosmographic system that could get him there. Then it was gone – the figures and the knowledge.

He got slowly to his feet and went back to the fire and by this time there was a bed of coals. He found a stick and scratched out a hollow in the coals and put in the potatoes and the corn, still wrapped in its husks, and used the stick to scratch the coals back across the hollow. Breaking a green branch off a sapling, he used it as a fork to broil one of the steaks.

Squatted beside the fire, with the warmth of it upon his face and hands, he felt a smug contentment that seemed strangely out of place – the contentment of a man who had reduced his needs to the strictly basic – and with the contentment came a full-bodied confidence that was just as out of place. It seemed almost as if he could look ahead and see that everything would be all right. But it was not prescience. There were hunchers who had prescience or who seemed to have it, but he was not one of them. It was rather as if he could sense ahead of him the pattern of all rightness, but with no specific detail, with no idea of the future's shape, nor of its direction. An assurance only, something that was akin to a plain, old-fashioned hunch, a feeling for the future – but nothing more than that.

The steak was sizzling and he could smell the potato baking and he grinned at steak and baked potato as a breakfast menu. Although it was all right. There was nothing at the moment that was not all right.

He remembered Dalton slumped spineless in the chair, with the clenched cigar and the brush-pile hair, raging at the butcher plant as another outrage committed upon the businessman by the maliciousness of Fishhook. And he tried to recall from what planet of which sun the butcher plant had come, and the name, it seemed to him, should be at his command, although he could not put it on his tongue.

The butcher plant, he thought, and how many other things? What would be the total score if all of Fishhook's contributions should be totaled up?

There were the drugs, for one thing, an entire new pharmacopoeia brought from other stars to alleviate and to cure the ills of Man. And as a result of this, all of Man's old bugaboos, all of his old killers, were being held at bay. Given another generation – given, at the most, two more generations – and the entire concept of illness would be wiped off the human slate. The human race would then emerge as a people healthful both in body and in mind.

There were new fabrics and new metals and many different foodstuffs. There were new architectural ideas and materials; there were new perfumes, unfamiliar literatures, alien principles in art. And there was dimensino, an entertainment medium that had replaced all the standard human entertainment – the movies, radio and TV.

For in dimensino you did not merely see and hear; you participated. You became a part of the portrayed situation. You identified yourself with one of the characters, or with more than one of them, and you lived out the action and emotion. For a time you ceased to be yourself; you became the person of your choice in the drama dimensino created.

Almost every home had its dimensino room, rigged with the apparatus, which picked up the weird, alien impulses that made you someone else – that lifted you out of the commonplace, out of the humdrum rut of your ordinary life and sent you off on wild adventure or on strange assignments or pitched you headlong into exotic places and fantastic situations.

And all of these, the food, the fabrics, the dimensino, were monopolies of Fishhook.

For all of these, thought Blaine, Fishhook had gained the hatred of the people – the hatred of not understanding, of being left outside, of being helped as no other single agency had ever helped the human race.

The steak was done, and Blaine propped the greenwood stick against a bush while he dug into the coals to hook out the potatoes and the corn.

He sat beside the fire and ate as the sun came up and the breeze died down and the world, on the threshold of another day, appeared to hold its breath. The first sunlight came through the grove of cottonwoods and turned some of the leaves into golden coins, and the brook grew hushed as the day-time sounds took up – the bawling of the cattle on the hill above, the hum of cars passing on the road, the distant drone of a cruising plane far up in the sky.

On the road, down by the bridge, a closed panel truck pulled up and stopped. The driver got out and lifted the hood and crawled halfway under it. Then he crawled out again and went back to the cab. Inside of it he hunted until he found what he was looking for, then got out again. He placed a kit of tools on the fender and unwrapped it, and the clinking of the tools as he unwrapped them came clearly up the hill.

It was an ancient truck – gas engine and with wheels, but it had some jet assistance. There were not many such vehicles left, except, perhaps, in junk yards.

An independent operator, Blaine told himself. Getting along the best he could, competing with the big truck lines by cutting down his rates and keeping down his overhead in any way he could.

The truck's original paint had faded and peeled off in places, but painted over this, in sharp fresh color, were complicated hex signs, guaranteed, no doubt, to fend off the evil of the world.

The truck, Blaine saw, had an Illinois license.

The driver got his tools laid out, then crawled back beneath the hood. The sound of hammering and the screech of stubborn, rusty bolts floated up the hill.

Blaine finished off his breakfast. There were two steaks left and two potatoes and by now the coals were growing black. He stirred up the coals and put on more wood, speared the two steaks on the stick and broiled them carefully.

The pounding and the screeching kept on beneath the hood. A couple of times the man crept out and rested, then went back to work.

When the steaks were finished, Blaine put the two potatoes in his pocket and went marching down the hill, carrying the two steaks on their stick as another man might take a banner into battle.

At the sound of his footsteps crunching on the road, the driver came out from beneath the hood and turned around to face him.

'Good morning,' said Blaine, being as happy as he could. 'I saw you down here while I was getting breakfast.'

The driver regarded him with considerable suspicion.

I had some food left over,' Blaine told him, 'so I cooked it up for you. Although, perhaps, you've eaten.'

'No, I haven't,' said the driver, with a show of interest. 'I intended to in the town just down the road, but it was still closed tight.'

'Well, then,' said Blaine and handed him the stick with the two steaks impaled upon it

The man took the stick and held it as if he feared that it might bite him. Blaine dug in his pockets and pulled out the two potatoes.

'There was some corn,' he said, 'but I ate it all. There were only three ears of it.'

'You mean you're giving this to me?'

'Certainly,' said Blaine. 'Although you can throw it back into my face if that's the way you feel.'

The man grinned uneasily. 'I sure could use it,' he declared. 'The next town is thirty miles and with this,' he gestured at the truck, 'I don't know when I'll get there.'

'There isn't any salt,' said Blaine, 'but it's not so bad without it.'

'Well,' said the man, 'since you've been so kind ...'

'Sit down,' said Blaine, 'and eat. What's the matter with the engine?'

'I'm not sure. Could be the carburetor.'

Blaine took off his jacket and folded it. He laid it neatly on the fender. He rolled up his sleeves.

The man found a seat on a rock beside the road and began to eat.

Blaine picked up a wrench and climbed up on the fender.

'Say,' said the man, 'where did you get this stuff?'

Up on the hill,' said Blaine. 'The farmer had a lot of it.'

'You mean you stole it?'

'Well, what would you do if you were out of work and had no money and were trying to get home?'

'Whereabouts is home?'

'Up in South Dakota.'

The man took a big bite of steak, and his mouth became so full he could talk no longer.

Blaine ducked underneath the hood and saw that the driver had all but one bolt loose on the carburetor mounting. He put the wrench on it, and the bolt screeched metallic protest.

'Damn thing rusted tight,' said the driver, watching Blaine.

Blaine finally freed the bolt and lifted out the carburetor. He walked over with it and sat down beside the eating man.

'Rig's about ready to fall apart,' the driver said. 'Wasn't much to start with. Been having trouble with it all the way. My schedule's shot to hell.'

Blaine found a smaller wrench that fitted the bolts on the carburetor assembly and began to wrestle with the threads.

'Tried driving at night,' said the man, 'but not for me. Not after that first time. Too risky.'

'See something?'

'If it hadn't been for those signs I painted on the truck, I would have been a goner. I have a shotgun with me, but it doesn't do no good. Can't drive and handle a gun at the self-same time.'

'Probably wouldn't do you any good even if you could.'

'I tell you, mister,' said the driver. 'I am set for them. I have a pocket full of shells loaded up with silver shot.'

'Expensive, isn't it?'

'Sure. But you have to be prepared.'

'Yeah,' said Blaine. 'I suppose you do.'

'It's getting worse,' declared the man, 'every blessed year. There is this preacher up north.'

'I hear there are a lot of preachers.'

'Yes, a lot of them. But all they do is talk. This one, he is all set to get some action on it.'

'There she is,' said Blaine, loosening the last bolt. He broke open the carburetor and looked at it.

'There it is,' he said.

The man bent over and looked where Blaine was pointing.

'Damned if it ain't,' he said.

'Have it fixed and back in place in another fifteen minutes. You got an oil can we can squirt these threads?'

The driver got up and wiped his hands on the seat of his trousers. 'I'll look it up,' he said.

He started for the truck, then turned back. He held out his hand. 'My name is Buck,' he said. 'Buck Riley.'

'Blaine. You can call me Shep.'

They shook.

Riley stood undecided, shuffling his feet.

'You say you're heading for Dakota.'

Blaine nodded.

'I'm damn near out of my mind,' said Riley. 'I need someone to help me.'

'Anything I can do to help?' asked Blaine. 'Would you drive at night?'

'Hell, yes,' said Blaine.

'You could drive and I could have the shotgun ready.'

'You'll need to get some sleep.'

'We'll manage that, the both of us, somehow or other. We have to keep this wagon rolling. I've lost too much time for comfort.'

'You're going South Dakota way?'

Riley nodded. 'You'll go with me, then?'

'Glad to,' said Blaine. 'It beats walking any time.'

'There'll be some money in it for you. Not much …'

'Forget about the money. I just want the ride.'

13

Northeastward out of the southwest they traveled, driving day and night but not driving all the time; driving, more than likely, not more than half the time. For the truck was no better than a rolling junk heap. They fought with the balky engine, they battled with the old and worn-out tires, they nursed the shaky chassis – and they made some mileage, but not so very much.

The roads were bad, as all roads now were bad. Dead for many years was the old concept of smooth, hard-surfaced, almost polished highways, for they were no longer needed. The traffic in this day was made up almost entirely of cars and trucks that were half planes; there was no need of good roads for vehicles which in their operation never touched the ground.

The old highway surfacing was broken and full of chuckholes. It was rough on tires, and the tires were not too good. Nor were the new ones, even if Riley had been able to afford them, easy to obtain. The demand for tires of the type used by his battered truck had dropped to almost nothing, and it was only by the greatest luck that they could be found.

There also was another ever-present worry – the finding of gasoline to put into the tank. For there were no service stations; there had been no service stations for almost fifty years. There was no need of service stations when highway traffic moved on atomic power. So, at each town they hunted for a farm service store or a co-operative tank farm to obtain their fuel, for the bulk of farm machinery still used gasoline.

They slept as they could, snatching catnaps whenever the chance came up. They ate on the run, usually out of a paper bag of sandwiches or of dough-nuts, with coffee in an old tin pail they carried.

Thus the two of them found their way along the ancient highways, used now by the modern traffic only because the engineering of those highways had been good, only because they represented the easiest, shortest distances between two points.

'I never should have took this job,' said Riley, 'but there was good pay in it and I don't mind telling you that I need the money.'

'You'll probably make out all right on it,' Blaine reassured him. 'You may be a few days late, but we'll get through all right.'

'If I have any truck left.'

'You didn't,' Blaine pointed out, 'have very much to start with.'

Riley mopped his face with a faded handkerchief that at one time had been turkey red.

'It's not only the truck and all the work,' he said. 'It's the wear and tear on a man himself.'

For Riley was a frightened man – and the fright, Blaine saw, went down to the bone and core of him.

It was not, Blaine told himself, watching the man, the simple emotional mechanics of a man frightened by the horrific menagerie of mischief and of evil from which, because he had believed in it for his entire life, he could conjure up with no effort whatsoever the terrible fantasies of an age gone past. It was something more than that; it was more immediate than latent night-time fears.

To Blaine the man was an oddity, a human specimen out of some medieval museum; a man who feared the dark and the imagined forms with which he peopled it; a man who placed reliance in a painted hex sign and in a shotgun loaded with a charge of silver buckshot. He had heard of men like this but had never met one. If there had been any such as this among the people that he met in Fishhook, they had kept it closely hidden behind a sophisticated mask.

But if Riley was a curiosity to Blaine, Blaine was likewise one to him.

'You are not afraid?' he'd ask.

Blaine would shake his head.

'You do not believe these things?'

'To me,' Blaine would tell him, 'they have always seemed just a little foolish.'

Riley would protest: 'They are not foolish, friend. I can assure you that. I've known too many people; I've heard too many tales that I know are true. There was an old man when I was a boy back in Indiana. He was found tangled in a fence with his throat ripped out. And there were tracks around the body and the smell of sulfur.'

If it were not this particular story, then it was another, just as gruesome, just as starkly mystic, just as ancient-dark.

And what could one do with that? Blaine wondered. Where would one find an answer? For the belief – the will to believe – was engrained deeply in the human fiber. Not entirely, either, in the matrix of the present situation, but in the blood and bone of Man clear back to the caves. There was in the soul of Man a certain deadly fascination with all things that were macabre. The situation as it stood had been grasped willingly, almost eagerly, by men for whom the world had become a rather tame and vapid place with no terror in it beyond the brute force terror of atomic weapons and the dread uncertainty of unstable men in power.

It had all begun quite innocently as the people grabbed at the new principles of PK for their entertainment and their enjoyment. Almost overnight the fact of mental power had become a fad that had overwhelmed the world. Night clubs had changed their names, there had been startling fashion trends, new teenage cants had risen, TV had gone overboard with its horror films, and the presses had poured out billions of volumes dealing with the supernatural. There had been new cults, and older cults had flourished. The Ouija board came back after two centuries of hiding in the mists of an earlier age which had played with ghosts for kicks but had given up when it had found that you could not play with the spirit world. You either believed in it or you didn't and there was no middle ground.

There had been quacks and there had been earnest men, considerably deluded, who had made names and fortunes from the fad. Manufacturers had turned out carload after carload of novelties and equipment for the pursuance of this new fad, or new hobby, or new study or religion – the specific term would apply in direct proportion to the seriousness with which each individual might consider it.

It all had been wrong, of course – for paranormal kinetics was not supernatural. Nor was it macabre, nor did it deal with ghost or devil or any of the other of the hordes of forgotten things which came charging happily out of the Middle Ages. It was, instead, a new dimension to Man's abilities – but the enamored people, agog at this new toy, had adopted it wholeheartedly in all misinterpretation.

As they always did, they had overdone it. They had played so hard at their misinterpretation that they had forgotten, despite warning after warning, that it was misinterpretation. They finally had come to believe in all the weirdness and all the fantasy; they finally regarded it as the gospel truth. Where there had been fun there now were leering fauns; where there had been gags there now were goblins and ghosts.

So the reaction had set in, the inevitable reaction of fanatical reformers, accompanied by the grim, horse-faced cruelty and blindness that goes with all fanatical reform. Now a grim and frightened people hunted down, as a holy mission, their paranormal neighbors.

There were a lot of these, but they were in hiding now or in masquerade. There had always been a lot of them through all the human ages, but mostly unsuspecting, never dreaming that they had powers within themselves fit to reach the stars. They were the people who had been just a little queer, a bit discombobulated and had been regarded tolerantly as harmless by their neighbors. There had been a few, of course, who had been in part effective, but even in their effectiveness they had not believed, or believing, they had used their strange powers poorly, for they could not understand them. And in the later years, when they might have understood it, none of them had dared, for the tribal god of science had called it all damn foolishness.

But when the stubborn men in Mexico had demonstrated that it was not all damn foolishness, then the people dared. Those who had the abilities then felt free to use them, and developed them by use. Others who never suspected that they had them found to their surprise they did and they used them, too. In some cases the abilities were used to good and solid purpose, but in other cases they were wrongly used or used for shallow purpose. And there were those, as well, who practiced this new-found art of theirs for unworthy ends, and a very few, perhaps, who used it in all evil.

Now the good gray moralists and the pulpit-pounding, crag-browed, black-attired reformers were out to quash PK for the evil it had done. They used the psychology of fear; they played upon the natural superstitions; they used the rope and brand and the quick shot in the night and they spread a fear across the land that one could smell in the very air – a thick, foul scent that clogged the nostrils and brought water to the eyes.

'You are lucky,' Riley said to Blaine. 'Not fearing them, you may be safe from them. A dog will bite a man who is afraid of it, but lick the hand of one who is not afraid.'

'The answer's easy, then,' Blaine told him. 'Do not be afraid.'

But it was impossible advice to a man like Riley.

Night after night he sat on the right-hand seat as Blaine drove through the darkness, shivering in terror like a spooky hound grasping the gun loaded with its silver buckshot.

There were alarms and frights – the swoop of owl, the running of a fox across the road, an imagined roadside shadow, all became an evil out of some darker night, while the howling of coyotes became the wailing of a banshee, hunting for a victim.

But there was more than imagined terror. There was the shadow shaped like a man, but a man no longer, twisting and turning in a lazy dance from a high branch above the thicket; there was the blackened ruins of the roadside farm, with the smoke-streaked chimney standing like an accusing finger pointing up to heaven; there was the smoke from the tiny campfire that Blaine stumbled on as he followed up a creek hunting down a spring while Riley wrestled with the balky spark plugs. Blaine had been moving quietly, and they had heard him just too late to vanish before he caught sight of them, fleeing like wraiths up the timbered slopes of the looming mountain spur.

He had stepped into the tiny, tramped-down circle of the camp site, with its small cooking fire and the skillet on its side, with four half-cooked trout lying in the trampled grass, with the wadded blankets and the comforter that had served as beds, with the rudely built brush shelter as refuge from the rain.

He had knelt beside the fire and righted the skillet. He had picked up the fish and brushed the twigs and grass off them and replaced them in the pan.

And he had thought to call out to the hiders, to try to reassure them, but he knew that it was useless, for they were past all trust.

They were hunted animals. Hunted animals in this great United States which for years had valued freedom, which in its later years had stood as a forthright champion, before the entire world, for the rights of man.

He knelt there, torn by an anger and a pity, and he felt the smarting of his eyes. He bunched up his fists and rubbed at his eyes, and the moist knuckles smeared streaks of dirt across his face.

He had stayed there for a while, but finally he had risen and gone down the creek again, forgetting that he had hunted for a spring, which no doubt had been only a few feet from the camp.

When he got back to the truck, he did not mention what he'd found to Riley.

They drove across the deserts and labored across the mountains and finally came to the great high plains where the wind came knifing down without a hill to stop it, without a tree to break it, a naked stretch of land that lay flat and hard to a far horizon.

Blaine rode in the seat alongside Riley, slouched and relaxed against the jolting of the truck. The sun beat down, and the wind was dry, and off to the north dust devils rose and spun above a dried-up river bed.

Riley drove hunched tight against the wheel, with his arms braced against the chuckholes and the ruts. His face was tense and at times a nervous tic twitched the muscles of his cheek.

Even in the daytime. Blaine thought, the man is still afraid, still runs his endless race with darkness.

Had it to do, he wondered, with the cargo in the truck? Not once had Riley said what he was hauling, not once had he inspected it. There was a heavy padlock on the rear door of the rig, and the padlock clanged and jangled as the truck lumbered on the road.

There had been a time or two when Blaine had been on the verge of asking, but there had been a certain reticence that had prevented it. Not anything, perhaps, that Riley had said or done or any way he'd acted, but, rather, his studied casualness in all these areas.

And after all, Blaine told himself, it was none of his affair. He did not care what might be in the truck. His only interest was in the truck itself; with every turn of a wheel it was carrying him where he had to go.

Riley said: 'If we get a good run tonight, we'll reach the river in the morning.'

'The Missouri?'

Riley nodded. 'If we don't break down again. If we make good time.'

But that night they met the witches.

14

The first they saw of them was a flicker in the fan of light the headlamps threw out along the road and then they saw them flying in the moonlight. Not flying, actually, for they had no wings, but moving through the air as a fish would move through water, and graceful as only flying things can be.

There was a moment when they might have been moths flying in the lights or night-swooping birds diving in the sky, but once the mind had its instant of utter disbelief and after that, of human rationalization, there was no doubt of what they were.

They were humans flying. They were levitators. They were witches and there was a coven of them.

In the seat beside him, Blaine saw Riley thrust the shotgun out the open window. Blaine slammed on the brakes.

The gun went off, the sound of the report blasting in the cab like a thunderbolt.

The car skidded to a halt, slantwise across the road. Blaine grabbed at Riley's shoulder and jerked him off his balance. With the other hand he jerked the gun away.

He caught a glimpse of Riley's face, and the man was yammering. His jaw went up and down in a devil's tattoo and there were little flecks of foam at each corner of his mouth. His eyes were wild and rolling and his face was stiff, with the muscles bunched and tensed, like a grotesque mask. His hooked fingers made clawing motions to get back the gun.

'Snap out of it!' roared Blaine. 'They're only levitators.'

But the word meant nothing to a man like Riley. All reason and all understanding were lost in the roll of fearful thunder that hammered in his brain.

And even as he spoke to Riley, Blaine became aware of voices in the night – soundless voices reaching out to him, a medley of voices that were talking to him.

Friend – one of us is hit (a line of oozing red across a shapely shoulder) – not bad – he has (a gun with its muzzle limp and drooping and turning suddenly into a rather melancholy and very phallic symbol). Safe – our friend has the gun. Let us get the other (a snarling dog backed into a corner, a skunk with its tail uplifted, a rattler coiled and set to strike).

Wait, yelled Blaine. Wait! Everything's all right. There'll be no more shooting.

He pressed down with his elbow against the door latch, and the door swung open. He pushed Riley from him and half fell out of the cab, still clutching the gun. He broke the weapon, and the shells jumped out; he threw the gun into the road and backed against the truck.

Suddenly the night was deadly silent except for the sounds of moaning and of wailing that came from Riley in the cab.

Everything is clear, said Blaine. *There is no more danger.*

They came plunging down out of the sky, as if they might be jumping from some hidden platform, but they landed lightly on their feet.

They moved slowly forward, catfooted in the night, and they were silent now.

That was a damn fool thing to do, Blaine told them. *Next time one of you will get your head blown off (a headless human walking casually with the stump of neck frothing furiously).*

He saw that they were young, not out of their teens, and that they wore what appeared to be bathing suits and he caught the sense of fun and the scent of prank.

They moved in cautiously, and he sought for other signs, but there were no other signs.

Who are you? one asked.

Shepherd Blaine of Fishhook.

And you are going?

Up to South Dakota.

In this truck?

And with this man, said Blaine. *I want him left alone.*

He took a shot at us. He hit Marie.

Not bad, said Marie. *Just a scratch is all.*

He's a frightened man, said Blaine. *He's using silver shot.*

He sensed the merriment of them at the thought of silver shot.

And caught the weirdness of the situation, the moonlit night and the deserted road, the car slewed across the highway, the lonely wind that moaned across the prairie, and the two of them, he and Riley, encircled, not by Sioux nor by Comanche nor by Blackfeet, but by a ring of paranormal teenagers out on a midnight lark.

And who was there to blame or censure them? he asked himself. If in this small action of defiance they found some measure of self-assertion in their hunted lives, if in this manner they snatched at something resembling human dignity, it was then no more than a very human action and not to be condemned.

He studied the faces, the ones that he could see, indistinct in the moon-and-headlamp-light, and there was indecision in them – faces on hair trigger.

From the cab still came the moaning of a man in mental agony.

Then: Fishhook? (The towered buildings on the hill, the acre upon acre of them, massive, majestic, inspiring ...)

That is right, said Blaine.

A girl moved out of the huddled group and walked close to Blaine. She held out her hand.

Friend, she said. We had not expected one. All of us are sorry that we troubled you.

Blaine put out his hand and felt the firm, strong pressure of young fingers.

We do not often find someone on the road at night, said another one.

Just having fun, another said. *There's little chance for fun.*

I know how little chance, said Blaine. *I've seen how little chance.*

We halloween, still another said.

Halloween? Oh, yes, I see. (A first banging on a closed shutter, a garden gate hanging in a tree, a hex sign upside down.)

It's good for them. They've got it coming to them.

I agree, said Blaine. *But it's dangerous.*

Not very. They are all too scared.

But it doesn't help the situation.

Mister, there is nothing that can help.

But Fishhook? asked the girl who stood in front of Blaine.

He studied her and saw that she was beautiful – blue eyes and golden hair and the sort of shape that in the ancient days would have won her beauty contests, one of the old paganisms that had been happily forgotten in the rush to PK fads.

I cannot tell you, said Blaine. *I'm sorry, I can't tell you.*

Trouble? Danger?

Not at the moment, no.

We could help.

No need, making it as casual as he could, as unworried as he could.

We could take you anywhere you wished!

I'm not a levitator.

No need for you to be. We could (himself flying through the air, dragged along by two levitators, each hanging to an arm).

Blaine shuddered. *No, thanks. I think I'd rather not.*

Someone opened up the door of the cab, and another one reached in and hurled Riley to the ground.

The trucker crawled along the ground on hands and knees and sobbed.

Leave him alone! yelled Blaine.

The girl turned around. Her thoughts were level, sharp: *Keep away from him! Don't touch him! Don't do a thing to him.*

But, Anita ...

Not a thing, she said.

He's a dirty reefer. He's using silver shot.

No!

They backed away.

We'll have to go, Anita said to Blaine. *Will you be all right?*

With him, you mean?

She nodded.

I can handle him, he told her.

My name is Anita Andrews. I live in Hamilton. My phone number is 276. Tattoo it.

Tattooed, said Blaine, showing her the words and numbers.

If you need help …

I'll call

Promise?

Promise (cross upon a throbbing heart).

Riley lunged and had the gun, was staggering to his feet, a hand groping in his pocket for a shell.

Blaine flattened in a dive. He caught the man just above the knees, his shoulder slamming hard, one arm about the body, the other slashing at the gun and missing.

And as he leaped, he yelled: *Get out of here! Every one of you!*

He hit the ground and skidded, face down, on the broken pavement. He felt the shattered blacktop scraping on his flesh, tearing at his clothes. But he still kept his grip on Riley and dragged the man down with him.

The skidding stopped, and Blaine groped blindly for the gun, and the gun barrel came lashing down out of the darkness and struck him across the ribs. He swore and grasped for it, but Riley had it raised again for another blow. Blaine punched out desperately in the darkness, and his fist caught yielding flesh that grunted at the blow. The gun thudded down, missing his face by a fraction of an inch.

His hand snaked out and grasped it and jerked, twisting as he jerked, and the gun came free.

Blaine rolled, carrying the gun with him, and scrambled to his feet.

Out at the edge of light, he saw Riley coming in a bull rush with his arms outspread, with his shoulders bunched, his mouth a snarling slit slashed across his face.

Blaine lifted the gun and flung it out into the darkness with Riley almost on him. He sidestepped, but not quite far enough. One of Riley's hamlike hands caught him on the hip. Blaine spun with the hand and sidestepped again. Riley tried to check his rush but seemed unable to. He twisted his body frantically, but his momentum drove him forward and he slammed with a resounding whack into the front end of the truck.

He folded then and slid into a heap. Blaine stood watching him and there was no motion in the man.

The night was silent. There were just the two of them. All the rest had gone. He and Riley were alone with the battered truck.

Blaine swung around and looked into the sky and there was nothing there but the moon and stars and the lonesome prairie wind.

He turned back to Riley, and the man was alive, he saw. He had hauled himself into a sitting position, braced against the front end of the truck. There was a cut across his forehead where he had struck on metal and there was no fight left in him. He was out of breath and panting and there was a wild glare in his eyes.

Blaine took a pace toward him.

'You damn fool,' he said. 'If you'd fired at them again, they'd have been on top of us. They'd have torn us to pieces.'

Riley stared at him, and his mouth was working but no words came out – just the one word: 'You – you – you.'

Blaine stepped forward and held out a hand to help him to his feet, but Riley shrank away from him, pressing his body tight against the truck as if he would intrude into the very metal.

'You're one of them!' he shouted. 'I guessed it days ago …'

'You're crazy!'

'But you are! You are afraid of being seen. You stick close to the truck. I always am the one who goes for the eats and coffee. You won't ever go. I always bargain for the gas. It is never you.'

'It's your truck,' said Blaine. 'You have money and I don't. You know I am dead broke.'

'The way you came to me,' wailed Riley. 'Walking from the woods. You must have spent the night in them there woods! And you never believed in nothing, the way ordinary people do.'

'I'm not a fool,' said Blaine. 'That's the only reason. I'm no more PK than you are. If I were, do you think I'd have ridden this far in your junk heap of a truck?'

He strode forward and seized Riley and jerked him to his feet. He shook him so his head bobbed back and forth.

'Snap out of it!' yelled Blaine. 'We're safe. Let's get out of here.'

'The gun! You threw away the gun!'

'The hell with the gun. Get into that truck.'

'But you talked with them! I heard you talking to them!'

'I never said a word.'

'Not with your mouth,' said Riley. 'Not with your tongue. But I heard you talking with them. Not all of what you said. Just pieces of it. I tell you that I heard you.'

Blaine pushed him back against the truck and held him with one hand while with the other he opened the cab door.

'Get in there and shut up,' Blaine said, bitterly. 'You and your God-damned gun! You and your silver shot! You and your hearing things!'

For it was too late, he told himself. It would be useless telling him. It would be a waste of time to show him or to try to help. Perhaps if he ever guessed the truth, he might lose his last thin fingerhold on reason and finally go insane, wallowing in a morass of guilt associations.

Blaine walked around the truck and got in on the other side. He started the engine and wheeled the vehicle back into a highway lane.

They drove for an hour in silence, with Riley hunched into his corner. Blaine felt his watching eyes.

Finally Riley said: 'I'm sorry, Blaine. I guess that you were right back there.'

'Sure I was,' said Blaine. 'If you had started shooting—'

'That's not what I meant,' said Riley. 'If you'd been one of them, you'd have thrown in with them. They could have whisked you anywhere you wanted quicker than this rig.'

Blaine chuckled. 'Just to prove it to you, I'll pick up the eats and coffee in the morning. If you'll trust me with the money, that is.'

15

Blaine sat on the stool in the hamburger joint, waiting for the man to bag a half-dozen sandwiches and fill the pail with coffee. There were only two other customers in the place, and they paid no attention to him. One had finished eating and was reading a paper. The other, poised above his plate, was shoveling in a gooey mess that originally had been eggs and fried potatoes but now looked like some new kind of dog food from being thoroughly mixed together.

Blaine turned from looking at the men and stared out the massive slab of glass which comprised two sides of the building.

The morning street was quiet, with only a few cars moving and only one man walking.

Probably it had been foolish, he told himself, to come out like this in an utterly mad and perhaps rather useless attempt to throw Riley off his guard, to attempt to reassure him. For it was more than likely that no matter what he did and no matter what Riley said, the trucker would continue to carry some suspicion.

But, Blaine thought, it would not be for long, for they must be near the river, and Pierre must be just a few miles to the north. And a funny thing, he thought – Riley had never told him where he had been going. Although it was not queer; it fit in with all the rest of it – the man's evident fright and his secrecy concerning what he carried.

He swung back from the window and watched the man put the hamburgers in the sack and fill the pail with coffee. He paid with the five-dollar bill Riley had given him and pocketed the change.

He went out into the street and headed for the bulk oil station where Riley and the truck were waiting. It was too early yet for anyone to be at the station, and they'd eat their breakfast while waiting for someone to show up. Then they'd fill the tank and be on their way, and this, thought Blaine, might be the last day he'd be with the truck.

For once they hit the river, he'd get off and start heading north for Pierre.

The morning was cool almost to the point of chill, and the air burned in his nose as he breathed it in. It was going to be another good day, he knew – another moment of October with its winelike air and its smoky sky.

As he came to the street where the bulk station was located, the truck was not in sight.

Perhaps, he told himself, Riley might have moved it. But even as he thought it, he knew it was not right. He knew he had been ditched.

At the cost of a few dollars, at the cost of finding someplace else to get a tank of gas, the trucker had rid himself of Blaine.

It came to Blaine as no great shock, for he realized that he'd been expecting it, although not admitting to himself that he had expected it. After all, from Riley's point of view, it was an astoundingly simple solution to his suspicions of the night before.

To convince himself to make sure there was no mistake, Blaine walked around the block.

The truck was not in sight. And he was on his own.

In just a little while the town would be coming to life, and before that happened he must be out of sight. He must find a place where he could hide out for the day.

He stood for a moment to orient himself.

The nearer edge of town, he was certain, lay to the east, for they had driven through the southern edge of it for a mile or two.

He started out, walking as fast as was possible, but not so fast, he hoped, as would attract attention. A few cars went by along the street, once a man came out of his house to pick up the morning paper, once he met another man with a lunch bucket swinging from his hand. No one paid attention to him.

The houses dwindled out, and he reached the last street in the town. Here the prairie ended and the land began to tumble down, in a jumble of wooded hills and knolls, each one lower than the last, and he knew that the Missouri lay beyond. Somewhere down there where the last hill ended, the mighty stream gurgled on its way with its shifting sand bars and its willow islands.

He made his way across a field and climbed a fence and went down the bank of a steep ravine and at the bottom of it was a tiny creek that chuckled at its banks and just beyond was a pool with a clump of willows growing close beside it.

Blaine got down on his hands and knees and crawled beneath the willows. It was a perfect hideout. It was outside the town and there was nothing to bring anybody here – the stream was too small to fish and it was too late for swimming. He would not be disturbed.

There would be no one to sense the flashing mirror he carried in his mind; there'd be no one to yell 'Parry!' And come night he could move on.

He ate three of the hamburgers and drank some of the coffee.

The sun came up and filtered through the willows to make a dappled pattern of sunshine and shadow.

From the town came far-off sounds – the rumble of a truck, the purring of an engine, the barking of some dogs, the calling of a mother rounding up the kids.

It had been a long road from that night in Fishhook, Blaine told himself, sitting in the willow shade and poking with a stick into the sandy ground. A long ways from Charline's and from Freddy Bates. And up until this moment he'd had no time to even think about it.

There had been a question then, and there was still a question now: whether it had been smart to run away from Fishhook; whether, despite all Godfrey Stone had said, it might not have been the wiser course to stay and take his chances of whatever Fishhook might have had in store.

He sat there and thought about it and he went back to the bright blue room where all had been set in motion. And he saw the room again as if it were only yesterday – better than if it were only yesterday. The alien stars were shining faintly down on this room which had no roof, and the bright blue floor was smooth beneath the rolling of his wheels, and the room was filled with the weird fabricated pieces that might have been furniture or art objects or appliances or almost anything at all.

It all came alive for him as it should not come alive – clear and concise, with no rough edges and nothing blurred, with not a thing put in and not a thing left out.

The Pinkness was sprawling at its ease and it roused and said to him: *So you came back again!*

And he was really there.

Without machine or body, without any outward trappings, with nothing but his naked mind, Shepherd Blaine had come back to the Pinkness.

16

You cannot see a mind.

But the Pinkness saw it, or sensed it – or at least it knew that the mind was there.

And to Shepherd Blaine there was no surprise and no alienness. It seemed almost as if he were coming home, for the bright blue of the room was much more homelike and familiar than it had seemed that first time.

Well, the Pinkness said, looking the mind up and down, *you make a pretty pair!*

And that was it, of course, thought the part of the mind that still was Shepherd Blaine – he, or at least a part of him, perhaps as much as half of him, had come home, indeed. For he was, in some percentage not yet determined, perhaps impossible to determine, a part of the alien he faced. He was Shepherd Blaine, traveler from Earth, and likewise a carbon copy of this thing that dwelt in the bright blue room.

And how are you getting on? the alien asked most affably. As if he didn't know.

There is just one thing, said Blaine, hurrying to get it in against the time when he might be forced to go from here. *There is just one thing. You've made us like a mirror. We bounce back at people.*

Why of course, the alien told him. *That is the only way to do it. On an alien planet you would need some shielding. You don't want intelligences prying round in you. So you bounce back their prying. Here at home, of course, there would be no need ...*

But you don't understand, protested Blaine. *It doesn't protect us. It attracts attention to us. It almost got us killed.*

There is no such thing, the alien told Blaine, gruffly. *There is no such thing as killed. There is no such thing as death. It is such a horrid waste. Although I may be wrong. It seems to me that there was a planet, very long ago ...*

One could almost hear him riffling through the dry filing cases of his cluttered memory.

Yes, he said, *there was a planet. There were several planets. And it was a shame. I cannot understand it. It makes no sense at all.*

I can assure you, Blaine told him, *that on my planet there is death for everything. For every single thing ...*

For everything?

Well, I can't be sure. Perhaps ...

You see, the creature said. *Even on your planet it is not universal.*

I do not know, said Blaine. *It seems to me that I remember there are death-less things.*

Normal things, you mean.

Death has a purpose, Blaine persisted. *It is a process, a function that has made the development of species and the differentiation of species possible on my planet. It averts the dead end. It is an eraser that wipes out mistakes, that provides for new beginnings.*

The Pinkness settled down. You could sense it settling down – smugly, primly getting set for a long and satisfactory exchange of ideas and, perhaps, an argument.

It may be so, it said, *but it's very primitive. It goes back to the ooze. There are better ways. There even is a point where there is no further need of this improvement that you speak of.*

But, first of all, he asked, *are you satisfied?*

Satisfied?

Well, you're an improved thing yourself. An expanded thing. You are part yourself and you are partly me.

And you are partly me as well.

The Pinkness seemed to chuckle. *But there are just the two of you – yourself and me – and I am so many things I cannot begin to tell you. I have done a lot of visiting and I've picked up a lot of things, including many minds, and some of them, I don't mind telling you, were hardly worth the trading. But do you know, for all the visiting I've done, almost no one ever visits me. I cannot tell you how I appreciate this visit. There was a being once who came to visit me quite often, but it was so long ago it's a bit hard to recall. By the way, you meas-ure time, don't you – surface time, that is?*

Blaine told him how humans measure time.

Hm, now, let's see, the creature said, doing rapid mental calculation, *that would make it about ten thousand of your years ago.*

That this creature came to visit you?

That is right, the Pinkness said. *You are the first since them And you came visiting me. You didn't wait for me to visit you. And you had that machine ...*

How come, Blaine asked, *you had to ask me about our count of time? You had it all. You traded minds with me. You have everything I know.*

Of course, the Pinkness mumbled. *Of course I had it. But I hadn't dug it out. You wouldn't believe me if I told you how cluttered up I am.*

And that was true, Blaine thought. Even with just one extra mind, he was cluttered up. He wondered ...

Yes, of course, the Pinkness told him. *You'll get it straightened out in time.*

It takes a little while. You'll become one mind, not two. You'll get together. You'll make a team. You like it this way, don't you?

It's been a little rough, this mirror business.

I'm not bent on causing trouble, said the Pinkness. *only do the best I can. So I make mistakes. So I fix it up. I take the mirror off, I cancel it. O.K.?*

O.K., said Blaine.

I sit here, said the Pinkness, *and I go visiting. Without stirring from this place, I go anyplace I wish and you'd be surprised how few minds I find that I'd care to trade for.*

In ten thousand years, however, you'd pick up a lot of them.

Ten thousand years, said the creature, startled. *Ten thousand years, my friend, is only yesterday.*

He sat there, mumbling, reaching back and back and not reaching the beginning and he finally gave it up.

And there are so few of them, he complained, *that can handle a second mind. I must be careful of them. There are a lot of them that think they are possessed. Some of these would go insane if I traded with them. You perhaps, can understand.*

Readily, said Blaine.

Come, said the Pinkness, *and sit down here beside me.*

I'm scarcely, Blaine explained, *in a condition to do much sitting.*

Oh, yes, I see, the creature said. *I should have thought of that. Well, then, move over closer. You came for a visit, I presume.*

Naturally, said Blaine, not knowing what to say.

Then, said the creature grimly, *leave us start to visit.*

Certainly, said Blaine, moving somewhat closer.

Now, where shall I start? the creature asked. *There are so many places and so many times and so many different creatures. It always is a problem. I suppose it comes because of a desire for neatness, an orderliness of mind. The thought persists to plague me that if I could put it all together I might arrive at something of significance. You would not mind, I presume, if I should tell you about those strange creatures that I ran into out at the edge of the galaxy.*

Not at all, said Blaine.

They are rather extraordinary, said the Pinkness, *in that they did not develop machines as your culture did, but became, in effect, machines themselves ...*

Sitting there in the bright blue room, with the alien stars flaming overhead, with the faint, far-off sound of the raging desert wind a whisper in the room, the Pinkness talked – not only of the machine entities, but of many others. Of the insect tribes that piled up over endless centuries huge reserves of food for which they had no need, slaving on an endless treadmill of a blind economic mania. Of the race that made their art forms the basis of a weird religion. Of the listening posts manned by garrisons of a galactic empire that had long since been forgotten by all except the garrisons themselves. Of the fantastic and complicated sexual arrangements of yet another race of beings who, faced with the massive difficulties of procreation, thought of little else. Of planets that never had known life but rolled along their courses as gaunt and raw and naked as the day they had been formed. And of other planets that were a boiling brew pot of chemical reactions which stretched the mind to think on, let alone to understand, and of how these chemical reactions of themselves gave rise to an unstable, ephemeral sort of sentience that was life one moment and just failed of life another. This – and yet a great deal more.

Blaine, listening, realized the true fantastic measure of this creature which he had stumbled on – an apparently deathless thing, which had no memory of its beginning, no concept of an end; a creature with a roving mind that had mentally explored, over billions of years, millions of stars and planets for millions of light years, in this present galaxy and in some of the neighbor ones; a mind that had assembled a gigantic grab box of assorted information, but information which it had made no effort to put to any use. That it, more than likely, had no idea of how to put to use, yet troubled by a vague idea that this store of knowledge should not be lying fallow.

The sort of creature that could sit in the sun for endless time and spin eccentric yarns of all that it had seen.

And for the human race, thought Blaine, here squatted an encyclopedia of galactic knowledge, here lounged an atlas that had mapped uncounted cubic light years. Here was the sort of creature that the tribe of Man could use. Here was a running off of mouth that would pay human dividends – dividends from an entity which seemed without emotion, other than a certain sense of friendliness – an entity that, perhaps, in years of armchair observation, had had all emotions, if any had existed, worn away until they were so much dust – who had not used any of the knowledge it had gained, but had not been the loser. For in all its observation, in its galactic window-peeping, it had gained a massive tolerance and an understanding, not of its own nature, not of human nature, but of every nature, an understanding of life itself, of sentience and intelligence. And a sympathy of all motives and all ethics, and of each ambition, no matter how distorted in the eyes of other life.

And all of this, as well. Blaine realized with a start, was likewise stored in the mind of one human being, of one Shepherd Blaine, if he could only separate it and classify and store it and then could dig it out and put it to proper use.

Listening, Blaine lost all sense of time, lost all knowing of what he was or where he was or why he might be there, listening as a boy might listen to some stupendous tale spun by an ancient mariner from far and unknown land.

The room became familiar and the Pinkness was a friend and the stars were no longer alien and the far-off howling of the desert wind was a cradle song that he had always known.

It was a long time before he realized he was listening only to the wind and that the stories of far away and long ago had ceased.

He stirred, almost sleepily, and the Pinkness said: *That was a nice visit that we had. I think it was the best that I have ever had.*

There is one thing, said Blaine, *one question—*

If it is the shield, the Pinkness said, *you needn't worry. I took it away. There is nothing to betray you.*

It wasn't that, said Blaine. *It was time. I – that is, the two of us – have some control of time. Twice it saved my life …*

It is there, the Pinkness said. *The understanding's in your mind. You only have to find it.*

But, time—

Time, the creature said, *is the simplest thing there is. I'll tell you …*

17

Blaine lay for a long time, soaking in the feel of body, for now he had a body. He could feel the pressure on it, he could sense the movement of the air as it touched the skin, knew the hot damp of perspiration prickle along his arms and face and chest.

He was no longer in the blue room, for there he had no body and there was no longer the far-off sound of the desert wind. There was, instead, a regular rasping sound that had a slobber in it. And there was a smell, an astringent smell, an aggressively antiseptic odor that filled not only the nostrils, but the entire body.

He let his eyelids come up slowly against possible surprise, set to snap them shut again if there should be a need. But there was only whiteness, plain and unrelieved. There was no more than the whiteness of a ceiling.

His head was on a pillow and there was a sheet beneath him and he was dressed in some sort of garment that had a scratchiness.

He moved his head and he saw the other bed and upon it lay a mummy.

Time, the creature on that other world had said, time is the simplest thing there is. And it had said that it would tell him, but it hadn't told him, for he hadn't stayed to hear.

It was like a dream, he thought – thinking back on it, it had the unreal, flat-planed quality of a dream, but it had not been any dream. He had been in the blue room once again and he'd talked with the creature that was its habitant. He had heard it spin its yarns and he still retained within his mind the details of those yarns. There was no fading of the detail as there would have been if it had been a dream.

The mummy lay upon the bed swathed in bandages. There were holes in the bandages for the nostrils and the mouth but no holes for the eyes. And as it breathed it slobbered.

The walls were of the same whiteness as the ceiling, and the floors were covered with ceramic tile and there was a sterility about the place that shrieked its identity.

He was in a hospital room with a slobbering mummy.

Fear moved in on him, a sudden wash of fear, but he lay there quietly while it washed over him. For even in the fear, he knew that he was safe. There was some reason he was safe. There was some reason if he could think of it.

Where had he been? he wondered; where had he been other than the blue room? His mind went tracking back and he remembered where he'd been – in the willow thicket in the gully beyond the edge of town.

There were footsteps in the hall outside, and a man with a white jacket came into the room.

The man stopped inside the door and stood there looking at him.

'So you've come around at last,' the doctor said. 'Just how do you feel?'

'Not too bad,' said Blaine, and actually he felt fine. There didn't seem to be a thing the matter. 'Where did you pick me up?'

The doctor did not answer. He asked another question. 'Did anything like this ever happen to you before?'

'Like what?'

'Blacking out,' said the doctor. 'Falling into a coma.'

Blaine rocked his head from side to side upon the pillow. 'Not that I recall.'

'Almost,' the doctor said, 'as if you were the victim of a spell.'

Blaine laughed. 'Witchcraft, Doctor?'

The doctor grimaced. 'No, I don't imagine so. But one never knows. The patient sometimes thinks so.'

He crossed the room and sat down on the edge of the bed. 'I'm Dr Wetmore,' he told Blaine. 'You've been here two days. Some boys were hunting rabbits east of town. They found you. You had crawled underneath some willows. They thought that you were dead.'

'And so you hauled me in.'

'The police did. They went out and got you.'

'And what is wrong with me?'

Wetmore shook his head. 'I don't know.'

'I haven't any money. I can't pay you, Doctor.'

'That,' the doctor told him, 'is not of any moment.'

He sat there, looking at him. 'There is one thing, however. There were no papers on you. Do you remember who you are?'

'Sure. I'm Shepherd Blaine.'

'And you live where?'

'Nowhere,' said Blaine. 'I just wander around.'

'How did you get to this town?'

'I don't somehow recall.' He sat up in bed. 'Look, Doctor, how about getting out of here? I'm taking up a bed.'

The doctor shook his head. 'I'd like you to stick around. There are several tests—'

'It'll be a lot of trouble.'

'I've never run across a case like yours,' the doctor said. 'You'd be doing me a favor. There was nothing wrong with you. Nothing organically, that is. Your heartbeat was retarded. Your breathing a little shallow. Your temperature off a point or two. But otherwise all right, except that you were out. No way of waking you.'

Blaine jerked his head toward the mummy. 'He's in bad shape, isn't he?'

'Highway accident,' the doctor said.

'That's a bit unusual. Not many any more.'

'Unusual circumstances,' the doctor explained. 'Driving an old truck. Tire blew when he was going fast. One of the curves above the river.'

Blaine looked sharply at the man on the other bed, but there was no way to tell. None of him was showing. His breath went slobbering in and out and there was a rasping to it, but there was no way to tell who he might be.

'I could arrange another room,' the doctor offered.

'No need. I won't be around too long.'

'I wish you'd stay awhile. You might flop over once again. And not be found this time.'

'I'll think on it,' Blaine promised.

He lay back on the bed.

The doctor rose and went to the other bed. He bent over it and listened to the breathing. He found a wad of cotton and dabbed it at the lips. He murmured at the man who lay there, then he straightened up.

'Anything you need?' he inquired of Blaine. 'You must be getting hungry.'

Blaine nodded. Now that he thought of it, he was.

'No hurry, though,' he said.

'I'll speak to the kitchen,' said the doctor. 'They'll find something for you.'

He turned about and walked briskly from the room, and Blaine lay listening to his crisp, quick footsteps going down the hall.

And suddenly he knew – or remembered – why he now was safe. The flashing signal light was gone, for the creature of the far star had taken it from him. Now there was no longer need to skulk, no need of hiding out.

He lay there and thought about it and felt a bit more human – although, to tell the truth, he had never felt anything but human. Although now, for the first time, beneath the humanness, he felt the quick, tense straining of new knowledge of a deep strata of new knowledge that was his to tap.

Across, in the other bed, the mummy wheezed and rasped and slobbered.

'Riley!' whispered Blaine.

There was no break in the breathing, no sign of recognition.

Blaine swung on the bed and thrust out his feet. He sat on the edge of the bed and let his feet down to the floor, and the patterned tile was chill. He stood up, and the scratchy hospital gown hung obscenely around his shanks.

At the other bed, he bent close above the white-swathed thing that lay there.

'Riley! Is it you? Riley, do you hear me?'

The mummy stirred.

The head tried to turn toward him but it couldn't. The lips moved with an effort. The tongue fought to frame a sound.

'Tell …' it said, dragging out the word with the effort of its saying.

It tried again. 'Tell Finn,' it said.

There was more to say. Blaine could sense that there was more to say. He waited. The lips moved again, laboriously, and yet again. The tongue writhed heavily inside the slobbering cavern. But there was nothing more.

'Riley!' But there was no answer.

Blaine backed away until the edge of his bed caught him back of the knees and he sat down upon it.

He stayed there, staring at the swathed figure motionless on the bed.

And the fear, he thought, had caught up with the man at last, the fear that he had raced across half a continent. Although, perhaps, not the fear he ran from, but another fear and another danger.

Riley gasped and panted.

And there he lay, thought Blaine, a man who had some piece of information to pass on to a man named Finn. Who was Finn and where? What had he to do with Riley?

Finn?

There had been a Finn. Once, long ago, he'd known the name of Finn. Blaine sat stiff and straight upon the bed, remembering what he knew of Finn.

Although it might be a different Finn.

For Lambert Finn had been a Fishhook traveler, too, although he'd disappeared, even as Godfrey Stone had disappeared, but many years before Stone had disappeared, long before Blaine himself had ever come to Fishhook.

And now he was a whispered name, a legend, a chilling character in a chilling story, one of the few Fishhook horror tales.

For, so the story ran, Lambert Finn had come back from the stars one day a screaming maniac!

18

Blaine lay back upon the bed and stared up at the ceiling. A breeze came sniffing through the window, and leaf shadows from a tree outside played fitfully upon the wall. It must be a stubborn tree, Blaine thought, among the last to lose its leaves, for it was late October now.

He listened to the muffled sounds that came from the hushed corridors beyond the room, and the biting antiseptic smell was still hanging in the air.

He must get out of here, he thought; he must be on his way. But on his way to where? On his way to Pierre, of course – to Pierre and Harriet, if Harriet were there. But Pierre itself was dead end. So far as he might know, there was no purpose in it. So far as he could know, it was just a place to run to.

For he was running still, in blind and desperate flight. He'd been running since that moment when he'd returned from his mission to the stars. And worst of all, running without purpose, running only to be safe, just to get away.

The lack of purpose hurt. It made him an empty thing. It made him a wind-blown striving that had no free will of its own.

He lay there and let the hurt sink in – and the bitterness and wonder, the wonder if it had been wise to run from Fishhook, if it had been the thing to do. Then he remembered Freddy Bates and Freddy's painted smile and the glitter in his eyes and the gun in Freddy's pocket. And he knew there was no doubt about it: it had been the thing to do.

But somewhere there must be something he could lay his fingers on, something he could grasp, some shred of hope or promise he could cling to. He must not go on forever floating without purpose. The time must come when he could stop his running, when he could set his feet, when he could look around.

On the bed Riley gasped and wheezed and gurgled and was silent.

There was no sense in staying, Blaine told himself, as the doctor wished. For there was nothing that the doc could find and nothing Blaine could tell him and there was no profit in it for either one of them.

He got off the bed again and walked across the room to the door that more than likely led into a closet.

He opened the door and it was a closet and his clothes hung there. There was no sign of underwear, but his pants and shirt were hanging there and his shoes sat underneath them. His jacket had fallen off the hook and lay in a crumpled heap upon the floor.

He stripped off the hospital gown and reached for his trousers. He stepped into them and cinched them tight about his middle.

He was reaching for the shirt when the stillness struck him – the peaceful, mellow stillness of an autumn afternoon. The peace of yellow leaf and the mellowness of the haze upon the distant hills and the winelike richness of the season.

But the stillness was all wrong.

There should be a gasping and a bubbling from the man upon the bed.

With his shoulders hunched, as if against a blow, Blaine waited for the sound and there was no sound.

He spun around and took a step toward the bed, then halted. For there was no reason for going near the bed. Riley's swathed body lay still and quiet, and the bubble on the lips was frozen there.

'Doctor!' Blaine yelled, 'Doctor!' running to the door, knowing even as he ran and yelled that he was being foolish, that his reaction was irrational.

He reached the door and stopped. He put his hands against the jambs and leaned forward to thrust his head out into the corridor.

The doctor was coming down the hall, hurrying, but not running.

'Doctor,' whispered Blaine.

The doctor reached the door. He put out a hand and pushed Blaine back into the room. He strode over to the bed.

He stooped with his stethoscope placed against the mummy, then stepped back from the bed.

He looked hard at Blaine.

'And you are going where?' he asked.

'He's dead,' said Blaine. 'His breathing stopped and it was a long time—'

'Yes, he's dead. He never had a chance. Even with gobathian he didn't have a chance.'

'Gobathian? That was what you used? That was why he was all wrapped up?'

'He was broken,' said the doctor. 'Like a toy someone had thrown on the floor and jumped on. He was …'

He stopped and for a long, hard moment looked at Blaine.

'What do you know about gobathian?' he asked.

'I've heard of it,' said Blaine.

And he'd heard of it, all right, he thought.

'An alien drug,' the doctor said. Used by an insect race. A warring insect race. And it's done miracles. It can patch up a smashed and broken body. It can repair bones and organs. It can grow new tissue.'

He glanced down at the swathed deadness, then looked back at Blaine.

'You've read the literature?' he asked.

'A popularization,' Blaine lied. 'In a magazine.'

And he could see again the seething madness of that jungle planet where

94

he had stumbled on this drug the insects used – although in very truth they were not insects nor was it a drug they used.

Although, he told himself, there was no need to quibble. Terminology, always difficult, had become impossible with the going to the stars. You used approximations and let it go at that. You did the best you could.

'We'll move you to another room,' the doctor told him.

'No need of that,' said Blaine. 'I was just about to leave.'

'You can't,' said the doctor, flatly. 'I will not allow it. I won't have you on my conscience. There's something wrong with you, something very wrong. There's no one to look after you – no friends, no people.'

'I'll get along. I always have before.'

The doctor moved closer.

'I have a feeling,' he said, 'that you're not telling me the truth – not the entire truth.'

Blaine walked away from him. He reached the closet and got his shirt and put it on. He scuffed into his shoes. He picked up his jacket and shut the closet door, then turned around.

'Now,' he said, 'if you'll just move aside, I'll be going out.'

There was someone coming down the corridor. Perhaps, Blaine thought, someone with the food the doctor promised, and maybe he should wait until the food arrived, for he needed it.

But there was more than one person coming down the corridor – there were at least a pair of footsteps. Perhaps someone who had heard him yelling for the doctor, bearing down upon the room to see if help were needed.

'I wish that you would change your mind,' the doctor said. 'Aside from the feeling you need help, there also is the matter of formalities ...'

Blaine heard no more of what he had to say, for the walkers had reached the door and were standing just outside of it, looking in the room.

Harriet Quimby, cool as ice, was saying: 'Shep, how did you wind up here? We've been looking everywhere for you.'

And the telepathic undertone hit him like a whiplash: *Give! Quick! Fill me in!*

Just claim me, that is all (ferocious woman dragging errant urchin behind her with no ceremony). If you do that, they'll let me go. Found me lying underneath a willow tree ...

(Drunk who had somehow climbed into a garbage can and can't get out of it, top hat tilted on one ear, nose snapping and flashing like an advertising sign, crossed eyes registering a rather mild surprise.)

No, not that, Blaine pleaded. Just stretched out underneath the tree, dead to all the world. He thinks there's something wrong with me ...

There is ...

But not what he—

And Godfrey Stone was saying, smoothly, friendly, with a half-relieved, half-worried smile: 'So you've been having the old trouble. Too much liquor, I suppose. You know the doctor told you—'

'Ah, hell,' protested Blaine, 'just a snort or two. Not enough ...'

'Aunt Edna has been wild,' said Harriet. 'She imagined all sorts of things. You know what an imaginer she is. She was convinced you were gone for good and all this time.'

Godfrey! Godfrey! Oh, my God, three years ...

Take it easy, Shep. No time now. Get you out of here.

Dr Wetmore said: 'You people know this man? A relative of yours?'

'Not relatives,' said Stone. 'Just friends. His Aunt Edna—'

'Well, let's go,' said Blaine.

Stone glanced questioningly at the doctor, and Wetmore nodded.

'Stop at the desk,' he said, 'and pick up his release. I'll phone it down. They'll want your names.'

'Gladly,' said Stone. 'And thank you very much.'

'It's quite all right.'

Blaine stopped at the door and turned back to the doctor. 'I'm sorry,' he said. 'I didn't tell the truth. I am not proud of it.'

'All of us,' the doctor said, 'have moments in which we can take no pride. You are not alone.'

'Good-bye, Doctor.'

'So long,' said the doctor. 'Take care of yourself.' Then they were going down the corridor, the three of them abreast.

Who was in that other bed? asked Stone.

A man by the name of Riley.

Riley!

A truck driver.

Riley! He was the man we were looking for. We just ran into you.

Stone halted and half turned to go back.

No use, said Blaine. *He's dead.*

And his truck?

Smashed. He ran off the road.

'Oh, Godfrey!' Harriet cried.

He shook his head at her. 'No use,' he said. 'No use.'

Hey, what is going on?

We'll tell you all of it. First, let's get out of here.

Stone seized him by the elbow and hustled him along.

Just one thing. How is Lambert Finn mixed up in all of this?

'Lambert Finn,' Stone said vocally, 'is the most dangerous man in the world today.'

19

'Don't you think we should drive a little farther?' Harriet asked, 'If that doctor should get suspicious …'

Stone wheeled the car into the drive.

'Why should he get suspicious?'

'He'll get to thinking. He's puzzled by what happened to Shep and he'll get to wondering. After all, our story had a lot of holes in it.'

'For one thought up on the moment, I thought we did real well.'

'But we're only ten miles out of town.'

'I'll want to go back tonight. I have to do some checking on what became of Riley's truck.'

He braked the car to a halt in front of the unit marked 'Office'.

'Run your head into a noose, you mean,' said Harriet. The man who had been sweeping off the steps walked over to the car.

'Welcome, folks,' he said, heartily. 'What can the Plainsman do for you?'

'Have you two connecting?'

'It just so happens,' said the man, 'we have. Nice weather we been having.'

'Yes, very splendid weather.'

'Might turn cold, though. Any day. It is getting late. I can remember when we had snow—'

'But not this year,' said Stone.

'No, not this year. You were saying you wanted two connecting.'

'If you don't mind.'

'Drive right on, straight ahead. Numbers ten and eleven. I'll get the keys and be right along.'

Stone lifted the car on gentle jets and slid down the roadway. Other cars were parked cozily against their units. People were unloading trunks. Others were sitting in chairs on the little patios. Down at the far end of the parkway a foursome of old codgers were loudly pitching horseshoes.

The car skidded into the space before No. 10 and settled easily to the ground.

Blaine got out and held the door for Harriet.

And it was good, he thought, it was almost like home to be with these two again – with two who had been lost and now were here again. No matter what might happen, he was with his own once more.

The motel sat atop the bluffs above the river, and from where he stood he could see the wide sweep of terrain north and east – the bald, brown bluffs and the erosion of the timbered gullies and ravines that ran down to the river valley, where a tangled expanse of ragged woods hemmed in the chocolate-flowing stream which meandered with an uneasiness of purpose, as if it could not quite make up its mind where it wished to go, leaving behind it, as landmarks of its indecision, isolated ponds and lakes and crazily winding sloughs as erratic in their course as the river ever could be.

There was a cleanness and a roominess that caught one's imagination. There was a breath of freshness and the sense of space.

The manager came trotting down the walk, jangling a couple of keys. He unlocked the doors and flung them open.

'You'll find everything O.K.,' he said. 'We are very careful. There are shutters for all windows, and the locks throughout are the best available. You'll find a supply of hex signs and good luck charms in the supply cabinet. We used to have them installed, but we found our guests have their own ideas on how they are best used.'

That,' said Stone, 'is very thoughtful of you.'

'It is good,' said the manager, 'to be snug and under cover.'

'You said a mouthful, pal,' said Stone.

'And we have a restaurant up front ...'

'We'll be using it,' said Harriet. 'I am almost starved.'

'You can stop on your way,' said the manager, 'and sign the register, if you would.'

'Of course,' said Harriet.

He handed her the keys and went jogging up the walk, bobbing and bowing in merry hostship to the occupants of the other units.

'Let's get inside,' said Stone.

He held the door for Harriet and Blaine, then stepped in himself and closed the door behind him.

Harriet tossed the keys down on a dresser and turned around to look about the room.

'And you,' she said to Blaine. 'Whatever happened to you? I went back to that place on the border and the town was in a stew. Something dreadful had happened. I never found out what. I never had a chance to learn. I had to get out fast.'

'I got away,' Blaine told her.

Stone held out his hand. 'You did it better than I did. You got clean away.'

Blaine's hand was engulfed in Stone's great fist and held there – not shaken up and down, but held there.

'It's good to have you here,' said Stone.

'You phoned that night,' said Blaine, 'or I'd have been caught flat-footed. I remembered what you said. I didn't wait around for them to put the finger on me.'

Stone let go of his hand and they stood facing one another and it was a different Stone who stood there than the one that Blaine remembered. Stone had always been a big man and he was still a big man, but now the bigness was not only physical and external – there was a bigness of the spirit and of purpose that one must sense immediately at the sight of him. And a hardness that had not been there before.

'I am not sure,' Blaine told him, 'that I've done you any favor, showing up like this. I traveled slow and awkward. By now Fishhook more than likely has a hounder on me.'

Stone made a motion to dismiss the thought, almost a motion of impatience, as if Fishhook could not matter here, as if Fishhook mattered nowhere any more.

He moved across the room and sat down in a chair.

'What happened to you, Shep?'

I got contaminated.'

'So did I,' said Stone.

He was silent for a moment, as if he might be thinking back to that time when he had fled from Fishhook.

'I turned from the phone,' he said, 'and they were waiting for me. I went along with them. There was nothing else to do. They took me to a place … '
(A great sprawling place set upon a sea-coast, with one huge rambling house – white, so white it glistened – with the sky so blue above it that the blueness hurt one's eyes, a blue that picked up and reflected back the brightness of the sun, and yet a blue with depth that one could gaze into so far that he was lost in distance. And around the sprawling building, other buildings that fell short of the sprawling big house only because of their lack of size. A sweep of lawn that one knew instantly could grow so lushly only by virtue of constant watering. Beyond the green of lawn lay a snow-white strip of sandy beach and the green-blue of the ocean with the froth of spray thrown high into the air where the surf came hammering in on the rocks beyond the beach. And upon the beach the gypsy color of many umbrellas …)

'It was, I found out later, in Baja California. A perfect wilderness of a place with this fabulous resort planted in the wilderness … ' *(The golf course flags flapping in the ocean breeze, the flat white rectangles of the tennis court, the patio with the guests sitting idly and talking, waiting for the liquor carts and the sandwich trays and dressed in vacation costumes that were impeccable.)* 'There was fishing such as you had never dreamed of and hunting in the hills and swimming the entire year around …'

'Hard to take,' said Harriet, idly.

'No,' said Stone, 'not hard to take at all. Not for six weeks. Not even for six months. There was everything a man might want. There was food and drink and women. Your slightest wish was filled. Your money was no good. Everything was free.'

'But I can see,' said Blaine, 'how a man might—'

'Of course you can,' said Stone. 'The utter uselessness. As if someone had taken you, a man, and turned you back into a boy, with nothing left but play. And yet Fishhook was being kind. Even as you hated it and resented it and rebelled against it, you could see their point. They had nothing against us, really. There had been no crime, no negligence of duty – that is, with most of us there hadn't. But they couldn't take the chance of continuing to use us and they could not turn us loose, for there must, you understand, be no blot upon the Fishhook name. It never must be said of them that they turned loose upon the world a man with a streak of alienness, with a mind or an emotion that deviated even by a hairsbreadth from the human viewpoint. So they gave us a long vacation – an endless vacation – in the kind of place that millionaires inhabit.

'And it was insidious. You hated it and still you could not leave, for common sense would tell you that you were a fool to leave it. You were living safe and high. There was no question of security. You really had it made. You thought about escaping – although you could scarcely think of it as escape, for there was nothing really holding you. That is, until you tried. Then you found out about the guards and outposts. Only then you learned that every trail and road was covered. This despite the fact that a man afoot would have been committing suicide to go charging out into the land. You found out, by slow degrees, about the men who watched you all the time – the men who posed as guests but were really Fishhook agents who kept an eye on every one of you, waiting for the sign that you were getting set, or even thinking of getting out of there.

'But the bars that held you, the bars that kept you in were the luxury and soft living. It is hard to walk out on a thing like that. And Fishhook knows it is. It is, I tell you, Shep, the tightest, hardest prison man has yet devised.

'But, like any other prison, it made you tough and hard. It made you fight to get tough and hard, to get tough enough to make up your mind, and hard enough, once you'd made it up, to carry out your plan. When you learned about the spies and guards, you got sly and clever, and those very spies and guards were the ones who gave you purpose. Fishhook overplayed its hand by building in any security at all, for none was really needed. Left to yourself, you might have escaped every second week, but come trailing back when you found how rough it was outside. But when you found that there were physical barriers – when you found out about the men and guns and dogs – then you had a challenge and it became a game and it was your life you were shoving out into the pot …'

'But,' said Blaine, 'there couldn't have been too many escapes, not even many tries. Otherwise Fishhook would have dreamed up new angles. They'd never let it stand.'

Stone grinned wolfishly. 'You're right. There were not many who ever made it. There were few who even tried.'

'You and Lambert Finn.'

'Lambert,' Stone said, dryly, 'was a daily inspiration for me. He'd escaped some years before I was taken there. And there was one other, years before Lambert. No one knows to this day what ever happened to him.'

'Well, O.K.,' asked Blaine, 'what does happen to a man who escapes from Fishhook, who runs away from Fishhook? Where does he end up? Here I am, with a couple of dollars in my pocket that aren't even mine, but belong to Riley, without identity, without a profession or a trade. How do I—?'

'You sound as if you might regret having run away.'

'There are times I have. Momentarily, that is. If I had it to do over, I'd do it differently. I'd have it planned ahead. I'd transfer some funds to some other country. I'd have a new identity all worked out and pat. I'd have boned up on something that would turn me into an economic asset—'

'But you never really believed that you'd have to run. You knew it had happened to me, but you told yourself it couldn't happen to yourself.'

'I guess that is about the size of it.'

'You feel,' said Stone, 'that you've turned into a misfit.'

Blaine nodded.

'Welcome to the club,' said Stone.

'You mean—'

'No, not me. I have a job to do. A most important job.'

'But—'

'I'm speaking,' Stone told him, 'of a vast segment of all mankind. I have no idea how many million people.'

'Well, of course, there always were—'

'Wrong again,' said Stone. 'It's the parries, man, the parries. The parries who are not in Fishhook. You couldn't have traveled almost a thousand miles and—'

'I saw,' said Blaine, a cold shudder building in him, an icelike quality that was neither fear nor hate, but a part of both. 'I saw what was happening.'

'It's a waste,' said Stone. 'A terrible waste, both to the parry and the human race. Here are people who are being hunted down, people who are forced into ghettos, people who are reviled and hated – and all the time, within them lies the hope of humankind.

'And I tell you something else. It is not only these intolerant, bigoted, ignorant savages who think of themselves as normal human beings who are to blame for the situation. It is Fishhook itself; Fishhook which must bear part of the blame. For Fishhook has institutionalized paranormal kinetics for its own selfish and particular purpose. It has taken care, most excellent care, of those parries like you and I, handpicking us to carry on their work. But they've turned their face against the others. They have given not a sign that they might care what might happen to them. All they'd have to do is stretch out their hand and yet they fail to do it and they leave the other parries in the position of wild animals running in the woods.'

'They are afraid—'

'They just don't give a damn,' said Stone. 'The situation as it stands suits them to the ground. Fishhook started as a human crusade. It has turned into one of the greatest monopolies the world has ever known – a monopoly that is unhampered by a single line of regulation or restriction, except as they may choose to impose upon themselves.'

'I am hungry,' Harriet announced.

Stone paid her no attention. He leaned forward in his chair.

'There are millions of these outcasts,' he declared. 'Untrained. Persecuted when they should be given all encouragement. They have abilities at this very moment that mankind, also at this very moment, needs most desperately. They have untrained and latent talents that would prove if exercised, greater than anything that Fishhook ever has attained.

'There was a time when there was a need for Fishhook. No matter what may happen, no matter what event, the world owes Fishhook more than it ever can repay. But the time has come when we no longer have any need of Fishhook. Fishhook today, so long as it ignores the parries who are not within its fold, has become a brake upon the advancement of the human race. The utilization of PK must no longer remain a monopoly of Fishhook.'

'But there is this terrible prejudice,' Blaine pointed out. 'This blind intolerance—'

'Granted,' Stone told him, 'and part of it was earned. PK was abused and used, most shamefully used for selfish and ignoble reasons. It was taken and forced into the pattern of the old world that now is dead. And for that reason the parries have a guilt complex. Under this present persecution and their own deep-rooted sense of guilt they cannot operate effectively, either for their own good or for the benefit of humanity. But there is no question that if they could operate openly and effectively, without the pressure of public censure, they could do far more than Fishhook, as it now is constituted, ever can accomplish. And if they were allowed to do this, if they could only be allowed to show that non-Fishhook PK could operate for human betterment, then they'd become accepted and instead of censure would have support and encouragement, and in that day, Shep, Man would have taken a great step forward.

'But we must show the world that PK is a human ability and not a Fishhook ability. And furthermore – if this could be done, then the entire human race would return to sanity and would regain its old-time self-respect.'

'You're talking in terms,' Blaine told him, 'of cultural evolution. It is a process that will take some time. In the end, of course, it may work out naturally – another hundred years.'

'We can't wait!' cried Stone.

'There were the old religious controversies,' Blaine pointed out. 'War between Protestant and Catholic, between Islam and Christianity. And where is it all now? There was the old battle between the Communist dictatorships and the democracies …'

'Fishhook helped with that. Fishhook became a powerful third force.'

'Something always helps,' said Blaine. 'There can be no end to hope. Conditions and events become so ordered that the quarrel of yesterday becomes an academic problem for historians to chew on.'

'A hundred years,' said Stone. 'You'd wait a hundred years?'

'You won't have to,' Harriet told him. 'You have it started now. And Shep will be a help.'

'Me?'

'Yes, you.'

'Shep,' said Stone, 'please listen.'

'I am listening,' said Blaine, and the shudder was growing in him once again, and the sense of alienness, for there was danger here.

'I have made a start.' said Stone. 'I have a group of parries – call them underground, call them cadre, call them a committee – a group of parries who are working out preliminary plans and tactics for certain experiments and investigations that will demonstrate the effective action which the free, non-Fishhook parries can contribute to their fellow men …'

'Pierre!' exclaimed Blaine, looking at Harriet.

She nodded.

'And this is what you had in mind from the very start. At Charline's party you said old pal, old friend …'

'Is it so bad?' she asked.

'No, I don't suppose it is.'

'Would you have gone along,' she asked, 'if you'd known of it?'

'I don't know. Harriet, I honestly don't know.'

Stone rose from his chair and walked the step or two to Blaine. He put out both his hands and dropped them on Blaine's shoulders. His fingers tightened hard.

'Shep,' he said, solemnly. 'Shep, this is important. This is necessary work. Fishhook can't be the only contact Man has with the stars. One part of the human race cannot be free of Earth and the rest remain earthbound.'

In the dim light of the room his eyes had lost their hardness. They became mystical, with the shine of unshed tears.

His voice was soft when he spoke again. 'There are certain stars,' he said, almost whispering, as if he might be talking to himself, 'that men must visit. To know what heights the human race can reach. To save their very souls.'

Harriet was busily gathering up her handbag and her gloves.

'I don't care,' she announced. 'I am going out to eat. I am simply starved. You two coming with me?'

'Yes,' said Blaine, 'I'll go.'

Then suddenly remembered.

She caught the thought and laughed softly.

'It'll be on us,' she said. 'Let us say in part payment for the times you fed the both of us.'

'No need to be,' said Stone. 'He's already on the payroll. He's got himself a job. How about it, Shep?'

Blaine said nothing.

'Shep, are you with me? I need you. I can't do without you. You're the difference I need.'

'I am with you,' Blaine said simply.

'Well, now,' said Harriet, 'since that is settled, let us go and eat.'

'You two go along.' said Stone. 'I'll hold the fort.'

'But, Godfrey—'

'I've got some thinking that I have to do. A problem or two …'

'Come along,' Harriet said to Blaine. 'He wants to sit and think.'

Puzzled, Blaine went along with her.

20

Harriet settled herself resolutely and comfortably in her chair as they waited for their orders.

'Now tell me all about it,' she demanded. 'What happened in that town? And what has happened since? How did you get in that hospital room?'

'Later,' Blaine objected. 'There'll be time later on to tell you all of that. First tell me what is wrong with Godfrey.'

'You mean him staying back in the room to think?'

'Yes, that. But there is more than that. This strange obsession of his. And the look in his eyes. The way he talks about men going to the stars to save their souls. He is like an old-time hermit who has seen a vision.'

'He has,' said Harriet. 'That is exactly it.'

Blaine stared.

'It happened on that last exploratory trip,' said Harriet. 'He came back touched. He had seen something that had shaken him.'

'I know,' said Blaine. 'There are things out there ...'

'Horrible, you mean.'

'Horrible, sure. That is part of it. Incomprehensible is a better word. Processes and motives and mores that are absolutely impossible in the light of human knowledge and morality. Things that make no sense at all, that you can't figure out. A stone wall so far as human understanding is concerned. And it scares you. You have no point of orientation. You stand utterly alone, surrounded by nothing that was ever of your world.'

'And yet you stand up to it?'

'I always did,' said Blaine. 'It takes a certain state of mind – a state of mind that Fishhook drills into you everlastingly.'

'With Godfrey it was different. It was something that he understood and recognized. Perhaps he recognized it just a bit too well. It was goodness.'

'Goodness!'

'A flimsy word,' said Harriet. 'A pantywaist of a word. A sloppy kind of word, but the only word that fits.'

'Goodness,' Blaine said again, as if he were rolling the word about, examining it for texture and for color.

'A place,' said Harriet, 'where there was no greed, no hate, no driving personal ambition to foster either hate or greed. A perfect place with a perfect race. A social paradise.'

'I don't see ...'

'Think a minute and you will. Have you ever seen a thing, an object, a painting, a piece of statuary, a bit of scenery, so beautiful and so perfect you ached when you looked at it?'

'Yes. A time or two.'

'Well, then – a painting or a piece of statuary is a thing outside the human life, your life. It is an emotional experience only. It actually has nothing at all to do with you yourself. You could live very well the rest of your life if you never saw it again, although you would remember it every now and then and the ache would come again at the memory of it. But imagine a form of life, a culture, a way of life, a way you, yourself could live, so beautiful that it made you ache just like the painting, but a thousandfold more so. That's what Godfrey saw, that is what he talked with. That is why he came back touched. Feeling like a dirty little boy from across the tracks looking through the bars into fairyland – a real, actual, living fairyland that he could reach out and touch but never be part of.'

Blaine drew in a long breath and slowly let it out.

'So that is it,' he said. 'That is what he wants.'

'Wouldn't you?'

'I suppose. If I had seen it.'

'Ask Godfrey. He will tell you. Or, come to think of it, don't ask him. He'll tell you anyhow.'

'He told you?'

'Yes.'

'And you are impressed?'

'I am here,' she said.

The waitress came with their orders – great sizzling steaks, with baked potatoes and a salad. She set a coffee bottle in the center of the table.

'That looks good,' said Harriet. 'I am always hungry. Remember, Shep, that first time you took me out?'

Blaine smiled. 'I'll never forget it. You were hungry that time, too.'

'And you bought me a rose.'

'It seems to me I did.'

'You're a sweet guy, Shep.'

'If I recall correctly, you're a newspaper gal. How come—'

'I'm still working on a story.'

'Fishhook,' said Blaine. 'Fishhook is your story.'

'Part of it,' she said, returning to her steak.

They ate for a while with very little talk.

'There is one other thing,' Blaine finally said. 'Just what gives with Finn? Godfrey said he was dangerous.'

'What do you know of Finn?'

'Not much of anything. He was out of Fishhook before I tied up with it. But the story went around. He came back screaming. Something happened to him.'

'Something did,' said Harriet. 'And he's been preaching it up and down the land.'

'Preaching?'

'Hell and brimstone preaching. Bible-pounding preaching, except there is no Bible. The evil of the stars. Man must stay on Earth. It's the only safe place for him. There is evil out there. And it has been the parries who have opened up the gates to this spawn of evil ...'

'And the people swallow that?'

'They swallow it,' said Harriet. 'They wallow in it clear up to their middles. They absolutely love it. They can't have the stars, you see. So there's satisfaction to them that the stars are evil.'

'And the parries, I suspect, are evil, too. They are ghouls and werewolves ...'

'And goblins,' said Harriet. 'And witches. And harpies. You name it and they're it.'

'The man's a mountebank.'

Harriet shook her head. 'Not a mountebank. He's as serious as Godfrey. He believes the evil. Because, you see, he saw the evil.'

'And Godfrey saw the good.'

'That's it. It's as simple as all that. Finn is just as convinced Man has no business among the stars as Godfrey is convinced he'll find salvation there.'

'And both of them are fighting Fishhook.'

'Godfrey wants to end the monopoly but retain the structure. Finn goes farther. Fishhook's incidental to him. PK is his target. He wants to wipe it out.'

'And Finn's been fighting Stone.'

'Harassing him,' said Harriet. 'There's no way to fight him, really. Godfrey shows little for anyone to hit at. But Finn found out about him and sees him as the one key figure who can prop the parries on their feet. If he can, he'll knock him out.'

'You don't seem too worried.'

'Godfrey's not worried. Finn's just another problem, another obstacle.'

They left the restaurant and walked down the strip of pavement that fronted on the units.

The river valley lay in black and purple shadow with the river a murky bronze in the dying light of day. The tops of the bluffs across the valley still were flecked with sunlight, and far up in the sky a hawk still wheeled, wings a silver flash as he tilted in the blue.

They reached the door of the unit, and Blaine pushed it open and stood aside for Harriet, then followed. He had just crossed the threshold when she bumped into him as she took a backward step.

He heard the sharp gasp in her throat, and her body, pressed against his, went hard and tense.

Looking over her shoulder, he saw Godfrey Stone, face downward, stretched upon the floor.

21

Even as he bent above him, Blaine knew that Stone was dead. There was a smallness to him, a sort of essential withering of the human form, as if life had been a basic dimension that had helped to fill him out. Now he was something less than six feet of limp body clothed in crumpled cloth, and the stillness of him was somehow very dreadful.

Behind him, he heard Harriet pulling shut the door and shooting home the bolts. And in the clatter of the bolts he thought he heard a sob.

He bent down for a closer look and in the dimness could make out the darker shine of hair where the blood had oozed out of the skull.

The window shutters creaked and groaned, sliding home with a clatter as Harriet shoved the lever that controlled them. 'Maybe, now,' he said, 'we can have a little light.'

'Just a minute, Shep.'

The lighting toggle clicked and light sprang from the ceiling, and in the glare of it Blaine could see how a heavy blow had crushed in the skull.

There was no need to hunt for pulse, no need to listen for a heartbeat. No man could live with a skull so out of shape.

Blaine rocked back and teetered, crouched upon his toes, marveling at the ferocity and, perhaps, the desperation, which must have driven the arm that had delivered such a blow.

He looked at Harriet and nodded quietly, wondering at her calmness, then remembering, even as he wondered, that in her reporting days violent death could have been no stranger to her.

'It was Finn,' she said, her voice quiet and low, so quiet that one could sense the checkrein she'd put upon herself. 'Not Finn, himself, of course. Someone that he hired. Or someone that volunteered. One of his wide-eyed followers. There are a lot of people who'd do anything for him.'

She came across the room and squatted across the corpse from Blaine. Her mouth was set in a straight, grim line. Her face was pinched and stern. And there was a streak down her face where a single tear had run.

'What do we do now?' he asked. 'The police, I would imagine.'

She made a restraining motion with her arm.

'Not the police,' she said. 'We can't afford to get tangled up in this. That would be exactly what Finn and his crew would want. What do you bet that someone has phoned the police already?'

'You mean the killer?'

'Certainly. Why not? Just a voice saying that a man has been killed in unit number ten out at The Plainsman. Then hang up real quick.'

'To put us on the spot?'

'To put whoever was with Godfrey on the spot. They maybe even know exactly who we are. That doctor—'

'I don't know,' said Blaine. 'He may have.'

'Listen, Shep, I'm positive from all that's happened that Finn is in Belmont.'

'Belmont?'

That town we found you in.'

'So that's the name of it.'

'There's something happening,' she said. 'Something happening right here. Something important going on. There was Riley and the truck and—'

'But what are we to do?'

'We can't let them find Godfrey here.'

'We could pull the car out back and take him out the back door.'

'There's probably someone watching. Then they'd have us cold.'

She beat her hands together in exasperation.

'If Finn has a free hand now,' she said, 'he probably can pull off whatever he is planning. We can't let him put us out of action. We have got to stop him.'

'We?'

'You and I. You step into Godfrey's shoes. Now it's up to you.'

'But I—'

Her eyes blazed suddenly. 'You were his friend. You heard his story. You told him you were with him.'

'Sure I did,' said Blaine. 'But I am starting cold. I don't know the score.'

'Stop Finn,' she said. 'Find out what he's doing and stop him in his tracks. Fight a delaying action ...'

'You and your military thinking. Your delaying actions and your lines of retreat laid out.' (*A very female general with enormous jackboots and a flock of medals pendant from very spearlike breasts*)

Cut that out!

A newspaper gal. And you are objective.

'Shep,' she said, 'shut up. How can I be objective? I believed in Godfrey. I believed in what he was doing.'

'I suppose that I do, too. But it is all so new, so quick ...'

'Maybe we should just cut and run.'

'No! Wait a minute. If we cut and run, we'd be out of it as surely as if they caught us here.'

'But, Shep, there is no way.'

'There just might be,' he told her. 'Is there a town around here by the name of Hamilton?'

110

'Why, yes, just a mile or two away. Down by the river.'

He sprang to his feet and glanced about the room. The phone sat on the night table between the single beds.

'What—'

'A friend,' said Blaine. 'Someone that I met. Someone who might help us. A mile or two away?'

'Yes, Hamilton is. If that is what—'

'It is,' said Blaine.

He stepped swiftly across the room and picked the handpiece out of the cradle. He dialed for operator.

'I want to get a number in Hamilton. How do I go about it?'

'What is the number, sir?'

'276.'

I will ring it for you.'

He turned his head toward Harriet. 'Is it getting dark outside?'

'It was getting dark when I closed the shutters.'

He heard the purring of the signal on the wire.

'They'll need some darkness,' he said. They couldn't come in—'

'I don't know,' said Harriet, 'what you could be up to.'

'Hello,' said a voice in the phone.

'Is Anita there?'

'Right here,' said the voice. 'Just a moment.' *Anita, for you. A man.*

And that was impossible, Blaine thought wildly: you simply couldn't do it. Perhaps he'd imagined it.

'Hello,' said Anita Andrews. 'Who is this?'

Blaine. Shepherd Blaine. Remember? I was with the man who had the shotgun. With the silver shot.

Yes, I remember you.

And it was true, he thought. He had not imagined it. You could use telepathy on the telephone!

You said that if I ever needed help.

Yes, I told you that.

I need help now. (A body on the floor; police car coming down the road, red light flashing, siren howling; a speedometer and clock that had sprouted legs and were racing for a tape; the sign that said The Plainsman, the unit number on the door) *I swear to you, Anita. This is on the level. I can't explain right now. But this is on the level. I can't let them find him here.*

We'll take him off your hands.

On faith?

On faith alone. You were square with us that night.

Hurry!

Right away. I'll bring some others.

Thanks, Anita. But she was already gone.

He stood there, holding the receiver out from his face, staring at it, then slowly put it in the cradle.

'I caught part of that,' said Harriet. 'It isn't possible.'

'Of course it's not,' said Blaine. 'Telly transmission on a wire. You don't have to tell me.'

He stared down at the man lying on the floor. 'It's one of the things he talked about. Greater than Fishhook could ever be, he said.'

Harriet didn't answer.

'I wonder how much else they have?' said Blaine.

'She said they'd come for Godfrey. How will they come for him? How soon?' There was a hint of hysteria in her voice.

'They fly,' he told her. 'They are levitators. Witches.' He made a bitter laugh.
'But you—'

'How did I know them? They ambushed us one night. Just out to raise some hell. Riley had a shotgun ...'

'Riley!'

The man in the hospital room, remember? The man who died. He was in an accident.'

'But, Shep, were you with Riley? How did you come to be with him?'

'I hitched a ride. He was scared at night. He wanted someone with him. We nursed that ramshackle truck ...'

She was staring at him, a startled look about her.

'Wait a minute,' he said. 'You said something back there in the hospital. You said you were—'

'Looking for him. Godfrey had hired him and he was late and—'

'But ...'

'What is it, Shep?'

'I talked to him just before he died. He tried to give me a message, but he couldn't get it out. The message was for Finn. That was the first I heard of Finn.'

'Everything went wrong,' said Harriet. 'Every blessed thing. There was the star machine ...'

She stopped what she was saying and came across the room to stand beside him. 'But you don't know about the star machine. Or do you?'

He shook his head. 'Like the ones in Fishhook? The ones that helped us to the stars?'

She nodded. 'That's what Riley was hauling in his truck. Godfrey had arranged to get it and he had to get it moved to Pierre somehow. So he hired Riley ...'

'A bootleg star machine!' said Blaine, a little awed. 'You know that every nation in the world has laws against possessing them. They're only legal if they are in Fishhook.'

'Godfrey knew all that. But he needed one. He tried to build one, but he couldn't. There aren't any blueprints.'

'You bet your life there aren't.'

'Shep, what is wrong with you?'

'I don't know. There's really nothing wrong. A bit confused, perhaps. At how, all along the line, I was pitchforked into this.'

'You can always run.'

'Harriet, you know better. I am through with running. There's no place for me to go.'

'You could always approach some business group. They'd be glad to have you. They'd give you a job, pay you plenty for what you know of Fishhook.'

He shook his head, thinking back to Charline's party, with Dalton sitting there, long legs outstretched, his hair a rumpled mouse nest, his mouth mangling the cigar. And Dalton saying: 'In a consultive capacity you'd be worth a lot of money.'

'Well, you could,' said Harriet.

'I couldn't stomach it Besides, I made a promise. I told Godfrey I was with him. And I don't like the way that things are going. I don't like the people taking me out to hang me because I am a parry. I don't like some of the things I saw along the road and—'

'You're bitter,' she said. 'You have a right to be.'

'And you?'

'Not bitter. Just scared. Scared down to the marrow.'

You scared! A tough newspaper gal ...

He turned toward her, remembering something – the place where the old blind woman sold the roses. That night, he had seen the mask slip from Harriet Quimby and this was the second time.

Her face told him the truth – the tough newspaper gal also, at times, could be a frightened woman.

He half lifted his arms, and she crossed the little space between them. He held her close against him, and she was soft and pliant, not hard, not made of steely purpose, but very human flesh.

It'll be all right, he said. Everything will be all right.

And wondered at the sudden tenderness and protectiveness he felt, which certainly was alien in any relation he might have with this girl within his arms.

But the truck is wrecked and the trucker's dead and the police, or maybe even Finn, have the star machine. And now Godfrey's lying dead and the police are coming ...

We'll lick them all, he told her. There's nothing that can stop us ...

A siren sounded from far off, a wail torn by the prairie wind.

She sprang away from him. 'Shep, they're coming!'

'The back door!' Blaine said, quickly. 'Run toward the river. We'll get down into the breaks.'

He sprang toward the door, and as his fingers found the bolt, there was a tapping on it.

He threw back the bolt and jerked open the door and standing in the fan of light that came pouring from the room was Anita Andrews and back of her other youthful faces.

'Just in time,' said Blaine.

'This body?'

'Over there,' he said.

They came in with a rush.

The siren was much closer.

'He was a friend of ours,' said Harriet, uncertainly. 'This seems a dreadful way—'

'Miss,' Anita said, 'we'll take care of him. We'll give him every honor ...'

The siren was a steady howl that seemed to fill the room.

Quick! Anita said. Fly low. You don't want to silhouette against the sky.

Even as she spoke the room was emptying and there was no body on the floor.

She hesitated for a moment, looking at the two of them.

Someday you'll tell me what this is all about?

Someday, said Blaine. And thanks.

Any time, she said. *We parries stick together. We have to stick together. They'll smash us if we don't.*

She swung toward Blaine, and he felt the touch of her, mind against mind, and there was suddenly the sense of fireflies in the evening dusk and the smell of lilacs drifting in the softness of a river fog.

Then she was gone and the front door was closing and someone was hammering at the front.

Sit down, Blaine said to Harriet. Act as naturally as you can. Unconcerned. Relaxed. We were just sitting here and talking. Godfrey had been with us, but he went into town. Someone came and he rode into town with them. We don't know who it was. He should be back in an hour or two.

Check, said Harriet.

She sat down in a chair and folded her hands in her lap sedately,

Blaine went to the door to let in the law.

22

Belmont was beginning to close up. All the houses, as they drove past, had been tightly shuttered, and in the business district, as they drove into it, the shop lights were going out.

Up the street a block or two, the marquee of the hotel still gleamed brightly in the dusk and just this side of it was a flashing sign that proclaimed the Wild West Bar still was willing to take on a customer.

'I don't think,' said Harriet, 'that we fooled those police too much.'

Blaine agreed. 'Maybe not. But we had them stopped. There was nothing they could find.'

'I thought for a while they would pull us in.'

'So did I. But you sat there making gentle fun of them. That was hard to take. They were glad to get away. They must have felt like fools.'

He motioned at the flashing bar sign. 'Maybe we should start with that.'

'As good a place as any. Likewise, about the only place there is.'

The bar was empty when they came into the place. The bartender had an elbow propped and was idly dabbing with a cloth at imaginary wet spots.

Blaine and Harriet hoisted themselves onto stools opposite the man.

'What'll it be?' he demanded of them.

They told him.

He got glasses and reached for bottles. 'Little slow tonight,' said Blaine.

'Almost closing time,' said the man. 'They don't stick around. Soon as it gets dark folks get under cover. Everyone in this town.'

'Bad town?'

'No, not especially. It's the curfew law. This place has got a tough one. Patrols all over the place and them cops are tough. They really make it stick.'

'How about yourself?' asked Harriet.

'Oh, I am all right, miss. The boys, they know me. They know the circumstances. They know I got to stick around just in case a late customer, like you, drops in. From the hotel mostly. They know I got to get the place tucked in and turn out the lights. They give me extra minutes.'

'Sounds tough, all right,' said Blaine.

The barkeep wagged his head. 'For your own protection, mister. Folks ain't got no sense. If it wasn't for the curfew, they'd stay out to all hours where anything could get them.'

He stopped what he was doing.

'I just happened to think,' he announced. 'I got something new. You might like to try it.'

'Like what?' asked Harriet.

He reached back and got the bottle, held it up to show them.

'Something new,' he said. 'Straight out of Fishhook. They picked it up some outlandish place. Sap of a tree or something. Probably loaded with a lot of hydrocarbons. I got a couple of bottles off the factor at the Trading Post. Just to try, you know. Thought there might be some folks who might like it.'

Blaine shook his head. 'Not for me. God knows what is in it.'

'Me, neither,' said Harriet.

The barkeep set the bottle back regretfully.

'I don't blame you folks,' he said, giving them the drinks he'd made. 'I took a nip of it myself. Just to test it out, you see, because I'm no drinking man.

'Not,' he added, quickly and parenthetically, 'that I have anything against it.'

'Of course not,' Harriet sympathized.

'It was funny tasting stuff,' he said. 'Not bad, you know. Not good, either. Had a musty tang. You might get to like it if you had a drink or two.'

He stood in silence for a moment, with his hands planted solidly on the bar. 'You know what I been thinking?' he demanded.

'Not the least,' said Harriet.

'I been wondering all this afternoon if that factor down at the Trading Post concocted that stuff up himself. Just as a sort of stinking joke, you see.'

'Oh, he wouldn't dare.'

'Well, I imagine you are right, miss. But all of them factors are funny sorts of jerks. Folks don't have much to do with them – socially, at least – but even so they manage to know more of what is going on than anyone in town. They must be listening all the time, for they have all the latest gossip.

'And,' said the barkeep, laying emphasis upon this horrid crime and this social failing, 'they don't never tell you nothing.'

'Ain't it a fact,' Harriet agreed, enthusiastically.

The barkeep subsided into brooding silence.

Blaine took a wild shot in the dark. 'Lots of folks in town,' he said. 'Big doings?'

The barkeeper settled down into solid conversational stance and his voice dropped to a confidential level.

'You mean you ain't heard about it?'

'No. Just got in town a couple of hours ago.'

'Well, mister, you won't believe this – but we got a star machine.'

'A what?'

'A star machine. It's one of them contraptions that parries use to travel to the stars.'

'Never heard of them.'

'No reason that you should. The only place they're legal is in Fishhook.'

'You mean this one is illegal?'

'Couldn't be no more illegal. The state police, they've got it down in the old highway shed. You know, the one on the west edge of town. Maybe you drove by it coming in tonight.'

'I don't remember it.'

'Well, anyhow, it's there. And then, on top of that, who should show up but Lambert Finn.'

'You don't mean the Lambert Finn?'

'No one else. He's up there, in the hotel right now. He's going to have a big mass meeting out by the highway shed tomorrow. I hear the police have agreed to haul out the star machine so he can preach about it, with it standing there, right out in plain sight of all the people. I tell you, mister, that will be something worth your while to listen. He'll spout more brimstone than you ever heard before. He'll lay it on them parries. He'll take the hide clean off them. They won't dare to show their faces.'

'Not many of them around, most likely, in a town like this.'

'Well,' the bartender said, drawing out the word, 'not many in the town itself. But there's a place just a ways from here, down by the river. A place called Hamilton. It's all parry. It's a new town the parries built. Parries from all over. There's a name for a place like that – I should know the name, but I can't remember it. Like the place they used to keep the Jews in Europe.'

'Ghetto.'

The bartender smote the bar with a disgusted hand. 'Now, why couldn't I think of that? Yes, mister, that's the word. Ghetto. Except in the old days it was in the poor part of a city and now it's out in the country, in the poor part of the country. That land down by the river don't amount to shucks. No place to build a town. But them parries like it down there. Long as they don't bother no one, no one bothers them. Long as they stay in line, we leave them alone. And we know where they are, and they know we know. Any time things start going wrong, we know right where to look.'

He glanced at the clock. 'If you folks want me to start another round, you'll have time to gulp it down.'

'No, thanks,' said Blaine. He laid two bills on the bar. 'Let it ride,' he said.

'Why, thank you, sir. I thank you very much.'

As they slid off the stools, he said: 'If I were you, I'd get under cover as soon as possible. The cops will be down on top of you if they catch you out.'

'We will,' said Harriet. 'And thanks for the conversation.'

'Pleasure,' said the barkeep. 'Pleasure any time.'

Outside the bar, Blaine held the car door for Harriet, then walked around it to get in on the other side.

'The highway shed?' he asked.

'Shep, what would you do there? We'd just get into trouble.'

'I'll figure out a way. We simply can't leave that machine there for Finn to preach a sermon over.'

'So I suppose you figure you'll just haul it off.'

'No, I guess not. It's too big and clumsy. But there has to be a way. We have to put a crimp in Finn. Somehow, we've got to manage.'

'They'll have a guard.'

'I don't think so, Harriet. Locked and bolted, but no guard. There isn't anyone who would stand on guard. This town is plenty scared.'

'You're just like Godfrey,' she said. 'Both of you go around sticking out your necks.'

'You thought a lot of Godfrey.'

'Yes, a lot,' she said.

He started up the engine and swung the car out into the street.

The old highway shed was black and silent and there was nothing to indicate there was anyone around. They rode past it twice to look it over, moving slowly, and it was the same each time – just the big shed standing there, a relic of the days when there were highways to maintain, when there was need of road machinery to keep their surfaces in shape.

Blaine pulled the car off the road and threaded it easily through a willow thicket, set it down and turned off the lights.

Silence closed down on them; the darkness pulsed with quietness.

'Harriet,' said Blaine.

'Yes, Shep.'

'You stay here. Don't move. I am going up there.'

'You won't be long? There's nothing you can do.'

'I won't be long,' he said. 'Have we got a flashlight?'

'There's one in the glove compartment.'

He heard her fumbling in the dark. The catch on the door of the compartment clicked and the tiny light inside came on. The flashlight lay amid a clutter of road maps, of sunglasses, of other odds and ends.

She handed it to him. He snapped it on to test it, and it worked. He shut it off again and got out of the car.

'Sit tight,' he told her.

'And you,' she warned, 'be careful.'

23

The shed was larger than it had appeared to be when seen from the highway. It was surrounded by a high, rank growth of dead, dried weeds that rustled with stealthy sound in the slightest movement of the air. It was built of the corrugated metal sheets which had been much in use for buildings of this sort before the introduction, some three-score years before, of the putty-plastic from Aldebaran VII. Occasional windows, begrimed with dirt and ancient spider webs, broke the smooth expanse of metal. Two great upward-folding doors filled almost the entire front exposure.

To the east lay the dark outline of the town, silhouetted against the faint flush in the sky which told of a moon about to rise.

Cautiously, Blaine made a circuit of the building, looking for a way that might allow him to get in. He found nothing that was easy. The two folding doors were locked. There were a few sheets of metal that had loosened at the bottom, but the material was too heavy to allow one to bend it upward and thus create a rathole for a man to sneak inside.

There was, he realized, only one way to get in.

He went to the corner of the building nearest to the road and stood listening. Except for the harsh whispering of the weeds there was nothing to be heard. The highway was deserted and, he knew, most likely would remain so. There was no sign of light – no lamp, no glitter through a distant window. It was as if he and the shed stood in a world where there was no life at all.

He stared for a time at the willow thicket by the road, but there was no glint, no shine, nothing to indicate that a car was hidden there.

He stepped quickly from the corner and moved along the wall of metal until he came to a window. He took off his tattered jacket and wrapped it about his fist and forearm.

Then he struck a blow, and the window shattered. He struck other blows to remove the glass that was still hanging in the frame. Carefully he picked out the remaining splinters that would slash a man trying to crawl in.

Then he went back to the corner and stood there for a moment. The night still was motionless and silent.

Back at the window, he crawled into the shed, let himself down carefully, felt the floor beneath his feet. He took the flashlight from his pocket and turned it on. He swept a swath of light across the empty cavern of the shed's interior.

And there, close to the door, was the battered, broken truck which had found its rest at last, and the gleaming star machine that it had carried.

Walking as softly as he could, Blaine moved across the floor and stood beside the machine, shining his light upon it. And it was something that he knew well, it was a machine that back in Fishhook he had known intimately. There was a strange beauty in it, he told himself as he stood and looked at it, almost as if one could see, reflected in its surface, the far reaches of the universe to which it could help a man to go.

But it was old – one of the older models that Fishhook had replaced some ten years or so ago, and there was little doubt, he knew that it had somehow come from Fishhook. There must be many of the older models such as this stacked away in some almost forgotten storehouse, stored there more than likely because it was easier to store them than it was to break them up. For something such as this must either be stored under lock and key or it must be broken up, for they could not be simply thrown away. In this machine lay the key to Fishhook's monopoly and there must be no possibility that one of them should fall into any other hands.

But one of them had fallen into other hands and here it lay tonight, mute evidence of one of the smartest, slickest bits of intrigue to which Fishhook, intrigue-ridden as it was, had ever been unwitting party.

Blaine tried to imagine how Stone had ever managed, and thinking of it, his admiration for the man rose a notch or two. It had taken money, surely, and it had taken trusted agents and it had required a plan of operation which would countenance no slip-up.

He wondered vaguely, as he stood there, how much Harriet might have had to do with it. Certainly, he told himself, she had had no qualms, in the process of smuggling him from Fishhook, of getting out herself. She was, he thought, just the kind of woman who could engineer a thing like this – self-possessed and calm and with a sure and certain knowledge of all those inner workings which made Fishhook keep on ticking. And with a mind that operated with the fine precision of a good Swiss watch.

Stone had had great hopes of this machine and now the hopes were gone. Now Stone was dead and the star machine lay here in this abandoned shed, a showpiece bit of evidence for a man so filled with hate that he would destroy paranormal kinetics, root and branch and leaf.

And Finn could make much of this machine, for while it might be called machine, it was not the kind of machine to which the human mind for centuries has become accustomed. It had no moving parts and it had no function that was discernible. It was designed to work upon nothing more material than the human mind and senses. It worked with symbolism rather than with energy – and yet it worked. Just as a rosary in the hands of the devout had worked for centuries before there had ever been a thought of such a thing as a paranormal human.

If the hope were gone, thought Blaine, then the machine could not remain. If he owed Stone nothing else, he owed him that much at least. He owed him, he reminded himself, some slight repayment for that night he'd phoned.

There was a way – there was a way, he knew, if out of the frothing sea of alien knowledge which surged inside of him he could only pull it forth.

He sought for it and found it and in the finding of it he touched on other knowledge, all neatly docketed and primly pigeonholed, as if some filing clerk had been busily at work within his cluttered mind.

He stood weak and trembling at the discovery of this pigeonholing, for he had not known, had had no inkling that it was going on. But it was the human way, he told himself – it was an evidence of human rebellion against the piecemeal disorderliness of the mass of data which had been dumped into his mind by the creature on that distant planet.

The creature still was with him, or the essence of the creature, and he hunted for it among the pigeonholes, but it was not there; there was no sign of it as such, but there was something else; there was something very wrong.

Startled, he went scrambling on the trail of wrongness and he caught and held it, muzzling it with a nose of horror – for it was simply this: his mind no longer was an entirely human mind. And in the edge of terror was the terrible wonder of how he still retained enough pure humanity to know this was the case.

He put out his hand in a blind and groping way and caught a corner of the star machine and held tightly on to it.

It all spelled out, he suspected, to the simple fact that he remained human, or mostly human, on the surface, while beneath that surface was a fusion of two individuals, of the knowledge and perhaps the ethics and the motives of two different forms of life. And that made sense when one thought of it, for the Pinkness had not changed, it had stayed its sprawling, slobby self; there had been no trace of human in it, although inside of it was a certain portion of humanity and God knew what else besides.

He released the grip he had upon the star machine and ran his hand against the glasslike smoothness of its metal structure.

There was a way – if he could only do it. He had the knowledge now, but did he have the technique?

Time, the Pinkness had told him – time is the simplest thing there is. But still, Blaine told himself, not as easily handled as the creature had made out.

He stood there thinking, and the thing that he must do became very clear indeed.

The past was a worthless path to follow, for the machine was in the past already. It had left a long and nebulous trail clear across the past.

But the future was a different matter. If it could be moved into the future, this present moment and all succeeding present moments would then become its past and all that would remain would be the ghostly track of it – and a laughter and a mocking and a thing of magic which would make no proper subject for a rabble-rousing sermon by a man named Lambert Finn.

And more than that, thought Blaine, it would, more than likely, scare the hell right out of him.

He reached out with his mind to encircle the machine and it was no use. His mind would open up and reach, but there was a lack of stretch in it and he could not take in all of the machine. So he rested and then he tried again.

There was a strangeness and an alienness in the shed he had not noticed, and there was an unknown menace in the scraping of the weeds outside the broken window, and the air held a sharpness and a tang that raised bristles on his neck. It was most confusing, for suddenly it seemed that he had lost all rapport with this world in which he found himself and that nothing, not the earth he stood on nor the air he breathed or even the body that he wore was anything he'd ever known before and there was a horror in this lack of familiarity, in this shift from the known which he no longer could remember into this unknown for which he had no focal points. But it would be all right, it all would come aright if he could move this strange artifact he held within his mind, for it had been for this purpose that he had been called forth from the darkness and the warmness and the snug security and if he got the job done he could go back again, back to his memories of other days and his slow assimilation of new data and the miser-satisfaction of counting up the new facts, one by one, as he piled them in neat stacks.

The artifact, for all its strangeness, was an easy thing to handle. Its roots did not run back too far and the co-ordinates were falling very satisfactorily into place and he almost had it made. But he must not hurry despite his screaming need to hurry; he must somewhere snare some patience. So he waited for the co-ordinates to go clicking into place and he made exact and unhurried measurement of the temporal strain and he gave the thing a twitch at just the right degree of twist and it was exactly where he had wanted it.

Then he dived back home again, back into the dark and warmness, and Blaine stood shorn of all but his human self in a place of foggy nothingness.

There was nothing there – nothing but himself and the star machine. He reached out his hand and touched the star machine and it was very solid. It was, so far as he could see, the only solid thing there was.

For the fog itself, if fog were what it was, had an unreal quality, as if it were striving to camouflage its very fact of being.

Blaine stood quietly, afraid to move – afraid that any movement might plunge him into some pit of black foreverness.

For this, he realized, was the future. It was a place without a single feature of the space-time matrix that he knew. It was a place where nothing yet had happened – an utter emptiness. There was neither light nor dark; there was nothing here but emptiness. There had never been anything in this place, nor was anything ever intended to occupy this place – until this very moment when he and his machine had been thrust upon it, intruders who have overstepped their time.

He let his breath out slowly and breathed in again – and there was nothing to breathe in!

Blackness rushed in upon him, and the throbbing of his heartbeat was loud within his head, and he reached out desperately to grab at something – at anything – in this place where there was not a thing to grab.

Even as he did, the alienness came back, a startled, frightened alienness, and a hodgepodge of queer symbolic figures, which even in his agony of mind, he took to be some outre mathematics, went flooding through his brain.

There was air again to breathe and there was solid floor beneath his feet and he smelled the mustiness of the inside of the highway shed.

He was back home again and so was the alienness, for it was gone from him. Back, he told himself, to the darkness and the warmth inside his very brain.

He stood erect and mentally checked himself and he was all right. He opened his eyes slowly, for they somehow had been closed, and there was only darkness until he remembered the flashlight still clutched in his hand. And yet not as dark as it had been before. Now light from a newly risen moon poured through the broken window.

He lifted the flashlight and shoved the contact button, and the light sprang out and the machine was there before him, but strange and unsubstantial – the ghost of a machine, the trail that it had left behind it when it had moved into the future.

He lifted his free arm and used his jacket sleeve to wipe his forehead dry. For it was over now. He had done what he had come to do. He'd struck the blow for Stone; he'd stopped Finn in his tracks.

There was here no object lesson; there was no longer any text for Finn to preach upon. There was, instead, a mocking jeer from the very magic that Finn had fought for years.

Behind him he sensed a movement and he swung around so hurriedly that his fingers loosened on the flashlight and it fell upon the floor and rolled.

Out of the darkness a voice spoke.

'Shep,' it said, with full heartiness, 'that was very neatly done.'

Blaine froze and hopelessness flooded in.

For this was the end, he knew. He had come as far as he was going to. He had finally run his race.

He knew that hearty voice. He never could forget it.

The man standing in the darkness of the shed was his old friend, Kirby Rand!

24

Rand was a blacker blob in the darkness as he stepped forward and picked the flashlight off the floor. He pivoted to turn the light full upon the star machine and in the flood of brightness tiny little dust motes could be seen dancing in the heart of the machine.

'Yes,' said Rand, 'very neatly done. I don't know how you did it and I don't know why you did it, but you most certainly have taken care of it.'

He turned the flashlight off and for a moment they stood silent in the darkness, relieved by the streaks of moonlight that came through the windows.

Then Rand said: 'I suppose you know that Fishhook owes you a vote of thanks for this.'

'Come off of it,' Blaine told him, roughly. 'You know very well it was not done for Fishhook.'

'Nevertheless,' said Kirby, 'it happens that in this particular area our interests coincide. We could not let this machine stay lost. We could not allow it to remain in improper hands. You understand, of course.'

'Perfectly,' said Blaine.

Rand sighed. 'I had expected trouble and if there is anything Fishhook doesn't want, it's trouble. Particularly when that trouble is out in the hinterlands.'

'There's not been any trouble,' Blaine told him, 'that needs to worry Fishhook.'

'I am glad to hear it. And you, Shep? How are you getting on.'

'Not too badly, Kirby.'

'That is nice,' said Kirby. 'That is very nice. It makes me feel so good. And now, I would imagine, we should get out of here.'

He led the way across the floor back to the broken window and stood aside.

'You first,' he said to Blaine, 'and I'll be right behind you. I would ask, as one friend to another, that you not try to run away.'

'No need to fear,' Blaine told him dryly, then climbed quickly through the window.

He could run, of course, he told himself, but that would be extremely foolish, for there was no doubt Rand would have a gun and he would be quite efficient with it, even in the moonlight. And more than that, if there were any shooting, Harriet might come running to be of what help she could, and if she got involved in this, then he'd be truly friendless. Otherwise, he told himself, almost prayerfully, Harriet would stay hidden in the willow clump. She would see what happened and in just a little while she'd have an angle figured out.

Harriet was, he told himself, the only hope he had.

He dropped out of the window and stood to one side for Rand to clamber through.

Rand hit the ground and turned toward him, just a bit too quickly, too much like a hunter, then he relaxed and chuckled,

'It was a slick trick, Shep,' he said. 'Efficiently engineered. Someday you'll have to tell me exactly how you did it. To steal a star machine is not an easy thing.'

Blaine gulped down his astonishment and hoped the moonlight hid the look he knew must be upon his face.

Rand reached out a hand and took him companionably by the elbow.

'The car's down here,' he said. 'Right down by the road.'

They walked together across the patch of rustling weeds, and the land lay different now, no longer dark and fearsome, but a place of painted magic stretched out in the moonlight. To their right lay the town, a mass of darkened houses that looked more like mounds than houses, with the faint tracery of nude trees standing up like ragged paintbrushes reared against the eastern sky. To the west and north lay the silver prairie land, flat and featureless and made immense by its very lack of features.

And just down the road was the clump of willows.

Blaine shot a quick glance at the clump and there were only willows. There was no glint of moonlight bouncing off metal. He walked a pace or two, then took another look and this time, he knew, there could be no mistake. There was no car in that clump of willows. Harriet was gone.

Good girl, he thought. She had a lot of sense. She'd probably gotten out of there as soon as Rand showed up. She'd figure, more than likely, that the one way she'd be most valuable would be to make a getaway against another day.

'I don't suppose,' said Rand, 'that you have a place to stay.'

'No,' said Blaine, 'I haven't.'

'Bad town,' Rand told him. 'They take this witchcraft-werewolf business seriously indeed. Cops stopped me twice. Warned me under cover. Told me very sternly it was for my own protection.'

'They're all wrought up,' said Blaine. 'Lambert Finn is here.'

'Oh, yes,' Rand said carelessly. 'An old friend of ours.'

'Not of mine. I never met the man.'

'A charming soul,' said Rand. 'A very charming one.'

Blaine said: I know very little of him. Just what I have heard.'

Rand grunted. 'I would suggest,' he said, 'that you spend the night at the Post. The factor will be able to find some place to bed you down. I wouldn't be surprised if he could dig up a bottle, too. I suddenly feel the need of a monstrous slug of booze.'

'I could stand one myself,' Blaine told him.

For there was no sense of fighting now, no more sense than running. You went along with them and waited for your chance. They tried to throw you off your balance and you tried to throw them off theirs. And all along you knew, both of you might know, that it was a most polite but very deadly game.

Although he wondered why he bothered. After the last few weeks, he told himself, Fishhook would seem an engaging place. Even if they sent him to the detention resort in Baja California, it would be better than the prospect he faced in this Missouri river town.

They reached the car that sat beside the road, and Blaine waited for Rand to get underneath the wheel, then crawled in himself.

Rand started the engine but did not switch on the lights. He pulled the machine out into the roadway and went drifting down it.

'The police can't really do much more,' he said, 'than run you under cover, but there seems to me no point in getting tangled up with them if you can avoid it.'

'None at all,' said Blaine.

Rand avoided the center of the town, went sneaking down the side streets. Finally he cut back and went sliding up an alley, swung into a parking lot and stopped.

'Here we are,' he said. 'Let's go get that drink.'

The back door opened to his knock and they walked into the back room of the Trading Post. Most of the place, Blaine saw, was used as storage space, but one corner of it served as a living room. There was a bed and stove and table. There was a massive stone fireplace with a wood fire burning in it and comfortable chairs ranged in front of it.

Up near the door that went into the front part of the store stood a massive boxlike structure, and Blaine, although he'd never seen one, recognized it immediately as a transo – the matter transference machine which made the vast network of Trading Posts stretched around the globe an economic possibility. Through that box could come, with a moment's notice, any of the merchandise for which any of the thousands of retail outlets might find itself in need.

This was the machine that Dalton had talked about that night at Charline's party – the machine which he had said could wipe out the world's transportation interests if Fishhook ever chose to put it in public use.

Rand waved a hand at one of the chairs. 'Make yourself comfortable,' he said to Blaine. 'Grant will rustle up a bottle. You have one, don't you, Grant?'

The factor grinned. 'You know I do. How else could I live in a place like this?'

Blaine sat down in one of the chairs before the fire, and Rand took one facing him. He rubbed his hands together.

'We parted over a bottle,' he reminded Blaine. 'I'd say it was only fitting to renew our acquaintance over one.'

Blaine felt a tenseness growing in him, the sense of being trapped, but he grinned at Rand.

'You know the margin that I had that night?' he asked. 'Eight lousy little minutes. That was all I had.'

'You miscalculated, Shep. You had exactly twelve. The boys were a little slow in getting out the tape.'

'And Freddy. Who'd ever thought that Freddy worked for you?'

'You'd be surprised,' Rand told him blandly, 'at some of the people I have working for me.'

They sat easily before the blazing fire of apple wood, measuring one another.

Finally Rand said: 'Why don't you tell me, Shep? I haven't all the answers. I can't get it figured out. You ran into that situation out beyond the Pleiades and you got it buttoned up ...'

'Buttoned up?'

'Sure. Buttoned up. Exclusive. We knew that you had something and we sent some others out there and your creature sits and stares at them and that is all it does. They try to talk with it and it's absolutely dumb. It pretends it doesn't hear them. It makes out not to understand ...'

'Brotherhood,' said Blaine. 'We went through the rites. You wouldn't understand.'

'I think I do,' said Rand. 'How alien are you, Shep?'

'Try me out and see.'

Rand shuddered. 'No, thanks. You see, I've followed up your trail. It began with Freddy and got weirder as it went along.'

'And what do you intend to do about it?'

'Damned if I know,' said Rand.

The factor brought a bottle and two glasses. 'None for yourself?' asked Rand.

Grant shook his head. 'I've got some stock arranging up front. If you don't mind ...'

'Of course not,' Rand told him. 'Go on with your work. One thing ...'

'What, sir?'

'I wonder if Mr Blaine could spend the night here.'

'Certainly. Although it's pretty crude.'

'I don't mind,' said Blaine.

'I'd offer you my bed, sir, but frankly it's no bargain. Once you get used to it, you can live with it, but to start out with—'

'I wouldn't think of taking it.'

'I could get some blankets and you could bed down on the floor. Believe me, it would be better than the bed.'

'Anything,' said Blaine. 'I'll be thankful for anything at all.'

Rand picked up the bottle and uncorked it.

'I'll bring out the blankets in a little while,' the factor told them.

'Thank you, Grant,' said Rand.

The man left. The door that led into the front part of the store sighed softly shut behind him.

Rand poured out the liquor.

'Actually,' he said, 'unless you want to, you don't have to stay here.'

'No?'

'I'm going back to Fishhook. Through the transo. You could come along.'

Blaine was silent. Rand handed him the drink.

'Well, what do you say?' he asked.

Blaine laughed. 'You're making it too easy.'

'Perhaps I am,' said Rand.

He took a drink and settled back into the chair.

'The alien part I can understand,' he said. 'That is an occupational hazard faced by every traveler. But how does the star machine tie up? You were in cahoots with Stone, of course.'

'You know that Stone is dead.'

'No, I haven't heard that.' But he was unconvincing.

And suddenly, from the quality of Rand's voice, from some intuition, Blaine knew that Rand did not care that Stone was dead or that Finn might be in town. It was all one with him. Or it might be even more than that. It might be that Rand was quite satisfied to know that Stone was dead, that he might approve in good part with what Finn was doing. For Fishhook's monopoly rested upon a non-parry world, upon all the millions of people in the world being forced to look to Fishhook for the commerce with stars. And so Fishhook and Rand, Blaine realized with something of a shock, might even be quite willing to see Finn's crusade go rolling ahead to its inevitable conclusion.

And if that was true, could it have been Fishhook instead of Finn which had struck the lethal blow at Stone?

He recoiled at the thought, but it clung inside his brain – for the situation was revealing itself as more than just a simple struggle between Finn and Stone.

It might be best, he told himself, to disclaim immediately any connection whatsoever with the star machine. Perhaps he should have made the disclaimer back there at the shed when Rand first had mentioned it. But if he told the truth, if he told Rand now that he had not known of the star machine until just hours ago, he conceivably might lose a bargaining point of uncertain value. And even if he told him, Rand more than likely would refuse to believe him, for he, after all, had helped Riley nurse the truck which had carried it almost all the way from Mexico.

'It took you plenty long,' said Blaine, 'to catch up with me. Are you, maybe, losing your grip? Or were you just amused?'

Rand frowned. 'We almost lost you, Shep. We had you pegged in that town where they were about to hang you.'

'You were even there that night?'

'Well, not personally,' said Rand, 'but I had some men there.'

'And you were about to let me hang?'

'Well, I tell you honestly, we were of divided mind. But you took the decision right out of our hands.'

'But if not ... '

'I think most likely we would have let you hang. There was the possibility, of course, that if we grabbed you off, you could have led us to the star machine. But we were fairly confident, at that point, we could spot it for ourselves.' He crashed his glass down on the table. 'Of all the crazy things!' he yelled, 'Hauling a machine like that in the rattletrap you used. Whatever—'

'Simple,' said Blaine, answering for Stone. 'And you know the answer just as well as I do. No one would be that crazy. If you had stolen something very valuable, you'd get it as far away and as fast as possible ...'

'Anybody would,' said Rand.

He saw Blaine grinning at him and grinned back.

'Shep,' he said, 'come clean with me. We were good friends once. Maybe, for all I know, we're still the best of friends.'

'What do you want to know?'

'You took that machine someplace just now.'

Blaine nodded.

'And you can get it back again.'

'No,' Blaine told him. 'I'm pretty sure I can't. I was – well, just sort of playing a joke on someone.'

'On me, perhaps?'

'Not you. On Lambert Finn.'

'You don't like Finn, do you?'

'I've never met the man.'

Rand picked up the bottle and filled the glasses once again. He drank half of the liquor in his glass and then stood up.

'I have to leave,' he said, looking at his watch. 'One of Charline's parties. Wouldn't miss it for the world. You're sure that you won't come? Charline would be glad to have you.'

'No, thanks. I'll stay right here. Give Freddy my regards.'

'Freddy,' said Rand, 'isn't with us any more.'

Blaine got up and walked with Rand over to the transo. Rand opened the door. The inside of it looked something like a freight elevator.

'Too bad,' said Rand, 'we can't use these out in space. It would free a lot of manpower.'

'I suppose,' Blaine said, 'that you are working on it.'

'Oh, certainly,' Rand told him. 'It's just a matter of refining the controls.' He held out his hand. 'So long, Shep. I'll be seeing you.'

'Good-bye, Kirby,' said Blaine. 'Not if I can help it.'

Rand grinned and stepped into the machine and closed the door. There was no flashing light – nothing to show the machine had operated.

And yet by now, Blaine knew, Kirby Rand was back in Fishhook.

He turned from the transo and started back for the chair beside the fire.

The door from the store up front swung open, and Grant came into the room. He had a striped robe folded on his arm. 'I've got just the thing,' he announced. 'I had forgotten that I had it.'

He lifted the robe off his arm and shook it out. 'Isn't it a beauty?' he demanded.

It was all of that. It was a fur of some sort and there was something about the fur itself that made it glitter in the firelight, as if someone had dusted it with tiny diamond fragments. It was a golden yellow with black stripes that ran diagonally and it had the look of silk rather than of fur.

'It's been around for years,' said Grant. 'There was this man camping on the river and he came in and ordered it. Fishhook had a bit of trouble locating one immediately, but they finally delivered. As you know, sir, they always do.'

'Yes, I know,' said Blaine.

'Then the man never did show up. But the fur was so beautiful I could never send it back. I kept it on inventory, pretending that someday I'd have a chance to sell it. I never will, of course. It costs too much money for a one-horse town like this.'

'What is it?'

'The warmest, lightest, softest fur in the universe. Campers carry it. Better than a sleeping bag.'

'I couldn't use it,' protested Blaine. 'Just an ordinary blanket—'

'But you must,' Grant told him. 'As a favor to me, sir. My accommodations are so poor, I feel deeply shamed. But if I knew you were sleeping in a luxury item ...'

Blaine laughed and held out his hand.

'All right,' he said. 'And thanks.'

Grant gave him the robe, and Blaine weighed it in his hand, not quite believing it could be so light.

'I've still got a little work,' the factor told him. 'If you don't mind, I'll go back and finish it. You can bed down anywhere.'

'Go ahead,' said Blaine. 'I'll finish up my drink and then turn in. Would you have one with me?'

'Later on,' the factor said. 'I always have a snort before I go to bed.'

'I'll leave the bottle for you.'

'Good night, sir,' the factor said. 'See you in the morning.'

Blaine went back to the chair and sat down in it, with the robe lying in his lap. He stroked it with his hand and it was so soft and warm that it gave the illusion of being still alive.

He picked up the glass and worked leisurely on the liquor and puzzled over Rand.

The man was probably the most dangerous man on Earth, despite what Stone had said of Finn – the most dangerous personally, a silky, bulldog danger, a bloodhound of a man who carried out the policies of Fishhook as if they had been holy orders. No enemy of Fishhook was ever safe from Rand.

And yet he had not insisted that Blaine go back with him. He had been almost casual in his invitation, as if it had been no more than a minor social matter, and he had displayed no resentment nor no apparent disappointment upon Blaine's refusal. Nor had he made a move toward force, although that, Blaine told himself, was more than likely due to his lack of knowledge with what he might be dealing. Along the trail, apparently, he had happened on enough to put him on his guard, to know that the man he followed had some secret abilities entirely new to Fishhook.

So he'd move slowly and cautiously, and he'd cover up with a nonchalance that fooled no one at all. For Rand, Blaine knew, was a man who would not give up.

He had something up his sleeve, Blaine knew – something so well hidden that no corner of it showed.

There was a trap all set and baited. There was no doubt of it.

Blaine sat quietly in his chair and finished off the liquor in his glass.

Perhaps it was foolish of him to remain here in the Post. Perhaps it would be better if he just got up and left. And yet that might be the very thing Rand would have figured him to do. Perhaps the trap was outside the door and not in the Post at all. It could be very likely that this room was the one safe place in all the world for him to spend the night.

He needed shelter, but he did not need the sleep. Perhaps the thing to do was stay here, but not to go to sleep. He could lie on the floor, with the robe wrapped tight about him and pretend to sleep, but keeping watch on Grant. For if there were a trap in this room, Grant was the one to spring it.

He put his glass back on the table beside the one that Rand had used, still a quarter full of liquor. He moved the bottle over to make a set piece out of the bottle and the glasses, the three of them together. He bundled the robe underneath his arm and walked over to the fire. He picked up the poker and pushed the burning logs together to revive their dying flame.

He'd bed down here, he decided, just before the fire, so that the light of it would be back of him, out into the room.

He spread the robe carefully on the floor, took off his jacket and folded it for a pillow. He kicked off his shoes and lay down on the robe. It was soft and yielding, almost like a mattress despite its lack of thickness. He pulled it over him and it fell together smoothly, like a sleeping bag. There was a comfort in it that he had not felt since those days when he had been a boy and had snuggled down into his bed, underneath the blankets, in his room on the coldest winter nights.

He lay there, staring out into the darkness of the storeroom beyond the living quarters. He could see the faint outlines of barrels and bales and boxes. And lying there in the silence, unbroken except by the occasional crackle of the fire behind him, he became aware of the faint scent which perfumed the room – the indescribable odor of things alien to the Earth. Not an offensive scent, nor exotic, not in any way startling at all, but a smell such as was not upon the Earth, the compounded smell of spice and fabric, of wood and food, of all the many other things which were gathered from the stars. And only a small stock of it here, he knew, only the staples considered necessary for one of the smaller Posts. But a Post with the entire resources of the massive Fishhook warehouses available within a moment's notice, thanks to the transo standing in its corner.

And this was only a small part of that traffic with the stars – this was only the part that you could put your hands upon, the one small part of it that one could buy or own.

There was also that greater unseen, almost unrealized part of the Fishhook operation – the securing and collecting (and the hoarding, as well) of ideas and of knowledge snared from the depths of space. In the universities of Fishhook, scholars from all parts of the world sifted through this knowledge and sought to correlate and study it, and in some cases to apply it, and in the years to come it would be this knowledge and these ideas which would shape the course and the eventual destiny of all humanity.

But there was more to it than that. There was, first of all, the revealed knowledge and ideas, and secondly, the secret files of learning and the facts kept under lock and key or at the very best reviewed by most confidential boards and panels.

For Fishhook could not, in the name of humanity as well as its own self-interest, release everything it found.

There were certain new approaches, philosophies, ideas, call them what you might, which, while valid in their own particular social structures, were not human in any sense whatever, nor by any stretch of imagination adaptable to the human race and the human sense of value. And there were those others which, while applicable, must be studied closely for possible side effects on human thinking and the human viewpoint before they could be introduced, no matter how obliquely, into the human cultural pattern. And there still were others, wholly applicable, which could not be released for perhaps another hundred years – ideas so far ahead, so revolutionary that they must wait for the human race to catch up with them.

And in this must have lain something of what Stone had been thinking when he had started his crusade to break the monopoly of Fishhook, to bring to the paranormal people of the world outside of Fishhook some measure of the heritage which was rightly theirs by the very virtue of their abilities.

In that Blaine could find agreement with him, for it was not right, he told himself, that all the results of PK should be forever funneled through the tight controls of a monopoly that in the course of a century of existence had somehow lost the fervor of its belief and its strength of human purpose in a welter of commercialism such as no human being, nor any age, had ever known before.

By every rule of decency, parakinesis belonged to Man himself, not to a band of men, not to a corporation, not even to its discoverers nor the inheritors of its discoverers – for the discovery of it, or the realization of it, no matter by what term one might choose to call it, could not in any case be the work of one man or one group of men alone. It was something that must lay within the public domain. It was a truly natural phenomena – more peculiarly a natural resource than wind or wood or water.

Behind Blaine the logs, burning to the point of collapse, fell apart in a fiery crash. He turned to look at them –

Or tried to turn.

But he could not turn.

There was something wrong.

Somehow or other, the robe had become wrapped too tightly –

He pushed his hands out from his side to pull it loose, but he could not push his hands and it would not loosen.

Rather, it tightened. He could feel it tighten.

Terrified, he tried to thrust his body upward, trying to sit up. He could not do it.

The robe held him in a gentle but unyielding grasp.

He was as effectively trussed as if he'd been tied with rope. The robe, without his knowing it, had become a strait jacket that held him close and snug.

He lay quietly on his back and while a chill went through his body, sweat poured down his forehead and ran into his eyes.

For there had been a trap.

He had been afraid of one.

He had been on guard against it.

And yet, of his own free will and unsuspecting, he had wrapped the trap about him.

25

Rand had said, 'I'll be seeing you,' when he had shaken hands and stepped into the transo. He had sounded cheerful and very confident. And he'd had a right to sound that way, Blaine thought ruefully, for he'd had it all planned out. He had known exactly what would happen and he'd planned it letter perfect – the one way to apprehend a man you happened to be just a little scared of, not knowing exactly what to expect from him.

Blaine lay on the floor, stretched out, held stretched out and motionless by the encircling robe – except, of course, it was not a robe. It was, more than likely, one of those weird discoveries which Fishhook, for purposes of its own, had found expedient to keep under very careful cover. Foreseeing, no doubt, that certain unique uses might be found for it.

Blaine searched his memory and there was nothing there – nothing that even hinted of a thing like this, some parasitic life, perhaps, which for time on end could lie quiet and easy, making like a robe, but which came to deadly life once it was exposed to something warm and living.

It had him now and within a little while it might start feeding on him, or whatever else it might plan to do with him. There was no use, he knew, to struggle, for at every movement of his body the thing would only close the tighter.

He searched his mind again for a clue to this thing and all at once he found a place – he could see a place – a murky, tumbled planet with tangled forestation and weird residents that flapped and crawled and shambled. It was a place of horror, seen only mistily through the fogs of memory, but the most startling thing about it was that he was fairly certain, even as he dredged it up, he had no such memory. He had never been there and he'd never talked to one who had, although it might have been something he'd picked up from dimensino – from some idle hour of many years before, buried deep within his mind and unsuspected until this very moment.

The picture grew the brighter and the clearer, as if somewhere in his brain someone might be screwing at a lens to get a better picture, and now he could see in remarkable and mind-chilling detail the sort of life that lived within the welter of chaotic jungle. It was horrendous and obscene and it crawled and crept and there was about it a studied, cold ferociousness, the cruelty of the uncaring and unknowing, driven only by a primal hunger and a primal hate.

Blaine lay frozen by the pitlike horror of the place, for it was almost as if he actually were there, as if a part of him lay on the floor before the fireplace while the other half was standing, in all reality, within the loathsome jungle.

He seemed to hear a noise, or this other half of him seemed to hear a noise, and this other half of him looked upward into what might have been a tree, although it was too gnarled, too thorned and too obnoxious to be any proper tree, and looked up, he saw the robe, hanging from a branch, with the shattered diamond dust sparkling in its fur, about to drop upon him.

He screamed, or seemed to scream, and the planet and its denizens faded out, as if the hand within his brain had turned the viewing lens out of proper focus.

He was back, entire, in the land of fireplace and of storeroom, with the transo machine standing in its corner. The door that went into the store was opening, and Grant was coming through.

Grant moved out into the room and eased the door behind him to its closed position. Then he swung around and stood silently, huge and stolid, staring at the man upon the floor.

'Mr Blaine,' he said, speaking softly. 'Mr Blaine, are you awake?'

Blaine did not answer.

'Your eyes are open, Mr Blaine. Is there something wrong with you?'

'Not a thing,' said Blaine. 'I was just lying here and thinking.'

'Good thoughts, Mr Blaine?'

'Very good, indeed.'

Grant moved forward slowly, catfooted, as if he might be stalking something. He reached the table and picked up the bottle. He put it to his mouth and let it gurgle.

He put the bottle down.

'Mr Blaine, why don't you get up? We could sit around and talk and have a drink or two. I don't get to talk to people much. They come here and buy, of course, but they don't talk to me no more than they just have to.'

'No, thanks,' said Blaine. 'I'm quite comfortable.'

Grant moved from the table and sat down in one of the chairs before the fireplace.

'It was a shame,' he said, 'you didn't go back to Fishhook with Mr Rand. Fishhook is an exciting place to be.'

'You're quite right,' Blaine told him, replying automatically, not paying much attention.

For now he knew – he knew where he'd got that memory, where he'd picked up the mental picture of that other planet. He had gotten it from the neat stacks of information he'd picked up from the Pinkness. He, himself, of course, had never visited the planet, but the Pinkness had.

And there was more to the memory than just the magic-lantern picture of the place. There was, as well, a file of data about the planet and its life. But disorderly, not yet sorted out, and very hard to get at.

Grant leaned back into his chair, smirking just a little.

Grant reached out a hand and tapped his fingers on the robe. It gave forth a sound like a muted drum.

'Well?' he demanded. 'How do you like it, Mr Blaine?'

'I'll let you know,' Blaine told him, 'when I get my hands on you.'

Grant got up from the chair and walked back to the table, following an exaggerated, mocking path around the stretched-out Blaine. He picked up the bottle and had another slug.

'You won't get your hands on me,' he said, 'because in just another minute I'm going to shove you into the transo over there and back you go to Fishhook.'

He took another drink and set the bottle back.

'I don't know what you done,' he said. 'I don't know why they want you. But I got my orders.'

He half lifted the bottle, then thought better of it. He shoved it back to the center of the table. He walked forward and stood towering over Blaine.

There was another picture, of another planet, and there was a thing that walked along what might have been a road. The thing was nothing such as Blaine had ever seen before. It looked something like a walking cactus, but it was not a cactus and there was every doubt that it was vegetable. But neither the creature nor the road were too significant. What was significant was that following at the creature's heels, gamboling awkwardly along the could-be road, were a half dozen of the robes.

Hunting dogs, thought Blaine. The cactus was a hunter and these were his hunting dogs. Or he was a trapper and these things were his traps. Robes, domesticated from that other jungle planet, perhaps picked up by some space-going trader, tough enough to survive stellar radiation, and brought to this planet to be bartered for something else of value.

Perhaps, Blaine thought wildly, it was from this very planet that the robe now wrapped about him had been found and taken back to Fishhook.

There was something else pounding in his brain – some sort of phrase, a very alien phrase, perhaps a phrase from the cactus language. It was barbarous in its twisting of the tongue and it made no sense, but as Grant stooped with his hands outstretched to lift him, Blaine shouted out the phrase with all his strength.

And as he shouted, the robe came loose. It no longer held him. Blaine rolled, with a powerful twist of his body, against the legs of the man who was bending over him.

Grant went over, face forward on the floor, with a roar of rage. Blaine, clawing his way to his hands and knees, broke free and lunged to his feet out beyond the table.

Grant swarmed off the floor. Blood dripped slowly from his nose where it had struck against the boards. One hand was raw with blood oozing from the knuckles where his hand had scraped.

He took a quick step forward and his face was twisted with a double fear – the fear of a man who could free himself from the clutches of the robe, the fear of having failed his job.

Then he lunged, head lowered, arms outthrust, fingers spread, driving straight for Blaine. He was big and powerful and he was driven by an utter desperation that made him doubly dangerous since he would be careless of any danger to himself.

Blaine pivoted to one side – not quite far enough. One of Grant's outstretched hands caught at his shoulder, slipped off it, the fingers dragging, clawing wildly, and closing on Blaine's shirt. The cloth held momentarily throwing Blaine off balance, then the fabric parted and ripped loose with a low-pitched screeching.

Grant swung around, then flung forward once again, a snarl rising in his throat. Blaine, his heels dug into the floor, brought his fist up fast, felt the jolt of it hitting bone and flesh, sensed the shiver that went through Grant's body as the big man staggered back,

Blaine swung again and yet again, following Grant, blows that started from his knees and landed with an impact that made his arm a dead thing from the elbow down – blows that shook and staggered Grant and drove him back, ruthlessly and relentlessly.

It was not anger that drove Blaine, although there was anger in him, nor fear, nor confidence, but a plain and simple logic that this was his only chance, that he had to finish the man in front of him or himself be finished.

He had gotten in one lucky blow and he must never stop. No rough-and-tumble fighter, he would lose everything he'd gained if he let Grant regain his balance, if he ever gave him a chance to rush him again or land a solid blow.

Grant tottered blindly, hands clawing frantically at the air, groggy with the blows. Deliberately, mercilessly, Blaine aimed at the chin.

The blow smacked hollowly, and Grant's head snapped back, pivoting to one side. His body became a limp thing without any bone or muscle that folded in upon itself. Grant slumped and hit the floor, lying like a rag doll robbed of its inner strength of sawdust,

Blaine let his arms fall to his side. He felt the stinging of the cuts across his knuckles and the dead, dull ache that went through his punished muscles.

A faint surprise ran through him – that he should have been able to do a thing like this; that he, with his own two fists, should have beaten this big brute of a man into a bloody pulp.

He'd got in the first good blow and that had been nothing but pure and simple luck. And he had found the key that unlocked the robe and had that been a piece of luck as well?

He thought about it and he knew that it had not been luck, that it had been good and solid information plucked from the file of facts dumped into his brain when the creature on that planet five thousand lights years distant had traded minds with him. The phrase had been a command to the robe to get its clutches off whatever it had trapped. Sometime in its mental wanderings across unimagined space, the Pinkness had soaked up a wondrous amount of information about the cactus people. And out of this incredible junk heap of miscellaneous facts the terribly discerning brain that belonged to human-kind had been able to select the one undistinguished fact which at a given moment had high survival value.

Blaine stood and stared at Grant and there was still no movement in the man.

And what did he do now? Blaine wondered.

He got out of here, of course, as quickly as he could. For in just a little while someone from Fishhook would be stepping from the transo, wonder-ing why he had not been delivered, all neatly trussed and gentle.

He would run again, of course, Blaine told himself with bitterness. Run-ning was the one thing he could do really well. He'd been running now for weeks on end and there seemed no end to it.

Someday, he knew, he would have to stop the running. Somewhere he'd have to make a stand, for the salvation of his self-respect if for no other reason.

But that time had not yet come. Tonight he'd run again, but this time he'd run with purpose. This night he'd gain something for the running.

He turned to get the bottle off the table and as he moved, he bumped into the robe, which was humping slowly on the floor. He kicked it savagely and it skidded weakly, almost wetly, into a lump in the fireplace corner.

Blaine grabbed the bottle in his fist and went across the room to the pile of goods stacked in the warehouse section.

He found a bale of goods and prodded it and it was soft and dry. He poured the contents of the bottle over it, then threw the bottle back into the corner of the room.

Back at the fireplace, he lifted the screen away, found the shovel and scooped up flaming coals. He dumped the coals on top the liquor-wetted goods, then flung the shovel from him and stepped back.

Little blue flames licked along the bale. They spread and grew. They crack-led. It was all right, Blaine knew.

Given five good minutes and the place would be in flames. The warehouse would be an inferno and there'd be nothing that could stop it. The transo would buckle and melt down, and the trail to Fishhook would be closed.

He bent and grasped the collar of Grant's shirt and tugged him to the door. He opened the door and hauled the man out into the yard, some thirty feet distant from the building.

Grant groaned and tried to get to hands and knees, then collapsed upon the ground again. Blaine bent and tugged him another ten feet along the ground and let loose of him. Grant muttered and thrashed, but he was too beaten to get up.

Blaine walked to the alley and stood for a minute, watching. The windows of the Post were filling very satisfactorily with the red of roaring flames.

Blaine turned and padded softly down the alley.

Now, he told himself, would be a splendid time to make a call on Finn. In just a little while the town would be agog with the burning of the Post and the police much too busy and officious to bother with a man out on the street in violation of the curfew.

26

A group of people were standing on the hotel steps, looking at the fire, which roared into the nighttime sky just two blocks away. They paid Blaine no notice. There was no sign of police.

'Some more reefer business,' said one man to another.

The other nodded. 'You wonder how their minds work,' he said. 'They'll go and trade there in the daytime, then sneak back and burn the place at night.'

'I swear to God,' said the first man, 'I don't see why Fishhook puts up with it. They needn't simply stand and take it.'

'Fishhook doesn't care,' the other told him. 'I spent five years in Fishhook. I tell you, the place is weird.'

Newsmen, Blaine told himself. A hotel crammed full of newsmen come to cover what Finn would say tomorrow. He looked at the man who had spent five years in Fishhook, but he did not recognize him.

Blaine went up the steps and into the empty lobby. He jammed his fists into his jacket pockets so that no one could spot the bruised and bloody knuckles.

The hotel was an old one and its lobby furnishings, he judged, had not been changed for years. The place was faded and old-fashioned and it had the faint, sour smell of many people who had lived short hours beneath its roof.

A few people sat here and there, reading papers or simply sitting and staring into space, with the bored look of waiting imprinted on their faces.

Blaine glanced at the clock above the desk and it was 11:30.

He went on past the desk, heading for the elevator and the stairs beyond.

'Shep!'

Blaine spun around.

A man had heaved himself out of a huge leather chair and was lumbering across the lobby toward him.

Blaine waited until the man came up and all the time there were little insect feet running on his spine.

The man stuck out his hand.

Blaine took his right hand from his pocket and showed it to him.

'Fell down,' he said. 'Stumbled in the dark.' The man looked at the hand. 'You better get that washed up,' he said.

'That's what I intend to do.'

'You know me, don't you?' the man demanded. 'Bob Collins. Met you a couple of times in Fishhook. Down at the Red Ghost Bar.'

'Yes, of course,' Blaine said, uncomfortably. 'I know you now. You slipped my mind at first. How are you?'

'Getting along all right. Sore that they pulled me out of Fishhook, but you get all sorts of breaks, mostly lousy, in this newspaper racket.'

'You're out here to cover Finn?'

Collins nodded. 'How about yourself?'

'I'm going up to see him.'

'You'll be lucky if you get to see him. He's up in 210. Got a big tough bruiser sitting just outside his door.'

'I think he'll see me.'

Collins cocked his head. 'Heard you took it on the lam. Just grapevine stuff.'

'You heard it right,' said Blaine.

'You don't look so good,' said Collins. 'Don't be offended, but I got an extra buck or two ...'

Blaine laughed.

'A drink, perhaps?'

'No. I must hurry and see Finn.'

'You with him?'

'Well, not exactly ...'

'Look, Shep, we were good pals back there in Fishhook. Can you give me what you know? Anything at all. Do a good job on this one, they might send me back to Fishhook. There's nothing I want worse.'

Blaine shook his head.

'Look, Shep, there are all sorts of rumors. There was a truck went off the road down by the river. There was something in that truck, something that was terribly important to Finn. He leaked it to the press. He'd have a sensational announcement to the press. He had something he wanted us to see. There's a rumor it's a star machine. Tell me, Shep, could it be a star machine? No one knows for sure.'

'I don't know a thing.'

Collins moved closer, his voice dropping to a husky whisper. 'This is big, Shep. If Finn can nail it down. He thinks he has hold of something that will blow the parries – every single parry, the whole concept of PK – clear out of the water. You know he's worked for that for years. In a rather hateful way, of course, but he has worked for it for years. He's preached hate up and down the land. He's a first-class rabble-rouser. He needs just this one to cinch his case. Give him a good one now and the entire world tips to him. Give him that clincher and the world will shut its eyes to the way he did it. They'll be out howling, out after parry blood.'

'You forgot that I'm a parry.'

'So was Lambert Finn – at one time.'

'There's too much hate,' Blaine said wearily. 'There are too many derogatory labels. The reformers call the paranormal people parries, and the parries call the reformers reefers. And you don't give a damn. You don't care which way it goes. You wouldn't go out and hunt someone to his death. But you'll write about it. You'll spread the blood across the page. And you don't care where it comes from, just so it is blood.'

'For the love of God, Shep …'

'So I will give you something. You can say that Finn hasn't anything to show, not a word to say. You can say that he is scared. You can say he stubbed his toe …'

'Shep, you're kidding me!'

'He won't dare show you what he's got.'

'What is it that he's got?'

'Something that, if he showed it, would make him out a fool. I tell you, he won't dare to show it. Tomorrow morning Lambert Finn will be the most frightened man the world has ever known.'

'I can't write that. You know I can't …'

'Tomorrow noon,' Blaine told him, 'everyone will be writing it. If you start right now, you can catch the last morning editions. You'll scoop the world – if you've got the guts to do it.'

'You're giving me straight dope? You're—'

'Make up your mind,' said Blaine. 'It's true, every word of it. It is up to you. Now I've got to get along.'

Collins hesitated. 'Thanks, Shep,' he said. 'Thanks an awful lot.'

Blaine left him standing there, went past the elevator and turned up the stairs.

He came to the second floor and there, at the end of the left-hand corridor, a man sat in a chair tilted back against the wall.

Blaine paced purposefully down the corridor. As he came closer, the guard tilted forward in his chair and came to his feet.

He put his hand out against Blaine's chest.

'Just a minute, mister.'

'It's urgent I see Finn.'

'He ain't seeing no one, mister.'

'You'll give him a message?'

'Not at this hour, I won't.'

'Tell him I'm from Stone.'

'But Stone—'

'Just tell him I'm from Stone.'

The man stood undecided. Then he let his arm drop.

'You wait right here,' he said. 'I'll go in and ask him. Don't try no funny stuff.'

'That's all right. I'll wait.'

He waited, wondering just how smart he was to wait. In the half-dark, rancid corridor he felt the ancient doubt. Maybe, he told himself, he should simply turn around and walk rapidly away.

The man came out.

'Stand still,' he commanded. 'I've got to run you down.' Expert hands went over Blaine, seeking knife or gun. The man nodded, satisfied. 'You're clean,' he said. 'You can go on in. I'll be right outside the door.'

'I understand,' Blaine told him.

The guard opened the door, and Blaine went through it.

The room was furnished as a living room. Beyond it was a bedroom.

There was a desk across the room, and a man stood behind the desk. He was clad in funeral black with a white scarf at this throat and he was tall. His face was long and bony and made one think of a winter-gaunted horse, but there was a hard, stern purpose to him that was somehow frightening.

Blaine walked steadily forward until he reached the desk. 'You are Finn,' he said.

'Lambert Finn,' said the man in a hollow voice, the tone of an accomplished orator who never can quite stop being an orator even when at rest.

Blaine brought his hands out of his pockets and rested his knuckles on the desk. He saw Finn looking at the blood and dirt.

'Your name,' said Finn, 'is Shepherd Blaine and I know all about you.'

'Including that someday I intend to kill you?'

'Including that,' said Finn. 'Or at least a suspicion of it.'

'But not tonight,' said Blaine, 'because I want to see your face tomorrow. I want to see if you can take it as well as dish it out.'

'And that's why you came to see me? That's what you have to tell me?'

'It's a funny thing,' Blaine told him, 'but at this particular moment, I can think of no other reason. I actually can't tell why I bothered to come up.'

'To make a bargain, maybe?'

'I hadn't thought of that. There's nothing that I want that you can give me.'

'Perhaps not, Mr Blaine, but you have something that I want. Something for which I'd pay most handsomely.' Blaine stared at him, not answering.

'You were in on the deal with the star machine,' said Finn. 'You could provide the aims and motives. You could connect up the pieces. You could tell the story. It would be good evidence.'

Blaine chuckled at him. 'You had me once,' he said. 'You let me get away.'

'It was that sniveling doctor,' Finn said ferociously. 'He was concerned there would be a rumpus and his hospital would somehow get bad publicity.'

'You should pick your people better, Finn.'

Finn growled. 'You haven't answered me.'

'About the deal, you mean? It would come high. It would come awfully high.'

'I am prepared to pay,' said Finn. 'And you need the money. You are running naked with Fishhook at your heels.'

'Just an hour ago,' Blaine told him, 'Fishhook had me trussed up for the kill.'

'So you got away,' Finn said, nodding. 'Maybe the next time, too. And the time after that as well. But Fishhook never quits. As the situation stands, you haven't got a chance.'

'Me especially, you mean? Or just anyone? How about yourself?'

'You especially,' said Finn. 'You know a Harriet Quimby?'

'Very well,' said Blaine.

'She,' Finn said, levelly, 'is a Fishhook spy.'

'You're staring mad!' yelled Blaine.

'Stop and think of it,' said Finn. 'I think you will agree.'

They stood looking at one another across the space of desk, and the silence was a live thing, a third presence in the room.

The red thought rose up inside Blaine's brain: why not kill him now?

For the killing would come easy. He was an easy man to hate. Not on principle alone, but personally, clear down to his guts.

All one had to do was think of the hate that rode throughout the land. All one had to do was close one's eyes and see the slowly turning body, half masked by the leaves; the deserted camp with the propped-up quilts for shelters and the fish for dinner laid out in the pan; the flame-scarred chimney stark against the sky.

He half lifted his hands off the table, then put them down again.

Then he did a thing quite involuntarily, without thinking of it, without a second's planning or an instant's thought. And even as he did it, he knew it was not he who did it, but the other one, the lurker in the skull.

For he could not have done it. He could not have thought of doing it. No human being could.

Blaine said, very calmly: 'I trade with you my mind.'

27

The moon rode high above the knobby bluffs that hemmed in the river valley, and down in the valley a dismal owl was hooting and chuckling to himself
in between the hoots. The chuckling of the owl carried clearly in the sharp
night air that held the hint of frost.

Blaine halted at the edge of the clump of scraggly cedars that hugged the
ground like gnarled and bent old men, and stood tense and listening. But
there was nothing except the chuckling of the owl and the faint sound of the
stubborn leaves still clinging to a cottonwood downhill from him, and
another sound so faint that one wondered if one really heard it – the remote
and faery murmur which was the voice of the mighty river flowing stolidly
below the face of the moonlit bluffs.

Blaine lowered himself and squatted close against the ground, huddling
against the tumbled darkness of the cowering cedars and told himself again
that there was no follower, that no one hunted him. Not Fishhook, for with
the burning of the Post the way to Fishhook was temporarily closed. And not
Lambert Finn. Right at this moment, Finn would be the last to hunt him.

Blaine squatted there, remembering, without a trace of pity in him, the
look that had come into Finn's eyes when he'd traded minds with him – the
glassy stare of terror at this impertinent defilement, at this deliberate befoul-
ment of the mighty preacher and great prophet who had cloaked his hate
with a mantle that was not quite religion, but as close to it as Finn had dared
to push it.

'What have you done!' he'd cried in cold and stony horror. 'What have you
done to me!'

For he had felt the biting chill of alienness and the great inhumanity and
he'd tasted of the hatred that came from Blaine himself.

'Thing!' Blaine had told him. 'You're nothing but a thing! You're no longer
Finn. You're only partly human. You are a part of me and a part of something
that I found five thousand light years out. And I hope you choke on it.'

Finn had opened up his mouth, then had closed it like a trap.

'Now I must leave,' Blaine had said to him, 'and just so there's no misunderstanding, perhaps you should come along. With an arm about my
shoulder as if we were long-lost brothers. You'll talk to me like a valued and
an ancient friend, for if you fail to do this, I'll manage to make it known
exactly what you are.'

Finn had hesitated.

'Exactly what you are,' said Blaine again, 'with all of those reporters hearing every word I say.'

That had been enough for Finn – more than enough for him.

For here was a man, thought Blaine, who could not afford to be tainted with any magic mumbo jumbo even if it worked. Here was the strait-laced, ruthless, stone-jawed reformer who thought of himself as the guardian of the moral values of the entire human race and there must be no hint of scandal, no whisper of suspicion.

So the two of them had gone down the corridor and down the stairs and across the lobby, arm in arm, and talking, with the reporters watching them as they walked along.

They'd gone down into the street, with the burning Post still red against the sky, and had walked along the sidewalk, as if they moved aside for some final word.

Then Blaine had slipped into an alley and had run, heading toward the east, toward the river bluffs.

And here he was, he thought, on the lam again, and without a single plan – just running once again. Although, in between his runnings, he'd struck a blow or two – he'd stopped Finn in his tracks. He'd robbed him of his horrible example of the perfidy of the parries and of the danger in them; he had diluted a mind that never again, no matter what Finn did, could be as narrow and as egomaniac as it had been before.

He squatted listening, and the night was empty except for the river and the owl and the leaves on the cottonwood.

He came slowly to his feet and as he did there was another sound, a howling that had the sound of teeth in it, and for an instant he stood paralyzed and cold. Out of the centuries the sound struck a chord of involuntary fear – out of the caves and beyond the caves to that other day when man had lived in terror of the night.

It was a dog, he told himself, or perhaps a prairie wolf. For there were no werewolves. He knew there were no werewolves.

And yet there was an instinct he barely could fight down – the instinct to run, madly and without reason, seeking for a shelter, for any kind of shelter, against the slavering danger that loped across the moonlight.

He stood, tensed, waiting for the howl again, but it did not come again. His body loosened up, knotted muscle, and tangled nerve, and he was almost himself again.

He would have run, he realized, if he had believed, if he'd even half-believed. It was an easy thing – first to believe and then to run. And that was what made men like Finn so dangerous. They were working on a human instinct that lay just beneath the skin – the instinct of fear, and after fear, of hate.

He left the clump of cedar and walked carefully along the bluff. The footing, he had learned, was tricky in the moonlight. There were rocks, half-hidden, that rolled beneath the foot, shadow-hidden holes and humps that were ankle traps.

He thought again of the one thing that bothered him – that had bothered him ever since that moment he had talked with Finn.

Harriet Quimby, Finn had said, was a Fishhook spy.

And that was wrong, of course, for it had been Harriet who had helped him escape from Fishhook.

And yet – she had been with him in that town where he had been nearly hanged. She had been with him while Stone was being killed. She had been with him when he'd gone into the highway shed and there been trapped by Rand.

He thrust the catalog of thoughts back into his mind, but they would not stay there. They kept creeping out to plague him.

It was ridiculous. Harriet was no spy. She was a top-notch news hen and a damn good pal to have and she was capable and cool and hard. She could be, Blaine admitted to himself, a good spy if she only wanted to – but it was alien to her nature. There was no subterfuge in her.

The bluff broke into a steep ravine that went plunging down toward the river and on the lip of it was a small clump of twisted trees.

Blaine walked around to the lower side of the clump and sat down on the ground.

Below him the river surged along, the blackness of its waters flecked with silver, and the frost of the river valley blacker than the river, while the bluffs marched up on either side like silver, humpbacked ghosts.

The owl had fallen silent, but the murmur of the river had grown louder now and if one listened closely he could hear the gurgle of the water as it swept around the sand and forced its liquid way through the tree that had toppled from the bank and hung there, its roots still anchored, its topknot in the water.

This would not, thought Blaine, be a bad place to stop the night. He'd have no quilt or blanket, but the tree would shelter him and hide him. And he'd be safer than he'd been anyplace this day.

He crawled back into the thicket that grew underneath the trees and rooted out a nest. There was a stone or two to move, there was a broken branch to be pushed out of the way. Feeling in the darkness, he scraped a pile of leaves together and it was not until he'd done all this that he thought of rattlesnakes. Although, he told himself, the season was a bit too late for many rattlesnakes.

He curled himself into a ball atop the pile of leaves and it was not as comfortable as he had hoped it might be. But it was passable and he'd spend not too many hours here. The sun would soon be up.

He lay quietly in the dark, and the happenings of the day began their remorseless march across his screen of consciousness – a mental summing up that he tried to put a stop to, but with no success.

Relentlessly, the endless reels ran on, snatches and impressions of a day that had been full, and charged with the unrealism of all post-mortem mental reviews.

If he could only stop them somehow, if he could think of something else.

And there was something else – the mind of Lambert Finn.

Gingerly he dug down into it and it hit him in the face, a cold, unrelenting tangle of hate and fear and plotting that writhed like a pail of worms. And in the center of the mass, stark horror – the horror of that other planet which had turned its human viewer into a screaming maniac who had come surging up out of his star machine with drooling mouth and staring eyes and fingers hooked like claws.

It was repulsive and obscene. It was bleak and raw. It was everything that was the opposite of humanity. It gibbered and it squawked and howled. It leered with an alien death's-head; was nothing clear or clean; there was no detail, but an overriding sense of abysmal evil.

Blaine jerked away with a scream exploding in his brain, and the scream wiped out the central core of horror.

But there was another thought – an incongruous, fleeting thought.

The thought of Halloween.

Blaine grabbed tight hold of it, fighting to keep the core of alien horror from being added to the footage of the endless film,

Halloween – the soft October night with the thin layers of leaf smoke floating in the street, lighted by the street lamps or the great full moon which hung just above the naked tree tops, larger than one ever had remembered it, as if it might have drawn a little closer to the Earth to spy on all the fun. The high, shrill, childish voices rang along the street and there was the continual patter of little racing feet as the goblin bands made their merry round, shrieking with delight or calling back and forth. The lights above the doors were all turned on in genial invitation to the trick-or-treaters, and the shrouded figures came and went, clutching bags which bulged the bigger and the heavier as the evening passed.

Blaine could remember it in detail – almost as if it were only yesterday and he was a happy child running in the town. But it was, in actuality, he thought, very long ago.

It was before the terror had grown foul and thick – when the magic still was a fading fad and there still was fun in it and Halloween was happy. And parents had no fear of their children being out at night.

Today such a Halloween would be unthinkable. Now Halloween was a time for the double-barring of the doors, of the tight-stuffed chimney, of the extra-potent hex sign nailed above the lintel.

It was too bad, he thought. It had been such a lot of fun. There had been that night he and Charlie Jones had rigged up the tick-tack beside Old Man Chandler's window and the old man had come roaring out in simulated anger with a shotgun in his hand and they had got out of there so fast they fell into the ditch back of the Lewis house.

And there had been that other time – and that other time – hanging to it hard so he could think of nothing else.

28

He woke cramped and cold and confused, not remembering where he was. For the branches intertwined above him and were like nothing he'd ever seen before. He lay with his body aching from rough ground and the cold, staring at the branches, and slowly the knowledge soaked into him – who he was and where. And why.

And the thought of Halloween.

He sat bolt upright and bumped his head upon the branches. For now there was more than just the thought of Halloween. There was the plot of Halloween!

He sat cold and frozen, while the fury and the fear raged inside of him.

It was diabolic and so simple – it was the very kind of gambit a man like Lambert Finn would plan.

It was something that could not be allowed to happen. For if it did, a new onslaught of public animosity would be roused against the parries and once the fierce reaction had worn off, there'd be new restrictive laws. Although the laws might not be needed, for it might set off a pogrom that would wipe out thousands of the parries. Such a plan of Halloween would result in a storm of public outrage such as the world had seldom known.

There was just one chance, he knew. He had to get to Hamilton, for it was the nearest place where he could find some help. Surely the folks of Hamilton would help him, for Hamilton was a parry village that lived by sufferance alone. If a thing like this should happen, then Hamilton would die.

And Halloween, unless he had lost count, was the day after tomorrow. No, that was wrong, for this was tomorrow. Starting now, there were just two days to stop it.

He crawled out of the thicket and saw that the sun was no more than a handbreadth above the eastern hills. There was a sharp, clean tang in the morning air, and the sloping bluff ran smooth, with the blond of sun-cured grass, down to the brown flood of the river. He shivered in the chill and beat his hands together to try to get them warm.

Hamilton would be north along the river, for The Plainsman motel had been on the road that ran north from Belmont, and Hamilton, from there, had been only a mile or two away.

He went angling down the slope, and the movement of his body drove away the chill. The climbing sun seemed to gather strength and there was more warmth in it.

He reached a sand bar that ran out into the river and walked out on it. The water was brown with sand and clay and it rumbled angrily as it swirled around the sand bar's end.

Blaine walked to the edge of the bar and squatted down. He put down cupped hands and dipped, and the trapped water came up roiled with sand. He raised the cupped hands to his face and drank and the water had a dark brown taste – the taste of silted clay and of ancient vegetation. When he closed his mouth, his teeth gritted on the sand.

But it was water. It was wet. He dipped and drank again, the water running through his fingers, no matter how tightly pressed together, leaving little for his throat.

He squatted in the stillness and sensed the loneliness and peace, as if this moment might be no later than the next day after the world had first been made – as if the earth lay new and clean and there'd been as yet no time to build up the historic backlog of worry and of greed and of all the other things which plagued the race of Man.

A splash broke the silence and he rose swiftly to his feet. There was nothing to be seen, either on the shore or on the river itself or the willow island which lay just beyond the sand bar. An animal, he thought. A mink or muskrat, an otter or a beaver, or perhaps a fish.

The splash came again, and a boat nosed around the island and came toward the bar. In its stern sat a man muffled in a cloak, swinging the paddle with an awkwardness that was embarrassing to watch. The bow was raised out of the water by the weight of the man and the canted outboard motor fastened to the stern.

The boat came lumbering around and there was something hauntingly familiar in the man who swung the paddle. Somewhere, sometime, Blaine knew, he had met this man; somehow their lives had touched.

He walked out into the shallows and grabbed the bow as the craft drew close and dragged it onto the sand.

'God be with you,' said the boatman. 'And how are you this morning?'

'Father Flanagan!' cried Blaine.

The old priest grinned, a very human, almost sunny grin.

'You,' Blaine told him, 'are very far from home.'

'I go,' said Father Flanagan, 'where the good Lord sends me.'

He reached forward and patted the seat in front of him.

'Why don't you come and sit awhile?' he invited. 'God forgive me, but I'm all beat up and weary.'

Blaine pulled the boat up harder on the sand and got into it. He took the seat the priest had patted and held out his hand. Father Flanagan took it in both his arthritis-crippled but very gentle paws.

'It's good to see you, Father.'

'And I,' the Father told him, 'am covered with confusion. For I must confess that I've been following you.'

'It would seem to me,' Blaine said, half amused, half frightened, 'that a man of your persuasion might find better things to do.'

The priest put Blaine's hand away, not forgetting to give it a placid pat.

'Ah, my son,' he said, 'but that is it. There can be, for me, no better occupation than keeping on your trail.'

'I'm sorry, Father. I don't quite understand.'

Father Flanagan leaned forward, capping each of his knees with a crippled fist.

'It is important,' he said, 'that you understand. You will listen carefully. You will not get angry. You'll let me have my time.'

'Most certainly,' said Blaine.

'You have heard, perhaps,' said Father Flanagan, 'that Holy Mother Church is inflexible and rigid, that she clings to old custom and to ancient thought, that she changes slowly if she changes at all. That the Church is stern and dogmatized and—'

'I've heard all that,' said Blaine.

'But it is not true. The church is modern and it changes. If it had been opposed to change, God save us, it would not have endured in all its greatness and its glory. It is not swayed by the winds of public utterance, it can stand against the groundswell of changing human mores. But it does adapt, although it does so slowly. But that slowness is because it must be very sure.'

'Father, you can't mean—'

'But I do. I asked you, if you will remember, if you were a warlock and you thought it very funny … '

'Of course I did.'

'It was a basic question,' said Father Flanagan, 'a much too simple question, purposely made simple so it could be answered with a yes or no.'

'I'll answer once again, then. I am not a warlock.'

The old priest sighed. 'You persist,' he complained, 'in making the telling of what I have to tell you very difficult.'

'Go ahead,' said Blaine. 'I'll restrain myself.'

'The Church must know,' said Father Flanagan, 'whether parakinesis is a true human ability or if it may be magic. One day, perhaps many years from now, it must make a ruling. It must take a stand as it historically has taken positions on all moral values through the centuries. It is no secret that a committee of theologians have had the matter under study …'

'And you?' asked Blaine.

'I am only one of many who has been assigned an investigatory role. We simply gather evidence which in due time will come under the scrutiny of the theologians.'

'And I am part of your evidence.'

Father Flanagan nodded solemnly.

'There's one thing I fail to understand,' said Blaine, 'and that is why your faith should have any doubts at all. You have your miracles, completely documented. And what, I ask you, are miracles if they don't involve PK? Somewhere in the universe human power and divine power must link. Here may be your bridge.'

'You really believe this, son?'

'I'm not a religico ...'

'I know you're not. You told me you were not. But answer me: is this what you believe?'

'I rather think it is.'

'I do not know,' said Father Flanagan, 'if I can quite agree with you. The idea has the smell of heresy. But that's neither here nor there. The point is that there's a certain strangeness in you, a strangeness I've not found in any of the others.'

'I'm half alien,' Blaine told him bitterly. 'No other man has ever been given that distinction. You talk not only with me, but with a being not remotely human – a being that sits on a planet five thousand light years distant. He has lived a million years or more. He'll live another million or maybe more than that. He sends out his mind to visit other planets and he is a very lonely being for all his visiting. Time is no mystery to him. I doubt there's very much that is. And all he knows I know and can put to better use than he – when I get the time, if I ever get the time, to get it all dug out and leveled and stacked along the shelves inside my brain.'

The priest drew his breath in slowly. 'I thought it might be something of that sort.'

'So do your job,' said Blaine. 'Get out the holy water. Sprinkle me with it and I'll go up in a puff of dirty smoke.'

'You mistake me,' said Father Flanagan. 'You mistake my purpose. And my attitude. If there is no evil in the power that sent you to the stars, then there can be no more than incidental evil in what you may absorb there.'

One crippled hand reached out and grasped Blaine's arm in a crushing grip which one would have sworn was not within its strength.

'You have a great power,' said the priest, 'and great knowledge. You have an obligation to use it for the glory of God and the good of all mankind, I, a feeble voice, charge you with that burden and that responsibility. It is not often that such a load is put upon one man. You must not waste it, son. You must not use it wrongly. Nor can you simply let it lie on fallow ground. It was given to you – perhaps by the intervention of some divine power neither of us can understand for a purpose neither of us know. Such things, I am certain, do not come about by pure happenstance.'

'The finger of God,' said Blaine, meaning to jest, but not quite able to make a proper jest, sorry that he'd said it as soon as the words were out.

'The finger of God,' said Father Flanagan, 'laid upon your heart.'

'I did not ask for it,' said Blaine. 'If anyone had asked me, I would have told them no.'

'Tell me about it,' said Father Flanagan. 'From the very start, as a favor to me.'

'In return for a favor of your own.'

'And what is that?' asked Father Flanagan.

'You say you followed me. How could you follow me?'

'Why, bless your soul,' said Father Flanagan. 'I thought you might have guessed. You see, I am one of you. I'm a quite efficient hounder.'

29

Hamilton dreamed beside the river. It had a certain hazy quality and the mellowness of old river towns, for all that it was new. Above it rose the tawny hills and below the hills the checked fields that came up to the town. Lazy morning smoke rose from the chimneys, and each picketed fence had in its corner a clump of hollyhocks.

'It looks a peaceful place,' said Father Flanagan. 'You know what you are doing?'

Blaine nodded. 'And you, Father? What about yourself?'

'There is an abbey down the river. I will be welcome there.'

'And I'll see you again.'

'Perhaps. I'll be going back to my border town. I'll be a lonely picket on the borderland of Fishhook.'

'Watching for others who may be coming through?'

The priest nodded. He cut the motor's speed and turned the boat for shore. It grated gently on the sand and pebbles, and Blaine jumped out of it.

Father Flanagan raised his face toward the western sky and sniffed. 'There is weather making.' he declared, looking like a hound-dog snuffling a cold trail. 'I can smell the edge of it.'

Blaine walked back through water that came up to his ankles and held out his hand.

'Thanks for the lift,' he said. 'It would have been tough walking. And it saved a lot of time.'

'Good-bye, my son. God go with you.'

Blaine pushed the boat out into the water. The priest speeded up the motor and swept the boat around. Blaine stood watching as he headed down the stream. Father Flanagan lifted his hand in a last farewell, and Blaine waved back.

Then he waded from the water and took the path up to the village.

He came up to the street and he knew it to be home.

Not his home, not the home he once had known, no home he'd ever dreamed of, but home for all the world. It had the peace and surety, the calmness of the spirit, the feel of mental comfort – the sort of place a man could settle down and live in, merely counting off the days, taking each day as it came and the fullness of it, without a thought of future.

There was no one on the street, which was flanked by trim, neat houses, but he could feel them looking at him from out the windows of each house – not spying on him or suspicious of him, but watching with a kindly interest.

A dog came from one of the yards – a sad and lonely hound – and went along with him, walking by his side in good companionship.

He came to a cross-street and to the left was a small group of business houses. A group of men were sitting on the steps of what he took to be a general store.

He and the hound turned up the street and walked until they came up to the group. The men sat silently and looked at him.

'Good morning, gentlemen,' he said. 'Can any of you tell me where I can find a man named Andrews?'

They were silent for another heartbeat, then one of them said: 'I'm Andrews.'

'I want to talk with you,' said Blaine.

'Sit down,' said Andrews, 'and talk to all of us.'

'My name is Shepherd Blaine.'

'We know who you are,' said Andrews. 'We knew when that boat pulled into shore.'

'Yes, of course,' said Blaine. 'I should have realized.'

'This man,' Andrews said, 'is Thomas Jackson and over there is Johnson Carter and the other one of us is Ernie Ellis.'

'I am glad,' said Blaine, 'to know each one of you.'

'Sit down,' said Thomas Jackson. 'You have come to tell us something.'

Jackson moved over to make room for him, and Blaine sat down between him and Andrews.

'First of all,' said Blaine, 'maybe I should tell you that I'm a fugitive from Fishhook.'

'We know a little of you,' Andrews told him. 'My daughter met you several nights ago. You were with a man named Riley. Then only last night we brought a dead friend of yours here.'

'He's buried on the hill,' said Jackson. 'We held a rather hasty funeral for him, but at least a funeral. You see, he was not unknown to us.'

'Thank you, sir,' said Blaine.

'Last night, also,' said Andrews, 'there was some sort of ruckus going on in Belmont—'

'We're not too happy with such goings-on,' said Carter, interrupting. 'We're too apt to become involved.'

'I'm sorry if that's the case,' Blaine told them. 'I'm afraid I'm bringing you more trouble. You know of a man named Finn.' They nodded.

'I talked with Finn last night. I found out something from him. Something he had no intention, I might add, of ever telling me.'

They waited.

Tomorrow night is Halloween,' said Blaine. 'It's set to happen then.'

He saw them stiffen and went quickly on: 'Somehow or other – I'm not just sure how he managed to achieve it – Finn has set up a sort of feeble underground among the paranormal people. None of them, naturally, know that he's behind it. They view it as a sort of pseudo-patriotic movement, a sort of cultural protest movement. Not too successful or extensive, but it would not have to be extensive. All that he needs is to create a few incidents – a few horrible examples. For that is how he works, using horrible examples to whip up the public frenzy.

'And this underground of his, working through the teen-age paranormals, has arranged a series of PK demonstrations on the night of Halloween. A chance, they've been told, to demonstrate paranormal powers. A chance, perhaps, to pay off some old scores. God knows, there must be old scores a-plenty that need some paying off.'

He stopped and looked around at their stricken faces. 'You realize what a dozen of these demonstrations – a dozen in the entire world, given the kind of publicity Finn intends to give them – would do to the imagination of the normal population.'

'It would not be a dozen,' Andrews said, quietly. 'Worldwide, it might be a hundred or even several hundreds. The morning after they'd sweep us off the Earth.'

Carter leaned forward, intently. 'How did you find this out?' he asked. 'Finn would not have told you unless you were in with him.'

'I traded minds with him,' said Blaine. 'It's a technique I picked up among the stars. I gave him a pattern of my mind and took in exchange a duplicate of his. A sort of carbon copy business. I can't explain it to you, but it can be done.'

'Finn,' said Andrews, 'won't thank you for this. Yours must be a most disturbing mind to have inside his head.'

'He was quite upset,' said Blaine.

'These kids,' said Carter. 'They would make like witches. They would burst open doors. They would whisk cars to another place. Small buildings would be upset and demolished. Voices and wailings would be heard.'

'That's the idea,' Blaine told him. 'Just like an old-fashioned, hell-raising Halloween. But to the victims it would not be merely mischief. It would be all the forces of the ancient darkness let loose upon the world. It would be goblins and ghosts and werewolves. On its surface it would be bad enough, but in the imagination of the victims it would grow out of all proportion. There would be, by morning, guts strung along the fence and men with their throats slashed ragged and girl children carried off. Not here, not where it was being told, but always somewhere else. And the people would believe. They'd believe everything they heard.'

'But still,' said Jackson, 'you can't criticize the teen-age parries too harshly if they should want to do this. I tell you, mister, you can't imagine what they have been through. Snubbed and ostracized. Here, at the beginning of their lives, they find bars raised against them, fingers leveled at them—'

'I know,' Blaine said, 'but even so you have got to stop it. There must be a way to stop it. You can use telepathy on the telephone. Somehow or other—'

'A simple device,' said Andrews. 'Although ingenious. Developed about two years ago.'

'Use it then,' said Blaine. 'Call everyone you can. Urge the people you talk with to pass the warning on and the ones they talk with to pass the warning on. Set up a chain of communication—'

Andrews shook his head. 'We couldn't reach them all.'

'You can try,' Blaine shouted.

'We will try, of course,' said Andrews. 'We'll do everything we can. Don't think that we're ungrateful. Very far from that. We thank you. We never can repay you. But—'

'But what?'

'You can't stay here,' said Jackson. 'Finn is hunting you. Fishhook, too, perhaps. And they'll all come here to look. They'll figure you'd run to cover here.'

'My God,' yelled Blaine, 'I came here—'

'We are sorry,' Andrews told him. 'We know how you must feel. We could try to hide you out, but if you were found—'

'All right, then. You'll let me have a car.'

Andrews shook his head. Too dangerous. Finn would watch the roads. And they could trace the registration ...'

'What then? The hills?'

'Andrews nodded.

'You'll give me food?'

Jackson got up. 'I'll get you grub,' he said.

'And you can come back,' said Andrews. 'When this all blows over, we'll be glad to have you back.'

'Thanks a lot,' said Blaine.

30

He sat beneath a lone tree that stood on a lesser spur of one of the great bluffs and stared out across the river. A flock of mallards came winging down the valley, a black line against the sky above the eastern hills.

There had been a day, he thought, when this season of the year the sky had been blackened by the flights that came down from the north, scooting before the first boisterous outriders of the winter storms. But today there were few of them – shot out, starved out by the drying up of areas which had been their nesting places.

And once this very land had teemed with buffalo and there had been beaver for the taking in almost every stream. Now the buffalo were gone and almost all the beaver.

Man had wiped them out, all three of them, the wild fowl, the buffalo, the beaver. And many other things besides.

He sat there thinking of Man's capacity for the wiping out of species – sometimes in hate or fear, at other times for the simple love of gain.

And this, he knew, was what was about to happen in large measure to the parries if Finn's plan were carried out. Back there in Hamilton they would do their best, of course, but would it be enough? They had thirty-six hours in which to put together a vast network of warning. They could cut down the incidents, but could they call them off entirely? It seemed impossible.

Although, he told himself, he should be the last to worry, for they had thrown him out; they had run him off. His own people, in a town that felt like home, and they had run him off.

He leaned over and fastened the straps of the knapsack in which Jackson had packed the food. He lifted and set it and the canteen close beside him.

To the south he could see the distant chimney smoke of Hamilton and even in his half-anger at being thrown out, he seemed to feel again that strange sense of home which he had encountered as he walked its streets. Over the world there must be many such villages as that – ghettos of this latter-day, where paranormal people lived as quietly and as inconspicuously as was possible. They were the ones who huddled in the corners of the Earth, waiting for the day, if it ever came, when their children or their children's children might be free to walk abroad, equals of the people who still were only normal.

In those villages, he wondered, how much ability and genius might be lying barren, ability and genius that the world could use but would never know because of the intolerance and hate which was held against the very people who were least qualified as the targets of it.

And the pity of it was that such hate and such intolerance would never have been born, could never have existed, had it not been for men like Finn – the bigots and the egomaniacs; the harsh, stern Puritans; the little men who felt the need of power to lift them from their smallness.

There was little moderation in humanity, he thought. It either was for you or it was against you. There was little middle ground.

Take science, for example. Science had failed in the dream of space, and science was a bum. And yet, men of science still worked as they had always worked, for the benefit of all humanity. So long as Man might exist, there would be need of science. In Fishhook there were corps of scientists working on the discoveries and the problems that stemmed from the galaxy – and yet science, in the minds of the masses, was a has-been and a heel.

But it was time to go, he told himself. There was no use staying on. There was no use thinking. He must be moving on, for there was nothing else to do. He had sounded the warning and that was all the men of Hamilton had allowed.

He'd go up to Pierre and he'd ask for Harriet at the cafe with the elk horns nailed above the door. Perhaps he'd find some of Stone's men and they might find a place for him.

He rose and slung the knapsack and canteen from one shoulder. He stepped out from the tree.

Behind him there was a sudden rustle and he swung around short hairs rising on his neck.

The girl was settling to earth, feet just above the grass, graceful as a bird, beautiful as morning.

Blaine stood watching, caught up in her beauty, for this was the first time that he'd really seen her. Once before he'd seen her in the pale slash of light from the headlamps of the truck, and once again last night, but for no more than a minute, in a dimly lighted room.

Her feet touched ground and she came toward him.

'I just found out,' she said. 'I think that it is shameful. After all, you came to help us …'

'It's O.K.,' Blaine told her. 'I don't deny it hurts, but I can see their reasoning.'

'They've worked so hard,' she said, 'to keep us quiet, away from all attention. They have tried to make a decent life. They can't take any chances.'

'I know,' said Blaine. 'I've seen some who weren't able to make a decent life.'

'Us young folks are a worry to them. We shouldn't go out halloweening, but there's nothing we can do. We have to stay at home so much. And we don't do it often.'

'I'm glad you came out that night,' Blaine told her. 'If I hadn't known of you, Harriet and I would have been trapped with Stone dead upon the floor ...'

'We did what we could for Mr Stone. We had to hurry and we couldn't be too formal. But everyone turned out. He's buried on the hill.'

'Your father told me.'

'We couldn't put up a marker and we couldn't make a mound. We cut the sod and put it back exactly as it was before. No one would ever know. But all of us have the place tattooed on our minds.'

'Stone and I were friends from long ago.'

'In Fishhook?'

Blaine nodded.

Tell me about Fishhook, Mr Blaine.'

The name is Shep.'

'Shep, then. Tell me.'

'It is a big place and a tall place *(the towers on the hill, the plazas and the walks, the trees and mighty buildings, the stores and shops and dives, the people ...)*

Shep, why don't they let us come?

Let you come?

There were some of us who wrote them and they sent application blanks. Just application blanks, that's all. But we filled them out and mailed them. And we never heard.

There are thousands who want to get into Fishhook.

Then why don't they let us come? Why not take all of us? A Fishhook reservation. Where all the little frightened people can have some peace at last:

He didn't answer. He closed his mind to her.

Shep! Shep, what's wrong? Something that I said?

Listen, Anita. Fishhook doesn't want you people. Fishhook isn't what you think it is. It has changed. It's become a corporation.

But, we have always ...

I know. I KNOW. I KNOW. It has been the promised land. It has been the ultimate solution. The never-never land. But it's not like that at all. It is a counting house. It figures loss and profit. Oh, sure, it will help the world; it will advance mankind. It's theoretically, and even actually, the greatest thing that ever happened. But it has no kindness in it, no kinship with the other paranormals. If we want that promised land, we'll have to work it out ourselves. We have to fight our own fight, like stopping Finn and his Project Halloween ...

That's what I came to tell you, really. It isn't working out.

The telephoning ...

They let two calls get through. Detroit and Chicago. Then we tried New York and the operator couldn't get New York. Can you imagine that – couldn't get New York. We tried Denver and the line was out of order. So we got scared and quit ...

Quit! You can't quit!

We're using long tellies. We have a few of them. But it's hard to reach their contacts. There is little use for distance telepathy and it's not practiced much.

Blaine stood in a daze.

Couldn't get New York! Line to Denver out of order!

It was impossible that Finn should have such complete control.

Not complete control, Anita told him. But people spotted in strategic situations. For example, he probably could sabotage the world's entire communications network. And he has people all the time watching and monitoring settlements like ours. We don't make one long-distance call a month. When three came through in fifteen minutes, Finn's people knew there was something wrong, so they isolated us.

Blaine slid the knapsack and canteen off his shoulder, lowered them to the ground.

'I'm going back,' he said.

'It would do no good. You couldn't do a thing we aren't doing now.'

'Of course,' said Blaine. 'You're very probably right. There is one chance, however, if I can get to Pierre in time ... '

'Pierre was where Stone lived?'

'Why, yes. You knew of Stone?'

'Heard of him. That was all. A sort of parry Robin Hood. He was working for us.'

'If I could contact his organization, and I think I can ... '

'The woman lives there, too?'

'You mean Harriet. She's the one who can put me in contact with Stone's group. But she may not be there. I don't know where she is.'

'If you could wait till night, a few of us could fly you up there. It's too dangerous in the daytime. There are too many people, even in a place like this.'

'It can't be more than thirty miles or so. I can walk it.'

'The river would be easier. Can you handle a canoe?'

'Many years ago. I think I still know how.'

'Safer, too,' Anita said. 'There's not much traffic on the river. My cousin has a canoe, just upriver from the town. I'll show you where it is.'

31

The storm sneaked in. There was no warning of it except for the gradual graying of the day. At noon the slow-moving clouds blotted out the sun and by three o'clock the sky was closed in, horizon to horizon, by a fleecy grayness that seemed less cloud than the curdling of the sky itself.

Blaine bent to his paddle, driving furiously to eat up the miles. It had been years since he had used a paddle, years since he had done anything approaching strenuous labor. His arms became stiff and numb, and his shoulders ached, and across the upper back a steel band had settled down and was tightening with every stroke he took. His hands seemed one vast blister.

But he did not slow his strokes nor the power behind them, for every minute counted. When he got to Pierre, he knew, he might be unable to locate immediately the group of parries who had worked with Stone, and even if he found them they might refuse to help him. They might want to confirm his identity, they might want to check his story, they might quite rightly suspect him as a spy for Finn. If Harriet were there, she could vouch for him, although he was not sure what her status with the group might be nor what her word was worth. Nor was he even sure that she would be there.

But it was a last, long chance. It was the final hope he had and he could not shirk it. He must get to Pierre, he must find the group, he must make them understand the urgency of the situation.

For if he failed, it spelled the end of Hamilton and of all the other Hamiltons that might be in the world. And it meant as well the end for the other parries who were not in the Hamiltons, but who lived out precarious, careful lives in the midst of normal neighbors.

Not all of them, of course, would die. But all, or nearly all, would be scattered to the winds, to hide in whatever social and economic nooks and crannies they might be able to devise. It would mean that the parries would lose on a world-wide basis whatever tacit accommodations or imperfect understandings they had been able to establish with their normal neighbors. It would mean another generation of slowly coming back, of regaining, item after painful item, what they would have lost. It would mean, perhaps, another fifty years to ride out the storm of rage, to await the growth of another generation's tolerance.

And in the long picture that stretched ahead, Blaine could see no sign of help – of either sympathy or assistance. For Fishhook, the one place that

could help, simply would not care. He had gained at least that much understanding of the situation from his contact with Kirby Rand.

The thought left the taste of bitter ashes in his mind, for it took away the
last comfort that he had in all the world – the memory of his days in Fishhook. He had loved Fishhook; he had fought against his fleeing from it; he
had regretted that he'd left it; at times he'd wondered if he should not have
stayed. But now he knew that he had stayed too long, that perhaps he never
should have joined it – for his place was here, out here in the bitter world of
the other parries. In them, he realized, lay the hope of developing paranormal kinetics to their full capacity.

They were the misfits of the world, the outcasts, for they deviated from the
norm of humanity as established through all of history. Yet it was this very
deviation which made them the hope of all mankind. Ordinary human
beings – the kind of human beings who had brought the race this far – were
not enough today. The ordinary humans had pushed the culture forward as
far as they could push it. It had served its purpose; it had brought the ordinary human as far as he could go. Now the race evolved. Now new abilities had
awoke and grown – exactly as the creatures of the Earth had evolved and
specialized and then evolved again from that first moment when the first
feeble spark of life had come into being in the seething chemical bath of a
new and madcap planet.

Twisted brains, the normal people called them; magic people, dwellers of
the darkness – and could anyone say no to this? For each people set its standards for each generation and these standards and these norms were not set by
any universal rule, by no all-encompassing yardstick, but by what amounted
to majority agreement, with the choice arrived at through all the prejudice
and bias, all the faulty thinking and the unstable logic to which all intelligence is prone.

And he, himself, he wondered – how did he fit into all of this? For his
mind, perhaps, was twisted more than most. He was not even human.

He thought of Hamilton and of Anita Andrews and his heart cried out to
both – but could he demand of any town, of any woman, that he become a
part of either?

He bent to the paddle, trying to blot out the thinking that bedeviled him,
trying to smother the rat race of questions that were twisting in his brain.

The wind, which had been a gentle breeze no more than an hour before, had
shifted and settled somewhat west of north and had taken on an edge. The
surface of the river was rippled with the driving wind and on the long,
straight stretches of water there was a hint of whitecaps.

The sky came down, pressing on the Earth, a hazy sky that stretched from
bluff to bluff, roofing in the river and shutting out the sun so that birds flew
with uneasy twitterings in the willows, puzzled at the early fall of night.

Blaine remembered the old priest, sitting in the boat and sniffing the sky. There was weather making, he had said; he could smell the edge of it.

But weather could not stop him, Blaine thought fiercely, digging at the water frantically with the paddle. There was nothing that could stop him. No force on Earth could stop him; he couldn't let it stop him.

He felt the first wet sting of snow upon his face and up ahead the river was disappearing in a great, gray curtain that came sweeping downstream toward him. He could hear distinctly the hissing of the snow as it struck the water and behind it the hungry moaning of the wind, as if some great animal were running on a track, moaning in the fear that it would not catch the thing that ran ahead.

Shore was no more than a hundred yards away, and Blaine knew that he must get there and travel the rest of the way on foot. For even in his desperate need of speed, in his frantic fight with time, he realized that he could not continue on the river.

He twisted the paddle hard to head the canoe for shore and even as he did the wind struck and the snow closed in and his world contracted to an area only a few feet in diameter. There was only snow and the running waves that fled beneath the wind, tossing the canoe in a crazy dance. The shore was gone and the bluffs above it. There was nothing but the water and the wind and snow.

The canoe bucked wildly, spinning, and Blaine in an instant lost all sense of direction. In the ticking of a single second he was lost upon the river, with not the least idea of where the shore might lie. He lifted the paddle and laid it across the thwarts, hanging on tightly, trying to keep the craft trim as it tossed and yawed.

The wind had a sharpness and a chill it had not had before and it struck his sweaty body like an icy knife. The snow clotted on his eyebrows, and streams of water came trickling down his face as it lodged in his hair and melted.

The canoe danced wildly, running with the waves, and Blaine hung grimly on, lost, not knowing what to do, overwhelmed by this assault that came roaring down the river.

Suddenly a snow-shrouded clump of willows loomed out of the grayness just ahead of him, not more than twenty feet away, and the canoe was bearing straight toward it.

Blaine only had time to get set for the crash, crouched above the seat, legs flexed, hands gripping the rails.

The canoe tore into the willows with a screeching sound that was muffled by the wind and caught up and hurled away. The craft hit and drove on into the willow screen, then hung up and slowly tipped, spilling Blaine out into the water.

Struggling blindly, coughing and sputtering, he gained his feet on the soft and slippery bottom, hanging tight to the willows to keep himself erect.

The canoe, he saw, was useless. A hidden snag had caught its bottom and had ripped a long and jagged tear across the canvas. It was filling with water and slowly going down.

Slipping, half-falling. Blaine fought his way through the willow screen to solid ground. And it was not until he left the water that he realized the water had been warm. The wind, striking through the wetness of his clothes, was like a million icy needles.

Blaine stood shivering, staring at the tangled clump of willows that thrashed wildly in the gale.

He must find a protected spot, he knew. He must start a fire. Otherwise, he'd not last out the night. He brought his wrist close up before his face, and the watch said that it was only four o'clock.

He had, perhaps, another hour of light and in that hour he must find some shelter from the storm and cold.

He staggered off, following the shore – and suddenly it struck him that he could not start a fire. For he had no matches, or he didn't think he had, and even if he did they would be soaked and useless. Although, more than likely, he could dry them, so he stopped to look. He searched frantically through all his sopping pockets. And he had no matches.

He plunged on. If he could find snug shelter, he might be able to survive even with no fire. A hole beneath the roots of a tipped-over tree, perhaps, or a hollow tree into which he could squeeze himself – any confined space where he'd be sheltered from the wind, where his body's heat might have a chance to partially dry out his clothing and be held in to warm him.

There were no trees. There was nothing but the everlasting willows, whipping like demented things in the gusty wind.

He stumbled on, slipping and falling, tripping over unseen chunks of driftwood left stranded by high water. He was covered with mud from his many falls, his clothes were freezing stiff, and still he blundered on. He had to keep on moving; he must find a place in which to hide; if he stood still, if he failed to move, he would freeze to death.

He stumbled again and pulled himself to his knees and there, at the water's edge, jammed in among the willows, floated a swamped canoe, rocking heavily in the storm-driven wash of water.

A canoe!

He wiped his face with a muddy hand to try to clear his vision. It was the same canoe, for there would be no other! It was the canoe he'd left to beat his way along the shore. And here he was, back at it again!

He fought with his muddled brain to find an answer – and there was an answer, the only answer that was possible.

He was trapped on a tiny willow island!

There was nothing here but willows. There were no honest trees, tipped-over, hollow, or in any other wise. He had no matches, and even if he had, there was no fuel except the scattered driftwood and not too much of that.

His trousers were like boards, frozen stiff and crackling as he bent his knees. Every minute, it seemed to him, the temperature was dropping – although there was no way to know; he was too cold to tell.

He came slowly to his feet and stood straight, faced into the cutting wind, with the hiss of snow driving through the willows, with the angry growl of the storm-lashed river and the falling dark, and there was another answer to a question yet unasked.

He could not live the night on this island and there was no way to leave it. It might be, for all he knew, no more than a hundred feet from shore, but even if it were, what difference would it make? Ten to one he'd be little better off on shore than he was right here.

There had to be a way, he insisted to himself. He could not die on this stinking little dot of real estate, this crummy little island. Not that his life was worth so much – perhaps not even to himself. But he was the one man who could get to Pierre for help.

And that was a laugh. For he'd never get to Pierre. He'd not get off the island. In the end, he'd simply stay right where he was and it was more than likely that he'd not be found.

When the spring floods came, he'd go down the river with all the other debris that the stream would collect and carry in its raging torrent.

He turned and went back a ways from the water's edge. He found a place where he was partially shielded from the wind by the thickness of the willows and deliberately sat down, with his legs stuck out straight before him. He turned up the collar of his jacket and it was a gesture only, for it did no good. He folded his arms tight across his chest and pinched half-frozen hands into the feeble warmth of armpits and stared straight ahead into the ghostly twilight.

This was wrong, he knew. When a man got caught in a fix like this, he kept on the move. He kept the blood flowing in his veins. He fought off sleep. He beat and flailed his arms. He stamped his feet. He fought to keep alive.

But it was no use, he thought. A man could go through all the misery of the fight and still die in the end.

There must be another way, a better way than that.

A real smart man would think of a better way than that.

The problem, he told himself, trying to divorce himself from the situation for the sake of objectivity – the problem was to get himself, his body, off this island and not only off this island, but to a place of safety.

But there was no place of safety.

Although suddenly there was.

There was a place that he could go. He could go back to that bright-blue living room where the Pinkness dwelled.

But no! That would be no better than staying on the island, for if he went he'd only go in mind and leave his body here. When he returned, the body, more than likely, would be unfit for use. If he could take his body there, it would be all right. But he couldn't take his body.

And even if he could, it might be very wrong and very likely deadly.

He tried to recall the data on that distant planet and it had escaped him. So he went digging after it and hauled it up from the deep recesses where he had buried it and regarded it with horror.

He'd not live a minute if he went there in his body!

It was pure and simple poison for his kind of life.

But there must be other places. There would be other places if only he could go there – if all of him could go there.

He sat hunched against the cold and wet and didn't even feel the cold and wet.

He sought the Pinkness in him and he called it and there was no answer.

He called again and yet again and there was no answer. He probed and searched and hunted and he found no sign of it and he knew, almost as if a voice had spoken out and told him, that there was no use of further call or hunting, for he would not find it. He would never find it now, for he was a part of it. The two of them had run together and there was no longer either a Pinkness or a human, but some strange alloy that was the two of them.

To go on hunting for it would be like hunting for himself.

Whatever he would do, he must do himself, by the total power of whatever he'd become.

There were data and ideas, there was knowledge, there was know-how and there was a certain dirtiness that was Lambert Finn.

He went down into his mind, into the shelves and pigeonholes, into the barrels and bins and boxes, into the still incredible junk heap that was as yet unsorted, the tangled billions of odds and ends that had been dumped helter-skelter into him by a helter-skelter being.

He found items that startled him and some that disgusted him and others that were swell ideas, but which in no way applied to his present problem.

And all the time, like some persistent busybody, running underfoot, the mind of Lambert Finn, unabsorbed as yet, perhaps never to be absorbed but always to remain dodging in and out of corners, kept getting in the way.

He pushed it to one side, he shoved it from his path, he swept it under rugs and he kept on searching – but the dirty thoughts and concepts and ideas, the thoughts of Finn, the unraveling subject matter of that core of raging horror from Finn's nightmare of a planet, still kept popping up.

And as, for the hundredth time, he swept the dirtiness away, he caught a hint of what he wanted and went scrabbling after it – scrabbling after it through all the obscenity and evil of that core of writhing horror which he had wrested from Finn's mind. For it was there he found it – not in the bright array of junk he'd inherited from the Pinkness, but in the mass of garbage he had stole away from Finn.

It was an alien knowledge and a crooked, slimy knowledge, and he knew it had its origin on the planet that had sent Finn home a maniac and as he held it in his mental hands and saw the way it worked, how simply it worked, how logical the concepts, he grasped at least a corner of the guilt and fear which had sent Finn in raging hate up and down the land.

For with this kind of know-how the stars lay open, physically open, to all the life in the universe. And to Finn's unbalanced mind that could mean one thing only – that Earth lay open, too. And most specifically that it lay open to the planet which had held the knowledge. Not thinking of how other races might make use of it, not recognizing it as a tool the human race could use to its benefit, he'd seen it simply as a bridge between the place he'd found and the planet he called home. And he had fought with all he had to pull the old home planet back to its former smallness, to break its contact with the stars, to starve and strangle Fishhook by wiping out the parries who in the future might be drafted or invited to carry on the work of Fishhook.

For Finn had reasoned, Blaine thought, with Finn's reasoning an open book before him, that if Earth stayed obscure and small and attracted no attention, the universe would pass it by and it would then be safe.

But however that might be, he held within his mind the technique to go in body to the stars – and a way to save his life.

But now he must find a planet where he could safely go – a planet which would not poison him or drown him or crush him, a place where he could live.

He dipped again into his mind and there, hauled from the junk heap and neatly catalogued, were thousands of planets the Pinkness at one time had visited.

He searched and found a hundred different kinds of planets and each one deadly to unprotected human life. And the horror grew – that with a way of going, he could find no planet soon enough where it would be safe to go.

The howling of the storm intruded on him, breaking through the fierce concentration of his search, and he knew that he was cold – far colder than he'd known. He tried to move a leg and could barely move it. The wind shrieked at him, mocking, as it went fleeing down the river and in between the gusts of wind he could hear the dry, rattling sound of hard snow pellets shotgunning through the willows.

He retreated from the wind and snow and cold, from the shrieking and the rattle – and there was the planet, the one he had been seeking.

He checked the data twice and it was satisfactory. He tattooed the coordinates. He got the picture in his mind. Then slowly, piece by piece, he fed in the long-hop method – and the sun was warm.

He was lying on his face and beneath him was grass and the smell of grass and earth. The howling of the storm was gone and there was no rattle in the willows.

He rolled over and sat up.

He held his breath at what he saw.

He was in paradise!

32

The sun had passed the midday mark and was slanting down the western sky when Blaine came striding down the bluff above the town of Hamilton, walking in the slush and mud after the first storm of the season.

Here he was, he thought, almost too late again – not quite soon enough. For when the sun slipped behind the horizon All Hallows Eve would start.

He wondered how many parry centers the folks of Hamilton had been able to contact. And it was possible, he told himself, that they had done better than anyone could hope. Perhaps they had been lucky. Perhaps they'd hit the jackpot.

And he thought of another thing, of the old priest saying: the finger of God stretched out to touch your heart.

Someday, he thought, the world would look back and wonder at the madness of this day – at the blindness and the folly and the sheer intolerance. Someday there would be vindication. Someday sanity. Someday the Church in Rome would recognize the paranormal as no practicer of witchcraft, but as the natural development of the human race in the grace of God. Someday there would be no social or economic barriers between the parry and the normal – if by that time there should be any normals left. Someday there'd be no need of Fishhook. Even, perhaps, someday there'd be no need of Earth.

For he had found the answer. Failing to reach Pierre, he still had found the answer. He had been forced (by the finger of God, perhaps?) – he had been forced to find the answer.

It was a better answer than the one that Stone had sought. It was a better technique than even Fishhook had. For it did away entirely with the concept of machines. It made a human whole and the master of himself and of the universe.

He strode on down the bluff and struck the trail that ran into Hamilton. In the sky a few scattered, tattered clouds still flew across the valley, the rearguard of the storm. Pools of melt stood along the token roadway and despite the brightness of the sun the wind out of the west had not lost its teeth.

He plodded up the street that led to the center of the town and from a block or two away he could see them waiting for him in the square before the stores – not just a few as had been the case before, but a crowd of them. More than likely, he figured, here was most of Hamilton.

He walked across the square and the crowd was quiet. He flicked a look at it, searching for Anita, but he did not see her.

On the steps four men waited, the same four he had met before.

He stopped before them.

'Good afternoon,' he said,

'We heard you coming,' Andrews told him,

'I didn't get to Pierre,' said Blaine. 'I tried to get there to find some help for us. But the storm caught me on the river.'

Jackson said: 'They blocked us on the phone. But we used long tellies. We got through to some of the other groups and they have spread the word. We don't know how far.'

'Nor how well,' said Andrews.

'Your tellies still can contact these groups?' asked Blaine. Andrews nodded.

Jackson said: 'Finn's men never showed. And it has us worried. Finn ran into trouble ...'

'They should have showed,' said Andrews. 'They should have turned us inside out in their hunt for you.'

'Perhaps they don't want to find me.'

'Perhaps,' Jackson told him coldly, 'you're not what you say you are.'

Blaine's temper flared. 'To hell with you,' he shouted. 'I damn near died for you. Go on and save yourselves.'

He turned on his heel and walked away, with the anger surging in him.

It was not his fight. Not personally his fight. No more his fight than any one of them. But he had made it his. Because of Stone, because of Rand and Harriet, because of the priest who'd hounded him across half the continent, he had tried to make a fight of it. And perhaps, as well, because of something undefinable, unknown to himself, unsuspected in himself – some crazy idealism, some deep-rooted sense of justice, some basic aversion to bullies and bigots and reformers.

He had come to this village with a gift – he had hurried here so he could give it to them. And they had stood and questioned his integrity and purpose.

To hell with them, he said.

He had been pushed far enough. He would be pushed no further.

There was just one thing left that was worth the doing and he would go and do it and from that moment on, he told himself, there would be nothing more that mattered, for him or anyone.

'Shep!'

He kept on walking. 'Shep!'

He stopped and turned around. Anita was walking from the crowd. 'No,' he said.

'But they are not the only ones,' she said. 'There are the rest of us. We will listen to you.' And she was right, of course. There were the rest of them.

Anita and all the rest of them. The women and the children and those other men who were not in authority. For it was authority that turned men suspicious and stern-faced. Authority and responsibility which made them not themselves, but a sort of corporate body that tried to think as a corporate body rather than a person.

And in this a parry or a community of parries was no different from a normal person or a community of normal persons. Paranormal ability, after all, did not change the person. It merely gave him a chance to become a better person.

'You failed,' Anita said. 'We could not expect that you would succeed. You tried and that's enough.'

He took a step toward her. 'But I didn't fail,' he said.

They were coming toward him now, all of them, a mass of people walking slowly and silently toward him. And in front of them walked Anita Andrews.

She reached him and stood in front of him and looked up into his face.

She kept her voice low. 'Where have you been?' she asked. 'Some of us went out and scouted on the river. We located the canoe.'

He reached out an arm and caught her and swung her to his side and held her tight against him.

'I'll tell you,' he said, 'in just a little while. What about these people?'

'They are scared,' she said. 'They'll grab at any hope.'

The crowd came to a halt a dozen feet away, and a man in front said: 'You're the man from Fishhook.'

Blaine nodded. 'I was from Fishhook. I'm not with them any longer.'

'Like Finn?'

'Like Finn,' admitted Blaine.

'Like Stone, too,' Anita said. 'Stone was from Fishhook, too.'

'You are afraid,' said Blaine. 'You're afraid of me and Finn and of the entire world. But I've found a place where you'll never need to think of fear again. I've found a new world for you and if you want it, it is yours.'

'What kind of a world, mister? One of the alien worlds?'

'A world like the best of Earth,' said Blaine. 'I've just come from there ...'

'But you came walking down the bluff. We saw you walking down the bluff ...'

'Shut up, you fools!' Anita screamed. 'Give him a chance to tell you.'

'I found a way,' said Blaine. 'I stole a way, call it what you will – for one to go to the stars in both mind and body. I went out to the stars last night. I came back this morning. No machine is needed. All you need is a little understanding.'

'But how can we tell—'

'You can't,' said Blaine. 'You gamble, that is all.'

'But even Fishhook, mister—'

'Last night,' Blaine said, slowly, 'Fishhook became obsolete. We don't need Fishhook any more. We can go anywhere we wish. We don't need machines. We just need our minds. And that is the goal of all paranormal research. The machines were never more than just a crutch to help our limping mind. Now we can throw away that crutch. We have no need for it.'

A gaunt-faced woman pushed through the crowd.

'Let's cut out all this talk,' she said. 'You say you found a planet?'

'That I did.'

'And you can take us there?'

'No one needs to take you. You can go yourself.'

'You are one of us, young man. You have an honest face. You wouldn't lie to us?'

Blaine smiled. 'I wouldn't lie to you.'

'Then tell us how to go.'

Someone cried out: 'Can we take some stuff with us?'

Blaine shook his head. 'Not much. A mother could take her baby if she held it in her arms. You could pack a knapsack and strap it on your back, you could sling a bag across your shoulder. You could take along a pitchfork and an ax and another tool or two.'

A man stirred out of line and said: 'We'll have to go about this right. We'll have to figure out what we want to take. We'll need food and garden seed and some clothes and tools.'

'You can come back for more,' said Blaine, 'any time you like. There's nothing hard about it.'

'Well,' said the gaunt-faced woman, 'let's not be standing here. Let us get about it. Why don't you tell us, sir?'

'There's just one thing,' said Blaine. 'You have long tellies here?'

'I'm one of them,' the woman told him. 'Me and Myrtle over there and Jim back in the crowd and—'

'You'll have to pass the word along to as many as you can. And the ones you pass it on to will have to pass it on to others. We have to open the gates to as many as we can.'

The woman nodded. 'You just tell it to us.'

There was a murmur in the crowd and they all were moving forward, flowing in on Blaine and Anita to form a ring around them.

'All right,' said Blaine, 'catch on.'

He felt them catching on, gently closing in upon his mind, almost as if they were becoming one with him.

But that wasn't it at all, he thought. He was becoming one with them. Here in the circle the many minds had become one mind. There was one big mind alone and it was warm and human and full of loving kindness. There was a hint of springtime lilac and the smell of nighttime river fog stealing up the land and the sense of autumn color when the hills were painted purple by an Indian summer. There was the crackling of a wood fire burning on the hearth, and the dog lay there sleeping by the fire and the croon of wind as it crawled along the eaves. There was a sense of home and friends, of good mornings and good nights, of the neighbor across the way and the sound of church bells ringing.

He could have stayed there, floating, but he swept it all away.

Here are the co-ordinates of the planet you are going to, he told them.

He gave them the co-ordinates and repeated them again so there'd be no mistake.

And here is how you do it.

He brought out the slimy alien knowledge and held it for them to see until they became accustomed to it, then step by step he showed them the technique and the logic, although there really was no need, for once one had seen the body of the knowledge, the technique and the logic became self-evident.

Then he repeated it again so there'd be no misunderstanding.

The minds drew back from him, and he stood alone with Anita at his side.

He saw them staring at him as they drew away.

What's the matter now? he asked Anita.

She shuddered. *It was horrible.*

Naturally. But I've seen worse.

And that was it, of course, He'd seen worse, but these people never had. They'd lived all their life on Earth; they knew nothing but the Earth. They had never really touched an alien concept, and that was all this concept was. It was not really as slimy as it seemed. It was only alien. There were a lot of alien things that could make one's hair stand up on end while in their proper alien context they were fairly ordinary.

Will they use it? Blaine asked.

The gaunt-faced woman said to him: *I overheard that, young man. It's dirty, but we'll use it. What else is there for us to do?*

You can stay here.

We'll use it, said the woman.

And you'll pass it along?

We'll do the best we can.

They began to move away. They were uneasy and embarrassed as if someone had told a particularly dirty joke at the church's ice-cream social.

And you? Blaine asked Anita.

She turned slowly from his side to face him. *You had to do it, Shep. There was no other way. You never realized how it would seem to them.*

No, I never did. I've lived so long with alien things. I'm part alien, really. I'm not entirely human …

Hush, she said. *Hush, I know just what you are.*

Are you sure, Anita?

Very sure, she said.

He drew her to him and held her tight against him for a moment, then he held her from him and peered into her face, seeing the tears that were just behind the smile inside her eyes.

'I have to leave,' he told her. 'There's one thing else to do.'

'Lambert Finn?'

He nodded.

'But you can't,' she cried. 'You can't!'

'Not what you think,' he told her. 'Although, God knows, I'd like to. I would like to kill him. Up to this very moment, that was what I had intended.'

'But is it safe – going back like this?'

'I don't know. We'll have to see. I can buy some time. I'm the only man who can. Finn's afraid of me.'

'You'll need a car?'

'If you can find me one.'

'We'll be leaving, probably shortly after dark. You'll be back by then?'

'I don't know,' he said.

'You'll come back to go with us? You'll come back to lead us?'

'Anita, I can't promise. Don't try to make me promise.'

'If we're gone, you'll follow?'

He only shook his head. He could give no answer.

33

The hotel lobby was quiet and almost empty. One man was dozing in a chair. Another read a paper. A bored clerk stood behind the desk, staring across the street and snapping his fingers absent-mindedly.

Blaine crossed the lobby and went down the short corridor toward the stairs. The elevator operator lounged beside the open cage.

'Lift, sir?' he asked.

'No bother,' Blaine told him. 'It's just one short flight.'

He turned and started up the stairs and he felt the skin tightening on his back and there was a prickling of the hairs at the base of his skull. For he might very well, he knew, be walking straight to death.

But he had to gamble.

The carpet on the tread muffled his footfalls so that he moved up the stairs in silence except for the nervous whistling of his breath.

He reached the second floor and it was the same as it had been before. Not a thing had changed. The guard still sat in the chair tilted back against the wall. And as Blaine came toward him, he tilted forward and sat spraddle-legged, waiting.

'You can't go in now,' the guard told Blaine. 'He chased everybody out. He said he'd try to sleep.'

Blaine nodded. 'He had a real tough time.'

The guard said, confidentially: 'I never seen a man hit quite so hard. Who do you figure done it?'

'Some more of this damn magic.'

The guard nodded sagely. 'Although he wasn't himself even before it happened. He was all right that first time you saw him, but right after that, right after you left, he was not himself.'

'I didn't see any difference in him.'

'Like I told you, he was all right. He came back all right. An hour or so later I looked in and he was sitting in his chair, staring at the door. A funny kind of stare. As if he maybe hurt inside. And he didn't even see me when I looked. Didn't know that I was there until I spoke to him.'

'Maybe he was thinking.'

'Yeah, I suppose. But yesterday was awful. There was all the crowd here, come to hear him speak, and all of them reporters, and they went out to the shed where he had this star machine ...'

'I wasn't here,' said Blaine, 'but I heard about it. It must have been quite a shock.'

'I thought he'd die right there,' said the guard. 'Right there on the spot. He got purple in the face and—'

'What do you say,' suggested Blaine, 'if we just look in? If he's asleep, I'll leave. But if he's still awake, I'd like a quick word with him. It's really quite important.'

'Well, I guess that would be all right. Seeing you're his friend.'

And that, thought Blaine, was the final pay-off in this fantastic game. Finn had not breathed a word about him, for he'd not dared to breathe a word about him. Finn had let it be presumed that he was a friend, for such a presumption was a shield for Finn himself. And that was why there'd been no hunt for him. That was why Finn's hoods had not turned Hamilton inside out in a frantic search for him.

This was the pay-off, then – unless it was a trap.

He felt his muscles tensing and he forced them to relax.

The guard was getting up and fumbling for the key.

'Hey, wait a minute there,' said Blaine. 'You'd better shake me down.'

The guard grinned at him. 'No need of that,' he said. 'You was clean before. You and Finn went out of here arm in arm. He told me you was an old friend he hadn't seen in years.'

He found the key and unlocked the door.

'I'll go in first,' he said. 'I'll see if he's asleep.'

He swung the door open quietly and moved across the threshold, Blaine following close behind.

The guard stopped so abruptly that Blaine bumped into him.

The guard was making funny noises deep inside his throat.

Blaine put out a hand and pushed him roughly to one side,

Finn was lying on the floor.

And there was about him a strange sense of alienness.

His body was twisted as if someone had taken it and twisted it beyond the natural ability of a body to contort itself. His face, resting on one cheek, was the visage of a man who had glimpsed the fires of hell and had smelled the stench of bodies that burned eternally. His black clothing had an obscene shine in the light from the lamp that stood beside a chair not far from the body. There was a wide blot of darkness in the carpeting about his head and chest. And there was the horror of a throat that had been slashed wide open.

The guard still was standing to one side of the door and the noises in his throat had changed to gagging noises.

Blaine walked close to Finn and there, beside the out-flung hand, was the instrument of death – an old-fashioned, straightedge razor that should have been safely tucked away in a museum.

Now, Blaine knew, all hope was gone. There could be no bargain made. For Lambert Finn was beyond all bargaining.

To the very last the man had stayed in character, had remained his harsh, stern self. No easy way for him, but the toughest way of all for a man to take his life.

But even so, Blaine thought, staring in chilled horror at the red gash in the throat, there had been no need to do the job so thoroughly, to keep on slashing with the razor even as he died.

Only a man of hate would do that, a man insane with the hate of self – a man who despised and loathed what he had become.

Unclean – unclean with an alien mind inside his antiseptic skull. A thing like that would drive a man like Finn to death; a fastidious fanatic who could become obsessed with his self-conceived idea of a perfect state could not live with nor survive the disorderly enigma of an alien mind.

Blaine turned on his heel and walked out of the room. In the corridor the guard was in a corner, doubled over, retching.

'You stay here,' Blaine told him. 'I'll call the cops.'

The man turned around. His eyes were glazed with horror. He wiped feebly at his chin.

'My God,' he said, 'I ask you, did you ever see a mess—'

'Sit down,' said Blaine, 'and take it easy. I'll be right back.'

Although he wouldn't be. Now was the time to blow. He needed time and he'd get a little time. For the guard was too shaken to do anything for quite a little while.

But as soon as the news was known, all hell was bound to break.

God help the parry, Blaine thought, who is caught this night!

He went swiftly down the corridor and ran down the stairs. The lobby still was empty and he set out across it briskly.

As he reached the door, it came open suddenly and someone came through it, walking briskly, too.

A purse clattered to the floor, and Blaine's hands reached out to steady the woman who had come through the doorway.

Harriet! Get out of here! Get out!

My purse!

He stooped to scoop it up and as he lifted it, the catch came open and something black and heavy fell. His free hand snapped at it and had it and he worked it back along his palm so that it was hidden

Harriet had turned around and was going out the door. Blaine hurried after her and caught her by the elbow, urging her along.

He reached his car and stooped to open the door. He pushed her to the seat.

But, Shep, my car is just a block—

No time. We're getting out of here.

He ran around the car and got in. He jerked it from the curb and out into the street. Moving far more slowly than he wanted, he eased it down the block, turned at the intersection, heading for the highway.

Just ahead stood the gutted structure of the Trading Post. He had been holding the purse in his lap and now he gave it to her.

'How about the gun?' he asked.

'I was going to kill him,' she shouted. 'I was going to shoot him dead.'

'No need to do that now. He is already dead.'

She turned toward him quickly.

'You!'

'Well, now, I guess that you could say so.'

'But, Shep, you know. You either killed him or you—'

'All right,' he said. 'I killed him.'

And it was no lie. No matter by what hand Lambert Finn had died, he, Shepherd Blaine, had killed him. 'I had reason to,' he said. 'But you?'

'He had Godfrey killed. That itself would have been enough.'

'You were in love with Godfrey.'

'Yes, I suppose I was. He was such a great guy, Shep.'

'I know how great he was. We were friends in Fishhook.'

'It hurts,' said Harriet. 'Oh, Shep, how it hurts!'

'And that night ...'

'There was no time for tears,' she said. 'There's never time for tears.'

'You knew about all this ...'

'For a long time. It was my job to know.'

He reached the highway and turned down it, back toward Hamilton. The sun had set. Twilight had crept across the land and in the east one star was twinkling, just above the prairie.

'And now?' he asked.

'Now I have a story. As much of it as I ever can.'

'You're going to write it. Will your paper run it?'

'I don't know,' she said. 'But I have to write it. You understand that I have to write it. I'm going to New York ...'

'Wrong,' he said. 'You're going to Fishhook. Not by car. From the nearest airport.'

'But, Shep—'

'It's not safe,' Blaine told her. 'Not for anyone who has the faintest hint of parry. Even minor telepaths, like you.'

'I can't do it, Shep. I—'

'Listen, Harriet. Finn had set up a Halloween outbreak by the parries, a sort of counterintelligence move. The other parries, when they learned about it, tried to stop it. They did stop part of it, but I don't know to what extent.

Whatever happens will be happening tonight. He would have used the outbreak to step up intolerance, to trigger rigid legislation. There would have been some violence, of course, but that was not, by and large, Finn's purpose. But now, with Finn dead ...'

Harriet drew in her breath. 'They'll wipe us out,' she said.

'They'll do their best. But there is a way ...'

'Knowing this, you still killed Finn!'

'Look, Harriet, I didn't really kill him. I went to bargain with him. I found a way to take the parries off Earth. I was going to promise to clean every parry off the Earth, clean out of his way, if he'd hold off his dogs for a week or two ...'

'But you said you killed him.'

'Maybe,' said Blaine, 'I better fill you in. So when you come to write your story you can write it all.'

34

Hamilton was silent. And so empty you could feel the emptiness.

Blaine stopped the car in the square and got out of it.

Not a light was showing, and the soft sound of the river came clearly to his ear.

'They are gone,' he said.

Harriet got out of the car and came around it to stand beside him. 'All right, pal,' she said. 'Get onto your horse.'

He shook his head.

'But you have to go. You have to follow them. You belong with them.'

'Someday,' said Blaine. 'Someday, years from now. There's still work to do. There'll be pockets of parries all up and down the land. Fearful and in hiding. I have to search them out. I have to save as many as I can.'

'You'll never live to do it. You'll be a special target. Finn's men will never rest ...'

'If the pressure gets too bad, I'll go. I'm no hero, Harriet. Basically, I'm a coward.'

'You'll promise that?' she asked.

'Of course. Cross my heart. And you're going back to Fishhook. You'll be safe in Fishhook. Straight to the airport up in Pierre.'

She turned and went back to his car, started to get in, then turned back again. 'But you'll need the car.'

He chuckled. 'If I need one, there's a village full of cars. I can pick the one I want. They couldn't take their cars.'

She got behind the wheel and turned her head to say good-bye.

'One thing,' said Blaine. 'What happened to you when I was in the shed?'

Her laughter had a sharpness to it. 'When Rand drove up, I pulled out. I went to get some help. I figured I should get on the phone to Pierre. There'd been men up there who'd helped us.'

'But?'

'The police stopped me and threw me into jail. They let me out the morning after, and I've been looking for you since.'

'Stout gal,' he said, and there was a faint throbbing in the air – a noise from far away.

Blaine stiffened, listening. The noise grew louder, deeper – the sound of many cars.

'Quick,' he said. 'No lights. Slant across the bluff. You'll hit the road up north.'

'Shep, what's got into you?'

'That noise you hear is cars. A posse coming here. They know that Finn is dead.'

'You, Shep?'

'I'll be all right. Get going.'

She started the motor.

'Be seeing you,' she said.

'Get moving, Harriet! And thanks a lot. Thanks for everything. Tell Charline hello.'

'Good-bye, Shep,' she said, and the car was moving, swinging in a circle to head up a street that led toward the bluff.

She'll make it all right, he told himself. Anyone who could drive those blind mountains out of Fishhook would have no trouble here.

'Good-bye, Harriet,' he had said. 'Tell Charline hello.' And why had he said that? he wondered. A hail and farewell to the old life, more than likely – a reaching out to touch hands with the past. Although there'd be no past in Fishhook. Charline would go on having parties, and the most peculiar people would continue showing up without having been invited. For Fishhook was a glamour and a glitter and a ghost. Without knowing it, Fishhook now was dead. And it was a pity. For Fishhook had been one of the greatest, one of the giddiest, one of the gladdest things that had ever happened to the human race.

He stood lonely in the square and listened to the furious sound of the coming cars. Far to the west he saw the flashing of their lights. A chill breeze came off the river and tugged at his trouser legs and jacket sleeves.

All over the world, he thought. All over the world tonight there'd be screaming cars and the slavering mobs and the running people.

He put his hand into a jacket pocket and felt the shape and the weight of the gun that had fallen from Harriet's purse. His fingers closed around it – but that, he thought, was not the way to fight them.

There was another way to fight them, a long-range way to fight them. Isolate them and strangle them in their own mediocrity. Give them what they wanted – a planet full of people who were merely normal. A planet full of people who could huddle here and rot – never knowing space, never getting to the stars, never going anyplace or doing anything. Like a man who rocked away his life sitting in a rocking chair on a porch of some little dying town.

Without recruits from outside, Fishhook itself would falter in another hundred years, come to a dead stop within still another hundred. For the parries on the other planets would recruit from Fishhook even as they winnowed through the world to rescue their own kind.

But it wouldn't matter in another hundred years, for the human race would then be safe on the other planets, building the kind of life and the kind of culture they'd been denied upon the Earth.

He started to move across the square, heading toward the bluffs. For he must be out of town, or nearly out of town, before the cars came in.

And he was, he knew, on a lonely path once more. But not so lonely now, for now he had a purpose. A purpose, he told himself with a sudden flickering of pride, he had hewn out himself.

He straightened his shoulders against the dullness of the wind and moved a bit more briskly. For there was work to do. A lot of work to do.

Something moved in the shadow of the trees off to the left, and Blaine, catching the movement with one corner of his mind, wheeled swiftly.

The movement came toward him, slowly, just a bit uncertainly.

'Shep?'

'Anita!' he cried. 'You little fool! Anita!'

She came running from the darkness and was in his arms.

I wouldn't go,' she said. 'I wouldn't go without you. I knew you would come back.'

He crushed her to him and bent to kiss her and there was nothing in the world, nothing in the universe, but the two of them. There was blood and lilacs and the shining star and the wind upon the hilltop and the two of them and that was all there was.

Except the screaming of the cars as they came tearing down the road.

Blaine jerked away from her. 'Run!' he cried. 'You must, Anita!'

'Like the wind,' she said. They ran.

'Up the bluff,' she said. 'There's a car up there. I took it up as soon as it got dark.'

Halfway up the bluff they stopped and looked back.

The first flames were beginning to run in the huddled blackness of the village, and screams of futile rage came drifting up the slope. Gunfire rattled hollowly, torn by the wind.

They're shooting at shadows,' said Anita. 'There is nothing down there. Not even dogs or cats. The kids took them along.'

But in many other villages, thought Blaine, in many other places, there would be more than shadows. There would be fire and gunsmoke and the knotted rope and the bloody knife. And there might be as well the pattering of rapid feet and the dark shape in the sky and a howling on the hills.

'Anita,' he asked, 'are there really werewolves?'

'Yes,' she told him. 'Your werewolves are down there.'

And that was right, he thought. The darkness of the mind, the bleakness of the thought, the shallowness of purpose. These were the werewolves of the world.

The two of them turned their backs upon the village and headed up the slope.

Behind them the flames of hate grew taller, hotter. But ahead, above the bluff top, the distant stars glowed with certain promise.

WAY STATION

1

The noise was ended now. The smoke drifted like thin, grey wisps of fog above the tortured earth and the shattered fences and the peach trees that had been whittled into toothpicks by the cannon fire. For a moment silence, if not peace, fell upon those few square miles of ground where just a while before men had screamed and torn at one another in the frenzy of old hate and had contended in an ancient striving and then had fallen apart, exhausted.

For endless time, it seemed, there had been belching thunder rolling from horizon to horizon and the gouted earth that had spouted in the sky and the screams of horses and the hoarse bellowing of men; the whistling of metal and the thud when the whistle ended; the flash of searing fire and the brightness of the steel; the bravery of the colours snapping in the battle wind.

Then it all had ended and there was a silence.

But silence was an alien note that held no right upon this field or day, and it was broken by the whimper and the pain, the cry for water, and the prayer for death – the crying and the calling and the whimpering that would go on for hours beneath the summer sun. Later the huddled shapes would grow quiet and still and there would be an odour that would sicken all who passed, and the graves would be shallow graves.

There was wheat that never would be harvested, trees that would not bloom when spring came round again, and on the slope of land that ran up to the ridge the words unspoken and the deed undone and the sodden bundles that cried aloud the emptiness and the waste of death.

There were proud names that were the prouder now, but now no more than names to echo down the ages – the Iron Brigade, the 5th New Hampshire, the Ist Minnesota, the 2nd Massachusetts, the 16th Maine.

And there was Enoch Wallace.

He still held the shattered musket and there were blisters on his hands. His face was smudged with powder. His shoes were caked with dust and blood.

He was still alive.

2

Dr Erwin Hardwicke rolled the pencil back and forth between his palms, an irritating business. He eyed the man across the desk from him with some calculation.

'What I can't figure out,' said Hardwicke, 'is why you should come to us.'

'Well, you're the National Academy and I thought ...'

'And you're Intelligence.'

'Look, Doctor, if it suits you better, let's call this visit unofficial. Pretend I'm a puzzled citizen who dropped in to see if you could help.'

'It's not that I wouldn't like to help, but I don't see how I can. The whole thing is so hazy and so hypothetical.'

'Damn it, man,' Claude Lewis said, 'you can't deny the proof – the little that I have.'

'All right, then,' said Hardwicke, 'let's start over once again and take it piece by piece. You say you have this man ...'

'His name,' said Lewis, 'is Enoch Wallace. Chronologically, he is one hundred and twenty-four years old. He was born on a farm a few miles from the town of Millville in Wisconsin, 22 April 1840, and he is the only child of Jedediah and Amanda Wallace. He enlisted among the first of them when Abe Lincoln called for volunteers. He was with the Iron Brigade, which was virtually wiped out at Gettysburg in 1863. But Wallace somehow managed to get transferred to another fighting outfit and fought down across Virginia under Grant. He was in on the end of it at Appomattox ...'

'You've run a check on him.'

'I've looked up his records. The record of enlistment at the State Capitol in Madison. The rest of it, including discharge, here in Washington.'

'You say he looks like thirty.'

'Not a day beyond it. Maybe even less than that.'

'But you haven't talked with him.'

Lewis shook his head.

'He may not be the man. If you had fingerprints ...'

'At the time of the Civil War,' said Lewis, 'they'd not thought of fingerprints.'

'The last of the veterans of the Civil War,' said Hardwicke, 'died several years ago. A Confederate drummer boy, I think. There must be some mistake.'

Lewis shook his head. 'I thought so myself, when I was assigned to it.'

'How come you were assigned? How does Intelligence get involved in a deal like this?'

'I'll admit,' said Lewis, 'that it's a bit unusual. But there were so many implications ...'

'Immortality, you mean.'

'It crossed our mind, perhaps. The chance of it. But only incidentally. There were other considerations. It was a strange set-up that bore some looking into.'

'But Intelligence ...'

Lewis grinned. 'You are thinking, why not a scientific outfit? Logically, I suppose it would have been. But one of our men ran afoul of it. He was on vacation. Had relatives back in Wisconsin. Not in that particular area, but some thirty miles away. He heard a rumour – just the vaguest rumour, almost a casual mention. So he nosed around a bit. He didn't find out too much, but enough to make him think there might be something to it.'

'That's the thing that puzzles me,' said Hardwicke. 'How could a man live for one hundred and twenty-four years in one locality without becoming a celebrity that the world would hear about? Can you imagine what the newspapers could do with a thing like this?'

'I shudder,' Lewis said, 'when I think about it.'

'You haven't told me how.'

'This,' said Lewis, 'is a bit hard to explain. You'd have to know the country and the people in it. The south-western corner of Wisconsin is bounded by two rivers, the Mississippi on the west, the Wisconsin on the north. Away from the rivers there is flat, broad prairie land, rich land, with prosperous farms and towns. But the land that runs down to the river is rough and rugged; high hills and bluffs and deep ravines and cliffs, and there are certain areas forming bays or pockets that are isolated. They are served by inadequate roads and the small, rough farms are inhabited by a people who are closer, perhaps, to the pioneer days of a hundred years ago than they are to the twentieth century. They have cars, of course, and radios, and some day soon, perhaps, even television. But in spirit they are conservative and clannish – not all the people, of course, not even many of them, but these little isolated neighbourhoods.

'At one time there were a lot of farms in these isolated pockets, but today a man can hardly make a living on a farm of that sort. Slowly the people are being squeezed out of the areas by economic circumstances. They sell their farms for whatever they can get for them and move somewhere else, to the cities mostly, where they can make a living.'

Hardwicke nodded. 'And the ones that are left, of course, are the most conservative and clannish.'

'Right. Most of the land now is held by absentee owners who make no pretence of farming it. They may run a few head of cattle on it, but that is all. It's not too bad as a tax write-off for someone who needs that sort of thing. And in the land-bank days a lot of the land was put into the bank.'

'You're trying to tell me these backwoods people – is that what you'd call them? – engaged in a conspiracy of silence.'

'Perhaps not anything,' said Lewis, 'as formal or elaborate as that. It is just their way of doing things, a holdover from the old, stout pioneer philosophy. They minded their own business. They didn't want folks interfering with them and they interfered with no one else. If a man wanted to to be a thousand, it might be a thing of wonder, but it was his own damned business. And if he wanted to live alone and be let alone while he was doing it, that was his business, too. They might talk about it among themselves, but to no one else. They'd resent it if some outsider tried to talk about it.

'After a time, I suppose, they came to accept the fact that Wallace kept on being young while they were growing old. The wonder wore off it and they probably didn't talk about it a great deal, even among themselves. New generations accepted it because their elders saw in it nothing too unusual – and anyhow no one saw much of Wallace because he kept strictly to himself.

'And in the near-by areas the thing, when it was thought of at all, grew to be just a sort of legend – another crazy tale that wasn't worth looking into. Maybe just a joke among those folks down Dark Hollow way. A Rip Van Winkle sort of business that probably didn't have a word of truth in it. A man might look ridiculous if he went prying into it.'

'But your man looked into it.'

'Yes. Don't ask me why.'

'Yet he wasn't assigned to follow up the job.'

'He was needed somewhere else. And besides he was known back there.'

'And you?'

'It took two years of work.'

'But now you know the story.'

'Not all of it. There are more questions now than there were to start with.'

'You've seen this man.'

'Many times,' said Lewis. 'But I've never talked with him. I don't think he's ever seen me. He takes a walk each day before he goes to get the mail. He never moves off the place, you see. The mailman brings out the little stuff he needs. A bag of flour, a pound of bacon, a dozen eggs, cigars, and sometimes liquor.'

'But that must be against the postal regulations.'

'Of course it is. But mailmen have been doing it for years. It doesn't hurt a thing until someone screams about it. And no one's going to. The mailmen probably are the only friends he has ever had.'

'I take it this Wallace doesn't do much farming.'

'None at all. He has a little vegetable garden, but that is all he does. The place has gone back pretty much to wilderness.'

'But he has to live. He must get money somewhere.'

'He does,' said Lewis. 'Every five or ten years or so he ships off a fistful of gems to an outfit in New York.'

'Legal?'

'If you mean, is it hot, I don't think so. If someone wanted to make a case of it, I suppose there are illegalities. Not to start with, when he first started sending them, back in the old days. But laws change and I suspect both he and the buyer are in defiance of any number of them.'

'And you don't mind?'

'I checked on this firm,' said Lewis, 'and they were rather nervous. For one thing, they'd been stealing Wallace blind. I told them to keep on buying. I told them that if anyone came around to check, to refer them straight to me. I told them to keep their mouths shut and not to change anything.'

'You don't want anyone to scare him off,' said Hardwicke.

'You're damned right, I don't. I want the mailman to keep on acting as a delivery boy and the New York firm to keep on buying gems. I want everything to stay just the way it is. And before you ask me where the stones come from, I'll tell you I don't know.'

'He maybe has a mine.'

'That would be quite a mine. Diamonds and rubies and emeralds, all out of the same mine.'

'I would suspect, even at the prices that he gets from them, he picks up a fair income.'

Lewis nodded. 'Apparently he only sends a shipment in when he runs out of cash. He wouldn't need too much. He lives rather simply, to judge from the grub he buys. But he subscribes to a lot of daily papers and news magazines and to dozens of scientific journals. He buys a lot of books.'

'Technical books?'

'Some of them, of course, but mostly keeping up with new developments. Physics and chemistry and biology – all that sort of stuff.'

'But I don't ...'

'Of course you don't. Neither do I. He's no scientist. Or at least he has no formal education in the sciences. Back in the days when he went to school there wasn't much of it – not in the sense of today's scientific education. And whatever he learned then would be fairly worthless now in any event. He went through grade school – one of those one-room country schools – and spent one winter at what was called an academy that operated for a year or two down in Millville village. In case you don't know, that was considerably better than par back in the 1850s. He was, apparently, a fairly bright young man.'

Hardwicke shook his head. 'It sounds incredible. You've checked on all of this?'

'As well as I could. I had to go at it gingerly. I wanted no one to catch on.

And one thing I forgot – he does a lot of writing. He buys these big, bound record books, in lots of a dozen at the time. He buys ink by the pint.'

Hardwicke got up from his desk and paced up and down the room.

'Lewis,' he said, 'if you hadn't shown me your credentials and if I hadn't checked on them, I'd figure all of this to be a very tasteless joke.'

He went back and sat down again. He picked up the pencil and started rolling it between his palms once more.

'You've been on the case two years,' he said. 'You have no ideas?'

'Not a one,' said Lewis. 'I'm entirely baffled. That is why I'm here.'

'Tell me more of his history. After the war, that is.'

'His mother died,' said Lewis, 'while he was away. His father and the neighbours buried her right there on the farm. That was the way a lot of people did it then. Young Wallace got a furlough, but not in time to get home for the funeral. There wasn't much embalming done in those days and the travelling was slow. Then he went back to the war. So far as I can find, it was his only furlough. The old man lived alone and worked the farm, batching it and getting along all right. From what I can pick up, he was a good farmer, an exceptionally good farmer for his day. He subscribed to some farm journals and was progressive in his ideas. He paid attention to such things as crop rotation and the prevention of erosion. The farm wasn't much of a farm by modern standards, but it made him a living and a little extra he managed to lay by.

'Then Enoch came home from the war and they farmed the place together for a year or so. The old man bought a mower – one of those horse-drawn contraptions with a sickle bar to cut hay or grain. It was the progressive thing to do. It beat a scythe all hollow.

'Then one afternoon the old man went out to mow a hay-field. The horses ran away. Something must have scared them. Enoch's father was thrown off the seat and forward, in front of the sickle bar. It was not a pretty way to die.'

Hardwicke made a grimace of distaste. 'Horrible,' he said.

'Enoch went out and gathered up his father and got the body to the house. Then he took a gun and went hunting for the horses. He found them down in the corner of the pasture and he shot the two of them and he left them. I mean exactly that. For years their skeletons lay there in the pasture, where he'd killed them, still hitched to the mower until the harness rotted.

'Then he went back to the house and laid his father out. He washed him and he dressed him in the good black suit and laid him on a board, then went out to the barn and carpentered a coffin. And after that, he dug a grave beside his mother's grave. He finished it by lantern-light, then went back to the house and sat up with his father. When morning came, he went to tell the nearest neighbour and that neighbour notified the others and someone went to get a preacher. Late in the afternoon they had the funeral, and Enoch went back to the house. He has lived there ever since, but he never farmed the land. Except the garden, that is.'

'You told me these people wouldn't talk to strangers. You seem to have learned a lot.'

'It took two years to do it. I infiltrated them. I bought a beat-up car and drifted into Millville and I let it out that I was a ginseng hunter.'

'A what?'

'A ginseng hunter. Ginseng is a plant.'

'Yes, I know. But there's been no market for it for years.'

'A small market and an occasional one. Exporters will take on some of it. But I hunted other medicinal plants as well and pretended an extensive knowledge of them and their use. "Pretended" isn't actually the word; I boned up plenty on them.'

'The kind of simple soul,' said Hardwicke, 'those folks could understand. A sort of cultural throwback. And inoffensive, too. Perhaps not quite right in the head.'

Lewis nodded. 'It worked even better than I thought. I just wandered around and people talked to me. I even found some ginseng. There was one family in particular – the Fisher family. They live down in the river bottoms below the Wallace farm, which sits on the ridge above the bluffs. They've lived there almost as long as the Wallace family, but a different stripe entirely. The Fishers are a coon-hunting, catfishing, moonshine-cooking tribe. They found a kindred spirit in me. I was just as shiftless and no-account as they were. I helped them with their moonshine, both in the making and the drinking and once in a while the peddling. I went fishing with them and hunting with them and I sat around and talked and they showed me a place or two where I might find some ginseng – "sang" is what they call it. I imagine a social scientist might find a gold mine in the Fishers. There is one girl – a deaf-mute, but a pretty thing, and she can charm off warts ...'

'I recognize the type,' said Hardwicke. 'I was born and raised in the southern mountains.'

'They were the ones who told me about the team and mower. So one day I went up in that corner of the Wallace pasture and did some digging. I found a horse's skull and some other bones.'

'But no way of knowing if it was one of the Wallace horses.'

'Perhaps not,' said Lewis. 'But I found part of the mower as well. Not much left of it, but enough to identify.'

'Let's get back to the history,' suggested Hardwicke. 'After the father's death, Enoch stayed on at the farm. He never left it?'

Lewis shook his head. 'He lives in the same house. Not a thing's been changed. And the house apparently has aged no more than the man.'

'You've been in the house?'

'Not in it. At it. I will tell you how it was.'

3

He had an hour. He knew he had an hour, for he had timed Enoch Wallace during the last ten days. And from the time he left the house until he got back with his mail, it had never been less than an hour. Sometimes a little longer, when the mailman might be late, or they got to talking. But an hour, Lewis told himself, was all that he could count on.

Wallace had disappeared down the slope of ridge, heading for the point of rocks that towered above the bluff face, with the Wisconsin River running there below. He would climb the rocks and stand there, with the rifle tucked beneath his arm, to gaze across the wilderness of the river valley. Then he would go back down the rocks again and trudge along the wooded path to where, in proper season, the pink lady's-slippers grew, and from there up the hill again to the spring that gushed out of the hillside just below the ancient field that had lain fallow for a century or more, and then along the slope until he hit the almost overgrown road and so down to the mailbox.

In the ten days that Lewis had watched him, his route had never varied. It was likely, Lewis told himself, that it had not varied through the years. Wallace did not hurry. He walked as if he had all the time there was. And he stopped along the way to renew acquaintances with old friends of his – a tree, a squirrel, a flower. He was a rugged man and there still was much of the soldier in him – old tricks and habits left from the bitter years of campaigning under many leaders. He walked with his head held high and his shoulders back and he moved with the easy stride of one who had known hard marches.

Lewis came out of the tangled mass of trees that once had been an orchard and in which a few trees, twisted and gnarled and grey with age, still bore their pitiful and bitter crop of apples.

He stopped at the edge of the copse and stood for a moment to stare up at the house on the ridge above, and for a single instant it seemed to him the house stood in a special light, as if a rare and more distilled essence of the sun had crossed the gulf of space to shine upon this house and to set it apart from all other houses in the world. Bathed in that light, the house was somehow unearthly, as if, indeed, it might be set apart as a very special thing. And then the light, if it ever had been there, was gone and the house shared the common sunlight of the fields and woods.

Lewis shook his head and told himself that it had been foolishness, or perhaps a trick of seeing. For there was no such thing as special sunlight and the house was no more than a house, although wondrously preserved.

It was the kind of house one did not see too often in these days. It was rectangular; long and narrow and high, with old-fashioned gingerbread along the eaves and gables. It had a certain gauntness that had nothing to do with age; it had been gaunt the day it had been built – gaunt and plain and strong, like the people that it sheltered. But gaunt as it might be, it stood prim and neat, with no peeling paint, with no sign of weathering, and no hint of decay.

Against one end of it was a smaller building, no more than a shed, as if it were an alien structure that had been carted in from some other place and shoved against its end, covering the side door of the house. Perhaps the door, thought Lewis, that led into the kitchen. The shed undoubtedly had been used as a place to hang outdoor clothing and to leave overshoes and boots, with a bench for milk cans and buckets, and perhaps a basket in which to gather eggs. From the top of it extended some three feet of stovepipe.

Lewis went up to the house and around the shed and there, in the side of it, was a door ajar. He stepped up on the stoop and pushed the door wide open and stared in amazement at the room.

For it was not a simple shed. It apparently was the place where Wallace lived.

The stove from which the stovepipe projected stood in one corner, an ancient cookstove, smaller than the old-fashioned kitchen range. Sitting on its top was a coffee pot, a frying pan, and a griddle. Hung from hooks on a board behind it were other cooking implements. Opposite the stove, shoved against the wall, was a three-quarter-size four-poster bed, covered with a lumpy quilt, quilted in one of the ornate patterns of many pieces of many-coloured cloth, such as had been the delight of ladies of a century before. In another corner was a table and a chair, and above the table, hung against the wall, a small open cupboard in which were stacked some dishes. On the table stood a kerosene lantern, battered from much usage, but with its chimney clean, as if it had been washed and polished as recently as this morning.

There was no door into the house, no sign there had ever been a door. The clapboard of the house's outer wall ran unbroken to form the fourth wall of the shed.

This was incredible, Lewis told himself – that there should be no door, that Wallace should live here, in this shed, when there was a house to live in. As if there were some reason he should not occupy the house, and yet must stay close by it. Or perhaps that he might be living out a penance of some sort, living here in this shed as a medieval hermit might have lived in a woodland hut or in a desert cave.

He stood in the centre of the shed and looked around him, hoping that he might find some clue to this unusual circumstance. But there was nothing, beyond the bare, hard fact of living, the very basic necessities of living – the stove to cook his food and heat the place, the bed to sleep on, the table to eat on, and the lantern for its light. Not even so much as an extra hat (although, come to think of it, Wallace never wore a hat) or an extra coat.

No sign of magazines or papers, and Wallace never came home from the mailbox empty-handed. He subscribed to the *New York Times*, the *Wall Street Journal*, the *Christian Science Monitor*, and the Washington *Star*, as well as many scientific and technical journals. But there was no sign of them here, nor of the many books he bought. No sign, either, of the bound record books. Nothing at all on which a man could write.

Perhaps, Lewis told himself, this shed, for some baffling reason, was no more than a show place, a place staged most carefully to make one think that this was where Wallace lived. Perhaps, after all, he lived in the house. Although, if that were the case, why all this effort, not too successful, to make one think he didn't?

Lewis turned to the door and walked out of the shed. He went around the house until he reached the porch that led up to the front door. At the foot of the steps, he stopped and looked around. The place was quiet. The sun was midmorning-high and the day was warming up and this sheltered corner of the Earth stood relaxed and hushed, waiting for the heat.

He looked at his watch and he had forty minutes left, so he went up the steps and across the porch until he came to the door. Reaching out his hand, he grasped the knob and turned – except he didn't turn it; the knob stayed exactly where it was and his clenched fingers went half around it in the motion of a turn.

Puzzled, he tried again and still he didn't turn the knob. It was as if the knob were covered with some hard, slick coating, like a coat of brittle ice, on which the fingers slipped without exerting any pressure on the knob.

He bent his head close to the knob and tried to see if there were any evidence of coating, and there was no evidence. The knob looked perfectly all right – too all right, perhaps. For it was clean, as if someone had wiped and polished it. There was no dust upon it, and no weather specks.

He tried a thumbnail on it, and the thumbnail slipped but left no mark behind it. He ran his palm over the outer surface of the door and the wood was slick. The rubbing of the palm set up no friction. The palm slid along the wood as if the palm were greased, but there was no sign of grease. There was no indication of anything to account for the slickness of the door.

Lewis moved from the door to the clapboard and the clapboard also was slick. He tried palm and thumbnail on it and the answer was the same. There was something covering this house which made it slick and smooth – so smooth that dust could not cling upon its surface nor could weather stain it.

He moved along the porch until he came to a window, and now, as he stood facing the window, he realized something he had not noticed before, something that helped make the house seem gaunter than it really was. The windows were black. There were no curtains, no drapes, no shades; they were simply black rectangles, like empty eyes staring out of the bare skull of the house.

He moved closer to the window and put his face up to it, shading the sides of his face, next to the eyes, with his upheld hands to shield out the sunlight. But even so, he could not see into the room beyond. He stared, instead, into a pool of blackness, and the blackness, curiously enough, had no reflective qualities. He could not see himself reflected in the glass. He could see nothing but the blackness, as if the light hit the window and was absorbed by it, sucked in and held by it. There was no bouncing back of light once it had hit that window.

He left the porch and went slowly around the house, examining it as he went. The windows were all blank, black pools that sucked in the captured light, and all the exterior was slick and hard.

He pounded the clapboard with his fist, and it was like the pounding of a rock. He examined the stone walls of the basement where they were exposed, and the walls were smooth and slick. There were mortar gaps between the stones and in the stones themselves one could see uneven surfaces, but the hand rubbed across the wall could detect no roughness.

An invisible something had been laid over the roughness of the stone, just enough of it to fill in the pits and uneven surfaces. But one could not detect it. It was almost as if it had no substance.

Straightening up from his examination of the wall, Lewis looked at his watch. There were only ten minutes left. He must be getting on.

He walked down the hill towards the tangle of old orchard. At its edge he stopped and looked back, and now the house was different. It was no longer just a structure. It wore a personality, a mocking, leering look, and there was a malevolent chuckle bubbling inside of it, ready to break out.

Lewis ducked into the orchard and worked his way in among the trees. There was no path and beneath the trees the grass and weeds grew tall. He ducked the drooping branches and walked around a tree that had been uprooted in some windstorm of many years before.

He reached up as he went along, picking an apple here and there, scrubby things and sour, taking a single bite of each one of them, then throwing it away, for there was none of them that was fit to eat, as if they might have taken from the neglected soil a certain basic bitterness.

At the far side of the orchard he found the fence and the graves that it enclosed. Here the weeds and grass were not so high and the fence showed signs of repair made rather recently, and at the foot of each grave, opposite the three crude native limestone headstones, was a peony bush, each a great straggling mass of plants that had grown, undisciplined, for years.

Standing before the weathered picketing, he knew that he had stumbled on the Wallace family burial plot.

But there should have been only the two stones. What about the third?

He moved around the fence to the sagging gate and went into the plot. Standing at the foot of the graves, he read the legends on the stones. The carving was angular and rough, giving evidence of having been executed by unaccustomed hands. There were no pious phrases, no lines of verse, no carvings of angels or of lambs or of other symbolic figures such as had been customary in the 1860s. There were just the names and dates.

On the first stone: Amanda Wallace 1821–63

And on the second stone: Jedediah Wallace 1816–66

And on the third stone –

4

'Give me that pencil, please,' said Lewis.

Hardwicke quit rolling it between his palms and handed it across.

'Paper, too?' he asked.

'If you please,' said Lewis.

He bent above the desk and drew rapidly.

'Here,' he said, handing back the paper.

Hardwicke wrinkled his brow.

'But it makes no sense,' he said. 'Except for that figure underneath.'

'The figure eight, lying on its side. Yes, I know. The symbol for infinity.'

'But the rest of it?'

'I don't know,' said Lewis. 'It is the inscription on the tombstone. I copied it …'

'And you know it now by heart.'

'I should. I've studied it enough.'

'I've never seen anything like it in my life,' said Hardwicke.

'Not that I'm an authority. I really know little at all in this field.'

'You can put your mind at rest. It's nothing that anyone knows anything about. It bears no resemblance, not even the remotest, to any language or any known inscription. I checked with men who know. Not one, but a dozen of them. I told them I'd found it on a rocky cliff. I am sure that most of them think I am a crackpot. One of those people who are trying to prove that the Romans or the Phoenicians or the Irish or whatnot had pre-Colombian settlements in America.'

Hardwicke put down the sheet of paper.

'I can see what you mean,' he said, 'when you say you have more questions now than when you started. Not only the question of a young man more than a century old, but likewise the matter of the slickness of the house and the third gravestone with the undecipherable inscription. You say you've never talked with Wallace?'

'No one talks to him. Except the mailman. He goes out on his daily walks and he packs this gun.'

'People are afraid to talk with him?'

'Because of the gun, you mean?'

'Well, yes, I suppose that was in the back of my mind. I wondered why he carried it.'

Lewis shook his head. 'I don't know. I've tried to tie it in, to find some reason he always has it with him. He has never fired the rifle so far as I can find. But I don't think the rifle is the reason no one talks with him. He's an anachronism, something living from another age. No one fears him, I am sure of that. He's been around too long for anyone to fear him. Too familiar. He's a fixture of the land, like a tree or boulder. And yet no one feels quite comfortable with him, either. I would imagine that most of them, if they should come face to face with him, would feel uncomfortable. For he's something they are not – something greater than they are and at the same time a good deal less. As if he were a man who had walked away from his own humanity. I think that, secretly, many of his neighbours may be a bit ashamed of him, shamed because he has, somehow, perhaps ignobly, side-stepped growing old, one of the penalties, but perhaps, as well, one of the rights of all human kind. And perhaps this secret shame may contribute in some part to their unwillingness to talk about him.'

'You spent a good deal of time watching him?'

'There was a time I did. But now I have a crew. They watch on regular shifts. We have a dozen spots we watch from, and we keep shifting them around. There isn't an hour, day in, day out, that the Wallace house isn't under observation.'

'This business really has you people bugged.'

'I think with reason,' Lewis said. 'There is still one other thing.'

He bent over and picked up the briefcase he had placed beside his chair. Unsnapping it, he took out a sheaf of photographs and handed them to Hardwicke.

'What do you make of these?' he asked.

Hardwicke picked them up. Suddenly he froze. The colour drained out of his face. His hands began to tremble and he laid the pictures carefully on the desk. He had looked at only the top one; not any of the others.

Lewis saw the question in his face.

'In the grave,' he said. 'The one beneath the headstone with the funny writing.'

5

The message machine whistled shrilly, and Enoch Wallace put away the book in which he had been writing and got up from his desk. He walked across the room to the whistling machine. He punched a button and shoved a key and the whistling stopped.

The machine built up its hum and the message began to form on the plate, faint at first and then becoming darker until it stood out clearly. It read:

NO. 406301 TO STATION 18327. TRAVELLER AT 16097.38. NATIVE THUBAN VI. NO BAGGAGE. NO. 3 LIQUID TANK. SOLUTION 27. DEPART FOR STATION 12892 AT 16439.16. CONFIRM.

Enoch glanced up at the great galactic chronometer hanging on the wall. There was almost three hours to go.

He touched a button, and a thin sheet of metal bearing the message protruded from the side of the machine. Beneath it the duplicate fed itself into the record file. The machine chuckled and the message plate was clear once more and waiting.

Enoch pulled out the metal plate, threaded the holes in it through the double filing spindle and then dropped his fingers to the keyboard and typed: NO. 406301 RECEIVED. CONFIRM MOMENTARILY. The message came into being on the plate and he left it there.

Thuban VI? Had there been, he wondered, one of them before? As soon as he got his chores done, he would go to the filing cabinet and check.

It was a liquid tank case and those, as a rule, were the most uninteresting of all. They usually were hard ones to strike up a conversation with, because too often their concept of language was too difficult to handle. And as often, too, their very thinking processes proved too divergent to provide much common ground for communication.

Although, he recalled, that was not always true. There had been that tank traveller several years ago, from somewhere in Hydra (or had it been the Hyades?), he'd sat up the whole night with and almost failed of sending off on time, yarning through the hours, their communication (you couldn't call it words) tumbling over one another as they packed into the little time they had a lot of fellowship and, perhaps, some brotherhood.

He, or she, or it – they'd never got around to that – had not come back again. And that was the way it was, thought Enoch; very few came back. By far the greater part of them were just passing through.

But he had he, or she, or it (whichever it might be) down in black and white, as he had all of them, every single blessed one of them, down in black and white. It had taken him, he remembered, almost the entire following day, crouched above his desk, to get it written down; all the stories he'd been told, all the glimpses he had caught of a far and beautiful and tantalizing land (tantalizing because there was so much of it he could not understand), all the warmth and comradeship that had flowed between himself and this mis-shapen, twisted, ugly living being from another world. And any time he wished, any day he wished, he could take down the journal from the row of journals and relive that night again. Although he never had. It was strange, he thought, how there was never time, or never seemed to be the time, to thumb through and reread in part what he'd recorded through the years.

He turned from the message machine and rolled a No. 3 liquid tank into place beneath the materializer, positioning it exactly and locking it in place. Then he pulled out the retracting hose and thumbed the selecter over to No. 27. He filled the tank and let the hose slide back into the wall.

Back at the machine, he cleared the plate and sent off his confirmation that all was ready for the traveller from Thuban, got back double confirmation from the other end, then threw the machine to neutral, ready to receive again.

He went from the machine to the filing cabinet that stood next to his desk and pulled out a drawer jammed with filing cards. He looked and Thuban VI was there, keyed to 22 August 1931. He walked across the room to the wall filled with books and rows of magazines and journals, filled from floor to ceiling, and found the record book he wanted. Carrying it, he walked back to his desk.

22 August 1931, he found, when he located the entry, had been one of his lighter days. There had been one traveller only, the one from Thuban VI. And although the entry for the day filled almost a page in his small, crabbed writing, he had devoted no more than one paragraph to the visitor.

Came today [it read] *a blob from Thuban VI. There is no other way in which one might describe it. It is simply a mass of matter, presumably of flesh, and this mass seems to go through some sort of rhythmic change in shape, for periodically it is globular, then begins to flatten out until it lies in the bottom of the tank, somewhat like a pancake. Then it begins to contract and to pull in upon itself, until finally it is a ball again. This change is rather slow and definitely rhythmic, but only in the sense that it follows the same pattern. It seems to have no relation to time. I tried timing it and could detect no time pattern. The shortest period needed to complete the cycle was seven minutes and the longest was eighteen. Perhaps over a longer period one might be able to detect a time rhythm, but I didn't have the time. The semantic translator did not work with it, but it did emit for me a series of sharp clicks, as if it might be clicking claws together, although it had no claws that I could see. When I looked this up in the pasimology manual I learned that what it was trying to say was that it was all right, that it needed no attention, and please leave it alone. Which I did thereafter.*

And at the end of the paragraph, jammed into the little space that had been left, was the notation: *See Oct. 16, 1931.*

He turned the pages until he came to October 16 and that had been one of the days, he saw, that Ulysses had arrived to inspect the station.

His name, of course, was not Ulysses. As a matter of fact, he had no name at all. Among his people there was no need of names; there was other identifying terminology which was far more expressive than mere names. But this terminology, even the very concept of it, was such that it could not be grasped, much less put to use, by human beings.

'I shall call you Ulysses,' Enoch recalled telling him, the first time they had met. 'I need to call you something.'

'It is agreeable,' said the then strange being (but no longer strange). 'Might one ask why the name Ulysses?'

'Because it is the name of a great man of my race.'

'I am glad you chose it,' said the newly christened being. 'To my hearing it has a dignified and noble sound and, between the two of us, I shall be glad to bear it. And I shall call you Enoch, for the two of us shall work together for many of your years.'

And it had been many years, thought Enoch, with the record book open to that October entry of more than thirty years ago. Years that had been satisfying and enriching in a way that one could not have imagined until it had all been laid out before him.

And it would go on, he thought, much longer than it already had gone on – for many centuries more, for a thousand years, perhaps. And at the end of that thousand years, what would he know then?

Although, perhaps, he thought, the knowing was not the most important part of it.

And none of it, he knew, might come to pass, for there was interference now. There were watchers, or at least a watcher, and before too long whoever it might be might start closing in. What he'd do or how he'd meet the threat, he had no idea until that moment came. It was something that had been almost bound to happen. It was something he had been prepared to have happen all these years. There was some reason to wonder, he knew, that it had not happened sooner.

He had told Ulysses of the danger of it that first day they'd met. He'd been sitting on the steps that led up to the porch, and thinking of it now, he could remember it as clearly as if it had been only yesterday.

6

He was sitting on the steps and it was late afternoon. He was watching the great white thunderheads that were piling up across the river beyond the Iowa hills. The day was hot and sultry and there was not a breath of moving air. Out in the barnyard a half a dozen bedraggled chickens scratched listlessly, for the sake, it seemed, of going through the motions rather than from any hope of finding food. The sound of the sparrows' wings, as they flew between the gable of the barn and the hedge of honeysuckle that bordered the field beyond the road, was a harsh, dry sound, as if the feathers of their wings had grown stiff with heat.

And here he sat, he thought, staring at the thunderheads when there was work to do – corn to be ploughed and hay to be gotten in and wheat to reap and shock.

For despite whatever might have happened, a man still had a life to live, days to be gotten through the best that one could manage. It was a lesson, he reminded himself, that he should have learned in all its fullness in the last few years. But war, somehow, was different from what had happened here. In war you knew it and expected it and were ready when it happened, but this was not the war. This was the peace to which he had returned. A man had a right to expect that in the world of peace there really would be peace fencing out the violence and the horror.

Now he was alone, as he'd never been alone before. Now, if ever, could be a new beginning; now, perhaps, there had to be a new beginning. But whether it was here, on the homestead acres, or in some other place, it still would be a beginning of bitterness and anguish.

He sat on the steps, with his wrists resting on his knees, and watched the thunderheads piling in the west. It might mean rain and the land could use the rain – or it might be nothing, for above the merging river valleys the air currents were erratic and there was no way a man could tell where those clouds might flow.

He did not see the traveller until he turned in at the gate. He was a tall and gangling one and his clothes were dusty and from the appearance of him he had walked a far way. He came up the path and Enoch sat waiting for him, watching him, but not stirring from the steps.

'Good day, sir,' Enoch finally said. 'It's a hot day to be walking. Why don't you sit a while.'

'Quite willingly,' said the stranger. 'But first, I wonder, could I have a drink of water?'

Enoch got up to his feet. 'Come along,' he said. 'I'll pump a fresh one for you.'

He went down across the barnyard until he reached the pump. He unhooked the dipper from where it hung upon a bolt and handed it to the man. He grasped the handle of the pump and worked it up and down.

'Let it run a while,' he said. 'It takes a time for it to get real cool.'

The water splashed out of the spout, running on the boards that formed the cover of the well. It came in spurts as Enoch worked the handle.

'Do you think,' the stranger asked, 'that it is about to rain?'

'A man can't tell,' said Enoch. 'We have to wait and see.'

There was something about this traveller that disturbed him. Nothing, actually, that one could put a finger on, but a certain strangeness that was vaguely disquieting. He watched him narrowly as he pumped and decided that probably this stranger's ears were just a bit too pointed at the top, but put it down to his imagination, for when he looked again they seemed to be all right.

'I think,' said Enoch, 'that the water should be cold by now.'

The traveller put down the dipper and waited for it to fill. He offered it to Enoch. Enoch shook his head.

'You first. You need it worse than I do.'

The stranger drank greedily and with much slobbering.

'Another one?' asked Enoch.

'No, thank you,' said the stranger. 'But I'll catch another dipperful for you if you wish me to.'

Enoch pumped, and when the dipper was full the stranger handed it to him. The water was cold and Enoch, realizing for the first time that he had been thirsty, drank it almost to the bottom.

He hung the dipper back on its bolt and said to the man, 'Now, let's get in that sitting.'

The stranger grinned. 'I could do with some of it,' he said.

Enoch pulled a red bandanna from his pocket and mopped his face. 'The air gets close,' he said, 'just before a rain.'

And as he mopped his face, quite suddenly he knew what it was that had disturbed him about the traveller. Despite his bedraggled clothes and his dusty shoes, which attested to long walking, despite the heat of this time-before-a-rain, the stranger was not sweating. He appeared as fresh and cool as if he had been lying at his ease beneath a tree in springtime.

Enoch put the bandanna back into his pocket and they walked back to the steps and sat there, side by side.

'You've travelled a far way,' said Enoch, gently prying.

'Very far, indeed,' the stranger told him. 'I'm a right smart piece from home.'

'And you have a far way yet to go?'

'No,' the stranger said, 'I believe that I have gotten to the place where I am going.'

'You mean ...' asked Enoch, and left the question hanging.

'I mean right here,' said the stranger, 'sitting on these steps. I have been looking for a man and I think that man is you. I did not know his name nor where to look for him, but yet I knew that one day I would find him.'

'But me,' Enoch said, astonished. 'Why should you look for me?'

'I was looking for a man of many different parts. One of the things about him was that he must have looked up at the stars and wondered what they were.'

'Yes,' said Enoch, 'that is something I have done. On many nights, camping in the field, I have lain in my blankets and looked up at the sky, looking at the stars and wondering what they were and how they'd been put up there and, most important of all, why they had been put up there. I have heard some say that each of them is another sun like the sun that shines on Earth, but I don't know about that. I guess there is no one who knows too much about them.'

'There are some,' the stranger said, 'who know a deal about them.'

'You, perhaps,' said Enoch, mocking just a little, for the stranger did not look like a man who'd know much of anything.

'Yes, I,' the stranger said. 'Although I do not know as much as many others do.'

'I've sometimes wondered,' Enoch said, 'if the stars are other suns, might there not be other planets and other people, too.'

He remembered sitting around the campfire of a night, jawing with the other fellows to pass away the time. And once he'd mentioned this idea of maybe other people on other planets circling other suns and the fellows all had jeered him and for days afterward had made fun of him, so he had never mentioned it again. Not that it mattered much, for he had no real belief in it himself; it had never been more than campfire speculation.

And now he'd mentioned it again and to an utter stranger. He wondered why he had.

'You believe that?' asked the stranger.

Enoch said, 'It was just an idle notion.'

'Not so idle,' said the stranger. 'There are other planets and there are other people. I am one of them.'

'But you ...' cried Enoch, then was stricken into silence.

For the stranger's face had split and began to fall away and beneath it he caught the glimpse of another face that was not a human face.

And even as the false human face sloughed off that other face, a great sheet of lightning went crackling across the sky and the heavy crash of thunder seemed to shake the land and from far off he heard the rushing of the rain as it charged across the hills.

7

That was how it started, Enoch thought, almost a hundred years ago. The campfire fantasy had turned into fact and the Earth now was on galactic charts, a way station for many different peoples travelling star to star. Strangers once, but now there were no strangers. There were no such things as strangers. In whatever form, with whatever purpose, all of them were people.

He looked back at the entry for 16 October 1931, and ran through it swiftly. There, near the end of it was the sentence:

Ulysses says the Thubans from planet VI are perhaps the greatest mathematicians in the galaxy. They have developed, it seems, a numeration system superior to any in existence, especially valuable in the handling of statistics.

He closed the book and sat quietly in the chair, wondering if the statisticians of Mizar X knew of the Thubans' work. Perhaps they did, he thought, for certainly some of the math they used was unconventional.

He pushed the record book to one side and dug into a desk drawer, bringing out his chart. He spread it flat on the desk before him and puzzled over it. If he could be sure, he thought. If he only knew the Mizar statistics better. For the last ten years or more he had laboured at the chart, checking and rechecking all the factors against the Mizar system, testing again and again to determine whether the factors he was using were the ones he should be using.

He raised a clenched fist and hammered at the desk. If he only could be certain. If he could only talk with someone. But that had been something that he had shrunk from doing, for it would be equivalent to showing the very nakedness of the human race.

He still was human. Funny, he thought, that he should stay human, that in a century of association with these beings from the many stars he should have, through it all, remained a man of Earth.

For in many ways, his ties with Earth were cut. Old Winslowe Grant was the only human he ever talked with now. His neighbours shunned him, and there were no others, unless one could count the watchers, and those he seldom saw – only glimpses of them, only the places they had been.

Only old Winslowe Grant and Mary and the other people from the shadow who came occasionally to spend lonely hours with him.

That was all of Earth he had, old Winslowe and the shadow people and the homestead acres that lay outside the house – but not the house itself, for the house was alien now.

He shut his eyes and remembered how the house had been in the olden days. There had been a kitchen, in this same area where he was sitting, with the iron cookstove, black and monstrous, in its corner, showing its row of fiery teeth along the slit made by the grate. Pushed against the wall had been the table where the three of them had eaten, and he could remember how the table looked, with the vinegar cruet and the glass that held the spoons and the Lazy Susan with the mustard, horseradish, and chili sauce sitting in a group, a sort of centrepiece in the middle of the red checkered cloth that the table wore.

There had been a winter night and he had been, it seemed, no more than three or four. His mother was busy at the stove with supper. He was sitting on the floor in the centre of the kitchen, playing with some blocks, and outside he could hear the muffled howling of the wind as it prowled along the eaves. His father had come in from milking at the barn, and a gust of wind and a swirl of snow had come into the room with him. Then he'd shut the door and the wind and snow were gone, shut outside this house, condemned to the outer darkness and the wilderness of night. His father had set the pail of milk that he had been carrying on the kitchen sink and Enoch saw that his beard and eyebrows were coated with snow and there was frost on the whiskers all around his mouth.

He held that picture still, the three of them like historic manikins posed in a cabinet in a museum – his father with the frost upon his whiskers and the great felt boots that came up to his knees; his mother with her face flushed from working at the stove and with the lace cap upon her head, and himself upon the floor, playing with the blocks.

There was one other thing that he remembered, perhaps more clearly than all the rest of it. There was a great lamp sitting on the table, and on the wall behind it hung a calendar, and the glow of the lamp fell like a spotlight upon the picture on the calendar. There was old Santa Claus, riding in his sleigh along a woodland track and all the little woodland people had turned out to watch him pass. A great moon hung above the trees and there was thick snow on the ground. A pair of rabbits sat there, gazing soulfully at Santa, and a deer beside the rabbits, with a raccoon just a little distance off, ringed tail wrapped about his feet, and a squirrel and chickadee side by side upon an overhanging branch. Old Santa had his whip raised high in greeting and his cheeks were red and his smile was merry and the reindeer hitched to his sled were fresh and spirited and proud.

Through all the years this mid-nineteenth-century Santa had ridden down the snowy aisles of time, with his whip uplifted in happy greeting to the woodland creatures. And the golden lamplight had ridden with him, still bright upon the wall and the checkered tablecloth.

So, thought Enoch, some things do endure – the memory and the thought and the snug warmness of a childhood kitchen on a stormy winter night.

But the endurance was of the spirit and the mind, for nothing else endured. There was no kitchen now, nor any sitting-room with its old-fashioned sofa and the rocking chair; no back parlour with its stuffy elegance of brocade and silk, no guest bedroom on the first and no family bedrooms on the second floor.

It all was gone and now one room remained. The second-storey floor and all partitions had been stripped away. Now the house was one great room. One side of it was the galactic station and the other side the living space for the keeper of the station. There was a bed over in one corner and a stove that worked on no principle known on Earth and a refrigerator that was of alien make. The walls were lined with cabinets and shelves, stacked with magazines and books and journals.

There was just one thing left from the early days, the one thing Enoch had not allowed the alien crew that had set up the station to strip away – the massive old fireplace of brick and native stone that had stood against one wall of the sitting-room. It still stood there, the one reminder of the days of old, the one thing left of Earth, with its great, scarred oak mantel that his father had carved out with a broadaxe from a massive log and had smoothed by hand with plane and draw-shave.

On the fireplace mantel and strewn on shelf and table were articles and artifacts that had no earthly origin and some no earthly names – the steady accumulation through the years of the gifts from friendly travellers. Some of them were functional and others were to look at only, and there were other things that were entirely useless because they had little application to a member of the human race or were inoperable on Earth, and many others of the purpose of which he had no idea, accepting them, embarrassed, with many stumbling thanks, from the well-meaning folks who had brought them to him.

And on the other side of the room stood the intricate mass of machinery, reaching well up into the open second storey, that wafted passengers through the space that stretched from star to star.

An inn, he thought, a stopping place, a galactic crossroads.

He rolled up the chart and put it back into the desk. The record book he put away in its proper place among all the other record books upon the shelf.

He glanced at the galactic clock upon the wall and it was time to go.

He pushed the chair tight against the desk and shrugged into the jacket that hung upon the chair back. He picked the rifle off the supports that held it on the wall and then he faced the wall itself and said the single word that he had to say. The wall slid back gently and he stepped through into the little shed with its sparse furnishings. Behind him the section of the wall slid back and there was nothing there to indicate it was anything but a solid wall.

Enoch stepped out of the shed and it was a beautiful late summer day. In a few weeks now, he thought, there'd be the signs of autumn and a strange chill in the air. The first golden rods were blooming now and he'd noticed, just the day before, that some of the early asters down in the ancient fence-row had started to show colour.

He went around the corner of the house and headed towards the river, striding down the long deserted field that was overrun with hazel brush and occasional clumps of trees.

This was the Earth, he thought – a planet made for Man. But not for Man alone, for it was as well a planet for the fox and owl and weasel, for the snake, the katydid, the fish, for all the other teeming life that filled the air and earth and water. And not these natives alone, but for other beings that called other earths their home, other planets that far light years distant were basically the same as Earth. For Ulysses and the Hazers and all the rest of them who could live upon this planet, if need be, if they wished, with no discomfort and no artificial aids.

Our horizons are so far, he thought, and we see so little of them. Even now, with flaming rockets striving from Canaveral to break the ancient bonds, we dream so little of them.

The ache was there, the ache that had been growing, the ache to tell all mankind those things that he had learned. Not so much specific things, although there were some of them that mankind well could use, but the general things, the unspecific, central fact that there was intelligence throughout the universe, that Man was not alone, that if he only found the way he need never be alone again.

He went down across the field and through the strip of woods and came out on the great out-thrust of rock that stood atop the cliff that faced the river. He stood there, as he had stood on thousands of other mornings, and stared out at the river, sweeping in majestic blue-and-silverness through the wooded bottom land.

Old, ancient water, he said, talking silently to the river, you have seen it happen – the mile-high faces of the glaciers that came and stayed and left, creeping back towards the pole inch by stubborn inch, carrying the melting water from those very glaciers in a flood that filled this valley with a tide such as now is never known; the mastodon and the sabretooth and the bear-sized beaver that ranged these olden hills and made the night clamorous with trumpeting and screaming; the silent little bands of men who trotted in the woods or clambered up the cliffs or paddled on your surface, woods-wise and water-wise, weak in body, strong in purpose, and persistent in a way no other thing ever was persistent, and just a little time ago that other breed of men who carried dreams within their skulls and cruelty in their hands and the awful sureness of an even greater purpose in their hearts. And before that, for this is ancient country beyond what is often found, the other kinds of life and the many turns of climate and the changes that came upon the Earth itself. And what think you of it? he asked the river. For yours is the memory and the perspective and the time and by now you should have the answers, or at least some of the answers.

As Man might have some of the answers had he lived for several million years – as he might have the answers several million years from this very summer morning if he still should be around.

I could help, thought Enoch. I could not give the answers, but I could help Man in his scramble after them. I could give him faith and hope and I could give purpose such as he has not had before.

But he knew he dare not do it.

Far below a hawk swung in lazy circles above the highway of the river. The air was so clear that Enoch imagined, if he strained his eyes a little, he could see every feather in those outspread wings.

There was almost a fairy quality to this place, he thought. The far look and the clear air and the feeling of detachment that touched almost on greatness of the spirit. As if this were a special place, one of those special places that each man must seek out for himself, and count himself lucky if he ever found it, for there were those who sought and never found it. And worst of all, there were even those who never hunted for it.

He stood upon the rock and stared out across the river, watching the lazy hawk and the sweep of water and the green carpeting of trees, and his mind went up and out to those other places until his mind was dizzy with the thought of it. And then he called it home.

He turned slowly and went back down the rock and moved off among the trees, following the path he'd beaten through the years.

He considered going down the hill a way to look in on the patch of pink lady's-slippers, to see how they might be coming, to try to conjure up the beauty that would be his again in June, but decided that there'd be little point to it, for they were well hidden in an isolated place, and nothing could have harmed them. There had been a time, a hundred years ago, when they had bloomed on every hill and he had come trailing home with great armloads of them, which his mother had put in the great brown jug she had, and for a day or two the house had been filled with the heaviness of their rich perfume. But they were hard to come by now. The trampling of pastured cattle and flower-hunting humans had swept them from the hills.

Some other day, he told himself, some day before first frost, he would visit them again and satisfy himself that they'd be there in the spring.

He stopped a while to watch a squirrel as it frolicked in an oak. He squatted down to follow a snail which had crossed his path. He stopped beside a massive tree and examined the pattern of the moss that grew upon its trunk. And he traced the wanderings of a silent, flitting songbird as it fluttered tree to tree.

He followed the path out of the woods and along the edge of field until he came to the spring that bubbled from the hillside.

Sitting beside the spring was a woman and he recognized her as Lucy Fisher, the deaf-mute daughter of Hank Fisher, who lived down in the river bottoms.

He stopped and watched her and thought how full she was of grace and beauty, the natural grace and beauty of a primitive and lonely creature.

She was sitting by the spring and one hand was uplifted and she held in it, at the tips of long and sensitive fingers, something that glowed with colour. Her head was held high, with a sharp look of alertness, and her body was straight and slender, and it also had that almost startled look of quiet alertness.

Enoch moved slowly forward and stopped not more than three feet behind her, and now he saw that the thing of colour on her fingertips was a butterfly, one of those large gold and red butterflies that come with the end of summer. One wing of the insect stood erect and straight, but the other was bent and crumpled and had lost some of the dust that lent sparkle to the colour.

She was, he saw, not actually holding the butterfly. It was standing on one fingertip, the one good wing fluttering very slightly every now and then to maintain its balance.

But he had been mistaken, he saw, in thinking that the second wing was injured, for now he could see that somehow it had been simply bent and distorted in some way. For now it was straightening slowly and the dust (if it ever had been gone) was back on it again, and it was standing up with the other wing.

He stepped around the girl so that she could see him and when she saw him there was no start of surprise. And that, he knew, would be quite natural, for she must be accustomed to it – someone coming up behind her and suddenly being there.

Her eyes were radiant and there was, he thought, a holy look upon her face, as if she had experienced some ecstasy of the soul. And he found himself wondering again, as he did each time he saw her, what it must be like for her, living in a world of two-way silence, unable to communicate. Perhaps not entirely unable to communicate, but at least barred from that free flow of communication which was the birthright of the human animal.

There had been, he knew, several attempts to establish her in a state school for the deaf, but each had been a failure. Once she'd run away and wandered days before being finally found and returned to her home. And on other occasions she had gone on disobedience strikes, refusing to co-operate in any of the teaching.

Watching her as she sat there with the butterfly, Enoch thought he knew the reason. She had a world, he thought, a world of her very own, one to which she was accustomed and knew how to get along in. In that world she was no cripple, as she most surely would have been a cripple if she had been pushed, part way, into the normal human world.

What good to her the hand alphabet or the reading of the lips if they should take from her some strange inner serenity of spirit?

She was a creature of the woods and hills, of springtime flower and autumn flight of birds. She knew these things and lived with them and was, in some strange way, a specific part of them. She was one who dwelt apart in an old and lost apartment of the natural world. She occupied a place that Man long since had abandoned, if, in fact, he'd ever held it.

And there she sat, with the wild red and gold of the butterfly poised upon her finger, with the sense of alertness and expectancy and, perhaps, accomplishment shining on her face. She was alive, thought Enoch, as no other thing he knew had ever been alive.

The butterfly spread its wings and floated off her finger and went fluttering, unconcerned, unfrightened, up across the wild grass and the golden rod of the field.

She pivoted to watch it until it disappeared near the top of the hill up which the old field climbed, then she turned to Enoch. She smiled and made a fluttery motion with her hands, like the fluttering of the red and golden wings, but there was something else in it, as well – a sense of happiness and an expression of well-being, as if she might be saying that the world was going fine.

If, Enoch thought, I could only teach her the pasimology of my galactic people – then we could talk, the two of us, almost as well as with the flow of words on the human tongue. Given the time, he thought, it might not be too hard, for there was a natural and logical process to the galactic sign language that made it almost instinctive once one had caught the underlying principle.

Throughout the Earth as well, in the early days, there had been sign languages, and none so well developed as that one which obtained among the aborigines of North America, so that an Amerindian, no matter what his tongue, could express himself among many other tribes.

But even so the sign language of the Indian was, at best, a crutch that allowed a man to hobble when he couldn't run. Whereas that of the galaxy was in itself a language, adaptable to many different means and methods of expression. It had been developed through millennia, with many different peoples making contributions, and through the centuries it had been refined and shaken down and polished until today it was a communications tool that stood on its own merits.

There was need for such a tool, for the galaxy was Babel. Even the galactic science of pasimology, polished as it might be, could not surmount all the obstacles, could not guarantee, in certain cases, the basic minimum of communication. For not only were there millions of tongues, but those other languages as well which could not operate on the principle of sound because the races were incapable of sound. And even sound itself failed of efficiency when the race talked in ultrasonics others could not hear. There was telepathy, of course, but for every telepath there were a thousand races that had telepathic blocks. There were many who got along on sign languages alone and others who could communicate only by a written or pictographic system, including some who carried chemical blackboards built into their bodies. And there was that sightless, deaf, and speechless race from the mystery stars of the far side of the galaxy who used what was perhaps the most complicated of all the galactic languages – a code of signals routed along their nervous systems.

Enoch had been at the job almost a century, and even so, he thought, with the aid of the universal sign language and the semantic translator, which was little more than a pitiful (although complicated) mechanical contrivance, he still was hard put at times to know what many of them said.

Lucy Fisher picked up a cup that was standing by her side – a cup fashioned of a strip of folded birch bark – and dipped it in the spring. She held it out to Enoch and he stepped close to take it, kneeling down to drink from it. It was not entirely watertight, and water ran from it down across his arm, wetting the cuff of shirt and jacket.

He finished drinking and handed back the cup. She took it in one hand and reached out the other, to brush across his forehead with the tip of gentle fingers in what she might have thought of as a benediction. He did not speak to her. Long ago he had ceased talking to her, sensing that the movement of his mouth, making sounds she could not hear, might be embarrassing.

Instead he put out a hand and laid his broad palm against her cheek, holding it there for a reassuring moment as a gesture of affection. Then he got to his feet and stood staring down at her and for a moment their eyes looked into the other's eyes and then turned away.

He crossed the little stream that ran down from the spring and took the trail that led from the forest's edge across the field, heading for the ridge. Halfway up the slope, he turned around and saw that she was watching him. He held up his hand in a gesture of farewell and her hand gestured in reply.

It had been, he recalled, twelve years or more ago that he first had seen her, a little fairy person of ten years or so, a wild thing running in the woods.

They had become friends, he recalled, only after a long time, although he saw her often, for she roamed the hills and valley as if they were a playground for her – which, of course, they were.

Through the years he had watched her grow and had often met her on his daily walks, and between the two of them had grown up an understanding of the lonely and the outcast, but understanding based on something more than that – on the fact that each had a world that was their own and worlds that had given them an insight into something that others seldom saw. Not that either, Enoch thought, ever told the other, or tried to tell the other, of these private worlds, but the fact of these private worlds was there, in the consciousness of each, providing a firm foundation for the building of a friendship.

He recalled the day he'd found her at the place where the pink lady's-slippers grew, just kneeling there and looking at them, not picking any of them, and how he'd stopped beside her and been pleased she had not moved to pick them, knowing that in the sight of them, the two, he and she, had found a joy and a beauty that was beyond possession.

He reached the ridge top and turned down the grass-grown road that led down to the mailbox.

And he'd not been mistaken back there, he told himself, no matter how it may have seemed on second look. The butterfly's wing had been torn and crumpled and drab from the lack of dust. It had been a crippled thing and then it had been whole again and had flown away.

8

Winslowe Grant was on time.

Enoch, as he reached the mailbox, sighted the dust raised by his old jalopy as it galloped along the ridge. It had been a dusty year, he thought, as he stood beside the box. There had been little rain and the crops had suffered. Although, to tell the truth, there were few crops on the ridge these days. There had been a time when comfortable small farms had existed, almost cheek by jowl, all along the road, with the barns all red and the houses white. But now most of the farms had been abandoned and the houses and the barns were no longer red or white, but grey and weathered wood, with all the paint peeled off and the ridge-poles sagging and the people gone.

It would not be long before Winslowe would arrive and Enoch settled down to wait. The mailman might be stopping at the Fisher box, just around the bend, although the Fishers, as a rule, got but little mail, mostly just the advertising sheets and other junk that was mailed out indiscriminately to the rural boxholders. Not that it mattered to the Fishers, for sometimes days went by in which they did not pick up their mail. If it were not for Lucy, they perhaps would never get it, for it was mostly Lucy who thought to pick it up.

The Fishers were, for a fact, Enoch told himself, a truly shiftless outfit. Their house and all the buildings were ready to fall in upon themselves and they raised a grubby patch of corn that was drowned out, more often than not, by a flood rise of the river. They mowed some hay off a bottom meadow and they had a couple of raw-boned horses and a half-dozen scrawny cows and a flock of chickens. They had an old clunk of a car and a still hidden out somewhere in the river bottoms and they hunted and fished and trapped and were generally no-account. Although, when one considered it, they were not bad neighbours. They tended to their business and never bothered anyone except that periodically they went around, the whole tribe of them, distribut- ing pamphlets and tracts through the neighbourhood for some obscure fundamentalist sect that Ma Fisher had become a member of at a tent revival meeting down in Millville several years before.

Winslowe didn't stop at the Fisher box, but came boiling around the bend in a cloud of dust. He braked the panting machine to a halt and turned off the engine.

'Let her cool a while,' he said.

The block crackled as it started giving up its heat.

'You made good time today,' said Enoch.

'Lots of people didn't have any mail today,' said Winslowe. 'Just went sailing past their boxes.'

He dipped into the pouch on the seat beside him and brought out a bundle tied together with a bit of string for Enoch – several daily papers and two journals.

'You get a lot of stuff,' said Winslowe, 'but hardly ever letters.'

'There is no one left,' said Enoch, 'who would want to write to me.'

'But,' said Winslowe, 'you got a letter this time.'

Enoch looked, unable to conceal surprise, and could see the end of an envelope peeping from between the journals.

'A personal letter,' said Winslowe, almost smacking his lips. 'Not one of them advertising ones. Nor a business one.'

Enoch tucked the bundle underneath his arm, beside the rifle stock.

'Probably won't amount to much,' he said.

'Maybe not,' said Winslowe, a sly glitter in his eyes.

He pulled a pipe and pouch from his pocket and slowly filled the pipe. The engine block continued its crackling and popping. The sun beat down out of a cloudless sky. The vegetation alongside the road was coated with dust and an acrid smell rose from it.

'Hear that ginseng fellow is back again,' said Winslowe, conversationally, but unable to keep out a conspiratorial tone. 'Been gone for three, four days.'

'Maybe off to sell his sang.'

'You ask me,' the mailman said, 'he ain't hunting sang. He's hunting something else.'

'Been at it,' Enoch said, 'for a right smart time.'

'First of all,' said Winslowe, 'there's barely any market for the stuff and even if there was, there isn't any sang. Used to be a good market years ago. Chinese used it for medicine, I guess. But now there ain't no trade with China. I remember when I was a boy we used to go hunting it. Not easy to find, even then. But most days a man could locate a little of it.'

He leaned back in the seat, puffing serenely at his pipe.

'Funny goings on,' he said.

'I never saw the man,' said Enoch.

'Sneaking through the woods,' said Winslowe. 'Digging up different kinds of plants. Got the idea myself he maybe is a sort of magic-man. Getting stuff to make up charms and such. Spends a lot of his time yarning with the Fisher tribe and drinking up their likker. You don't hear much of it these days, but I still hold with magic. Lots of things science can't explain. You take that Fisher girl, the dummy, she can charm off warts.'

'So I've heard,' said Enoch.

And more than that, he thought. She can fix a butterfly.

Winslowe hunched forward in his seat.

'Almost forgot,' he said. 'I have something else for you.'

He lifted a brown paper parcel from the floor and handed it to Enoch.

'This ain't mail,' he said. 'It's something that I made for you.'

'Why, thank you,' Enoch said, taking it from him.

'Go ahead,' Winslowe said, 'and open it up.'

Enoch hesitated.

'Ah, hell,' said Winslowe, 'don't be bashful.'

Enoch tore off the paper and there it was, a full-figure wood carving of himself. It was in a blond, honey-coloured wood and some twelve inches tall. It shone like golden crystal in the sun. He was walking, with his rifle tucked beneath his arm and a wind was blowing, for he was leaning slightly into it and there were wind-flutter ripples on his jacket and his trousers.

Enoch gasped, then stood staring at it.

'Wins,' he said, 'that's the most beautiful piece of work I have ever seen.'

'Did it,' said the mailman, 'out of that piece of wood you gave me last winter. Best piece of whittling stuff I ever ran across. Hard and without hardly any grain. No danger of splitting or of nicking or of shredding. When you make a cut, you make it where you want to and it stays the way you cut it. And it takes polish as you cut. Just rub it up a little is all you need to do.'

'You don't know,' said Enoch, 'how much this means to me.'

'Over the years,' the mailman told him, 'you've given me an awful lot of wood. Different kinds of wood no one's ever seen before. All of it top-grade stuff and beautiful. It was time I was carving something for you.'

'And you,' said Enoch, 'have done a lot for me. Lugging things from town.'

'Enoch,' Winslowe said, 'I like you. I don't know what you are and I ain't about to ask, but anyhow I like you.'

'I wish that I could tell you what I am,' said Enoch.

'Well,' said Winslowe, moving over to plant himself behind the wheel, 'it don't matter much what any of us are, just so we get along with one another. If some of the nations would only take a lesson from some small neighbourhood like ours – a lesson in how to get along – the world would be a whole lot better.'

Enoch nodded gravely. 'It doesn't look too good, does it?'

'It sure don't,' said the mailman, starting up the car.

Enoch stood and watched the car move off, down the hill, building up its cloud of dust as it moved along.

Then he looked again at the wooden statuette of himself.

It was as if the wooden figure were walking on a hilltop, naked to the full force of the wind and bent against the gale.

Why? He wondered. What was it the mailman had seen in him to portray him as walking in the wind?

9

He laid the rifle and the mail upon a patch of dusty grass and carefully rewrapped the statuette in the piece of paper. He'd put it, he decided, either on the mantelpiece or, perhaps better yet, on the coffee table that stood beside his favourite chair in the corner by the desk. He wanted it, he admitted to himself, with some quiet embarrassment, where it was close at hand, where he could look at it or pick it up any time he wished. And he wondered at the deep, heartwarming, soul-satisfying pleasure that he got from the mailman's gift.

It was not, he knew, because he was seldom given gifts. Scarcely a week went past that the alien travellers did not leave several with him. The house was cluttered and there was a wall of shelves down in the cavernous basement that were crammed with the stuff that had been given to him. Perhaps it was, he told himself, because this was a gift from Earth, from one of his own kind.

He tucked the wrapped statuette beneath his arm and, picking up the rifle and the mail, headed back for home, following the brush-grown trail that once had been the wagon road leading to the farm.

Grass had grown into thick turf between the ancient ruts, which had been cut so deep into the clay by the iron tyres of the old-time wagons that they still were no more than bare, impacted earth in which no plant as yet had gained a root-hold. But on each side the clumps of brush, creeping up the field from the forest's edge, grew man-high or better, so that now one moved down an aisle of green.

But at certain points, quite unexplainably – perhaps due to the character of the soil or to the mere vagaries of nature – the growth of brush had faltered, and here were vistas where one might look out from the ridge-top across the river valley.

It was from one of these vantage points that Enoch caught the flash from a clump of trees at the edge of the old field, not too far from the spring where he had found Lucy.

He frowned as he saw the flash and stood quietly on the path, waiting for its repetition. But it did not come again.

It was one of the watchers, he knew, using a pair of binoculars to keep watch upon the station. The flash he had seen had been the reflection of the sun upon the glasses.

Who were they? he wondered. And why should they be watching? It had been going on for some time now but, strangely, there had been nothing but the watching. There had been no interference. No one had attempted to approach him, and such approach, he realized, could have been quite simple and quite natural. If they – whoever they might be – had wished to talk with him, a very casual meeting could have been arranged during any one of his morning walks.

But apparently as yet they did not wish to talk.

What, then, he wondered, did they wish to do? Keep track of him, perhaps. And in that regard, he thought, with a wry inner twinge of humour, they could have become acquainted with the pattern of his living in their first ten days of watching.

Or perhaps they might be waiting for some happening that would provide them with a clue to what he might be doing. And in that direction there lay nothing but certain disappointment. They could watch for a thousand years and gain no hint of it.

He turned from the vista and went plodding up the road, worried and puzzled by his knowledge of the watchers.

Perhaps, he thought, they had not attempted to contact him because of certain stories that might be told about him. Stories that no one, not even Winslowe, would pass on to him. What kind of stories, he wondered, might the neighbourhood by now have been able to fabricate about him – fabulous folk tales to be told in bated breath about the chimney corner?

It might be well, he thought, that he did not know the stories, although it would seem almost a certainty that they would exist. And it also might be as well that the watchers had not attempted contact with him. For so long as there was no contact, he still was fairly safe. So long as there were no questions, there need not be any answers.

Are you really, they would ask, that same Enoch Wallace who marched off in 1861 to fight for old Abe Lincoln? And there was one answer to that, there could only be one answer. Yes, he'd have to say, I am that same man.

And of all the questions they might ask him that would be the only one of all he could answer truthfully. For all the others there would necessarily be silence or evasion.

They would ask how come that he had not aged – how he could stay young when all mankind grew old. And he could not tell them that he did not age inside the station, that he only aged when he stepped out of it, that he aged an hour each day on his daily walks, that he might age an hour or so working in his garden, that he could age for fifteen minutes sitting on the steps to watch a lovely sunset. But that when he went back indoors again the ageing process was completely cancelled out.

He could not tell them that. And there was much else that he could not tell them. There might come a time, he knew, if they once contacted him, that he'd have to flee the questions and cut himself entirely from the world, remaining isolated within the station's walls.

Such a course would constitute no hardship physically, for he could live within the station without any inconvenience. He would want for nothing, for the aliens would supply everything he needed to remain alive and well. He had bought human food at times, having Winslowe purchase it and haul it out from town, but only because he felt a craving for the food of his own planet, in particular those simple foods of his childhood and his campaigning days.

And, he told himself, even these foods might well be supplied by the process of duplication. A slab of bacon or a dozen eggs could be sent to another station and remain there as a master pattern for the pattern impulses, being sent to him on order as he needed them.

But there was one thing the aliens could not provide – the human contacts he'd maintained through Winslowe and the mail. Once shut inside the station, he'd be cut off completely from the world he knew, for the newspapers and the magazines were his only contact. The operation of a radio in the station was made impossible by the interference set up by the installations.

He would not know what was happening in the world, would know no longer how the outside might be going. His chart would suffer from this and would become largely useless; although, he told himself, it was nearly useless now, since he could not be certain of the correct usage of the factors.

But aside from all of this, he would miss this little outside world that he had grown to know so well, this little corner of the world encompassed by his walks. It was the walks, he thought, more than anything, perhaps, that had kept him human and a citizen of Earth.

He wondered how important it might be that he remain, intellectually and emotionally, a citizen of Earth and a member of the human race. There was, he thought, perhaps no reason that he should. With the cosmopolitanism of the galaxy at his fingertips, it might even be provincial of him to be so intent upon his continuing identification with the old home planet. He might be losing something by this provincialism.

But it was not in himself, he knew, to turn his back on Earth. It was a place he loved too well – loving it more, most likely, than those other humans who had not caught his glimpse of far and unguessed worlds. A man, he told himself, must belong to something, must have some loyalty and some identity. The galaxy was too big a place for any being to stand naked and alone.

A lark sailed out of a grassy plot and soared high into the sky, and seeing it, he waited for the trill of liquid song to spray out of its throat and drip out of the blue. But there was no song, as there would have been in spring.

He plodded down the road and now, ahead of him, he saw the starkness of the station, reared upon its ridge.

Funny, he thought, that he should think of it as station rather than as home, but it had been a station longer than it had been a home.

There was about it, he saw, a sort of ugly solidness, as if it might have planted itself upon that ridge-top and meant to stay for ever.

It would stay, of course, if one wanted it, as long as one wanted it. For there was nothing that could touch it.

Even should he be forced some day to remain within its walls, the station still would stand against all of mankind's watching, all of mankind's prying. They could not chip it and they could not gouge it and they could not break it down. There was nothing they could do. All his watching, all his speculating, all his analysing, would gain Man nothing beyond the knowledge that a highly unusual building existed on that ridge-top. For it could survive anything except a thermonuclear explosion – and maybe even that.

He walked into the yard and turned around to look back towards the clump of trees from which the flash had come, but there was nothing now to indicate that anyone was there.

10

Inside the station, the message machine was whistling plaintively.

Enoch hung up his gun, dropped the mail and statuette upon his desk and strode across the room to the whistling machine. He pushed the button and punched the lever and the whistling stopped.

Upon the message plate he read:

NO. 406302 TO STATION 18327. WILL ARRIVE EARLY EVENING YOUR TIME. HAVE THE COFFEE HOT. ULYSSES.

Enoch grinned. Ulysses and his coffee! He was the only one of the aliens who had ever liked any of Earth's foods or drinks. There had been others who had tried them, but not more than once or twice.

Funny about Ulysses, he thought. They had liked each other from the very first, from that afternoon of the thunderstorm when they had been sitting on the steps and the mask of human form had peeled off the alien's face.

It had been a grisly face, graceless and repulsive. The face, Enoch had thought, of a cruel clown. Wondering, even as he thought it, what had put that particular phrase into his head, for clowns were never cruel. But here was one that could be – the coloured patchwork of the face, the hard, tight set of jaw, the thin slash of the mouth.

Then he saw the eyes and they cancelled all the rest. They were large and had a softness and the light of understanding in them, and they reached out to him, as another being might hold out its hands in friendship.

The rain had come hissing up the land to thrum across the machine-shed roof, and then it was upon them, slanting sheets of rain that hammered angrily at the dust which lay across the yard, while surprised, bedraggled chickens ran frantically for cover.

Enoch sprang to his feet and grasped the other's arm, pulling him to the shelter of the porch.

They stood facing one another, and Ulysses had reached up and pulled the split and loosened mask away, revealing a bullet head without a hair upon it – and the painted face. A face like a wild and rampaging Indian, painted for the warpath, except that here and there were touches of the clown, as if the entire painting job had been meant to point up the inconsistent grotesqueries of war. But even as he stared, Enoch knew it was not paint, but the natural coloration of this thing which had come from somewhere among the stars.

Whatever other doubt there was, or whatever wonder, Enoch had no doubt at all that this strange being was not of the Earth. For it was not human. It might be in human form, with a pair of arms and legs, with a head and face. But there was about it an essence of inhumanity, almost a negation of humanity.

In olden days, perhaps, he thought, it might have been a demon, but the days were past (although, in some areas of the country, not entirely past) when one believed in demons or in ghosts or in any of the others of that ghastly tribe which, in man's imagination, once had walked the Earth.

From the stars, he'd said. And perhaps he was. Although it made no sense. It was nothing one ever had imagined even in the purest fantasy. There was nothing to grab hold of, nothing to hang on to. There was no yardstick for it and there were no rules. And it left a sort of blank spot in one's thinking that might fill in, come time, but now was no more than a tunnel of great wonder that went on and on for ever.

'Take your time,' the alien said. 'I know it is not easy. And I do not know of a thing that I can do to make it easier. There is, after all, no way for me to prove I am from the stars.'

'But you talk so well.'

'In your tongue, you mean. It was not too difficult. If you only knew of all the languages in the galaxy, you would realize how little difficult. Your language is not hard. It is a basic one and there are many concepts with which it need not deal.'

And, Enoch conceded, that could be true enough.

'If you wish,' the alien said, 'I can walk off somewhere for a day or two. Give you time to think. Then I could come back. You'd have thought it out by then.'

Enoch smiled, woodenly, and the smile had an unnatural feel upon his face.

'That would give me time,' he said, 'to spread alarm throughout the countryside. There might be an ambush waiting for you.'

The alien shook its head. 'I am sure you wouldn't do it. I would take the chance. If you want me to ...'

'No,' said Enoch, so calmly he surprised himself. 'No, when you have a thing to face, you face it. I learned that in the war.'

'You'll do,' the alien said. 'You will do all right. I did not misjudge you and it makes me proud.'

'Misjudge me?'

'You do not think I just came walking in here cold? I know about you, Enoch. Almost as much, perhaps, as you know about yourself. Probably even more.'

'You know my name?'

'Of course I do.'

'Well, that is fine,' said Enoch. 'And what about your own?'

'I am seized with great embarrassment,' the alien told him. 'For I have no name as such. Identification, surely, that fits the purpose of my race, but nothing that the tongue can form.'

Suddenly, for no reason, Enoch remembered that slouchy figure perching on the top rail of a fence, with a stick in one hand and a jack-knife in the other, whittling placidly while the cannon balls whistled overhead and less than half a mile away the muskets snarled and crackled in the billowing powder smoke that rose above the line.

'Then you need a name to call you by,' he said, 'and it shall be Ulysses. I need to call you something.'

'It is agreeable,' said the strange one. 'But might one ask why the name Ulysses?'

'Because it is the name,' said Enoch, 'of a great man of my race.'

It was a crazy thing, of course. For there was no resemblance between the two of them – that slouchy Union general whittling as he perched upon the fence and this other who stood upon the porch.

'I am glad you chose it,' said this Ulysses, standing on the porch. 'To my hearing it has a dignified and noble sound and, between the two of us, I shall be glad to bear it. And I shall call you Enoch, as friends of the first names, for the two of us shall work together for many of your years.'

It was beginning to come straight now and the thought was staggering. Perhaps it was as well, Enoch told himself, that it had waited for a while, that he had been so dazed it had not come on him all at once.

'Perhaps,' said Enoch, fighting back the realization that was crowding in on him, crowding in too fast, 'I could offer you some victuals. I could cook up some coffee ...'

'Coffee,' said Ulysses, smacking his thin lips. 'Do you have the coffee?'

'I'll make a big pot of it. I'll break in an egg so it will settle clear ...'

'Delectable,' Ulysses said. 'Of all the drinks that I have drank on all the planets I have visited, the coffee is the best.'

They went into the kitchen and Enoch stirred up the coals in the kitchen range and then put in new wood. He took the coffee-pot over to the sink and ladled in some water from the water pail and put it on to boil. He went into the pantry to get some eggs and down into the cellar to bring up the ham.

Ulysses sat stiffly in a kitchen chair and watched him as he worked.

'You eat ham and eggs?' asked Enoch.

'I eat anything,' Ulysses said. 'My race is most adaptable. That is the reason I was sent to this planet as a – what do you call it? – a looker-out, perhaps.'

'A scout,' suggested Enoch.

'That is it, a scout.'

He was an easy thing to talk with, Enoch told himself – almost like another person, although, God knows, he looked little like a person. He looked, instead, like some outrageous caricature of a human being.

'You have lived here, in this house,' Ulysses said, 'for a long, long time. You feel affection for it.'

'It has been my home,' said Enoch, 'since the day that I was born. I was gone from it for almost four years, but it was always home.'

'I'll be glad,' Ulysses told him, 'to be getting home again myself. I've been away too long. On a mission such as this one, it always is too long.'

Enoch put down the knife he had been using to cut a slice of ham and sat down heavily in a chair. He stared at Ulysses, across the table from him.

'You?' he asked. 'You are going home?'

'Why, of course,' Ulysses told him. 'Now that my job is nearly done. I have got a home. Did you think I hadn't?'

'I don't know,' said Enoch weakly. 'I had never thought of it.'

And that was it, he knew. It had not occurred to him to connect a being such as this with a thing like home. For it was only human beings that had a place called home.

'Some day,' Ulysses said, 'I shall tell you about my home. Some day you may even visit me.'

'Out among the stars,' said Enoch.

'It seems strange to you now,' Ulysses said. 'It will take a while to get used to the idea. But as you come to know us – all of us – you will understand. And I hope you like us. We are not bad people, really. Not any of the many different kinds of us.'

The stars, Enoch told himself, were out there in the loneliness of space and how far they were he could not even guess, nor what they were nor why. Another world, he thought – no, that was wrong – many other worlds. There were people there, perhaps many other people; a different kind of people, probably, for every different star. And one of them sat here in this very kitchen, waiting for the coffee-pot to boil, for the ham and eggs to fry.

'But why?' he asked. 'But why?'

'Because,' Ulysses said, 'we are a travelling people. We need a travel station here. We want to turn this house into a station and you to keep the station.'

'This house?'

'We could not build a station, for then we'd have people asking who was building it and what it might be for. So we are forced to use an existing structure and change it for our needs. But the inside only. We leave the outside as it is, in appearance, that is. For there must be no questions asked. There must be—'

'But travelling ...'

'From star to star,' Ulysses said. 'Quicker than the thought of it. Faster than a wink. There is what you would call machinery, but it is not machinery – not the same as the machinery you think of.'

'You must excuse me,' Enoch said, confused. 'It seems so impossible.'

'You remember when the railroad came to Millville?'

'Yes, I can remember that. I was just a kid.'

'Then think of it this way. This is just another railroad and the Earth is just another town and this house will be the station for this new and different railroad. The only difference is that no one on Earth but you will know the railroad's here. For it will be no more than a resting and a switching point. No one on the Earth can buy a ticket to travel on the railroad.'

Put that way, of course, it had a simple sound, but it was, Enoch sensed, very far from simple.

'Railroad cars in space?' he asked.

'Not railroad cars,' Ulysses told him. 'It is something else. I do not know how to begin to tell you …'

'Perhaps you should pick someone else. Someone who would understand.'

'There is no one on this planet who could remotely understand. No, Enoch, we'll do with you as well as anyone. In many ways, much better than with anyone.'

'But …'

'What is it, Enoch?'

'Nothing,' Enoch said.

For he remembered now how he had been sitting on the steps thinking how he was alone and about a new beginning, knowing that he could not escape a new beginning, that he must start from scratch and build his life anew.

And here, suddenly, was that new beginning – more wondrous and fearsome than anything he could have dreamed even in an insane moment.

11

Enoch filed the message and sent his confirmation:

NO. 406302 RECEIVED. COFFEE ON THE FIRE. ENOCH.

Clearing the machine, he walked over to the No. 3 liquid tank he'd prepared before he left. He checked the temperature and the level of the solution and made certain once again that the tank was securely positioned in relation to the materializer.

From there he went to the other materializer, the official and emergency materializer, positioned in the corner, and checked it over closely. It was all right, as usual. It always was all right, but before each of Ulysses' visits he never failed to check it. There was nothing he could have done about it had there been something wrong other than send an urgent message to Galactic Central. In which case someone would have come in on the regular materializer and put it into shape.

For the official and emergency materializer was exactly what its name implied. It was used only for official visits by personnel of Galactic Centre or for possible emergencies and its operation was entirely outside that of the local station.

Ulysses, as an inspector for this and several other stations, could have used the official materializer at any time he wished without prior notice. But in all the years that he had been coming to the station he had never failed, Enoch remembered with a touch of pride, to message that he was coming. It was, he knew, a courtesy which all the other stations on the great galactic network might not be accorded, although there were some of them which might be given equal treatment.

Tonight, he thought, he probably should tell Ulysses about the watch that had been put upon the station. Perhaps he should have told him earlier, but he had been reluctant to admit that the human race might prove to be a problem to the galactic installation.

It was a hopeless thing, he thought, this obsession of his to present the people of the Earth as good and reasonable. For in many ways they were neither good nor reasonable; perhaps because they had not as yet entirely grown up. They were smart and quick and at times compassionate and even understanding, but they failed lamentably in many other ways.

But if they had the chance, Enoch told himself, if they ever got a break, if they only could be told what was out in space, then they'd get a grip upon themselves and they would measure up and then, in the course of time, would be admitted into the great confraternity of the people of the stars.

Once admitted, they would prove their worth and would pull their weight, for they were still a young race and full of energy – at times, maybe, too much energy.

Enoch shook his head and went across the room to sit down at his desk. Drawing the bundle of mail in front of him, he slid it out of the string which Winslowe had used to tie it all together.

There were the daily papers, a news weekly, two journals – *Cosmos* and *Science* – and the letter.

He pushed the paper and the journals to one side and picked up the letter. It was, he saw, an air mail sheet and was postmarked London and the return address bore a name that was unfamiliar to him. He puzzled as to why an unknown person should be writing him from London. Although, he reminded himself, anyone who wrote from London, or indeed from anywhere, would be an unknown person. He knew no one in London nor elsewhere in the world.

He slit the air sheet open and spread it out on the desk in front of him, pulling the desk lamp close so the light would fell upon the writing.

Dear Sir [he read], *I would suspect I am unknown to you. I am one of the several editors of the British journal,* Cosmos, *to which you have been a subscriber for these many years. I do not use the journal's letterhead because this letter is personal and unofficial and perhaps not even in the best of taste.*

You are, it may interest you to know, our eldest subscriber. We have had you on our mailing lists for more than eighty years.

While I am aware that it is no appropriate concern of mine, I have wondered if you, yourself, have subscribed to our publication for this length of time, or if it might be possible that your father or someone close to you may have been the original subscriber and you simply have allowed the subscription to continue in his name.

My interest undoubtedly constitutes an unwarranted and inexcusable curiosity and if you, sir, choose to ignore the query it is entirely within your rights and proper that you do so. But if you should not mind replying, an answer would be appreciated.

I can only say in my own defence that I have been associated for so long with our publication that I feel a certain sense of pride that someone has found it worth the having for more than eighty years. I doubt that many publications can boast such long time interest on the part of any man.

May I assure, you, sir, of my utmost respect.

Sincerely yours.

And then the signature.

Enoch shoved the letter from him.

And there it was again, he told himself. Here was another watcher, although discreet and most polite and unlikely to cause trouble.

But someone else who had taken notice, who had felt a twinge of wonder at the same man subscribing to a magazine for more than eighty years.

As the years went on, there would be more and more. It was not only the watchers encamped outside the station with whom he must concern himself, but those potential others. A man could be as self-effacing as he well could manage and still he could not hide. Soon or late the world would catch up with him and would come crowding around his door, agog to know why he might be hiding.

It was useless, he knew, to hope for much further time. The world was closing in.

Why can't they leave me alone? he thought. If he only could explain how the situation stood, they might leave him alone. But he couldn't explain to them. And even if he could, there would be some of them who'd still come crowding in.

Across the room the materializer beeped for attention and Enoch swung around.

The Thuban had arrived. He was in the tank, a shadowy globular blob of substance, and above him, riding sluggishly in the solution, was a cube of something.

Luggage, Enoch wondered. But the message had said there would be no luggage.

Even as he hurried across the room, the clicking came to him – the Thuban talking to him.

'Presentation to you,' said the clicking. 'Deceased vegetation.'

Enoch peered at the cube floating in the liquid.

'Take him,' clicked the Thuban. 'Bring him for you.'

Fumblingly, Enoch clicked out his answer, using tapping fingers against the glass side of the tank: 'I thank you, gracious one.' Wondering as he did it, if he were using the proper form of address to this blob of matter. A man, he told himself, could get terribly tangled up on that particular point of etiquette. There were some of these beings that one addressed in flowery language (and even in those cases, the floweriness would vary) and others that one talked with in the simplest, bluntest terms.

He reached into the tank and lifted out the cube and he saw that it was a block of heavy wood, black as ebony and so close-grained it looked very much like stone. He chuckled inwardly, thinking how, in listening to Winslowe, he had grown to be an expert in the judging of artistic wood.

He put the wood upon the floor and turned back to the tank.

'Would you mind,' clicked the Thuban, 'revealing what you do with him? To us, very useless stuff.'

Enoch hesitated, searching desperately through his memory. What, he wondered, was the code for 'carve'?

'Well?' the Thuban asked.

'You must pardon me, gracious one. I do not use this language often. I am not proficient.'

'Drop, please, the "gracious one". I am a common being.'

'Shape it,' Enoch tapped. 'Into another form. Are you a visual being? Then I show you one.'

'Not visual,' said the Thuban. 'Many other things, not visual.'

It had been a globe when it had arrived and now it was beginning to flatten out.

'You,' the Thuban clicked, 'are a biped being.'

'That is what I am.'

'Your planet. It is a solid planet?'

Solid? Enoch wondered. Oh, yes, solid as opposed to liquid.

'One-quarter solid,' he tapped. 'The rest of it is liquid.'

'Mine almost all liquid. Only little solid. Very restful world.'

'One thing I want to ask you,' Enoch tapped.

'Ask,' the creature said.

'You are a mathematician. All you folks, I mean.'

'Yes,' the creature said. 'Excellent recreation. Occupies the mind.'

'You mean you do not use it?'

'Oh, yes, once use it. But no need for use any more. Got all we need to use, very long ago. Recreation now.'

'I have heard of your system of numerical notation.'

'Very different,' clicked the Thuban. 'Very better concept.'

'You can tell me of it?'

'You know notation system used by people of Polaris VII?'

'No, I don't,' tapped Enoch.

'Then no use to tell you of our own. Must know Polaris first.'

So that was that, thought Enoch. He might have known. There was so much knowledge in the galaxy and he knew so little of it, understood so little of the little that he knew.

There were men on Earth who could make sense of it. Men who would give anything of their very lives to know the little that he knew, and could put it all to use.

Out among the stars lay a massive body of knowledge, some of it an extension of what mankind knew, some of it concerning matters which Man had not yet suspected, and used in ways and for purposes that Man had not as yet imagined. And never might imagine, if left on his own.

Another hundred years, thought Enoch. How much would he learn in another hundred years? In another thousand?

'I rest now,' said the Thuban. 'Nice to talk with you.'

12

Enoch turned from the tank and picked up the block of wood. A little puddle of liquid had drained off it and lay glistening on the floor.

He carried the block across the room to one of the windows and examined it. It was heavy and black and close-grained and at one corner of it a bit of bark remained. It had been sawn. Someone had cut it into a size that would fit the tank where the Thuban rested.

He recalled an article he had read in one of the daily papers just a day or two before in which a scientist had contended that no great intelligence ever could develop on a liquid world.

But that scientist was wrong, for the Thuban race had so developed and there were other liquid worlds which were members of the galactic confraternity. There were a lot of things, he told himself, that Man would have to unlearn, as well as things to learn, if he ever should become aware of the galactic culture.

The limitation of the speed of light, for one thing.

For if nothing moved faster than the speed of light, then the galactic transport system would be impossible.

But one should not censure Man, he reminded himself, for setting the speed of light as a basic limitation. Observations were all that Man – or anyone, for that matter – could use as data upon which to base his premises. And since human science had so far found nothing which consistently moved faster than the speed of light, then the assumption must be valid that nothing could or did consistently move faster. But valid as an assumption only and no more than that.

For the impulse patterns which carried creatures star to star were almost instantaneous, no matter what the distance.

He stood and thought about it and it still was hard, he admitted to himself, for a person to believe.

Moments ago the creature in the tank had rested in another tank in another station and the materializer had built up a pattern of it – not only of its body, but of its very vital force, the thing that gave it life. Then the impulse pattern had moved across the gulfs of space almost instantaneously to the receiver of this station, where the pattern had been used to duplicate the body and the mind and memory and the life of that creature now lying dead many light years distant. And in the tank the new body and the new mind and memory and life had taken almost instant form – an entirely new being, but exactly like the old one, so that the identity continued and the consciousness (the very thought no more than momentarily interrupted), so that to all intent and purpose the being was the same.

There were limitations to the impulse patterns, but this had nothing to do with speed, for the impulses could cross the entire galaxy with but little lag in time. But under certain conditions the patterns tended to break down and this was why there must be many stations, many thousands of them. Clouds of dust or gas or areas of high ionization seemed to disrupt the patterns and in those sectors of the galaxy where these conditions were encountered, the distance jumps between the stations were considerably cut down to keep the pattern true. There were areas that had to be detoured because of high concentrations of the distorting gas and dust.

Enoch wondered how many dead bodies of the creature that now rested in the tank had been left behind at other stations – in the course of the journey it was making – as this body in a few hours' time would lie dead within this tank when the creature's pattern was sent out again, riding on the impulse waves.

A long trail of dead, he thought, left across the stars, each to be destroyed by a wash of acid and flushed into deep-lying tanks, but with the creature itself going on and on until it reached its final destination to carry out the purpose of its journey.

And those purposes, Enoch wondered – the many purposes of the many creatures who passed through the stations scattered wide in space? There had been certain instances when, chatting with the travellers, they had told their purpose, but with the most of them he never learned the purpose – nor had he any right to learn it. For he was the keeper only.

Mine host, he thought, although not every time, for there were many creatures that had no use for hosts. But the man, at any rate, who watched over the operation of the station and who kept it going, who made ready for the travellers and who sent them on their way again when that time should come. And who performed the little tasks and courtesies of which they might stand in need.

He looked at the block of wood and thought how pleased Winslowe would be with it. It was very seldom that one came upon a wood that was as black or fine-grained as this.

What would Winslowe think, he wondered, if he could only know that the statuettes he carved were made of woods that had grown on unknown planets many light years distant? Winslowe, he knew, must have wondered many times where the wood came from and how his friend could have gotten it. But he had never asked. And he knew as well, of course, that there was something very strange about this man who came out to the mailbox every day to meet him. But he had never asked that, either.

And that was friendship, Enoch told himself.

This wood, too, that he held in his hands, was another evidence of friendship – the friendship of the stars for a very humble keeper of a remote and backwoods station stuck out in one of the spiral arms, far from the centre of the galaxy.

The word had spread, apparently, through the years and throughout space, that this certain keeper was a collector of exotic woods – and so the woods came in. Not only from those races he thought of as his friends, but from total strangers, like the blob that now rested in the tank.

He put the wood down on a table top and went to the refrigerator. From it he took a slab of aged cheese that Winslowe had bought for him several days ago, and a small package of fruit that a traveller from Sirrah X had brought the day before.

'Analysed,' it had told him, 'and you can eat it without hurt. It will play no trouble with your metabolism. You've had it before, perhaps? So you haven't. I am sorry. It is most delicious. Next time, you like it, I shall bring you more.'

From the cupboard beside the refrigerator he took out a small, flat loaf of bread, part of the ration regularly provided him by Galactic Central. Made of a cereal unlike any known on Earth, it had a distinctly nutty flavour with the faintest hint of some alien spice.

He put the food on what he called the kitchen table, although there was no kitchen. Then he put the coffee maker on the stove and went back to his desk.

The letter still lay there, spread out, and he folded it together and put it in a drawer.

He stripped the brown folders off the papers and put them in a pile. From the pile he selected the *New York Times* and moved to his favourite chair to read.

NEW PEACE CONFERENCE AGREED UPON, said the lead-off headline.

The crisis had been boiling for a month or more, the newest of a long series of crises which had kept the world on edge for years. And the worst of it, Enoch told himself, was that the most of them were manufactured crises, with one side or the other pushing for advantage in the relentless chess game of power politics which had been under way since the end of World War II.

The stories in the *Times* bearing on the conference had a rather desperate, almost fatalistic, ring, as if the writers of the stories, and perhaps the diplomats and all the rest involved, knew the conference would accomplish nothing – if, in fact, it did not serve to make the crisis deeper.

Observers in this capital [wrote one of the *Times'* Washington bureau staff] *are not convinced the conference will serve, in this instance, as similar conferences sometimes have served in the past, to either delay a showdown on the issues or to advance the prospects for a settlement. There is scarcely concealed concern in many quarters that the conference will, instead, fan the flames of controversy higher without, by way of compensation, opening any avenues by which a compromise might seem possible. A conference is popularly supposed to provide a time and place for the sober weighing of the facts and points of argument, but there are few who see in the calling of this conference any indications that this may be the case.*

The coffee maker was going full blast now and Enoch threw the paper down and strode to the stove to snatch it off. From the cupboard he got a cup and went to the table with it.

But before he began to eat, he went back to the desk and, opening a drawer, got out his chart and spread it on the table. Once again he wondered just how valid it might be, although in certain parts of it, at times, it seemed to make a certain sort of sense.

He had based it on the Mizar theory of statistics and had been forced, because of the nature of his subject, to shift some of the factors, to substitute some values. He wondered now, for the thousandth time, if he had made an error somewhere. Had his sifting and substitution destroyed the validity of the system? And if so, how could he correct the errors to restore validity?

Here the factors were, he thought: the birth rate and the total population of the Earth, the death rate, the values of currencies, the spread of living costs, attendance at places of worship, medical advances, technological developments, industrial indices, the labour market, world trade trends – and many others, including some that at first glance might not seem too relevant: the auction price of art objects, vacation preferences and movements, the speed of transportation, the incidence of insanity.

The statistical method developed by the mathematicians of Mizar, he knew, would work anywhere, on anything, if applied correctly. But he had been forced to twist it in translating an alien planet's situation to fit the situation here on Earth – and in consequence of that twisting, did it still apply?

He shuddered as he looked at it. For if he'd made no mistake, if he'd handled everything correctly, if his translations had done no violence to the concept, then the Earth was headed straight for another major war, for a holocaust of nuclear destruction.

He let loose of the corners of the chart and it rolled itself back into a cylinder.

He reached for one of the fruits the Sirrah being had brought him and bit into it. He rolled it on his tongue, savouring the delicacy of the taste. It was, he decided, as good as that strange, birdlike being had guaranteed it would be.

There had been a time, he remembered, when he had held some hope that the chart based on the Mizar theory might show, if not a way to end all war, at least a way to keep the peace. But the chart had never given any hint of the road to peace. Inexorably, relentlessly, it had led the way to war.

How many other wars, he wondered, could the people of the Earth endure?

No man could say, of course, but it might be just one more. For the weapons that would be used in the coming conflict had not as yet been measured and there was no man who could come close to actually estimating the results these weapons would produce.

War had been bad enough when men faced one another with their weapons in their hands, but in any present war great pay-loads of destruction would go hurtling through the skies to engulf whole cities – aimed not at military concentrations, but at total populations.

He reached out his hand for the chart again, then pulled it back. There was no further need of looking at it. He knew it all by heart. There was no hope in it. He might study it and puzzle over it until the crack of doom and it would not change a whit. There was no hope at all. The world was thundering once again, in a blind red haze of fury and of helplessness, down the road to war.

He went on with his eating and the fruit was even better than it had been at first bite. 'Next time,' the being had said, 'I will bring you more.' But it might be a long time before he came again, and he might never come. There were many of them who passed through only once, although there were a few who showed up every week or so – old, regular travellers who had become close friends.

And there had been, he recalled, that little group of Hazers who, years ago, had made arrangements for extra long stopovers at the station so they could sit around this very table and talk the hours away, arriving laden with hampers and with baskets of things to eat and drink, as if it were a picnic.

But finally they had stopped their coming and it had been years since he'd seen any one of them. And he regretted it, for they'd been the best of companions.

He drank an extra cup of coffee, sitting idly in the chair, thinking about those good old days when the band of Hazers came.

His ears caught the faint rustling and he glanced quickly up to see her sitting on the sofa, dressed in the demure hoop skirts of the 1860s.

'Mary!' he said, surprised, rising to his feet.

She was smiling at him in her very special way and she was beautiful, he thought, as no other woman ever had been beautiful.

'Mary,' he said, 'it's so nice to have you here.'

And now, leaning on the mantelpiece, dressed in Union blue, with his belted sabre and his full black moustache, was another of his friends.

'Hello, Enoch,' David Ransome said. 'I hope we don't intrude.'

'Never,' Enoch told him. 'How can two friends intrude?'

He stood beside the table and the past was with him, the good and restful past, the rose-scented and unhaunted past that had never left him.

Somewhere in the distance was the sound of fife and drum and the jangle of the battle harness as the boys marched off to war, with the colonel glorious in his full-dress uniform upon the great black stallion, and the regimental flags snapping in the stiff June breeze.

He walked across the room and over to the sofa. He made a little bow to Mary.

'With your permission, ma'am,' he said.

'Please do,' she said. 'If you should happen to be busy ...'

'Not at all,' he said. 'I was hoping you would come.'

He sat down on the sofa, not too close to her, and he saw her hands were folded, very primly, in her lap. He wanted to reach out and take her hands in his and hold them for a moment, but he knew he couldn't.

For she wasn't really there.

'It's been almost a week,' said Mary, 'since I've seen you. How is your work going, Enoch?'

He shook his head. 'I still have all the problems. The watchers still are out there. And the chart says war.'

David left the mantel and came across the room. He sat down in a chair and arranged his sabre.

'War, the way they fight it these days,' he declared, 'would be a sorry business. Not the way we fought it, Enoch.'

'No,' said Enoch, 'not the way we fought it. And while a war would be bad enough itself, there is something worse. If Earth fights another war, our people will be barred, if not for ever, at least for many centuries, from the confraternity of space.'

'Maybe that's not so bad,' said David. 'We may not be ready to join the ones in space.'

'Perhaps not,' Enoch admitted. 'I rather doubt we are. But we could be some day. And that day would be shoved far into the future if we fight another war. You have to make some pretence of being civilized to join those other races.'

'Maybe,' Mary said, 'they might never know. About a war, I mean. They go no place but this station.'

Enoch shook his head. 'They would know. I think they're watching us. And anyhow, they would read the papers.'

'The papers you subscribe to?'

'I save them for Ulysses. That pile over in the corner. He takes them back to Galactic Central every time he comes. He's very interested in Earth, you know, from the years he spent here. And from Galactic Central, once he's read them, I have a hunch they travel to the corners of the galaxy.'

'Can you imagine,' David asked, 'what the promotion departments of those newspapers might have to say about it if they only knew their depth of circulation.'

Enoch grinned at the thought of it.

'There's that paper down in Georgia,' David said, 'that covers Dixie like the dew. They'd have to think of something that goes with galaxy.'

'Glove,' said Mary quickly. 'Covers the galaxy like a glove. What do you think of that?'

'Excellent,' said David.

'Poor Enoch,' Mary said contritely. 'Here we make our jokes and Enoch has his problems.'

'Not mine to solve, of course,' Enoch told her. 'I'm just worried by them. All I have to do is stay inside the station and there are no problems. Once you close the door here, the problems of the world are securely locked outside.'

'But you can't do that.'

'No, I can't,' said Enoch.

'I think you may be right,' said David, 'in thinking that these other races may be watching us. With an eye, perhaps, to someday inviting the human race to join them. Otherwise, why would they have wanted to set up a station here on Earth?'

'They're expanding the network all the time,' said Enoch. 'They needed a station in this solar system to carry out their extension into this spiral arm.'

'Yes, that's true enough,' said David, 'but it need not have been the Earth. They could have built a station out on Mars and used an alien for a keeper and still have served their purpose.'

'I've often thought of that,' said Mary. 'They wanted a station on the Earth and an Earthman as its keeper. There must be a reason for it.'

'I had hoped there was,' Enoch told her, 'but I'm afraid they came too soon. It's too early for the human race. We aren't grown up. We still are juveniles.'

'It's a shame,' said Mary. 'We'd have so much to learn. They know so much more than we. Their concept of religion, for example.'

'I don't know,' said Enoch, 'whether it's actually a religion. It seems to have few of the trappings we associate with religion. And it is not based on faith. It doesn't have to be. It is based on knowledge. These people know, you see.'

'You mean the spiritual force.'

'It is there,' said Enoch, 'just as surely as all the other forces that make up the universe. There is a spiritual force, exactly as there is time and space and gravitation and all the other factors that make up the immaterial universe. It is there and they can establish contact with it ...'

'But don't you think,' asked David, 'that the human race may sense this? They don't know it, but they sense it. And are reaching out to touch it. They haven't got the knowledge, so they must do the best they can with faith. And that faith goes back a far way. Back, perhaps, deep into the prehistoric days. A crude faith, then, but a sort of faith, a grasping for a faith.'

'I suppose so,' Enoch said. 'But it actually wasn't the spiritual force I was thinking of. There are all the other things, the material things, the methods, the philosophies that the human race could use. Name almost any branch of science and there is something there for us, more than what we have.'

But his mind went back to that strange business of the spiritual force and the even stranger machine which had been built eons ago, by means of which the galactic people were able to establish contact with the force. There was a name for that machine, but there was no word in the English language which closely approximated it. 'Talisman' was the closest, but Talisman was too crude a word. Although that had been the word that Ulysses had used when, some years ago, they had talked of it.

There were so many things, so many concepts, he thought, out in the galaxy which could not be adequately expressed in any tongue on Earth. The Talisman was more than a talisman and the machine which had been given the name was more than a mere machine. Involved in it, as well as certain mechanical concepts, was a psychic concept, perhaps some sort of psychic energy that was unknown on Earth. That and a great deal more. He had read some of the literature on the spiritual force and on the Talisman and had realized, he remembered, in the reading of it, how far short he fell, how far short the human race must fall, in an understanding of it.

The Talisman could be operated only by certain beings with certain types of minds and something else besides (could it be, he wondered, with certain kinds of souls?). 'Sensitives' was the word he had used in his mental translation of the term for these kinds of people, but once again he could not be sure if the word came close to fitting. The Talisman was placed in the custody of the most capable, or the most efficient, or the most devoted (whichever it might be) of the galactic sensitives, who carried it from star to star in a sort of eternal progression. And on each planet the people came to make personal and individual contact with the spiritual force through the intervention and the agency of the Talisman and its custodian.

He found that he was shivering at the thought of it – the pure ecstasy of reaching out and touching the spirituality that flooded through the galaxy and, undoubtedly, through the universe. The assurance would be there, he thought, the assurance that life had a special place in the great scheme of existence, that one, no matter how small, how feeble, how insignificant, still did count for something in the vast sweep of space and time.

'What is the trouble, Enoch?' Mary asked.

'Nothing,' he said. 'I was just thinking. I am sorry. I will pay attention now.'

'You were talking,' David said, 'about what we could find in the galaxy.

There was, for one thing, that strange sort of math. You were telling us of it once and it was something ...'

'The Arcturus math, you mean,' said Enoch. 'I know little more than when I told you of it. It is too involved. It is based on behaviour symbolism.'

There was some doubt, he told himself, that you could even call it math, although, by analysis, that was probably what it was. It was something that the scientists of Earth, no doubt, could use to make possible the engineering of the social sciences as logically and as efficiently as the common brand of math had been used to build the gadgets of the Earth.

'And the biology of that race out in Andromeda,' Mary said. 'The ones who colonized all those crazy planets.'

'Yes, I know. But Earth would have to mature a bit in its intellectual and emotional outlook before we'd venture to use it as the Andromedans did. Still, I suppose that it would have its applications.'

He shuddered inwardly as he thought of how the Andromedans used it. And that, he knew, was proof that he still was a man of Earth, kin to all the bias and the prejudice and the shibboleths of the human mind. For what the Andromedans had done was only common sense. If you cannot colonize a planet in your present shape, why, then you change your shape. You make yourself into the sort of being that can live upon the planet and then you take it over in that alien shape into which you have changed yourself. If you need to be a worm, then you become a worm – or an insect or a shellfish or what-ever it may take. And you change not your body only, but your mind as well, into the kind of mind that will be necessary to live upon that planet.

'There are all the drugs,' said Mary, 'and the medicines. The medical know-ledge that could apply to Earth. There was that little package Galactic Central sent you.'

'A packet of drugs,' said Enoch, 'that could cure almost every ill on Earth. That, perhaps, hurts me most of all. To know they're up there in the cup-board, actually on this planet, where so many people need them.'

'You could mail out samples,' David said, 'to medical associations or to some drug concern.'

Enoch shook his head. 'I thought of that, of course. But I have the galaxy to consider. I have an obligation to Galactic Central. They have taken great precautions that the station not be known. There is Ulysses and all my other alien friends. I cannot wreck their plans. I cannot play the traitor to them. For when you think of it, Galactic Central and the work it's doing is more important than the Earth.'

'Divided loyalties,' said David with slight mockery in his tone.

'That is it, exactly. There had been a time, many years ago, when I thought of writing papers for submission to some of the scientific journals. Not the medical journals, naturally, for I know nothing about medicine. The drugs are there, of course, lying on the shelf, with directions for their use, but they are merely so many pills or powders or ointments, or whatever they may be. But there were other things I knew of, other things I'd learned. Not too much about them, naturally, but at least some hints in some new directions. Enough that someone could pick them up and go on from there. Someone who might know what to do with them.'

'But look here,' David said, 'that wouldn't have worked out. You have no technical nor research background, no educational record. You're not tied up with any school or college. The journals just don't publish you unless you can prove yourself.'

'I realize that, of course. That's why I never wrote the papers. I knew there was no use. You can't blame the journals. They must be responsible. Their pages aren't open to just anyone. And even if they had viewed the papers with enough respect to want to publish them, they would have had to find out who I was. And that would have led straight back to the station.'

'But even if you could have gotten away with it,' David pointed out, 'you'd still not have been clear. You said a while ago you had a loyalty to Galactic Central.'

'If,' said Enoch, 'in this particular case I could have got away with it, it might have been all right. If you just threw out ideas and let some Earth scientists develop them, there'd be no harm done to Galactic Central. The main problem, of course, would be not to reveal the source.'

'Even so,' said David, 'there'd be little you actually could tell them. What I mean is that generally you haven't got enough to go on. So much of this galactic knowledge is off the beaten track.'

'I know,' said Enoch. 'The mental engineering of Mankalinen III, for one thing. If the Earth could know of that, our people undoubtedly could find a clue to the treatment of the neurotic and the mentally disturbed. We could empty all the institutions and we could tear them down or use them for something else. There'd be no need of them. But no one other than the people out on Mankalinen III could ever tell us of it. I only know they are noted for their mental engineering, but that is all I know. I haven't the faintest inkling of what it's all about. It's something that you'd have to get from the people out there.'

'What you are really talking of,' said Mary, 'are all the nameless sciences – the ones that no human has ever thought about.'

'Like us, perhaps,' said David.

'David!' Mary cried.

'There is no sense,' said David angrily, 'in pretending we are people.'

'But you are,' said Enoch tensely. 'You are people to me. You are the only people that I have. What is the matter, David?'

'I think,' said David, 'that the time has come to say what we really are. That

242

we are illusion. That we are created and called up. That we exist only for one purpose, to come and talk with you, to fill in for the real people that you cannot have.'

'Mary,' Enoch cried, 'you don't think that way, too! You can't think that way!'

He reached out his arms to her and then he let them drop – terrified at the realization of what he'd been about to do. It was the first time he'd ever tried to touch her. It was the first time, in all the years, that he had forgotten.

'I am sorry, Mary. I should not have done that.'

Her eyes were bright with tears.

'I wish you could,' she said. 'Oh, how I wish you could!'

'David,' he said, not turning his head.

'David left,' said Mary.

'He won't be back,' said Enoch.

Mary shook her head.

'What is the matter, Mary? What is it all about? What have I done?'

'Nothing,' Mary said, 'except that you made us too much like people. So that we became more human, until we were entirely human. No longer puppets, no longer pretty dolls, but really actual people. I think David must resent it – not that he is people, but that being people, he is still a shadow. It did not matter when we were dolls or puppets, for we were not human then. We had no human feeling.'

'Mary, please,' he said. 'Mary, please forgive me.'

She leaned toward him and her face was lighted by deep tenderness. 'There is nothing to forgive,' she said. 'Rather, I suppose, we should thank you for it. You created us out of a love of us and a need of us and it is wonderful to know that you are loved and needed.'

'But I don't create you any more,' Enoch pleaded. 'There was a time, long ago, I had to. But not any longer. Now you come to visit me of your own free will.'

How many years? he wondered. It must be all of fifty. And Mary had been the first, and David had been second. Of all the others of them, they had been the first and were the closest and the dearest.

And before that, before he'd even tried, he'd spent other years in studying that nameless science stemming from the thaumaturgists of Alphard XXII.

There had been a day and a state of mind when it would have been black magic, but it was not black magic. Rather, it was the orderly manipulation of certain natural aspects of the universe as yet quite unsuspected by the human race. Perhaps aspects that Man never would discover. For there was not, at least at the present moment, the necessary orientation of the scientific mind to initiate the research that must precede discovery.

'David felt,' said Mary, 'that we could not go on for ever, playing out our little sedate visits. There had to be a time when we faced up to what we really are.'

'And the rest of them?'

'I am sorry, Enoch. The rest of them as well.'

'But you? How about you, Mary?'

'I don't know,' she said. 'It is different with me. I love you very much.'

'And I ...'

'No, that's not what I mean. Don't you understand! I'm in love with you.'

He sat stricken, staring at her, and there was a great roaring in the world, as if he were standing still and the world and time were rushing swiftly past him.

'If it only could have stayed,' she said, 'the way it was at first. Then we were glad of our existence and our emotions were so shallow and we seemed to be so happy. Like little happy children, running in the sun. But then we all grew up. And I think I the most of all.'

She smiled at him and tears were in her eyes.

'Don't take it so hard, Enoch. We can ...'

'My dear,' he said, 'I've been in love with you since the first day that I saw you. I think maybe even before that.'

He reached out a hand to her, then pulled it back, remembering.

'I did not know,' she said. 'I should not have told you. You could live with it until you knew I loved you, too.' He nodded dumbly.

She bowed her head. 'Dear God, we don't deserve this. We have done nothing to deserve it.'

She raised her head and looked at him. 'If I could only touch you.'

'We can go on,' he said, 'as we have always done. You can come to see me any time you want. We can ...'

She shook her head. 'It wouldn't work,' she said. 'There could neither of us stand it.'

He knew that she was right. He knew that it was done. For fifty years she and the others had been dropping in to visit. And they'd come no more. For the fairyland was shattered and the magic spell was broken. He'd be left alone – more alone than ever, more alone than before he'd ever known her.

She would not come again and he could never bring himself to call her up again, even if he could, and his shadow world and his shadow love, the only love he'd ever really had, would be gone for ever.

'Good-bye, my dear,' he said.

But it was too late. She was already gone.

And from far off, it seemed, he heard the moaning whistle that said a message had come in.

13

She had said that they must face up to the kind of things they were.

And what were they? Not, what did he think they were, but what were they, actually? What did they think themselves to be? For perhaps they knew much better than did he.

Where had Mary gone? When she left this room, into what kind of limbo did she disappear? Did she still exist? And if so, what kind of an existence would it be? Would she be stored away somewhere as a little girl would store away her doll in a box pushed back into the closet with all the other dolls?

He tried to imagine limbo and it was a nothingness, and if that were true, a being pushed into limbo would be an existence within a non-existence. There would be nothing – not space nor time, nor light, nor air, no colour and no vision, just a never ending nothing that of necessity must lie at some point outside the universe.

Mary! he cried inside himself. *Mary, what have I done to you?*

And the answer lay there, hard and naked.

He had dabbled in a thing which he had not understood. And had, furthermore, committed that greater sin of thinking that he did understand. And the fact of the matter was that he had just barely understood enough to make the concept work, but had not understood enough to be aware of its consequences.

With creation went responsibility and he was not equipped to assume more than the moral responsibility for the wrong that he had done, and moral responsibility, unless it might be coupled with the ability to bring about some mitigation, was an entirely useless thing.

They hated him and resented him and he did not blame them, for he'd led them out and shown them the promised land of humanity and then had led them back. He had given them everything that a human being had with the one exception of that most important thing of all – the ability to exist within the human world.

They all hated him but Mary, and for Mary it was worse than hate. For she was condemned, by the very virtue of the humanity he had given her, to love the monster who had created her.

Hate me, Mary, he pleaded. *Hate me like the others!*

He had thought of them as shadow people, but that had been just a name he'd thought up for himself, for his own convenience, a handy label that he had tagged them with so that he would have some way of identifying them when he thought of them.

But the label had been wrong, for they were not shadowy or ghostlike. To the eyes they were solid and substantial, as real as any people. It was only when you tried to touch them that they were not real – for when you tried to touch them, there was nothing there.

A figment of his mind, he'd thought at first, but now he was not sure. At first they'd come only when he'd called them up, using the knowledge and the techniques that he had acquired in his study of the work done by the thaumaturgists of Alphard XXII. But in recent years he had not called them up. There had been no occasion to. They had anticipated him and come before he could call them up. They sensed his need of them before he knew the need himself. And they were there, waiting for him, to spend an hour or evening.

Figments of his mind in one sense, of course, for he had shaped them, perhaps at the time unconsciously, not knowing why he shaped them so, but in recent years he'd known, although he had tried not to know, would have been the better satisfied if he had not known. For it was a knowledge that he had not admitted, but kept pushed back, far within his mind. But now, when all was gone, when it no longer mattered, he finally did admit it.

David Ransome was himself, as he had dreamed himself to be, as he had wished himself to be – but, of course, as he had never been. He was the dashing Union officer, of not so high a rank as to be stiff and stodgy, but a fair cut above the man of ordinary standing. He was trim and debonair and definitely dare-devilish, loved by all the women, admired by all the men. He was a born leader and a good fellow all at once, at home alike in the field or drawing-room.

And Mary? Funny, he thought, he had never called her anything but Mary. There had never been a surname. She had been simply Mary.

And she was at least two women, if not more than that. She was Sally Brown, who had lived just down the road – and how long had it been he wondered, since he'd thought of Sally Brown? It was strange, he knew, that he had not thought of her, that he now was shocked by the memory of a one-time neighbour girl named Sally Brown. For the two of them once had been in love, or only thought, perhaps, that they had been in love. For even in the later years, when he still remembered her, he had never been quite certain, even through the romantic mists of time, if it had been love or no more than the romanticism of a soldier marching off to war. It had been a shy and fumbling, an awkward sort of love, the love of the farmer's daughter for the next-door farmer's son. They had decided to be married when he came home from war, but a few days after Gettysburg he had received the letter, then more than three weeks written, which told him that Sally Brown was dead of diphtheria. He had grieved, he now recalled, but he could not recall how deeply, although it probably had been deeply, for to grieve long and deeply was the fashion in those days.

So Mary very definitely was partly Sally Brown, but not entirely Sally. She was as well that tall, stately daughter of the South, the woman he had seen for a few moments only as he marched a dusty road in the hot Virginia sun. There had been a mansion, one of those great plantation houses, set back from the road, and she had been standing on the portico, beside one of the great white pillars, watching the enemy march past. Her hair was black and her complexion whiter than the pillar and she had stood so straight and proud, so defiant and imperious, that he had remembered her and thought of her and dreamed of her – although he never knew her name – through all the dusty, sweaty, bloody days of war. Wondering as he thought and dreamed of her if the thinking and the dreaming might be unfaithful to his Sally. Sitting around the campfire, when the talk grew quiet, and again, rolled in his blankets, staring at the stars, he had built up a fantasy of how, when the war was ended, he'd go back to that Virginia house and find her. She might be there no longer, but he still would roam the South and find her. But he never did; he had never really meant to find her. It had been a campfire dream.

So Mary had been both of these – she had been Sally Brown and the unknown Virginia belle standing by the pillar to watch the troops march by. She had been the shadow of them and perhaps of many others as yet unrealized by him, a composite of all he had ever known or seen or admired in women. She had been an ideal and perfection. She had been his perfect woman, created in his mind. And now, like Sally Brown, resting in her grave; like the Virginia belle, lost in the mists of time; like all the others who may have contributed to his moulding of her, she was gone from him.

And he had loved her, certainly, for she had been a compounding of his loves – a cross section, as it were, of all the women he had ever loved (if he actually had loved any) or the ones he had thought he loved, even in the abstract.

But that she should love him was something that had never crossed his mind. And until he knew her love for him, it had been quite possible to nurse his love of her close inside the heart, knowing that it was a hopeless love and impossible, but the best that he could manage.

He wondered where she might be now, where she had retreated – into the limbo he had attempted to imagine or into some strange non-existence, waiting all unknowing for the time she'd come to him again.

He put up his hands and lowered his head in them and sat in utter misery and guilt, with his face cupped in his fingers.

She would never come again. He prayed she'd never come. It would be better for the both of them if she never came.

If he only could be sure, he thought, of where she might be now. If he only could be certain that she was in a semblance of death and untortured by her thoughts. To believe that she was sentient was more than one could bear.

He heard the hooting of the whistle that said a message waited and he took his head out of his hands. But he did not get up off the sofa.

Numbly his hand reached out to the coffee table that stood before the sofa, its top covered with some of the more colourful of the gewgaws and gimcracks that had been left as gifts by travellers.

He picked up a cube of something that might have been some strange sort of glass or of translucent stone – he had never been able to decide which it was, if either – and cupped it in his hands. Staring into it, he saw a tiny picture, three-dimensional and detailed, of a faery world. It was a prettily grotesque place set inside what might have been a forest glade surrounded by what appeared to be flowering toadstools, and drifting down through the air, as if it might have been a part of the air itself, came what looked for all the world like a shower of jewelled snow, sparkling and glinting in the violet light of a great blue sun. There were things dancing in the glade and they looked more like flowers than animals, but they moved with a grace and poetry that fired one's blood to watch. Then the faery place was wiped out and there was another place – a wild and dismal place, with grim, gaunt, beetling cliffs rearing high against a red and angry sky, while great flying things that looked like flapping dishrags beat their way up and down the cliffs, and there were others of them roosting, most obscenely, upon the scraggly projections that must have been some sort of misshapen trees growing from the very wall of rock. And from far below, from some distance that one could only guess, came the lonesome thundering of a rushing river.

He put the cube back upon the table. He wondered what it was that one saw within its depths. It was like turning the pages of a book, with each page a picture of a different place, but never anything to tell where that place might be. When he first had been given it, he had spent fascinated hours, watching the pictures change as he held it in his hands. There had never been a picture that looked even faintly like any other picture and there was no end to them. One got the feeling that these were not pictures, actually, but that one was looking at the scene itself and that at any moment one might lose his perch upon wherever he was roosting and plunge head first down into the place itself.

But it had finally palled upon him, for it had been a senseless business, gawking at a long series of places that had no identity. Senseless to him, of course, he thought, but not senseless, certainly, to that native of Enif V who had given it to him. It might, for all he knew, Enoch told himself, be of great significance and a treasure of great value.

That was the way it was with so many of the things he had. Even the ones that had given pleasure, he knew, he might be using wrongly, or, at least, in a way that had not been intended.

But there were some – a few, perhaps – that did have a value he could understand and appreciate, although in many instances their functions were of little use to him. There was the tiny clock that gave the local times for all the sectors of the galaxy, and while it might be intriguing, and even essential under certain circumstances, it had little value to him. And there was the perfume mixer, which was as close as he could come in naming it, which allowed a person to create the specific scent desired. Just get the mixture that one wanted and turn it on and the room took on that scent until one should turn it off. He'd had some fun with it, remembering that bitter winter day when, after long experimenting, he had achieved the scent of apple blossoms, and had lived a day in spring while a blizzard howled outside.

He reached out and picked up another piece – a beautiful thing that always had intrigued him, but for which he had never found a use – if, indeed, it had a use. It might be, he told himself, no more than a piece of art, a pretty thing that was meant to look at only. But it had a certain feel (if that were the word) which had led him to believe that it might have some specific function.

It was a pyramid of spheres, succeeding smaller spheres set on larger spheres. Some fourteen inches tall, it was a graceful piece, with each of the spheres a different colour – and not just a colour painted on, but each colour so deep and true that one knew instinctively the colour was intrinsic to each sphere, that the entire sphere, from the centre of it out to the surface, was all of its particular colour.

There was nothing to indicate that any gluelike medium had been used to mount the spheres and hold them in their places. It looked for all the world as if someone had simply piled the spheres, one atop the other, and they had stayed that way.

Holding it in his hands, he tried to recall who had given it to him, but he had no memory of it.

The whistle of the message machine still was calling and there was work to do. He could not sit here, he told himself, mooning the afternoon away. He put the pyramid of spheres back on the table top, and rising, went across the room.

The message said:

NO. 406302 TO STATION 18327. NATIVE OF VEGA XXI ARRIVING AT 16532.82, DEPARTURE INDETERMINATE. NO LUGGAGE. CABINET ONLY, LOCAL CONDITIONS. CONFIRM.

Enoch felt a glow of happiness, looking at the message. It would be good to have a Hazer once again. It had been a month or more since one had passed through the station.

He could remember back to that first day he had ever met a Hazer, when the five of them had come. It must have been, he thought, back in 1914 or maybe 1915. World War I, which everyone then was calling the Great War, was under way, he knew.

The Hazer would be arriving at about the same time as Ulysses and the three of them could spend a pleasant evening. It was not too often that two good friends ever visited here at once.

He stood a bit aghast at thinking of the Hazer as a friend, for more than likely the being itself was one he had never met. But that made little difference, for a Hazer, any Hazer, would turn out to be a friend.

He got the cabinet in position beneath a materializer unit and double-checked to be sure that everything was exactly as it should be, then went back to the message machine and sent off the confirmation.

And all the time his memory kept on nagging at him. Had it been 1914, or perhaps a little later?

At the catalogue cabinet, he pulled out a drawer and found Vega XXI and the first date listed was 12 July 1915. He found the record book on the shelf and pulled it out and brought it to the desk. He leafed through it rapidly until he found the date.

14

12 July 1915 – Arrived this afternoon (3.20 pm) five beings from Vega XXI, the first of their kind to pass through this station. They are biped and humanoid, and one gains the impression that they are not made of flesh – that flesh would be too gross for the kind of things they are – but, of course, they are made of flesh the same as anyone. They glow, not with a visible light, but there is about them an aura that goes with them wherever they may be.

They were, I gathered, a sexual unit, the five of them, although I am not so certain I understand, for it is most confusing. They were happy and friendly and they carried with them an air of faint amusement, not at anything in particular, but at the universe itself, as if they might have enjoyed some sort of cosmic and very private joke that was known to no one else. They were on a holiday and were en route to a festival (although that may not be the precise word for it) on another planet, where other life forms were gathering for a week of carnival. Just how they had been invited or why they had been invited I was unable to determine. It must surely have been a great honour for them to be going there, but so far as I could see they did not seem to think so, but took it as their right. They were very happy and without a care and extremely self-assured and poised, but thinking back on it, I would suppose that they are always that way. I found myself just a little envious at not being able to be as carefree and gay as they were, and trying to imagine how fresh life and the universe must seem to them, and a little resentful that they could be, so unthinkingly, as happy as they were.

I had, according to instructions, hung hammocks so that they could rest, but they did not use them. They brought with them hampers that were filled with food and drink and sat down at my table and began to talk and feast. They asked me to sit with them and they chose two dishes and a bottle; which they assured me would be safe for me to eat and drink, the rest of their fare being somewhat doubtful for a metabolism such as mine. The food was delicious and of a kind I had never tasted – one dish being rather like the rarest and most delicate of old cheeses, and the other of a sweetness that was heavenly. The drink was somewhat like the finest of brandies, yellow in colour and no heavier than water.

They asked me about myself and about my planet and they were courteous and seemed genuinely interested and they were quick of understanding in the things I told them. They told me they were headed for a planet the name of which I had not heard before, and they talked among themselves, gaily and happily, but in such a way that I did not seem to be left out. From their talk I gained the fact that some form of art was being presented at the festival on this planet. The art form was not alone of music or painting, but was composed of sound and colour and emotion and form and other qualities for which there seem to be no words in the language of the Earth, and which I do not entirely recognize, only gaining the very faintest inkling of what they were talking of in this particular regard. I gained the impression of a three-dimensional symphony, although this is not entirely the right expression, which had been composed, not by a single being, but by a team of beings. They talked of the art form enthusiastically and I seemed to understand that it would last for not only several hours, but for days, and that it was an experience rather than a listening or seeing and that the spectators or audience did not merely sit and listen, but could, if they wished, and must, to get the most out of it, be participants. But I could not understand how they participated and felt I should not ask. They talked of the people they would meet and when they had met them last and gossiped considerably about them, although in kindly fashion, leaving the impression that they and many other people went from planet to planet for some happy purpose. But whether there was any purpose other than enjoyment in their going, I could not determine. I gathered that there might be.

They spoke of other festivals and not all of them were concerned with the one art form, but with other more specialized aspects of the arts, of which I could gain no adequate idea. They seemed to find a great and exuberant happiness in the festivals and it seemed to me that some certain significances aside from the art itself contributed to that happiness. I did not join in this part of their conversation, for, frankly, there was no opportunity. I would have liked to ask some questions, but I had no chance. I suppose that if I had, my questions must have sounded stupid to them, but given the chance, that would not have bothered me too much. And yet in spite of this, they managed somehow to make me feel I was included in their conversation. There was no obvious attempt to do this, and yet they made me feel I was one with them and not simply a station keeper they would spend a short time with. At times they spoke briefly in the language of their planet, which is one of the most beautiful I have ever heard, but for the most part they conversed in the vernacular used by a number of the humanoid races, a sort of pidgin language made up for convenience, and I suspect that this was done out of courtesy to me, and a great courtesy it was. I believe that they were truly the most civilized people I have ever met.

I have said they glowed and I think by that I mean they glowed in spirit. It seemed that they were accompanied, somehow, by a sparkling golden haze that made happy everything it touched – almost as if they moved in some special world that no one else had found. Sitting at the table with them, I seemed to be included in this golden haze and I felt strange, quiet, deep currents of happiness flowing in my veins. I wondered by what route they and their world had arrived at this golden state and if my world could, in some distant time, attain it.

But back of this happiness was a great vitality, the bubbling, effervescent spirit with an inner core of strength and a love of living that seemed to fill every pore of them and every instant of their time.

They had only two hours' time and it passed so swiftly that I had to finally warn them it was time to go. Before they left, they placed two packages on the table and said they were for me and thanked me for my table (what a strange way for them to put it) then they said good-bye and stepped into the cabinet (the extra-large one) and I sent them on their way. Even after they were gone, the golden haze seemed to linger in the room and it was hours before all of it was gone. I wished that I might have gone with them to that other planet and its festival.

One of the packages they left contained a dozen bottles of the brandy-like liquor and the bottles themselves were each a piece of art, no two of them alike, being formed of what I am convinced is diamond, but whether fabricated diamond or carved from some great stones, I have no idea. At any rate, I would estimate that each of them is priceless, and each carved in a disturbing variety of symbolisms, each of which, however, has a special beauty of its own. And in the other box was a – well, I suppose that, for lack of other name, you might call it a music box. The box itself is ivory, old yellow ivory that is as smooth as satin, and covered by a mass of diagrammatic carving which must have some significance which I do not understand. On the top of it is a circle set inside a graduated scale and when I turned the circle to the first graduation there was music and through all the room an interplay of many-coloured light, as if the entire room was filled with different kinds of colour, and through it all a far-off suggestion of that golden haze. And from the box came, too, perfumes that filled the room, and feeling, emotion – whatever one may call it – but something that took hold of one and made one sad or happy or whatever might go with the music and the colour and perfume. Out of that box came a world in which one lived out the composition or whatever it might be – living it with all that one had in him, all the emotion and belief and intellect of which one is capable. And here, I am quite certain, was a recording of that art form of which they had been talking. And not one composition alone, but 206 of them, for that is the number of the graduation marks and for each mark there is a separate composition. In the days to come I shall play them all and make notes upon each of them and assign them names, perhaps, according to their characteristics, and from them, perhaps, can gain some knowledge as well as entertainment.

15

The twelve diamond bottles, empty long ago, stood in a sparkling row upon the fireplace mantel. The music box, as one of his choicest possessions, was stored inside one of the cabinets, where no harm could come to it. And Enoch thought rather ruefully, in all these years, despite regular use of it, he had not as yet played through the entire list of compositions. There were so many of the early ones that begged for a replaying that he was not a great deal more than halfway through the graduated markings.

The Hazers had come back, the five of them, time and time again, for it seemed that they found in this station, perhaps even in the man who operated it, some quality that pleased them. They had helped him learn the Vegan language and had brought him scrolls of Vegan literature and many other things, and had been, without any doubt, the best friends among the aliens (other than Ulysses) that he had ever had. Then one day they came no more and he wondered why, asking after them when other Hazers showed up at the station. But he had never learned what had happened to them.

He knew far more now about the Hazers and their art forms, their traditions and their customs and their history, than he'd known that first day he'd written of them, back in 1915. But he still was far from grasping many of the concepts that were commonplace with them.

There had been many of them since that day in 1915 and there was one he remembered in particular – the old, wise one, the philosopher, who had died on the floor beside the sofa.

They had been sitting on the sofa, talking, and he even could remember the subject of their talk. The old one had been telling of the perverse code of ethics, at once irrational and comic, which had been built up by that curious race of social vegetables he had encountered on one of his visits to an off-track Planet on the other side of the galactic rim. The old Hazer had a drink or two beneath his belt and he was in splendid form, relating incident after incident with enthusiastic gusto.

Suddenly, in mid-sentence, he had stopped his talking, and had slumped quietly forward. Enoch, startled, reached for him, but before he could lay a hand upon him, the old alien had slid slowly to the floor.

The golden haze had faded from his body and slowly flickered out and the body lay there, angular and bony and obscene, a terribly alien thing there upon the floor, a thing that was at once pitiful and monstrous. More monstrous, it seemed to Enoch, than anything in alien form he had ever seen before.

In life it had been a wondrous creature, but now, in death, it was an old bag of hideous bones with a scaly parchment stretched to hold the bones together. It was the golden haze, Enoch told himself, gulping, in something near to horror, that had made the Hazer seem so wondrous and so beautiful, so vital, so alive and quick, so filled with dignity. The golden haze was the life of them and when the haze was gone, they became mere repulsive horrors that one gagged to look upon.

Could it be, he wondered, that the goldenness was the Hazers' life force and that they wore it like a cloak, as a sort of over-all disguise? Did they wear their life force on the outside of them while all other creatures wore it on the inside?

A piteous little wind was lamenting in the gingerbread high up in the gables and through the windows he could see battalions of tattered clouds fleeing in ragged retreat across the moon, which had climbed halfway up the eastern sky.

There was a coldness and a loneliness in the station – a far-reaching loneliness that stretched out and out, farther than mere Earth loneliness could go.

Enoch turned from the body and walked stiffly across the room to the message machine. He put in a call for a connection direct with Galactic Central, then stood waiting; gripping the sides of the machine with both his hands.

GO AHEAD, said Galactic Central.

Briefly, as objectively as he was able, Enoch reported what had happened.

There was no hesitation and there were no questions from the other end. Just the simple directions (as if this was something that happened all the time) of how the situation should be handled. The Vegan must remain upon the planet of its death, its body to be disposed of according to the local customs obtaining on that planet. For that was the Vegan law, and, likewise, a point of honour. A Vegan, when he fell, must stay where he fell, and that place became, for ever, a part of Vega XXI. There were such places, said Galactic Central, all through the galaxy.

THE CUSTOM HERE [typed Enoch] IS TO INTER THE DEAD.
THEN INTER THE VEGAN.
WE READ A VERSE OR TWO FROM OUR HOLY BOOK.
READ ONE FOR THE VEGAN, THEN. YOU CAN DO ALL THIS?
YES. BUT WE USUALLY HAVE IT DONE BY A PRACTITIONER OF RELIGION. UNDER THE PRESENT CIRCUMSTANCES, HOWEVER, THAT MIGHT BE UNWISE.
AGREED [said Galactic Central] YOU CAN DO AS WELL YOURSELF?
I CAN.

IT IS BEST, THEN, THAT YOU DO.

WILL THERE BE RELATIVES OR FRIENDS ARRIVING FOR THE RITES?

NO.

YOU WILL NOTIFY THEM?

FORMALLY, OF COURSE. BUT THEY ALREADY KNOW.

HE ONLY DIED A MOMENT OR TWO AGO.

NEVERTHELESS, THEY KNOW.

WHAT ABOUT A DEATH CERTIFICATE?

NONE IS NEEDED. THEY KNOW OF WHAT HE DIED.

HIS LUGGAGE? THERE IS A TRUNK.

KEEP IT. IT IS YOURS. IT IS A TOKEN FOR THE SERVICES YOU PERFORM FOR THE HONOURED DEAD. THAT ALSO IS THE LAW.

BUT THERE MAY BE IMPORTANT MATTERS IN IT.

YOU WILL KEEP THE TRUNK. TO REFUSE WOULD INSULT THE MEMORY OF THE DEAD.

ANYTHING ELSE? [asked Enoch] THAT IS ALL?

THAT IS ALL. PROCEED AS IF THE VEGAN WERE ONE OF YOUR OWN.

Enoch cleared the machine and went back across the room. He stood above the Hazer, getting up his nerve to bend and lift the body to place it on the sofa. He shrank from touching it. It was so unclean and terrible, such a travesty on the shining creature that had sat there talking with him.

Since he met the Hazers he had loved them and admired them, had looked forward to each visit by them – by any one of them. And now he stood, a shivering coward who could not touch one dead.

It was not the horror only, for in his years as keeper of the station, he had seen much of pure visual horror as portrayed in alien bodies. And yet he had learned to submerge that sense of horror, to disregard the outward appearance of it, to regard all life as brother life, to meet all things as people.

It was something else, he knew, some other unknown factor quite apart from horror, that he felt. And yet this thing, he reminded himself, was a friend of his. And as a dead friend, it demanded honour from him, it demanded love and care.

Blindly he drove himself to the task. He stooped and lifted it. It had almost no weight at all, as if in death it had lost a dimension of itself, had somehow become a smaller thing and less significant. Could it be, he wondered, that the golden haze might have a weight all of its own?

He laid the body on the sofa and straightened it as best he could. Then he went outside and, lighting the lantern in the shed, went down to the barn.

It had been years since he had been there, but nothing much had changed.

Protected by a tight roof from the weather, it had stayed snug and dry. There were cobwebs hanging from the beams and dust was everywhere. Straggling clumps of ancient hay, stored in the mow above, hung down through the cracks in the boards that floored the mow. The place had a dry, sweet, dusty smell about it, all the odours of animals and manure long gone.

Enoch hung the lantern on the peg behind the row of stanchions and climbed the ladder to the mow. Working in the dark, for he dared not bring the lantern into this dust heap of dried-out hay, he found the pile of oaken boards far beneath the eaves.

Here, he remembered, underneath these slanting eaves, had been a pretended cave in which, as a boy, he had spent many happy rainy days when he could not be outdoors. He had been Robinson Crusoe in his desert island cave, or some now nameless outlaw hiding from a posse, or a man holed up against the threat of scalp-hunting Indians. He had had a gun, a wooden gun that he had sawed out of a board, working it down later with draw-shave and knife and a piece of glass to scrape it smooth. It had been something he had cherished through all his boyhood days – until that day, when he had been twelve, that his father, returning home from a trip to town, had handed him a rifle for his very own.

He explored the stack of boards in the dark, determining by feel the ones that he would need. These he carried to the ladder and carefully slid down to the floor below.

Climbing down the ladder, he went up the short flight of stairs to the granary, where the tools were stored. He opened the lid of the great tool chest and found that it was filled with long deserted mice nests. Pulling out handfuls of the straw and hay and grass that the rodents had used to set up their one-time housekeeping, he uncovered the tools. The shine had gone from them, their surface greyed by the soft patina that came from long disuse, but there was no rust upon them and the cutting edges still retained their sharpness.

Selecting the tools he needed, he went back to the lower part of the barn and fell to work. A century ago, he thought, he had done as he was doing now, working by lantern-light to construct a coffin. And that time it had been his father lying in the house.

The oaken boards were dry and hard, but the tools still were in shape to handle them. He sawed and planed and hammered and there was the smell of sawdust. The barn was snug and silent, the depth of hay standing in the mow drowning out the noise of the complaining wind outside.

He finished the coffin and it was heavier than he had figured, so he found the old wheelbarrow, leaning against the wall back of the stalls that once had been used for horses, and loaded the coffin on it. Laboriously, stopping often to rest, he wheeled it down to the little cemetery inside the apple orchard.

And here, beside his father's grave, he dug another grave, having brought a shovel and a pickaxe with him. He did not dig it as deep as he would have liked to dig, not the full six feet that was decreed by custom, for he knew that if he dug it that deep he never would be able to get the coffin in. So he dug it slightly less than four, labouring in the light of the lantern, set atop the mound of dirt to cast its feeble glow. An owl came up from the woods and sat for a while, unseen, somewhere in the orchard, muttering and gurgling in between its hoots. The moon sank towards the west and the ragged clouds thinned out to let the stars shine through.

Finally it was finished, with the grave completed and the casket in the grave and the lantern flickering, the kerosene almost gone, and the chimney blacked from the angle at which the lantern had been canted.

Back at the station, Enoch hunted up a sheet in which to wrap the body. He put a Bible in his pocket and picked up the shrouded Vegan and, in the first faint light that preceded dawn, marched down to the apple orchard. He put the Vegan in the coffin and nailed shut the lid, then climbed from the grave.

Standing on the edge of it, he took the Bible from his pocket and found the place he wanted. He read aloud, scarcely needing to strain his eyes in the dim light to follow the text, for it was from a chapter that he had read many times:

In my Father's house are many mansions; if it were not so, I would have told you ...

Thinking, as he read it, how appropriate it was; how there must need be many mansions in which to house all the souls in the galaxy – and of all the other galaxies that stretched, perhaps interminably, through space. Although if there were understanding, one might be enough.

He finished reading and recited the burial service, from memory, as best he could, not being absolutely sure of all the words. But sure enough, he told himself, to make sense out of it. Then he shovelled in the dirt.

The stars and moon were gone and the wind had died. In the quietness of the morning, the eastern sky was pearly pink.

Enoch stood beside the grave, with the shovel in his hand.

'Good-bye, my friend,' he said.

Then he turned and, in the first flush of the morning, went back to the station.

16

Enoch got up from his desk and carried the record book back to the shelf and slid it into place.

He turned around and stood hesitantly.

There were things that he should do. He should read his papers. He should be writing up his journal. There were a couple of papers in the latest issues of the *Journal of Geophysical Research* that he should be looking at.

But he didn't feel like doing any of them. There was too much to think about, too much to worry over, too much to mourn.

The watchers still were out there. He had lost his shadow people. And the world was edging in towards war.

Although, perhaps, he should not be worrying about what happened to the world. He could renounce the world, could resign from the human race any time he wished. If he never went outside, if he never opened up the door, then it would make no difference to him what the world might do or what might happen to it. For he had a world. He had a greater world than anyone outside this station had ever dreamed about. He did not need the Earth.

But even as he thought it, he knew he could not make it stick. For, in a very strange and funny way, he still did need the Earth.

He walked over to the door and spoke the phrase and the door came open. He walked into the shed and it closed behind him.

He went around the corner of the house and sat down on the steps that led up to the porch.

This, he thought, was where it all had started. He had been sitting here that summer day of long ago when the stars had reached out across vast gulfs of space and put the finger on him.

The sun was far down the sky towards the west and soon it would be evening. Already the heat of the day was falling off, with a faint, cool breeze creeping up out of the hollow that ran down to the river valley. Down across the field, at the edge of the woods, crows were wheeling in the sky and cawing.

It would be hard to shut the door, he knew, and keep it shut. Hard never to feel the sun or wind again, to never know the smell of the changing seasons as they came across the Earth. Man, he told himself, was not ready for that. He had not as yet become so totally a creature of his own created environment that he could divorce entirely the physical characteristics of his native planet. He needed sun and soil and wind to remain a man.

He should do this oftener, Enoch thought, come out here and sit, doing nothing, just looking, seeing the trees and the river to the west and the blue of the Iowa hills across the Mississippi, watching the crows wheeling in the skies and the pigeons strutting on the ridge-pole of the barn.

It would be worth while each day to do it, for what was another hour of ageing? He did not need to save his hours – not now he didn't. There might come a time when he'd become very jealous of them and when that day came, he could hoard the hours and minutes, even the seconds, in as miserly a fashion as he could manage.

He heard the sound of the running feet as they came around the farther corner of the house, a stumbling, exhausted running, as if the one who ran might have come a far way.

He leapt to his feet and strode out into the yard to see who it might be and the runner came stumbling towards him, with her arms outstretched. He put out an arm and caught her as she came close to him, holding her close against him so she would not fall.

'Lucy!' he cried. 'Lucy! What has happened, child?'

His hands against her back were warm and sticky and he took one of them away to see that it was smeared with blood. The back of her dress, he saw, was soaked and dark.

He grabbed her by the shoulders and shoved her away from him so he could see her face. It was wet with crying and there was terror in the face – and pleading with the terror.

She pulled away from him and turned around. Her hands came up and slipped her dress off her shoulders and let it slide halfway down her back. The flesh of the shoulders were ribboned by long slashes that still were oozing blood.

She pulled the dress up again and turned to face him. She made a pleading gesture and pointed backward down the hill, in the direction of the field that ran down to the woods.

There was motion down there, someone coming through the woods, almost at the edge of the old deserted field.

She must have seen it, too, for she came close against him, shivering, seeking his protection.

He bent and lifted her in his arms and ran for the shed. He spoke the phrase and the door came open and he stepped into the station. Behind him he heard the door go sliding shut.

Once inside, he stood there, with Lucy Fisher cradled in his arms, and knew that what he'd done had been a great mistake – that it was something that, in a sober moment, he never would have done, that if he'd given it a second thought, he would not have done it.

But he had acted on an impulse, with no thought at all. The girl had asked protection and here she had protection, here nothing in the world ever could get at her. But she was a human being and no human being, other than himself, should have ever crossed the threshold.

But it was done and there was no way to change it. Once across the threshold, there was no way to change it.

He carried her across the room and put her on the sofa, then stepped back. She sat there, looking up at him, smiling very faintly, as if she did not know if she were allowed to smile in a place like this. She lifted a hand and tried to brush away the tears that were upon her cheeks.

She looked quickly around the room and her mouth made an O of wonder.

He squatted down and patted the sofa and shook a finger at her, hoping that she might understand that he meant she should stay there, that she must go nowhere else. He swept an arm in a motion to take in all the remainder of the station and shook his head as sternly as he could.

She watched him, fascinated, then she smiled and nodded, as if she might have understood.

He reached out and took one of her hands in his own, and holding it, patted it as gently as he could, trying to reassure her, to make her understand that everything was all right if she only stayed exactly where she was.

She was smiling now, not wondering, apparently, if there were any reason that she should not smile.

She reached out her free hand and made a little fluttering gesture toward the coffee table, with its load of alien gadgets.

He nodded and she picked up one of them, turning it admiringly in her hand.

He got to his feet and went to the wall to take down the rifle.

Then he went outside to face whatever had been pursuing her.

17

Two men were coming up the field towards the house and Enoch saw that one of them was Hank Fisher, Lucy's father. He had met the man, rather briefly, several years ago, on one of his walks. Hank had explained, rather sheepishly and when no explanation had been necessary, that he was hunting for a cow which had strayed away. But from his furtive manner, Enoch had deduced that his errand, rather than the hunting of a cow, had been somewhat on the shady side, although he could not imagine what it might have been.

The other man was younger. No more, perhaps, than sixteen or seventeen. More than likely, Enoch told himself, he was one of Lucy's brothers.

Enoch stood by the porch and waited.

Hank, he saw, was carrying a coiled whip in his hand, and looking at it, Enoch understood those wounds on Lucy's shoulders. He felt a swift flash of anger, but tried to fight it down. He could deal better with Hank Fisher if he kept his temper.

The two men stopped three paces or so away.

'Good afternoon,' said Enoch.

'You seen my gal?' asked Hank.

'And if I have?' asked Enoch.

'I'll take the hide off her,' yelled Hank, flourishing the whip.

'In such a case,' said Enoch, 'I don't believe I'll tell you anything.'

'You got her hid,' charged Hank.

'You can look around,' said Enoch.

Hank took a quick step forward, then thought better of it.

'She got what she had coming to her,' he yelled. 'And I ain't finished with her yet. There ain't no one, not even my own flesh and blood, can put a hex on me.'

Enoch said nothing. Hank stood, undecided.

'She meddled,' he said. 'She had no call to meddle. It was none of her damn' business.'

The young man said, 'I was just trying to train Butcher. Butcher,' he explained to Enoch, 'is a coon hound pup.'

'That is right,' said Hank. 'He wasn't doing nothing wrong. The boys caught a young coon the other night. Took a lot of doing. Roy, here, had staked out the coon – tied it to a tree. And he had Butcher on a leash. He was letting Butcher fight the coon. Not hurting anything. He'd pull Butcher off before

262

any damage could be done and let them rest a while. Then he'd let Butcher at the coon again.'

'It's the best way in the world,' said Roy, 'to get a coon dog trained.'

'That is right,' said Hank. 'That is why they caught the coon.'

'We needed it,' said Roy, 'to train this Butcher pup.'

'This all is fine,' said Enoch, 'and I am glad to hear it. But what has it got to do with Lucy?'

'She interfered,' said Hank. 'She tried to stop the training. She tried to grab Butcher away from Roy, here.'

'For a dummy,' Roy said, 'she is a mite too uppity.'

'You hush your mouth,' his father told him sternly, swinging around on him.

Roy mumbled to himself, falling back a step.

Hank turned back to Enoch.

'Roy knocked her down,' he said. 'He shouldn't have done that. He should have been more careful.'

'I didn't mean to,' Roy said. 'I just swung my arm out to keep her away from Butcher.'

'That is right,' said Hank. 'He swung a bit too hard. But there wasn't any call for her doing what she did. She tied Butcher up in knots so he couldn't fight that coon. Without laying a finger on him, mind you, she tied him up in knots. He couldn't move a muscle. That made Roy mad.'

He appealed to Enoch, earnestly, 'Wouldn't that have made you mad?'

'I don't think it would,' said Enoch. 'But then, I'm not a coon-dog man.'

Hank stared in wonder at this lack of understanding.

But he went on with his story. 'Roy got real mad at her. He'd raised that Butcher. He thought a lot of him. He wasn't going to let no one, not even his own sister, tie that dog in knots. So he went after her and she tied him up in knots, just like she did to Butcher. I never seen a thing like it in all my born days. Roy just stiffened up and then he fell down to the ground and his legs pulled up against his belly and he wrapped his arms around himself and he laid there on the ground, pulled into a ball. Him and Butcher, both. But she never touched that coon. She never tied him in no knots. Her own folks is all she touched.'

'It didn't hurt,' said Roy. 'It didn't hurt at all.'

'I was sitting there,' said Hank, 'braiding this here bull whip. Its end had frayed and I fixed a new one on it. And I seen it all, but I didn't do a thing until I saw Roy there, tied up on the ground. And I figured then it had gone far enough. I am a broad-minded man; I don't mind a little wart-charming and other piddling things like that. There have been a lot of people who have been able to do that. It ain't no disgrace at all. But this thing of tying dogs and people into knots …'

'So you hit her with the whip,' said Enoch.

'I did my duty,' Hank told him solemnly. 'I ain't about to have no witch in any family of mine. I hit her a couple of licks and her making that dumb show of hers to try to get me stopped. But I had my duty and I kept on hitting. If I did enough of it, I figured, I'd knock it out of her. That was when she put the hex on me. Just like she did on Roy and Butcher, but in a different way. She turned me blind – she blinded her own father! I couldn't see a thing. I just stumbled around the yard, yelling and clawing at my eyes. And then they got all right again, but she was gone. I saw her running through the woods and up the hill. So Roy and me, we took out after her.'

'And you think I have her here?'

'I know you have,' said Hank.

'O.K.,' said Enoch. 'Have a look around.'

'You can bet I will,' Hank told him grimly. 'Roy, take the barn. She might be hiding there.'

Roy headed for the barn. Hank went into the shed, came out almost immediately, strode down to the sagging chicken house.

Enoch stood and waited, the rifle cradled on his arm.

He had trouble here, he knew – more trouble than he'd ever had before. There was no such thing as reasoning with a man of Hank Fisher's stripe. There was no approach, right now, that he would understand. All that he could do, he knew, was to wait until Hank's temper had cooled off. Then there might be an outside chance of talking sense to him.

The two of them came back.

'She ain't nowhere around,' said Hank. 'She is in the house.'

Enoch shook his head. 'There can't anyone get into that house.'

'Roy,' said Hank, 'climb them there steps and open up that door.'

Roy looked fearfully at Enoch.

'Go ahead,' said Enoch.

Roy moved forward slowly and went up the steps. He crossed the porch and put his hand upon the front door knob and turned. He tried again. He turned around.

'Pa,' he said, 'I can't turn it. I can't get it open.'

'Hell,' said Hank, disgusted, 'you can't do anything.'

Hank took the steps in two jumps, paced wrathfully across the porch. His hand reached out and grasped the knob and wrenched at it powerfully. He tried again and yet again. He turned angrily to face Enoch.

'What is going on here?' he yelled.

'I told you,' Enoch said, 'that you can't get in.'

'The hell I can't!' roared Hank.

He tossed the whip to Roy and came down off the porch, striding over to the woodpile that stood beside the shed. He wrenched the heavy, double-bitted axe out of the chopping block. 'Careful with that axe,' warned Enoch. 'I've had it for a long time and I set store by it.'

Hank did not answer. He went up on the porch and squared off before the door.

'Stand off,' he said to Roy. 'Give me elbow room.'

Roy backed away.

'Wait a minute,' Enoch said. 'You mean to chop down that door?'

'You're damned right I do.'

Enoch nodded gravely.

'Well?' asked Hank.

'It's all right with me if you want to try.'

Hank took his stance, gripping the handle of the axe. The steel flashed swiftly, up over his shoulder, then down in a driven blow.

The edge of the steel struck the surface of the door and turned, deflected by the surface, changed its course, bouncing from the door. The blade came slicing down and back. It missed Hank's spraddled leg by no more than an inch and the momentum of it spun him half around.

He stood there, foolishly, arms outstretched, hands still gripping the handle of the axe. He stared at Enoch.

'Try again,' invited Enoch.

Rage flowed over Hank. His face was flushed with anger.

'By God, I will!' he yelled.

He squared off again and this time he swung the axe, not at the door, but at the window set beside the door.

The blade struck and there was a high singing sound as pieces of sun-bright steel went flying through the air.

Ducking away, Hank dropped the axe. It fell to the floor of the porch and bounced. One blade was broken, the metal sheared away in jagged breaks. The window was intact. There was not a scratch upon it.

Hank stood there for a moment, staring at the broken axe, as if he could not quite believe it.

Silently he stretched out his hand and Roy put the bull whip in it.

The two of them came down the stairs.

They stopped at the bottom of them and looked at Enoch. Hank's hand twitched on the whip.

'If I were you,' said Enoch, 'I wouldn't try it, Hank. I can move awfully fast.'

He patted the gun butt. 'I'd have the hand off you before you could swing that whip.'

Hank breathed heavily. 'There's the devil in you, Wallace,' he said. 'And there's the devil in her, too. You're working together, the two of you. Sneaking around in the woods, meeting one another.'

Enoch waited, watching the both of them.

'God help me,' cried Hank. 'My own daughter is a witch!'

'I think,' said Enoch, 'you should go back home. If I happen to find Lucy, I will bring her there.'

Neither of them made a move.

'You haven't heard the last of this,' yelled Hank. 'You have my daughter somewhere and I'll get you for it.'

'Any time you want,' said Enoch, 'but not now.'

He made an imperative gesture with the rifle barrel.

'Get moving,' he said. 'And don't come back. Either one of you.'

They hesitated for a moment, looking at him, trying to gauge him, trying to guess what he might do next.

Slowly they turned and, walking side by side, moved off down the hill.

18

He should have killed the two of them, he thought. They were not fit to live.

He glanced down at the rifle and saw that his hands had such a tense grip on the gun that his fingers stood out white and stiff against the satin brownness of the wood.

He gasped a little in his effort to fight down the rage that boiled inside him, trying to explode. If they had stayed here any longer, if he'd not run them off, he knew he'd have given in to that towering rage.

And it was better, much better, the way that it had been. He wondered a little dully how he had managed to hold in.

And was glad he had. For even as it stood, it would be bad enough.

They would say he was a madman; that he had run them off at gunpoint. They might even say that he had kidnapped Lucy and was holding her against her will. They would stop at nothing to make him all the trouble that they could.

He had no illusions about what they might do, for he knew the breed, vindictive in their smallness – little vicious insects of the human race.

He stood beside the porch and watched them down the hill wondering how a girl so fine as Lucy could spring from such decadent stock. Perhaps her handicap had served as a bulwark against the kind of folks they were; had kept her from becoming another one of them. Perhaps if she could have talked with them or listened, she would in time have become as shiftless and as vicious as any one of them.

It had been a great mistake to get mixed up in a thing like this. A man in his position had no business in an involvement such as this. He had too much to lose; he should have stood aside.

And yet what could he have done? Could he have refused to give Lucy his protection, with the blood soaking through her dress from the lashes that lay across her shoulders? Should he have ignored the frantic, helpless pleading in her face?

He might have done it differently, he thought. There might have been other, smarter ways in which to handle it. But there had been no time to think of any smarter way. There only had been time to carry her to safety and then go outside to meet them.

And now that he thought of it, perhaps the best thing would have been not to go outside at all. If he'd stayed inside the station, nothing would have happened.

It had been impulsive, that going out to face them. It had been, perhaps, the human thing to do, but it had not been wise. But he had done it and it was over now and there was no turning back. If he had it to do again, he would do it differently, but you got no second chance.

He turned heavily around and went back inside the station.

Lucy was still sitting on the sofa and she held a flashing object in her hand. She was staring at it raptly and there was in her face again that same vibrant and alert expression he had seen that morning when she'd held the butterfly.

He laid the rifle on the desk and stood quietly there, but she must have caught the motion of him, for she looked quickly up. And then her eyes once more went back to the flashing thing she was holding in her hands.

He saw that it was the pyramid of spheres and now all the spheres were spinning slowly, in alternating clockwise and counterclockwise motions, and that as they spun they shone and glittered, each in its own particular colour, as if there might be, deep inside each one of them, a source of soft, warm light.

Enoch caught his breath at the beauty and the wonder of it – the old, hard wonder of what this thing might be and what it might be meant to do. He had examined it a hundred times or more and had puzzled at it and there had been nothing he could find that was of significance. So far as he could see, it was only something that was meant to be looked at, although there had been that persistent feeling that it had a purpose and that, perhaps, somehow, it was meant to operate.

And now it was in operation. He had tried a hundred times to get it figured out and Lucy had picked it up just once and had got it figured out.

He noticed the rapture with which she was regarding it. Was it possible, he wondered, that she knew its purpose?

He went across the room and touched her arm and she lifted her face to look at him and in her eyes he saw the gleam of happiness and excitement.

He made a questioning gesture towards the pyramid, trying to ask if she knew what it might be. But she did not understand him. Or perhaps she knew, but knew as well how impossible it would be to explain its purpose. She made that happy, fluttery motion with her hand again, indicating the table with its load of gadgets and she seemed to try to laugh – there was, at least, a sense of laughter in her face.

Just a kid, Enoch told himself, with a box heaped high with new and wondrous toys. Was that all it was to her? Was she happy and excited merely because she suddenly had become aware of all the beauty and the novelty of the things stacked there on the table?

He turned wearily and went back to the desk. He picked up the rifle and hung it on the pegs.

She should not be in the station. No human being other than himself should ever be inside the station. Bringing her here, he had broken that unspoken understanding he had with the aliens who had installed him as a keeper. Although, of all the humans he could have brought, Lucy was the one who could possibly be exempt from the understood restriction. For she could never tell of the things that she had seen.

She could not remain, he knew. She must be taken home. For if she were not taken, there would be a massive hunt for her, a lost girl – a beautiful deaf-mute.

A story of a missing deaf-mute girl would bring in newspapermen in a day or two. It would be in all the papers and on television and on radio and the woods would be swarming with hundreds of searchers.

Hank Fisher would tell how he'd tried to break into the house and couldn't and there'd be others who would try to break into the house and there'd be hell to pay.

Enoch sweated, thinking of it.

All the years of keeping out of people's way, all the years of being unobtrusive would be for nothing then. This strange house upon a lonely ridge would become a mystery for the world, and a challenge and a target for all the crackpots of the world.

He went to the medicine cabinet, to get the healing ointment that had been included in the drug packet provided by Galactic Central.

He found it and opened the little box. More than half of it remained. He'd used it through the years, but sparingly. There was, in fact, little need to use a great deal of it.

He went across the room to where Lucy sat and stood back of the sofa. He showed her what he had and made motions to show her what it was for. She slid her dress off her shoulders and he bent to look at the slashes.

The bleeding had stopped, but the flesh was red and angry.

Gently he rubbed ointment into the stripes that the whip had made.

She had healed the butterfly, he thought; but she could not heal herself.

On the table in front of her the pyramid of spheres still was flashing and glinting, throwing a flickering shadow of colour all about the room.

It was operating, but what could it be doing?

It was finally operating, but not a thing was happening as a result of that operation.

19

Ulysses came as twilight was deepening into night. Enoch and Lucy had just finished with their supper and were sitting at the table when Enoch heard his footsteps.

The alien stood in shadow and he looked, Enoch thought, more than ever like the cruel clown. His lithe, flowing body had the look of smoked, tanned buckskin. The patchwork colour of his hide seemed to shine with a faint luminescence and the sharp, hard angles of his face, the smooth baldness of his head, the flat, pointed ears pasted tight against the skull lent him a vicious fearsomeness.

If one did not know him for the gentle character that he was, Enoch told himself, he would be enough to scare a man out of seven years of growth.

'We had been expecting you,' said Enoch. 'The coffee pot is boiling.'

Ulysses took a slow step forward, then paused.

'You have another with you. A human, I would say.'

'There is no danger,' Enoch told him.

'Of another gender. A female, is it not? You have found a mate?'

'No,' said Enoch. 'She is not my mate.'

'You have acted wisely through the years,' Ulysses told him. 'In a position such as yours, a mate is not the best.'

'You need not worry. There is a malady upon her. She has no communication. She can neither hear nor speak.'

'A malady?'

'Yes, from the moment she was born. She has never heard or spoken. She can tell of nothing here.'

'Sign language?'

'She knows no sign language. She refused to learn it.'

'She is a friend of yours.'

'For some years,' said Enoch. 'She came seeking my protection. Her father used a whip to beat her.'

'This father knows she's here?'

'He thinks she is, but he cannot know.'

Ulysses came slowly out of the darkness and stood within the light.

Lucy was watching him, but there was no terror on her face. Her eyes were level and untroubled and she did not flinch.

'She takes me well,' Ulysses said. 'She does not run or scream.'

'She could not scream,' said Enoch, 'even if she wished.'

'I must be most repugnant,' Ulysses said, 'at first sight to any human.'

'She does not see the outside only. She sees inside of you as well.'

'Would she be frightened if I made a human bow to her?'

'I think,' said Enoch, 'she might be very pleased.'

Ulysses made his bow, formal and exaggerated, with one hand upon his leathery belly, bowing from the waist.

Lucy smiled and clapped her hands.

'You see,' Ulysses cried, delighted, 'I think that she may like me.'

'Why don't you sit down, then,' suggested Enoch, 'and we all will have some coffee.'

'I had forgotten of the coffee. The sight of this other human drove coffee from my mind.'

He sat down at the place where the third cup had been set and waiting for him. Enoch started around the table, but Lucy rose and went to get the coffee.

'She understands?' Ulysses asked.

Enoch shook his head. 'You sat down by the cup and the cup was empty.'

She poured the coffee, then went over to the sofa.

'She will not stay with us?' Ulysses asked.

'She's intrigued by that tableful of trinkets. She set one of them to going.'

'You plan to keep her here?'

'I can't keep her,' Enoch said. 'There'll be a hunt for her. I'll have to take her home.'

'I do not like it,' Ulysses said.

'Nor do I. Let's admit at once that I should not have brought her here. But at the time it seemed the only thing to do. I had no time to think it out.'

'You've done no wrong,' said Ulysses softly.

'She cannot harm us,' said Enoch. 'Without communication ...'

'It's not that,' Ulysses told him. 'She's just a complication and I do not like further complications. I came tonight to tell you, Enoch, that we are in trouble.'

'Trouble? But there's not been any trouble.'

Ulysses lifted his coffee cup and took a long drink of it.

'That is good,' he said. 'I carry back the bean and make it at my home. But it does not taste the same.'

'This trouble?'

'You remember the Vegan that died here several of your years ago.'

Enoch nodded. 'The Hazer.'

'The being has a proper name ...'

Enoch laughed. 'You don't like our nicknames.'

'It is not our way,' Ulysses said.

'My name for them,' said Enoch, 'is a mark of my affection,'

'You buried this Vegan.'

'In my family plot,' said Enoch. 'As if he were my own. I read a verse above him.'

'That is well and good,' Ulysses said. 'That is as it should be. You did very well. But the body's gone.'

'Gone! It can't be gone!' cried Enoch.

'It has been taken from the grave.'

'But you can't know,' protested Enoch. 'How could you know?'

'Not I. It's the Vegans. The Vegans are the ones who know.'

'But they're light years distant ...'

And then he was not too sure. For on that night the wise old one had died and he'd messaged Galactic Central, he had been told that the Vegans had known the moment he had died. And there had been no need for a death certificate, for they knew of what he died.

It seemed impossible, of course, but there were too many impossibilities in the galaxy which turned out, after all, to be entirely possible for a man to ever know when he stood on solid ground.

Was it possible, he wondered, that each Vegan had some sort of mental contact with every other Vegan? Or that some central census bureau (to give a human designation to something that was scarcely understandable) might have some sort of official linkage with every living Vegan, knowing where it was and how it was and what it might be doing?

Something of the sort, Enoch admitted, might indeed be possible. It was not beyond the astounding capabilities that one found on every hand throughout the galaxy. But to maintain a similar contact with the Vegan dead was something else again.

'The body's gone,' Ulysses said. 'I can tell you that and know it is the truth. You're held accountable.'

'By the Vegans?'

'By the Vegans, yes. And the galaxy.'

'I did what I could,' said Enoch hotly. 'I did what was required. I filled the letter of the Vegan law. I paid the dead my honour and the honour of my planet. It is not right that the responsibility should go on for ever. Not that I can believe the body can be really gone. There is no one who would take it. No one who knew of it.'

'By human logic,' Ulysses told him, 'you, of course, are right. But not by Vegan logic. And in this case Galactic Central would tend to support the Vegans.'

'The Vegans,' Enoch said testily, 'happen to be friends of mine. I have never met a one of them that I didn't like or couldn't get along with. I can work it out with them.'

'If only the Vegans were concerned,' said Ulysses, 'I am quite sure you could. I would have no worry. But the situation gets complicated as you go along. On the surface it seems a rather simple happening, but there are many factors. The Vegans, for example, have known for some time that the body had been taken and they were disturbed, of course. But out of certain considerations, they had kept their silence.'

'They needn't have. They could have come to me. I don't know what could have been done …'

'Silent not because of you. Because of something else.'

Ulysses finished off his coffee and poured himself another cup. He filled Enoch's half-filled cup and set the pot aside.

Enoch waited.

'You may not have been aware of it,' said Ulysses, 'but at the time this station was established, there was considerable opposition to it from a number of races in the galaxy. There were many reasons cited, as is the case in all such situations, but the underlying reason, when you get down to basics, rests squarely on the continual contest for racial or regional advantage. A situation akin, I would imagine, to the continual bickering and manœuvring which you find here upon the Earth to gain an economic advantage for one group or another, or one nation and another. In the galaxy, of course, the economic considerations only occasionally are the underlying factors. There are many factors other than the economic.'

Enoch nodded. 'I had gained a hint of this. Nothing recently. But I hadn't paid too much attention to it.'

'It's largely a matter of direction,' Ulysses said. 'When Galactic Central began its expansion into this spiral arm, it meant there was no time or effort available for expansions in other directions. There is one large group of races which has held a dream for many centuries of expanding into some of the near-by globular clusters. It does make a dim sort of sense, of course. With the techniques that we have, the longer jump across space to some of the closer clusters is entirely possible. Another thing – the clusters seem to be extraordinarily free of dust and gas, so that once we got there we could expand more rapidly throughout the cluster than we can in many parts of the galaxy. But at best, it's a speculative business, for we don't know what we'll find there. After we've made all the effort and spent all the time we may find little or nothing, except possibly some more real estate. And we have plenty of that in the galaxy. But the clusters have a vast appeal for certain types of minds.'

Enoch nodded. 'I can see that. It would be the first venturing out of the galaxy itself. It might be the first short step on the route that could lead us to other galaxies.'

Ulysses peered at him. 'You, too,' he said. 'I might have known.'

Enoch said smugly: 'I am that type of mind.'

'Well, anyhow, there was this globular-cluster faction – I suppose you'd call it that – which contended bitterly when we began our move in this direction. You understand – certainly you do – that we've barely begun the expansion into this neighbourhood. We have less than a dozen stations and we'll need a hundred. It will take centuries before the network is complete.'

'So this faction is still contending,' Enoch said. 'There still is time to stop this spiral-arm project.'

'That is right. And that's what worries me. For the faction is set to use this incident of the missing body as an emotion-charged argument against the extension of this network. It is being joined by other groups that are concerned with certain special interests. And these special interest groups see a better chance of getting what they want if they can wreck this project.'

'Wreck it?'

'Yes, wreck it. They will start screaming, as soon as the body incident becomes open knowledge, that a planet so barbaric as the Earth is no fit location for a station. They will insist that this station be abandoned.'

'But they can't do that!'

'They can,' Ulysses said. 'They will say it is degrading and unsafe to maintain a station so barbaric that even graves are rifled, on a planet where the honoured dead cannot rest in peace. It is the kind of highly emotional argument that will gain wide acceptance and support in some sections of the galaxy. The Vegans tried their best. They tried to hush it up, for the sake of the project. They have never done a thing like that before. They are a proud people and they feel a slight to honour – perhaps more deeply than many other races – and yet, for the greater good, they were willing to accept dishonour. And would have if they could have kept it quiet. But the story leaked out somehow – by good espionage, no doubt. And they cannot stand the loss of face in advertised dishonour. The Vegan who will be arriving here this evening is an official representative charged with delivering an official protest.'

'To me?'

'To you, and through you, to the Earth.'

'But the Earth is not concerned. The Earth doesn't even know.'

'Of course it doesn't. So far as Galactic Central is concerned, you are the Earth. You represent the Earth.'

Enoch shook his head. It was a crazy way of thinking. But, he told himself, he should not be surprised. It was the kind of thinking he should have expected. He was too hidebound, he thought, too narrow. He had been trained in the human way of thinking and, even after all these years, that way of thought persisted. Persisted to a point where any way of thought that conflicted with it must automatically seem wrong.

This talk of abandoning Earth station was wrong, too. It made no sort of sense. For abandoning the station would not wreck the project. Although, more than likely, it would wreck whatever hope he'd held for the human race.

'But even if you have to abandon Earth,' he said, 'you could go out to Mars. You could build a station there. If it's necessary to have a station in this solar system there are other planets.'

'You don't understand,' Ulysses told him. 'This station is just one point of attack. It is no more than a toehold, just a bare beginning. The aim is to wreck the project, to free the time and effort that is expended here for some other project. If they can force us to abandon one station, then we stand discredited. Then all our motives and our judgement come up for review.'

'But even if the project should be wrecked,' Enoch pointed out, 'there is no surety that any group would gain. It would only throw the question of where the time and energy should be used into an open debate. You say that there are many special interest factions banding together to carry on the fight against us. Suppose that they do win. Then they must turn around and start fighting among themselves.'

'Of course that's the case,' Ulysses admitted, 'but then each of them has a chance to get what they want, or think they have a chance. The way it is they have no chance at all. Before any of them has a chance this project must go down the drain. There is one group on the far side of the galaxy that wants to move out into the thinly populated sections of one particular section of the rim. They still believe in an ancient legend which says that their race arose as the result of immigrants from another galaxy who landed on the rim and worked their way inward over many galactic years. They think that if they can get out to the rim they can turn that legend into history to their greater glory. Another group wants to go into a small spiral arm because of an obscure record that many eons ago their ancestors picked up some virtually undecipherable messages which they believed came from that direction. Through the years the story has grown, until today they are convinced a race of intellectual giants will be found in that spiral arm. And there is always the pressure, naturally, to probe deeper into the galactic core. You must realize that we have only started, that the galaxy still is largely unexplored, that the thousands of races who form Galactic Central still are pioneers. And as a result, Galactic Central is continually subjected to all sorts of pressures.'

'You sound,' said Enoch, 'as if you have little hope of maintaining this station, here on Earth.'

'Almost no hope at all,' Ulysses told him. 'But so far as you yourself are concerned, there will be an option. You can stay here and live out an ordinary life on Earth or you can be assigned to another station. Galactic Central hopes that you would elect to continue on with us.'

'That sounds pretty final.'

'I am afraid,' Ulysses said, 'it is. I am sorry, Enoch, to be the bearer of bad news.'

Enoch sat numb and stricken. Bad news! It was worse than that. It was the end of everything.

He sensed the crashing down of not only his own personal world, but of all the hopes of Earth. With the station gone, Earth once more would be left in the backwaters of the galaxy, with no hope of help, no chance of recognition, no realization of what lay waiting in the galaxy. Standing alone and naked, the human race would go on in its same old path, fumbling its uncertain way towards a blind, mad future.

20

The Hazer was elderly. The golden haze that enveloped him had lost the sparkle of its youthfulness. It was a mellow glow, deep and rich – not the blinding haze of a younger being. He carried himself with a solid dignity, and the flaring topknot that was neither hair nor feathers was white, a sort of saintly whiteness. His face was soft and tender, the softness and the tenderness which in a man might have been expressed in kindly wrinkles.

'I am sorry,' he told Enoch, 'that our meeting must be such as this. Although, under any circumstances, I am glad to meet you. I have heard of you. It is not often that a being of an outside planet is the keeper of a station. Because of this, young being, I have been intrigued with you. I have wondered what sort of creature you might turn out to be.'

'You need have no apprehension of him,' Ulysses said, a little sharply. 'I will vouch for him. We have been friends for years.'

'Yes, I forgot,' the Hazer said. 'You are his discoverer.'

He peered around the room. 'Another one,' he said. 'I did not know there were two of them. I only knew of one.'

'It's a friend of Enoch's,' Ulysses said.

'There has been contact, then. Contact with the planet.'

'No, there has been no contact.'

'Perhaps an indiscretion.'

'Perhaps,' Ulysses said, 'but under provocation that I doubt either you or I could have stood against.'

Lucy had risen to her feet and now she came across the room, moving quietly and slowly, as if she might be floating.

The Hazer spoke to her in the common tongue. 'I am glad to meet you. Very glad to meet you.'

'She cannot speak,' Ulysses said. 'Nor hear. She has no communication.'

'Compensation,' said the Hazer.

'You think so?' asked Ulysses.

'I am sure of it.'

He walked slowly forward and Lucy waited.

'It – she, the female form, you called it – she is not afraid.'

Ulysses chuckled. 'Not even. Of me,' he said.

The Hazer reached out his hand to her and she stood quietly for a moment, then one of her hands came up and took the Hazer's fingers, more like tentacles than fingers, in its grasp.

It seemed to Enoch, for a moment, that the cloak of golden haze reached out to wrap the Earth girl in its glow. Enoch blinked his eyes and the illusion, if it had been illusion, was swept away, and it only was the Hazer who had the golden cloak.

And how was it, Enoch wondered, that there was no fear in her, either of Ulysses or the Hazer? Was it because, in truth, as he had said, she could see beyond the outward guise, could somehow sense the basic humanity (God help me, I cannot think, even now, except in human terms!) that was in these creatures? And if that were true, was it because she herself was not entirely human? A human, certainly, in form and origin, but not formed and moulded into the human culture – being, perhaps, what a human would be if he were not hemmed about so closely by the rules of behaviour and outlook that through the years had hardened into law to comprise a common human attitude.

Lucy dropped the Hazer's hand and went back to the sofa.

The Hazer said, 'Enoch Wallace.'

'Yes.'

'She is of your race?'

'Yes, of course she is.'

'She is most unlike you. Almost as if there were two races.'

'There is not two races. There is only one.'

'Are there many others like her?'

'I would not know,' said Enoch.

'Coffee,' said Ulysses to the Hazer. 'Would you like some coffee?'

'Coffee?'

'A most delicious brew. Earth's one great accomplishment.'

'I am not acquainted with it,' said the Hazer. 'I don't believe I will.'

He turned ponderously to Enoch.

'You know why I am here?' he asked.

'I believe so.'

'It is a matter I regret,' said the Hazer. 'But I must ...'

'If you'd rather,' Enoch said, 'we can consider that the protest has been made. I would so stipulate.'

'Why not?' Ulysses said. 'There is no need, it seems to me, to have the three of us go through a somewhat painful scene.'

The Hazer hesitated.

'If you feel you must,' said Enoch.

'No,' the Hazer said. 'I am satisfied if an unspoken protest be generously accepted.'

'Accepted,' Enoch said, 'on just one condition. That I satisfy myself that the charge is not unfounded. I must go out and see.'

'You do not believe me?'

'It is not a matter of belief. It is something that can be checked. I cannot accept either for myself or for my planet until I have done that much.'

'Enoch,' Ulysses said, 'the Vegan has been gracious. Not only now, but before this happened. His race presses the charge most reluctantly. They suffered much to protect the Earth and you.'

'And the feeling is that I would be ungracious if I did not accept the protest and the charge on the Vegan statement.'

'I am sorry, Enoch,' said Ulysses. 'That is what I mean.'

Enoch shook his head. 'For years I've tried to understand and to conform to the ethics and ideas of all the people who have come through this station. I've pushed my own human instincts and training to one side. I've tried to understand other viewpoints and to evaluate other ways of thinking, many of which did violence to my own. I am glad of all of it, for it has given me a chance to go beyond the narrowness of Earth. I think I gained something from it all. But none of this touched Earth; only myself was involved. This business touches Earth and I must approach it from an Earthman's viewpoint. In this particular instance I am not simply the keeper of a galactic station.'

Neither of them said a word. Enoch stood waiting and still there was nothing said.

Finally he turned and headed for the door.

'I'll be back,' he told them.

He spoke the phrase and the door started to slide open.

'If you'll have me,' said the Hazer quietly, 'I'd like to go with you.'

'Fine,' said Enoch. 'Come ahead.'

It was dark outside and Enoch lit the lantern. The Hazer watched him closely.

'Fossil fuel,' Enoch told him. 'It burns at the tip of a saturated wick.'

The Hazer said, in horror, 'But surely you have better.'

'Much better now,' said Enoch. 'I am just old-fashioned.'

He led the way outside, the lantern throwing a small pool of light. The Hazer followed.

'It is a wild planet,' said the Hazer.

'Wild here. There are parts of it that are tame.'

'My own planet is controlled,' the Hazer said. 'Every foot of it is planned.'

'I know. I have talked to many Vegans. They described the planet to me.'

They headed for the barn.

'You want to go back?' asked Enoch.

'No,' said the Hazer. 'I find it exhilarating. Those are wild plants over there?'

'We call them trees,' said Enoch.

'The wind blows as it wishes?'

'That's right,' said Enoch. 'We do not know as yet how to control the weather.'

The spade stood just inside the barn door and Enoch picked it up. He headed for the orchard.

'You know, of course,' the Hazer said, 'the body will be gone.'

'I'm prepared to find it gone.'

'Then why?' the Hazer asked.

'Because I must be sure. You can't understand that, can you?'

'You said back there in the station,' the Hazer said, 'that you tried to understand the rest of us. Perhaps, for a change, at least one of us should try understanding you.'

Enoch led the way down the path through the orchard. They came to the rude fence enclosing the burial plot. The sagging gate stood open. Enoch went through it and the Hazer followed.

'This is where you buried him?'

'This is my family plot. My mother and my father are here and I put him with them.'

He handed the lantern to the Vegan and, armed with the spade, walked up to the grave. He thrust the spade into the ground.

'Would you hold the lantern a little closer, please?'

The Hazer moved up a step or two.

Enoch dropped to his knees and brushed away the leaves that had fallen on the ground. Underneath them was the soft, fresh earth that had been newly turned. There was a depression and a small hole at the bottom of the depression. As he brushed at the earth, he could hear the clods of displaced dirt falling through the hole and striking on something that was not the soil.

The Hazer had moved the lantern again and he could not see. But he did not need to see. He knew there was no use of digging; he knew what he would find. He should have kept a watch. He should not have put up the stone to attract attention – but Galactic Central had said, 'As if he were your own'. And that was the way he'd done it.

He straightened, but remained upon his knees, felt the damp of the earth soaking through the fabric of his trousers.

'No one told me,' said the Hazer, speaking softly.

'Told you what?'

'The memorial. And what is written on it. I was not aware that you knew our language.'

'I learned it long ago. There were scrolls I wished to read. I'm afraid it's not too good.'

'Two misspelled words,' the Hazer told him, 'and one little awkwardness. But those are things which do not matter. What matters, and matters very much, is that when you wrote, you thought as one of us.'

Enoch rose and reached out for the lantern.

'Let's go back,' he said sharply, almost impatiently. 'I know now who did this. I have to hunt him out.'

21

The treetops far above moaned in the rising wind. Ahead, the great clump of canoe birch showed whitely in the dim glow of the lantern's light. The birch clump, Enoch knew, grew on the lip of a small cliff that dropped twenty feet or more and here one turned to the right to get around it and continue down the hillside.

Enoch turned slightly and glanced over his shoulder. Lucy was following close behind. She smiled at him and made a gesture to say she was all right. He made a motion to indicate that they must turn to the right, that she must follow closely. Although, he told himself, it probably wasn't necessary; she knew the hillside as well, perhaps even better, than he did himself.

He turned to the right and followed along the edge of the rocky cliff, came to the break and clambered down to reach the slope below. Off to the left he could hear the murmur of the swiftly running creek that tumbled down the rocky ravine from the spring below the field.

The hillside plunged more steeply now and he led a way that angled across the steepness.

Funny, he thought, that even in the darkness he could recognize certain natural features – the crooked white oak that twisted itself, hanging at a crazy angle above the slope of hill; the small grove of massive red oaks that grew out of a dome of tumbled rock, so placed that no axeman had even tried to cut them down; the tiny swamp, filled with cattails, that fitted itself snugly into a little terrace carved into the hillside.

Far below he caught the gleam of window light and angled down towards it. He looked back over his shoulder and Lucy was following close behind.

They came to a rude fence of poles and crawled through it and now the ground became more level.

Somewhere below a dog barked in the dark and another joined him. More joined in and the pack came sweeping up the slope towards them. They arrived in a rush of feet, veered around Enoch and the lantern to launch themselves at Lucy – suddenly transformed, at the sight of her, into a welcoming committee rather than a company of guards. They reared upward, a tangled mass of dogs. Her hands went out and patted at their heads. As if by signal, they went rushing off in a happy frolic, circling to come back again.

A short distance beyond the pole fence was a vegetable garden and Enoch led the way across, carefully following a path between the rows. Then they were in the yard and the house stood before them, a tumble-down, sagging structure, its outlines swallowed by the darkness, the kitchen windows glowing with a soft, warm lamplight.

Enoch crossed the yard to the kitchen door and knocked. He heard feet coming across the kitchen floor.

The door came open and Ma Fisher stood framed against the light, a great, tall, bony woman clothed in something that was more sack than dress.

She stared at Enoch, half frightened, half belligerent. Then, back of him, she saw the girl.

'Lucy!' she cried.

The girl came forward with a rush and her mother caught her in her arms.

Enoch set his lantern on the ground, tucked the rifle underneath his arm, and stepped across the threshold.

The family had been at supper, seated about a great round table set in the centre of the kitchen. An ornate oil lamp stood in the centre of the table. Hank had risen to his feet, but his three sons and the stranger still were seated.

'So you brung her back,' said Hank.

'I found her,' Enoch said.

'We quit hunting for her just a while ago,' Hank told him. 'We was going out again.'

'You remember what you told me this afternoon?' asked Enoch.

'I told you a lot of things.'

'You told me that I had the devil in me. Raise your hand against that girl once more and I promise you I'll show you just how much devil there is in me.'

'You can't bluff me,' Hank blustered.

But the man was frightened. It showed in the limpness of his face, the tightness of his body.

'I mean it,' Enoch said. 'Just try me out and see.'

The two men stood for a moment, facing one another, then Hank sat down.

'Would you join us in some victuals?' he inquired.

Enoch shook his head.

He looked at the stranger. 'Are you the ginseng man?' he asked.

The man nodded. 'That is what they call me.'

'I want to talk with you. Outside.'

Claude Lewis stood up.

'You don't have to go,' said Hank. 'He can't make you go. He can talk to you right here.'

'I don't mind,' said Lewis. 'In fact, I want to talk with him. You're Enoch Wallace, aren't you?'

'That's who he is,' said Hank. 'Should of died of old age fifty years ago. But look at him. He's got the devil in him. I tell you, him and the devil has a deal.'

'Hank,' Lewis said, 'shut up.'

Lewis came around the table and went out the door.

'Good night,' Enoch said to the rest of them.

'Mr Wallace,' said Ma Fisher, 'thanks for bringing back my girl. Hank won't hit her again. I can promise you. I'll see to that.'

Enoch went outside and shut the door. He picked up the lantern. Lewis was out in the yard. Enoch went to him.

'Let's walk off a ways,' he said.

They stopped at the edge of the garden and turned to face one another.

'You been watching me,' said Enoch.

Lewis nodded.

'Official? Or just snooping?'

'Official, I'm afraid. My name is Claude Lewis. There is no reason I shouldn't tell you – I'm C.I.A.'

'I'm not a traitor or a spy,' Enoch said.

'No one thinks you are. We're just watching you.'

'You know about the cemetery?'

Lewis nodded.

'You took something from a grave.'

'Yes,' said Lewis. 'The one with the funny headstone.'

'Where is it?'

'You mean the body. It's in Washington.'

'You shouldn't have taken it,' Enoch said, grimly. 'You've caused a lot of trouble. You have to get it back. As quickly as you can.'

'It will take a little time,' said Lewis. 'They'll have to fly it out. Twenty-four hours, maybe.'

'That's the fastest you can make it?'

'I might do a little better.'

'Do the very best you can. It's important that you get that body back.'

'I will, Wallace. I didn't know ...'

'And, Lewis.'

'Yes.'

'Don't try to play it smart. Don't add any frills. Just do what I tell you. I'm trying to be reasonable because that's the only thing to be. But you try one smart move ...'

He reached out a hand and grabbed Lewis' shirt front, twisting the fabric tight.

'You understand me, Lewis?'

Lewis was unmoved. He did not try to pull away.

'Yes,' he said. 'I understand.'

'What the hell ever made you do it?'

'I had a job.'

'Yeah, a job. Watching me. Not robbing graves.'

He let loose of the shirt.

'Tell me,' said Lewis, 'that thing in the grave. What was it?'

'That's none of your damn' business,' Enoch told him, bitterly. 'Getting back that body is. You're sure that you can do it? Nothing standing in your way?'

Lewis shook his head. 'Nothing at all. I'll phone as soon as I can reach a phone. I'll tell them that it's imperative.'

'It's all of that,' said Enoch. 'Getting that body back is the most important thing you've ever done. Don't forget that for a minute. It affects everyone on Earth. You and me and everyone. And if you fail, you'll answer to me for it.'

'With that gun?'

'Maybe,' Enoch said. 'Don't fool around. Don't imagine that I'd hesitate to kill you. In this situation, I'd kill anyone – anyone at all.'

'Wallace, is there something you can tell me?'

'Not a thing,' said Enoch.

He picked up the lantern.

'You're going home?'

Enoch nodded.

'You don't seem to mind us watching you.'

'No,' Enoch told him. 'Not your watching. Just your interference. Bring back that body and go on watching if you want to. But don't push me any. Don't lean on me. Keep your hands off. Don't touch anything.'

'But good God, man, there's something going on. You can tell me something.'

Enoch hesitated.

'Some idea,' said Lewis, 'of what this is all about. Not the details, just …'

'You bring the body back,' Enoch told him, slowly, 'and maybe we can talk again.'

'It will be back,' said Lewis.

'If it's not,' said Enoch, 'you're as good as dead right now.'

Turning, he went across the garden and started up the hill.

In the yard, Lewis stood for a long time, watching the lantern bobbing out of sight.

22

Ulysses was alone in the station when Enoch returned. He had sent the Thuban on his way and the Hazer back to Vega.

A fresh pot of coffee was brewing and Ulysses was sprawled out on the
sofa, doing nothing.

Enoch hung up the rifle and blew out the lantern. Taking off his jacket, he
threw it on the desk. He sat down in a chair across from the sofa.

'The body will be back,' he said, 'by this time tomorrow.'

'I sincerely hope,' Ulysses said, 'that it will do some good. But I'm inclined
to doubt it.'

'Maybe,' said Enoch bitterly, 'I should not have bothered.'

'It will show good faith,' Ulysses said. 'It might have some mitigating effect
in the final weighing.'

'The Hazer could have told me,' Enoch said, 'where the body was. If he
knew it had been taken from the grave, then he must have known where it
could be found.'

'I would suspect he did,' Ulysses said, 'but, you see, he couldn't tell you. All
that he could do was to make his protest. The rest was up to you. He could
not lay aside his dignity by suggesting what you should do about it. For the
record, he must remain the injured party.'

'Sometimes,' said Enoch, 'this business is enough to drive one crazy. Despite the briefings from Galactic Central, there are always some surprises,
always yawning traps for you to tumble into.'

'There may come a day,' Ulysses said, 'when it won't be like that. I can look
ahead and see, in some thousands of years, the knitting of the galaxy together
into one great culture, one huge area of understanding. The local and the
racial variations still will exist, of course, and that is as it should be, but overriding all of these will be a tolerance that will make for what one might be
tempted to call a brotherhood.'

'You sound,' said Enoch, 'almost like a human. That is the sort of hope that
many of our thinkers have held out.'

'Perhaps,' Ulysses said. 'You know that a lot of Earth seems to have rubbed
off on me. You can't spend as long as I did on your planet without picking up
at least a bit of it. And by the way, you made a good impression on the Vegan.'

'I hadn't noticed it,' Enoch told him. 'He was kind and correct, of course,
but little more.'

'That inscription on the gravestone. He was impressed by that.'

'I didn't put it there to impress anyone. I wrote it out because it was the way I felt. And because I like the Hazers. I was only trying to make it right for them.'

'If it were not for the pressure from the galactic factions,' Ulysses said, 'I am convinced the Vegans would be willing to forget the incident and that is a greater concession than you can realize. It may be that, even so, they may line up with us when the showdown comes.'

'You mean they might save the station?'

Ulysses shook his head. 'I doubt anyone can do that. But it will be easier for all of us at Galactic Central if they threw their weight with us.'

The coffee-pot was making sounds and Enoch went to get it. Ulysses had pushed some of the trinkets on the coffee table to one side to make room for two coffee cups. Enoch filled them and set the pot upon the floor.

Ulysses picked up his cup, held it for a moment in his hands, then put it back on the table top.

'We're in bad shape,' he said. 'Not like in the old days. It has Galactic Central worried. All this squabbling and haggling among the races, all the pushing and the shoving.'

He looked at Enoch. 'You thought it was all nice and cosy.'

'No,' said Enoch, 'not that. I knew that there were conflicting viewpoints and I knew there was some trouble. But I'm afraid I thought of it as being on a fairly lofty plane – gentlemanly, you know, and good-mannered.'

'That was the way it was at one time. There always have been differing opinions, but they were based on principles and ethics, not on special interests. You know about the spiritual force, of course – the universal spiritual force.'

Enoch nodded. 'I've read some of the literature. I don't quite understand, but I'm willing to accept it. There is a way, I know, to get in contact with the force.'

'The Talisman,' said Ulysses.

'That's it. The Talisman. A machine, of sorts.'

'I suppose,' Ulysses agreed, 'you could call it that. Although the word, "machine", is a little awkward. More than mechanics went into the making of it. There is just the one. Only one was ever made, by a mystic who lived ten thousand of your years ago. I wish I could tell you what it is or how it is constructed, but there is no one, I am afraid, who can tell you that. There have been others who have attempted to duplicate the Talisman, but no one has succeeded. The mystic who made it left no blueprints, no plans, no specifications, not a single note. There is no one who knows anything about it.'

'There is no reason, I suppose,' said Enoch, 'that another should not be made. No sacred taboos, I mean. To make another one would not be sacrilegious.'

'Not in the least,' Ulysses told him. 'In fact, we need another badly. For now we have no Talisman. It has disappeared.'

Enoch jerked upright in his chair.

'Disappeared?' he asked.

'Lost,' said Ulysses. 'Misplaced. Stolen. No one knows.'

'But I hadn't ...'

Ulysses smiled bleakly. 'You hadn't heard. I know. It is not something that we talk about. We wouldn't dare. The people must not know. Not for a while, at least.'

'But how can you keep it from them?'

'Not too hard to do. You know how it worked, how the custodian took it from planet to planet and great mass meetings were held, where the Talisman was exhibited and contact made through it with the spiritual force. There had never been a schedule of appearances; the custodian simply wandered. It might be a hundred of your years or more between the visits of the custodian to any particular planet. The people hold no expectations of a visit. They simply know there'll be one, sometime; that some day the custodian will show up with the Talisman.'

'That way you can cover up for years.'

'Yes,' Ulysses said. 'Without any trouble.'

'The leaders know, of course. The administrative people.'

Ulysses shook his head. 'We have told very few. The few that we can trust. Galactic Central knows, of course, but we're a close-mouthed lot.'

'Then why ...'

'Why should I be telling you. I know; I shouldn't. I don't know why I am. Yes, I guess I do. How does it feel, my friend, to sit as a compassionate confessor?'

'You're worried,' Enoch said. 'I never thought I would see you worried.'

'It's a strange business,' Ulysses said. 'The Talisman has been missing for several years or so. And no one knows about it – except Galactic Central and the – what would you call it? – the hierarchy, I suppose, the organization of mystics who take care of the spiritual set-up. And yet, even with no one knowing, the galaxy is beginning to show wear. It's coming apart at the seams. In time to come, it may fall apart. As if the Talisman represented a force that all unknowingly held the races of the galaxy together, exerting its influence even when it remained unseen.'

'But even if it's lost, it's somewhere,' Enoch pointed out. 'It still would be exerting its influence. It couldn't have been destroyed.'

'You forget,' Ulysses reminded him, 'that without its proper custodian, without its sensitive, it is inoperative. For it's not the machine itself that does the trick. The machine merely acts as an intermediary between the sensitive and the spiritual force. It is an extension of the sensitive. It magnifies the capability of the sensitive and acts as a link of some sort. It enables the sensitive to perform his function.'

'You feel that the loss of the Talisman has something to do with the situation here?'

'The Earth station. Well, not directly, but it is typical. What is happening in regard to the station is symptomatic. It involves the sort of petty quarrelling and mean bickering that has broken out through many sections of the galaxy. In the old days it would have been – what did you say, gentlemanly and on a plane of principles and ethics.'

They sat in silence for a moment, listening to the soft sound that the wind made as it blew through the gable gingerbread.

'Don't worry about it,' Ulysses said. 'It is not your worry. I should not have told you. It was indiscreet to do so.'

'You mean I shouldn't pass it on. You can be sure I won't.'

'I know you won't,' Ulysses said. 'I never thought you would.'

'You really think relations in the galaxy are deteriorating?'

'Once,' Ulysses said, 'the races all were bound together. There were differences, naturally, but these differences were bridged, sometimes rather artificially and not too satisfactorily, but with both sides striving to maintain the artificial bridging and generally succeeding. Because they wanted to, you see. There was a common purpose, the forging of a great confraternity of all intelligences. We realized that among us, among all the races, we had a staggering fund of knowledge and of techniques – that working together, by putting together all this knowledge and capability, we could arrive at something that would be far greater and more significant than any race, alone, could hope of accomplishing. We had our troubles, certainly, and as I have said, our differences, but we were progressing. We brushed the small animosities and the petty differences underneath the rug and worked only on the big ones. We felt that if we could get the big ones settled, the small ones would become so small they would disappear. But it is becoming different now. There is a tendency to pull the pettiness from underneath the rug and blow it beyond its size, meanwhile letting the major and the important issues fall away.'

'It sounds like Earth,' said Enoch.

'In many ways,' Ulysses said. 'In principle, although the circumstances would diverge immensely.'

'You've been reading the papers I have been saving for you?'

Ulysses nodded. 'It doesn't look too happy.'

'It looks like war,' said Enoch bluntly.

Ulysses stirred uneasily.

'You don't have wars,' said Enoch.

'The galaxy, you mean. No, as we are set up now we don't have wars.'

'Too civilized?'

'Stop being bitter,' Ulysses told him. 'There has been a time or two when we came very close, but not in recent years. There are many races now in the confraternity that in their formative years had a history of war.'

'There is hope for us, then. It's something you outgrow.'

'In time, perhaps.'

'But not a certainty?'

'No, I wouldn't say so.'

'I've been working on a chart,' said Enoch. 'Based on the Mizar system of statistics. The chart says there is going to be war.'

'You don't need the chart,' Ulysses said, 'to tell you that.'

'But there was something else. It was not just knowing if there'd be a war. I had hoped that the chart might show how to keep the peace. There must be a way. A formula, perhaps. If we could only think of it or know where to look or whom to ask or ...'

'There is a way,' Ulysses said, 'to prevent a war.'

'You mean you know ...'

'It's a drastic measure. It only can be used as a last resort.'

'And we've not reached that last resort?'

'I think, perhaps, you have. The kind of war that Earth would fight could spell an end to thousands of years of advancement, could wipe out all the culture, everything but the feeble remnants of civilizations. It could, just possibly, eliminate most of the life upon the planet.'

'This method of yours – it has been used?'

'A few times.'

'And worked?'

'Oh, certainly. We'd not even consider it if it didn't work.'

'It could be used on Earth?'

'You could apply for its application.'

'I?'

'As a representative of the Earth. You could appear before Galactic Central and appeal for us to use it. As a member of your race, you could give testimony and you would be given a hearing. If there seemed to be merit in your plea, Central might name a group to investigate and then, upon the report of its findings, a decision would be made.'

'You said I. Could anyone on Earth?'

'Anyone who could gain a hearing. To gain a hearing, you must know about Galactic Central and you're the only man of Earth who does. Besides, you're a part of Galactic Central's staff. You have served as a keeper for a long time. Your record has been good. We would listen to you.'

'But one man alone! One man can't speak for an entire race.'

'You're the only one of your race who is qualified.'

'If I could consult some others of my race.'

'You can't. And even if you could, who would believe you?'

'That's true,' said Enoch.

Of course it was. To him there was no longer any strangeness in the idea of a galactic confraternity, of a transportation network that spread among the stars – a sense of wonder at times, but the strangeness had largely worn off. Although, he remembered, it had taken years. Years even with the physical evidence there before his eyes, before he could bring himself to a complete acceptance of it. But tell it to any other Earthman and it would sound like madness.

'And this method?' he asked, almost afraid to ask it, braced to take the shock of whatever it might be. 'Stupidity,' Ulysses said.

Enoch gasped. 'Stupidity? I don't understand. We are stupid enough, in many ways, right now.'

'You're thinking of intellectual stupidity and there is plenty of that, not only on Earth, but throughout the galaxy. What I am talking about is a mental incapacity. An inability to understand the science and the technique that makes possible the kind of war that Earth would fight. An inability to operate the machines that are necessary to fight that kind of war. Turning the people back to a mental position where they would not be able to comprehend the mechanical and technological and scientific advances they have made. Those who know would forget. Those who didn't know could never learn. Back to the simplicity of the wheel and lever. That would make your kind of war impossible.'

Enoch sat stiff and straight, unable to speak, gripped by an icy terror, while a million disconnected thoughts went chasing one another in a circle through his brain.

'I told you it was drastic,' Ulysses said. 'It has to be. War is something that costs a lot to stop. The price is high.'

'I couldn't!' Enoch said. 'No one could.'

'Perhaps you can't. But consider this: If there is a war ...'

'I know. If there is a war, it could be worse. But it wouldn't stop war. It's not the kind of thing I had in mind. People still could fight, still could kill.'

'With clubs,' said Ulysses. 'Maybe bows and arrows. Rifles, so long as they still had rifles, and until they ran out of ammunition. Then they wouldn't know how to make more powder or how to get the metal to make the bullets or even how to make the bullets. There might be fighting, but there'd be no holocaust. Cities would not be wiped out by nuclear warheads, for no one could fire a rocket or arm the warhead – perhaps wouldn't even know what a rocket or a warhead was. Communications as you know them would be gone. All but the simplest transportation would be gone. War, except on a limited local scale, would be impossible.'

'It would be terrible,' Enoch said.

'So is war,' Ulysses said. 'The choice is up to you.'

'But how long?' asked Enoch. 'How long would it last? We wouldn't have to go back to stupidity for ever?'

'Several generations,' said Ulysses. 'By that time the effect of – what shall we call it? the treatment? – would gradually begin wearing off. The people slowly would shake off their moronic state and begin their intellectual climb again. They'd be given, in effect, a second chance.'

'They could,' said Enoch, 'in a few generations after that arrive at exactly the same situation that we have today.'

'Possibly. I wouldn't expect it, though. Cultural development would be most unlikely to be entirely parallel. There'd be a chance that you'd have a better civilization and a more peaceful people.'

'It's too much for one man ...'

'Something hopeful,' Ulysses said, 'that you might consider. The method is offered only to those races which seem to us to be worth the saving.'

'You have to give me time,' said Enoch.

But he knew there was no time.

23

A man would have a job and suddenly be unable to perform it. Nor could the men around him carry on their jobs. For they would not have the knowledge or the backgrounds to do the tasks that they had been doing. They might try, of course – they might keep on trying for a time, but perhaps for not too long. And because the jobs could not be done, the business or the corporation or factory or whatever it might be, would cease its operation. Although the going out of business would not be a formal nor a legal thing. It would simply stop. And not entirely because the jobs could not be done, because no one could muster the business sense to keep it operating, but also because the transportation and communications which made the business possible also would have stopped.

Locomotives could not be operated, nor could planes and ships, for there would be no one who would remember how to operate them. There would be men who at one time had possessed all the skills that had been necessary for their operation, but now the skills would have disappeared. There might be some who still would try, with tragic consequences. And there still might be a few who could vaguely remember how to operate the car or truck or bus, for they were simple things to run and it would be almost second nature for a man to drive them. But once they had broken down, there would be no one with the knowledge of mechanics to repair them and they'd not run again.

In the space of a few hours' time the human race would be stranded in a world where distance once again had come to be a factor. The world would grow the larger and the oceans would be barriers and a mile would be long once more. And in a few days' time there would be a panic and a huddling and a fleeing and a desperation in the face of a situation that no one could comprehend.

How long, Enoch wondered, would it take a city to use the last of the food stacked in its warehouses and then begin to starve? What would happen when electricity stopped flowing through the wires? How long, under a situation such as this, would a silly symbolic piece of paper or a minted coin still retain its value?

Distribution would break down; commerce and industry would die; government would become a shadow, with neither the means nor the intelligence to keep it functioning; communications would cease; law and order would disintegrate; the world would sink into a new barbaric framework and would begin to slowly readjust. That readjustment would go on for years and in the process of it there would be death and pestilence and untold misery and despair. In time it would work out and the world would settle down to its new way of life, but in the process of shaking down there'd be many who would die and many others who would lose everything that had spelled out life for them and the purpose of that life.

But would it, bad as it might be, be as bad as war?

Many would die of cold and hunger and disease (for medicine would go the way of all the rest), but millions would not be annihilated in the fiery breath of nuclear reaction. There would be no poison dust raining from the skies and the waters still would be as pure and fresh as ever and the soil remain as fertile. There still would be a chance, once the initial phases of the change had passed, for the human race to go on living and rebuild society.

If one were certain, Enoch told himself, that there would be a war, that war was inescapable, then the choice might not be hard to make. But there was always the possibility that the world could avoid war, that somehow a frail, thin peace could be preserved, and in such a case the desperate need of the galactic cure for war would be unnecessary. Before one could decide, he told himself, one must be sure; and how could one be sure? The chart lying in the desk drawer said there would be a war; many of the diplomats and observers felt that the upcoming peace conference might serve no other purpose than to trigger war. Yet there was no surety.

And even if there were, Enoch asked himself, how could one man – one man, alone – take it upon himself to play the role of God for the entire race? By what right did one man make a decision that affected all the rest, all the billions of others? Could he, if he did, ever be able, in the years to come, to justify his choice?

How could a man decide how bad war might be and, in comparison, how bad stupidity? The answer seemed to be he couldn't. There was no way to measure possible disaster in either circumstance.

After a time, perhaps, a choice either way could be rationalized. Given time, a conviction might develop that would enable a man to arrive at some sort of decision which, while it might not be entirely right, he nevertheless could square with his conscience.

Enoch got to his feet and walked to the window. The sound of his footsteps echoed hollowly in the station. He looked at his watch and it was after midnight.

There were races in the galaxy, he thought, who could reach a quick and right decision on almost any question, cutting straight across all the tangled lines of thought, guided by rules of logic that were more specific than anything the human race might have. That would be good, of course, in the sense that it made a decision possible, but in arriving at a decision would it not tend to minimize, perhaps ignore entirely, some of those very facets of the situation that might mean more to the human race than the decision would itself?

Enoch stood at the window and stared out across the moonlit fields that ran down to the dark line of the woods. The clouds had blown away and the night was peaceful. This particular spot, he thought, always would be peaceful, for it was off the beaten track, distant from any possible target in atomic war. Except for the remote possibility of some ancient and non-recorded, long forgotten minor conflict in prehistoric days, no battle ever had been fought here or ever would be fought. And yet it could not escape the common fate of poisoned soil and water if the world should suddenly, in a fateful hour of fury, unleash the might of its awesome weapons. Then the skies would be filled with atomic ash, which would come sifting down, and it would make little difference where a man might be. Soon or late, the war would come to him, if not in a flash of monstrous energy, then in the snow of death falling from the skies.

He walked from the window to the desk and gathered up the newspapers that had come in the morning mail and put them in a pile, noticing as he did so that Ulysses had forgotten to take with him the stack of papers which had been saved for him. Ulysses was upset, he told himself, or he'd not have forgotten the papers. God save us both, he thought; for we have our troubles.

It had been a busy day. He had done no more, he realized, than read two or three of the stories in the *Times*, all touching on the calling of the conference. The day had been too full, too full of direful things.

For a hundred years, he thought, things had gone all right. There had been the good moments and the bad, but by and large his life had gone on serenely and without alarming incident. Then today had dawned and all the serene years had come tumbling down all about his ears.

There once had been a hope that Earth could be accepted as a member of the galactic family, that he might serve as the emissary to gain that recognition. But now that hope was shattered, not only by the fact that the station might be closed, but that its very closing would be based upon the barbarism of the human race. Earth was being used as a whipping boy, of course, in galactic politics, but the brand, once placed, could not soon be lifted. And in any event, even if it could be lifted, now the planet stood revealed as one against which Galactic Central, in the hope of saving it, might be willing to apply a drastic and degrading action.

There was something he could salvage out of all of it, he knew. He could remain an Earthman and turn over to the people of the Earth the information that he had gathered through the years and written down, in meticulous detail, along with personal happenings and impressions and much other trivia, in the long rows of record books which stood on the shelves against the wall. That and the alien literature he had obtained and read and hoarded.

And the gadgets and the artifacts which came from other worlds. From all of this the people of the Earth might gain something which could help them along the road that eventually would take them to the stars and to that further knowledge and that greater understanding which would be their heritage – perhaps the heritage and right of all intelligence. But the wait for that day would be long – longer now, because of what had happened on this day, than it had ever been before. And the information that he held, gathered painfully over the course of almost a century, was so inadequate compared with that more complete knowledge which he could have gathered in another century (or a thousand years) that it seemed a pitiful thing to offer to his people.

If there could only be more time, he thought. But, of course, there never was. There was not the time right now and there would never be. No matter how many centuries he might be able to devote, there'd always be so much more knowledge than he'd gathered at the moment that the little he had gathered would always seem a pittance.

He sat down heavily in the chair before the desk and now, for the first time, he wondered how he'd do it – how he could leave Galactic Central, how he could trade the galaxy for a single planet, even if that planet still remained his own.

He drove his haggard mind to find the answer and the mind could find no answer.

One man alone, he thought.

One man alone could not stand against both Earth and galaxy.

24

The sun streaming through the window woke him and he stayed where he was, not stirring for a moment, soaking in its warmth. There was a good, hard feeling to the sunlight, a reassuring touch, and for a moment he held off the worry and the questioning. But he sensed its nearness and he closed his eyes again. Perhaps if he could sleep some more it might go away and lose itself somewhere and not be there when he awakened later.

But there was something wrong, something besides the worry and the questioning.

His neck and shoulders ached and there was a strange stiffness in his body and the pillow was too hard.

He opened his eyes again and pushed with his hands to sit erect and he was not in bed. He was sitting in a chair and his head, instead of resting on a pillow, had been laid upon the desk. He opened and shut his mouth to taste it, and it tasted just as bad as he knew it would.

He got slowly to his feet, straightening and stretching, trying to work out the kinks that had tied themselves into joints and muscles. As he stood there, the worry and the trouble and the dreadful need of answers seeped back into him, from wherever they'd been hiding. But he brushed them to one side, not an entirely successful brush, but enough to make them retreat a little and crouch there, waiting to close in again.

He went to the stove and looked for the coffee-pot, then remembered that last night he'd set it on the floor beside the coffee table. He went to get it. The two cups still stood on the table, the dark brown dregs of coffee covering the bottoms of them. And in the mass of gadgets that Ulysses had pushed to one side to make room for the cups, the pyramid of spheres lay tilted on its side, but it still was sparkling and glinting, each successive sphere revolving in an opposite direction to its fellow spheres.

Enoch reached out and picked it up. His fingers carefully explored the base upon which the spheres were set, seeking something – some lever, some indentation, some trip, some button – by which it might be turned either on or off. But there was nothing he could find. He should have known, he told himself, that there would be nothing. For he had looked before. And yet yesterday Lucy had done something that had set it operating and it still was operating. It had operated for more than twelve hours now and no results had been obtained. Check that, he thought – no results that could be recognized.

He set it back on the table on its base and stacked the cups, one inside the other, and picked them up. He stooped to lift the coffee-pot off the floor. But his eyes never left the pyramid of spheres.

It was maddening, he told himself. There was no way to turn it on and yet, somehow, Lucy had turned it on. And now there was no way to turn it off – although it probably did not matter if it were off or on.

He went back to the sink with the cups and coffee-pot.

The station was quiet – a heavy, oppressive quietness; although, he told himself, the impression of oppressiveness probably was no more than his imagination.

He crossed the room to the message machine and the plate was blank. There had been no messages during the night. It was silly of him, he thought, to expect there would be, for if there were, the auditory signal would be functioning, would continue to sound off until he pushed the lever.

Was it possible, he wondered, that the station might already have been abandoned, that whatever traffic that happened to be moving was being detoured around it? That, however, was hardly possible, for the abandonment of Earth station would mean as well that those beyond it must also be abandoned. There were no shortcuts in the network extending out into the spiral arm to make rerouting possible. It was not unusual for many hours, even for a day, to pass without any traffic. The traffic was irregular and had no pattern to it. There were times when scheduled arrivals had to be held up until there were facilities to take care of them, and there were other times when there would be none at all, when the equipment would sit idle, as it was sitting now.

Jumpy, he thought. I am getting jumpy.

Before they closed the station, they would let him know. Courtesy, if nothing else, would demand that they do that.

He went back to the stove and started the coffee-pot. In the refrigerator he found a package of mush made from a cereal grown on one of the Draconian jungle worlds. He took it out, then put it back again and took out the last two eggs of the dozen that Wins, the mailman, had brought out from town a week or so ago.

He glanced at his watch and saw that he had slept later than he thought. It was almost time for his daily walk.

He put the skillet on the stove and spooned in a chunk of butter. He waited for the butter to melt, then broke in the eggs.

Maybe, he thought, he'd not go on the walk today. Except for a time or two when a blizzard had been raging, it would be the first time he had ever missed his walk. But because he always did it, he told himself, contentiously, was no sufficient reason that he should always take it. He'd just skip the walk and later on go down and get the mail. He could use the time to catch up on all the things he'd failed to do yesterday. The papers still were piled upon the desk, waiting for his reading. He'd not written in his journal, and there was a lot to write, for he must record in detail exactly what had happened and there had been a good deal happening.

It had been a rule he'd set himself from the first day that the station had begun its operation – that he never skimped the journal. He might be a little late at times in getting it all down, but the fact that he was late or that he was pressed for time had never made him put down one word less than he had felt might be required to tell all there was to tell.

He looked across the room at the long rows of record books that were crowded on the shelves and thought, with pride and satisfaction, of the completeness of that record. Almost a century of writing lay between the covers of those books and there was not a single day that he had ever skipped.

Here was his legacy, he thought; here was his bequest to the world; here would be his entrance fee back into the human race; here was all he'd seen and heard and thought for almost a hundred years of association with those alien peoples of the galaxy.

Looking at the rows of books, the questions that he had shoved aside came rushing in on him and this time there was no denying them. For a short space of time he had held them off, the little time he'd needed for his brain to clear, for his body to become alive again. He did not fight them now. He accepted them, for there was no dodging them.

He slid the eggs out of the skillet on to the waiting plate. He got the coffee-pot and sat down to his breakfast.

He glanced at his watch again.

There still was time to go on his daily walk.

25

The ginseng man was waiting at the spring.

Enoch saw him while still some distance down the trail and wondered, with a quick flash of anger, if he might be waiting there to tell him that he could not return the body of the Hazer, that something had come up, that he had run into unexpected difficulties.

And thinking that, Enoch remembered how he'd threatened the night before to kill anyone who held up the return of the body. Perhaps, he told himself, it had not been smart to say that. Wondering whether he could bring himself to kill a man – not that it would be the first man he had ever killed. But that had been long ago and it had been a matter then of kill or be killed.

He shut his eyes for a second and once again could see that slope below him, with the long lines of men advancing through the drifting smoke, knowing that those men were climbing up the ridge for one purpose only, to kill himself and those others who were atop the ridge.

And that had not been the first time nor had it been the last, but all the years of killing boiled down in essence to that single moment – not the time that came after, but that long and terrible instant when he had watched the lines of men purposefully striding up the slope to kill him.

It had been in that moment that he had realized the insanity of war, the futile gesture that in time became all but meaningless, the unreasoning rage that must be nursed long beyond the memory of the incident that had caused the rage, the sheer illogic that one man, by death or misery, might prove a right or uphold a principle.

Somewhere, he thought, on the long backtrack of history, the human race had accepted an insanity for a principle and had persisted in it until today that insanity-turned-principle stood ready to wipe out, if not the race itself, at least all of those things, both material and immaterial, that had been fashioned as symbols of humanity through many hard-won centuries.

Lewis had been sitting on a fallen log and now, as Enoch neared, he rose.

'I waited for you here,' he said. 'I hope that you don't mind.'

Enoch stepped across the spring.

'The body will be here some time in early evening,' Lewis said. 'Washington will fly it out to Madison and truck it here from there.'

Enoch nodded. 'I am glad to hear that.'

'They were insistent,' Lewis said, 'that I should ask you once again what the body is.'

'I told you last night,' said Enoch, 'that I can't tell you anything. I wish I could. I've been figuring for years how to get it told, but there's no way of doing it.'

'The body is something from off this Earth,' said Lewis. 'We are sure of that.'

'You think so,' Enoch said, not making it a question.

'And the house,' said Lewis, 'is something alien, too.'

'The house,' Enoch told him, shortly, 'was built by my father.'

'But something changed it,' Lewis said. 'It is not the way he built it.'

'The years change things,' said Enoch.

'Everything but you.'

Enoch grinned at him. 'So it bothers you,' he said. 'You figure it's indecent.'

Lewis shook his head. 'No, not indecent. Not really anything. After watching you for years, I've come to an acceptance of you and everything about you. No understanding, naturally, but complete acceptance. Sometimes I tell myself I'm crazy, but that's only momentary. I've tried not to bother you. I've worked to keep everything exactly as it was. And now that I've met you, I am glad that is the way it was. But we're going at this wrong. We're acting as if we were enemies, as if we were strange dogs – and that's not the way to do it. I think that the two of us may have a lot in common. There's something going on and I don't want to do a thing that will interfere with it.'

'But you did,' said Enoch. 'You did the worst thing that you could when you took the body. If you'd sat down and planned how to do me harm, you couldn't have done worse. And not only me. Not really me, at all. It was the human race you harmed.'

'I don't understand,' said Lewis. 'I'm sorry, but I don't understand. There was the writing on the stone …'

'That was my fault,' said Enoch. 'I should never have put up that stone. But at the time it seemed the thing to do. I didn't think that anyone would come snooping around and …'

'It was a friend of yours?'

'A friend of mine? Oh, you mean the body. Well, not actually. Not that particular person.'

'Now that it's done,' Lewis said, 'I'm sorry.'

'Sorry doesn't help,' said Enoch.

'But isn't there something – isn't there anything that can be done about it? More than just bringing back the body?'

'Yes,' Enoch told him, 'there might be something. I might need some help.'

'Tell me,' Lewis said, quickly. 'If it can be done …'

'I might need a truck,' said Enoch. 'To haul away some stuff. Records and other things like that. I might need it fast.'

'I can have a truck,' said Lewis. 'I can have it waiting. And men to help you load.'

'I might want to talk to someone in authority. High authority. The President. Secretary of State. Maybe the U.N. I don't know. I have to think it out. And not only would I need a way to talk to them, but some measure of assurance that they would listen to what I had to say.'

'I'll arrange,' said Lewis, 'for mobile short-wave equipment. I'll have it standing by.'

'And someone who will listen?'

'That's right,' said Lewis. 'Anyone you say.'

'And one thing more.'

'Anything,' said Lewis.

'Forgetfulness,' said Enoch. 'Maybe I won't need any of these things. Not the truck or any of the rest of it. Maybe I'll have to let things go just as they're going now. And if that should be the case, could you and everyone else concerned forget I ever asked?'

'I think we could,' said Lewis. 'But I would keep on watching.'

'I wish you would,' said Enoch. 'Later on I might need some help. But no further interference.'

'Are you sure,' asked Lewis, 'that there is nothing else?'

Enoch shook his head. 'Nothing else. All the rest of it I must do myself.'

Perhaps, he thought, he'd already talked too much. For how could he be sure that he could trust this man? How could he be sure he could trust anyone?

And yet, if he decided to leave Galactic Central and cast his lot with Earth, he might need some help. There might be some objection by the aliens to his taking along his records and the alien gadgets. If he wanted to get away with them, he might have to make it fast.

But did he want to leave Galactic Central? Could he give up the galaxy? Could he turn down the offer to become the keeper of another station on some other planet? When the time should come, could he cut his tie with all the other races and all the mysteries of the other stars?

Already he had taken steps to do those very things. Here, in the last few moments, without too much thought about it, almost as if he already had reached his decision, he had arranged a set-up that would turn him back to Earth.

He stood there, thinking, puzzled at the steps he'd taken.

'There'll be someone here,' said Lewis. 'Someone at this spring. If not myself, then someone else who can get in touch with me.'

Enoch nodded absent-mindedly.

'Someone will see you every morning when you take your walk,' said Lewis. 'Or you can reach us here any time you wish.'

Like a conspiracy, thought Enoch. Like a bunch of kids playing cops and robbers.

'I have to be getting on,' he said. 'It's almost time for mail. Wins will be wondering what has happened to me.'

He started up the hill.

'Be seeing you,' said Lewis.

'Yeah,' said Enoch. 'I'll be seeing you.'

He was surprised to find the warm glow spreading in him – as if there had been something wrong and now it was all right, as if there had been something lost that now had been recovered.

26

Enoch met the mailman halfway down the road that led into the station. The old jalopy was travelling fast, bumping over the grassy ruts, swishing through the overhanging bushes that grew along the track.

Wins braked to a halt when he caught sight of Enoch and sat waiting for him.

'You got on a detour,' Enoch said, coming up to him. 'Or have you changed your route?'

'You weren't waiting at the box,' said Wins, 'and I had to see you.'

'Some important mail?'

'Nope, it isn't mail. It's old Hank Fisher. He is down in Millville, setting up the drinks in Eddie's tavern and shooting off his face.'

'It's not like Hank to be buying drinks.'

'He's telling everyone that you tried to kidnap Lucy.'

'I didn't kidnap her,' Enoch said. 'Hank had took a bull whip to her and I hid her out until he got cooled down.'

'You shouldn't have done that, Enoch.'

'Maybe. But Hank was set on giving her a beating. He already had hit her a lick or two.'

'Hank's out to make you trouble.'

'He told me that he would.'

'He says you kidnapped her, then got scared and brought her back. He says you had her hid out in the house and when he tried to break in and get her, he couldn't do it. He says you have a funny sort of house. He says he broke an axe blade on a window pane.'

'Nothing funny about it,' Enoch said. 'Hank just imagines things.'

'It's all right so far,' said the mailman. 'None of them in broad daylight and their right senses, will do anything about it. But come night they'll be liquored up and won't have good sense. There are some of them might be coming up to see you.'

'I suppose he's telling them I've got the devil in me.'

'That and more,' said Wins. 'I listened for a while before I started out.'

He reached into the mail pouch and found the bundle of papers and handed them to Enoch.

'Enoch, there's something that you have to know. Something you may not realize. It would be easy to get a lot of people stirred up against you – the way you live and all. You are strange. No, I don't mean there's anything wrong with you – I know you and I know there isn't – but it would be easy for people who didn't know you to get the wrong ideas. They've let you alone so far because you've given them no reason to do anything about you. But if they get stirred up by all that Hank is saying ...'

He did not finish what he was saying. He left it hanging in mid-air.

'You're talking about a posse,' Enoch said.

Wins nodded, saying nothing.

'Thanks,' said Enoch. 'I appreciate your warning me.'

'Is it true,' asked the mailman, 'that no one can get inside your house?'

'I guess it is,' admitted Enoch. 'They can't break into it and they can't burn it down. They can't do anything about it.'

'Then, if I were you, I'd stay close tonight. I'd stay inside. I'd not go venturing out.'

'Maybe I will. It sounds like a good idea.'

'Well,' said Wins, 'I guess that about covers it. I thought you'd ought to know. Guess I'll have to back out to the road. No chance of turning around.'

'Drive up to the house. There's room there.'

'It's not far back to the road,' said Wins. 'I can make it easy.'

The car started backing slowly.

Enoch stood watching.

He lifted a hand in solemn salute as the car began rounding a bend that would take it out of sight. Wins waved back and then the car was swallowed by the scrub that grew close against both sides of the road.

Slowly Enoch turned around and plodded back towards the station.

A mob, he thought – good God, a mob!

A mob howling about the station, hammering at the doors and windows, peppering it with bullets, would wipe out the last faint chance – if there still remained a chance – of Galactic Central standing off the move to close the station. Such a demonstration would add one more powerful argument to the demand that the expansion into the spiral arm should be abandoned.

Why was it, he wondered, that everything should happen all at once? For years nothing at all had happened and now everything was happening within a few hours' time. Everything, it seemed, was working out against him.

If the mob showed up, not only would it mean that the fate of the station would be sealed, but it might mean, as well, that he would have no choice but to accept the offer to become the keeper of another station. It might make it impossible for him to remain on Earth, even if he wished. And he realized, with a start, that it might just possibly mean that the offer of another station for him might be withdrawn. For with the appearance of a mob howling for his blood, he, himself, would become involved in the charge of barbarism now levelled against the human race in general.

Perhaps, he told himself, he should go down to the spring and see Lewis once again. Perhaps some measures could be taken to hold off the mob. But if he did he knew, there'd be an explanation due and he might have to tell too much. And there might not be a mob. No one would place too much credence in what Hank Fisher said and the whole thing might peter out without any action being taken.

He'd stay inside the station and hope for the best. Perhaps there'd be no traveller in the station at the time the mob arrived – if it did arrive – and the incident would pass with no galactic notice. If he were lucky it might work out that way. And by the law of averages, he was owed some luck. Certainly he'd had none in the last few days.

He came to the broken gate that led into the yard and stopped to look up at the house, trying, for some reason he could not understand, to see it as the house he had known in boyhood.

It stood the same as it had always stood, unchanged, except that in the olden days there had been ruffled curtains at each window. The yard around it had changed with the slow growth of the years, with the clump of lilacs thicker and more rank and tangled with each passing spring, with the elms that his father had planted grown from six-foot whips into mighty trees, with the yellow rose bush at the kitchen corner gone, victim of a long-forgotten winter, with the flower beds vanished and the small herb garden, here beside the gate, overgrown and smothered out by grass.

The old stone fence that had stood on each side of the gate now was little more than a humpbacked mound. The heaving of a hundred frosts, the creep of vines and grasses, the long years of neglect, had done their work and in another hundred years, he thought, it would be level, with no trace of it left. Down in the field, along the slope where erosion had been at work, there were long stretches where it had entirely disappeared.

All of this had happened and until this moment he had scarcely noticed it. But now he noticed it and wondered why he did. Was it because he now might be returning to the Earth again – he who had never left its soil and sun and air, who had never left it physically, but who had, for a longer time than most men had allotted to them, walked not one, but many planets, far among the stars?

He stood there, in the late summer sun, and shivered in the cold wind that seemed to be blowing out of some unknown dimension of unreality, wondering for the first time (for the first time he ever had been forced to wonder at it) what kind of man he was. A haunted man who must spend his days neither completely alien nor completely human, with divided loyalties, with old ghosts to tramp the years and miles with him no matter which life he might choose, the Earth life or the stars? A cultural half-breed, understanding neither Earth nor stars, owing a debt to each, but paying neither one?

A homeless, footless, wandering creature who could recognize neither right nor wrong from having seen so many different (and logical) versions of the right and wrong?

He had climbed the hill above the spring, filled with the rosy inner glow of a regained humanity, a member of the human race again, linked in a boylike conspiracy with a human team. But could he qualify as human – and if he qualified as human, or tried to qualify, then what about the implied hundred years' allegiance to Galactic Central? Did he, he wondered, even want to qualify as human?

He moved slowly through the gate, and the questions still kept hammering in his brain, that great, ceaseless flow of questions to which there were no answers. Although that was wrong, he thought. Not no answers, but too many answers.

Perhaps Mary and David and the rest of them would come visiting tonight and they could talk it over – then he suddenly remembered.

They would not be coming. Not Mary, not David, nor any of the others. They had come for years to see him, but they would come no longer, for the magic had been dimmed and the illusion shattered and he was alone.

As he had always been alone, he told himself, with a bitter taste inside his brain. It all had been illusion; it never had been real. For years he'd fooled himself – most eagerly and willingly he had fooled himself into peopling the little corner by the fireplace with these creatures of his imagination. Aided by an alien technique, driven by his loneliness for the sight and sound of human-kind, he had brought them into a being that defied every sense except the solid sense of touch.

And defied as well every sense of decency.

Half-creatures, he thought. Poor pitiful half-creatures, neither of the shadow or the world.

Too human for the shadows, too shadowy for Earth.

Mary, if I had only known – if I had known, I never would have started. I'd have stayed with loneliness.

And he could not mend it now. There was nothing that would help.

What is the matter with me? he asked himself.

What has happened to me?

What is going on?

He couldn't even think in a straight line any more. He'd told himself that he'd stay inside the station to escape the mob that might be showing up – and he couldn't stay inside the station, for Lewis, some time shortly after dark, would be bringing back the Hazer's body.

And if the mob showed up at the same time Lewis should appear, bringing back the body, there'd be unsheeted hell to pay.

Stricken by the thought, he stood undecided.

If he alerted Lewis to the danger, then he might not bring the body. And he had to bring the body. Before the night was over the Hazer must be secure within the grave.

He decided that he would have to take a chance.

The mob might not show up. Even if it did, there had to be a way that he could handle it.

He'd think of something, he told himself.

He'd have to think of something.

27

The station was as silent as it had been when he'd left it. There had been no messages and the machinery was quiet, not even muttering to itself, as it sometimes did.

Enoch laid the rifle across the desk top and dropped the bundle of papers beside it. He took off his jacket and hung it on the back of the chair.

There were still the papers to be read, not only today's, but yesterday's as well, and the journal to be gotten up, and the journal, he reminded himself, would take a lot of time. There would be several pages of it, even if he wrote it close, and he must write it logically and chronologically, so that it would appear he had written the happenings of yesterday yesterday and not a full day late. He must include each event and every facet of each happening and his own reactions to it and his thoughts about it. For that was the way he'd always done it and that was the way he must do it now. He'd always been able to do it that way because he had created for himself a little special niche, not of the Earth, nor of the galaxy, but in that vague condition which one might call existence, and he had worked inside the framework of that special niche as a medieval monk had worked inside his cell. He had been an observer only, an intensely interested observer who had not been content with observance only, but who had made an effort to dig into what he had observed, but still basically and essentially an observer who was not vitally nor personally involved in what had gone on about him. But in the last two days, he realized, he had lost that observer status. The Earth and the galaxy had both intruded on him, and his special niche was gone and he was personally involved. He had lost his objective viewpoint and no longer could command that correct and coldly factual approach which had given him a solid basis upon which to do his writing.

He walked over to the shelf of journals and pulled out the current volume, fluttering its pages to find where he had stopped. He found the place and it was very near the end. There were only a few blank pages left, perhaps not enough of them to cover the events of which he'd have to write. More than likely, he thought, he'd come to an end of the journal before he had finished with it and would have to start a new one.

He stood with the journal in his hand and stared at the page where the writing ended, the writing that he'd done the day before yesterday. Just the day before yesterday and it now was ancient writing; it even had a faded look about it. And well it might, he thought, for it had been writing done in another age. It had been the last entry he had made before his world had come crashing down about him.

And what, he asked himself, was the use of writing further? The writing now was done, all the writing that would matter. The station would be closed and his own planet would be lost – no matter whether he stayed on or went to another station on another planet, the Earth would now be lost.

Angrily he slammed shut the book and put it back into its place upon the shelf. He walked back to the desk.

The Earth was lost, he thought, and he was lost as well, lost and angry and confused. Angry at fate (if there were such a thing as fate) and at stupidity. Not only the intellectual stupidity of the Earth, but at the intellectual stupidity of the galaxy as well, at the petty bickering which could still the march of the brotherhood of peoples that finally had extended into this galactic sector. As on Earth, so in the galaxy, the number and complexity of the gadget, the noble thought, the wisdom and erudition might make for a culture, but not for a civilization. To be truly civilized, there must be something far more subtle than the gadget or the thought.

He felt the tension in him, the tension to be doing something – to prowl about the station like a caged and pacing beast, to run outside and shout incoherently until his lungs were empty, to smash and break, to work off, somehow, his rage and disappointment.

He reached out a hand and snatched the rifle off the desk. He pulled out a desk drawer where he kept the ammunition, and took out a box of it, tearing it apart, emptying the cartridges into his pocket.

He stood there for a moment, with the rifle in his hand, and the silence of the room seemed to thunder at him and he caught the bleakness and the coldness of it and he laid the rifle back on the desk again.

What childishness, he thought, to take out his resentment and his rage on an unreality. And when there was no real reason for resentment or for rage. For the pattern of events was one that should be recognized and thus accepted. It was the kind of thing to which a human being should long since have become accustomed.

He looked around the station and the quietness and the waiting still was there, as if the very structure might be marking time for an event to come along on the natural flow of time.

He laughed softly and reached for the rifle once again.

Unreality or not, it would be something to occupy his mind, to snatch him for a while from this sea of problems which was swirling all about him.

And he needed the target practice. It had been ten days or more since he'd been on the rifle range.

28

The basement was huge. It stretched out into a dim haze beyond the lights which he had turned on, a place of tunnels and rooms, carved deep into the rock that folded up to underlie the ridge.

Here were the massive tanks filled with the various solutions for the tank travellers; here the pumps and the generators, which operated on a principle alien to the human manner of generating electric power, and far beneath the floor of the basement itself those great storage tanks which held the acids and the soupy matter which once had been the bodies of those creatures which came travelling to the station, leaving behind them, as they went on to some other place, the useless bodies which then must be disposed of.

Enoch moved across the floor, past the tanks and generators, until he came to a gallery that stretched out into the darkness. He found the panel and pressed it to bring on the lights, then walked down the gallery. On either side were metal shelves which had been installed to accommodate the overflow of gadgets, of artifacts, of all sorts of gifts which had been brought him by the travellers. From floor to ceiling the shelves were jammed with a junkyard accumulation from all the corners of the galaxy. And yet, thought Enoch, perhaps not actually a junkyard, for there would be very little of this stuff that would be actual junk. All of it was serviceable and had some purpose, either practical or aesthetic, if only that purpose could be learned. Although perhaps not in every instance a purpose that would be applicable to humans.

Down at the end of the shelves was one section of shelving into which the articles were packed more systematically and with greater care, each one tagged and numbered, with cross-filing to a card catalogue and certain journal dates. These were the articles of which he knew the purpose and, in certain instances, something of the principles involved. There were some that were innocent enough and others that held great potential value and still others that had, at the moment, no connection whatsoever with the human way of life – and there were, as well, those few, tagged in red, that made one shudder to even think upon.

He went down the gallery, his footsteps echoing loudly as he trod through this place of alien ghosts.

Finally the gallery widened into an oval room and the walls here were padded with a thick grey substance that would entrap a bullet and prevent a ricochet.

Enoch walked over to a panel set inside a deep recess sunk into the wall. He reached in and thumbed up a tumbler, then stepped quickly out into the centre of the room.

Slowly the room began to darken, then suddenly it seemed to flare and he was in the room no longer, but in another place, a place he had never seen before.

He stood on a little hillock and in front of him the land sloped down to a sluggish river bordered by a width of marsh. Between the beginning of the marsh and the foot of the hillock stretched a sea of rough, tall grass. There was no wind, but the grass was rippling and he knew that the rippling motion of the grass was caused by many moving bodies, foraging in the grass. Out of it came a savage grunting, as if a thousand angry hogs were fighting for choice morsels in a hundred swill troughs. And from somewhere farther off, perhaps from the river, came a deep, monotonous bellowing that sounded hoarse and tired.

Enoch felt the hair crawling on his scalp and he thrust the rifle out and ready. It was puzzling. He felt and knew the danger and as yet there was no danger. Still, the very air of this place – wherever it might be – seemed to crawl with danger.

He spun around and saw that close behind him the thick, dark woods climbed down the range of river hills, stopping at the sea of grass which flowed around the hillock on which he found himself. Off beyond the hills, dark purple in the air, loomed a range of mighty mountains that seemed to fade into the sky, but purple to their peaks, with no sign of snow upon them.

Two things came trotting from the woods and stopped at the edge of it. They sat down and grinned at him, with their tails wrapped neatly round their feet. They might have been wolves or dogs, but they were neither one. They were nothing he had ever seen or heard of. Their pelts glistened in the weak sunshine, as if they had been greased, but the pelts stopped at their necks, with their skulls and faces bare. Like evil old men, off on a masquerade, with their bodies draped in the hides of wolves. But the disguise was spoiled by the lolling tongues which spilled out of their mouths, glistening scarlet against the bone-white of their faces.

The woods were still. There were only the two gaunt beasts sitting on their haunches. They sat and grinned at him, a strangely toothless grin.

The woods were dark and tangled, the foliage so dark green that it was almost black. All the leaves had a shine to them, as if they had been polished to a special sheen.

Enoch spun around again, to look back towards the river, and crouched at the edge of the grass was a line of toad-like monstrosities, six feet long and standing three feet high, their bodies the colour of a dead fish belly, and each with a single eye, or what seemed to be an eye, which covered a great part of the area just above the snout. The eyes were faceted and glowed in the dim sunlight, as the eyes of a hunting cat will glow when caught in a beam of light.

The hoarse bellowing still came from the river and in between the bellowing there was a faint, thin buzzing, an angry and malicious buzzing, as if a mosquito might be hovering for attack, although there was a sharper tone in it than in the noise of a mosquito.

Enoch jerked up his head to look into the sky and far in the depths of it he saw a string of dots, so high that there was no way of knowing what kind of things they were.

He lowered his head to look back at the line of squatting, toad-like things, but from the corner of his eye he caught the sense of flowing motion and swung back towards the woods.

The wolf-like bodies with the skull-like heads were coming up the hill in a silent rush. They did not seem to run. There was no motion of their running. Rather they were moving as if they had been squirted from a tube.

Enoch jerked up his rifle and it came into his shoulder, fitting there, as if it were a part of him. The bead settled in the rear-sight notch and blotted out the skull-like face of the leading beast. The gun bucked as he squeezed the trigger and, without waiting to see if the shot had downed the beast, the rifle barrel was swinging towards the second as his right fist worked the bolt. The rifle bucked again and the second wolf-like being somersaulted and slid forward for an instant, then began rolling down the hill, flopping as it rolled.

Enoch worked the bolt again and the spent brass case glittered in the sun as he turned swiftly to face the other slope.

The toad-like things were closer now. They had been creeping in, but as he turned they stopped and squatted, staring at him.

He reached a hand into his pocket and took out two cartridges, cramming them into the magazine to replace the shells he'd fired.

The bellowing down by the river had stopped, but now there was a honking sound that he could not place. Turning cautiously, he tried to locate what might be making it, but there was nothing to be seen. The honking sound seemed to be coming from the forest, but there was nothing moving.

In between the honking he still could hear the buzzing and it seemed louder now. He glanced into the sky and the dots were larger and no longer in a line. They had formed into a circle and seemed to be spiralling downward, but they were still so high that he could not make out what kind of things they were.

He glanced back towards the toad-like monsters and they were closer than they had been before. They had crept up again.

Enoch lifted the rifle and, before it reached his shoulder, pressed the trigger, shooting from the hip. The eye of one of the foremost of them exploded, like the splash a stone would make if thrown into water. The creature did not jump or flop. It simply settled down, flat upon the ground, as if someone had put his foot upon it and had exerted force enough to squash it flat. It lay there, flat, and there was a big round hole where the eye had been and the hole was filling with a thick and ropy yellow fluid that may have been the creature's blood.

The others backed away, slowly, watchfully. They backed all the way off the hillock and only stopped when they reached the grass edge.

The honking was closer and the buzzing louder and there could be no doubt that the honking was coming from the hills.

Enoch swung about and saw it, striding through the sky, coming down the ridge, stepping through the trees and honking dolefully. It was a round and black balloon that swelled and deflated with its honking, and jerked and swayed as it walked along, hung from the centre of four stiff and spindly legs that arched above it to the joint that connected this upper portion of the leg arrangement with the downward-spraddling legs that raised it high above the forest. It was walking jerkily, lifting its legs high to clear the massive tree-tops before putting them down again. Each time it put down a foot, Enoch could hear the crunching of the branches and the crashing of the trees that it broke or brushed aside.

Enoch felt the skin along his spine trying to roll up his back like a window shade, and the bristling of the hair along the base of his skull, obeying some primordial instinct in its striving to raise itself erect into a fighting ruff.

But even as he stood there, almost stiff with fright, some part of his brain remembered that one shot he had fired and his fingers dug into his pocket for another cartridge to fill the magazine.

The buzzing was much louder and the pitch had changed. The buzzing was now approaching at tremendous speed.

Enoch jerked up his head and the dots no longer were circling in the sky, but were plunging down towards him, one behind the other.

He flicked a glance towards the balloon, honking and jerking on its stilt-like legs. It still was coming on, but the plunging dots were faster and would reach the hillock first.

He shifted the rifle forward, outstretched and ready to slap against his shoulder, and watched the falling dots, which were dots no longer, but hideous streamlined bodies, each carrying a rapier that projected from its head. A bill of sorts, thought Enoch, for these things might be birds, but a longer, thinner, larger, more deadly bird than any earthly bird.

The buzzing changed into a scream and the scream kept mounting up the scale until it set the teeth on edge and through it, like a metronome measuring off a beat, came the hooting of the black balloon that strode across the hills.

Without knowing that he had moved his arms, Enoch had the rifle at his shoulder, waiting for that instant when the first of the plunging monsters was close enough to fire.

They dropped like stones out of the sky and they were bigger than he had thought they were – big and coming like so many arrows aimed directly at him.

The rifle thudded against his shoulder and the first one crumpled, lost its arrow shape, folding up and falling, no longer on its course. He worked the bolt and fired again and the second one in line lost its balance and began to tumble – and the bolt was worked once more and the trigger pressed. The third skidded in the air and went off at a slant, limp and ragged, fluttering in the wind, falling towards the river.

The rest broke off their dive. They made a shallow turn and beat their way up into the sky, great wings that were more like windmill vanes than wings thrashing desperately.

A shadow fell across the hillock and a mighty pillar came down from somewhere overhead, driving down to strike to one side of the hillock. The ground trembled at the tread and the water that lay hidden by the grass squirted high into the air.

The honking was an engulfing sound that blotted out all else and the great balloon was zooming down, cradled on its legs.

Enoch saw the face, if anything so grotesque and so obscene could be called a face. There was a beak and beneath it a sucking mouth and a dozen or so other organs that might have been the eyes.

The legs were like inverted V's, with the inner stroke somewhat shorter than the outer and in the centre of these inner joints hung the great balloon that was the body of the creature, with its face on the underside so that it could see all the hunting territory that might be beneath it.

But now auxiliary joints in the outer span of legs were bending to let the body of the creature down so it could seize its prey.

Enoch was not conscious of putting up the rifle or of operating it, but it was hammering at his shoulder and it seemed to him that a second part of him stood off, apart, and watched the firing of the rifle – as if the figure that held and fired the weapon might be a second man.

Great gouts of flesh flew out of the black balloon and jagged rents suddenly tore across it and from these rents poured out a cloud of liquid that turned into a mist, with black droplets raining from it.

The firing pin clicked on an empty breech and the gun was empty, but there was no need of another shot. The great legs were folding, and trembling as they folded, and the shrunken body shivered convulsively in the heavy mist that was pouring out of it. There was no hooting now, and Enoch could hear the patter of the black drops falling from that cloud as they struck the short grass on the hill.

There was a sickening odour and the drops, where they fell on him, were sticky, running like cold oil, and above him the great structure that had been the stiltlike creature was toppling to the ground.

Then the world faded swiftly and was no longer there.

Enoch stood in the oval room in the faint glow of the bulbs. There was the heavy smell of powder and all about his feet, glinting in the light, lay the spent and shining cases that had been kicked out of the gun.

He was back in the basement once again. The target shoot was over.

29

Enoch lowered the rifle and drew in a slow and careful breath. It always was like this, he thought. As if it were necessary for him to ease himself, by slow degrees, back to this world of his after the season of unreality.

One knew that it would be illusion when he kicked on the switch that set into motion whatever was to happen and one knew it had been illusion when it all had ended, but during the time that it was happening it was not illusion. It was as real and as substantial as if it all were true.

They had asked him, he remembered, when the station had been built, if he had a hobby – if there was any sort of recreational facility they could build into the station for him. And he had said that he would like a rifle range, expecting no more than a shooting gallery with ducks moving on a chain or clay pipes rotating on a wheel. But that, of course, would have been too simple for the screwball architects, who had designed, and the slap-happy crew of workmen who had built the station.

At first they had not been certain what he meant by a rifle range and he'd had to tell them what a rifle was and how it operated and for what it might be used. He had told them about hunting squirrels on sunny autumn mornings and shaking rabbits out of brush piles with the first coming of the snow (although one did not use a rifle, but a shotgun, on the rabbits), about hunting coons of an autumn night, and waiting for the deer along the run that went down to the river. But he was dishonest and he did not tell them about that other use to which he'd put a rifle during four long years.

He'd told them (since they were easy folks to talk with) about his youthful dream of some day going on a hunt in Africa, although even as he told them he was well aware of how unattainable it was. But since that day he'd hunted (and been hunted by) beasts far stranger than anything that Africa could boast.

From what these beasts might have been patterned, if indeed they came from anywhere other than the imagination of those aliens who had set up the tapes which produced the target scene, he had no idea. There had not, so far in the thousands of times that he had used the range, been a duplication either in the scene nor in the beasts which rampaged about the scene. Although, perhaps, he thought, there might be somewhere an end of them, and then the whole sequence might start over and run its course once more. But it would make little difference now, for if the tapes should start rerunning there'd be but little chance of his recalling in any considerable detail those adventures he had lived so many years ago.

He did not understand the techniques nor the principle which made possible this fantastic rifle range. Like many other things, he accepted it without the need of understanding. Although, some day, he thought, he might find the clue which in time would turn blind acceptance into understanding – not only of the range, but of many other things.

He had often wondered what the aliens might think about his fascination with the rifle range, with that primal force that drove a man to kill, not for the joy of killing so much as to negate a danger, to meet force with a greater and more skilful force, cunning with more cunning. Had he, he wondered, given his alien friends concern in their assessment of the human character by his preoccupation with the rifle? For the understanding of an alien, how could one draw a line between the killing of other forms of life and the killing of one's own? Was there actually a differential that would stand up under logical examination between the sport of hunting and the sport of war? To an alien, perhaps, such a differentiation would be rather difficult, for in many cases the hunted animal would be more closely allied to the human hunter in its form and characteristics than would many of the aliens.

Was war an instinctive thing, for which each ordinary man was as much responsible as the policy makers and the so-called statesmen? It seemed impossible, and yet, deep in every man was the combative instinct, the aggressive urge, the strange sense of competition – all of which spelled conflict of one kind or another if carried to conclusion.

He put the rifle underneath his arm and walked over to the panel. Sticking from a slot in the bottom of it was a piece of tape.

He pulled it out and puzzled out the symbols. They were not reassuring. He had not done so well.

He had missed that first shot he had fired at the charging wolf-thing with the old man's face, and back there somewhere, in that dimension of unreality, it and its companion were snarling over the tangled, torn mass of ribboned flesh and broken bone that had been Enoch Wallace.

30

He went back through the gallery, with its gifts stacked there as other gifts, in regular human establishments, might be stacked away in dry and dusty attics.

The tape nagged at him, the little piece of tape which said that while he had made all his other shots, he had missed that first one back there on the hillock. It was not often that he missed. And his training had been for that very type of shooting – the you-never-know-what-will-happen-next, the totally unexpected, the kill-or-be-killed kind of shooting that thousands of expeditions into the target area had taught him. Perhaps, he consoled himself, he had not been as faithful in his practice lately as he should have been. Although there actually was no reason that he should be faithful, for the shooting was for recreation only and his carrying of the rifle on his daily walks was from force of habit only and for no other reason. He carried the rifle as another man might take along a cane or walking stick. At the time he had first done it, of course, it had been a different kind of rifle and a different day. It then was no unusual thing for a man to carry a gun while out on a walk. But today was different and he wondered, with an inner grin, how much talk his carrying a gun might have furnished the people who had seen him with it.

Near the end of the gallery he saw the black bulk of a trunk projecting from beneath the lower shelf, too big to fit comfortably beneath it, jammed against the wall, but with a foot or two of it still projecting out beyond the shelf.

He went on walking past it, then suddenly turned around. That trunk, he thought – that was the trunk which had belonged to the Hazer who had died upstairs. It was his legacy from that being whose stolen body would be brought back to its grave this evening.

He walked over to the shelving and leaned his rifle against the wall. Stooping, he pulled the trunk clear of its resting place.

Once before, prior to carrying it down the stairs and storing it here beneath the shelves, he had gone through its contents, but at the time, he recalled, he'd not been too interested. Now, suddenly, he felt an absorbing interest in it.

He lifted the lid carefully and tilted it back against the shelves.

Crouching above the open trunk, and without touching anything to start with, he tried to catalogue the upper layer of its contents.

There was a shimmering cloak, neatly folded, perhaps some sort of ceremonial cloak, although he could not know. And atop the cloak lay a tiny bottle that was a blaze of reflected light, as if someone had taken a large-sized diamond and hollowed it out to make a bottle of it. Beside the cloak lay a nest of balls, deep violet and dull, with no shine at all, looking for all the world like a bunch of table-tennis balls that someone had cemented together to make a globe. But that was not the way it was, Enoch remembered, for that other time he had been entranced by them and had picked them up, to find that they were not cemented, but could be freely moved about although never outside the context of their shape. One ball could not be broken from the mass, no matter how hard one might try, but would move about, as if buoyed in a fluid, among all the other balls. One could move any, or all, of the balls, but the mass remained the same. A calculator of some sort, Enoch wondered, but that seemed only barely possible, for one ball was entirely like another, there was no way in which they could be identified. Or at least, no way to identify them by the human eye. Was it possible, he wondered, that identification might be possible to a Hazer's eye? And if a calculator, what kind of a calculator? Mathematical? Or ethical? Or philosophical? Although that was slightly foolish, for who had ever heard of a calculator for ethics or philosophy? Or, rather, what human had ever heard? More than likely it was not a calculator, but something else entirely. Perhaps a sort of game – a game of solitaire?

Given time, a man might finally get it figured out. But there was no time and no incentive at the moment to spend upon one particular item any great amount of time when there were hundreds of other items equally fantastic and incomprehensible. For while one puzzled over a single item, the edges of his mind would always wonder if he might not be spending time on the most insignificant of the entire lot.

He was a victim of museum fatigue, Enoch told himself, overwhelmed by the many pieces of the unknown scattered all about him.

He reached out a hand, not for the globe of balls, but for the shining bottle that lay atop the cloak. As he picked it up and brought it closer, he saw that there was a line of writing engraved upon the glass (or diamond?) of the bottle. Slowly he studied out the writing. There had been a time, long ago, when he had been able to read the Hazer language, if not fluently at least well enough to get along. But he had not read it for some years now and he had lost a good deal of it and he stumbled haltingly from one symbol to another. Translated very freely, the inscription on the bottle read: *To be taken when the first symptoms occur.*

A bottle of medicine! To be taken when the first symptoms occur. The symptoms, perhaps, that had come so quickly and built up so rapidly that the owner of this bottle could make no move to reach it and so had died, falling from the sofa.

Almost reverently, he put the bottle back in its place atop the cloak, fitting it back into the faint impression it had made from lying there.

So different from us in so many ways, thought Enoch, and then in other little ways so like us that it is frightening. For that bottle and the inscription on its face was an exact parallel of the prescription bottle that could be compounded by any corner drugstore.

Beside the globe of balls was a box, and he reached out and lifted it. It was made of wood and had a rather simple clasp to hold it shut. He flipped back the lid and inside he saw the metallic sheen of the material the Hazers used as paper.

Carefully he lifted out the first sheet and saw that it was not a sheet, but a long strip of the material folded in accordion fashion. Underneath it were more strips, apparently of the same material.

There was writing on it, faint and faded, and Enoch held it close to read it.

To my —, — friend: (although it was not 'friend'. 'Blood brother,' perhaps, or 'colleague'. And the adjectives which preceded it were such as to escape his sense entirely.)

The writing was hard to read. It bore some resemblance to the formalized version of the language, but apparently bore the imprint of the writer's personality, expressed in curlicues and flourishes which obscured the form. Enoch worked his way slowly down the paper, missing much of what was there, but picking up the sense of much that had been written.

The writer had been on a visit to some other planet, or possibly just some other place. The name of the place or planet was one that Enoch did not recognize. While he had been there he had performed some sort of function (although exactly what it was was not entirely clear) which had to do with his approaching death.

Enoch, startled, went back over the phrase again. And while much of the rest of what was written was not clear, that part of it was. *My approaching death,* he had written, and there was no room for mistranslation. All three of the words were clear.

He urged that his good (friend?) do likewise. He said it was a comfort and made clear the road.

There was no further explanation, no further reference. Just the calm declaration that he had done something which he felt must be arranged about his death. As if he knew that death was near and was not only unafraid, but almost unconcerned.

The next passage (for there were no paragraphs) told about someone he had met and how they'd talked about a certain matter which made no sense at all to Enoch, who found himself lost in a terminology he did not recognize.

And then: *I am most concerned about the mediocrity* (incompetence? inability? weakness?) *of the recent custodian of* (and then that cryptic symbol which could be translated, roughly, as the Talisman). *For* (a word, which from the context, seemed to mean a great length of time), *ever since the death of the last custodian, the Talisman has been but poorly served. It has been, in all reality* (another long time term), *since a true* (sensitive?) *has been found to carry out its purpose. Many have been tested and none has qualified, and for the lack of such a one the galaxy has lost its close identification with the ruling principle of life. We here at the* (temple? sanctuary?) *all are greatly concerned that without a proper linkage between the people and* (several words that were not decipherable) *the galaxy will go down in chaos* (and another line that he could not puzzle out).

The next sentence introduced a new subject – the plans that were going forward for some cultural festival which concerned a concept that, to Enoch, was hazy at the best.

Enoch slowly folded up the letter and put it back into the box. He felt a faint uneasiness in reading what he had, as if he'd pried into a friendship that he had no right to know. *We here at the temple,* the letter had said. Perhaps the writer had been one of the Hazer mystics, writing to his old friend, the philosopher. And the other letters, quite possibly, were from that same mystic – letters that the dead old Hazer had valued so highly that he took them along with him when he went travelling.

A slight breeze seemed to be blowing across Enoch's shoulders; not actually a breeze, but a strange motion and a coldness to the air.

He glanced back into the gallery and there was nothing stirring, nothing to be seen.

The wind had quit its blowing, if it had ever blown. Here one moment, gone the next. Like a passing ghost, thought Enoch.

Did the Hazer have a ghost?

The people back on Vega XXI had known the moment he had died and all the circumstances of his death. They had known again about the body disappearing. And the letter had spoken calmly, much more calmly than would have been in the capacity of most humans, about the writer's near approach to death.

Was it possible that the Hazers knew more of life and death than had ever been spelled out, Or had it been spelled out, put down in black and white, in some depository or depositories in the galaxy?

Was the answer there? he wondered.

Squatting there, he thought that perhaps it might be, that someone already knew what life was for and what its destiny. There was a comfort in the thought, a strange sort of personal comfort in being able to believe that some intelligence might have solved the riddle of that mysterious equation of the universe. And how, perhaps, that mysterious equation might tie in with the spiritual force that was idealistic brother to time and space and all those other elemental factors that held the universe together.

322

He tried to imagine what one might feel if he were in contact with the force, and could not. He wondered if even those who might have been in contact with it could find the words to tell. It might, he thought, be impossible. For how could one who had been in intimate contact all his life with space and time tell what either of these meant to him or how they felt?

Ulysses, he thought, had not told him all the truth about the Talisman. He had told him that it had disappeared and that the galaxy was without it, but he had not told him that for many years its power and glory had been dimmed by the failure of its custodian to provide a proper linkage between the people and the force. And all that time the corrosion occasioned by that failure had eaten away at the bonds of the galactic confraternity. Whatever might be happening now had not happened in the last few years; it had been building up for a longer time than most aliens would admit. Although, come to think of it, most aliens probably did not know.

Enoch closed the box lid and put it back into the trunk. Some day, he thought, when he was in the proper frame of mind, when the pressure of events made him less emotional, when he could dull the guilt of prying, he would achieve a scholarly and conscientious translation of those letters. For in them, he felt certain, he might find further understanding of that intriguing race. He might, he thought, then be better able to gauge *their* humanity – not humanity in the common and accepted sense of being a member of the human race of Earth, but in the sense that certain rules of conduct must underlie all racial concepts even as the thing called humanity in its narrow sense underlay the human concept.

He reached up to close the lid of the trunk and then he hesitated.

Some day, he had said. And there might not be a some day. It was a state of mind to be always thinking *some day*, a state of mind made possible by the conditions inside this station. For here there were endless days to come, for ever and for ever there were days to come. A man's concept of time was twisted out of shape and reason and he could look ahead complacently down a long, almost never ending, avenue of time. But that might be all over now. Time might suddenly snap back into its rightful focus. Should he leave this station, the long procession of days to come would end.

He pushed back the lid again until it rested against the shelves. Reaching in, he lifted out the box and set it on the floor beside him. He'd take it upstairs, he told himself, and put it with the other stuff that he must be prepared immediately to take along with him if he should leave the station.

If? he asked himself. Was there a question any longer? Had he, somehow, made that hard decision? Had it crept upon him unaware, so that he now was committed to it?

And if he had actually arrived at that decision, then he must, also, have arrived at the other one. If he left the station, then he could no longer be in a position to appear before Galactic Central to plead that Earth be cured of war.

You are the representative of the Earth, Ulysses had told him. You are the only one who can represent the Earth. But could he, in reality, represent the Earth? Was he any longer a true representative of the human race? He was a nineteenth-century man and how could he, being that, represent the twentieth? How much, he wondered, does the human character change with each generation? And not only was he of the nineteenth century, but he had, as well, lived for almost a hundred years under a separate and a special circumstance.

He knelt there, regarding himself with awe, and a little pity too, wondering what he was, if he were even human, if, unknown to himself, he had absorbed so much of the mingled alien viewpoint to which he had been subjected that he had become some strange sort of hybrid, a queer kind of galactic half-breed.

Slowly he pulled the lid down and pushed it tight. Then he shoved the trunk back underneath the shelves.

He tucked the box of letters underneath his arm and rose, picking up his rifle, and headed for the stairs.

31

He found some empty cartons stacked in the kitchen corner, boxes that Winslowe had used to bring out from town the supplies that he had ordered, and began to pack.

The journals, stacked neatly in order, filled one large box and a part of another. He took a stack of old newspapers and carefully wrapped the twelve diamond bottles off the mantel and packed them in another box, thickly padded, to guard against their breakage. Out of the cabinet he got the Vegan music box and wrapped it as carefully. He pulled out of another cabinet the alien literature that he had and piled it in the fourth box. He went through his desk, but there wasn't too much there, only odds and ends tucked here and there throughout the drawers. He found his chart and, crumpling it, threw it in the wastebasket that stood beside his desk.

The already filled boxes he carried across the room and stacked beside the door for easy reaching. Lewis would have a truck, but once he let him know he needed it, it still might take a while for it to arrive. But if he had the important stuff all packed, he told himself, he could get it out himself and have it waiting for the truck.

The important stuff, he thought. Who could judge importance? The journals and the alien literature, those first of all, of course. But the rest of it? Which of the rest of it? It was all important; every item should be taken. And that might be possible. Given time and with no extra complications, it might be possible to haul it all away, all that was in this room and stored down in the basement. It all was his and he had a right to it, for it had been given him. But that did not mean, he knew, that Galactic Central might not object most strenuously to his taking any of it.

And if that should happen, it was vital that he should be able to get away with those most important items. Perhaps he should go down into the basement and lug up those tagged articles of which he knew the purpose. It probably would be better to take material about which something might be known than a lot of stuff about which there was nothing known.

He stood undecided, looking all about the room. There were all the items on the coffee table and those should be taken, too, including the little flashing pyramid of globes that Lucy had set to working.

He saw that the Pet once again had crawled off the table and fallen on the floor. He stooped and picked it up and held it in his hands. It had grown an extra knob or two since the last time he had looked at it and it was now a faint and delicate pink, whereas the last time he had noticed it had been a cobalt blue.

He probably was wrong, he told himself, in calling it the Pet. It might not be alive. But if it were, it was a sort of life he could not even guess at. It was not metallic and it was not stone, but very close to both. A file made no impression on it and he'd been tempted a time or two to whack it with a hammer to see what that might do, although he was willing to bet it would have no effect at all. It grew slowly, and it moved, but there was no way of knowing how it moved. But leave it and come back and it would have moved – a little, not too much. It knew it was being watched and it would not move while watched. It did not eat so far as he could see and it seemed to have no wastes. It changed colours, but entirely without season and with no visible reason for the change.

A being from somewhere in the direction of Sagittarius had given it to him just a year or two ago, and the creature, Enoch recalled, had been something for the books. He probably wasn't actually a walking plant, but that was what he'd looked like – a rather spindly plant that had been shorted on good water and cheated on good soil, but which had sprouted a crop of dime-store bangles that rang like a thousand silver bells when he made any sort of motion.

Enoch remembered that he had tried to ask the being what the gift might be, but the walking plant had simply clashed its bangles and filled the place with ringing sound and didn't try to answer.

So he had put the gift on one end of the desk and hours later, after the being was long gone, he found that it had moved to the other end of the desk. But it had seemed too crazy to think that a thing like that could move, so he finally convinced himself that he was mistaken as to where he'd put it. It was not until days later that he was able to convince himself it moved.

He'd have to take it when he left and Lucy's pyramid and the cube that showed you pictures of other worlds when you looked inside of it and a great deal of other stuff.

He stood with the Pet held in his hand and now, for the first time, he wondered at why he might be packing.

He was acting as if he'd decided he would leave the station, as if he'd chosen Earth as against the galaxy. But when and how, he wondered, had he decided it? Decision should be based on weighing and on measuring and he had weighed and measured nothing. He had not posed the advantages and the disadvantages and tried to strike a balance. He had not thought it out. Somehow, somewhere, it had sneaked up on him – this decision which had seemed impossible, but now had been reached so easily.

Was it, he wondered, that he had absorbed, unconsciously, such an odd mixture of alien thought and ethics that he had evolved, unknown to himself, a new way in which to think, perhaps some subconscious way of thought that had lain inoperative until now, when it had been needed?

There was a box or two out in the shed and he'd go and get them and finish up the packing of what he'd pick out here. Then he'd go down into the basement and start lugging up the stuff that he had tagged. He glanced towards the window and realized, with some surprise, that he would have to hurry, for the sun was close to setting. It would be evening soon.

He remembered that he'd forgotten lunch, but he had no time to eat. He could get something later.

He turned to put the Pet back on the table and as he did a faint sound caught his ear and froze him where he stood.

It was the slight chuckle of a materializer operating and he could not mistake it. He had heard the sound too often to be able to mistake it.

And it must be, he knew, the official materializer, for no one could have travelled on the other without the sending of a message.

Ulysses, he thought. Ulysses coming back again. Or perhaps some other member of Galactic Central. For if Ulysses had been coming, he would have sent a message.

He took a quick step forward so he could see the corner where the materializer stood and a dark and slender figure was stepping out from the target circle.

'Ulysses!' Enoch cried, but even as he spoke he realized it was not Ulysses.

For an instant he had the impression of a top hat, of white tie and tails, of a jauntiness, and then he saw that the creature was a rat that walked erect, with sleek, dark fur covering its body and a sharp, axe-like rodent face. For an instant, as it turned its head towards him, he caught the red glitter of its eyes. Then it turned back towards the corner and he saw that its hand was lifted and was pulling out of a harnessed holster hung about its middle something that glinted with a metallic shimmer even in the shadow.

There was something very wrong about it. The creature should have greeted him. It should have said hello and come out to meet him. But instead it had thrown him that one red-eyed glance and then turned back to the corner.

The metallic object came out of the holster and it could only be a gun, or at least some sort of weapon that one might think of as a gun.

And was this the way, thought Enoch, that they would close the station? One quick shot, without a word, and the station keeper dead upon the floor. With someone other than Ulysses, because Ulysses could not be trusted to kill a longtime friend.

The rifle was lying across the desk top and there wasn't any time.

But the rat-like creature was not turning towards the room. It still was facing towards the corner and its hand was coming up, with the weapon glinting in it.

An alarm twanged within Enoch's brain and he swung his arm and yelled, hurling the Pet towards the creature in the corner, the yell jerked out of him involuntarily from the bottom of his lungs.

For the creature, he realized, had not been intent on the killing of the keeper, but the disruption of the station. The only thing there was to aim at in the corner was the control complex, the nerve centre of the station's operation. And if that should be knocked out, the station would be dead. To set it in operation once again it would be necessary to send a crew of technicians out in a spaceship from the nearest station – a trip that would require many years to make.

At Enoch's yell, the creature jerked around, dropping towards a crouch, and the flying Pet, tumbling end for end, caught it in the belly and drove it back against the wall.

Enoch charged, arms outspread to grapple with the creature. The gun flew from the creature's hand and pinwheeled across the floor. Then Enoch was upon the alien and even as he closed with it, his nostrils were assailed by its body stench – a sickening wave of nastiness.

He wrapped his arms about it and heaved, and it was not as heavy as he had thought it might be. His powerful wrench jerked it from the corner and swung it around and sent it skidding out across the floor.

It crashed against a chair and came to a stop and then like a steel coil it rose off the floor and pounced for the gun.

Enoch took two great strides and had it by the neck, lifting it and shaking it so savagely that the recovered gun flew from its hand again and the bag it carried on a thong across its shoulder pounded like a vibrating trip hammer against its hairy ribs.

The stench was thick, so thick that one could almost see it, and Enoch gagged on it as he shook the creature. And suddenly it was worse, much worse, like a fire raging in one's throat and a hammer in one's head. It was like a physical blow that hit one in the belly and shoved against the chest. Enoch let go his hold upon the creature and staggered back, doubled up and retching. He lifted his hands to his face and tried to push the stench away, to clear his nostrils and his mouth, to rub it from his eyes.

Through a haze he saw the creature rise and, snatching up the gun, rush towards the door. He did not hear the phrase that the creature spoke, but the door came open and the creature spurted forward and was gone. And the door slammed shut again.

32

Enoch wobbled across the room to the desk and caught at it for support. The stench was diminishing and his head was clearing and he scarcely could believe that it all had happened. For it was incredible that a thing like this should happen. The creature had travelled on the official materializer, and no one but a member of Galactic Central could travel by that route. And no member of Galactic Central, he was convinced, would have acted as the rat-like creature had. Likewise, the creature had known the phrase that would operate the door. No one but himself and Galactic Central would have known that phrase.

He reached out and picked up his rifle and hefted it in his fist.

It was all right, he thought. There was nothing harmed. Except that there was an alien loose upon the Earth and that was something that could not be allowed. The Earth was barred to aliens. As a planet which had not been recognized by the galactic confraternity, it was off-limit territory.

He stood with the rifle in his hand and knew what he must do – he must get that alien back, he must get it off the Earth.

He spoke the phrase aloud and strode towards the door and out and around the corner of the house.

The alien was running across the field and had almost reached the line of woods.

Enoch ran desperately, but before he was halfway down the field, the rat-like quarry had plunged into the woods and disappeared.

The woods were beginning to darken. The slanting rays of light from the setting sun still lighted the upper canopy of the foliage, but on the forest floor the shadows had begun to gather.

As he ran into the fringe of the woods, Enoch caught a glimpse of the creature angling down a small ravine and plunging up the other slope, racing through a heavy cover of ferns that reached almost to its middle.

If it kept on in that direction, Enoch told himself, it might work out all right, for the slope beyond the ravine ended in a clump of rocks that lay above an out-thrust point that ended in a cliff, with each side curving in, so that the point and its mass of boulders lay isolated, a place hung out in space. It might be a little rough to dig the alien from the rocks if it took refuge there, but at least it would be trapped and could not get away. Although, Enoch reminded himself, he could waste no time, for the sun was setting and it would soon be dark.

Enoch angled slightly westward to go around the head of the small ravine, keeping an eye on the fleeing alien. The creature kept on up the slope and Enoch, observing this, put on an extra burst of speed. For now he had the alien trapped. In its fleeing, it had gone past the point of no return. It could no longer turn around and retreat back from the point. Soon it would reach the cliff edge and then there'd be nothing it could do but hole up in the patch of boulders.

Running hard, Enoch crossed the area covered by the ferns and came out on the sharper slope some hundred yards or so below the boulder clump. Here the cover was not so dense. There was a scant covering of spotty under-brush and a scattering of trees. The soft loam of the forest floor gave way to a footing of shattered rock which through the years had been chipped off the boulders by the winters' frost, rolling down the slope. They lay there now, covered with thick moss, a treacherous place to walk.

As he ran, Enoch swept the boulders with a glance, but there was no sign of the alien. Then, out of the corner of his vision, he saw the motion, and threw himself forward to the ground behind a patch of hazel brush, and through the network of the bushes he saw the alien outlined against the sky, its head pivoting back and forth to sweep the slope below, the weapon half lifted and set for instant use.

Enoch lay frozen, with his outstretched hand gripping the rifle. There was a slash of pain across one set of knuckles and he knew that he had skinned them on the rock as he had dived for cover.

The alien dropped from sight behind the boulders and Enoch slowly pulled the rifle back to where he would be able to handle it should a shot present itself.

Although, he wondered, would he dare to fire? Would he dare to kill an alien?

The alien could have killed him back there at the station, when he had been knocked silly by the dreadful stench. But it had not killed him; it had fled instead. Was it, he wondered, that the creature had been so badly fright-ened that all that it could think of had been to get away? Or had it, perhaps, been as reluctant to kill a station keeper as he himself was to kill an alien?

He searched the rocks above him and there was no motion and not a thing to see. He must move up that slope, and quickly, he told himself, for time would work against him and to the advantage of the alien. Darkness could not be more than thirty minutes off and before dark had fallen this issue must be settled. If the alien got away, there'd be little chance to find it.

And why, asked a second self, standing to one side, should you worry about alien complications? For are you yourself not prepared to inform the

Earth that there are alien peoples in the galaxy and to hand to Earth, unauthorized, as much of that alien lore and learning as may be within your power? Why should you have stopped this alien from the wrecking of the station, insuring its isolation for many years – for if that had been done, then you'd have been free to do as you might wish with all that is within the station? It would have worked to your advantage to have allowed events to run their course.

But I couldn't, Enoch cried inside himself. *Don't you see I couldn't? Don't you understand?*

A rustle in the bushes to his left brought him around with the rifle up and ready.

And there was Lucy Fisher, not more than twenty feet away.

'Get out of here!' he shouted, forgetting that she could not hear him.

But she did not seem to notice. She motioned to the left and made a sweeping motion with her hand and pointed towards the boulders.

Go away, he said underneath his breath. *Go away from here.*

And made rejection motions to indicate that she should go back, that this was no place for her.

She shook her head and sprang away, in a running crouch, moving farther to the left and up the slope.

Enoch scrambled to his feet, lunging after her, and as he did the air behind him made a frying sound and there was the sharp bite of ozone in the air.

He hit the ground, instinctively, and farther down the slope he saw a square yard of ground that boiled and steamed, with the ground cover swept away by a fierce heat and the very soil and rock turned into a simmering pudding.

A laser, Enoch thought. The alien's weapon was a laser, packing a terrific punch in a narrow beam of light.

He gathered himself together and made a short rush up the hillside, throwing himself prone behind a twisted birch clump.

The air made the frying sound again and there was an instant's blast of heat and the ozone once again. Over on the reverse slope a patch of ground was steaming. Ash floated down and settled on Enoch's arms. He flashed a quick glance upward and saw that the top half of the birch clump was gone, sheared off by the laser and reduced to ash. Tiny coils of smoke rose lazily from the severed stumps.

No matter what it may have done, or failed to do, back there at the station, the alien now meant business. It knew that it was cornered and it was playing vicious.

Enoch huddled against the ground and worried about Lucy. He hoped that she was safe. The little fool should have stayed out of it. This was no place for her. She shouldn't even have been out in the woods at this time of day. She'd have old Hank out looking for her again, thinking she was kidnapped. He wondered what the hell had gotten into her.

The dusk was deepening. Only the far peak of the treetops caught the last rays of the sun. A coolness came stealing up the ravine from the valley far below and there was a damp, lush smell that came out of the ground. From some hidden hollow a whippoorwill called out mournfully.

Enoch darted out from behind the birch clump and rushed up the slope. He reached the fallen log he'd picked as a barricade and threw himself behind it. There was no sign of the alien and there was not another shot from the laser gun.

Enoch studied the ground ahead. Two more rushes, one to that small pile of rock and the next to the edge of the boulder area itself, and he'd be on top of the hiding alien. And once he got there, he wondered, what was he to do?

Go in and rout the alien out, of course.

There was no plan that could be made, no tactics that could be laid out in advance. Once he got to the edge of the boulders, he must play it all by ear, taking advantage of any break that might present itself. He was at a disadvantage in that he must not kill the alien, but must capture it instead and drag it back, kicking and screaming, if need be, to the safety of the station.

Perhaps, here in the open air, it could not use its stench defence as effectively as it had in the confines of the station, and that, he thought, might make it easier. He examined the clump of boulders from one edge to the other and there was nothing that might help him to locate the alien.

Slowly he began to snake around, getting ready for the next rush up the slope, moving carefully so that no sound would betray him.

Out of the tail of his eye he caught the moving shadow that came flowing up the slope. Swiftly he sat up, swinging the rifle. But before he could bring the muzzle round, the shadow was upon him, bearing him back, flat upon the ground, with one great splay-fingered hand clamped upon his mouth.

'Ulysses!' Enoch gurgled, but the fearsome shape only hissed at him in a warning sound.

Slowly the weight shifted off him and the hand slid from his mouth.

Ulysses gestured towards the boulder pile and Enoch nodded.

Ulysses crept closer and lowered his head towards Enoch's. He whispered with his mouth inches from the Earthman's ear: 'The Talisman! He has the Talisman!'

'The Talisman!' Enoch cried aloud, trying to strangle off the cry even as he made it, remembering that he should make no sound to let the watcher up above know where they might be.

From the ridge above a loose stone rattled as it was dislodged and began to roll, bouncing down the slope. Enoch hunkered closer to the ground behind the fallen log.

'Down!' he shouted to Ulysses. 'Down! He has a gun.'

But Ulysses' hand gripped him by the shoulder.

'Enoch!' he cried. 'Enoch, look!'

Enoch jerked himself erect and atop the pile of rock, dark against the skyline, were two grappling figures.

'Lucy!' he shouted.

For one of them was Lucy and the other was the alien.

She sneaked up on him, he thought. The damn' little fool, she sneaked up on him! While the alien had been distracted with watching the slope, she had slipped up close and then had tackled him. She had a club of some sort in her hand, an old dead branch, perhaps, and it was raised above her head, ready for a stroke, but the alien had a grip upon her arm and she could not strike.

'Shoot,' said Ulysses, in a flat, dead voice.

Enoch raised the rifle and had trouble with the sights because of the deepening darkness. And they were so close together! They were too close together.

'Shoot!' yelled Ulysses.

'I can't,' sobbed Enoch. 'It's too dark to shoot.'

'You have to shoot,' Ulysses said, his voice tense and hard. 'You have to take the chance.'

Enoch raised the rifle once again and the sights seemed clearer now and he knew the trouble was not so much the darkness as that shot which he had missed back there in the world of the honking thing that had strode its world on stilts. If he had missed then, he could as well miss now.

The bead came to rest upon the head of the rat-like creature, and then the head bobbed away, but was bobbing back again.

'Shoot!' Ulysses yelled.

Enoch squeezed the trigger and the rifle coughed and up atop the rocks the creature stood for a second with only half a head and with tattered gouts of flesh flying briefly like dark insects zooming against the half-light of the western sky.

Enoch dropped the gun and sprawled upon the earth, clawing his fingers into the thin and mossy soil, sick with the thought of what could have happened, weak with the thankfulness that it had not happened, that the years on that fantastic rifle range had at last paid off.

How strange it is, he thought, how so many senseless things shape our destiny. For the rifle range had been a senseless thing, as senseless as a billiard table or a game of cards – designed for one thing only, to please the keeper of the station. And yet the hours he'd spent there had shaped towards this hour and end, to this single instant on this restricted slope of ground.

The sickness drained away into the earth beneath him and a peace came stealing in upon him – the peace of trees and woodland soil and the first faint hush of nightfall. As if the sky and stars and very space itself had leaned close above him and was whispering his essential oneness with them. And it seemed for a moment that he had grasped the edge of some great truth and with this truth had come a comfort and a greatness he'd never known before.

'Enoch,' Ulysses whispered. 'Enoch, my brother ...'

There was something like a hidden sob in the alien's voice and he had never, until this moment, called the Earthman brother.

Enoch pulled himself to his knees and up on the pile of tumbled boulders was a soft and wondrous light, a soft and gentle light, as if a giant firefly had turned on its lamp and had not turned it off, but had left it burning.

The light was moving down across the rocks towards them and he could see Lucy moving with the light, as if she were walking towards them with a lantern in her hand.

Ulysses' hand reached out of the darkness and closed hard on Enoch's arm.

'Do you see?' he asked.

'Yes, I see. What is ...'

'It is the Talisman,' Ulysses said, enraptured, his breath rasping in his throat. 'And she is our new custodian. The one we've hunted through the years.'

33

You did not become accustomed to it, Enoch told himself as they tramped up through the woods. There was not a moment you were not aware of it. It was something that you wanted to hug close against yourself and hold it there forever, and even when it was gone from you, you'd probably not forget it, ever.

It was something that was past all description – a mother's love, a father's pride, the adoration of a sweetheart, the closeness of a comrade, it was all of these and more. It made the farthest distance near and turned the complex simple and it swept away all fear and sorrow, for all of there being a certain feeling of deep sorrow in it, as if one might feel that never in his lifetime would he know an instant like this, and that in another instant he would lose it and never would be able to hunt it out again. But that was not the way it was, for this ascendant instant kept going on and on.

Lucy walked between them and she held the bag that contained the Talisman close against her breast, with her two arms clasped about it, and Enoch, looking at her, in the soft glow of its light, could not help but think of a little girl carrying her beloved pussy cat.

'Never for a century,' said Ulysses, 'perhaps for many centuries, perhaps never, has it glowed so well. I myself cannot remember when it was like this. It is wonderful, is it not?'

'Yes,' said Enoch, 'it is wonderful.'

'Now we shall be one again,' Ulysses said. 'Now we shall feel again. Now we shall be a people instead of many people.'

'But the creature that had it …'

'A clever one,' Ulysses said. 'He was holding it for ransom.'

'It had been stolen, then.'

'We do not know all the circumstances,' Ulysses told him. 'We will find out, of course.'

They tramped on in silence through the woods and far in the east one could see, through the treetops, the first flush in the sky that foretold the rising moon.

'There is something,' Enoch said.

'Ask me,' said Ulysses.

'How could that creature back there carry it and not feel – feel no part of it? For if he could have, he would not have stolen it.'

'There is only one in many billions,' Ulysses said, 'who can – how do you say it? – tune in on it, perhaps. To you and I it would be nothing. It would not respond to us. We could hold it in our hands for ever and there would nothing happen. But let that one in many billions lay a finger on it and it becomes alive. There is a certain rapport, a sensitivity – I don't know how to say it – that forms a bridge between this strange machine and the cosmic spiritual force. It is not the machine, itself, you understand, that reaches out and taps the spiritual force. It is the living creature's mind, aided by the mechanism, that brings the force to us.'

A machine, a mechanism, no more than a tool – technological brother to the hoe, the wrench, the hammer – and yet as far a cry from these as the human brain was from that first amino acid which had come into being on this planet when the Earth was very young. One was tempted, Enoch thought, to say that this was as far as a tool could go, that it was the ultimate in the ingenuity possessed by any brain. But that would be a dangerous way of thinking, for perhaps there was no limit, there might, quite likely, be no such condition as the ultimate; there might be no time when any creature or any group of creatures could stop at any certain point and say, this is as far as we can go, there is no use of trying to go farther. For each new development produced, as side effects, so many other possibilities, so many other roads to travel, that with each step one took down any given road there were more paths to follow. There'd never be an end, he thought – no end to anything.

They reached the edge of the field and headed up across it towards the station. From its upper edge came the sound of running feet.

'Enoch!' a voice shouted out of the darkness. 'Enoch, is that you?'

Enoch recognized the voice.

'Yes, Winslowe. What is wrong?'

The mailman burst out of the darkness and stopped, panting with his running, at the edge of light.

'Enoch, they are coming! A couple of carloads of them. But I put a crimp in them. Where the road turns off into your lane – that narrow place, you know. I dumped two pounds of roofing nails along the ruts. That'll hold them for a while.'

'Roofing nails?' Ulysses asked.

'It's a mob,' Enoch told him. 'They are after me. The nails …'

'Oh, I see,' Ulysses said. 'The deflation of the tyres.'

Winslowe took a slow step closer, his gaze riveted on the glow of the shielded Talisman.

'That's Lucy Fisher, ain't it?'

'Of course it is,' said Enoch.

'Her old man came roaring into town just a while ago and said she was gone again. Up until then everything had quieted down and it was all right.

But old Hank, he got them stirred up again. So I went down to the hardware store and got them roofing nails and I beat them here.'

'This mob?' Ulysses asked. 'I don't—'

Winslowe interrupted him, gasping in his eagerness to tell all his information. 'That ginseng man is up there, waiting at the house for you. He has a panel truck.'

'That,' said Enoch, 'would be Lewis with the Hazer's body.'

'He is some upset,' said Winslowe. 'He said you were expecting him.'

'Perhaps,' suggested Ulysses, 'we shouldn't just be standing here. It seems to my poor intellect that many things, indeed, may be coming to a crisis.'

'Say,' the mailman yelled, 'what is going on here? What is that thing Lucy has and who's this fellow with you?'

'Later,' Enoch told him. 'I'll tell you later. There's no time to tell you now.'

'But, Enoch, there's the mob.'

'I'll deal with them,' said Enoch grimly, 'when I have to deal with them. Right now there's something more important.'

They ran up the slope, the four of them, dodging through the waist-high clumps of weeds. Ahead of them the station reared dark and angular against the evening sky.

'They're down there at the turnoff,' Winslowe gasped, wheezing with his running. 'That flash of light down the ridge. That was the headlights of a car.'

They reached the edge of the yard and ran towards the house. The black bulk of the panel truck glimmered in the glow cast by the Talisman. A figure detached itself from the shadow of the truck and hurried out towards them.

'Is that you, Wallace?'

'Yes,' said Enoch. 'I'm sorry that I wasn't here.'

'I was a bit upset,' said Lewis, 'when I didn't find you waiting.'

'Something unforeseen,' said Enoch. 'Something that must be taken care of.'

'The body of the honoured one?' Ulysses asked. 'It is in the truck?'

Lewis nodded. 'I am happy that we can restore it.'

'We'll have to carry him down to the orchard,' Enoch said. 'You can't get a car in there.'

'The other time,' Ulysses said, 'you were the one who carried him.'

Enoch nodded.

'My friend,' the alien said, 'I wonder if on this occasion I could be allowed the honour.'

'Why, yes, of course,' said Enoch. 'He would like it that way.'

And the words came to his tongue, but he choked them back, for it would not have done to say them – the words of thanks for lifting from him the necessity of complete recompense, for the gesture which released him from the utter letter of the law.

At his elbow, Winslowe said: 'They are coming. I can hear them down the road.'

He was right.

From down the road came the soft sound of footsteps padding in the dust, not hurrying, with no need to hurry, the insulting and deliberate treading of a monster so certain of its prey that it need not hurry.

Enoch swung around and half lifted his rifle, training it towards the padding that came out of the dark.

Behind him, Ulysses spoke softly: 'Perhaps it would be most proper to bear him to the grave in the full glory and unshielded light of our restored Talisman.'

'She can't hear you,' Enoch said. 'You must remember she is deaf. You will have to show her.'

But even as he said it, a blaze leaped out that was blinding in its brightness.

With a strangled cry Enoch half turned back to face the little group that stood beside the truck, and the bag that had enclosed the Talisman, he saw, lay at Lucy's feet and she held the glowing brightness high and proudly so that it spread its light across the yard and the ancient house, and some of it as well spilled out into the field.

There was a quietness. As if the entire world had caught its breath and stood attentive and in awe, waiting for a sound that did not come, that would never come but would always be expected.

And with the quietness came an abiding sense of peace that seemed to seep into the very fibre of one's being. It was no synthetic thing – not as if someone had invoked a peace and peace then was allowed to exist by sufferance. It was a present and an actual peace, the peace of mind that came with the calmness of a sunset after a long, hot day, or the sparkling, ghost-like shimmer of a springtime dawn. You felt it inside of you and all about you, and there was the feeling that it was not only here but that the peace extended on and out in all directions, to the farthest reaches of infinity, and that it had a depth which would enable it to endure until the final gasp of all eternity.

Slowly, remembering, Enoch turned back to face the field and the men were there, at the edge of the light cast by the Talisman, a grey, huddled group, like a pack of chastened wolves that slunk at the faint periphery of a campfire's light.

And as he watched, they melted back – back into the deeper dark from which they had padded in the dust track of the road.

Except for one who turned and bolted, plunging down the hill in the darkness towards the woods, howling in maddened terror like a frightened dog.

'There goes Hank,' said Winslowe. 'That is Hank running down the hill.'

'I am sorry that we frightened him,' said Enoch soberly. 'No man should be afraid of this.'

'It is himself that he is frightened of,' the mailman said. 'He lives with a terror in him.'

And that was true, thought Enoch. That was the way with Man; it had always been that way. He had carried terror with him. And the thing he was afraid of had always been himself.

34

The grave was filled and mounded and the five of them stood for a moment more, listening to the restless wind that stirred in the moon-drenched apple orchard, while from far away, down in the hollows above the river valley, the whippoorwills talked back and forth through the silver night.

In the moonlight Enoch tried to read the graven line upon the rough-hewn tombstone, but there was not light enough. Although there was no need to read it; it was in his mind:

Here lies one from a distant star, but the soil is not alien to him, for in death he belongs to the universe.

When you wrote that, the Hazer diplomat had told him, just the night before, you wrote as one of us. And he had not said so, but the Vegan had been wrong. For it was not a Vegan sentiment alone; it was human, too.

The words were chiselled awkwardly and there was a mistake or two in spelling, for the Hazer language was not an easy one to master. The stone was softer than the marble or the granite most commonly used for gravestones and the lettering would not last. In a few more years the weathering of sun and rain and frost would blur the characters, and in some years after that they would be entirely gone, with no more than the roughness of the stone remaining to show that words had once been written there. But it did not matter, Enoch thought, for the words were graven on more than stone alone.

He looked across the grave at Lucy. The Talisman was in its bag once more and the glow was softer. She still held it clasped tight against herself and her face was still exalted and unnoticing – as if she no longer lived in the present world, but had entered into some other place, some other far dimension where she dwelled alone and was forgetful of all past.

'Do you think,' Ulysses asked, 'that she will go with us? Do you think that we can have her? Will the Earth ...'

'The Earth,' said Enoch, 'has not a thing to say. We Earth people are free agents. It is up to her.'

'You think that she will go?'

'I think so,' Enoch said. 'I think maybe this has been the moment she had sought for all her life. I wonder if she might not have sensed it, even with no Talisman.'

For she always had been in touch with something outside of human ken. She had something in her no other human had. You sensed it, but you could not name it, for there was no name for this thing she had. And she had fumbled with it, trying to use it, not knowing how to use it, charming off the warts and healing poor hurt butterflies and only God knew what other acts that she performed unseen.

'Her parent?' Ulysses asked. 'The howling one that ran away from us?'

'I'll handle him,' said Lewis. 'I'll have a talk with him. I know him fairly well.'

'You want her to go back with you to Galactic Central?' Enoch asked.

'If she will,' Ulysses said, 'Central must be told at once.'

'And from there throughout the galaxy?'

'Yes,' Ulysses said. 'We need her very badly.'

'Could we, I wonder, borrow her for a day or two.'

'Borrow her?'

'Yes,' said Enoch. 'For we need her, too. We need her worst of all.'

'Of course,' Ulysses said. 'But I don't ...'

'Lewis,' Enoch asked, 'do you think our government – the Secretary of State, perhaps – might be persuaded to appoint one Lucy Fisher as a member of our peace conference delegation?'

Lewis stammered, made a full stop, then began again: 'I think it could possibly be managed.'

'Can you imagine,' Enoch asked, 'the impact of this girl and the Talisman at the conference table?'

'I think I can,' said Lewis. 'But the Secretary undoubtedly would want to talk with you before he arrived at his decision.'

Enoch half turned towards Ulysses, but he did not need to phrase his question.

'By all means,' Ulysses said to Lewis. 'Let me know and I'll sit in on the meeting. And you might tell the good Secretary, too, that it would not be a bad idea to begin the formation of a world committee.'

'A world committee?'

'To arrange,' Ulysses said, 'for the Earth becoming one of us. We cannot accept a custodian, can we, from an outside planet?'

35

In the moonlight the tumbled boulder pile gleamed whitely, like the skeleton of some prehistoric beast. For here, near the edge of the cliff that towered above the river, the heavy trees thinned out and the rocky point stood open to the sky.

Enoch stood beside one of the massive boulders and gazed down at the huddled figure that lay among the rocks. Poor, tattered bungler, he thought, dead so far from home and, so far as he, himself, must be concerned, to so little purpose.

Although perhaps neither poor nor tattered, for in that brain, now broken and spattered beyond recovery, must surely have lain a scheme of greatness – the kind of scheme that the brain of an earthly Alexander or Xerxes or Napoleon may have held, a dream of some great power, cynically conceived, to be attained and held at whatever cost, the dimensions of it so grandiose that it shoved aside and cancelled out all moral considerations.

He tried momentarily to imagine what the scheme might be, but knew, even as he tested his imagination, how foolish it was to try, for there would be factors he was sure that he would not recognize and considerations that might lie beyond his understanding.

But however that might be, something had gone wrong, for in the plan itself Earth could have had no place other than as a hideout which could be used if trouble struck. This creature's lying here, then, was a part of desperation, a last-ditch gamble that had not worked out.

And, Enoch thought, it was ironic that the key of failure lay in the fact that the creature, in its fleeing, had carried the Talisman into the backyard of a sensitive, and on a planet, too, where no one would have thought to look for a sensitive. For, thinking back on it, there could be little doubt that Lucy had sensed the Talisman and had been drawn to it as truly as a magnet would attract a piece of steel. She had known nothing else, perhaps, than that the Talisman had been there and was something she must have, that it was something she had waited for in all her loneliness, without knowing what it was or without hope of finding it. Like a child who sees, quite suddenly, a shiny, glorious bauble on a Christmas tree and knows that it's the grandest thing on Earth and that it must be hers.

This creature lying here, thought Enoch, must have been able and resourceful. For it would have taken great ability and resourcefulness to have stolen the Talisman to start with, to keep it hidden for years, to have penetrated into the secrets and the files of Galactic Central. Would it have been possible he wondered, if the Talisman had been in effective operation? With an energetic Talisman would the moral laxity and the driving greed have been possible to motivate the deed?

But that was ended now. The Talisman had been restored and a new custodian had been found – a deaf-mute girl of Earth, the humblest of humans. And there would be peace on Earth and in time the Earth would join the confraternity of the galaxy.

There were no problems now, he thought. No decisions to be made. Lucy had taken the decisions from the hands of everyone.

The station would remain and he could unpack the boxes he had packed and put the journals back on the shelves again. He could go back to the station once again and settle down and carry on his work.

I am sorry, he told the huddled shape that lay among the boulders. *I am sorry that mine was the hand that had to do it to you.*

He turned away and walked out to where the cliff dropped straight down to the river flowing at its foot. He raised the rifle and held it for a moment motionless and then he threw it out and watched it fall, spinning end for end, the moonlight glinting off the barrel, saw the tiny splash it made as it struck the water. And far below, he heard the smug, contented gurgling of the water as it flowed past this cliff and went on, to the farther ends of Earth.

There would be peace on Earth, he thought; there would be no war. With Lucy at the conference table, there could be no thought of war. Even if some ran howling from the fear inside themselves, a fear and guilt so great that it overrode the glory and the comfort of the Talisman, there still could be no war.

But it was a long trail yet, a long and lonesome way, before the brightness of real peace would live in the hearts of man.

Until no man ran howling, wild with fear (any kind of fear), would there be actual peace. Until the last man threw away his weapon (any sort of weapon), the tribe of Man could not be at peace. And a rifle, Enoch told himself, was the least of the weapons of the Earth, the least of man's inhumanity to man, no more than a symbol of all the other and more deadly weapons.

He stood on the rim of the cliff and looked out across the river and the dark shadow of the wooded valley. His hands felt strangely empty with the rifle gone, but it seemed that somewhere, back there just a way, he had stepped into another field of time, as if an age or day had dropped away and he had come into a place that was shining and brand new and unsullied by any past mistakes.

The river rolled below him and the river did not care. Nothing mattered to the river. It would take the tusk of mastodon, the skull of sabretooth, the rib cage of a man, the dead and sunken tree, the thrown rock or rifle and would swallow each of them and cover them in mud or sand and roll gurgling over them, hiding them from sight.

A million years ago there had been no river here and in a million years to come there might be no river – but in a million years from now there would be, if not Man, at least a caring thing. And that was the secret of the universe, Enoch told himself – a thing that went on caring.

He turned slowly from the cliff edge and clambered through the boulders, to go walking up the hill. He heard the tiny scurrying of small life rustling through the fallen leaves and once there was the sleepy peeping of an awakened bird and through the entire woods lay the peace and comfort of that glowing light – not so intense, not so deep and bright and so wonderful as when it actually had been there, but a breath of it still left.

He came to the edge of the woods and climbed the field and ahead of him the station stood foursquare upon its ridge top. And it seemed that it was no longer a station only, but his home as well. Many years ago it had been a home and nothing more and then it had become a way station to the galaxy. But now, although way station still, it was home again.

36

He came into the station and the place was quiet and just a little ghostly in the quietness of it. A lamp burned on his desk and over on the coffee table the little pyramid of spheres was flashing, throwing its many-coloured lights, like the crystal balls they'd used in the Roaring Twenties to turn a dance hall into a place of magic. The tiny flickering colours went flitting all about the room, like the dance of a zany band of Technicolor fireflies.

He stood for a moment, indecisive, not knowing what to do. There was something missing and all at once he realized what it was. During all the years there'd been a rifle to hang upon its pegs or to lay across the desk. And now there was no rifle.

He'd have to settle down, he told himself, and get back to work. He'd have to unpack and put the stuff away. He'd have to get the journals written and catch up with his reading. There was a lot to do.

Ulysses and Lucy had left an hour or two before, bound for Galactic Central, but the *feeling* of the Talisman still seemed to linger in the room. Although, perhaps, he thought, not in the room at all, but inside himself. Perhaps it was a feeling that he'd carry with him no matter where he went.

He walked slowly across the room and sat down on the sofa. In front of him the pyramid of spheres was splashing out its crystal shower of colours. He reached out a hand to pick it up, then drew it slowly back. What was the use, he asked himself, of examining it again? If he had not learned its secret the many times before, why should he expect to now?

A pretty thing, he thought, but useless.

He wondered how Lucy might be getting on and knew she was all right. She'd get along, he told himself, anywhere she went.

Instead of sitting here, he should be getting back to work. There was a lot of catching up to do. And his time would not be his own from now on, for the Earth would be pounding at the door. There would be conferences and meetings and a lot of other things and in a few hours more the newspapers might be here. But before it happened, Ulysses would be back to help him, and perhaps there would be others, too.

In just a little while he'd rustle up some food and then he'd get to work. If he worked far into the night, he could get a good deal done.

Lonely nights, he told himself, were good for work. And it was lonely now, when it should not be lonely. For he no longer was alone, as he had thought he was alone just a few short hours before. Now he had the Earth and the galaxy, Lucy and Ulysses, Winslowe and Lewis and the old philosopher out in the apple orchard.

He rose and walked to the desk and picked up the statuette Winslowe had carved of him. He held it beneath the desk lamp and turned it slowly in his hands. There was, he saw now, a loneliness in that figure, too – the essential loneliness of a man who walked alone.

But he'd had to walk alone. There'd been no other way. There had been no choice. It had been a one-man job. And now the job was – no, not done, for there still was much that must be done. But the first phase of it now was over and the second phase was starting.

He set the statuette back on the desk and remembered that he had not given Winslowe the piece of wood the Thuban traveller had brought. Now he could tell Winslowe where all the wood had come from. They could go through the journals and find the dates and the origin of every stick of it. That would please old Winslowe.

He heard the silken rustle and swung swiftly round.

'Mary!' he cried.

She stood just at the edge of shadow and the flitting colours from the flashing pyramid made her seem like someone who had stepped from fairyland. And that was right, he was thinking wildly, for his lost fairyland was back.

'I had to come,' she said. 'You were lonely, Enoch, and I could not stay away.'

She could not stay away – and that might be true, he thought. For within the conditioning he'd set up there might have been the inescapable compulsion to come whenever she was needed.

It was a trap, he thought, from which neither could escape. There was no free will here, but instead the deadly precision of this blind mechanism he had shaped himself.

She should not come to see him and perhaps she knew this as well as he, but could not help herself. Would this be, he wondered, the way that it would be, for ever and for ever?

He stood there, frozen, torn by the need of her and the emptiness of her unreality, and she was moving towards him.

She was close to him and in a moment she would stop, for she knew the rules as well as he; she, no more than he, could admit illusion.

But she did not stop. She came so close that he could smell the apple-blossom fragrance of her. She put out a hand and laid it on his arm.

It was no shadow touch and it was no shadow hand. He could feel the pressure of her fingers and the coolness of them.

He stood rigid, with her hand upon his arm.

The flashing light! he thought. The pyramid of spheres!

For now he remembered who had given it to him – one of those aberrant races of the Aplhard system. And it had been from the literature of that system that he had learned the art of fairyland. They had tried to help him by giving him the pyramid and he had not understood. There had been a failure of communication – but that was an easy thing to happen. In the Babel of the galaxy, it was easy to misunderstand or simply not to know.

For the pyramid of spheres was a wonderful, and yet a simple, mechanism. It was the fixation agent that banished all illusion, that made a fairyland for real. You made something as you wanted it and then turned on the pyramid and you had what you had made, as real as if it had never been illusion.

Except, he thought, in some things you couldn't fool yourself. You knew it was illusion, even if it should turn real.

He reached out towards her tentatively, but her hand dropped from his arm and she took a slow step backward. In the silence of the room – the terrible, lonely silence – they stood facing one another while the coloured lights ran like playing mice as the pyramid of spheres twirled its everlasting rainbow.

'I am sorry,' Mary said, 'but it isn't any good. We can't fool ourselves.'

He stood mute and shamed.

'I waited for it,' she said. 'I thought and dreamed about it.'

'So did I,' said Enoch. 'I never thought that it would happen.'

And that was it, of course. So long as it could not happen, it was a thing to dream about. It was romantic and far-off and impossible. Perhaps it had been romantic only because it had been so far-off and so impossible.

'As if a doll had come to life,' she said, 'or a beloved Teddy bear. I am sorry, Enoch, but you could not love a doll or a Teddy bear that had come to life. You always would remember them the way they were before. The doll with the silly, painted smile; the Teddy bear with the stuffing coming out of it.'

'No!' cried Enoch. 'No!'

'Poor Enoch,' she said. 'It will be so bad for you. I wish that I could help. You'll have so long to live with it.'

'But you!' he cried. 'But you? What can you do now?'

It had been she, he thought, who had the courage. The courage that it took to face things as they were.

How, he wondered, had she sensed it? How could she have known?

'I shall go away,' she said. 'I shall not come back. Even when you need me, I shall not come back. There is no other way.'

'But you can't go away,' he said. 'You are trapped the same as I.'

'Isn't it strange,' she said, 'how it happened to us? Both of us victims of illusion …'

'But you,' he said. 'Not you.'

She nodded gravely. 'I, the same as you. You can't love the doll you made or I the toymaker. But each of us thought we did; each of us still think we should and are guilty and miserable when we find we can't.'

'We could try,' said Enoch. 'If you would only stay.'

'And end up by hating you? And, worse than that, by your hating me. Let us keep the guilt and misery. It is better than the hate.'

She moved swiftly and the pyramid of spheres was in her hand and lifted. 'No, not that!' he shouted. 'No, Mary ...'

The pyramid flashed, spinning in the air, and crashed against the fireplace. The flashing lights went out. Something – glass? metal? stone? – tinkled on the floor.

'Mary!' Enoch cried, striding forward in the dark.

But there was no one there.

'Mary!' he shouted, and the shouting was a whimper.

She was gone and she would not be back.

Even when he needed her, she would not be back.

He stood quietly in the dark and silence, and the voice of a century of living seemed to speak to him in a silent language.

All things are hard, it said. There is nothing easy.

There had been the farm girl living down the road, and the southern beauty who had watched him pass her gate, and now there was Mary, gone for ever from him.

He turned heavily in the room and moved forward, groping for the table. He found it and switched on the light.

He stood beside the table and looked about the room. In this corner where he stood there once had been a kitchen, and there, where the fireplace stood, the living-room, and it all had changed – it had been changed for a long time now. But he still could see it as if it were only yesterday.

All the days were gone and all the people in them.

Only he was left.

He had lost his world. He had left his world behind him.

And, likewise, on this day, had all the others – all the humans that were alive this moment.

They might not know it yet, but they, too, had left their world behind them. It would never be the same again.

You said good-bye to so many things, to so many loves, to so many dreams.

'Good-bye, Mary,' he said. 'Forgive me and God keep you.'

He sat down at the table and pulled the journal that lay upon its top in front of him. He flipped it open, searching for the pages he must fill.

He had work to do.

Now he was ready for it.

He had said his last good-bye.

A CHOICE OF GODS

1

Aug. 1, 2185: So we begin again. Actually, we began again fifty years ago, but did not know it then. There was hope, for a time, that there were more people left and that we could pick up where we had left off. We thought, somehow, that we could hang onto what we had, once the shock was over and we could think more clearly and plan more cleverly. By the end of the first year we should have known that it was impossible; by the end of five we should have been willing to admit it, but we weren't. At first we refused to face the fact and once we had to face it we became stubborn with a senseless sort of faith. The old way of life could not be revived; there were too few of us and none with special knowledge and the old technology was gone beyond all restoration. The technology had been too complex and too specialized and too regimented to be picked up and carried on without a large work force equipped with appropriate skills and knowledge that were necessary not only to operate the technology itself, but to produce the energy that went into it. We are now no more than scavengers feeding on the carcass of the past and some day we'll be down to the bare bones of it and will be finally on our own. But over the years we have been recovering or rediscovering, whichever it may be, some of the older and more basic technology geared to a simpler way of life and these basic rudimentary skills should keep us from sinking into utter savagery.

There is no one who knows what really happened, which does not, of course, deter some of us from formulating theories that might explain it all. The trouble is that all the theories boil down to simple guesses, in which all kinds of metaphysical misconceptions play a part. There are no facts other than two very simple facts and the first of these is that fifty years ago last month the greater fraction of the human race either went somewhere or was taken somewhere. Out of more than eight billion of us, which was certainly far too many of us, there are now, at most, a few hundred left. In this house in which I sit to write these words, there are sixty-seven humans, and only that many because on the night it happened we had invited some young guests to help us celebrate the coming of age of our twin grandsons, John and Jason Whitney. Of the Leech Lake Indians there may be as many as three hundred, although we now see little of them, for they have taken up again, quite happily and to their great advantage, or so it would seem to me, their old tribal wanderings. At times rumors reach us of the other little pockets of humanity still surviving (the rumors chiefly brought by some loose-footed robot), but when we've gone to hunt for them, they are never there, nor is there anything to indicate they ever had been there. This, of course, proves nothing. It stands to reason that elsewhere on the Earth there must be others left, although we have no idea where. We hunt for them no longer, even when the rumors come, for it seems to us that we no longer have any need of them. In the intervening years we have become content, settling down into the routine of a bucolic life.

The robots still are with us and we have no idea how many there may be. All the robots that were ever in existence must still remain. They did not go or were not taken as was the human race. Over the years a number of them have come to settle in with us, doing all the work and chores necessary for our comfortable existence, becoming, in all truth, a part of our community. Some of them at times may leave and go elsewhere for a while and there are occasions when new ones float in and stay, either for good or for varying periods. It might seem to someone unacquainted with the situation that in the robots we had the labor force we needed to keep at least a small sector of the more vital parts of the old technology alive. It is possible the robots could have been taught the necessary skills, but the rub here is that we had no one who was equipped to teach them. Even if we'd had, I have some well-founded doubt that it would have worked. The robots are not technologically minded. They were not built to be. They were built to bolster human vanity and pride, to meet a strange longing that seems to be built into the human ego – the need to have other humans (or a reasonable facsimile of other humans) to minister to our wants and needs, human slaves to be dominated, human beings over which a man or woman (or a child) can assert authority, thus building up a false feeling of superiority. They were built to serve as cooks, gardeners, butlers, maids, footmen (I have never got quite straight in my mind what a footman is) – servants of all kinds. They were the flunkeys and the inferior companions, the yea-sayers, the slaves. In a manner of speaking, in their services to us, I suppose they still are slaves. Although I doubt the robots think of it as slavery; their values, while supplied by human agency, are not entirely human values. They serve us most willingly; thankful of a chance to serve, they press their services upon us, apparently glad to find new masters to replace the old. This is the situation as it applies to us; with the Indians it is different. The robots do not feel at ease with the Indians and the Indians, in turn, regard them with an emotion that borders upon loathing. They are a part of the white man's culture and are readily acceptable to us upon the basis of our one-time preoccupation with machines. To the Indians they are unclean, something that is repulsively foul and alien. They will have no part of them. Any robot stumbling into an Indian camp is summarily hustled off. A few of the robots serve us. There must be many thousands more. Those that are not with us we have fallen into the habit of calling wild robots, although I doubt they, in any sense, are wild. Often, from our windows or while sitting on the patio, or while out walking, we see bands of wild robots hurrying along as if they had an urgent destination or were involved in some great purpose. We have never been able to determine where the destination or what might be the purpose. There are certain stories of them that we hear at times, but nothing more than stories and with no evidence, and not worth repeating here.

I said there were two facts and then got lost in the telling of the first. This is the second fact: our lives are much longer now. In some strange way which no one pretends to understand, the process of aging, if not halted, has been slowed. I have not seemed to age at all, nor have any of the others, in these last fifty years. If there are a few more white hairs I cannot detect them; if I walk a little slower after fifty years I am not aware of it. I was sixty then and I still am sixty. The youngsters develop to maturity in the usual manner and the normal course of time, but once they reach maturity, the aging seems to stop. Our twin grandsons, whose twenty-first birthday we observed fifty years ago, still are twenty-one. They are, to all physical appearances, the same age as their sons and their oldest grandsons and at times this becomes somewhat disconcerting to someone like myself, who has lived his entire life with aging, and with the expectation of it. But disconcerting as it may be, I do not quibble with it, for with the inhibition of aging has come, as well, unbelievable good health. That was something that had worried us to start with – with all the people gone, what would we do for doctors or hospital care if we should happen to fall ill? Luckily, perhaps, the chronological years during which a woman remains capable of bearing children are about the same as they were before the span of life was lengthened. The female reproductive system apparently exhausts its supply of potential egg cells within some thirty years or so, as it did before.

There can be little doubt that the disappearance of the human race and the inhibiting of aging must somehow be connected. And while none of us can help but be grateful for this longer life and, perhaps as well, for the lifting of the social pressure which came with the overpopulation of the planet, the more thoughtful of us sometimes worry about the implications which may lie behind it all. In the dark of night we lie unsleeping in our beds and think of it and although the shock has faded with the years, we are sometimes frightened.

So on this August morning near the end of the twenty-second century since the birth of Jesus, I begin this record in which I shall set down, in detail, my remembrance of what has happened. It is a job that someone should do and, as the oldest member of this house, in my hundred and tenth chronological year, it seems only meet and proper that mine should be the hand to put down the words. Without a record of this sort, inscribed while human memory serves with some faithfulness, what happened to the race would become, in time, a myth ...

2

He could not forget that last bear but, strangely, could not remember exactly what had happened. Trying to remember, trying to be sure, had occupied his thoughts for the last few days and he was no nearer to an answer than he had ever been. The beast, rearing up from a deep-cut stream bed, had caught him off his guard and there had been no chance to run, for the bear was far too close. The arrow had not killed it, he was sure of that, for there was little time to shoot and the shaft had been badly placed. Yet the bear had died, lunging forward to skid almost to his feet. And in that fractured moment before the bear had died, something had happened and it was this something that had happened that he could not remember. It was, he was certain, something he had done, but there was no clue to what it might have been. There had been times when the answer had welled almost to awareness and then been driven back, deep into his mind, as if it were something he was not supposed to know, or that he would be better off not knowing, something that his inner, hidden mind would not let him know.

He dropped his pack beside him and leaned the bow against it Staring out across the wide expanse of bluff-rimmed, autumn-painted valley where the two great rivers met, he saw that it was exactly as he had been told it would be by the buffalo-hunting band he'd met in the great high plains almost a moon before. He smiled to himself as he thought of them, for they had been pleasant people. They had asked him to stay and he very nearly had. There had been a girl who had laughed with him, the laughter deep inside her throat, and a young man who had laid his hand upon his arm with the touch of brotherhood. But in the end he could not stay.

The sun was coming up and the maples along the rim of the farther bluff, caught in its rays, flamed with sudden red and gold. And there, on the rocky headland that reared above the river's junction, stood the huge block of masonry that they had told him of, with its many chimneys pointing stubby fingers at the sky.

The young man lifted a pair of binoculars off his chest and set them to his eyes. Disturbed by the movement of the strap, the bear claws of his necklace clicked together.

Jason Whitney came to the end of his morning walk and it had been, he told himself, the best walk he'd ever had – although he recalled that he always thought that each morning as he came up the slight slope toward the patio, with the smell of frying bacon and of morning eggs wafting from the kitchen, where Thatcher made them ready. But this morning had been good, he insisted to himself. It had been so fresh, with just a nip of chill until the rising sun dispelled it, and the leaves, he thought – the leaves were at their best. He had stood out on the point of rocks and had watched the rivers and they had been (perhaps to complement the autumn colors through which they flowed) a deeper blue than usual. A flock of ducks had been flying across the bottom land, close above the treetops, and in one of the little ponds which dotted the flood plain a moose had stood knee-deep, putting his head down into the water to feed upon the lilies, the water cascading off his mighty antlers when he raised his head. Even from where he stood, Jason had imagined he could hear that sound of cascading water, although he knew it was too far to hear.

The two dogs that had gone with him had hurried on ahead and now were waiting on the patio, not for him, although he would have liked to think so, but for their plates of food. Bowser, full of many years, had walked heavily and sedately beside him as they'd gone down across the land, while Rover, the foolish pup, had treed an early-foraging squirrel in the walnut grove and had flushed a covey of quail out of the corn shocks and pumpkins of an autumn field.

The door opened on the patio and Martha came out, carrying plates for the two dogs. She stooped and set them on the stones, while the dogs waited, respectfully and politely, with their tails swinging slowly and their ears pricked forward. Straightening, she came off the patio and down the slope to meet him. She gave him her morning kiss and linked her arm in his.

'While you were on your walk,' she said, 'I had a talk with Nancy.'

He knitted his brow, trying to remember. 'Nancy?' he asked.

'Why, of course,' she said. 'You know. She is Geoffrey's oldest child. It has been so long since I have talked with her.'

'I place her now,' he said. 'And where might Nancy be?'

'Out Polaris way,' said Martha. 'They moved just recently. They're on the nicest planet ...'

Evening Star, crouched in the lodge, put the finishing touches to the talismanic doll. She had worked hard on it to make it nice and this was the day she'd take it as an offering to the oak. It was a good day for it, she told herself – fair and soft and warm. These were the kind of days that one must treasure, close against the heart, for the painted days were few. Soon would come the dreary days, with the cold mist slanting ghostlily through the naked trees and after that the frigid sweep of northern winds and snow. Outside she heard the camp come to morning life – the ring of ax on wood, the clatter of the cooking pots, the call of friend to friend, the happy barking of a dog.

Later in the day the work of clearing the old fields would take up again, grubbing out the brush, clearing away the stones heaved up by the frosts of other years, the raking and burning of the weeds, leaving the ground bare and ready for the springtime plowing and the planting. Everyone would be busy (as she herself would be expected to be) and it would be easy for her to leave the camp unnoticed and to get back again before anyone should remark her absence.

She must let no one know, she reminded herself – not her father or mother and least of all Red Cloud, the first chieftain of the band and her own grandfather, many times removed. For it was not proper that a woman should have a guardian spirit. Except that to her it seemed entirely right. On that day seven years ago the signs of guardianship had been too plain to doubt. The tree had spoken to her and she had spoken to the tree and it was as if a father and a daughter had bespoken one another. It was not, she thought, as if she had sought the relationship. It had been the last thing in her mind. But when a tree speaks to one, what is one to do?

On this day, she wondered, would the tree speak to her again? After so long an absence, would the tree remember?

Hezekiah sat on the marble bench beneath the drooping branches of the ancient willow tree and pulled the coarse brown robe close about his metal frame – and this was pretense and pride, he thought, and unworthy of him, for he did not need to sit and he did not need the robe. A yellow leaf fluttered down from overhead and settled in his lap, a clear, almost transparent yellow against the brownness of the robe. He moved to brush it off and then he let it stay. For who am I, he thought, to interfere with or dispute even such a simple thing as the falling of a leaf.

He lifted his eyes from the leaf and over there, a mile or so away, beyond the monastery walls, the great house of stone stood solid on the rocky battlement that rose above the rivers – a mighty, sprawling house with its windows winking in the morning sun, the chimney's pleading hands lifted up to God.

They are the ones who should be here instead of us, he thought, the people in that house, and then, almost as soon as he thought of it, recalled that for many centuries there had been only two of them in residence, Jason Whitney and his good wife, Martha. At times some of the others came back from the stars to visit their old home or the old family home (whichever it might be, for some of them had been born far among the stars). And what business did they have, Hezekiah asked, with a touch of bitterness, to be out among the stars? Their concern should not be with the stars and all that they might find to amuse themselves out there; any human's one concern rightfully should be the condition of his immortal soul.

In the grove of music trees beyond the monastery walls the leaves were rustling gently, but as yet the trees were silent. Later in the day, sometime in the afternoon, they'd do some tuning up for the nightly concert. It would be, he thought, with some reluctance at the thought, a glorious thing to hear. At times he had imagined their music was that of some heavenly choir, but it was all, he knew, in his imagination; at times the kind of music they produced was anything but churchly. It was thoughts like this, he told himself, and the action of sitting on a bench and the wearing of a robe that made himself and his companions less fit to perform with faith the task they'd taken up. But a naked robot, he told himself, could not stand before the Lord; he must have about him some of the habiliments of man if he were to take the place of man, who had so utterly forgotten.

The old doubts and fears came flooding into him and he sat bowed against them. It would seem, he thought, one would become accustomed to them, for they'd been with him from the start (and with the others, too), but the sharpness of them had not dulled and they still cut him to the core. Rather than diminishing with familiarity, they had grown sharper as the years went on, with no answer found after centuries of poring over the meticulous commentaries and the extensive, searching writings of the human theologians. Was all of this, he asked himself in anguish, no more than a monstrous blasphemy? Could entities that had no souls minister to the Lord? Or might they, in their years of faith and work, have developed souls? He searched for a soul deep inside himself (and it was not the first time he had searched) and could find no soul. Even if there were one, he wondered, how could it be recognized? What ingredients went into the formation of a soul? Could one, in fact, be fashioned or need one be born with it – and if that should be the case, what genetic patterns were involved?

Were he and his fellow robots (his fellow monks?) usurping human rights? Were they, in sinful pride, aspiring to something reserved for the human race? Was it – had it ever been – within their province to attempt to maintain a human and a Godly institution that the humans had rejected and which even now God might not care about?

3

After breakfast, in the hushed quiet of the library, Jason Whitney sat at his desk and opened one of the bound record books which he had picked from a long row of its fellows on the shelf behind him. He saw that it had been more than a month since he had made an entry. Not, he thought, that there had been any real reason to make an entry then. Life ran so placidly that there were few ripples to record. Perhaps it would be better to put the book back on the shelf with nothing written in it, although it seemed, somehow, an act of faith to write an occasional paragraph at not too long an interval from the last one written. In the last month nothing of any consequence had happened – no one had come back to visit, there had been nothing but routine contacts from those out among the stars, there had been no word of the Indian bands, there had been no robots passing by and stopping, so there had been no news – although what the robots brought was rumor more often than it was news. There had been gossip, of course. Martha kept up a running conversation with others of the clan and when they sat on the patio to hear the nightly concert, she would fill him in on what had been said that day. But mostly it was woman talk and nothing to put down.

A narrow shaft of morning sun, slotted through the slit where the heavy drapes at one of the tall windows failed to come together, fell across him, lighting up the gray hair and the square and solid shoulders. He was a tall man, thin, but with a sense of strength that offset the thinness. His face was rugged, creased with tiny lines. The mustache bristled and was matched by the craggy brows that sat above the deep-sunken eyes that held a steely look in them. He sat in the chair, unmoving, looking at the room and wondering again at the quiet satisfaction that he always found within it, and at times more than satisfaction, as if the room, with its book-lined loftiness and vastness, carried a special benediction. The thoughts of many men, he told himself, resided in this space – all the great thinkers of the world held secure between the bindings of the volumes on the shelves, selected and placed there long ago by his grandfather so that in the days to come the essence of the human race, the heritage of recorded thought, would always be at hand. He recalled that he had often held the conceit that the essential characters of these ancient writers, the ghostly presence of the men themselves, had in the passing years settled on this room, and late at night, when all else was quiet, he had often found himself conversing with these olden men, who emerged from the dust of the past into the shadow of the present.

The tier of books ran all around the room, broken only by two doors and, on the river side, three windows. When the first tier ended a balcony began, guarded by a decorative metal railing, and on the balcony the second tier of books went all around the room. Above one of the doors a clock was mounted on the wall and for more than five thousand years, he reminded himself in wonder, the clock had kept on ticking, beating off the seconds century on century. The clock said 9:15 and how near, he wondered, was that to the correctness of the time as set up by men so many years ago. There was, he realized, no way that one might know, although it did not matter now. The world would be as well off if there were no clock.

Muffled sounds made their way into the room – the mournful lowing of a distant cow, the nearby barking of a dog, the insane cackling of a hen. The music trees still were silent – they'd not start tuning up until sometime in the afternoon. He wondered if they'd try one of the new compositions tonight. There had, of late, been a lot of them. If so, he hoped it would not be one of the experimental ones they had been trying lately. There were so many others they might play, so many of the old and favorite ones, but there was no sense to what they did. It seemed, he told himself, that it had been getting worse in the last few years since two of the older trees had shown some sign of dying. They had begun to lose some of their branches and each spring it seemed that their leaf output was smaller. There were young saplings to take their place, of course, and that might be the trouble. He put up his hand and brushed a finger across his mustache, worriedly. He wished for the thousandth time that he knew something about the care of trees. He had looked through some of the books, of course, but there seemed nothing there that would be of any help. And even if there were, one could not be sure that the music trees would respond to the treatment as would a tree of Earth.

At the sound of padding feet, he turned. The robot, Thatcher, was coming through the door.

'Yes, what is it, Thatcher?'

'It is Mr Horace Red Cloud, sir.'

'But Horace is up north. In the wild rice country.'

'It seems, sir, the band has moved. They are camped down by the river, in their old camping grounds. They plan to restore the old fields and put in a crop next spring.'

'You had a talk with him?'

'Sir,' said Thatcher, 'he is an old acquaintance and, naturally, I passed a few words with him. He brought a bag of rice.'

'I hoped you thanked him, Thatcher.'

'Oh, indeed I did, sir.'

'You should have brought him in.'

'He said he had no desire to disturb you, sir, if you happened to be busy.'

'I am never really busy. Surely you know that.'

'Then,' said Thatcher, 'I'll ask him to step in.'

Jason rose and walked around the desk, standing beside it, waiting for his friend. How long had it been, he wondered – four years, or five – it surely must be five. He'd gone down to the camp to bid his old friend good-bye and after the band had embarked, had stood for a long time on the shingle of the shore, watching the long line of canoes move swiftly up the river, paddles flashing in the sunlight.

Red Cloud was the same age as Jason, but had a younger look. When he came into the room and across the carpeting, his stride had a young man's spring. His hair was black, without a trace of gray; it was parted exactly down the center of his scalp and hung in two heavy braids across his shoulders to dangle on his chest. His face was weather-beaten but, except for a tiny network of crow's feet at the corner of his eyes, had not a wrinkle in it. He wore a buckskin shirt and leggings, with moccasins on his feet. The hand he held out to Jason was thick and calloused, with short, blunt fingers.

'It has been a long time, Horace,' Jason said. 'I am glad to see you.'

'You are the only one,' said Red Cloud, 'who still calls me Horace.'

'All right, then,' said Jason, 'shall I call you Chief? Or Cloud? Or maybe Red?'

Red Cloud grinned. 'From you, Jason, Horace sounds just fine. We were boys together. Surely you remember. And it brings back the times when we roamed the woods together. We nicked our wrists and held the cuts together so that our blood would mingle. Or at least we thought that it would mingle. I rather doubt it did. But that is neither here nor there. The important thing was the symbolism.'

'I remember,' Jason said. 'I can remember that first day, when your band came paddling down the river and saw the smoke rising from one of our chimneys. All of you, the whole kit and caboodle of you, came swarming up the hill to see what it was all about and for the first time both your band and the people at this house learned that they were not alone, but there still were others left.'

'We built big fires out on the lawn,' said Red Cloud, 'and we killed a beef or two and had a barbecue. We joined hands in a ring and danced around the fires, whooping and hollering. Your grandfather of blessed memory rolled out a keg of whiskey and we all got rather drunk.'

'That was when you and I first met,' said Jason. 'Two young sprouts out to show the world – except there was no world to show. We took to one another almost immediately. We went hunting and fishing together and we roamed the hills. And we chased the girls.'

'We caught some of them, as I recall,' said Red Cloud.

'They weren't hard to catch,' said Jason.

They stood, looking into one another's faces, silently, then Jason said, 'Let's sit down. There must be a lot we need to talk about.'

Red Cloud sat down in a chair and Jason took another and spun it around so he could face his friend.

'How long has it been?' he asked.

'Six years.'

'You just arrived?'

'A week ago,' said Red Cloud. 'We left the north after the wild rice harvest. We didn't travel fast. We stopped whenever we found a good camping place and loafed around and hunted. Some of our young men took the horses down west of the river and will hold them there until there is ice to cross. Later, when it gets colder, we'll cross over and hunt for winter meat. Buffalo and wild cattle. A runner came in last night and said there are a lot of them on the prairies.'

Jason frowned. 'A week, you say. You shouldn't have waited so long. If you didn't have time yourself, you should have sent a runner. I'd have come down to visit you.'

'The time went fast. There was much to do. We are trying to get the corn ground into shape. The fields have grown up to brush and weeds. We ran out of corn and got hungry for it. Tried to grow some up north, but the season was too short Got it in late and the frost caught it. Had some roasting ears, but that was all.'

'We have corn,' said Jason. 'A lot of it, ground and ready. I'll send some down to the camp before the day is over. What else do you need – bacon, eggs, flour? We have some good wheat flour. More by far than we can use. Cloth, if you want it. The wool has been good and the looms busy.'

'Jason, I didn't come begging ...'

'I know you didn't. For years we've shared things back and forth. I hate to think of how much meat and fish and berries and other things your folks packed up the hill for us in days gone by. Thatcher says you brought some rice ...'

'All right,' said Red Cloud. 'You'll not object to a supply of buffalo meat when we make the hunt?'

'Not at all,' said Jason.

'Better yet, how about coming along on the hunt?'

'There is nothing I'd like better.'

'Good! It will be like old times. We'll let the others do the work. We'll sit around the fire, you and I, and talk and eat hump meat.'

'You live a good life, Horace.'

'I think we do. There were so many ways we could have gone. We could have settled down. We could have taken over some good housing and good fields and put in crops and collected us some livestock. We could have become good farmers. But we didn't. We took up the old ways. I guess we never were too far from them. In the heart of each of us, we'd dreamed of them time and yet again. The pull was there. The call was there. Our ancestors had lived the life for thousands of years. We had only a few hundred years of the white man's way and they had been far from good years. We never fitted in, we never had a chance to. It was a relief to shuck off all of it and go back to the flowers, the trees, the clouds, the seasons and the weather, the running water, the creatures of the woods and prairies – to make them a part of us again, more a part of us than they'd ever been before. We learned something from the whites, that we can't deny – we'd have been stupid if we hadn't. And we used these white man's ways to make the old way of life an even better life. Sometimes I wonder if we made the right choice, then I see an autumn leaf – one leaf alone, not a lot of leaves – or hear the sound of a little stream of water running in the woods, or catch a forest scent, and then I know we were not wrong. We went back to the earth, linked ourselves with the hills and streams, and that is the way it should be. That is the way we were meant to live. Not back to the old tribal concept, but back to a way of life. We were a woodland tribe to start with, but now we are no longer woodland. Maybe we're simply Indian. We adopted the skin tepee of the Western plains tribes and, in large part, their way of dress and their use of horses. But we kept the birch bark canoe, the wild rice harvest and the maple sugar. It has been a good life. You and I, old friend, have caught the feel of life – I in my teepee, you in this stone house. You never went to the stars and you may be better off for never having gone. I suppose they find great things out there ...'

'A few things,' Jason said. 'Many interesting things. Perhaps even some useful items. But we put few of them to any use. We have seen them, observed them, even studied them, in some cases arrived at an understanding of what is going on. But we no longer are a technological race. We lost technology when we lost the manpower and the knowledge and the machines broke down and there was no one to start them up again and no energy to run them. We don't mourn that lost technology, as I think you know. At one time we might have, but not any longer. It would be a bother now. We have become competent observers and we gain our satisfaction from our observations, achieving minor triumphs when we are able to reach some solid understanding. Knowing is the goal, not the using. We aren't users. We have somehow risen above using. We can rest content to see resources lying idle; we might even think it shameful to try to use or harness them. And it's not only resources; it's ideas and ...'

'How much do you remember, Jason? How much, really, from the old days? Not how our tribe found your people, but all the rest of it.'

'I remember rather vividly,' said Jason. 'And so should you. You were a young man, with me, when it happened. We were both at the impressionable age. It should have made a great impact on us.'

Red Cloud shook his head. 'My memory is dim. There are too many other things. I can scarcely remember any other life than the one we live today.'

'My remembrance is in a book, or in many books,' said Jason, gesturing at the shelf behind the desk. 'It all is written down. My grandfather began it, some fifty years after it happened, writing it down so we'd not forget, so it would not become a myth. He wrote all that he could remember of what had happened and once that was finished, he made regular entries. When he finally died, I took up the work. It all is written down, from the day it happened.'

'And when you die,' asked Red Cloud, 'who then will do the writing?'

'I do not know,' said Jason.

'Jason, a thing I have often wondered, but have never asked. May I ask it now?'

'Certainly. Anything at all.'

'Why did you never go out to the stars?'

'Perhaps because I can't.'

'But you never tried. You never really wanted to.'

'The others went out one by one,' said Jason, 'until only Martha and I were left. It seemed that someone should stay. It seemed that we should not leave Earth entirely. Someone belonged here. An anchor man, perhaps, for the others who had gone. To keep the home fires burning. Be here to welcome the others back when they wanted to come home. To keep a place for them.'

'They do come back, of course. And you are here to welcome them.'

'Some of them,' said Jason. 'Not all. My brother, John, was one of the first to go. He has not been back. We've had no word of him. I often wonder where he is. If he is still alive.'

'You imply a responsibility to stay. But, Jason, that can't be the entire story.'

'It's part of it, I think. At one time more a part of it than it is now. John and I were the oldest. My sister, Janice, is younger. We still see her occasionally and Martha talks with her quite often. If John had stayed, Martha and I might have gone. I said maybe we didn't because we couldn't. I don't really believe that. The ability seems to be inherent. Man probably had it for a long time before he began to use it. For it to develop time was needed and the longer life gave us time. Perhaps it would have developed even without the longer life if we'd not been so concerned, so fouled up, with our technology. Somewhere we may have taken the wrong turning, accepted the wrong values and permitted our concern with technology to mask our real and valid purpose. The concern with technology may have kept us from knowing what we had. These abilities of ours could not struggle up into our consciousness through the thick layers of machines and cost estimates and all the rest of it. And when we talk about abilities, it's not simply going to the stars. Your people don't go to the stars. There may be no need of you to do so. You have become, instead, a part of your environment, living within its texture and understanding. It went that way for you …'

'But if you could go, why don't you? Surely you could be away for a little time. The robots would take care of things. They'd keep the home fires burning, keep the welcome ready for those who wanted to return.'

Jason shook his head. 'It is too late now. I fall increasingly in love with this house and with these acres as the years go on. I feel a part of it. I'd be lost without the house and land – and Earth. I couldn't live without them. A man can't walk the same land, live in the same house, for almost five thousand years—'

'I know,' said Red Cloud. 'The band, as its numbers increased, split up and scattered, becoming many bands. Some are on the prairies, others eastward in the forests. I stick to these two rivers …'

'I am guilty of bad manners,' Jason said. 'I should have asked first off. How is Mrs Cloud?'

'Happy. With a new camp to boss, she is in her glory.'

'And your sons and grandsons many times removed?'

'Only a few of the grandsons still are with us,' Red Cloud said. 'The sons and other grandsons are with other bands. We hear from them at times. Running Elk, my grandson thrice removed, was killed by a grizzly about a year ago. A runner came to tell us. Otherwise they all are well and happy.'

'I grieve for you,' said Jason. 'Running Elk was a grandson to be proud of.'

Red Cloud bowed his head in thanks. 'Mrs Jason, I gather, is in good health.'

Jason nodded. 'She spends a lot of time talking with the others. She is most proficient at it. Much more so than I am. Telepathy seems to be second nature to her. Each evening she has much news to tell. There are a lot of us now. I have no idea how many. Martha would know better than I do. She keeps it all in mind. All the relationships, who married whom and so on. Some thousands of us, surely.'

'You told me once before, many years ago, that some intelligences had been found in space, but none like us. In the years since we've been gone …'

'You're right,' said Jason. 'None like us. Some contacts. Some friendly, some not so friendly, some indifferent to us. The most of them so alien to us they set one's teeth on edge. And, of course, the wandering alien travelers that sometimes visit Earth.'

'And that is all? No cooperating …'

'No, that isn't all,' said Jason. 'Something has arisen that is most disturbing. A whiff of something most disturbing. Like a bad smell on the wind. From somewhere out in the center …'

'The center of what, Jason?'

'The center of the galaxy. The core. An intelligence of some sort We just sniffed the edge of it and that's enough ...'

'Hostile?'

'No, not hostile. Cold. Intelligent, too intelligent. Cold and indifferent. Analytical Oh, hell, I can't tell you. There's no way to tell you. As if an angle-worm could sniff the intelligence of a human. More than that More difference between it and us than there is between man and angleworm.'

'It's got you scared?'

'Scared? I guess so. Upset. Apprehensive. Only comfort is that we probably are beneath their notice.'

'Then why worry?'

'Not worrying too much. It isn't that. Just that a man feels unclean know-ing there is something like that in the galaxy With him. As if you stumbled across a pit of concentrated evil.'

'But it isn't evil.'

'I don't think so. I don't know what it is. Neither does anyone else. We just caught a whiff ...'

'You haven't detected it? You, yourself?'

'No. Some of the others. Two of the others out in the stars.'

'No need to worry, more than likely. Just stay out of the way. I wonder, though – could it have had something to do with the People leaving? It seems unlikely, though. You still have no idea, Jason, of why it happened, why all the People went away.'

'None at all,' said Jason.

'You were speaking of the aliens that came to Earth ...'

'Yes,' said Jason. 'It is strange how they come to Earth these days. Not many of them, of course. Not many that we know about. Two or three in the last century, although I guess, when you come to think of it, with all the space there is and the distances, that is quite a lot. But they never seemed to come before. It's only happened since the People left. Although it is possible they may have been coming in the old days and were never seen, or if seen, unrec-ognized for what they were. Maybe we didn't see them because we were unprepared to recognize them. Even if we'd seen them, we would have closed our eyes to them. We'd have felt uncomfortable in the presence of something that we couldn't understand and so, with one grand gesture, we'd have wiped them all away. We would have said they can't be here, they aren't here, we never saw them, and that would be the end of it.'

'That may have been it,' said Red Cloud. 'Or far fewer may have come. We were a turbulent planet, seething with intelligence and at times a rather terrifying kind of intelligence. On a smaller scale, maybe something like that intelligence of yours in the center of the galaxy. Surely not the sort of place a wandering alien would have chosen to sit down to seek a time of rest. For he would have had no rest. In those days there was no rest for anyone.'

'You are right, of course,' said Jason. 'We know it now. I don't suppose there was any way we could have known it then. We got ahead. We progressed ...'

'You have talked, I think,' said Red Cloud, 'with some of the wandering aliens.'

'Two of three of them. Once I traveled five hundred miles to talk with one of them, but it was gone by the time I got there. A robot brought the news. I'm not as good as Martha with this business of galactic telepathy, but I can talk with aliens. With some of them, that is. I seem to have the knack for it. Sometimes, though, there is no way of talking. They have no basis for recognizing sound waves as a means of communication and a human, on his part, may not even have the sense to recognize the signals or the mental waves they use for communication. With others of them, even if the means of communication is there, you can't do any talking. There's really nothing to talk about. No common grounds for talking.'

'This matter of wandering aliens,' said Red Cloud, 'is partly why I came. I'd have come anyhow, of course, the first day that I could. But I wanted to tell you we have an alien here. Up at the head of Cat Den Hollow. Little Wolf found him and came running and I went to have a look.'

So this was it, thought Jason; he should have known. All this careful, polite talking on everything except the one thing that Red Cloud had really come to tell him, and finally it was out. It was the way they were; one should expect it of them. The old unhurried way, the tribal protocol, the dignity. To never be excited, to not come charging in, to be leisurely and deliberate and to make ground for decency.

'You tried to talk with him?' he asked.

'No,' said Horace Red Cloud. 'I can talk with flowers and flowing rivers and they can talk back to me, but an alien – I'd not know how to start.'

'All right,' said Jason, 'I'll amble over and see what it has in mind, if it has anything in mind. That is, if I can talk with it. Was there any indication of how it might have come?'

'It's a teleporter, I would guess. There was no sign of any kind of ship.'

'Usually they are,' said Jason. 'The same as us. A machine of any sort is a cumbersome contraption. Star-roving is nothing new, of course, although at first we thought it was. We thought we had made such a wonderful discovery when the first of us began to develop and employ parapsychic powers. But it was not so wonderful; it was simply something that we'd been too busy, as a technological race, to take the time to look at. And even if someone had thought about it and had tried to talk about it, he would have been ridiculed.'

'None of us have star-roved,' Red Cloud said. 'I'm not sure any of us have any powers at all. We have been so occupied with the world we live in and the secrets that it holds that we may not have tapped the secret resources that we have, if there should be any. But now ...'

'I think you have powers and are using them,' Jason told him, 'to the best of purposes. You know your environment and mesh more closely with it than men ever have before. This must take some sort of psychic instinct. It may not be as romantic as star-roving, but it takes, perhaps, an even greater understanding.'

'I thank you for your kindness,' Red Cloud said, 'and there may be certain truth in what you say. I have a beautiful and very foolish granddaughter-many-times-removed who has only turned her nineteenth year. Perhaps you remember her – the Evening Star.'

'Why, of course I do,' Jason said, delighted. 'When you were away from camp or busy and I came visiting, she would take me over. We went on nature hikes and she showed me birds and flowers and other woodland wonders, and she chattered all the time, most delightfully.'

'She still chatters most delightfully, but I am somewhat concerned by her. I think, perhaps, she has some of the brand of psychic power that your clan may hold ...'

'You mean star-roving?'

Red Cloud crinkled up his face. 'I'm not sure. No, I don't think so. It may be something else. I sense a certain strangeness in her. I suppose I am disturbed by it, although I have no right to be. She has a thirst for knowledge such as I have never seen in any of my people. Not a thirst to know her world, although that is there as well, but a thirst to know outside her world. To know all that's ever happened, all that men have thought. She has read all the books that the band possesses and they are very few ...'

Jason raised his arm and swept it in an arc to indicate the room. 'There are books here,' he said, 'if she would come and read them. Down in the basement areas there are other rooms stacked to the ceilings with others of them. She is free to use any that she wishes, but I am reluctant to let any leave this house. Once lost, a book would be irreplaceable.'

'I had come prepared to ask,' said Red Cloud. 'I was leading up to it. Thank you for offering.'

'It pleases me there is someone who might wish to read them. It is a privilege to share them with her, I assure you.'

'I suppose,' said Red Cloud, 'we should have given thought to books, but it's a little late now to do anything about it There might still be books, of course, although time, I would imagine, has destroyed most of them. Weather and the rodents would have gotten at them. And our people hesitate to go looking for them. We have a great dislike for the ancient places. They are so old and musty and are filled with many ghosts – ghosts of the past that even now we do not like to think about. We have a few books, of course, and treasure them as an ancient heritage. And we make it a point of honor with the past each child is taught to read. But for most of them it is an unpleasant duty only. Until the Evening Star, there have been few who cared to read.'

'Would Evening Star,' asked Jason, 'be willing to come and live with us? For as long as she might like. It would brighten up the house to have a youngster in it and I would undertake to guide her in her reading.'

'I shall tell her,' Red Cloud said. 'She will be delighted. You know, of course, she calls you Uncle Jason.'

'No, I did not know,' said Jason. 'I am honored.' Silence fell upon the two men and they sat there for a moment, in the hush of the library. Upon the wall the clock ticked off the seconds, loudly in the silence.

Red Cloud stirred. 'Jason, you have kept track of time. Of the years, I mean. You even have a clock. We have no clocks and we've kept no count. We didn't bother to. We took each day as it came and lived it to the full. We live not with days, but seasons. And we have not counted seasons.'

'Here and there,' said Jason, 'we may have missed a day or two or added a day or two – I can't be sure of that. But we have kept count. It's been five thousand years. I'm as old, physically, as my grandfather was when he first wrote in the books. After that he lived for almost three thousand years. If I follow the same schedule, I'll live a full eight thousand years. It does not seem possible, of course. It seems a bit indecent for a man to live eight thousand years.'

'Some day,' said Red Cloud, 'we may know what brought about all this – where the people went to and why we live so long.'

'Perhaps,' said Jason, 'although I have no hope. I have been thinking, Horace ...'

'Yes?'

'I could round up a gang of robots and send them down to clear those cornfields for you. They're just messing around, not doing much of anything. I know how you feel about robots, of course ...'

'No. Thank you very much. We'll accept the corn and flour and all the rest of it, but we can't accept the help of robots.'

'What, actually, have you got against them? Don't you trust them? They won't hang around. They won't bother you. They'll just clear the fields, then leave.'

'We feel uneasy with them,' Red Cloud said. 'They don't fit in with us. They're a reminder of what happened to us when the white men came. When we broke, we broke completely. We kept only a few things. The simple metal tools, the plow, a better economic sense – we no longer feast one day and starve the next as the Indians did in many instances before the white men came. We went back to the old woods life, the old plains life. We went on our way; we have to keep it that way.'

'I think I understand.'

'I'm not entirely sure we trust them, either,' Red Cloud said. 'Not completely. Maybe the ones you have here, working in your fields for you and doing other things, may be all right. But I have my reservations about some of the wild ones. I told you, didn't I, that there is a gang of them up the river, at the site of some old city …'

'Yes, I remember that you did. Minneapolis and St. Paul. You saw them, many, many years ago. They were building something.'

'They still are building it,' said Red Cloud. 'We stopped on the way downstream and had a look – a far-off look. There are more of them than ever and they still are building. One great building, although it doesn't look like a building. The robots wouldn't be building a house, would they?'

'I don't think so. Not for themselves. They laugh at weather. They're made of some sort of almost indestructible alloy. It doesn't rust, it doesn't wear, it resists almost everything. Weather, temperature, rain … none of them mean a thing to them.'

'We didn't hang around too long,' said Red Cloud. 'We stayed a good ways off. We used glasses, but still couldn't see too much. We were scared, I guess. Uncomfortable. We got out of there once we had a look. I don't suppose there is any real danger, but we took no chances.'

4

Evening Star walked through the morning and talked with the friends she met. Be careful, rabbit, nibbling at your clover; a red fox has his den just across the hill. And why do you chatter, little bushy-tail, and stamp your feet at me: it is your friend who is walking past. You took all the hickory nuts from the three big trees at the hollow's mouth before I could get to them and have them stored away. You should be happy, for you're the most fortunate of squirrels. You have a deep den in a hollow oak where you'll be snug and happy when the winter comes and you have food hidden everywhere. Chickadee, you are out of place and time, swinging on the thistle stalk. You should not be here so soon. You come only when there are snowflakes in the air. Did you steal a march upon your fellows; you'll be lonesome here until the others come. Or are you like myself, cherishing the last few golden days before the chill moves down?

She walked through the sun of morning, with the colored pageant of the open woods burst into flame and gold about her. She saw the burnished metal of the goldenrod, the sky-blue of the asters. She walked upon the grass that once had been lush and green and now was turning tawny and was slippery beneath her moccasins. She knelt to brush her hand against the green and scarlet carpet of the lichen patches growing on an old, gray boulder and she sang within herself because she was a part of it – yes, even of the lichens, even of the boulder.

She came to the top of the ridge that she was climbing and below her lay the denser forest that cloaked the river hills. A hollow dipped down between the slopes rising on each side and she followed it. A spring flowed out of a limestone outcrop and she went on down the hollow, walking to the music of hidden, singing water flowing from the spring. Her memory winged back to that other day. It had been summer then, with the hills a froth of green and birds still singing in the trees. She clasped the doll she carried close against her breast and again she heard the words the tree had spoken to her. It all was wrong, of course, for no woman should make a compact with a thing so strong and lordly as a tree. A birch, perhaps, or a poplar, or one of the lesser, more feminine of trees – that, while it would be frowned upon still might be understandable. But the tree that had spoken to her had been an ancient white oak – a hunter's tree.

It stood just ahead of her, old and gnarled and strong, but despite all its girth and strength seeming to crouch against the ground, as if it were a thing embattled. Its leaves were brown and had begun to wither, but it had not lost them yet. It still clung to its warrior's cloak while some of the other trees nearby stood in nakedness.

She clambered down to reach it and, having reached it, found the rotted, flaking hollow that gouged into its massive trunk. Standing on tiptoe, she saw that the secret hollow place still held and guarded the doll she'd placed there all those years before – a little corncob doll dressed in scraps of woolen cloth. It had weathered and been darkened by the rain that had seeped into the hollow and soaked it time and time again, but it held its shape, it still clung against the tree.

Still standing on tiptoe, she placed the doll she carried into the hollow, settling it carefully beside the first doll. Then she stepped away.

'Old Grandfather,' she said, her eyes looking at the ground as a matter of respect, 'I went away, but I did not forget you. In the long nights and the bright noons I remembered you. Now I have come back again to tell you that I may go away again, although in a different way. But I'll never leave completely, because I love this world too much. And I shall always reach out to you, knowing you will know when I hold out my arms and I shall know that upon this land stands one I can believe and depend upon. I am truly grateful to you, Old Grandfather, for the strength you give me and for your understanding.'

She stopped and waited for an answer and there was no answer. The tree did not talk to her as it had that first time.

'I do not know where I'll be going,' she told the tree, 'or when I'll go or even if I'll go at all, but I came to tell you. To share with you a feeling I can share with no one else.'

She waited once again for the tree to answer and there were no words, but it seemed to her that the great oak stirred, as if arousing from a sleep, and she had the sense of great arms lifted and held above her head and there was something – benediction? – that came out from the tree and settled over her.

She backed away slowly, step by step, her eyes still upon the ground, then she turned and fled, running wildly up the hill, filled with that sense of something that had come forth from the tree and touched her.

She tripped on a surface root that looped out of the forest floor, caught herself against a huge fallen tree trunk, and sat down on it. Looking back, she saw that the ancient oak was no longer in sight. There were too many intervening trees.

The woods were quiet. Nothing stirred in the underbrush and there were no birds. In the spring and summer this place was filled with birds, but now there was none. They either had gone south or were elsewhere, flocking up, ready for the move. Down in the river bottoms vast flocks of ducks quarreled and chortled in the sloughs and the reed patches were filled with great flocks of blackbirds that went storming up into the sky like hurtling sleet. But here the gentler birds were gone and the woods were quiet, a solemn quietness that held a touch of loneliness.

She had told the tree that she might be going elsewhere and she wondered if she had said what she really meant or if she knew as much as she should know about this going elsewhere. It sometimes seemed that she might be going to another place – and it might not be that at all. There was in her a feeling of unease, of expectation, the prickling sensation that something most momentous was about to happen, but she could not define it. It was an unfamiliar thing, a rather frightening thing to someone who had lived all her life in a world she knew so intimately. The world was full of friends – not only human friends, but many other friends, the little scurriers of the woods and brush, the shy flowers hidden in their woodland nooks, the graceful trees that stood against the sky, the very wind and weather.

She patted the old decaying trunk as if it might be a friend as well and saw how the briars and high-growing forest plants had gathered all around it, rallying to its defense, hiding it in its hour of indignity and need.

She rose from the trunk and went on up the hill, going slowly now, no longer running. She had left the doll and the tree had not spoken as it had before, but it had done something else, performed some other act and everything was well.

She reached the crest of the steep river slope and started down the reverse side, heading for the camp, and as she started to angle down the hill realized, suddenly, without actually seeing, that she was not alone. She turned swiftly and there he stood, clad only in a breech clout, his bronzed body smooth and hard and shining in the sun, his pack beside him and the bow leaned against the pack. A pair of binoculars hung from their strap about his neck, half hiding the necklace that he wore.

'Do I intrude upon your land?' he asked, politely.

'The land is free,' she said.

She was fascinated by the necklace. She kept staring at it.

He touched it with his finger. 'Vanity,' he said.

'You killed the great white bear,' she said. 'More than one, from all the claws there are.'

'Also,' he said, 'a way to keep the count One claw, one bear. A claw from each.'

She drew in her breath. 'Your medicine is strong.'

He slapped the bow. 'My bow is strong: My arrows true and tipped with flint. Flint is better than anything except the finest steel and where now do you find the finest steel?'

'You came from the West,' she said. She knew that the great white bears lived only in the West. One of her kins people, Running Elk, had been killed by one just a year or so ago.

He nodded. 'Far from the West. From the place where there is big water. From the ocean.'

'How far is that?'

'Far? I cannot tell. Many moons upon the road.'

'You count by moons. Are you of my people?'

'No, I don't think so. Were it not for the sun, my skin is white. I met some of your people, hunting buffalo. They were the first people other than my own I had ever seen. I had not known there were other people. There were only robots, running wild.'

She made a motion of disdain. 'We have no traffic with the robots.'

'So I understand.'

'How much farther do you intend to go? To the east the prairie ends. It is only woods. Finally there is another ocean. I have seen the maps.'

He pointed at the house that stood on top the great headland. 'Maybe only that far. The people on the plains told me of a big house of stone with people living in it. I have seen many houses of stone, but with no one living in them. There are people living in it?'

'Two people.'

'That is all?'

'The others,' she said, 'have gone to the stars.'

'They told me that, too,' he said, 'and I have wondered of it. I could not believe. Who would want to go to the stars?'

'They find other worlds and live on them.'

'The stars are only bright lights shining in the sky.'

'They are other suns,' she said. 'Have you read no books?'

He shook his head. 'I saw one once. I was told it was a book. It was said to me that it would speak to me if one knew the way. But the person who showed it to me had lost the way.'

'You cannot read?'

'This reading is the way? The way a book will talk?'

'Yes, that's it,' she said. 'There are little marks. You read the marks.'

'Have you got a book?' he asked.

'A big box of books. I have read them all. But up there,' she gestured at the house, 'there are rooms filled with nothing but books. My grandfather-many-times-removed will ask today if I may read those books.'

'It is strange,' he said. 'You read the book. I kill the bear. I do not like the idea of a book. I was told the book would speak, but in olden magic, better left alone.'

'That is not true,' she said. 'You are a funny kind of man.'

'I came from far,' he said, as if that might explain it. 'Across high mountains, across great rivers, across places where there is only sand and too much sun.'

'Why did you do it? Why did you come so far?'

'Something in me said go and find. It did not say what I should find. Only go and find. No other of my people have ever gone to find. I feel something driving me, as if I cannot stay. When the people on the plains tell me of this great high house of stone, I think perhaps this is what I go to find.'

'You are going up there?'

'Yes, of course,' he said.

'And if it is what you set out to find, you will stay awhile?'

'Perhaps. I do not know. The thing inside me that drives me on will tell me. I thought awhile ago perhaps I had found what I came to find without going to the house. The great oak changed. You made the oak to change.'

She flared in anger. 'You spied on me. You sat there, spying.'

'I did not mean to spy,' he said. 'I was coming up the hill as you were coming down and I saw you at the tree. I hid so you wouldn't see me. I thought you would not want anyone to know. So I was quiet. I kept out of sight. I moved away, quietly, so you wouldn't know.'

'Yet you tell me.'

'Yes, I tell you. The oak was changed. It was a wondrous thing.'

'How did you know the oak had changed?'

He wrinkled his brow. 'I do not know. There was the bear as well. The bear that my arrow did not kill and yet it dropped dead at my feet. I am puzzled by all this. I do not know these things.'

'Tell me, how did the oak change?'

He shook his head. 'I only sensed it change.'

'You should not have spied.'

'I am ashamed I did. I will not speak of it.'

'Thank you,' she said, turning to go down the hill.

'Can I walk a way with you?'

'I go this way,' she said. 'You go to the house.'

'I'll see you again,' he said.

She went on down the hill. When finally she looked back, he was still standing there. The bear-claw necklace glittered in the sun.

5

The alien was a can of worms. It huddled among the boulders, close up against the clump of birch that grew from one side of the gorge, the trees bent and tilted to hang above the dry stream bed. Leaf-filtered sunlight shattered itself against the twisted alien and the substance of the alien's body refracted the rays so that it seemed to sit in a pool of broken rainbows.

Jason Whitney, sitting on a mossy bank, leaned back against a small ash tree, settling himself comfortably, letting himself relax. The faint, delicate smell of dying autumn leaves filled the glen.

It was a horror, he thought, and then tried to erase the horror from his mind. Some of them weren't bad; others of them were. This was the worst he had ever seen. If it would just be still, he thought, so a man could familiarize himself with it and thus become at least partially accustomed to it. But it wouldn't be still, it kept moving that can of worms around, the movement serving to emphasize its repulsiveness.

He started to put out his mind cautiously, reaching out to touch it, then, suddenly frightened, pulled back his mind and tucked it securely inside himself. He had to settle down before he tried to talk with this thing. An old alien hand like himself, he thought, should be up to almost anything, but this one had him down.

He sat quietly, smelling the dying leaves in the secluded silence, not letting himself think of much of anything at all. That was the way you did it – you sneaked up on it somehow, pretending not to notice.

But the alien didn't wait. It reached out and touched him with a mental probe that was firm and calm and warm, totally unlike the visual image of the thing.

– Welcome, it said, to this snug retreat. I trust I violate no convention in addressing myself to you and that I do not trespass. I know what you are. I have seen another of you. You are a human creature.

– Yes, said Jason, I am human. And you are most welcome here. You violate no convention, for we have few of them. And you do not trespass.

– You are one of the travelers, said the can of worms. You rest on your planet now, but at times you travel far.

– Not I, said Jason. Some of the others have, but I stay at home.

– Then truly I have arrived at my destination. This is the planet of the traveler I communicated with very far ago. I could not be sure.

– This is the planet Earth, said Jason.

– That is the designation, said the creature, happily. I could not recall it. This other described it to me and I sought it far and wide, having only a general idea of the direction that it lay. But I was sure when I arrived that it was the proper planet.

– You mean you sought our Earth? You aren't simply stopping off to rest?

– I came to seek a soul.

– You came to seek a what?

– A soul, the creature said. This other one I communicated with said that humans once had souls and probably still did have them, although he could not be sure, professing much ignorance of the matter. He piqued my interest with what he told of souls, but could give me no adequate idea of what a soul might be. I say to myself, quite secretly, of course, so wonderful a thing is worth the seeking of. So I began my search.

– It might interest you to know, said Jason, that many humans have sought their souls as assiduously as do you.

And, he wondered, by what strange combination of circumstances one of the clan might have come to talk with this creature about the concept of the soul. Surely not a likely topic, he told himself, and one in which there might be certain dangers. But more than likely it had not been serious talk, or certainly had not been meant to be, although this can of worms seemed to have taken it seriously enough to send it on a search of no one could guess how many years to track it to its source.

– I sense a strangeness in your response, the alien said. Can you tell me if you have a soul?

– No, I can't, said Jason.

– Surely if you had one, you'd be aware of it.

– Not necessarily, Jason told it.

– You sound, the creature said, very much like that one of your kind I sat with an entire afternoon on a hilltop of my own most lovely planet. We talked of many things, but the last half of our talk had much to do with souls. He didn't know if he had one, either, and was not sure that other humans had, now or in the past, and he could not tell me what a soul was or how a being, not having one, might go about the acquisition of a soul. He seemed to think he was acquainted with the advantages of possessing one, but I thought his talk on that point was somehow very hazy. It was, in many ways, a most unsatisfactory explanation that he gave me, but I thought I could detect a germ of truth in it. Surely, I thought, if I could win my way to his native planet there would be someone there who could supply the information that I seek.

– I am sorry, Jason said. Terribly sorry that you came so far and wasted so much time.

– There is nothing you can tell me? There is no one else?

– There might be, Jason told him, adding quickly, I can't be really sure.

He had made a slip and knew it. He couldn't turn Hezekiah loose on a thing like this. Loopy as Hezekiah was, he would go hog wild.

– But there must be others.

– There are only two of us.

– You must be mistaken, said the alien. There were two others came. Neither one was you. They stood and looked at me and then they went away. They did not notice when I tried to communicate.

– They could not hear you, Jason said. They could not have answered. They use their minds for other things. They were the ones who told me. They knew I could talk with you.

– Then there only is one other who can communicate.

– That is all. The rest of us are gone, far among the stars. It was one of them who you talked with.

– This other one?

– I do not know, said Jason. She has never talked with people other than her own. She talks well with them, no matter how distant they may be.

– Then you are the only one. And you can tell me nothing.

– Look, said Jason, it is an old idea. There was never any proof. There was only faith. I have a soul, one would tell himself. He believed it because he had been told by others. Told authoritatively. Without any question. He was told so often and he told himself so often that there was no question in his mind that he had a soul. But there was never any evidence. There was never any proof.

– But honored sir, the alien pleaded, you will tell me, will you not, what a soul might be.

– I can tell you, Jason said, what it is supposed to be. It is a part of you. Unseen and undetectable. Not of your body. Not even of your mind. It lives on, eternally, after you are dead. Or, at least, it is supposed to live on eternally and the condition in which it finds itself once you are dead depends on what kind of creature you have been.

– Who judges what kind of creature you have been?

– A deity, said Jason.

– And this deity?

– I do not know, said Jason. I simply do not know.

– You have been honest with me, then. I must thank you most heartily for your honesty. You say much the same as the other one I talked with.

– There may be someone else, said Jason. If I can find him, I will talk with him;

– But you said …

– I know what I said. This is not another human. Another being that may be wiser than I am.

– I will talk with him?

– No, you cannot talk with him. There is no way you can talk with him. You'll have to leave it to me.

– I trust you, said the can of worms.

– In the meantime, said Jason, will you be my guest? I have a dwelling place. There is room for you. We would be glad to have you.

– I detect, the alien said, an uneasiness in you at the sight of me.

– I would not lie to you, said Jason. There is an uneasiness in me. But I tell myself there may be as well an uneasiness in you at the sight of me.

There was no use in lying, Jason knew. It did not take his words to tell the creature the uneasiness he felt.

– Not at all in me, the creature said. I am tolerant. But it might be best if we stay apart. I shall wait here for you.

– Is there anything you need? asked Jason. Anything you lack? Something that I could supply for nourishment or comfort?

– No, thank you. I am quite all right. I am sufficient to myself.

Jason rose and turned to leave.

– You have a lovely planet, said the alien. Such a restful place. And so filled with the strangeness of its beauty.

– Yes, said Jason, we think so, too. A very lovely planet. He clambered up the deep-cut path he had followed down into the gorge. The sun, he saw, had passed the zenith and was slanting toward the west. Great storm clouds boiled up far off and in a little time, he knew, the sun would be hidden by them. The coming of the clouds, it seemed, had deepened the silence of the woods. He could hear the little raining sounds made by the falling leaves as they came floating down to the forest floor. Somewhere, far to the left, a squirrel was cluttering, disturbed, more than likely, by some woodland fantasy that had crossed its fuzzy mind.

It had been a splendid day, he thought, a splendid day even if it rained – it still would be a splendid day in every way but one and it was a shame that it should be marred by the problem that had been thrust upon his shoulders.

To keep faith with the creature waiting in the glen, he should talk with Hezekiah, but if he talked with the self-styled robot-abbot, there was no telling what might happen. Although maybe the use of self-styled as a characterization of the robot might be a bit unfair. Who was there anymore to say that, lacking humans who were interested, robots had no grounds to assume the task of keeping alive the spark of mankind's ancient faith?

And what of that ancient faith? he wondered. Why had mankind turned away from it? It had still existed in some measure in that day when the human race had been taken elsewhere. There still were traces of it in the early writings that his grandfather had made in the first of the record books. Perhaps it existed, in a slightly different context, among the Indians, although his contact with them had never revealed it. Some, perhaps all, of the young men formed secret symbolic associations with objects in the natural world, but it was questionable that this sort of behavior could be described as any sort of faith. It was something that was never talked about and so, naturally, he had only the most meager information on it.

The wrong people had been left behind, he thought. Given another segment of the population untouched by whatever agency had carried off the human race, and the ancient human faith might still be flourishing, perhaps stronger than it had ever been. But among his people and the other people who had been in the big house above the rivers on that fateful night, the faith already had been eroded, remaining as no more than a civilized convention to which they had conformed in a lukewarm manner. There had been a time, perhaps, when it had been meaningful. In the centuries after it had been conceived in all its glory, it had been allowed to fade, to become a shadow of its former force and strength. It had been a victim of man's mismanagement, of his overwhelming concept of property and profit. It had been manifested in lordly buildings filled with pomp and glitter rather than being nourished in the human heart and mind. And now it came to this – that it was kept alive by beings that were not human, machines that had been accorded a measure of seeming humanness purely as a matter of man's technology and pride.

He gained the ridgetop and noticed, now that the woods fell away and his view was clear, that the storm clouds were piling even higher in the western sky and had engulfed the sun. The house lay ahead of him and he set out toward it at a somewhat more rapid rate than he was accustomed in his walking. He had opened the record book this morning and it was still lying open on his desk, but not written in. There had been nothing to write in it this morning, but now there would be much to write – the visit of Horace Red Cloud, the alien in the glen and its strange request, the wish of Evening Star to read the books and his invitation for her to come and live with him and Martha. He would get in some writing before the hour for dinner and after the evening concert would sit down at his desk again and finish his account of the happenings of the day.

The music trees were tuning up and there was one young sapling that was doing badly. Out back a robot blacksmith was hammering noisily on metal – more than likely he was working on a plow. Thatcher, he recalled, had told him that all the plowshares had been brought in for work against the coming of the spring and another planting season.

The door off the patio opened and Martha came out and down the path toward him. She was beautiful, he thought, watching her – more beautiful, in many ways, than that long-gone day when they had been married. Their life together had been good. A man couldn't ask for better. A warm glow of thankfulness for the fullness of their life surged through him.

'Jason,' she cried, hurrying to meet him. 'Jason, it is John! Your brother, John, is home!'

6

(Excerpt from journal entry of 2 September 2185) ... I often wonder how it happened we were missed. If the People were taken away, which seems far more likely than that they simply went away, by what quirk of fortune or of fate were the people in this house missed by the agency which caused the taking? The monks and brothers in the monastery a mile down the road were taken. The people in the agricultural station, a fair-sized village in itself, a half mile farther off, were taken. The great apartment complex five miles up the river, housing the workers who fished the rivers, was emptied. We alone were left.

I sometimes wonder if the social and financial privilege which had been my family's lot for the last century or more may still have been operative – that we, somehow, were above being touched even by this supernatural agency, even as we remained untouched (nay, were even benefited) by the misery and the restriction and the want which overpopulation visited upon the people of the Earth. It seems to be a social axiom that as misery and privation increase for the many, the few rise ever higher in luxury and comfort, feeding on the misery. Not aware, perhaps, that they feed upon the misery, not with any wish of feeding on it – but they do.

It is retrospective guilt, of course, which forces me to wonder this and I know it can't be true, for there were many families other than our own which fattened on the misery and they were not spared. If spared is the word. We have no idea, of course, what the taking meant. It may have meant death, or it might, as well, have spelled transference to some other place, or to many other places, and if that is true, the transference may have been a blessing. For the Earth was not, in that day, the kind of place the majority of the people would have elected to remain. The entire surface of the land, and a part of the sea as well, and the entire output of energy were utilized to maintain a bare existence for the hordes that peopled Earth. Bare existence is no idle phrase, for the people barely had enough to eat, barely room enough to live, barely fabric enough to cover their bodies for the sake of decency.

That my family, and other similar families, were allowed the privilege of retaining the relatively large amounts of living space they had fashioned for themselves well before the population pinch became as bad as it eventually became, is only one example of the inequities that existed. That the Leech Lake Indian tribe, which also was missed by the supernatural agency, had been living in a relatively large and uncrowded space can be explained in another way. The land into which they had been forced, centuries before, was largely worthless land, although throughout the years the original tract had been taken from them, bit by bit, by the relentless force of economic pressure and eventually all of it would have been taken and they would have been shoved into the anonymity of the global ghetto. Although, truth to tell, their lives had been, in some ways, a ghetto from the start.

At the time of the disappearance, the building of this house and the acquisition of the estate which surrounds it would have been impossible. For one thing, no such tract could have been found and even had it been available its price would have been such that even the most affluent of the families would not have been able to afford it. Furthermore, there would not have been the labor force or the materials available to construct the house, for the world economy was stretched to the breaking point to maintain eight billion people.

My great-grandfather built this house almost a century and a half ago. Even then the land was hard to come by and he was only able to obtain it because the monastery down the road had fallen on hard times and was forced to sell a part of its holdings to meet certain pressing obligations. In building the house, my great-grandfather ignored all modern trends and went back to the solidity and simplicity of the great country houses of some centuries before. He built it well and he often said that it would stand forever, and while this, of course, was an exaggeration, there is no question that it still will stand at a time when many other buildings have crumbled into mounds.

In our present situation we are fortunate to have such a house, so solid and so large. It even now accommodates the sixty-seven persons who are resident in it without any great inconvenience, although as our population grows we may have to look for other places where some of us can live. The habitations at the agricultural station now have fallen into disrepair, but the monastery buildings, much more stoutly built, are possibilities (and the four robots who now occupy them could make do with lesser space), and the great apartment complex up the river is another lesser possibility. The apartment buildings stand in some need of repair, having stood unoccupied all these fifty years, but our corps of robots, properly supervised, should be equal to the task.

Our livelihood is well taken care of, for we have simply taken over as much as we need of the great expanse of farmland formerly worked by the agricultural station. The robots form a work force that is fully equal to the situation and as the agricultural machines broke down beyond the possibility of repair, we have gone back to farming with horses for motive power and to the simple plow, mower and reaper, which our robots have built by cannibalizing the more modern and sophisticated implements.

We are now on what I like to think of as a manorial basis – the manor providing all those things of which we have any need. We have great flocks of sheep for wool and mutton, a dairy herd for milk, beef cattle for meat, hogs for pork and ham and bacon, poultry for eggs and eating, bees and cane for honey and for sorghum, grains for flour and extensive gardens to furnish a great array of vegetables. It is a simple existence and a quiet and most satisfactory one. There were times, to start with, when we missed the old life – or at least some of the younger people missed it, but now I believe that all of us are convinced that, in its way, the life that we have fashioned is a most satisfactory one.

I have one deep regret. I have wished many times that my son, Jonathon, and his lovely wife, Marie, the parents of our three grandchildren, might have lived to be here with us. The two of them, I know, would have enjoyed the life that we live now. As a boy Jonathon never wearied of tramping over the estate. He loved the trees and flowers, the few wild creatures that managed to still exist in our little patch of woodland, the free and uncluttered feeling that a little open space could give. Now the world (or all of it I know, and I suppose the rest of it) is going back into wilderness. Trees are growing on the old farmlands. Grass had crept into places where no grass had grown before. The wild flowers are coming back and spreading from the little, forgotten nooks where they had hidden out, and the wildlife is taking over. The river valleys, now fairly heavily wooded, swarm with squirrel and coon and occasionally there are deer, probably drifting down out of the north. I know of five covey of quail that are doing well and the other day I ran into a flock of grouse. Once again the migratory wildfowl each spring and fall fly in great Vs across the sky. With man's heavy hand lifted off the Earth the little, humble creatures are coming back into an olden heritage.

With certain modifications, the situation is analogous to the extinction of the dinosaurs at the close of the Cretaceous. The one important modification, of course, is that all the dinosaurs became extinct and there are a few humans still surviving. I may, however, be coming to a conclusion concerning this modification somewhat early. Triceratops, it is believed, may have been the last of the dinosaurs to disappear and it is entirely possible that small herds of Triceratops may have dragged out an existence spanning perhaps half a million years or more after the other dinosaurs had died before they, too, succumbed to the factors that had brought extinction to the others. In this light, the fact that a few hundred humans, the ragged remnants of a once mighty race, still exists may be of slight significance. We may be the Triceratops of the human species.

When the dinosaurs and many of the other reptiles died out, the mammals, which had existed in unknown numbers for millions of years, swarmed into the vacuum left by the dying reptiles and proliferated to take their places. Is this, then, another case of wiping out a certain mammalian population to give the other vertebrates a second chance, to lift from them the doom of man? Or is this facet of the situation only incidental? Has mankind, or the most of mankind, been removed to make way for a further evolutionary development? And if this should be the case, what and where is the new evolutionary creature? What bothers one when he thinks of this is the strange process of extinction. A change in climate, a shifting of geography, disease, a scrambling of ecological parameters, factors that limit the food supply – all of these are physically, biologically and geologically understandable. The extinction or the near extinction of the human race is not. Slow, gradual extinction is one thing, instantaneous extinction is another. An instantaneous extinction postulates the machination of an intelligence rather than a natural process.

If the extinction were the result of the operation of another intelligence, one finds himself forced to ask, not only where and what is this other intelligence, but more importantly, what could have been its purpose?

Is all life in the galaxy watched over by some great central intelligence that is alert to certain crimes that cannot be tolerated? Was the vanishing of the human race a punishment, an extermination, a death sentence passed because of what we'd done to planet Earth and to all the other creatures that had shared it with us? Or was it simply a removal, a cleansing – an action taken to ensure that a valuable planet would not be ruined utterly? Or, perhaps, in an even more far-reaching purpose, to give the planet a chance to replenish, over the next billion years or so, the natural resources of which it had been stripped – so that new coal fields might be laid down and new pools of oil created, so that ravaged soil could be rebuilt, new iron deposits come into being?

There is little purpose, I suppose, and less profit, to think of these things and to ask these questions. But man, being what he is, having obtained his short-lived dominance of the planet by virtue of his question-asking, will not be denied such speculation ...

7

Half the afternoon the thick cloud bank had piled up in the sky and Hezekiah, watching as it climbed, had told himself that it were as if there were a ladder in the sky and the clouds had kept climbing it, growing taller and higher and more threatening and impressive as they climbed. Then, almost immediately, he had rebuked himself for thinking so – for there was no ladder, it was God's will that the clouds came climbing. He was puzzled and ashamed at these flights of fancy, at this romanticism, which he should have conquered long ago, but which, in the last few years (or so it seemed) had come welling more often to the surface. Or was it, he wondered, that only in the last few years he had directed his attention the more to these flights of fancy, aghast that there could linger in him such foolish notions, so far afield from the serious considerations to which he should be dedicated.

In the study the other brothers were bent above the books. They had sat thus for years, dedicated to the task of collating and condensing down to elemental truths all that the creature, man, had written, all that he had thought and reasoned and speculated in the spiritual sense. Of the four of them only he, Hezekiah, had not tied himself to the written or the printed word, and that had been according to the agreement they had made, in that time long centuries past when they had planned their search of truth. Three of them studying all that had been written – rewriting it, reassembling it, reassessing it, as if one man, and one man alone, had thought it all and written all of it as a single body, not many men who strove to understand, but one man who had truly understood. Three of them to do their work and the fourth to read their evaluations and assessments and, from this basis, try to puzzle out the meaning that had escaped the grasp of man. It had been a glorious idea, Hezekiah reassured himself; it had seemed so sound and it still was sound, but the way to truth was longer and more difficult than they had imagined and they still held no real inkling of the truth. Faith was something else; through the years their faith had deepened and been strengthened by their work, but the deepening of faith had not led the way to truth. Could it be possible, Hezekiah asked himself, that there was no room for both the faith and truth, that they were mutually exclusive qualities that should not coexist? He shuddered as he thought of it, for if this should be the case, they had spent their centuries of devotion to but little purpose, pursuing a will-o'-the-wisp. Must faith be exactly that, the willingness and ability to believe in the face of a lack of evidence? If one could find the evidence, would then the faith be dead? If that were the situation, then which one did they want? Had it been, he wondered, that men had tried what they even now were trying and had realized that there was no such thing as truth, but only faith, and being unable to accept the faith without its evidence, had dropped the faith as well? There was nothing in the books to make one think this might be so, but while they had thousands of books, they did not have them all. Was there somewhere in the world, moldering away, or perhaps already moldered, a book (or several books) that would make it clear what man had really done, or had tried to do and failed?

He had been pacing in the garden all the afternoon and this was not unusual, for he often walked there. Pacing helped him think and, besides, he loved the garden for the beauty that was in it – the changing of the leaves and the flowering of the blooms in season, the miracle of life and death, the singing of the birds and the pattern of their flight, the haze of the river hills and, at times, the orchestration of the music trees – although he was not sure he approved entirely of the music trees. But now he went to the door of the chapter house and as he reached it, the storm broke, great sheets of rain sweeping across the garden, pounding on the roofs, filling the gutters, the walks almost instantly transformed into brimming creeks.

He opened the door and ducked inside, but stood within the entryway a moment, holding the door partly open to gaze out across the garden, swept by the torrents of rain that came down hissing against the grass and flowers. The ancient willow tree that stood beside the bench strained in the direction of the wind, as if it were trying to tug free of the roots that anchored it.

Somewhere something was banging and as he listened, he finally made out what it was. The great metal gate that stood in the outer wall had been forced open by the wind and was banging back and forth against the field stone wall. If it were not shut and fastened, it might beat itself to pieces.

Hezekiah stepped out of the door and closed it behind him. As he went down the brimming walk, the wind and water beat at him, sluicing off his body in streaming sheets. The walk turned the corner of the building and now he walked into the wind and it was as if a great hand had been placed against his metal chest and pushed to hold him back. His brown robe trailed behind him, snapping in the wind.

The gate was straight ahead, swinging through its hinged arc and slamming against the wall, the metal shuddering at each impact with the stone. It was not only the gate that caught his attention. Lying near the gate was a sprawled and huddled shape, half on the walk, half lying on the grass. Even through the blur of rain he could make out that it was a man. The figure lay upon its face and when he turned it over he saw the jagged cut that started at the, temple and ran down across the face, not bleeding, for the rain washed the blood away, but a livid streak of torn flesh.

He got his arms around the body and stood, lifting the man from where he lay, turning and moving back along the path, driving his feet hard against the ground to brace himself against the pressure of the wind which, if he had not fought against it, would have driven him at a headlong pace.

He reached the door of the chapter house and went in. With his heel, he kicked the door shut and went across the room to a bench against the wall and laid the man upon it. He saw that the man still breathed, his chest rising and falling. He was a young man, or seemed a young man, naked except for a breech clout and a necklace of bear claws and a pair of binoculars hung around his neck.

A stranger, Hezekiah thought, a human being who had come out of nowhere and who, by the grace of God, had sought refuge in this place against the breaking storm, only to be caught and knocked unconscious by the wildly swinging gate once he had unlatched it. This was the first time in all the years the robots had occupied the monastery that a human had ever come to this house for shelter and for aid. And that, he told himself, was meet, for historically such a place as this had stood for many centuries as a place of aid and refuge. He felt a shiver running through him, a shiver of excitement and of dedication. It was a charge they must accept, a duty and an obligation that must be fulfilled. There must be blankets to keep the young man warm, hot food, a fire, a bed – and there were in this place no such things as blankets or hot food or fires. There had not been for many years, for robots did not need them.

'Nicodemus,' he shouted. 'Nicodemus!'

His shouts boomed between the walls, as if olden echoes had been magically awakened, echoes that had waited for many, many years. He heard their running feet and a door burst open and they came running through.

'We have a guest,' said Hezekiah. 'He is hurt and we must care for him. Run, one of you, to the House and find Thatcher. Tell him we need food and blankets and a way of making fire. Another one of you break up some of the furniture and lay it in the fireplace. All the wood we might find outdoors is wet. But try to choose the pieces that have the lesser value. Some old stools, perhaps, a broken table or a chair.'

He heard them leave, heard the outer door bang as Nicodemus plunged out into the storm to go up to the House.

Hezekiah hunkered down beside the bench and kept his eyes upon the man. The breathing was regular and the face had lost some of its pallor, which had showed even through the tan. With no rain to wash it off, blood was oozing from the cut and running down the face. Hezekiah gathered up one corner of his rain-soaked robe and gently wiped it off.

Inside himself he sensed a deep, abiding peace, a sense of accomplishment, a compassion for and a dedication to this man who lay upon the bench. Was this, he wondered, the true function of the people – or the robots – who might dwell within this house? Not the vain unraveling of truth, but the succor of one's fellow men? Although that was not entirely true, he knew – not the way he said it. For this was not a fellow man lying on the bench, could not be a fellow man; a robot was not fellow to a man. But if a robot stood in place of man, if he took the place of man, if he followed in man's ways and tried to carry on the task that man had dropped, might he not, in some measure, be fellow to humanity?

And was aghast.

How could he think, even by the most clever argument, that a robot could be fellow to a man?

Vanity, he cried inside himself. An overweening vanity would be the death of him – the damnation of him, and was aghast again, for how could a robot think that he was worthy even of damnation?

He was nothing and a nothing and a nothing. And yet he aped a man. He wore a robe, he sat when there was no need of either robe or sitting; he fled a storm and there was no need for such as he to flee the wet and rain. He read the books that man had written and sought an understanding that man had failed to find. He worshiped God – and that, he thought, might be the greatest blasphemy of them all.

He hunkered on the floor, close beside the bench, the sorrow and the horror welling up in him.

8

He would not have known his brother, Jason told himself, if he'd met him unaware. The stature was there and the proud, hard bearing, but the face was hidden behind a dull and grizzled beard. There was something else as well – a coldness in the eyes, a tenseness in the face. Age had not mellowed John; it had tempered and toughened him and given him a sadness that had not been there before.

'John,' he said and stopped just inside the doorway. 'John, we have so often wondered …' and then stopped talking, staring at this stranger in the room.

'It's all right, Jason,' said his brother. 'Martha didn't know me, either. I have changed.'

'I would have,' Martha said. 'Given just a little time, I would have. It's the beard.'

Jason went quickly across the room, grasped his brother's outstretched hand, put an arm around his shoulder and drew him close, holding him hard. 'It's good to see you,' he said. 'So good to have you back. It has been so long.'

They stepped away from one another and stood for a moment, silent, staring at one another, each trying to see in the other man the man they had seen at their last meeting. Finally, John said, 'You look well, Jason. I knew I'd find you well. You always were one to look after yourself. And you have Martha, who looks after you. Some of the others that I met told me you had stayed home.'

'Someone had to,' Jason told him. 'It was not a hardship. We have made a good life. We've been happy here.'

'I asked about you often,' Martha said. 'I always asked about you. No one seemed to know.'

'I've been far out,' said John. 'Out toward the center. There was something out there that I had to find. I went farther toward the center than any of the others. There were others who told me what was out there, or rather what might be out there, for they did not really know, and it seemed someone should go and see, and none of these others were about to go. Someone had to go. Someone had to go just as someone had to stay at home.'

'Let's sit down,' said Jason. 'There's a lot you have to tell us, so let's be comfortable while you're telling it. Thatcher will bring in something and we can sit and talk. You are hungry, John?'

His brother shook his head.

'A drink, perhaps. All the old stuff's gone, but some of our robots are handy with moonshine of a sort. Properly aged and cared for, it is not too bad. We've tried to make wine, but this is not wine country. The soil's not right and the sun's not hot enough. It always turns out poor.'

'Later on,' said John. 'After I have told you. Then we can have a drink.'

'You went out to find the evil,' Jason said. 'That must be it. We know there's an evil out there. We got word of it quite some years ago. No one knew what it was – not even that it's really evil. All they knew was it had an evil smell.'

'Not an evil,' John told him. 'Something worse than evil. A great uncaring. An intellectual uncaring. An intelligence that has lost what we think of as humanity. Perhaps not lost it, for it may have never had it. But that's not all of it. I found the People.'

'The People!' Jason cried. 'You can't mean that. No one ever knew. No one had the least idea ...'

'Of course, no one ever knew. But I found them. They are on three planets, the planets close to one another, and they are doing well, perhaps somewhat too well. They haven't changed. They are the same as they were five thousand years ago. They have followed to its logical conclusion the course we all were following five thousand years ago and now they are coming back to Earth. They are on their way to Earth.'

A sudden wall of water splashed against the windows, driven by a wind that went howling in the eaves, far overhead.

'I do believe,' said Martha, 'that the storm has broken. It may be a bad one.'

9

She sat and listened to the voices of the books – or, rather, perhaps, to the voices of the men who had written all the books, strange, grave voices far off in time, speaking from the depths of time, the distant mumble of many cultivated voices, without words, but with meaning and with thought instead of words, and she had never thought, she told herself, it could be anything like this. The trees had words to speak and the flowers a meaning and the little people of the woods often talked to her and the river and the running streams had music and a magic that surpassed understanding. But this was because they were living things – yes, even the river and the brook could be thought of as living things. Could it be that books were living, too?

She had never known there could be so many books, a large room, floor to ceiling, lined with rows of books, and many times that number, she had been told by the funny little robot, Thatcher, stored away in basement rooms. But the strangest thing of all was that she could think of a robot as being a funny sort of creature – almost as if he were a man. No great black horror that stalked the evening skyline, no midnight wraith out of the place of dreams; if not a man at least a manlike being with a gentle voice. Perhaps it had been something he had said: 'Here you can trace and chart the path of man up from darkest night.' Saying it proudly, as if he were a man himself and alone, in terror and in hope, had trod that very path.

The voices of the books kept mumbling in the dimness of the room while rain ran down the windows – a companionable muttering that must keep on forever, the ghostly conversations of long-dead writers whose works lined the study walls. Was it all imagination, she asked herself, or did others hear them, too – did Uncle Jason sometimes hear them as he sat here by himself? Although she knew, even as she wondered it, that this was something she could never ask. Or could it be heard by no one but herself, hearing it as she had heard the voice of Old Grandfather Oak on that long-gone summer day before the tribe had gone into the wild rice country, as she this very day had sensed the lifting of the arms and the benediction?

As she sat there, at a small desk in one corner of the room, with the book opened on the desk (not the big desk where Uncle Jason sat to write the chronicles), listening to the wind running in the eaves, watching the rain sluice down the windows from which Thatcher had drawn the drapes with the passing of the morning sun, she moved into another place, or seemed to move into another place, although the room remained. In this place were many people, or at least the shadows of many people, and many other desks and far distant times and places, although the distance of the times and places seemed less than they should have been, as if the veils of time and space had grown very thin and were ready to dissolve, so that she sat, an observer to a great event – the running together of all time and space so that the both of them became almost nonexistent, no longer caging men and events into separate cells, but running them all together, as if everything had happened all at once and in the self-same area, with the past crowding close upon the future within the confines of a tiny point of existence that, for convenience, might be called the present. Frightened at what was happening, she nevertheless glimpsed for a terrible, sublime moment all the causes and effects, all the direction and the purpose, all the agony and glory that had driven men to write all the billions of words that stood stacked within the room. Glimpsed it all without understanding, with no time or capacity for an understanding, understanding only that what had happened in the minds of men to drive them to create all the mumbled, scribbled burning words had not been so much the work of many individual minds as the impact of a pattern of existence upon the minds of all mankind.

The spell (if it were no more than a spell) was broken almost immediately, with Thatcher coming through the door and padding across the room toward her, carrying a tray which he put down upon the desk.

'This is slightly delayed, miss,' he apologized. 'Just as I was about to bring it Nicodemus from the monastery came rushing in to say that hot soup and blankets and many other things were needed for the comfort of an injured pilgrim.'

A glass of milk, a jar of wild gooseberry jam, slices of buttered bread and a slab of honey cake rested on the tray. 'It is not elaborate,' said Thatcher. 'It is not as splendid as a guest of this house has reason to expect, but taking care of the monastery's needs, I did not have the time to do full justice to it.'

'It is more than adequate,' said Evening Star. 'I had not expected such a kindness. Busy as you were, you should not have bothered.'

'Miss,' said Thatcher, 'through the centuries it has been my pleasure and responsibility to operate this household according to certain standards that have not varied through all the days of my stewardship. I am only sorry that the procedure should, for the first time, have been upset on your first day here.'

'Never mind,' she told him. 'You said a pilgrim. Do pilgrims often come to the monastery? I have never heard of them.'

'This one,' Thatcher said, 'is the first there ever was. And I am not sure that he is a pilgrim, although that is what Nicodemus called him. A mere wanderer, no doubt, although that is memorable in itself, for never before has there been a human wanderer. A young man, almost naked, as Nicodemus tells it, with a bear-claw necklace encircling his throat.'

She sat stiff and straight, remembering the man who had stood that morning on the bluff top with her.

'Is he badly hurt?' she asked.

'I do not think so,' Thatcher told her. 'He sought refuge in the monastery from the storm. When he opened the gate, the wind caught it and it struck him. He is very much alive.'

'He is a good man,' said Evening Star, 'and a very simple man. He cannot even read. He thinks the stars are no more than points of light shining in the sky. But he can sense a tree …'

And stopped, confused, for she must not talk about the tree. She must learn to guard her tongue.

'Miss, you know this human?'

'No. I mean I do not know him. I saw him for a moment and talked with him this morning. He said he was coming here. He was seeking something and thought he might find it here.'

'All humans seek for something,' Thatcher said. 'We robots are quite different. We are content to serve.'

10

'To begin with,' said John Whitney, 'I simply wandered. It was wonderful to all of us, of course, but I think, somehow, most wonderful of all to me. The idea that man could be a free agent in the universe, that he could go wherever he might wish, was a bit of magic that was utterly beyond all comprehension, and that he could do this by himself, with no machinery, with no instruments, with nothing but his body and his mind, through a power that he held within himself and which no human had ever known before, was simply unbelievable, and I found myself exercising the power to prove to myself again and yet again that it could be really done, that it was a solid and ever-present ability that could be called upon at will and that it was never lost, and that it belonged to one by right of his humanity and not by some special dispensation that could be withdrawn at a moment's notice. You never tried it, Jason, neither you nor Martha?'

Jason shook his head. 'We found something else. Not as exhilarating, perhaps, but with a deep satisfaction of its own. A love of land and a feeling of continuity, a sense of heritage, even of being a substantial part of that heritage, an earth-bound certainty.'

'I think I can understand that,' said John. 'It's something that I never had and I suspect it was the lack of it that drove me on and on once the sheer exuberance of traveling from one star to another had worn somewhat thin. Although I still can become excited over a new place that I find – for there are never any of them that are exactly like another. The one amazing thing to me, the thing that continues to amaze me, is the great range of dissimilarities that can exist, even on those planets where the basic characteristics of their geology and history are very much the same.'

'But why did you wait so long, John? All these years without coming home. Without letting us know. You said you had met others and that they told you we were still on Earth, that we had never left.'

'I had thought of it,' said John. 'Many times I thought of it, of coming back to see you. But I'd have come back empty-handed, with not a thing to show for all the years of wanderlust. Not possessions, of course, for we know now they don't count. But nothing really learned, no great new understanding. A fistful of stories of where I'd been and what I'd seen, but that would have been the size of it. The prodigal coming home and I—'

'But it wouldn't have been that way. Your welcome always waited you. We've waited for years and asked of you.'

'What I don't understand,' said Martha, 'is why there was no word of you. You said you had met others and I talk all the time with our people out there and there never was a word about you, never any news. You just dropped out of sight.'

'I was far out, Martha. Much farther than most of the others ever got. I ran hard and fast. Don't ask me why. I sometimes asked myself and there was never any answer. Never any real answer. The others that I met, only two or three of them quite by accident, had run as hard as I. Like a bunch of kids, I suppose, who come to a new and wondrous place, and there is so much to see they're afraid they'll not get to see it all, so they run hard to see it all, telling themselves that once they've seen it all, they'll go back to the one place that is best, probably knowing that they never will, for that one best place is always, in their minds, just a little way ahead and they become obsessed with the idea that if they don't keep going they will never find it. I knew what I was doing and I knew it made no sense and it was some comfort to me when I met those other few who were the same as I.'

'But there was purpose in your running,' Jason said. 'Even if you didn't know it at the time, the purpose still was there. For you found the People. If you hadn't gone so far, I don't suppose you'd ever have found them.'

'That is true,' said John, 'but I had no sense of purpose. I simply stumbled on them. I had no word of them, no inkling they were there. I wasn't hunting them. I had sensed the Principle and I was hunting it.'

'The Principle?'

'I don't know how I can tell you, Jason. There aren't words to tell you. There is no way I can express exactly what it is, although I am certain I have a fairly good idea. Perhaps no man can ever know exactly what it is. You remember that you said there was an evil toward the center. That evil is the Principle. The people I met far out had sensed it, too, and somehow must have sent back word. But evil is not right; it is not really evil. Sensed, scented, become aware of from far off, it has the smell of evil because it is so different, so unhuman, so uncaring. By human standards blind and reasonless, and seeming blind and reasonless because there is about it not one single emotion, one single motive or purpose, one single thought process that can be equated with the human mind. A spider is blood brother and intellectual equal to us as compared to it. It sits there and it knows. It knows all there is to know. And its knowing is translated in such nonhuman terms that we could never even scratch the surface of the simplest of those terms. It sits there and knows and translates what it knows and that translation of its knowledge is so coldly correct that one shrinks away from it, for there is nothing that can be so right, without the slightest possibility of error. I've said it is unhuman and perhaps it is this ability to be so utterly right, so absolutely correct, that makes it so unhuman. For proud as we may be of our intellect and understanding, there is no one of us who can say with any honesty or any certainty that he is correct on any point of information or interpretation.'

'But you said that you found the People and they're coming back to Earth,' said Martha. 'Can't you tell us more about them and when they're coming back ...'

'My dear,' said Jason, softly, 'I think there's more that John wants to tell us, that he has to tell us before he talks about the People.'

John rose from the chair in which he had been sitting, walked to the rain-smeared window and looked out, then came back to face the two sitting on the davenport. 'Jason is right,' he said. 'There is more I have to tell. I've wanted for so long to tell it to someone, to share it all with someone. I may be wrong. I've thought about it for so long that I may have become confused. I'd like to have you two hear me out and tell me what you think.'

He sat down on the chair again. 'I'll try to present it as objectively as I can,' he said. 'You realize that I never saw this thing, this Principle. I may not have even gotten close to it. But close enough to know that it is there and to sense a little, perhaps as much as any man may sense, the sort of thing it is. Not understanding it, of course, not even trying to understand it, for you know you are too small and weak for understanding. That was the thing that hurt the most, perhaps – realizing how small and weak you were, and not only you yourself, but all humanity. Something that reduced the human race to microbe status, perhaps to less than microbe status. You know instinctively that you, as one human being, are beneath its notice, although there is evidence, or I think there may be evidence, that it could and did take notice of humanity.

'I got as close to it as my mind could bear. I cowered before it. I don't know what else I did. There is a part of all of this that tends to go foggy in the mind. Perhaps I got too close. But I had to know, you see. I had to be sure and I am sure. It is out there and it watches and it knows and if need be it can act, although I am inclined to think it would not be quick to act ...'

'Act – how?' asked Jason.

'I don't know,' John told him. 'You have to understand this is all impression. Intellectual impression. Nothing visual. Nothing that I saw or heard. It's the fact that it's all intellectual impression that makes it so hard to describe. How do you describe the reactions of the human mind? How do you blueprint the emotional impact of those reactions?'

'We had the report,' Jason said to Martha. 'You picked it up from someone. Do you remember who it was, who it might have been who was out as far as John, or almost as far as John ...'

'They wouldn't have had to be out as far as I was,' said John. 'They could have picked up the sense of it a good deal farther off. I deliberately tried to get in close to it.'

'I don't remember who it was,' said Martha. 'Two or three people told me of it. It was, I'm sure, all very second-hand. Maybe tenth- or twelfth-hand. Word that had been passed on from one person to another, from many persons to many other persons. Simply that there was something evil out near the center of the galaxy. That someone had been out there and had run into it. But no hint that anyone had investigated. Afraid to investigate, perhaps.'

'That would be right,' said John. 'I was very much afraid.'

'You call it a Principle,' said Jason. 'That is a funny thing to call it. Why the Principle?'

'It was what I thought when I was close to it,' said John. 'It didn't tell me. It didn't communicate at all. It probably was not even aware of me, didn't know that I existed. One tiny little microbe creeping up on it ...'

'But Principle? It was a thing, a creature, an entity. That is a strange designation to hang on a creature or an entity. There must have been a reason.'

'I'm not sure, Jason, that it is a creature or an entity. It is simply something. A mass of intelligence, perhaps. And what form would a mass of intelligence take? What would it look like? Could you even see it? Would it be a cloud, a wisp of gas, trillions of tiny motes dancing in the light of the center's suns. And the reason for calling it the Principle? I can't really tell you. There is no logic to it, no single reason I can put a finger on. Simply that I felt it was the basic principle of the universe, the director of the universe, the brain center of the universe, the thing that holds the universe together and makes it operate – the force that makes the electrons spin about the nucleus, that makes the galaxies rotate about their centers, that holds everything in place.'

'Could you pinpoint its location?' Jason asked.

John shook his head. 'No way that I could. No such thing as triangulation. The feel of the Principle was everywhere, it seemed; it came from everywhere. It closed in around you. It muffled and engulfed you; there was no sense of direction. And in any case, it would be difficult, for there are so many suns and so many planets. Jammed close together. Suns fractions of light years apart. Old, the most of them. Most of the planets dead. Some of them with the wreckage and ruin of what at one time must have been great civilizations, but now all of them are gone ...'

'Perhaps it was one of these civilizations ...'

'Perhaps,' said John. 'I thought so at first. That one of the ancient civilizations had managed to survive and that its intelligence evolved into the Principle. But since then I've come to doubt it. For more time would have been needed, I'm convinced, than the lifetime of a galaxy could afford. I can't begin to tell you, I don't know how to tell you, the sheer force of this intelligence, or the alienness of it. Not just the difference of it. Throughout all space you find scattered intelligences that are different and these differences make them alien. But not alien in the way the Principle is alien. And this terrible alienness hints at an origin not of the galaxy, of a time before the galaxy, of a place and time so different from the galaxy that it would be inconceivable. You are acquainted, I suppose, with the theory of the steady-state?'

'Yes, of course,' said Jason. 'The universe had no beginning and will never have an end, that it is in a state of continual creation, new matter being formed, new galaxies coming into being even as the old ones die. But the cosmologists, before the disappearance of the People, had fairly well established that the theory was untenable.'

'I know they did,' said John. 'But there was still one hope – you could call it hope, for there were certain people who, for philosophical reasons, clung stubbornly to the steady-state concept. It was so beautiful, so superb and awe-inspiring, that they would not let it go. And they said, suppose that the universe is far bigger than it seems to be, that what we see is only a local segment, one tiny local bubble on the skin of this greater universe and this local bubble is going through a phase that makes it appear not to be steady-state, but an evolving universe.'

'And you think that they were right?'

'I think they could be right. Steady-state would give the Principle the time that it needed to come into being. Before it came into being the universe may have been chaotic. The Principle may be the engineering force that put it all to right.'

'You believe all this?'

'Yes, I do believe it. I've had time to think of it and I put it all together and I did the job so well that I'm convinced of it. Not a shred of proof. Not a point of information. But it's fastened in my mind and I can't shake it free. I try to tell myself that the Principle, or certain features of the Principle, may have put it in my mind, might have planted it. I try to tell this to myself because it's the only way that I can explain it. And yet I know I must be wrong, for I am sure the Principle was entirely unaware of me. There was never any sign it was aware of me.'

'You got close to it, you say.'

'As close as I dared to get. I was frightened all the way. I went to a point where I had to break and run.'

'Somewhere along the way you found the People. So there was purpose after all. You never would have found them if you'd not gone chasing after this thing you call the Principle.'

'Jason,' Martha said, 'you don't sound too impressed. What's the matter with you? Here your brother has come back and ...'

'I am sorry,' Jason said. 'I would suppose I do not grasp it yet. It is too big to grasp. Maybe I'm deeply horrified and calling it "this thing" is simply a defense mechanism to hold it away from me.'

'I found the same reaction in myself,' John told Martha. 'That is, to begin with. I soon got over it. And, yes, I'd have never found the People if I'd not tracked down the Principle. It was blind luck I found them. I had started back, you see, and was planet hopping, but going on a different tack than the one I'd followed going in. You have to be extremely careful, as I suppose you know, in choosing the planets that you use. You can sense them and pick out the ones that seem the best and there are a lot of guidelines that serve you fairly well, but there always is a chance that a planet might have some characteristics that you have not detected or lack something that you took for granted and that simply isn't there, so you have to have an alternative or two, so that if anything goes sour with the planet you have chosen you can shift most hurriedly to another one. I had alternatives and I hit a planet that, if not deadly, was uncomfortable, so I switched quickly to another one and that's where I found the People. It was still fairly close to the Principle and I wondered how they stood it, how they could live so close to it and entirely disregard it, or pretend to disregard it. I thought perhaps they had become accustomed to it, although it did not seem the sort of thing one could very readily become accustomed to. It was only after a time that I realized they were unaware of it. They had not developed parapsychic abilities, as we have, and they were entirely deaf to it. They had no idea such a thing was there.

'I was fortunate. I materialized in an open field – materialized is not the word, of course; there is no word for it. It's insane that a man can do a thing and still have no word for what he does. Do you happen to know, Jason, if anyone has actually figured out what actually happens when we go star-traveling?'

'No, I don't,' said Jason. 'I would think not. Martha might know better than I do. She keeps up a running conversation with the stars. She hears all the news.'

'There have been those who've tried,' said Martha. 'They have gotten nowhere. That was earlier. I don't think anyone has bothered for a long, long time. They just accept it now. No one wonders anymore about how or why it works.'

'Perhaps it's just as well,' said John. 'But, the situation being as it is, I could have muffed it. I could have arrived at a place that teemed with people and someone might have seen me appearing out of nothing or I, seeing humans in numbers for the first time in centuries, or somehow recognizing them as the people who had been taken, might have rushed into their arms, elated at having finally found them, although I was not looking for them. It was the last thing in my mind.

'But I arrived in an open field and at some distance I saw other humans, or what I thought were humans – farmers working with big powered agricultural implements. And when I saw the implements, I knew that if they should be humans, they'd not be humans of our kind, for we've had nothing to do

398

with powered machines of any sort for millennia. The thought crossed my mind that if the creatures undeniably were humans, they might be the ones who were taken from the Earth and my knees went wobbly at the thought of it and I was filled with a great elation. Although I told myself that would be most unlikely and the only other alternative was that I'd found another race of humanoid creatures and that was unlikely, too, for in all the galaxy no one has ever found another human race. Or have they? I've been gone so long my information is much out of date.'

'No one has,' said Martha. 'Many other creatures, but no humanoids.'

'There was, too, the fact that they had machines. And I told myself that made the possibility even of less likelihood. For we've found new techno-logical races and of those the technology so weird that in many cases it was impossible for us to grasp the principle or the purpose of it. To find another humanoid race with machine technology seemed to me absurd. The only answer could be that here were the People. Realizing this, I became some-what cautious. We might be of the same blood, but there was five thousand years between us and I reminded myself that five thousand years might have made them as alien as anything we've found in space. And we've learned, if nothing else, that first contact with aliens must be managed adroitly.

'I will not try to tell you now all the things that happened. Later on, per-haps. But I rather think I managed very well. Although I guess, it was mostly luck. When I went up to the farmers I was mistaken for a wandering scholar from another of the three planets the human race inhabits – not quite right in the head and concerned with things no normal man would think worth consideration. Once I caught the drift of it, I went along with them. It covered up a lot of slips I made. My slips seemed no more than eccentricities to them. I think it may have been my clothing and my language that made them think I was a wanderer. Luckily, they spoke a sort of English, but changed consid-erably from the language that we speak. I would imagine that back on the old Earth of five thousand years ago our language, as we speak it now, would not be readily understood. Time and changing circumstance and sloppiness in speech bring about many changes in the spoken word. Under the guise of their mistake, I was able to get around enough to find out what was going on, to learn what sort of society had developed and some of their long-range planning.'

'And,' said Jason, 'it turned out not so pretty.'

John gave him a startled glance. 'How would you know that?'

'You said they still had a machine technology. I think that might be the key. I would guess they continued, once they got themselves sorted out, in about the same way they were going before they were snatched off Earth. And if that is the case, the picture would not be a pretty one.'

'You are right,' said John. 'It took them, apparently, not too long to get themselves, as you say, sorted out. Within a very few years after finding themselves, in a twinkling, on another planet, or on other planets, rather, in an unguessed part of space, they got their bearings and became organized and went on pretty much the way they had left off. They had to start from scratch, of course, but they had the technological knowledge and they had brand-new planets with untouched raw materials and they were very quickly on their way. And what was more, they have the same life expectancy, the same long life that we have. A lot of them died in those first few years while they struggled to get themselves adjusted, but there still were a lot of them left, and among those were people with all the skills that were needed to develop a new technology. Can you imagine what might happen if a skilled, trained engineer or a well-grounded, imaginative scientist lived for many centuries? The society did not lose needed skills by death, as had been the case before. Geniuses did not die, but continued being geniuses. Engineers did not build and plan for a few years only and then die or retire, but kept on building and planning. A man with a theory was given as many centuries as he needed to develop it to its full potentiality and retained the youth that was needed to continue with it. There is a great drawback to this, of course. The presence of men of great age and vast experience and in positions of importance would tend to have an inhibiting influence upon younger men and would make for a conservatism that would be blind to new ideas and in the end would stall all progress if it had not been recognized and compensated for. The People had the sense to recognize it and to build some compensatory features into the social structure.'

'Were you able to arrive at any idea of their time table? How swiftly did they get started again and how they may have progressed?'

'Roughly. Nothing definite, of course. But say a hundred years to get themselves established as a viable society, perhaps three hundred to rebuild an approximation of the kind of technological setup they had here on Earth. And from there they built on the basis of what they had, with the advantage of being able to drop a lot of ancient millstones they carried around their necks. They build from scratch and to start with there was no need to struggle with the obsolescence they were burdened with on Earth. Well before a thousand years had passed the groups living on the three different planets – all within less than a light year of one another – knew about the others and in a very little time spaceships had been developed and built and the human race was together once again. The physical contact and the commerce this made possible gave the technology a new shot in the arm, for during those thousand years or so they had been apart each had developed their technology a little differently, had gone probing in different directions. And also they had the resources of three planets rather than of one and that must have been a distinct advantage. What happened was the melding of three separate cultures into a sort of superculture that still had the advantage of having common roots.'

'They never developed parapsychic powers? No sign of them at all?'

John shook his head. 'They are as blind to them as they had been before. It's not only time that's needed to develop them, for now each of them, all of them, have as much time as we have. It must be that what is needed is a different outlook, a lifting of the pressures that a particular brand of technology imposes not only on a race, but on each human being.'

'And this brand of technology?'

'To you and me,' said John, 'it would be brutal. Knowing nothing else, seeing in it the goals they have striven for, it must seem wonderful to them. Satisfactory, if not wonderful. For them it represents freedom, the freedom of being lifted above and beyond the environment they have struggled to subdue and bend to their purposes; to us it would be stifling.'

'But they must think back,' said Martha. 'Their transfer from Earth must be recent enough that it is remembered. There must be records. They must have wondered all these years what happened to them and where the Earth may be.'

'Records, yes,' said John. 'Myth-haunted, for it was some time, many years, before anyone got around to putting anything on paper and by that time the incident had grown misty and no two men, most likely, could ever quite agree on what exactly happened. But they did think about it. It was forever in their minds. They tried to explain it and there are some marvelous theories and once again there is no agreement on one particular theory. The fuzziness of it all may seem difficult for us to understand, for you have your records, Jason, the ones Grandfather started. I suppose you keep them up.'

'Sporadically,' said Jason. 'Often there is not much to write about.'

'Our records,' said John, 'were written with clear deliberation, with a sense of calmness. We had no upheaval; we were simply left behind. But with the others there was upheaval. It is hard to imagine how it might have been. To be one second on familiar Earth, the next dumped on a planet that was, of course, much the same as Earth, but in many ways entirely different. To be dumped there without food, with no possessions, without shelter. To become pioneers at a moment's notice, under the most adverse circumstances. They were frightened and confused and, worst of all, entirely mystified. There is a great need for man to explain what happens to him or how a thing has happened and they had no way to arrive at any explanation. It was as if magic had been performed – a very vicious and unfeeling magic. The wonder is that any of them survived at all. Many of them didn't. And to this day they don't know why or how it happened. But I think I know the why of it, the reason. Maybe not the method, but the reason.'

'You mean the Principle?'

'The idea may be no more than fantasy,' said John. 'I may have arrived at it because there seemed no other explanation. If the People had parapsychic abilities and knew what I know, that the Principle exists, I have no doubt they would arrive at the same idea as I have. Which wouldn't mean that we were correct. I have said that I don't think the Principle was aware of me. I'm not sure it could become aware of any single human being – it would be akin to a human being becoming aware of a single microbe. Although it may have the power to focus down to very fine perception; it may have no limitations whatever. But in any case it would be more likely to pay attention to humans in a mass, to any sort of creature in a mass, being attracted, perhaps, to the social structure and the intellectual trend brought about by such a mass of beings rather than by the mere massiveness itself. To attract its attention, I would presume that any situation would have to be unique, and from what we ourselves have found so far in the galaxy, I would assume that the humanity of five millennia ago, in the full flower of its technological development and its materialistic point of view, must have seemed unique. The Principle may have studied us for a time and puzzled over us, maybe a bit apprehensive over the possibility that, given time, we could upset the orderliness and precision of the universe – which would have been something it would not have been willing to tolerate. So I think it did with us exactly what men of that day would have done if they'd found a new strain of virus that might just possibly be dangerous. Such a virus would have been placed in culture tubes and run through many tests, trying to determine what it might do under varying conditions. The Principle reached out and grabbed humanity and dumped it on three planets and then settled back to watch, wondering, perhaps, if there'd be divergence or if the strain ran true. By this time it must know that the strain runs true. The cultures on the three planets varied, certainly, but even in their variance all three were technological and materialistic, and once they became aware of one another they had no trouble pooling their characteristics to become a superculture, still materialistic, still technological.'

'I don't know why,' said Jason, 'but when you talk about the People I have the feeling that you are describing a monstrous alien race rather than humanity. Without knowing any of the details, they sound frightening.'

'They are to me,' said John. 'Not perhaps because of any single facet of their culture, for some of these facets can be very pleasant, but because of a sense of the irresistible arrogance implicit in it. Not the power so much, although the power is there, but the naked arrogance of a species that sees everything as property to be manipulated and used.'

'And yet,' said Martha, 'they are our people. The rest of us have wondered about them for so long, have worried over them, wondering what could have happened to them, fearful of what had happened to them. We should be happy that we found them, happy that they have done so well.'

'I suppose we should,' said Jason, 'but somehow I can't. If they'd stay where they are, I'd feel differently about it, I imagine. But John said they're coming back to Earth. We can't let them come. Can you imagine what it might be like? What they'd do to Earth and us?'

'We might have to leave,' said Martha.

'We can't do that,' said Jason. 'Earth is part of us. And not only you and I, but the others, too. Earth is the tie, the anchor. It holds us together – all of us, even those who have never been on Earth.'

'Why did they have to locate Earth?' asked Martha. 'How could they, lost among the stars, have located Earth?'

'I don't know,' said John. 'But they are clever. Far too clever, more than likely. Their astronomy, all their sciences, exceed anything that man of Earth had even dared to dream. Somehow they managed to sift among the stars until they found, and identified, the old ancestral sun. And they have the ships to get here. They've gone to many other, nearby suns, exploring and exploiting.'

'It may take them awhile to get here,' Jason said. 'We'll have some time to figure out what should be done.'

John shook his head. 'Not with the kind of ships they have, traveling many times the speed of light. The survey ship had been a year on its way when I found out about it. It could be here almost any time.'

11

(Excerpt from journal entry of 19 April 6135) ... Today we planted the trees that Robert brought back from one of the stars far out toward the Rim. We planted them most carefully on the little knoll halfway between the House and the monastery. The robots planted them, of course, but we were there to provide unneeded supervision, making, in effect, a quiet ceremony of it. There was Martha and myself and Robert and while we were about it, Andrew and Margaret and their children happened to drop in and Thatcher sent them out to us and we made quite a party of it.

I wonder, sitting here tonight, how the trees will thrive. It is not the first time we have tried to introduce an alien plant to the soil of Earth. There were, for example, the pocketful of cereal grains that Justin carried with him from out Polaris way and the tubers that Celia gathered in another of the Rim systems. Either one of them would have provided another welcome food plant to add to those we have, but in each case we lost them, although the grain dragged out through several seasons, producing less and less, until in the final year we planted the little that we had and it failed to germinate. There is, I suspect, lacking in our soil some vital factor, perhaps the absence of certain minerals, or perhaps the absence of an alien bacteria or little microscopic animal life forms that may be necessary to the growth of alien plants.

We shall lavish great care on the trees, of course, and shall watch them closely, for if we can keep them alive and thriving it will be a wondrous thing. Robert calls them music trees and says that on their native planet there are great groves of them and that in the evening hours they play their concerts, although why they should play a concert is very hard to tell, for there lives upon this planet no other form of life with an intellectual capacity to appreciate good music. Perhaps they play it for themselves, or perhaps for one another, with one grove listening in deep appreciation while its neighbor grove takes over for the evening.

I would suspect that there might be other reasons for the playing that Robert has not caught, being content to sit and listen and not disposed to inquire too deeply into the reason for the music. But when I try to think of those other possible reasons, there is not a single one that occurs to me. We are too limited, of course, in our experience and history, to attempt to understand the purposes of the other life forms that live within the galaxy.

Robert was able to bring to Earth only a half dozen of the trees, little saplings three feet high or so, which he had dug most carefully, using his clothing
to ball the roots, so that he arrived on Earth quite naked. My clothes are
somewhat large for him, but being the kind of man he is, always ready to
laugh, even at himself, he does not seem to mind. The robots are now engaged
in making him a wardrobe and he'll leave Earth much better equipped, gar-
mentwise, than he had been when he stripped himself to ball the trees.

We have no reasonable expectations, of course, that the trees will survive,
but the hope they will is good to think upon. Thinking back, it is so long
since I have heard music, of any sort, that it is difficult to remember what it
might be like. Neither Martha nor myself has any musical ability. Only a
couple of the others of the original group had a musical sense and they are
long gone from Earth. Years ago, seized with a great idea, I read enough
about music to understand some of the basics of its playing and made an
attempt to have the robots construct instruments, which did not turn out too
well, and then to play them, which turned out even worse. Apparently the
robots, or at least the ones on this farm, have no more musical ability than I.
In the days of our youth most of the music was electronically recorded and
since the Disappearance there has been no way in which it can be repro-
duced. As a matter of fact, my grandfather, realizing this when he collected
books and art, made no effort to collect any tapes, although I believe that in
one of the basement vaults there is a respectable collection of musical scores,
the old gentleman hoping, perhaps, that in the years to come there might be
those with some musical aptitude who would find use for them …

12

He knew of music and was entranced by it, sometimes imagining that he heard it in the wind blowing through the trees, or in the silvery tinkling of swift water running over stones, but never in his life had he heard music such as this.

There had been Old Jose, he remembered, hunkered of an evening at the doorway of his hut, tucking the fiddle underneath his chin and drawing the bow across the strings to make happiness or sadness or sometimes neither, but just a flow of sweetness. 'Although I can no longer do it well,' he'd say. 'My fingers no longer dance upon the strings with the nimbleness they should and my arm has grown too heavy to draw the bow with the lightness it should have. Like the wings of a butterfly across the strings – that's the way of it.' But to the boy, crouching in the sand, still warm from the sun, it had been wonderful. On the high hill behind the hut a coyote would point its nose into the sky and howl accompaniment, voicing the loneliness of hill and sea and beach, as if he and the old man with the fiddle and the crouching lad were all the life still left in this lonesome land, with the stubs and mounds of ancient shapes showing in the dust of twilight.

There had been, much later, the buffalo hunters on the plains with their drums and rattles and the deer-bone whistles, thumping out the beat to which he and others danced in the flickering campfire light, dancing with a high exhilaration that he sensed had its roots far back in time.

But this was neither fiddle nor deer-bone whistle, nor the thump of drum; this was music that filled the world and thundered at the sky, that caught one up and carried him, that drowned him, that made one forgetful of his body, welding his very being into the pattern that the music wrought.

One part of his brain was not caught, was not drowned, but held out against the magic of the sound in puzzled wonderment, saying over and over to itself: it is the trees that make the music. The little clump of trees standing on the knoll, ghostly in the evening so clean and fresh after the sweep of rain, white like birch, but larger than most birch. Trees with drum and fiddle and deer-bone whistle and much more than that, putting it all together until the very heavens talked.

He became aware that someone had moved up the garden and now stood beside him, but he did not turn to see who it might be, for there was something wrong out on the knoll. Despite all the beauty and power there was something there that was not exactly right, something that, if it could be fixed, would make the music perfect.

Hezekiah reached out and gently adjusted the bandage on the young man's cheek.

'Are you feeling all right now?' he asked. 'Are you feeling better?'

'It is beautiful,' said the young man, 'but there is something wrong.'

'There is nothing wrong,' said Hezekiah. 'We bandaged you and kept you warm and fed you and now you are all right.'

'Not me. The trees.'

'They are playing well,' said Hezekiah. 'They seldom have played better. And it is one of their old pieces, not one of their experimental—'

'There is a sickness in them.'

'Some of the trees are old and dying,' Hezekiah said. 'They do not perform perfectly, perhaps, not as they did in their younger days, but they still do well. And there are some young saplings that have not caught the knack.'

'Why does no one help them?'

'There is no way to help them. Or if there is, no one knows of it. All things grow old and die, you from oldness, I from rust. They are not trees of Earth. They were brought here many centuries ago by one of those who travel to the stars.'

And there, the young man thought, was the talk again of travelling to the stars. The buffalo hunters had told him there were men and women who traveled to the stars and again this morning the girl he had talked with had mentioned it again. Of them all, the girl might know, for she could talk with trees. Had she, he wondered, ever talked with the ghostly trees standing on the knoll?

She could talk with trees and he could kill the bears and suddenly the moment was with him once again when that last bear had reared up from the gully and had been far too close. But now, for some strange reason, it was not the bear at all, but the trees upon the knoll and in that instant the same thing happened as had happened with the bear, the same sense of going out and meeting. And the meeting of what? The bears? The trees?

Then it was all gone and he was back inside himself again and the wrongness of the trees was gone and everything was right. The music filled the world and thundered at the sky.

Hezekiah said, 'You must be wrong about the trees. There can be no sickness in them. It seems to me, right now, they do as well as I ever can remember.'

13

Jason woke in the night and could not go to sleep again. It was not his body that defied sleep, he knew; it was his mind, so filled with speculation, half numbed with apprehension, that it refused to rest.

Finally he got up and began to dress.

From her bed, Martha asked, 'What is the matter, Jason?'

'Can't sleep,' he told her. 'I am going for a walk.'

'Take your cape,' she said. 'The night wind might be chill. And try not to worry. It will work out all right.'

Going down the stairs, he knew that she was wrong and knew she must be wrong; she spoke the way she did in an attempt to cheer him. It would not work out all right. When the People returned to Earth, life would be changed, it would never be the same again.

As he came out on the patio, old Bowser came wobbling around the corner of the kitchen. There was no sign of the younger dog that usually accompanied him on his walks, or of any of the others. They were either asleep somewhere or out exploring for a coon or maybe nosing out the mice from among the corn shocks. The night was quiet and slightly chilly and had at once a frosty and a melancholy feel about it. A thin moon hung in the west, above the darkness of the wooded bluff across the Mississippi. The faint, sharp tang of dying leaves hung in the air.

Jason went down the path that led to the point of rocks above the meeting of the rivers. The old dog fell in behind him. The crescent moon shed but little light, although, Jason told himself, he scarcely needed light. He had walked this path so many times he could find it in the dark.

The Earth was quiet, he thought, not only here, but everywhere. Quiet and resting after the turbulent centuries when men cut down its trees, ripped out its minerals, plowed its prairies, built upon broad expanses of it and fished its waters. After this short rest, would it all begin again? The ship heading for the Earth from the human planets was only an exploratory probe, to find old Earth again, to make sure the astronomers were right in their calculations, to survey it and take back the word. And after that, Jason wondered, what would happen? Would the humans rest with having satisfied an intellectual curiosity, or would they reassert their ancient ownership – although he doubted very much that at any time man could have been said to have truly owned the Earth. Rather, they had taken it, wresting it from the other creatures that had as much right of ownership as they, but without the intelligence or the ingenuity or power to assert their rights. Man had been the pushy, arrogant interloper rather than the owner. He had taken over by the force of mind, which could be as detestable as the force of muscle, making his own rules, setting his own goals, establishing his own values in utter disregard of all other living things.

A shadow lifted out of a grove of oaks and sailed down into a deep ravine, to be swallowed by the shadow and the silence of which it was a part. An owl, Jason told himself. There were a lot of them, but no one but a night-roamer ever had a chance to see them, for they hid themselves by day. Something ran rustling through the leaves and Bowser cocked an ear at it and snuffled, but either knew too much or was too old and stiff to attempt a chase. A weasel more than likely, or possibly a mink, although this was a bit too far from water for a mink. Too big for a mouse, too silent for a rabbit or an otter.

A man got to know his neighbors, Jason told himself, when he no longer hunted them. In the old days he hunted them, and so had many of the others once the wildlife had been given the chance to grow back to numbers that made hunting reasonable. Sport, they called it, but that had been nothing more than a softer name for the bloodlust that man had carried with him from prehistoric days, when hunting had been a business of keeping life intact – man blood brother to the other carnivores. And man, he thought, the greatest carnivore of all. Now there was no need for such as he to prey upon his brothers of the woodland and the marsh. Meat was supplied by the herds and flocks, although even so he supposed that even this equated to a modified carnivorous mode of life. Even if one wanted to hunt he would have had to revert to the bow and arrow and the lance. The guns still rested in their cases and were meticulously cleaned and oiled by robotic hands, but the supply of powder had long been exhausted and no way, without much study and laborious effort, that it could be resupplied.

The path bent up the hill to the little field where the corn stood in scattered shocks, the pumpkins still upon the ground. In another day or two the robots would haul in the pumpkins for storage, but the corn probably would be left in the shocks until all the other work of autumn had been done. It could be brought in later or, more likely, shucked in the field even after snow lay upon the ground.

In the dim moonlight, the shocks reminded Jason of an Indian encampment and the sight made him wonder if the robots had taken down to Horace Red Cloud's camp the flour and corn meal, the bacon and all the other supplies that he had ordered taken. The chances were they had. The robots were most meticulous in all matters and he fell to wondering, as he had many times before, exactly what they got out of such an arrangement as caring for him and Martha, the house and farm. Or, for that matter, what any robot got out of anything at all ... Hezekiah and the others in the monastery, the robots at their mysterious building project up the river. This wonderment, he realized, grew out of the old profit motive which had been the obsession and the mainstay of the ancient human race. You didn't do a thing unless there was some material return. Which, of course, was wrong, but the old habit, the old way of thinking, sometimes still intruded and he felt a touch of shame that it should still intrude.

If the humans should repossess the Earth the old profit motive and the subsidiary philosophies that depended on it would be re-established, and the Earth, except for whatever benefits it might have gained from its five thousand years of rest from the human plague, would be no better off than it had been before. There was just a bare possibility, he knew, that there would be no move to repossess it. They would know, of course, that the bulk of its resources had been depleted, but even that consideration might not be taken into account. There might be (he could not be sure and John had said nothing about it) a yearning in many of them to return to the ancestral planet. Five thousand years should be a long enough span of time to make the planets on which they now resided seem like home, but one could not be certain. At the very best, Earth would be subjected, more than likely, to streams of tourists and of pilgrims coming back to pay sentimental homage to mankind's parent planet.

He passed the cornfield and went along a narrow ridge to the point of rocks that hung above the meeting of the rivers. The waning moon made the converging streams shining silver roads cutting through the dark woodlands of the valley. He sat down on the boulder where he always sat, wrapping his heavy cape around him against the chill night wind. Sitting in the silence and hushed loneliness, he was surprised to find himself untouched by the loneliness. For this was home, he thought, and no man could be lonely who stayed close within his home.

That was why, of course, he viewed with such horror the arrival of the People. He could not abide the invasion of his home, of the land that he had made his territory as truly as other animals marked out their territorial rights – not by virtue, however, but by the quiet procedure of simply living here. Not taking over, not contending with his little wildlife neighbors the right to use and walk the land, but by simply staying on in very simple peace.

It could not be allowed, he told himself. They could not be allowed to come back and spoil the Earth again. They could not, for a second time, contaminate it with their machines. He must find a way to stop them and even as he thought that he must find a way, he knew there was no way. One old and selfish man could not stand against all humanity; perhaps he had no right to stand against humanity. They had their three planets only, and the Earth would make a fourth, while the other small segment of humanity, those not taken in the net that had swept the others off the Earth, had all the galaxy, all the universe, perhaps, if the time ever came when they wished to spread throughout the universe.

Except that he'd not gone out into the galaxy, neither he nor Martha. This was their home, not just these few acres, but the entire Earth. And there were, as well, the others – the Leech Lake Indians. What of them? What would happen to them and their way of life if the others should come back? Another reservation? Another penning up?

Back on the ridge a stone was dislodged by something and went rolling down the slope. Jason sprang swiftly to his feet.

'Who's out there?' he demanded.

It might be a bear. It might be a deer. It was neither.

'It's Hezekiah, sir,' a voice said. 'I saw you leave the house and I followed you.'

'Come on in,' said Jason. 'Why did you follow me?'

'To give you thanks,' the robot said. 'My very heartfelt thanks.'

He came lumbering out of the darkness.

'Sit down,' said Jason. 'That boulder over there. It is comfortable.'

'I have no need of comfort. I have no need to sit.'

'And yet you do,' said Jason. 'I see you often sitting on the bench beneath the willow tree.'

'It is an affectation only,' Hezekiah said. 'An aping of my betters and a quite unworthy act. I feel great shame of it.'

'Continue in your shame,' said Jason, 'if you enjoy it, but please humor me. I have a need of comfort and a need to sit and shall feel most uncomfortable if you continue standing.'

'If you insist,' said Hezekiah.

'Indeed I do,' said Jason, 'and now what is this imaginary kindness for which you wish to thank me?'

'It concerns the pilgrim.'

'Yes, I know. Thatcher told me of him.'

'I am fairly certain,' the robot said, 'that he is not a pilgrim. Nicodemus, I know, told Thatcher that he was. Nicodemus got carried away. It is so easy, sir, to get carried away when you want something very much.'

'I can understand,' said Jason.

'It would have been so wonderful if he had been a pilgrim. It would have meant that the word had spread of the labor in which we are engaged. Not a robot pilgrim, you understand, but a human pilgrim ...'

Jason sat quietly. The wind fluttered the robe that the robot wore. Hezekiah picked at it, trying to wrap it more closely about himself.

'Pride,' he said. 'That's the thing to fight. Like sitting down when there is no need to sit. Wearing a robe when there is need of none. Pacing up and down the garden, thinking, when one could think as well if one were standing still.'

Jason sat unmoving, keeping his mouth tight shut when he wanted to scream questions: What about this pilgrim? Who is he? Where did he come from? What has he been doing all these years? But remembering with a sour amusement that up until a few moments ago the worry and the fret of the human race returning had blanketed out any real concern about the stranger at the monastery.

'The thing I want to say is this,' said Hezekiah. 'I know how long the humans at the House hunted for other humans in the world. I recall all the rumors that were brought and how, rumor by rumor, you were disappointed. Now a human does show up and you'd have been quite within your rights to have come hurrying down to claim him. And yet you did not do it. You stayed away. You let us have our human. You gave us our hour of glory.'

'We figured that it was your show,' said Jason. 'We talked about it and decided to stay away. We can talk with this man later. There is little likelihood that he will run off. He must have traveled far to get here.'

'Our hour of glory,' Hezekiah said, 'and an empty hour, for we know now we did no more than delude ourselves. I sometimes wonder if our whole life may not be delusion.'

'You'll not get me,' said Jason, 'to wallow on the ground with you in your game of martyr. You've sat down there for years, I know, and eaten out your hearts, wondering if you were doing right, if you might be engaged in blasphemy, if you should not be stricken dead for your presumption. Well, the answer is that you've not been stricken dead ...'

'You mean that you approve. That you, a human ...'

'No,' said Jason. 'Not approve, or disapprove. What basis do I have to judge?'

'But once upon a time—'

'Yes, I know. Once upon a time man made images out of sticks and clay and worshiped them. Once upon a time he thought the sun was God. How many times must man be mistaken before he learns the truth?'

'I see your point,' said Hezekiah. 'Do you think we may ever know the truth?'

'How much do you want to know the truth?'

'We seek it,' said Hezekiah, 'with all our energies. That's the purpose in us, is it not?'

'I don't know,' said Jason. 'I wish very much I did.'

He thought how ridiculous it was, sitting on this windy ridge in the dead of night, talking about the possibility of truth – of any truth, at all – with a fanatic robot. He could tell Hezekiah about the Principle that John had found. He could tell him about the alien who had come to seek a soul. And what good would it do if he told him either?

'I tell you my troubles,' Hezekiah said. 'You have troubles of your own. You walk the night thinking of your trouble.'

Jason grunted noncommittally. He might have suspected. The robots knew what was going on, sometimes, it seemed, before you knew of it yourself. They walked quietly when they wished and heard and, once heard, the news sprang from one to the other of them like an electric impulse. Thatcher would have heard the talk at dinner and later on the patio while they listened to the concert, with the evening clean and beautiful after the passing of the rain (and, come to think of it, there had been something very funny happened at the concert). But it was not only Thatcher. Thatcher, perhaps, less than all the rest of them. They always were around. They listened and they pried and later they talked it over interminably among themselves. There was nothing wrong in it, of course. There was nothing that one had any wish to hide. But their obsession with every little detail of the human world sometimes was disconcerting.

'I,' said Hezekiah, 'share your great concern.'

'How is that?' Jason asked, surprised.

'I understand how you must feel,' the robot told him. 'Perhaps not all the others, out among the stars. But you and Miss Martha, certainly the two of you ...'

'Not only us,' said Jason. 'How about the tribes? The lives of their ancestors were dislocated once. Must it happen again? They have made a new life for themselves. Must they give it up? And how about your people? Would you be happier if there were more humans? At times I think you would.'

'Some of us, perhaps,' said Hezekiah. 'Our function is to serve and there are so few to serve. If only the tribes ...'

'But you know they won't. They'll have none of you.'

'I was about to say,' said Hezekiah, 'that there is a certain segment of us who might not look kindly upon their coming back. I do not know too much about them, but they are engaged upon a project ...'

'You mean the installation up the river?'

The robot nodded. 'You might talk with them. You might find some help.'

'You think that they would help us, would be willing to?'

'There is talk,' said Hezekiah, 'of marvelous new ideas, of very cunning work. There is none of it I can understand.'

Jason sat hunched upon his boulder. He shivered and drew the cape close about his shoulders. The night suddenly seemed darker and lonely and perhaps a little frightening.

'Thank you,' he said. 'I'll see about it.'

In the morning he'd go down to the river landing and talk with Horace Red Cloud. Horace might know what could be done.

14

(Excerpt from journal of Sept. 18, 2185) ... Sometime after we had started our ambitious expeditions to get together a comprehensive library and to acquire at least a sampling of the arts, four robots came to see me. I did not recognize them – after all, there are few distinguishing marks by which a robot can be recognized. They may have been working about the farm for years or they may just then have wandered in. I am somewhat surprised, now that I write of it, that I did not question them more closely, but my best memory now is that I did not ask them about their origins, either then or since. It may have been that I was so astounded – and in a sense, upset – by what they had to ask that I was delinquent in my investigation of them.

They told me that their names were Hezekiah, Nicodemus, Jonathon and Ebenezer, and that if I had no objection they would like to occupy the monastery buildings down the road and devote their entire time to a study of Christianity. They seemed to have gotten the idea that man had stopped far short of the point he should have reached in his study of religion and that they, as objective students, might press the matter much beyond man's short-range venture into it. I could detect about them no sign of religious fervor, although I greatly fear that if they continue at it (they have been at it, at the time of this writing, almost thirty years) they will not be able to maintain an objective attitude and may develop unthinking religious fanaticism. I am not even now convinced (perhaps now less convinced than I was then) that I was right in raising no objections to their project. It may not have been right or wise to turn a group of robots loose upon so sensitive a subject. I suppose fanatics have their proper niche in all societies, but the thought of fanatic robots (fanatic on any subject, and religion somehow seems to breed fanatics) does not particularly enchant me. The entire business suggests a situation that can be really frightening. With the most of mankind gone and all the robots left, the robots in time may move to fill the vacuum thus created. They were made to serve us and they cannot, by the very nature of them, be idle. One wonders if, lacking men to serve, in time they will not somehow contrive to serve themselves. If that should be the case, what sort of motives might they have and what kind of purpose? Surely not human and for that, I would suppose, one might be duly grateful. But it is with what I tell myself is pardonable apprehension that one must view the rise of a new philosophy and a setting of new values by creatures that were created in their final form little more than a century ago, having no evolutionary period in which they could develop by the same slow process as man and the other creatures of the Earth (not forgetting that man, even with his long history, may have developed far too fast). It may be that they will take time to evolve, not consciously, of course, but because they will need the time to form, for themselves, a logical operating base. But the time will be short, I fear, and because of this the possibility of serious flaws exists. Evolution supplies the time for testing and rejecting and because of this has a way of straightening out the kinks in a way of life. For the robots there can be little in the way of evolution and thus many of the kinks will be carried over into their final thinking.

But I get beyond my story. To get back to the four who came to see me. If they were to carry on the work that they proposed, they said, they must have a large body of religious writings and they wondered if they could go along with us on our book-hunting expeditions, being willing to help us with the labor in return for our hauling back the books selected for their studies. The offer of labor was much beside the point, for we had all the robots that we needed for the actual work. But for some reason which I now do not understand (and may not have understood at the time) I agreed. Perhaps the agreement came because the thing they proposed to do seemed more ridiculous than it does now. I may even have chuckled at it then, although after further deliberations I have no chuckles for it.

The collection of our library proved a much harder task than I had anticipated. It was an easy matter, on the face of it, to sit down and write a list, saying that we need Shakespeare, Proust, Plato, Aristotle, Virgil, Gibbon, Locke, Euripides, Aristophanes, Tolstoy, Pascal, Chaucer, Montaigne, Hemingway, Wolfe, Steinbeck, Faulkner and all the others that would go on any list; that we needed texts on mathematics, engineering, chemistry, astronomy, biology, philosophy, psychology and many other branches of the arts and sciences, with the possible exception of medicine, which no longer seems necessary to those of us on Earth (although one can't be entirely sure of that), but how can one be sure he has not missed something that at sometime in the future will be, not sadly missed, for not knowing of it, it will not be missed, but which will not be there for use when there could be need of it. And how does one, obversely, know that much of what he does select may not, in time to come, be unworthy of the space it takes?

Over the years, of course, there may be opportunity to supply any deficit, to obtain what might have been overlooked. But as the years go on, it will be more difficult to do. Even when we collected the books we had great difficulties. The trucks we used required continual tinkering to keep them running and in many cases the roads had deteriorated, through flood and frost and other circumstances, to a point where they were often hard to travel. At some places, we were forced to make detours. The trucks, of course, are no longer usable; after a time even the most determined tinkering could not keep them running. The roads, I would presume, are now much farther gone to ruin, although they still possibly could be used by wagons. I can foresee a time (although we tried our best to guard against such an eventuality) when men, seeking a particular book or books, of which they might have found some reference, will be forced to strike out afoot or by pack train through the wilderness in hopes of finding a still existent library or some other repository where there still may exist the books we may have forgotten to place upon our list.

By that time, perhaps, the books no longer will exist. Even housed under the best circumstances in the long-deserted cities, the weather will get at them, and the rodents and the worms, and if nothing else, sheer time will take its toll.

We finally located and transported here all the books that we had listed. With the art objects we sought to salvage we encountered greater problems, principally because with them space was a greater consideration than it is with books. We had to painfully select and choose with the greatest care. How many Rembrandts, for example, could we allow ourselves, knowing that each extra Rembrandt would rob us of a Courbet or a Renoir? Because of the very lack of space, both in transportation and in storage, we were forced to choose the smaller canvas rather than the larger. The same criterion applied to all other categories of the arts.

There are times when I could weep, thinking of all the great endeavors and accomplishments of mankind we were forced to leave to be forever lost ...

15

Horace Red Cloud squatted by the fire for a long time after the two white men had left. He had watched them leave, going up the hollow that ran back into the hills, until a twisting of the hollow had hidden them from view, and after they were gone, had stayed by the fire, unmoving. The morning was far gone, but as yet the camp lay in shadow, the sun not having risen high enough into the sky to clear the towering bluffs that blocked its light. The camp was quiet, quieter than usual – the others knew something was afoot, but they would not intrude upon him, there beside the fire; they would not ask, but wait for him to tell them. The women went about their work as usual, but with less commotion, without a banging of the pans and yelling back and forth. The small fry huddled, quiet in groups, whispering to one another, bursting with excitement. The others were not in camp – perhaps working in the cornfields, although some of them would be fishing or out prowling. One could not expect a man, especially a young man, to spend an entire day at drudgery. Even the dogs were quiet.

The fire had burned to a gray ash, with some blackened sticks showing at its edges and a hint of heat lying in its heart, with only the smallest trickle of smoke rising from the ash and the ends of the blackened sticks. Slowly he put out his hands, holding them in the smoke, scrubbing them together, washing them with smoke. He did it absentmindedly and was somewhat amused when he saw what he was doing. A cultural reflex action, he wondered, still keeping his hands where they were, still washing them with smoke. Thus his far ancestors had washed their hands in smoke as a purification rite, one of the many senseless little gestures they went through when they stood upon the brink of magic, symbolically purifying themselves so they could deal in magic. And how much had he and the others lost when they had turned their backs on magic? Belief, of course, and there might be some value in belief, although there was, as well, delusion, and did a man want to pay for the value of belief in the coinage of delusion? Although we've lost very little, he told himself, and have gained a great deal more – an understanding of ourselves as a factor of ecology. We have learned to live with trees and water, with earth and sky and wind, with weather and the wild things, as if they were brothers to us. Using them as we need them, not abusing our need and use of them, respecting them, living with them, being one with them. Not using them as the white man did, not owning them, not ignoring them, with no contempt of them.

He got up slowly from the fire and went down the path toward the river. Where the path ended at the water's edge canoes were drawn up on the gravel beach and a yellowed willow tree, its branches drooping, dipped the gold of its leaves into the flowing stream. Upon the water were other floating leaves, the red and brown of oak, the scarlet of the maple, the yellow of the elm – the tributes of other trees farther up the stream, their offerings to the river that had supplied the water that they needed through the hot, dry days of summer. The river talked to him, not to him alone, he knew, but to the trees, the hills, the sky, a friendly mumbling gossip that ran down across the land.

He stooped and cupped his hands together, plunged them in the river and then lifted them. His hands were full, but the water ran between his fingers and escaped, leaving a little puddle of it where the edges of his palms were pressed together. He opened the hands and let the water go, back into the river. That was the way it should be, he told himself. The water and the air and earth ran away when you tried to grasp them. They would not be caught and held. They were not something one could own, but something one could live with. It had been so long ago in the first beginning, and then there had been men who had tried to own them, to hold them, to influence and coerce them, and after that there had been a new beginning and was that new beginning to come to an end again?

I shall call all the tribes together, he had told Jason, sitting at the fire. It is near the time to make the winter meat, but this is more important than the winter meat. It had, perhaps, been silly for him to say a thing like that, for he should have known – and did know – that a throng a thousand times as large as all the tribes would not prevail against the whites if they wanted to come back. Strength was not enough, determination would be futile, love of homeland and devotion to it stood as nothing against men who could cross between the stars on ships. They took one path, he thought, and we took another, from the very first, and ours was not the wrong path (indeed, it was the right one), but it made us weak against their rapacity, as everything was weak against their rapacity.

These had been good years since they had gone away. There had been time to find the old paths once again. Once again the wind blew free and the water ran untrammeled down the land. Once more the prairie grass grew thick and sweet and the forest was a forest once again and the sky was black in spring and fall with wildfowl.

He did not like the idea of visiting the robot installation; he recoiled against the robot, Hezekiah, riding in a canoe, sharing even temporarily this ancient way of life, but Jason was quite right – it was the only thing to do, it was the only chance they had.

He turned back up the path, toward the camp. They all were waiting and now he'd call them all together. The men would be picked to paddle canoes. Some of the young men would have to secure fresh meat and fish for the journey. The women must get together food and robes. There was much to do: they'd set out in the morning.

16

Evening Star was sitting on the patio when the young man with the binoculars and the bear-claw necklace showed up, coming up the path from the monastery.

He stopped in front of her. 'You are here to read the books,' he said. 'That is the correct word, is it not? To read?'

He wore a white bandage on his cheek. 'You have the word,' she said. 'Won't you please sit down. How are you feeling?'

'Very well,' he said. 'The robots took good care of me.'

'Well, then, sit down,' she said. 'Or are you going somewhere?'

'I have nowhere to go,' he said. 'I may go no farther.' He sat down in a chair beside her and laid the bow upon the flagstones. 'I had wanted to ask you about the trees that make the music. You know about the trees. Yesterday you spoke with the ancient oak ...'

'You told me,' she said, somewhat angrily, 'that you'd never mention that again. You spied upon me and you promised.'

'I am sorry, but I must,' he told her. 'I have never met a person who could talk with trees. I have never heard before a tree that could make music.'

'What have the two to do with one another?'

'There was something wrong with the trees last night. I thought perhaps you noticed. I think I did something to them.'

'You must be joking. Who could do anything with the trees? And there was nothing wrong with them. They played beautifully.'

'There was a sickness in them, or in some of them. They played not as well as they could play. And I did something with the bears as well. Especially that last bear. Maybe with all of them.'

'You told me that you killed them. And took one claw from each to put into the necklace. A way of keeping count, you said. And, if you ask me, a way of bragging, too.'

She thought he might get angry, but he only looked a little puzzled. 'I had thought all the time,' he said, 'that it was the bow. That I killed them because I could shoot the bow so well and the arrows were so finely fashioned. What if it were not the bow at all, or the arrows or my shooting of them, but something else entirely?'

'What difference does it make? You killed them, didn't you?'

'Yes, of course I killed them, but ...'

'My name is Evening Star,' she said, 'and you've never told me yours.'

'I am David Hunt.'

'And so, David Hunt, tell me about yourself.'

'There is not much to tell.'

'But there must be something. You have people and a home. You surely came from somewhere.'

'A home. Yes, I suppose so. Although we moved around a lot. We were always fleeing and the people leaving ...'

'Fleeing? What was there to flee from?'

'The Dark Walker. I see you do not know of it. You have not heard of it?'

She shook her head.

'A shape,' he said. 'Like a man and yet not like a man. Two-legged. Maybe that is the only way it is like a man. Never seen in daytime. Always seen at night. Always on a ridgetop, black against the sky. It was first seen on the night everyone was taken – that is, everyone but us, and I suppose, to say it right, everyone but us and the people here and those out on the plains. I am the first of our people to know there are other people.'

'You seem to think there is only one Dark Walker. Are you sure of that? Are you sure there really is a Dark Walker, or do you just imagine it? My people at one time imagined so many things that we now know were never true. Has it ever hurt any of your people?'

He frowned, trying to think. 'No, not that I know of. It hurt no one; it is only seen. It is horrible to see. We watch for it all the time and when we see it, we flee to somewhere else.'

'You never tried to track it down?'

'No,' he said.

'I thought perhaps that was what you were doing now. Trying to track it down and kill it. A great bowman such as you, who can kill the bears ...'

'You make fun of me,' he said, but without a show of anger.

'Perhaps,' she said. 'You are so proud of the killing of the bears. No one of my people has killed so many bears.'

'I doubt,' he said, 'that the Walker could be killed with arrows. Maybe it can not be killed at all.'

'There may be no Walker,' said the girl. 'Have you ever thought of that? Surely, if there were, we would have seen or heard of it. My people range far west to the mountains and there'd have been some word of it. And so far as that goes, how is it that all these years there has been no word of your people? For centuries the people in this house hunted other people, running down all sorts of rumors.'

'So did my people, I am told, in the early years. I have only heard of it, of course. Things that people talked about. I have, myself, only twenty summers.'

'We are the same age,' said Evening Star. 'I am just nineteen.'

'There are few young people among us,' said David Hunt. 'There are not many of us, all of us together, and we move around so much ...'

'It puzzles me,' she said, 'that there are only a few of you. If you are like the rest of us, you live for a long, long time and there is no sickness. From one small tribe, my people number many thousands. From a few people in this house there are thousands in the stars. There should be thousands of you. You should be strong and many ...'

'We could be many,' he said, 'but we go away.'

'I thought you told me—'

'Not to the stars, like these others. But across the water. There is a madness that sends many of us across the water. They build rafts and they set out across the water, toward the setting sun. It has been done for many years. I don't know why. I never have been told.'

'Perhaps fleeing from the Walker.'

'I don't think,' he said. 'I don't think those who go know why they are going or even that they're going until the madness seizes them.'

'Lemmings,' said Evening Star.

'What are lemmings?'

'Small animals. Rodents. I read about them once.'

'What have lemmings to do with us?'

'I am not sure,' she said.

'I ran away,' he said. 'Myself and Old Jose. We both feared the bigness of the water. We did not want to go if the few remaining people went. If we ran away, we said, the madness might not touch us. Jose saw the Walker, twice, after we had run away, and we ran again, from the Walker, very far and fast.'

'When Jose saw the Walker, did you ...'

'No. I've never seen it.'

'Do you think the other people went? Out across the water, after you and Jose left?'

'I do not know,' he said. 'Jose died. He was an old, old man. He remembered when the People disappeared. He was an old man even then. There came a day when his life ran out. I think that he was glad. It is not always good to live too long. When you live too long you too often are alone.'

'But he had you with him.'

'Yes, but there were too many years between us. We got along all right and we talked a lot, but he missed the people like himself. He would play the fiddle and I would listen and the coyotes would sit up on the hills and sing with the fiddle. Have you ever heard a coyote sing?'

'I've heard them bark and howl,' she said. 'I never heard one sing.'

'They sang every night when Old Jose would play. He'd play only in the evening. There were a lot of coyotes and I think they came to listen and to sing along. There were times when there'd be a dozen of them, sitting on the hilltops, singing. Jose said he couldn't play as well as he should. His fingers were no longer limber and his arm was heavy with the bow. I felt the death that was in him, death sitting on the hilltop and listening with the wolves. When he died I dug a deep hole and buried him, with the fiddle beside him, for it was no use to me and I thought he'd like it that way. Then I worked for days, carrying rocks, as big as I could pack, to pile upon the grave against the wolves. All the time I did this I was not lonesome, for somehow it seemed that I was still with Jose. Working for him was like being with him. But once I finished, I was lonely.'

'You could have gone back to find your people.'

'I thought of it,' he said, 'but I had no idea where they were and I still was afraid of the madness that might send me out with them upon the water. I had a feeling that the madness would not strike me if I were alone. It is – what would you call it? – a group madness. And, besides, there was something inside me that kept telling me to go toward the rising sun. I have wondered many times what it was that made me go. There seemed no reason that I should. It was as if I were hunting for something, although I did not know what it is I am supposed to hunt. I found your people out on the plains and I wanted to stay with them. They would have let me stay. But I couldn't. The call of the rising sun still was in me and I had to leave them. They told me of this great stone house and I wondered if that was what I had set out to find. There were many houses of stone that I found along the way, but I was afraid of them. My people never lived in houses. We were afraid of them. They made noises in the night and they were so empty and we thought that there were ghosts in them, maybe the ghosts of the people who had been taken when everyone disappeared.'

'You're here now,' said the girl. 'I hope you stay awhile. You'll find nothing to the east. It is only empty forest. A few of my people live there, but even so, it all is empty forest. And this house is not like the houses that you saw. It is not empty; it is lived in. It has the feel of people.'

'The robots would let me stay with them,' he said. 'They are kindly folks.'

'But,' she said, 'they aren't human. You'll want to be with humans. Uncle Jason and Aunt Martha, I am sure, would be glad to have you. Or, if you'd rather, there always would be a place for you in my people's camp.'

'Uncle Jason and Aunt Martha live in this house?'

'Yes, but they really aren't aunt and uncle to me. I call them that, but only to myself. They do not know I call them that. Uncle Jason and my grand-father-many-times-removed have been lifelong friends. They were young men at the Disappearance.'

'I may have to go on,' he said. 'The call of the rising sun may not have left me yet. But I'd be glad of a little time to rest. I came to ask you about your talking with the trees. You have not told me of it. Do you talk with all the trees, or just a certain tree?'

'You may not understand,' she said. 'We live close to the trees, the streams, the flowers, the animals and birds. We are one with them. Any one of us can talk with them.'

'And you the best of all.'

'I would not know. Among ourselves we do not discuss it. I can speak only for myself. I can go for a walk, into the woods or along a stream, and I am never lonely or alone, for I meet so many friends and I always talk with them.'

'And they talk back to you.'

'Sometimes they do,' she said.

'You talk with the trees and the others go out to the stars.'

'You still don't believe about the stars.'

'I am beginning to,' he said. 'Although it is hard to believe it. I asked the robots about it and they explained it to me, although I do not think I understood entirely. They said that of all the people once in this house, only two remain. The rest are out among the stars. They said that at times they come back from the stars for a visit. Is that so?'

'Yes, it is. There is one of them now back from the stars. Uncle Jason's brother. He brought disturbing word. He and Uncle Jason went down to the camp this morning to talk with my many-times-grandfather about the word he brought.'

She was running on too much, she thought. Perhaps Uncle Jason would not like her telling this to a perfect stranger, a man who had stumbled out of nowhere. It had just slipped out, as if he were a friend. And she did not really know him. She had met him only yesterday after he had spied on her and again this morning when he'd come up the road from the monastery. But it was, she thought, as if she'd known him for years. He was just a boy. What was it he had said about the many years that lay between himself and his old friend? Maybe that was it. There were no years to lie between the two of them.

'You think,' he asked, 'that your aunt and uncle would not mind my staying here? You could ask your aunt, perhaps.'

'Not now,' said Evening Star. 'She is talking with the stars. She has been talking all the morning. But we can ask her later – or my uncle when he returns from camp.'

17

He felt old and lonely. It was the first time in years that he had felt lonely, and the first time ever that he'd had a sense of being old.

'I debated telling you,' said Martha. 'Perhaps I should not have told you, Jason, but you had to know. They were all polite and understanding ...'

'And a bit amused,' he said.

'I don't think quite that,' she told him. 'But a little baffled as to why you should be so upset. Earth can't mean as much to them, of course, as it means to you and me. Some of them have never been here. To them Earth is only an old and beautiful story. And all of them pointed out that the others may have no intention of coming back and staying; it might simply be an exploratory trip to satisfy their curiosity.'

'The point is,' said Jason, 'that they don't really care. They have the stars; they don't need Earth. As you say, it's just a story to them. I had thought of calling a conference – some of the old and trusted friends, some of the younger ones to whom we've been the closest.'

'It still might be a good idea,' Martha said. 'They would come, I'm sure. All of them would come, I think, if we really needed them. It might do a lot of good. There are so many things that they have learned. We don't know of all the things they've learned.'

'I wouldn't count too much on what they've learned,' said John. 'Collectively, they have learned a great deal. Since they've gone to the stars the sum total of the knowledge they have gained probably is as great or greater than all that man had learned on Earth before the Disappearance. But this knowledge is superficial. They have learned the surface facts, that a certain thing is possible or that certain action will bring about a prescribed effect, but they've gained no real understanding for they have not sought the why and wherefore of it. And because of this, while they know many strange and unguessed things, the knowledge does them little good, for they cannot use it. And a lot of it, as well, is defiant of any human understanding. Much of it is so alien to the human concept of the universe that it can't be understood until a man has mastered alien viewpoints and intellectual processes and—'

'You need not go on,' said Jason, bitterly. 'I know how impossible it is.'

'I've not wanted to point this out,' said John, 'because I know you will not like it. But, if worse comes to worst, you and Martha can go to the stars.'

'John, you know I can't do that,' said Jason. 'And I don't think Martha could. Earth is in our bones. We've lived with it too long. It's too much a part of us.'

'I've often wondered what it would be like,' said Martha. 'I've talked to so many people and they've told me so much of it. But if it came to going, I don't think I could go.'

'You see,' said Jason, 'we're just two old selfish people.'

And that's the truth of it, he told himself. It's a selfish thing to hang onto Earth, to claim it, all of it, for one's own. When one came right down to it, the People had a right to return to Earth if that should be their wish. They'd not left Earth of their own free will; they had been abducted from it; they had been taken from it. If they could find their way back to it, there was no legal and no moral stricture barring their return. The worst thing about it all, he realized, would be their insistence on sharing with those still left on Earth all that they had learned and gained, all their technological advances, all their bright new concepts, all their shimmering knowledge, determined to give freehandedly to the benighted people left on Earth all the advantages of the continuing human heritage. And what of the tribes, who wanted none of this? And the robots, too? Although maybe the robots would welcome their return. He knew little of the robots or how they might feel about such a circumstance.

In a day or two he'd know how the robots felt about it. Tomorrow morning he and John and Hezekiah would set out up the river with Red Cloud and his men.

18

(Excerpt from journal of Oct. 9, 3935) … I have hesitated to accept the business of going to the stars. I knew it was being done; I knew it was possible; I saw them go and, after a time, return. And I talked with them about it; all of us have talked about it at great length and, being human, have sought to determine the mechanism that makes it possible and even at times, although less often now, have debated the desirability of this trait we discovered. And the use of that word, trait, is most revealing, for it lends emphasis to the fact that we know nothing whatever about how we do it or how it might have come about.

I say there has been some hesitancy on my part to accept going to the stars and that is, I know, a somewhat confusing statement and I am not sure at all that I can make it clear. I, of course, have accepted it intellectually and even emotionally in that I have been as excited about this seeming impossibility as have any of the others. But the acceptance is not total. It is as if I were shown some impossible animal or plant (impossible for any number of good and logical reasons). Seeing it, I would be forced to admit that it did, indeed, exist. But turning and walking away from it, I'd find myself doubting the evidence of my eyes and telling myself that I had not actually seen it, in consequence of which I'd have to go back and see it once again. And when I turned away from it the second time, and the third and fourth and fifth, I'd still find myself doubtful of what I had seen and have to turn back to reassure myself. Perhaps there is something more as well. Try as I may, I cannot make up my mind that this is a beneficial, or even a proper, thing for any human being to do. A built-in caution, perhaps, or a resistance to anything too revolutionary (an attitude not uncommon in one of my biological age) niggles at me continually, whispering warnings of catastrophe as a result of this new ability. The conservatism in me will not accept that so great a thing can be conferred upon the human race without the exaction of some sort of heavy payment. Feeling so, I suppose that unconsciously I have gone on the assumption that until I unreservedly admit that it is so, it cannot be so and that until it actually becomes so, the payment can be deferred.

All of this, of course, is egocentric and, more than that, plain foolish and I have felt at times, although everyone has been at great pains not to make it so appear, that I have made a great fool of myself. For the trips to the stars have been going on for some years now and by this time almost everyone has gone for at least one short trip. I have not gone, of course; my doubts and reservations no doubt would act as a psychological block to my going, which is something that is idle to speculate upon, for I don't intend to try. My grandson Jason and his excellent Martha are among the few who have not gone and my prejudice makes me very glad of this. I seem to see in Jason some of the same love of the ancestral acres that I have myself and I am inclined to believe that this love will keep him forever from the stars which, mistaken though I may be, I account no tragedy. His brother, John, however, was among the first to go and he has not come back. I have spent many hours of worry over him.

It is ridiculous, of course, for me to persist in this illogical attitude. Whatever I may say or think, man finally has severed, quite naturally and as a matter of course, his dependence on the Earth. And that may be the core of how I feel about it – an uneasiness that Man should, after long millennia, finally end his dependence on the Earth.

The house is filled with mementos from the stars. Amanda just this morning brought the beautiful bouquet of most strange flowers that sits upon my desk, plucked on a planet of which I now quite forget the name – although the name is not important, for it is not really its name (if it ever had a name) but a name by which two human beings, Amanda and her boyfriend, George, have designated it. It is out toward a bright star of which I now also forget the name – not a planet of that particular star, of course, but of a smaller neighbor, so much fainter that even if we had a large telescope we could not pick up its light. All about the house are strange objects – branches with dried berries, colorful rocks and pebbles, chunks of exotic wood, fantastic artifacts picked up from sites where intelligent creatures once had lived and built and fabricated the cultural debris that we now bring back. We have no photographs and that's a pity, for while we have the cameras, still in working condition, we have no film to load them with. Some day someone may develop a way of making film again and we'll have photographs. Strangely, I am the only one who has considered photographs; none of the others have any interest in them.

At first there was a fear that someone, returning from the stars, would coalesce, or otherwise come back together in their natural form, at the exact location of some solid object or, perhaps, another person, which in the last instance, would be extremely messy. I don't think there was ever any real need for apprehension, for as I understand it, the returning traveler, before he aims for his next point of materialization, peeps or scans or otherwise becomes aware of the situation and conditions of the location he is aiming at. I must admit that I am very bad at writing this, for despite being associated with it for a number of years, I do not understand what is going on, which may be due to the fact that the ability which the others have developed has bypassed me entirely.

Anyhow – and this is what I have been leading up to – the large ballroom on the third floor has been set aside as the area in which returning travelers materialize, with the area barred to all others and a rule set up that the entire room be kept clear of any object. Some of the younger people called the room the Depot, harking back to those virtually prehistoric days when buses and trains arrived and departed from depots, and the name has stuck. There was at first a great deal of hilarity over the name, for to some of the young folks it seemed very humorous. I must admit that I see no particular humor in it, although I can see no real harm in whatever they may call it.

I have pondered the development of the entire business and, despite some of the theories advanced by others who have actually traveled (and therefore assume they know more of it than I), I believe that what we may have here is a normal evolutionary process – at least, that is what I would like to think it is. Man rose from a lowly primate to intelligence, became a toolmaker, a hunter, a farmer, a controller of his environment – he had progressed steadily through the years and the progress most admittedly has not always been for the good, either to himself or others. But the point is that he has progressed and this going to the stars may be only another evolutionary point that marks a further logical progression …

19

Jason couldn't go to sleep. He couldn't quit thinking about the Principle. What had started him to thinking on it he did not know, and as an exercise that might shake him loose from it, he tried to backtrack in his mind to the point where he had first began his speculations, but the area was fogged and he could not get to the beginning of it and the wondering went on.

He should get to sleep, he told himself. Thatcher would wake him early in the morning and with John he'd set off down the path to Horace Red Cloud's camp. He looked forward to traveling up the river, for it would be interesting – it had been a long time since he had gone far from home – but no matter how interesting it might be, it would be a hard day for him and he needed sleep.

He tried counting sheep and tried adding a column of imaginary figures, but the sheep refused to jump and the figures faded off into the nothingness from which he'd summoned them and he was left with the worry and the wonder of the Principle.

If the universe were steady-state, if it had no beginning and would not have an end, if it had always existed and would continue to exist, at what point in this foreverness had the Principle come into being – or was it, as well as the universe, a foreverness? And if the universe were evolutionary, starting at a certain time and place and destined to come to an end at a certain time and place, had the Principle been there and waiting, a strangeness out of nothingness, or had it evolved only at a later time and from what it had evolved? And why this galaxy, he wondered – why had the Principle chosen to reside within this galaxy, when there were billions of other galaxies that could have been its home? Had it come into being in this galaxy and stayed here, and if that should be the case, what unique characteristics did this galaxy offer to trigger its appearance? Or was it a much larger thing than anyone might imagine, was the manifestation of it in this galaxy only an outpost of a much greater central unity?

It was all absurd, of course. There was no way in which he could find an answer; no means by which he could arrive at even a logical suspicion of what had really happened. He didn't have the data; no one had the data. The only one that would know would be the Principle itself. The whole procedure of his thinking, Jason knew, was an imbecilic exercise; there was no compelling reason for him to seek an answer. And yet his mind bored on and on and he could not stop it, hanging with desperation to an impossibility to which it never should have paid attention.

He turned over restlessly and tried to burrow his head deeper into the pillow.

'Jason,' said Martha, out of the darkness, 'are you asleep?'

He mumbled to her. 'Almost,' he said. 'Almost.'

20

He was polished and he shone in the morning light; he said his name was Stanley and he was glad that they had come. He recognized three of them – Hezekiah, Jason and Red Cloud, in that order – and he said that word and rumor of them had made its way into the Project. Introduced to John, he professed unusual pleasure at meeting a man from among the stars. He was suave and genteel and he glittered when he walked and he said it was neighborly of them to pay a visit, even after all the years, and that he was desolated he could offer neither food nor drink, since robots made no use of either.

Apparently a watch had been kept on them from the time of the flotilla's first appearance, coming up the river, for he had been waiting for them on the blufftop when they came climbing up the path, with the beached canoes and the men who had paddled them waiting on the shore below the bluff.

Above the blufftop towered the structure, whatever it might be – a huge and curving thinness that flared out, with a greater diameter at the top than at that point where it emerged from the ground, black with the shine of many metallic highlights that caught the morning sun, a huge and curving thinness that went up into the sky, more like a fantastic monument or a dreaming sculpture than it was like a structure, and, looking at it, it seemed to make no sense. Set in a circle, it did not quite complete the circle, but stood with a V-section of emptiness gaping on one side of it

From where they stood, at some distance beyond the flaring structure, lay the mounds of the ancient city, with here and there broken walls and the metallic skeletons of buildings still rising above the uneven ground, looking for all the world like the canted arms or the stiffened hands of corpses buried hurriedly and too shallowly for decency.

Across the river stood another mounded area, but here the disintegration of the buildings seemed somewhat less advanced, for at certain intervals great piles of masonry still emerged.

Stanley saw Jason looking at the structures. 'The old university,' he said. 'We have been at great pains to preserve some selected buildings.'

'You make use of them?'

'Of the contents of them. Certain instruments and libraries. Old workshops and laboratories. And what was missing in them we have transported, through the years, from other learning centers. Although,' he said with a touch of sadness, 'there's not much left elsewhere anymore.'

'You used the knowledge to build this,' said John, indicating the flaring structure with an upward sweep of his arm.

'We did,' the robot Stanley said. 'You came to hear of it?'

'That, in part,' said Jason. 'There is something more, however.'

'We have a place,' said Stanley, 'where you can be far more comfortable than standing on this windswept prairie. If you will follow me.'

Following him, they went along a beaten path until they came to a ramp that led down into the space enclosed by the flaring structure. As they walked down the ramp, they saw that less than half the structure stood above the ground, that its smooth sides went plunging down into a great hole that had been excavated to accommodate it. The ramp wound steeply downward, curving in a great sweep around the smooth wall of the flaring thing.

'We went down to bedrock to anchor it,' said Stanley. 'Down to the solid limestone.'

'And you call it the Project?' Red Cloud asked. It was the first time he had spoken. Jason had seen him stiffen in something close to outrage when the glittering robot had come out to meet them and had momentarily held his breath, afraid of what his old friend might feel compelled to say. But he had said nothing and Jason had felt for him a surge of affection and admiration. Over the years that Red Cloud had been coming to the house, there had developed between him and Thatcher something that resembled affectionate respect, but Thatcher was the only robot the old chief would give a second glance. And now here was this striding, competent, self-assured dandy of a robot performing as their host. Jason could imagine how the gorge must have risen in the old man's throat at the sight of him.

'That is what we call it, sir,' said Stanley. 'We called it that to start with and it got to be a habit and we never changed the name. Which is all right, of course. It is the only project that we have.'

'And the purpose of it? It must have a purpose?' The way that Red Cloud said it, it was quite apparent he rather doubted that it had.

'Once we get to the place of comfort,' the robot said, 'I shall tell you all you wish. We have no secrets here.'

They met other robots, going up the ramp, but they spoke no greeting and they did not stop. And here, thought Jason, as he went pacing down the ramp, was the explanation of all those hurrying, purposeful bands of so-called 'wild robots' they had seen through all the centuries – purposeful, dedicated bands setting off in all directions, and returning from all directions, to get the needed materials for the building of this place.

They finally reached the bottom of the ramp and here the circle of the structure was much smaller than at the top, and set in the space at the bottom of the pit was what appeared to be an open-sided house, a roof set on stout columns, housing tables, desks and chairs, along with filing cabinets and some rather strange machines. It was, Jason decided, a combination operations centre and construction shack.

'Gentlemen,' said Stanley, 'if you please will find a place to sit, I shall listen to your questions and endeavor to tell you all you wish. I have associates I can summon ...'

'One of you is enough,' said Red Cloud harshly.

'I think,' said Jason, hurrying to cover Red Cloud's words, 'we'll not need to bother any of the others. I take it you can answer for the others.'

'I have told you,' the robot said, 'that we have no secrets. And we're all of a single mind, or very nearly so. I can call the others if there is any need. It is not necessary to tell you, I suppose, that I recognized all of you except the gentleman who came from the stars. Your reputations had preceded you. The chief we know and have admired, although we are aware of the animosity that he and his people hold toward us. We can understand the basis of that attitude, although we do regret it, and we have made a point, sir,' he said to Red Cloud, 'not to intrude ourselves upon you.'

'Your tongue,' said Red Cloud, 'is smoother than it should be, but I grant you have kept out of our way.'

'Mr Jason,' said the robot, 'we have regarded as a good, great friend and we've been most proud of Hezekiah and the work that he has done.'

'If you felt that way,' asked Jason, 'why did you never come to visit us?'

'We had thought, somehow, that it might not be proper. You may be able to understand a little how we must have felt when suddenly there were no longer men to serve, when the very purpose of our existence was, in a moment, taken from us.'

'But others come to us,' said Jason. 'We are knee-deep in robots, for which we are quite thankful. They have taken splendid care of us.'

'That is true,' said Stanley, 'but you had all you needed. Perhaps far more than you needed. We had no wish to embarrass you.'

'Then I would take it,' said John, 'that you would be glad to hear the People may be coming back.'

'The People!' croaked the robot, shaken from the calm of his self-assurance. 'The People coming back?'

'They have only been away,' said John, 'on other planets. They have relocated Earth and a survey ship is on its way. It may be arriving very soon.'

Stanley struggled with himself. They could see him struggle. When he finally spoke, he was himself again. 'You are sure of this?' he asked.

'Very sure,' said John.

'You ask if we would be glad,' said Stanley. 'I do not think we would.'

'But you said—'

'That was in the beginning. That was five thousand years ago. In that length of time, there must be changes. You call us machines and I suppose we are.

434

But in five thousand years even a machine can change. Not mechanically, of course. But you made us machines with brains and brains can change. Viewpoints can shift. New values can be arrived at and accepted. Once we worked for men; it was our purpose and our life. Given a choice, we would not have changed the situation. We gained satisfaction from our servitude; we were built to gain satisfaction from a life of servitude. Loyalty was the love we gave the human race and we take no credit for it, for the loyalty was built into us.'

'But now,' said Hezekiah, 'you work for yourself.'

'You can understand that, Hezekiah. You and your companions now work for yourselves.'

'No,' said Hezekiah. 'We still work for Man.'

The robot Stanley paid no attention to what Hezekiah said. 'We were confused at first,' he said, 'and lost. Not we, of course, but each of us, each one separately. For we had never been one people; there had been no we; just each of us alone, doing what was expected of him, doing what he'd been fabricated for, and happy in the doing of it. We had no life of our own and I think that is what confused us so much when the People went away. For here suddenly, not we, but each of us alone, found that he did have a life of his own; that he could live without his human master, and that he still was capable of functioning had there been anything to do. Many of us stayed on for a time, in some cases a very long time, in the old households, performing the tasks we were supposed to do – as if our people had only gone off on a trip and would soon be coming back. Although even the stupidest of us, I think, knew this was not the case, for not only our own people, but everyone, had gone, and that was most peculiar, for never before had everyone gone away at once. I think that the most of us grasped immediately what had happened, but we kept on pretending that it wasn't so, that in time the people would all come home again and, true to our conditioning and training, we continued in the tasks that now were no tasks at all, but simply senseless motions. In time we gave up the pretence, not all of us at once, of course, but a few of us at first and others a little later and others after them. We took to wandering, hunting for new masters, for tasks that were not senseless. We found no humans, but we did find ourselves, we found one another. We talked with one another; we laid our little, short-range, meaningless plans by consultation with others of our kind. First we sought for humans and finally, when we knew there were no humans who would take us in – for your people, Mr Jason, had all the robots that you needed and your people, Chief Red Cloud, would have none of us, and there was a small band out West, on the coast, who were frightened of everything, even of us who tried to help them—'

Red Cloud said to Jason, 'That would be the tribe from which your wanderer came. What was it he said they were afraid of? The Dark Walker, wasn't it?'

'They were field workers to begin with,' Jason said. 'He didn't tell me this, perhaps he doesn't know, but from what he told me it is very plain. Agricultural people who worked continually in the fields, following the plantings, the tending and the harvest. Ground down in poverty, living hand to mouth, tied so close to the soil they became the very soil. They had no robots, of course. They may only have glimpsed robots from a distance, if at all. Even having seen them, they may not have fully understood exactly what they were. The robots were far better off than they. They would have been frightened of a robot.'

'They fled from us,' said Stanley. 'Not from me. I wasn't there. But from others of our people. We tried to make them understand. We tried to explain to them. But still they fled from us. We finally no longer followed them. We had no wish to frighten them.'

'What do you think they saw?' asked Red Cloud. 'This Dark Walker of theirs ...'

'Perhaps nothing,' Jason said. 'They would have had, I suspect, a long background of folklore. They would have been a superstitious people. To people such as they, superstition would have been an entertainment and perhaps a hope ...'

'But they might have seen something,' insisted Red Cloud. 'On that night when it happened, there might have been something on the Earth. There may have been netters who swept up the People. In times past my people had their stories of things that walked the Earth and we, in our new sophistication, are too ready to discount them. But when you live as close to the bosom of the Earth as we do you come to realize that some of the old stories may have some shreds of truth in them. We know, for example, that aliens on occasion now do visit Earth and in time past, before the white man came with his fury and his noise, when this continent was quieter and less boisterous than it became, who can say they did not visit then?'

Jason nodded. 'Old friend,' he said, 'you may well be right.'

'We came to a time,' said the robot Stanley, 'when we knew there were no humans we could serve and we stood with idle hands and there was nothing we could do. But through the centuries the idea grew, slowly at first and then with greater impact, that if we could not work for humans, we could work for ourselves. But what can a robot do for himself or for other robots? Build a civilization? A civilization would be meaningless for us. Build a fortune? What would we get a fortune from and what need would we have of it? We had no profit motive, we did not thirst for status. Education we might have been capable of and even have enjoyed, but it was a dead end, for except for a questionable self-satisfaction it might have given us, we had no use for it. Humans used education for their self-improvement, to earn a better living, to contribute to society, to assure themselves of more enjoyment of the arts. They called it self-improvement and that was a worthy goal for any human, but how could a robot improve himself? And to what purpose and what end? The answer seemed to be that we could not improve ourselves. No robot could make himself appreciably better than he already was. He had limitations built into him by his makers. His capabilities were predetermined by the materials and the programming that went into him. Considering the tasks he was designed to do, he served well enough. There was no need for a better robot. But there seemed no doubt that a better robot could be built. Once you thought of it, it became apparent that there was no limit to a robot. There was no place you had to stop and say, this is the best robot we can make. No matter how well a robot was designed, a better one was always possible. What would happen, we asked ourselves, if an open-ended robot should be built, one that was never really finished …'

'Are you trying to tell us,' Jason asked, 'that what you have here is your open-ended robot?'

'Mr Jason,' Stanley said, 'that is, indeed, what I have tried to say.'

'But what do you intend?'

'We do not know,' said Stanley.

'You don't know? You are the ones who are building …'

'Not any longer,' Stanley said. 'It has taken over now. It tells us what to do.'

'What use is it?' asked Red Cloud. 'It is anchored here. It can't move. It can't do anything.'

'It has a purpose,' said the robot, stubbornly. 'It must have a purpose …'

'Now, just a minute there,' said Jason. 'You say it tells you what to do. You mean that it has taken over the building of itself? That it tells you how to build it?'

Stanley nodded. 'It started twenty years or more ago. We have talked with it—'

'Talked with it. How?'

'By printout. We talk back and forth, like the old computers.'

'What you really have built is a big computer.'

'No. Not a computer. A robot. Another one of us, except it is so big it has no mobility.'

'We are talking to no point at all,' said Red Cloud. 'A robot is nothing more than a walking computer.'

'There are points of difference,' said Jason, gently. 'That, Horace, is what you have refused to see all these years. You've thought of a robot as a machine and it is not. It is a biological concept expressed mechanically—'

'You are quibbling,' Red Cloud said.

'I don't think we'll gain anything,' said John, 'even by the most good-natured argument. We didn't come here, actually, to find what might be building. We came to see how the robots would react to the People, perhaps, many of them, millions of them, coming back to Earth.'

'I can tell you, without any question, how the most of us would react to it,' said Stanley. 'We would view it with some apprehension. For they would take us back into their service or, perhaps worse than that, would have no need of us. Some of us, perhaps quite a number of us, would welcome being taken back into their service, for through all the years we have felt the lack of someone needing us. Some of us would welcome the old servitude, for to us it was never really servitude. But I think, as well, that the majority of us now feel we have started on a road along which we can work out for ourselves something approaching the destiny of mankind – not that precise kind of destiny, of course, for it would not fit us and we would not want it. For that reason we would not want the humans to come back. They would interfere. They could not help the interference; it is intellectually impossible for them not to interfere in any affairs that touch them, even most remotely. But that is not a decision we can make for ourselves alone. The decision is the province of the Project ...'

'You mean the monster you have built,' said Hezekiah.

Stanley, who had been standing all the time, slowly lowered himself into a chair. He swiveled his head around to stare at Hezekiah. 'You do not approve?' he asked. 'You do not understand? Of all these people, I would have thought you would.'

'You have committed sacrilege,' said Hezekiah, sternly. 'You have erected an abomination. You have chosen to elevate yourself above your creators. I have spent many lonely, terrible hours, wondering if I and my associates may not be committing sacrilege, devoting our time and utmost effort to a study and a task that should be mankind's study and its task, but at least we still are working for the good of mankind ... '

'Please,' said Jason. 'Let us not debate that now. How can any of us tell if we're right or wrong in any of our actions? Stanley says that it is up to the Project to decide ...'

'The Project will know,' said Stanley. 'It has far more background knowledge than any one of us. We have traveled widely through the years to obtain material that has been fed into its memory cores. We have given it all the knowledge it has been our fortune to lay our hands upon. It knows history, science, philosophy, the arts. And now it is adding to this knowledge on its own. It is talking with something very far in space.'

John jerked upright. 'How far in space?' he asked.

'We are not sure,' said Stanley. 'Something, we believe, in the center of the galaxy.'

21

He felt the crying need of the creature in the glen, the lack of something that it sought and the damnation of that lack. He stopped so quickly that Evening Star, walking close behind, bumped into him.

'What is it?' she whispered.

He stood rigid, feeling the lack and need, and he did not answer. The wash of feeling from the glen came pouring over him and into him – the hopelessness, the doubt, the longing and the need. The trees stood straight and silent in the breathless afternoon and for a moment everything in the forest – the birds, the little animals, the insects – fell into a silence. Nothing stirring, nothing making any noise, as if all of nature held its breath to listen to the creature in the glen.

'What's wrong?' asked Evening Star.

'There is something suffering,' he said. 'Can't you feel the suffering? It's just there ahead of us.'

'You can't feel suffering,' she said.

He moved ahead slowly and the silence held and there the creature was – a terrible can of worms crouched against the nest of boulders that lay beneath the arching birch. But he did not see the can of worms, he only heard the cry of need and something turned over in his mind and for a moment he held the need within his mental grip.

Evening Star recoiled and came up against the tough bark of an oak that stood beside the path. The can of worms kept changing, exactly as a can of worms would change, all the worms crawling over one another in the seething ferment of some nameless, senseless urge. And out of that seething mass came a cry of gladness and relief – a cry of gladness and relief that had no sound at all, and a cry that somehow was intertwined with a sense of compassion and of power that had nothing to do with the can of worms. And over all of this was spread, like a mantle of hope and understanding, what the great white oak had said, or tried to say, or failed to say, and within her mind the universe opened up like a flower awakened by the rising sun. For an instant she sensed and knew (not saw or heard or understood, for it all was beyond simple sight or understanding) the universe to its very core and out to its farthest edges – the mechanism of it and the purpose of its existence and the place that was held in it by everything that held the touch of life.

Only for an instant, a fractional second of realizing, of knowing, and then unknowing, then she was back again within herself, an incomplete, insignificant life form that crouched against the tree, feeling the rough bark of the massive oak against her shoulders and her back, with David Hunt standing in the path beside her and in the glen a squirming can of worms that seemed to shine with a holy light so bright and glittering that it was beautiful as no can of worms could ever be, and crying over and over inside her brain, with a meaning in the cry she could not comprehend.

'David,' she cried, 'what have we done? What happened?'

For there had been a great happening, she knew, or perhaps great happenings and she was confused, although in the confusion there was something that was at once a happiness and wonder. She crouched against the tree and the universe seemed to lean down above her and she felt hands fastening upon her and lifting her and she was in David's arms, clinging to him as she had never clung to anyone before, glad that he was there in what she sensed must be the great moment of her life, secure within the strength of his lean, hard body.

'You and I,' he was saying. 'You and I together. Between the two of us ...'

His voice faltered and she knew that he was frightened and she put her arms about him and held him with all the comfort that she had.

22

They waited on the riverbank, with the canoes drawn up on the rocky beach. Some of the canoemen were squatted about a tiny driftwood fire, broiling fish that they had caught, others were sitting about and talking, one of them lay fast asleep upon the river pebbles – which seemed to Jason, watching the sleeper, to be a most unsatisfactory bed.

The river was smaller here, much smaller than it was at the old camp from which they had started out. It was in a hurry here, its waters, sparkling in the sun of late afternoon, running between high bluffs that rose on either side, the stream sliding down an imperceptible chute.

Behind them rose the great flared structure of the Project, a black thin scroll of metal that seemed at once massive from its very size and yet so fragile that one wondered it did not flutter in the breeze.

'Did the same thought cross your mind,' John asked Jason, 'as occurred to me?'

'You mean whatever it might be the Project was talking with?'

'That's it,' said John. 'Do you think that it is possible? Could a super-robot, or a vastly sophisticated computer, or whatever that thing is up there, get in contact with the Principle?'

'It may only be listening to it, be aware of it, perhaps extracting some information from it. It may not actually be talking with it.'

'It does not have to be the Principle,' said John. 'It could be another race or other races. We have found a few of them and of these there are very few with whom we can communicate because we have no common ground for understanding. But a biological-mechanical contraption, such as that up there, might make ground for understanding. It may have a mind, if what it has can be called a mind, that is more flexible than ours. There is no question that it is the equal of mankind in its background for understanding. For hundreds of years the robots have pumped into its memory cores as much of human knowledge as they have been able to lay their hands upon. It probably is the best educated entity that has ever existed on the Earth. It has the equivalent of several hundred university or college educations. The sheer impact of the knowledge – all of which it would keep intact, not being subject to the forgetfulness of human beings – might have given it a broader outlook than any man has yet achieved.'

'Whatever it is talking with,' said Jason, 'it is one up on us. There are very few intelligences out there with which we have been able to set up any kind of communication, let alone a meaningful communication. And the communication this super-robot has set up, I gather, is very meaningful.'

'Perhaps meaningful for two reasons,' said John. 'First, it might be able to decipher the symbols of the language ...'

'The function of a good computer,' Jason pointed out.

'And, secondly, a good computer might have, not only a better and a different understanding, but a wider understanding. It might have a wider spectrum of understanding than is possible in a human. Our failure to achieve communication is due, in many instances, to our inability to comprehend a way of thought and a schedule of values different from our own.'

'It is taking a long time,' said Red Cloud. 'Do you think that monstrosity up there is having trouble making up its mind? Although I'm inclined to think it makes no difference what it says. I am doubtful it could be of help.'

'It is not a monstrosity, sir,' said Hezekiah. 'It is a logical construction for such as I to make, although I must hasten to say that such as I would never make it. Logical though it may be, it is an abomination built of sinful pride. But even so, I am certain that if it so decides, it can be of help. For, logically built, it would deal in logic ...'

'We'll soon know,' sad Jason, 'for Stanley is coming down the path.'

They got to their feet and waited for the glittering robot. He came down off the path and across the beach to stand in front of them. He looked from one to another of them. 'For you,' he finally said, 'the news is bad.'

'You won't help us, then,' said Jason.

'I am truly sorry,' the robot said. 'My personal inclination would be to cooperate with you in any way we could. But we built the Project as another one of us, as a greater one of us – perhaps I should say,' nodding to Horace Red Cloud, 'as the chief of us and in consequence must go along with the Project's judgment. For what is the sense of creating a chief if you do not trust and follow him?'

'But on what basis was the judgment made?' Jason asked. 'That you do not trust us, perhaps. Or that the problem, in your opinion, is somewhat less a problem than we had stated it?'

Stanley shook his head. 'Neither of those,' he said.

'You realize, of course, that if the People come they can take you over. And the Project, too.'

Hezekiah said, 'Surely you owe these gentlemen the courtesy—'

'You keep out of this,' said Stanley, speaking sharply.

'I will not keep out of it,' said Hezekiah, his words rasping with an uncharacteristic anger. 'These are the creatures that made us. They are our creators. Any loyalty that we have we owe to them. Even your Project owes them loyalty, for you used not only the intelligence that the humans gave you to conceive and build the Project, but you salvaged from their world the materials to build it, the knowledge to feed into it.'

'We no longer look for loyalty,' said Jason. 'Perhaps we never should have. I sometimes think we owe you an apology for ever having built you. We certainly gave you no world for which you have occasion to be thankful. But now, as it turns out, we're all in this together. If the People come back to occupy the planet, all of us will suffer.'

'What do you want?' asked Stanley.

'Your help, of course. But since you can't give us that, I think we have the right to ask why you are refusing help.'

'It will be no comfort to you.'

'Who said anything of comfort? It's not comfort we are looking for.'

'All right,' said Stanley. 'Since you insist. But I cannot tell you.'

He reached into the pouch suspended from his waist, took out a folded piece of paper, unfolded it and smoothed it out.

'This,' he said, 'is the answer that the Project gave us.'

He handed the piece of paper to Jason. There were three printed lines upon it. They read: *The situation outlined is immaterial to us. We could help humanity, but there is no reason that we should. Humanity is a transient factor and is none of our concern.*

23

Uncle Jason had said that, as a beginning, she should read history – starting with the general histories. This, he said, would provide a basis for an understanding of all the rest of it.

Now, sitting at the desk in the library, with the night wind muttering in the eaves and the thick candle burned almost to its socket, Evening Star wondered wearily at the need of understanding. Understanding would not take the lines of worry from Uncle Jason's face. It would not ensure, if the People came, that the forests and the buffalo plains would remain, unchanged, the province of her people. And it would not tell her what had happened to David Hunt.

The last consideration, she admitted to herself, was for her, personally, the most important one of all. He had held and kissed her on that day they'd found the creature in the glen and they'd walked back to the house together hand in hand. And that had been the last she had seen of him, the last that anyone had seen of him. She had walked the woods, hoping she would find him or some trace of where he might have gone, and she remembered with a rush of shame that she had gone down the road to the monastery to inquire if he'd been there. The robots had not cared; they had been courteous, but scarcely pleasant, and she had walked back to the house feeling, in a sense, degraded, as if she had shown her naked body to those uncaring men of metal.

Had he run from her? she wondered. Or had she read more into what had happened that day in the glen than had actually been there? Both of them, she realized, had been shaken by the events that had transpired in the glen and their flooding emotions may have found an outlet in one another that was, viewed in a sober moment, entirely without meaning. She didn't think, she told herself, that had been the case. She had thought about it since and the answer seemed to be that the events had no more than triggered something that she had known and felt, but had not entirely realized – that she loved this wanderer from the west. But had he, she wondered, asked the same question of himself and found another answer?

Had he run away? Or was there something that he still must seek – after all the months and miles of seeking, was he seeking still? Was he convinced that what he hunted – perhaps not really knowing what he hunted – did not lie in this house or in herself, and had he moved on towards the east in his endless quest?

She pushed the book away from her and sat in the quietness of the shadowed library, with all its tiers of books, with the candle guttering as it burned toward its end. Winter soon would come, she thought, and he would be cold. There were blankets she could have given him, there were robes that would have kept him warm. But he had not told her he was going and there was no way she could know.

Once again she lived over in her mind that day when they had found the creature. It all had been most confusing and she found that it still was impossible to put it all together, saying that, first, this happened, then another event took place, and after that, another. It was all jumbled up together, as if everything had happened all at once with no chinks of time between them, but she knew it had not been that way, that there had been a progression of events, although they had happened rather fast and had not been orderly. The oddest thing of all was that she had trouble separating what David had done and what she had done, and she wondered, once again, if, while they may not have done it all together, whether one of them alone could have made any of it happen, but that, rather, it took the two of them to do what each had done.

And what had she done? she wondered. What had happened to her? Trying to recall it, she could discover only fragments of it and she was sure that when it had happened there had been no fragmentation and that the fragments she could recall were no more than broken pieces of the whole. The world had opened out and so had the universe, or what she since had thought must have been the universe, lying all spread out before her, with every nook revealed, with all the knowledge, all the reasons there – a universe in which time and space had been ruled out because time and space were only put there, in the first place, to make it impossible for anyone to grasp the universe. Seen for a moment, half-sensed, a flash of insight that had been gone before there had been time for it to register on her brain, sensed and known for an instant only and then gone so quickly that it had left impression only, no certain memory and no solid knowledge, but impressions only, like a face seen in a lightning flash, and then the darkness closing in.

Was this – could this – be the realization of what she had tried to tell Grandfather Oak, knowing that there was something happening inside her, that change was about to come, but not knowing what it was and telling him instead that she might go away again, although in a different sense than she had gone to the wild rice country? If that were the case, she thought, if this were it, if this might be a new ability, like going to the stars, and not simply something that she had imagined, she'd never have to go anywhere again, for she was already there, she was any place that she might want to be.

It was the first time she had thought of it as an ability and she found herself confused and frightened, not so much at the implications of the thought as that she had thought of it at all, that she, even subconsciously, could have allowed herself to think of it. She sat stiff and straight, holding herself tense, and in the shadowed room flickering with the light of the dying candle, she seemed to hear again the muttering and stirring of all those ghosts that huddled there among their works, the one last place left to them on Earth.

24

(Excerpt from journal of Nov. 29, 5036) ... In the last few centuries I have experienced some physical deterioration and now there are days (like today) when I feel the weight of years upon me. I have a tiredness that cannot be accounted for by usual exertion, for I never have exerted myself too greatly and in late years almost not at all. My step has been reduced to shuffling and my hand, once firm, has lost some coordination, so that the writing in this journal has become shaky scrawling and there are times, as well, when I write a word I do not mean to write – a word very close to the one I meant to write, but not the one intended. There are other times when I cannot think of the word I want and must sit here sifting back through memory for it, saddened rather than irritated that I cannot think of it. I misspell a word at times, which is something I never used to do. I have become, I think, like an old dog sleeping in the sun, with the significant difference that the old dog expects nothing of itself.

Alison, my wife, passed away five hundred years ago and while I cannot recall a great deal now, I remember that her death was a peaceful dying and I would presume that mine may be the same. Living as a human being now lives, death comes by wearing out and not by the ravages of disease and this, more than the long life, I think, is the real blessing that has been conferred upon us. There are times when I wonder just how much a boon the longer life – the fabulously longer life – has been to humankind. Although such thoughts, I tell myself, are the crotchety views of an aging being, and in consequence to be given little credence.

One thing I do recall, and ever since that day it has haunted me. When Alison died many people came, from far among the stars, and we had a service for her, in the house, and at the graveside. There being no person of religious calling, my grandson Jason read from the Bible and said the words that custom decreed should be said and it all was very solemn and, in many ways, most satisfactory. The humans stood at the graveside, a great crowd of us, and at a little distance the robots stood, not that we had indicated in any way that they should stand apart, but of their own choosing and according to the ancient custom.

After it was all over, we went back to the house and after a time I retired into the library and sat there alone, no one intruding on me, for they understood my need to be alone. After a time there was a knock upon the door and when I called out for whoever it was to enter, in came Hezekiah of the monastery. He had come to tell me that he and his companions had not been at the funeral (a fact that I had failed to notice) because at the time those of the monastery had held a memorial service for her. Having told me this, he presented me with a copy of the service they had held. It was lettered on the sheets most legibly and beautifully, with colorful illustrative initials and decorations around the margins of the pages – the same careful, meticulous kind of manuscript as had been turned out in the scriptoriums of the Middle Ages. Frankly, I did not know how to respond. It was impudent of him, of course, and from my viewpoint not in the best of taste. But there was no question that what he and his companions had done had been with no thought of impudence nor impropriety, but from their own light, an act of utmost charity. So I thanked him and I fear I was somewhat curt in the thanks and I am certain he noted the curtness. At the time I did not record the incident in the journal and never spoke of it to anyone. I doubt that anyone, in fact, was aware that the robot had come calling on me. Over the years I have been most responsible in the writing of everything that happens. At first I started the journal so that the truth of what had happened to the human race would be placed upon the record and thus serve as a deterrent against the rise of myth and legend. I think that at the time I had no other reason and did not plan to continue with the journal, but by the time I had it all written down I had so acquired the habit of writing that I continued with it, putting down upon the pages all daily events, however small, as they took place – oftentimes writing down my thoughts as well as the events. Why I did not record at the time what took place between myself and Hezekiah has been a long, long puzzle to me. Surely it did not carry so great a significance, did not constitute so great a breach of etiquette, that it must be hidden. At first I put it out of my mind and when I happened to think of it, put it out of my mind again, but of late it has been with me overmuch.

In the last few years I have been able to ask myself many questions concerning the incident, for now the edge of the encounter has dulled and I can think of it objectively. The thought has occurred to me that we might have considered asking Hezekiah to officiate at the funeral, he rather than Jason reading the burial service and the words of comfort, although, shying from this even now, I know it would have been impossible then. And yet the fact remains that robot, rather than man, has kept not only Christianity, but the very idea of religion alive. This may not be entirely true, I realize, for Red Cloud's people undoubtedly do have a body of beliefs and a pattern of attitude that should be called religion, although as I understand it, it is not formalized, but is highly personal – which probably makes for a better practice and more common sense than the empty formalizations that other religions had become. But the point, it seems to me, is that we should either have held to our religion or have abandoned it entirely. What we did was let it die because we no longer cared and had grown very weary of pretending to believe. This does not apply to the last few thousand years alone. Even before the Disappearance our faith had been allowed to die and in this sense I use the word faith in a most restrictive sense, equating it with organized religion.

I have thought much on this the last number of years, sitting on the patio and watching the seasons pass. In the process I have become a student of the sky and know all the clouds there are and have firmly fixed in mind the various hues of blue that the sky can show – the washed-out, almost invisible blue of a hot, summer noon; the soft robin's egg, sometimes almost greenish blue of a late springtime evening, the darker, almost violet blue of fall. I have become a connoisseur of the coloring that the leaves take on in autumn and I know all the voices and the moods of the woods and river valley. I have, in a measure, entered into communion with nature, and in this wise have followed in the footsteps of Red Cloud and his people, although I am sure that their understanding and their emotions are more fine-tuned than mine are. I have seen, however, the roll of seasons, the birth and death of leaves, the glitter of the stars on more nights than I can number, and from all this as from nothing else I have gained a sense of a purpose and an orderliness which it does not seem to me can have stemmed from accident alone.

It seems to me, thinking of it, that there must be some universal plan which set in motion the orbiting of the electrons about the nucleus and the slower, more majestic orbit of the galaxies about one another to the very edge of space. There is a plan, it seems to me, that reaches out from the electron to the rim of the universe and what this plan may be or how it came about is beyond my feeble intellect. But if we are looking for something on which to pin our faith – and, indeed, our hope – the plan might well be it. I think we have thought too small and have been too afraid ...

25

The concert came to a crashing close and the music trees stood silent in the autumn moonlight. Down in the river valley owls were chuckling back and forth to one another and a faint breeze sent a rustle through the leaves. Jason stirred in his chair, glancing over his shoulder at the great antenna that had been installed upon the roof, then settled back again.

Martha rose from her chair. 'I am going in,' she said. 'Are you coming, Jason?'

'I think I'll stay here for a while,' he said. 'We don't get too many nights like this, this late in the year. It's a shame to miss it. Do you happen to know where John is? He didn't come out tonight.'

'John is getting restless with the waiting,' Martha said. 'One of these days he will be off to the stars again. He has found, I imagine, this is home no longer. He has been gone too long.'

Jason grumbled at her. 'No place is home to John. He hasn't got a home. He doesn't want a home. He simply wants to wander. He's like all the rest of them. None of them, no single one of them, cares what happens to the Earth.'

'They all are most sympathetic. All of those I talked with. If they could do anything, they said—'

'Knowing,' Jason said, 'there is nothing they can do.'

'I suppose so. Don't take it so hard, Jason. You may be worrying about something that will never come about.'

'It's not us I'm worried over,' he told her. 'It is Red Cloud's people and the robots. Yes, even the robots. They've made a new start of sorts. They should have their chance. There should be no interference.'

'But they refused to help.'

'They installed the radio and the beam,' he said.

'But no real help.'

'No real help,' he agreed. 'I can't understand the robots. I never have been able to.'

'Our own robots—'

'Our own robots are different,' Jason said. 'They are a part of us. They're doing what they were intended for. They have not changed, but the others have. Hezekiah, for example …'

'They had to change,' said Martha. 'They had no choice. They couldn't hunker down and wait.'

'I suppose you're right,' said Jason.

'I am going in now. Don't stay out too long. It will be getting cold soon ...'

'Where is Evening Star? She didn't come out, either. Just the two of us tonight.'

'Evening Star is worrying. About that funny boy. I don't know what she sees in him.'

'She has no idea what happened to him? Where he may have gone?'

'If she had, she'd not be worrying. I imagine that she thinks he ran away from her.'

'You talked with her?'

'Not about the boy.'

'He was a strange one,' Jason said.

'Well, I'm going in. You'll be coming soon?'

He sat and listened to her footsteps going across the patio, heard the door shut behind her.

Strange about the boy, he thought, strange that he should disappear. The alien in the glen had disappeared as well. He'd gone down to see it and talk with it again and there had been no sign of it, no matter how he'd hunted. Had it grown tired of waiting and gone away? he wondered. Or could there be some connection between its disappearance and that of David Hunt? It seemed impossible that there should be; David Hunt had not known about the creature in the glen. There was this story that the lad had told of the Dark Walker and it had been quite apparent he was afraid of it and, although he did not say so, he might have crossed the continent to get away from it, to shake it from his footsteps. He might be fleeing it still – from a thing that more than likely did not exist. But that was not strange, Jason told himself. He'd not be the first to flee from a nonexistent thing.

Could it be, he wondered, that his own fear was based upon a nonexistent premise? Might it be that a reconnaissance ship carrying representatives of the People posed no actual threat to Earth? And even should it carry the seeds of change for Earth, who was he to decide that it was a threat? But that must be wrong, he thought; it could be nothing but a threat. No threat, of course, to those people who had gone out to the stars, for they had cut their ties with Earth, they no longer cared for Earth and whatever might happen on the Earth would have no impact upon them. Learning this had been something of a shock, he admitted to himself. For all the years he had fostered the idea that he had been the anchor man of Earth, that he had held in trust the home base of humanity. Now it seemed that this had been a self-sustained illusion he had nourished carefully to bolster a sense of his own importance. So far as the people of this house might be concerned, there were only he and Martha who could be harmed if the People should decide to recolonize the Earth. And no matter how he might rebel against the thought of it, to the two of them it would not matter too much. So far as he and Martha were concerned, the People could be held at arm's length – certainly they could not interfere with this house and these few acres if it were amply apparent that they were not welcome. The very thought of them being here upon the planet would be gall upon his tongue, but that was selfishness, and utter arrogance and selfishness.

What did matter, he told himself, were the Indians, the descendants of the old aborigines who at one time had called this continent their home – and the robots as well as the Indians. Neither of them had asked for the kind of culture and civilization that had been forced upon them; the robots had not even asked for life. Enough injustice had been visited upon each of them in the past; it was more than decency could bear that they be made the victims of a new injustice. They had to have their chance. And if the People came they would have no chance.

What was this fatal disease that his own race carried? Fatal not to itself, but to all others that came in contact with it, although in the end, perhaps, fatal even to itself. It had all began, he told himself, when the first man had scratched the ground and planted seed, and must, therefore, secure to himself the ground in which to plant the seed. It had started with the concept of ownership – ownership of land, ownership of natural resources, ownership of labor. And perhaps from the concept of security as well, the erecting of fences against the adversities of life, the protection of one's station in life and the ambition to improve that station and, obtaining that improvement, to fortify it so well against one's neighbors that they could never wrest it from one. Thinking of it, he felt certain that the idea of security must, in its first instance, have risen from the concept of ownership. The two sprang from the same roots, really were the same. The man who owned was safe.

The Indians owned not one foot of ground, would spurn such ownership, for ownership would have meant they were tied to what they owned. And the robots, he wondered – did they in some manner which he had not noticed, have some idea of ownership? He doubted it very much. Their society must be even more a communistic one than the society of Red Cloud's people. It was only his own people who held to ownership, and that was the sickness in them. But it was from this sickness, built upon the basis of this sickness, that a most complicated social structure had been built up through the ages.

The social structure, swept away by the Disappearance, might be re-established now on Earth, and what could be done about it? What could he, Jason Whitney, do to prevent it being re-established? There was no answer, none that he could find.

The robots were a puzzle. Stanley had said that he and his fellows were deeply concerned, and yet when the Project had decided against offering help they had accepted the decision without question. Although they had been helpful in a most important way. They had supplied and installed the directional beam and the radio and batteries that operated them. Without such a setup it would have been impossible to contact the people when they arrived. Without the directional beam it would have been highly probable that they could arrive and leave without ever knowing there were people on the planet. They would land, perhaps at several places, make their surveys and then return to their new home planets to report that Earth was uninhabited. And it was important, Jason told himself – terribly important – that he have a chance to talk with them. What he could do by talking he had no idea, but at least he must have this chance to talk with those men on the ship that must, by now, be coming near to Earth. With the homing beam reaching out in space they would know there still were people here and would have means to seek them out.

Jason sat huddled in his chair. He felt lonely and forsaken; once again he wondered if he could be mistaken in all of this, and brushed the thought away. Mistaken for himself, perhaps, even mistaken for the robots, but certainly not mistaken for Red Cloud and his people – and perhaps not for himself or the robots, either.

He tried deliberately to wipe his mind clear of the whole affair. Perhaps if he could wipe it clean and keep it clean for a little while, he could think the clearer when the time came to think again. He sat as easily as he could, not thinking, willing the tenseness in him to soften and relax. He saw the moon glinting off the roofs of the monastery buildings and making slim white ghosts of the music trees. The last few nights, he thought, the trees had done much better, as good or even better than in the days of long ago. Their improvement had come about, he recalled, in the middle of the concert on the evening of the day his brother John had come home from the stars. He had noticed it then and had wondered over it for a little time, but there had been too much to do, too much to worry over, to think of it for long. On the night of the day John came home, he thought, but the fact of the homecoming could have not a thing to do with it. John's coming home could have made no difference to the music trees.

A foot crunched on the paving stones and Jason swung around in his chair. Thatcher was hurrying toward him.

'Mr Jason, sir,' the robot said, 'there is someone calling on the radio. I told him to wait and I would put you on.'

Jason rose from the chair. He was aware of a weakness in his knees, a goneness in his belly. This was it, he thought, this was it at last. He wasn't ready for it. He would never, he realized, have been ready for it.

'Thank you, Thatcher,' he said. 'There is something I'd like you to do for me.'

'Anything at all, sir.' Thatcher was excited. Jason looked at him curiously – he had never thought he'd see Thatcher excited.

'Would you please send one of the robots down to Red Cloud's camp. Tell him what has happened. Tell him that I need him. Ask him if he'll come.'

'Immediately,' said Thatcher. 'I'll make the trip myself.'

'That is fine,' said Jason. 'I had hoped you would. Horace knows you. He might resent any other robot yelling him awake.'

Thatcher turned and started off.

'Just a moment,' Jason said. 'There is something further. Would you ask Red Cloud to send someone up the river and fetch Stanley down. We should have him here. And Hezekiah, too. One of the other robots can rout out Hezekiah.'

26

He had killed that last bear when it had been so close that there had been no time to get off a decent shot. He had killed all the others, too – one bear for each of the claws in the necklace that hung about his throat. Some of the others, perhaps all of them, had been killed by the arrows he had fired – stout, true, well-fletched arrows driven by a powerful bow. But now he could not be sure, not absolutely sure, about the arrows.

Although it was not only killing. It was healing, too.

He had killed the bears, but he had healed the trees. He had thought so at the time and now he was sure he had. He had sensed something wrong with them and he had made it right, although he had never really known what had been wrong with them.

The alien came hobbling through the moonlit trees and squatted close to him. It made the worms go round and round and tumble all about. It had been following him for days and he was weary of it.

'Get out of here,' he yelled. 'Go away,' he shouted.

It paid no attention. It stayed there, redistributing the worms. He had been tempted at times to do to it whatever it was he had done to the bears. But he told himself that it would not be right to do it to the alien. The alien was no real threat, or at least he didn't think it was; it was just a nuisance.

The alien squirmed closer.

'I gave you what you wanted,' shouted David Hunt at it. 'I fixed up what was wrong with you. I took away the ache. Now leave me alone.'

The alien backed away.

David crouched at the foot of the mighty maple and tried to think it out – although, actually, there was not too much to think about. The record seemed quite clear: he had cured the trees, he had cured this strange creature which continually came sneaking up on him, he had cured the bird of its broken wing and an old black bear of an aching tooth and he had purged a bed of asters of a deadly thing that sucked the life from them (and was not quite easy in his mind on that one, for in helping the asters it appeared that he had killed some other form of life – a lowly life perhaps, but it still was life). As if a great compassion came rolling out of him to make all things well and whole and yet, quite strangely, he felt no great compassion. Rather, he felt an uneasiness when he sensed an unwell or aching thing and somehow he must make it right again. Right, perhaps, so he'd not be bothered with it. Was he to go through life, he wondered, sensing all the wrongness with the world? He had been all right until that night he had listened to the trees – until he had sensed the wrongness in them, he had been oblivious to wrongness, had not been aware of wrongness and quite carefree because he did not know of it. Something in the music, he wondered. Something in the robot that had stood beside him? And what did it mean, he wondered – that he must go stumbling through life aware of every little trouble, every little ill, and could get no rest or peace until he had fixed them all?

Out of the corner of his eye, David Hunt saw the alien creeping closer. He waved his hands at it in a pantomime of pushing it away.

'Get out of here!' he yelled.

27

Jason picked up the microphone and thumbed the switch. And what did one say? he wondered. Was there a convention of radio conversation? If so, he didn't know it.

He said, 'This is Jason Whitney of the planet Earth. Are you still out there?'

He waited and after a pause the voice came: 'Jason who? Please identify.'

'Jason Whitney.'

'Whitney. Are you a human? Or another robot?'

'I am human,' Jason said.

'Are you qualified to talk with us?'

'I am the only one who can. I'm the only human here.'

'The only—'

'There are other humans. Not many. Only a few of us. At the moment the others are not here.'

The voice was puzzled, but it said, 'Yes, we understand. We were told there were few humans. A few humans only and some robots.'

Jason sucked in his breath, cutting off the questions that came unbidden to his tongue. How would you know? Who told you there were humans? Certainly not John. And if any of the others out in space had found the People, they would come posting back to Earth to bring the news as quickly as they could, just as John had done. No one would have found the People and talked with them casually and then gone on without getting word to Earth.

Should he let them know, he wondered, that their coming had been anticipated? Like how come it took so long, we had expected you much sooner. That would set them back on their heels exactly as they had set him back on his. But he throttled the desire. He could tell them nothing now. It might be to Earth's advantage if they did not know.

'We had not expected,' said the voice, 'to find a directional beam or a radio. Once we found the beam, of course ...'

'Our robots,' Jason said, 'use radios to talk back and forth.'

'But the beam ...'

'I see no reason why you and I should argue,' Jason told them smoothly. 'Especially since I have no idea who you are.'

'But the beam ...'

'Just on the bare chance,' said Jason, 'that someone might want to visit us.

It takes little effort to keep it operational. Now please identify yourself. Tell me who you are.'

'We once lived on Earth,' the voice said. 'We were taken from it long ago. Now we are coming back.'

'Then,' said Jason, calmly, 'you must be the People. We had wondered, all these years, what could have happened to you.'

'The People?'

'That is what we called you – if you are the ones who disappeared from Earth.'

'We are the ones.'

'Well, welcome back,' said Jason.

He smiled quietly to himself. As if they'd just stepped across the road to visit friends and were late in getting back. It could not be the way they had expected it. What they had expected, more than likely, was a sort of gibbering joy that they had found their way back to Earth and that after all the years the poor creatures who had been left behind were united once again with others of their race.

'We had expected we would have to hunt for you,' the voice said. 'We had feared, in fact, that we would not find you.'

Jason chuckled. 'You have been spared that fear. Are you coming in to visit us? I don't quite see how you can. We have no landing field.'

'We need no field. We'll send down a boat, with two men. The boat can land anywhere. Just keep the beam going. The boat will ride it down.'

'There's a cornfield near the house,' said Jason. 'You'll recognize it by the corn shocks. You can manage there?'

'Very nicely.'

'When can we be expecting you?'

'By morning light.'

'In that case,' said Jason, 'we'll kill the fatted calf.'

Alarm sounded in the voice. 'You'll do what?' it asked.

'Never mind,' said Jason. 'Just a saying. We'll be seeing you.'

28

The oak log finally burned through and broke into two pieces, collapsing, sending up a shower of sparks that funneled up the chimney. The wind growled in the flue and from far off came the whining of the eaves. They sat by the fire and waited, the three of them – Martha, John and Jason.

'It worries me,' said Jason. 'How did they come to know? How could they have learned there was anybody here? It must have been quite natural for them to have assumed the entire race was taken. By rights, they should have thought they were coming to a planet with no inhabitants. They would have known, at least assumed, that the robots had been left behind and that they would have guessed the robots would persist. They might logically have imagined they'd find a robot civilization, but they couldn't know …'

'Don't worry about it,' said John. 'We'll get the answer soon enough. The important thing is that you handled it just right. You left them guessing. They must be mighty puzzled people. Your reactions were not typical to the situation and you've got them worried. They don't know what to think. They're up there psyching you right now.'

'No matter what,' said Martha, 'you shouldn't take on so. This is no life-and-death affair.'

'To me it is,' said Jason. 'And it is to Red Cloud. We can't let them ruin everything.'

'Maybe they won't,' said Martha.

'Another planet for them to take over,' Jason said. 'Do you think they'd miss a chance like that?'

'But a planet,' suggested John, 'with its resources stripped. They know the planet has been stripped; they stripped it.'

'Minerals, of course,' said Jason. 'The minerals are gone and most of the fossil fuels. Although they probably could salvage a lot of the minerals from the ruins – it's not all gone back to rust. And the cities would be quarries for building stone. Since the Disappearance the forests have grown up again. The forests today can't be much inferior to what they were when the Europeans took over the continent. The same would be true of the rest of the world. Back to primordial woodlands. Billions of board feet of lumber. The land has renewed itself. It's fertile once again, as it was before man first scratched the earth to plant a crop. The sea is full of fish.'

'We can bargain with them,' Martha said. 'We can talk with them.'

'We have nothing to bargain with,' said Jason, bitterly. 'We can appeal to their better nature, but I have no hope in that.'

Footsteps came clumping down the hall. Jason leaped to his feet.

'It's only Hezekiah,' Martha said. 'Thatcher sent him word.'

Hezekiah came into the room. 'There was no one,' he said, 'to announce my coming. I hope I do no wrong.'

'Of course you haven't,' Martha said. 'Thank you for coming. Won't you please sit down.'

'I do not need to sit,' said Hezekiah, primly.

'Damn it, Hezekiah,' Jason said, 'stop practicing your humility on us. In this house you're like any of the rest of us.'

'I thank you, Mr Jason,' Hezekiah said. He sat down on a sofa. 'I must admit that I have become partial to this human thing of sitting. In my case there is no earthly reason for it, but I enjoy it, although I suspect my enjoyment of it is something of a sin. I am told you have received word from the coming People. Aside from my realization of the problem posed by their imminent arrival, I am considerably intrigued at the opportunity to get from them some account of the development of their belief in the matter of religion. It would be a comfort—'

'You will find no comfort,' John told him. 'You can hope for nothing from them. I saw no evidence of any religious belief while I was on their planet.'

'No evidence at all, sir?'

'None at all,' said John. 'No churches, no places of worship, no inclination to worship. No ministers or preachers or priests. And don't act so startled. Certainly it would be possible for a society to exist, quite comfortably, without any kind of faith. In fact, even before the Disappearance, we almost did. And in case you are wondering, there is no evidence that the lack of faith had anything to do with the Disappearance.'

'I don't care too much about what they believe or don't believe,' said Jason. 'Let's not get off the track. How could the People have known there was anybody here? John, you didn't, by any chance ...'

'No,' said John. 'I am sure I didn't. I did my best not to give any inkling that I came from Earth. I'm almost positive I said nothing ...'

'How, then? No other of our people have been there. If they had been, they would have told us. It wouldn't be something that anyone would ignore. All these years we have wondered what happened to the People. It is a question that never has been too far from our thoughts.'

'Have you considered that the People may have heard it from some other intelligence? We've been at no pains, as we traveled in the galaxy, to hide where we are from or how we travel ...'

'Then you think they could know, as well, about our star-traveling?'

'It is possible,' said John. 'Remember, the People are star rovers, too. They have their ships. They may have visited many planets. I know they have made star trips. In the course of their traveling, they could have contacted some intelligences, probably among them some of the same we have contacted.'

'Our contacts have not been too satisfactory.'

'Nor, perhaps, have theirs. But if they developed any contact at all with the intelligences we have met, one of the first things they would learn would be that others like them had visited the planet and by an entirely different means than they used in getting there. These People are not stupid, Jason. They could put two and two together.'

'But you heard none of this. Nothing to hint at it. All the time you spent on their planet, you heard nothing at all.'

John shook his head. 'Only that they finally had relocated Earth and some months since had sent out a survey ship to visit it. You must realize, however, that I was in no position to reach into their governmental or scientific circles. All I heard was what the common people knew or could read in their publications.'

'You think if the government knew about it they might have kept their knowledge secret?'

'They could have. I don't know what the reason for secrecy could have been, but it's possible.'

Soft feet came down the hall toward the room in which they sat.

'That's Red Cloud,' said Jason. He rose and met his old friend as he came into the room.

'I'm sorry to rout you out, Horace,' he said, 'but they'll be here this morning.'

'I would not,' said Horace Red Cloud, 'have missed this wake for all the world.'

'Wake?'

'Certainly. The custom of old barbarians from across the sea. No Indian foolishness.'

'You mean sitting with the dead.'

'And this time,' said Horace, 'the dead are a planet and a people. My planet and my people.'

'They may have changed,' said Martha. 'They've had thousands of years to acquire some different viewpoints, a new morality, to mature a little. It might be a different culture.'

Red Cloud shook his head. 'John, from what he told us, doesn't seem to think so. He spent some time with them and it's the same old culture, a little smarter, maybe, a little slicker in its operations. These kind never change. A machine does something to a man. It brutalizes him. It serves as a buffer between himself and his environment and he is the worse for it. It arouses an opportunistic instinct and makes possible a greed that makes a man inhuman.'

'I'm frightened,' Jason said, 'if that's what you want to hear me say.'

'I sent a canoe up the river,' said Red Cloud, 'to carry word to Stanley – I think that is his name. Although why we bother with him I do not understand.'

'We're all in this together. He has a right to be here if he wants to come.'

'Remember what that contraption said? We are a transient factor ...'

'I suppose we are,' said Jason. 'The trilobites were a transient factor. So were the dinosaurs. I suppose the robots have the right to think – even good reason to believe – they'll outlive us all.'

'If they do,' said Red Cloud, 'it will serve them right.'

29

They arrived at dawn, their little craft landing softly in the cornfield. In coming to a landing, it knocked down and scattered a corn shock and smashed three pumpkins. The little band of four humans and one robot waited at the edge of the field. There were other robots about, Jason knew, but well hidden, peering out in awe at this machine that came down from the sky. When the hatch opened, two men stepped out. They were tall and heavy, dressed in plain gray pants and jackets, small caps on their heads.

Jason strode down to the field toward them. They came to meet him.

'You are Jason Whitney,' said one of them. 'The one who talked with us last night.'

'Yes, I am,' said Jason. 'Welcome back to Earth.'

'I am Reynolds,' said one of them, holding out his hand. 'My companion is Harrison.'

Jason shook hands with the two of them.

'We are not armed,' said Harrison, 'but we have protection.' It was almost as if the speech was ritual.

'You have no need of protection here,' said Jason. 'We are highly civilized. There is not an ounce of violence in all of us combined.'

'One never knows,' said Harrison. 'After all, we have been apart for some thousands of years, time enough for change. Not an alien encounter, of course, but with some aspects that are not too far from it. You tried last night, Mr Whitney, to throw us in confusion.'

'I do not understand,' said Jason.

'Your words are calculated to make us believe you had no notice of our coming. I don't know how you could have had, but it was apparent that you knew. You studiously showed no surprise and if you had not known, you would have been surprised. You attempted to make it seem our arrival was of little consequence.'

'Should it be of consequence?' asked Jason.

'We can offer much to you.'

'We are satisfied,' said Jason, 'with the little that we have.'

'There was the beam,' said Harrison. 'You would not have had a beam out if you had not believed there was someone out there. There is very little traffic in this part of the galaxy.'

'You gentlemen,' said Jason, 'seem to be sure enough of your deductions to allow for rudeness.'

'We do not mean to be rude,' Reynolds said. 'We do think there should be understanding. You attempted to mislead us and it might clear the way for further talk if we let you know that we realize the situation.'

'You are our guests,' said Jason. 'I don't intend to bicker with you. If you believe what you say, there is no possible way in which I could persuade you otherwise, and, indeed, no point in doing so.'

'We were somewhat surprised,' said Harrison, casually conversational, 'to learn, a little time ago, there were humans still on Earth. We had realized, of course, that there must be robots, for whatever it was that swept us away did not sweep the robots. But we had thought, of course, that there'd be no humans. We thought they got us all.'

'They?' asked Jason. 'Then you know who did it.'

'Not at all,' said Harrison. 'In saying they, I may be guilty of personalizing some force that was not personal at all. We had hoped you might have some idea. We know you've traveled far. Much farther than we have.'

So they knew, thought Jason, bleakly, about star-traveling. It had been too much to hope they wouldn't.

'Not I,' he said. 'I have never left the Earth. I have stayed at home.'

'But others have.'

'Yes,' said Jason. 'Many others.'

'And they talk? Telepathy?'

'Yes, of course,' said Jason.

There was no use denying it. They had learned the entire story. Maybe not heard it, not been told it. Perhaps only bits and pieces. And they'd put it all together. A handful of tiny facts and they would have the story. A new ability, he wondered – a better psychology, a sense of hunch, prognostication?

'We should have gotten together sooner,' said Harrison.

'I don't understand,' said Jason.

'Why, man,' said Harrison, 'you have got it made. So have we. The two of us together ...'

'Please,' said Jason. 'The others are waiting for us. We can't stand here, talking. After you have met them, there will be breakfast. Thatcher is cooking up some pancakes.'

30

(Excerpt from journal of Aug. 23, 5152) ... When a man gets old (and now I am getting old) it seems he climbs a mountain to leave everyone behind, although I would suspect, if he but stopped to think of it, he'd realize he was the one who was left behind. In my circumstance the situation is not really applicable, for I and all the rest of us were left behind 3,000 years ago. But in a normal human community such as existed before the Disappearance, the old were left behind. Their old friends died or moved away or simply went away, moving so quietly and so softly, like leaves dried to paper thinness blowing in the wind, that they were not missed until sometime after they were gone and the old man (or the old leaf), looking for them, would find with some astonishment and sadness that they were not anywhere, nor had they been for a long time in the past. He (the old man) might ask someone where they had gone or what had happened to them, and getting no answer, would not ask again. For the old do not really mind; in a strange way they become sufficient to themselves. They need so very little and they care so very little. They climb the mountain no one else can see and as they climb, the old, once-valued things they've carried all their lives tend to drop away, and as they climb higher the knapsack that they carry becomes emptier, but perhaps no less in weight than it had ever been, and the few things that are left in it, they find, with some amusement, are those few indispensable belongings which they've gathered in a long lifetime of effort and of seeking. They wonder greatly, if they think of it at all, how it was left to age to winnow out the chaff they've carried all the years, thinking that it was valuable when it was only chaff. When they reach the mountain top, they find they can see farther than they've ever seen before and with greater clarity and, if by this time they're not past all caring, may bemoan that they must approach the end of their lives before they can see with this marvelous clarity, which does little for them now, but might, in earlier years, have been of incalculable value.

Sitting here, I think of this and know there is not as much fantasy in such a notion as someone of more youthful years might believe. It seems to me that even now I can see farther and with greater clarity, although perhaps neither so far nor so clear as may be the case closer to the end. For, as yet, I cannot discern what I am looking for – the path and promise for the mankind that I know.

At the time of the Disappearance we took a different path than the one that

Man had followed through the ages. We were forced, in fact, to take another path. We no longer could continue as we had before. The old world came crashing down about us and there was little left. We thought, at first, that we were lost and indeed we were, if lostness means the losing of a culture we'd built up so laboriously through the years. And yet, in time, I think we came to know that the losing of it was not entirely bad – perhaps not bad at all, but good. For the loss had been the loss of many things we were better off without. Rather than losing, we gained a chance for a second start.

I must confess that I am still somewhat confused by what we did with this second start, or rather what the second start did to us. For certainly what we did came about through no conscious effort. It happened to us. Not to me, of course, but to the others. I was, I suspect, too old, too molded in that older, earlier life, for it to happen. I stood aside, not particularly because I wanted to, but because there was no choice.

The important aspect of the whole situation, it seems to me, is that this business of traveling to the stars and talking back and forth across the galaxy (Martha, at this moment, has spent a good part of the afternoon gossiping across light years) is no more than a bare beginning. It may be that star-traveling and telepathy are the easy part of what has happened to us. They may be only the first easy steps, as hammering out a stone fist ax was the first and easy step toward the great technology that was later hammered out.

What comes next? I ask myself, and I do not know. There seems to be no logical progression to this sort of thing, and the reason that there is no logic is that we are too new at it to have an understanding of what may be involved. The flint worker of prehistoric days had no idea why a stone would cleave in the fashion that he wished when he struck a blow in a certain place upon its face. He knew how, but not why, and he didn't spend much time, I would suppose, in figuring out the why. But as the cleaving of the flint came clear to men of later days, the mechanism of the parapsychic ability some millennia from now will come as clear to the men then living.

As it stands at the moment, I can only speculate. Speculation is a footless endeavor, I am well aware, but I cannot refrain from it. Standing on my mountain top, I strain my eyes to look into the future.

Will there come a time, perhaps, when a race of godlike men can manipulate the very fabric of the universe? Will they be able to rearrange the atoms, bending their structures and their energies to the will of mind alone? Will they be able to save a star tottering close to the nova stage from its natural evolutionary course and enable it to continue as a normal, stable star? Will they be able, by the power of mind alone, to engineer a planet, converting it from a useless mass of matter to an abode for life? Will they be able to alter the genetics of a life form, by the power of mind alone, refashioning it into a more significant and more satisfactory life form? Perhaps more importantly, will they be able to free the minds of universal intelligences from the chains and shackles that they carry from the olden days of their evolutionary cycle so that the intelligences become reasonable and compassionate intelligences?

It is good to dream and there could be the hope, of course, that this all might come about, man finally emerging as a factor in introducing even a great orderliness into the universe. But I cannot see the path to reach this time. I can see the beginning and can dream the hoped-for end, but the in-between escapes me. Before such a situation can obtain there must be certain progress made. It is the shape of this progress I cannot determine. We must, of course, not only know, but understand the universe before we can manipulate it and we must arrive at the ability for that manipulation by a road for which there is no map. All must necessarily come by slow degree; we shall travel that unmapped road foot by weary foot. We must grow into this new ability of ours to make things happen without the aid of silly mechanical contrivances and the growth will not be rapid.

In my far view from the mountain of my age, I seem to see an end to it, a point beyond which we cannot or, perhaps, would not wish to go. Beyond which we might not dare to go. But I do not think there will be an end to it any more than there was an end to technology, until that day something took a hand and put an end to it here on the planet of its origin. Let alone, man himself would not have ended it. Man must always take that extra or that final step, finding once he has taken it it is not a final step. Today I can imagine only so far into the future, not having the data to extend my imagery beyond a certain point. But by the time man reaches that point where my imagination fails, he will have the data to push the point far into the future. There will be no place to stop.

If man persists, there'll be no stopping him. The question, it seems to me, is not whether he will persist, but whether he has the right to. I shudder when I envision man, the prehistoric monster, continuing into a time and world where he has no place ...

31

'I do not know,' Harrison said to Jason, 'how I can talk reason to you. All we want is to send a small group of people here so they can learn the parapsychic abilities, in return for which—'

'I have already told you,' Jason said, 'that we cannot teach you the abilities. It's apparent you refuse to believe what I have told you.'

'I think,' said Harrison, 'that you are bluffing. So, all right, you're bluffing. What more do you want? Tell me what you want.'

'You have nothing that we want,' said Jason. 'That's something else you won't believe. Let me spell it out to you once again. You either are parapsychic or you aren't. You are technological or you aren't. You can't be both of them. They are mutually exclusive because so long as you remain technological, you can't be parapsychic and once you're parapsychic, you have no use for technology. We do not want any of you here under the pretense of learning what we know or can do, even if you think you want what we know or can do. A few of you, you say, and it would be a few at first, then more of you, and after that still more and once you understand there was no chance of going parapsychic, why, then, you'd settle in. It's the pattern of technology – to grab and hold, then grab and hold some more ...'

'But if we were sincere,' protested Reynolds. 'If we really meant it. And, of course, we do. We are being honest with you.'

'I have told you it can't be done,' said Jason. 'If you want to be parapsychic, you don't have to come to Earth. Let those people who want to be parapsychic strip themselves of everything they have, let them live thus stripped for two thousand years. At the end of that time it might happen to them, although I'll not guarantee it. We didn't know of it until it happened to us. It was easier for us than it would be for you. There'd be a difference in the attitude of people who set out deliberately to acquire the abilities and that difference in attitude might make it impossible.'

'What you are talking about,' said John, 'is a combination of your way of life with ours. You see a great advantage to the both of us if it could be done. If some of your people could only find the way, you'd figure that you had it made. But it wouldn't work. If some of your people could become parapsychic, they'd stand alien from you; they'd take the same attitude toward you that we are taking now.'

Harrison looked around the table slowly and deliberately, at each one sitting there. 'Your arrogance is appalling,' he said.

'We are not arrogant,' said Martha. 'We are so far from arrogant—'

'But you are,' said Harrison. 'You assume that you are better now than you were before. How better I don't know, but better. You hold technology in contempt. You view it with disdain, and perhaps alarm, forgetting that if it had not been for technology we'd all be squatting in a cave.'

'Perhaps not,' said Jason. 'If we'd not cluttered up our lives with machines —'

'But you don't know that.'

'No, of course I don't,' said Jason.

'So we should forget our squabbling,' said Harrison. 'Why can't we —'

'We've made our position clear,' said Jason. 'You must believe us when we say we can't teach you parapsychics. It's not something that can be taught. You must find it inside yourself. And you must believe us when we say we want nothing of technology. We people of this house have no need of it. The Indians dare not touch it, for it would ruin the kind of life they've fashioned. They live with nature, not on it. They take what nature gives; they do not rip their living out of nature. I can't speak for the robots, but I would suspect they have a technology of their own.'

'There's one of them here,' said Reynolds. 'You need not speak for them.'

'The one who is here,' said Jason, 'is more man than robot. He is doing mankind's work, has picked up something that we found too bulky or too inconvenient or not worthwhile to carry.'

'We seek the truth,' said Hezekiah. 'We work for faith.'

'This may all be true,' Reynolds said to Jason, ignoring Hezekiah, 'but there still remains your opposition to our resettling the Earth, colonizing it. There probably would not be many who would want to come, but you don't want even a few of us. You do not own the Earth. You cannot own it.'

'Except for an emotional revulsion at seeing another technological threat to Earth,' said Jason, 'I don't suppose that Martha and myself could raise logical objection, and of this house, we are the only two who matter. The others are among the stars. When Martha and I are gone this house will stand empty and I know now there would be few, if any, who would really care. Earth has gone back to its primitive heritage and I would hate to see it stripped and gutted again. We did that to it once and once should be enough. Earth should not stand in double jeopardy. To me the matter is emotional, but there are others to whom it really matters. The Indians owned this continent once and the whites took it from them. We slaughtered them and robbed them and pushed them into reservations and those who escaped the reservations we forced to live in ghettos. Now they have made a new life, based on the old – better than their old life because they learned from us – but still their life, not ours. Neither should they stand in double jeopardy. They should be left alone.'

'If we agreed,' said Harrison, 'to leave this continent alone, to only settle on the others ...'

'In the old days,' said Jason, 'we made treaties with the Indians. So long as the rivers flow, so long as the winds shall blow, we said, the treaties would be kept. They were never kept. And neither would your so-called agreements. A few hundred years perhaps, more likely less than that. No longer. Even from the first you would interfere. You'd want to set up trade. You would break your old agreements and then make new agreements, and each time the Indian would get less and less. It would be the same old story as it was before. A technological civilization is never satisfied. It is based on profit and progress, its own brand of progress. It must expand or die. You might make promises and be sincere in the making of them; you might intend to keep them, but you wouldn't and you couldn't.'

'We would fight you,' Red Cloud said. 'We would not want to fight, but we'd have to. We would lose, we know that even now. But we still would fight – once a plow was put into the ground, once a tree was felled, once a wheel had turned ...'

'You're insane!' shouted Harrison. 'You are all insane. You talk of fighting us! You? With spears and arrows!'

'I told you,' said Horace Red Cloud, 'that we know we'd lose.'

'And you close the planet to us,' said Harrison, grimly, turning to Jason. 'It's not your planet to close. It is ours as well as yours.'

'The planet is not closed,' said Jason. 'We have no legal, perhaps not even a moral right to stand upon. But I ask you, in the name of common decency, to stay away from us, to keep your hands off us. You have other planets, there are still others you can take ...'

'But this is our planet,' Reynolds said. 'It's been waiting all these years. You, a handful of people, can't keep the rest of the human race from taking what is theirs. We were taken from it; we did not desert it. All these years we have thought of it as home.'

'You can't possibly expect us to believe that,' Jason. 'Not the story of expatriates coming back, gratefully, to the old familiar shore. Let me tell you what I think.'

'Yes, please do,' said Reynolds.

'I think,' said Jason, 'that you may have known for years the location of the Earth, but you had no interest in it. You knew that it had little of value left, that it offered nothing but the room to live. And then, somehow, you heard a rumor about people left on Earth and how they could travel to the stars without any help at all – going anywhere they wished in the flicker of an eyelash – and how they talked telepathically across great distances. Perhaps not a true picture in the first rumor, but there were other rumors and the story built up and up. And you thought if only you could add this sort of ability to your technology you could progress the faster, that you'd increase your profits, that you'd have more power. And it wasn't until then that you thought of coming back to Earth.'

'I fail to see the point of what you say,' said Harrison. 'The fact is we are here.'

'The point is this,' said Jason. 'Don't use your threat to take over Earth in the belief that we are bluffing and will finally give in and give you what you want to keep you from colonizing Earth.'

'And if we still decide to colonize?'

'Then you'll colonize. There's no way we can stop you. Red Cloud's people will be swept away. The robotic dream may end. Two cultures that might have come to something will be cut off and you'll have a worthless planet on your hands.'

'Not worthless,' Reynolds said. 'You should give us credit for the progress we have made. With what we have now Earth would have economic value as an outpost, as a base, as an agricultural planet. It would be worth our while.'

The candles guttered in a wind that came out of nowhere and a silence fell – a silence, Jason thought, because all had been said that could be said and there was no use of saying further. This was the end of it, he knew. There was no compassion in these two men across the table; an understanding, perhaps, of what might be at stake, but a cold, hard understanding that they'd weigh to their own advantage. They'd been sent to do a job, these two here and the others up there in the ship orbiting the Earth – they had been sent to do a job and they meant to do it. It did not matter to them what might come about because they did the job – it had never mattered, neither now or in the years before. Societies had been smashed, cultures erased, human lives and hopes used up, all decency ignored. All was sacrificed to progress. And what, he wondered, might progress be? How did one define it? Was it merely naked power, or was there more to it than that?

Somewhere a door banged and a rush of chill autumn air came with the banging of the door. Feet came down the hall and through the doorway came a robot that glittered as he walked.

Jason came swiftly to his feet. 'Stanley,' he said, 'I'm glad that you could come, although I am afraid too late.'

Stanley gestured at the two across the table.

'Are these the ones?' he asked.

'They are, indeed,' said Jason. 'I would like to have you meet—'

The robot brushed aside the introduction.

'Gentlemen,' he said to them, 'I have a message for you.'

32

He came down the ridge that ran above the river, striding in the crisp, moonlit autumn night, and came to the edge of a cornfield where the shocks stood like ghostly wigwams. Behind him the mewling creature humped along, hurrying to keep pace with him, tagging at his heels. From somewhere across the field a coon made a lonesome whickering.

David Hunt was coming back to the great house that stood above the rivers; now he could come back because he knew the answer or at least the beginning of an answer. Evening Star would be waiting for him – at least, he hoped she would. He should, he realized, have told her of his going and the reason for it, but he'd not been able, for some reason he did not understand, to find the words and would have been embarrassed to speak even if he had known what to say.

He still carried the bow and the quiver of arrows was slung across his shoulder, although now he knew he carried them from habit; he no longer needed them. He wondered, as he strode along, how long he may have carried them beyond the time of need.

Above the trees he could see the topmost storeys and the chimney-studded roof of the great house, a blur of darkness against the night-time sky, and as he rounded a small tongue of timber that jutted out into the field, he saw the gleaming, metallic object that squatted there.

The sight of it brought him to a halt and he half crouched, as if the gleaming object might be an unknown danger, although even as he crouched, he knew what it was – a machine that brought men from the stars. Evening Star had told him of the threat posed to the Earth by such a ship that even then was heading toward the planet. And here it was; in the short time he'd been gone, it had arrived. But even so he felt a shiver of fear reach out and touch him and, touched by the fear, it seemed that he could see the indistinct outline of a shape that lurked behind the ship.

He moved backward a step, and at the step the shape moved out from behind the ship and it was strange that it should have been hidden by the ship, for it was larger than the ship. It was huge and, shadowy as it was, there was a brutality about it and as it lurched toward him he knew he had not outrun it, for all the miles he had covered. There was no outrunning it, he knew. He never should have tried.

The Dark Walker lurched another ponderous step and David turned to run, then spun back again to face the oncoming shadow-thing. If he ran now, he knew, he'd keep running and he would never quit. He'd go through life poised and set to run – as his people had run and run and run again.

Now, perhaps, there was no need to run.

It was closer now and he could see it better, although it still was indistinct – but now he had the impression of legs like tree trunks, a massive torso, a tiny head, clawed hands reaching out.

And in that moment it became, not the Dark Walker, but the grizzly bear rising from its bed and towering over him, too close to shoot, far too close to shoot. Without even thinking of it, his hand went back to grasp an arrow and the bow came up and his mind – or the thing inside his mind, the power inside his mind – went crashing out.

It did not drop as the grizzly had dropped. It faltered, bent forward, reaching for him, and the string came back, almost to the bowman's ear, with the arrow steady. The Walker dropped away and the arrow whistled and struck against the gleaming ship with a clanging sound. The Walker was no longer there.

David Hunt lowered the bow and stood shaking. He slumped to his knees and huddled, muscles twitching, nerves as taut as bowstrings. The can of worms moved closer to him, pressed hard against him, grew a tentacle and held him tight, broadcasting unheard comfort.

33

'Who is this person?' Reynolds asked Jason.

'His name is Stanley,' Jason told him. 'He is a robot from the Project. We told you of the Project, if you recall ...'

'Oh, yes,' said Harrison, 'a super-robot being built by all his little brothers.'

'I must protest your tone,' said Hezekiah, sharply. 'There is no reason for you to be supercilious. What this robot and his fellows do lies within the great tradition of your technology, to build bigger and better and with a greater imagination ...'

'I beg your pardon,' said Harrison. 'But he came rushing in here—'

'He was invited,' said Jason coldly. 'He had a long way to come. He has only now arrived.'

'With a message?'

'It is from the Project,' Stanley said.

'What is this message?' Harrison demanded.

'First I must explain it,' said Stanley. 'The Project, for some years now, has been in communication with intelligence somewhere in the central galaxy.'

'Yes,' said Reynolds. 'We have been told of that.'

'The message I carry,' Stanley said, 'is from that intelligence.'

'And it has to do with the situation here?' asked Reynolds. 'I find that ridiculous.'

'It has to do with you,' said Stanley.

'But how could it know? What would it know about the situation here? Certainly a great alien intelligence would not concern itself—'

'The message, directed to you and the rest of your party, is this: Leave Earth alone. No interference is allowed. It also is a part of the experiment.'

'But I don't understand,' Harrison said, angrily. 'What experiment? What is it talking about? It makes no sense at all. Certainly, we have the right to know.'

Stanley took a folded paper from a pouch. He tossed it across the table to Reynolds. 'There is a copy of the message, off the printer.'

Reynolds picked it up, glanced at it. 'That is what it says. But I don't see the point. If you're trying another bluff ...'

'It's the Principle,' said Jason, speaking quietly. 'That cinches it. We had wondered; now we know. The Project was talking with the Principle.'

'A Principle?' yelled Harrison. 'What is all this? We know of no Principle. It means nothing to us.'

John sighed. 'I don't suppose it does. We should have told you, but there was so much to tell. If you'll just settle back, I'll tell you about the Principle.'

'Another fairy story, no doubt,' Harrison said, angrily. 'A phony message and now a fairy story. You people must think that we are stupid …'

'It doesn't matter now,' said Jason. 'It doesn't matter what you think. It's out of our hands entirely and it is out of yours.'

John had been correct in his assumption, Jason told himself, that the people of the Earth had been made an experiment, in the same spirit and, perhaps, in much the same manner as a human bacteriologist or virologist would have experimented with a colony of bacteria or of virus. And if that were true, he realized with something of a shock, the people in this house and the little band of Indians and the other little group of people on the West Coast had not been missed. Rather, they deliberately had been left as a part of the experiment – as controls, perhaps.

John had said that by now the Principle would know that the strains of humanity ran true, but in the face of this new revelation, they must know as well that while in the mass humanity ran true, fragmented portions of it underwent mutation. For there were three human strains here – the people of this house and the Indians and the people on the coast. And of the three of them, two had been successful in their mutation and the third had gone to seed. Although, wait a minute, he told himself, that last conclusion is not true, for there was David Hunt. Thinking of him, he remembered how the music trees that evening of a week or two ago had suddenly regained their delicacy and poise and the incredible rumor he had heard from Thatcher this very afternoon. How was it, he wondered, the robots picked up the rumors before anyone else might be aware of them?

And the robots. Not three divergent strains, but four. Which was one up on the Principle, Jason thought with glee. He'd make any kind of bet (and be sure of winning) the Principle had not taken the robots into consideration. Although the robots, come to think of it, were a little frightening. What kind of contraption was this thing that could talk with the Principle and relay its message? And why had the Principle chosen it as spokesman? Simply because it had been there and handy? Or was there an affinity, an understanding, between the two of them that could not exist between the Principle and a human, or any other biologic form of life? He shivered at the thought of it.

'You remember,' he said to Stanley, 'that first you told us you could be of no help to us.'

'I remember that,' the robot said.

'But finally you were.'

'I am very glad,' said Stanley, 'that we were able to help you in the end. You and we, I think, have very much in common.'

'I sincerely hope we do,' said Jason, 'and I thank you from my heart.'

475

34

She was sitting at the desk, with the books spread out, when he came into the room. For a moment, in the feeble candlelight, she could not be sure that it was he; then she saw it was. She came swiftly to her feet. 'David!' she said.

He stood looking at her and she saw that he did not have the bow or quiver of arrows. And something else as well – the necklace of bear claws no longer lay upon his chest. Silly, she thought, that she should notice things like that when all that really mattered was that he was back.

'The necklace,' she said, feeling silly when she said it, not wanting to say it, but saying it just the same.

'I threw it away,' he said.

'But, David ...'

'I met the Walker. I did not need the bow. The arrow did not strike him; it only struck the ship.'

She did not answer.

'You thought the Walker was only a shadow in my mind.'

'Yes,' she said. 'A piece of folklore. An olden story ...'

'Perhaps it was,' he said. 'I don't know. Perhaps a shadow of that great race of builders who once lived here. The people not like us. Not like you and I. The shadow that they cast upon the land, that even after they were gone still remained upon the land.'

'A haunt,' she said. 'A ghost.'

'But it is gone now,' he said. 'It no longer walks.'

She stepped around the desk and he came quickly to meet her and had his arms about her and held her close against him. 'It is so strange about the two of us,' he said. 'I can make things well, I can cure the sick. You can see everything there is and make me see it, too; everything there is comes clear inside your mind.'

She did not answer. He was too close, too real; he was back again. There was no room for an answer.

But, within her mind, she told Grandfather Oak: It is a new beginning ...

'I'll be leaving soon,' said John. 'I won't remain away so long this time.'

'I hate to see you go,' said Jason. 'Do come back as soon as you are able. We were boys together ...'

'We had good times,' said John.

'There is something very special,' Jason said, 'about two men being brothers.'

'There is nothing to worry over now,' said John. 'The Earth is safe. We can continue as we have. The Indians and the robots can take any road they wish. The idea of the Principle may not be accepted in its entirety by the People. They'll think about it for a while, they'll mull it over, they'll talk it over. They'll figure, as Harrison said, it probably is no more than a fairy tale. They may make a try for Earth. I would think it's almost certain that they will. If they do, they'll get slapped down and then they will believe.'

Jason nodded. 'That is true. But there's the business of the Project.'

'What about the Project?'

'You mean you haven't thought of it?'

'You're talking riddles, Jason.'

'No, I'm not,' said Jason. 'It's just that you haven't seen it. No one saw it. They figured all the Principle did was use the Project for an errand boy.'

'Well, wasn't that what it was – now, wait a second, you can't be thinking ...'

'But I am,' said Jason. 'Not an errand boy for the Principle, but a spokesman for the Principle. What have the two in common? We wondered whether the Project might just be listening, but now we know it wasn't that. They were talking back and forth. The Project told the Principle what was going on and the Principle told it what to do ...'

'I think you may be right,' said John, 'but you must remember that we've met other intelligences and we've had slight success ...'

'The thing you don't realize,' said Jason, 'is that the Principle is not another alien, not just another intelligence you run into out in space. It could have talked to us, I think, to any one of us, if it had wanted to.'

John grunted. 'That raises a question, Jason. Like speaks to like. Would you suppose the Principle could be – no, it can't be that. It must be something else. The Principle is no machine. I can swear to that. I lived on the edge of it for days.'

'That's not the point,' said Jason. 'The Principle would have nothing to do with a mere machine. Could it be, I wonder, that the Project is no longer a machine? How far do you have to push a machine before it becomes something other than machine? How much does a machine need to evolve before it becomes something else – another form of life? Different than we are, it would have to be different than we are, but a life form just as surely—'

'You're letting your imagination run away with you,' said John. 'Even if you aren't, there's nothing we need fear. The robots are friends of ours. They have to be good friends – damn it, man, we made them.'

'I don't think it's all imagination,' Jason said. 'I think there is some basis for it, some evidence of it. I find myself wondering if the Principle, whatever it may be, has found a closer identification with the Project than it has with the human race. And that's the kind of thing that sends a shiver up my spine.'

'Even if it should be so,' said John, 'and I can't agree it is, it would make no difference to us. Except for you and Martha, we're out among the stars. In another few thousand years there'll be none of us who'll care particularly either about the Principle or Earth. We're free agents, going where we want to go, doing what we want to do. And this business of star-roving, I feel sure, is only a part of it, a beginning of it. In the centuries to come the race will develop other capabilities. I don't know what they'll be, but I know they will develop.'

'I may be short-sighted,' Jason admitted. 'I live too close to Earth. I never gained the perspective the others of you have. By the time the situation with the Project has developed to the point where it has any impact, Martha and I will be long gone. But the Indians will stay here and what about the Indians? Of all of us, they may be the most important segment of the human race.'

John chuckled. 'The Indians will get along all right. They've developed the most solid basis of any of us. They've made a compact with the planet. They've become a part of it.'

'I hope,' said Jason, 'you are right.'

They sat in silence, the fire flickering in the grate, the chimney making sighing noises. The wind plucked at the eaves and in the stillness of the night the old house moaned with its weight of years.

Finally John said, 'There's one thing I want to know and I want the truth. What about your alien?'

'It left,' said Jason. 'It went home. It stayed longer than it planned because it had to tell someone, had to thank someone. David was the man to thank, for David was the one who did it, but David never heard a single word it said. So it came to me and told me.'

'And you've told David? You passed along the thanks?'

Jason shook his head. 'No, not yet. If ever. He's not ready for it. It might frighten him. He might run off again. I told two people, you and Hezekiah.'

John frowned. 'Was it smart to tell Hezekiah?'

'I debated it,' said Jason, 'then finally I did. It seemed – well, it seemed to be in his department. He's so weighed down with imaginary, self-accusatory worry that I thought it might help him. Give him something solid to worry over for a change.'

'This wasn't really what I meant,' said John, 'when I asked the question. What worries me is this matter of a soul. Do you honestly think it possible this strange character out of the West could have given the alien a soul?'

'That's what the alien said.'

'Not the alien. You. What do you think?'

'I sometimes think,' said Jason, 'that the soul may be a state of mind.'

*

478

Hezekiah tramped, troubled, up and down the garden of the monastery.

It was impossible, he told himself, that what Mr Jason told him could be right. Mr Jason must have misunderstood. He wished the alien still were here, so that he could talk with it, although Mr Jason has said, even had it been here, he could not talk with it. There was no way for him to talk with it.

The night was silent and the stars far off. A winter wind came stealing up an autumn hill. Hezekiah shivered at the touch of it and was at once disgusted with himself and a little frightened. He should not shiver in the wind, he could not feel the wind. Could it be, he wondered, that he was turning human? Could he, in his humanness, really feel the wind? And he was even more frightened that he should think he might be human than he'd been frightened at shivering in the wind.

Pride, he thought – pride and vanity. Would he ever rid himself of his pride and vanity? And he might as well admit it – when would he be rid of doubt?

And now, as he asked himself that question, he could no longer hide from the thing he had been hiding from, the thought he had tried to keep himself from facing by thinking about the alien and its soul.

The Principle!

'No!' he shouted at himself, in sudden terror. 'No, it can't be so! There can be nothing to it. It is sacrilege to even think of it.'

In that area, he fiercely reminded himself, he could not be shaken.

God must be, forever, a kindly old (human) gentleman with a long, white, flowing beard.

If you've enjoyed these books and would like to read more, you'll find literally thousands of classic Science Fiction & Fantasy titles through the **SF Gateway**

✳

For the new home of Science Fiction & Fantasy . . .

✳

For the most comprehensive collection of classic SF on the internet . . .

✳

Visit the SF Gateway

www.sfgateway.com

CLIFFORD D. SIMAK (1904–1988)

Clifford Donald Simak was born in Wisconsin, in 1904. He attended the University of Wisconsin and spent his working life in the newspaper business. He flirted briefly with science fiction in the early '30s but did not start to write seriously until John W. Campbell's *Astounding Stories* began to rejuvenate the field in 1937. Simak was a regular contributor to *Astounding* throughout the Golden Age, producing a body of well regarded work. He won the Nebula and multiple Hugo Awards, and in 1977 was the third writer to be named a Grand Master by SFWA. He died in 1988.